Crying in the Morgue, Laughing in the Dark

Mary A. Allen

Inspiring Voices®

Author photo by Brandy Photos; www.BranyPhotos.com

Inspiring Voices books may be ordered through booksellers or by contacting:

Inspiring Voices
1663 Liberty Drive
Bloomington, IN 47403
www.inspiringvoices.com
1 (866) 697-5313

ISBN: 978-1-4624-1080-4 (sc)
ISBN: 978-1-4624-1079-8 (e)

Library of Congress Control Number: 2014921630

Printed in the United States of America.

Inspiring Voices rev. date: 12/11/2014

This book is dedicated to my husband, Bob Allen. You have walked with me through this incredible writing journey with love, encouragement and prayers. Have I told you today that I love you? I do, you know, with my whole heart.

Acknowledging the Ingredients

If there is anything praiseworthy in this book, then the glory should go to God for all He has done in and through my life. I am thankful for my walk with Jesus. I may veer from the path at times, but *He* never leaves *me*. He remains my constant companion.

Through my writing journey, I have discovered a lot of ingredients go into writing a book. I am grateful to the following people God brought into my life to help me with the book "recipe."

Loretta Sinclair, Jane S. Daly, and Michelle Murray who filled my bowl with main ingredients such as encouragement, love and instruction. (That's what critique groups do. Love and cheese, ladies.) Jodi Brown and Clareen Aseltine for the final edits that gave finishing touches to frost my completed creation.

John-Thomas Pryor for the cover design which garnishes the book with beauty and appeal. Elyse Allen, MA LMFT for her ability to stretch my creativity and make things palatable by keeping me real. Diana Symons for her honesty about my first draft and giving me the basic recipe for success. Dawn Kinzer for her friendship that walked me through the editing process, and challenged me to take chances with creative ingredients and methods in order to serve a more appetizing meal.

A Little Something Extra

My life is filled with people whose encouraging words will never fade from my memory. Their words are permanently etched upon my heart. Without them, this book may never have been written. This is a special thank you to *some* of those people. Chuck Grifasi, Jane Grifasi, Michelle Griffiths, Betty Harding, Maggie Hodge, Barb (Bee) Hunt, Deanne Karnaze, Linda Kral, James and Shirley McClure, Barb Ricotta, Gayle Roper and Vicki Quirarte.

And to my ordinary family for whom I have extraordinary love-I've been blessed and inspired by you: James, Jacob, Joy, Tony, Heather, Thomas, Isabella, Mary, Anna, Jacob F., Matthew, Jacob A., and Eleanor. I love you.

This story is a work of fiction based on a true story. (Mine.)

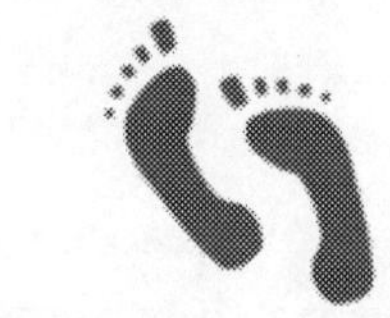

Chapter One

Present Day

All eyes were fixed on her. Myra Collins paused and scanned the small audience, her heart racing. She stared down at her notes. What compelled her to reveal a story that lay dormant for so many years? Would these fifty women understand how the tale impacted her? Would anyone understand? Could what she had to say help even one woman in this room?

Myra gave her audience a tentative smile. "I've lived like so many other people, getting out of bed every day, going about my business, doing my best to live a decent life."

She sighed. Her life seemed so routine, so mundane. She'd spent the majority of it without value or purpose, without goals, aimlessly living one day to the next, never believing she had anything to offer.

"To tell you the truth," she continued, "it never occurred to me that my life is filled with purpose, or that I could be of any use to anyone." The words written in her notes emboldened her. "But recently, a series of events radically altered me. Change is something I struggle with. But through it emerged purpose."

She glanced at the audience as memories of her mother drifted through her mind.

Myra's Mother, Stella
October 1955

The chill of the bathroom tiles seeped through Stella Grayson's threadbare nightgown as she rested her head on the wooden toilet seat. Tears stung her eyes as anger burned within her like a red-hot flame. No, she wouldn't cry. She was far too angry. And nauseous. And tired. It wasn't the stomach flu or food poisoning. If only it were. No, it was something far worse than a mere life-threatening bout with botulism. She was pregnant. Again.

She should have been done having babies. For goodness sake, she was forty! Her four boys already performed plenty of mischief and kept her on edge, both physically and emotionally. From the twelve-year-old to the two-year-old, each managed to challenge her sanity. Most days, she was a bundle of raw nerves. She woke before dawn exhausted, to prepare the day for her family. She cooked, cleaned, and kept the house running in smooth working order, and she was the last one to fall into bed at night, even more drained. Would it ever end? She should be looking forward to having grandchildren, but instead she'd face overflowing diaper pails, more laundry, larger meals, bigger grocery bills, and less time for herself.

Stella contemplated her options. There weren't any. No need to tell anyone of the pregnancy just yet. After all, she'd gained so much weight with the other kids no one would ever suspect she was pregnant. Maybe she would get lucky and lose this baby.

Stella shuffled to the sink to wash her face. She touched the crow's feet next to her eyes, the frown line around her lips. She felt old and haggard. The reflection in the mirror confirmed it. *I am old, I have always been old.* Never young, carefree, or without responsibility. Only two and a half when her mother died, Stella aged fast.

Stella didn't remember her mother, but a warm feeling possessed her when she pondered the days before the 1917 pandemic stole her mother away. Her father—an imposing man—wasn't prone to moments of warmth or tenderness. Shortly after her dear mother's death, Papa had lifted her into his large, black touring car. The cold evening wind had stung her cheeks. Stella didn't remember being in Papa's touring car before, and was afraid to ask where they were going. Unspoken words hung between them as fear threatened to strangle her and breathing became quick and shallow.

By the time they arrived at their destination, her stomach was in a tight knot. Papa set her down on the sidewalk in front of the large, frightening brick building, where she immediately threw up beside the car. Papa took hold of her wrist with great force and pulled her toward the massive, weather-beaten doors. She sobbed, desperate to know why she was being brought to this horrible place.

The door opened with a terrifying creak, and a stern-faced woman appeared in front of them. She wore a long, black dress with a funny black and white cape draped over her head. Papa handed her over to the woman and with a nod, turned and walked back to his motor car without looking back.

The horror of that moment washed over Stella now as she remembered. "Papa, I'm sorry. I won't throw up again. Come back, please, come back." Tears coursed down her face.

But the strange woman held her back with an iron grip. "That's enough," her words snapped.

As her father drove off into the blackness, Stella's heart shattered like an icicle falling to the ground.

The boys' laughter bounced through the house, filling each room with childish joy and exuberance. It pinged off the light fixtures, ricocheted from the ceiling, danced over the area rug, reflected off the mirrors, and settled over every surface in the house. But it didn't touch Stella. It never drew close to the dark corner of her world.

The ache in her stomach brought her back to the bathroom. Her throat burned from the bile forced into it from the dry heaves. Maybe she should eat something and make all this effort worthwhile.

The house became as silent as a winter morning in January. Indeed, the silence moved through the house like a cold front with frightening speed. Stella headed toward the boys' room fully expecting to come face-to-face with the usual midmorning disaster. She was not disappointed. Ribbons of toilet paper hung from every surface like streamers at a school dance.

"What are you boys doing? Clean this mess up right now." The boys were, as usual, about to unravel her nerves to the very end. *How do they do it?* She longed for the days before these four boys took over her very existence. *These boys are spoiled. They don't know how good they have it.*

"Stella, come here now!" The nun's voice was as sharp as a straight-edged razor. It had not dulled one bit in all the years that Stella live there.

Stella's presence in Sister Superior's office was immediate. She learned how to move fast and think quickly to avoid the swift rap on the knuckles given for poor performance. The room's hot, dusty air irritated Stella's throat, but she dared not cough. The old, dark furniture resembled the sister's personality—she never smiled or laughed. When she spoke, her words were like shards of glass from a shattered mirror. Stella dreaded the very thought of her.

"Yes, Sister." Stella was careful to modulate her voice to be neither too loud to offend the nun, nor too soft to force her to order Stella to speak up. She stood tall, but not at attention, so she would not be accused of being impertinent.

The nun crossed her arms in front of her and peered down her nose at Stella. "Your father has come for you." Stella glanced to the right. A tall, forbidding man and a sour, young woman stood there staring at her. The young woman could have been Sister Superior forty years ago. Her features were unmovable– as though carved into granite. Stella gazed beyond and to the left of the unfamiliar man with the stern, humorless face, but didn't see anyone else.

Stella remained silent.

"Go get your things. Hurry! We don't have all day." The nun's words landed on the floor like a rock.

Trembling, Stella left to prepare for her new life with these two strangers. She didn't have much to pack, even after almost six years in the orphanage.

Stella's stepmother's hardened features were actually pleasant compared to her personality. Stella became a servant, doing her stepmother's cooking and cleaning. Stella's body ached, and her hands burned and smelled of bleach when she finally crawled into bed at night. After completing assigned tasks, Stella was forced to sit by the hour, knitting and crocheting blankets and doilies for her dowry.

One such day, soon after turning twelve, Stella fought to keep her weary eyes from closing as her sore and reddened hands worked her knitting needles.

Her stepmother grabbed Stella's knitting, examined it, and threw it down. "I expect better than this. Your dowry needs to be extremely nice if you are to have any hope of ever finding someone to marry *you.*"

Stella's face burned with humiliation, her young heart again crashing to the ground, shattered.

"Stella, get in here." Her father's voice bellowed, shaking the walls like a passing trolley car.

She rushed in. Her father's anger filled the room. Her stepmother's smug expression created a vacuum, and Stella couldn't breathe. What was it this time? Was the breakfast toast a little too dark, did she miss a spot of dust, did the mail come late? Or did the granite woman just make up a new lie to tell Papa? *Shrew!*

Stella could not understand how her father could beat her for not getting the laundry off the clothesline by noon. They were still wet. He probably didn't hear that part of the story.

After two years of slavery, it was a rare day when Cora, granite woman, didn't tell Stella "Wait until your father gets home." Before Stella healed from one beating, her father gave her fresh wounds to lick. He wasn't fussy how he hit her. Sometimes a sharp slap to her face, other times a belt across the back of her bare legs. He used whatever was handy to "make his point." If there were a way for Stella to improve her behavior, she would. But her stepmother was unpredictable and unstable, leaving Stella's attempt to "be a better little girl" impotent.

Once her stepmother started having children, her personality soured noticeably. She was unbearable during her three pregnancies and a walking time bomb after the boys were born.

Stella longed to be remembered on her birthday or on Christmas with just one toy, one book, or even one handkerchief. The dream of her heart played over and over in her mind like a phonograph record skipping back over and over the same groove. They were the thoughts that kept her company in the loneliest moments of her childhood.

Two weeks before her thirteenth birthday, her stepmother went into labor with her fourth child. The screams from her bedroom were unbearable. Sweat ran down Stella's neck. Her head pounded from the tension of her clenched teeth. Her stepmother's screaming and cursing, combined with her father's never-ending pacing, and the midwife's darting back and forth from bed to door like a drug fiend in need of a fix, created chaos.

"Push, push!" The midwife's excited voice was followed by a loud grunt.

The one in labor released a long, bloodcurdling scream. A baby's cry followed. "Take it away. I don't want another boy." Cora's harsh, angry words landed like wet sand in the middle of Stella's room.

Her eyes grew wide anticipating her father's reaction. There was no reaction.

Silence, at last silence. Stella sighed with relief.

Hushed voices sounded outside her bedroom. A rapid, hollow knocking on her bedroom door startled her. Stella opened the door with apprehension, and there stood the midwife, baby in her arms. Without a word, the midwife handed the baby to her and walked away. No explanation. No training. At almost thirteen years old, Stella became a mother, by default.

Chapter Two

John, Myra's Dad

October 1955

The gentle click and sizzle from the wall heater filled the room with soothing sounds like a faraway symphony. John slumbered in a dream-like state, just at the edge of wakefulness. Even with the wall heater on low, the room offered a slight chill that rested lightly on his nose and ears. But the cozy warmth of his blankets beckoned him deeper. He sighed, content with the knowledge that Saturday offered him a few extra precious moments to remain enraptured between the fresh, crisp laundered sheets.

The room quaked as Stella bolted from bed, leaving John startled and unearthed from the warm covers. A cacophony of loathsome sounds assaulted his ears from the bathroom down the hall where Stella vomited with fierce effort. He closed his eyes against the assault, trying to recapture his dreamy state, but the sounds from the bathroom commanded his attention. After some time, Stella returned to the bed, and with a clumsy, jolting effort, plunged between the sheets again.

"Are you okay, Stella? Got a touch of the stomach flu?" He reached over and touched her back with tenderness.

"I'm not pregnant!" She jerked away from him.

Her words snatched away any intelligent thought that may have been lingering around the periphery of his brain. He hadn't considered that possibility at all. He pulled his hand back, searching for an appropriate response.

"Hope you feel better, Honey," he mumbled with limp sincerity.

Stella didn't reply. John felt somehow rebuked.

Her attitude continued to make him feel chastised. No matter hard he tried to be gentle and tender with her, she met him with resistance. For the remainder of the weekend, she wore an ironclad attitude of indifference toward him. He looked forward to the routine of Monday morning monotony. It was a welcome relief from the tension that settled between them.

At 5:30 a.m. on Monday, night slipped off its shroud of silence while it's long dark fingers still held a tenuous grip on the sky. John peered through the window, waiting for his ride. He was ready earlier than usual, anxious to leave the weekend behind. He saw the headlights moving with steady stealth through the semi-darkness. They stopped in front of his house, and the driver gave one quick piercing blast of his horn to announce his arrival.

He opened the car door with a sharp jerk, hoping he could fling some of the cigarette smoke lingering inside the car out with one quick motion. It never did, but his heart remained hopeful. He greeted the three men inside with a pleasant voice and took his usual seat in back.

The conversation drifted from topic to topic, until it finally settled on the woes of work. John's mind wandered in aimless directions as the other three men complained bitterly about working conditions at the factory, the union and its exorbitant dues, management's attitude towards workers, and how a strike would be a welcome event, as if it were a hospitable celebration of workplace camaraderie.

The conversation settled heavy in his gut like a large breakfast of pancakes swimming in syrup, making him queasy. His mind made a journey to Stella. He pondered their predicament, her silence and his confusion. Was she really pregnant? He hadn't understood her reaction Saturday and didn't know how to make things right. Where had he lost control?

At twenty-seven, John had not yet found the love of his life. But he was in active pursuit of the one perfect woman to stand by him. He tried several venues for his search–church, community college, social clubs, but none brought any positive result until the night he was at his buddy Ted's house. They had been sitting around shooting the breeze and sharing raucous laughter when Ted's sister walked into the room with their cousin, Stella. John was enamored.

For the remainder of the evening, he did everything he could to capture her attention. He told stories with animated gestures, cracked jokes that were successful in the past, and in general remained the center of attention. Ted and his sister were delighted with his antics. The room rang with laughter.

Stella, however, appeared to be somewhat reserved. John's enthusiasm was not deterred. He moved forward like a snowplow clearing a highway as he attempted to remove any obstacles that lay between him and Stella. His skin tingled with anticipation. At the end of the evening, Stella stood and announced her departure. John leaped up with eagerness and offered to walk her home. She gave a slight nod, a Mona Lisa smile fixed on her face.

The short walk down the block was filled with limited conversation and tense silence. Several houses from where she lived, Stella stopped and thanked John for his kindness, stating she would prefer he leave her now.

"My father would not understand your offer to walk me home." Her voice was so matter-of-fact it took John a moment to get past it.

"Okay." John paused a moment to digest her words. Undaunted, he continued. "May I have the pleasure of your company at a movie Friday evening?"

She looked puzzled.

"I'm asking you for a date," he said, eyebrows raised.

"You're a buffoon." Stella spun around and took several steps away, then stopped. She turned back and offered a sweet smile. "Pick me up at my cousin's house. I'll be there at 6:30."

Her answer shot through him like electricity. He loved the sweet flavor of victory that covered his tongue.

They entered the movie theater Friday evening, and the aroma of popcorn welcomed them.

They settled in their seats with popcorn to share, but John was too anxious to watch the movie. He planned this evening all week, rehearsing his words over and over until he had them right. Stella's eyes never left the screen, but John shot her a furtive glance out of the corner of his eye. He was ready. She was "the one."

The drive home felt stilted and uncomfortable, but John was quite motivated. When they arrived in front of Stella's cousin's house, he turned the car off and faced her. The rich May evening air cleared his head of any hesitancy, and he cleared his throat. As Stella reached for the car door handle, John forged ahead.

"Stella, here are my intentions. I'd like to get engaged and be married within six months."

She stared at John with a blank face, as if he had just given her the results of the 1912 World Series. Then she looked him in the eye. "Okay." Accepting his proposal was the first and only verbal response she'd given all evening. John was overwhelmed. He did it! He got engaged and was going to be married. He won her heart-however unremarkable her reaction. John leaned over and placed his lips on hers to seal the deal. They were warm, and it felt exhilarating. But, it only lasted for a wistful moment. Then John felt the swift, smart slap of her hand across his face. John jerked away in one sharp movement, confusion spreading through his body.

Stella reached for the car door handle again and turned to him. "Okay then, see you later." She got out of the car and left.

Chapter Three

Mark, Myra's Brother

December 1955

A flurry of animated energy burst out of the bedroom as the three brothers stampeded down the stairs and charged to the coat rack, arms and sleeves flinging simultaneously in every direction. The boy's excitement spilled from their mouths, each trying to speak over the other.

"Mom, the guys and me are going out to play ball," Mark roared through the house as the boys almost reached the front door. "See ya later." They flung the door open, sweeping in a current of snow-kissed air.

"Oh, no you don't. It's too cold out there to play baseball. You boys go upstairs and gather your dirty laundry and bring it to me."

"Awwww, Maaaaa," the boys chorused in agreement.

Stella entered the room as the last measure of their protest faded into disappointment. A moment of silent anticipation followed, as the boys waited for Stella to relent, and she waited for the boys to obey.

"Aw, Ma, please," Mark said, attempting one last appeal. "We don't want to waste a Saturday stuck inside. Please."

"Now." Stella's verbal gavel proclaimed the final verdict.

The boys flew up the stairs without further comment.

Stella stared after them, frustrated. She shook her head. It wouldn't be long before Billy joined them, torturing her for her parental duties.

She wished her little brother, Carl still lived with them. He was a big help with the boys. But, he joined the service the minute he turned eighteen, leaving Stella to deal with the boys and John on her own.

At nine years old, Mark was the leader and brains of the outfit, always luring his eleven-year- old brother, David, and his eight-year old brother, Danny, into mischief. Although mischievous, Mark had leadership skills. If Stella could recruit Mark for positive activities, the other two would follow. Danny wanted to emulate Mark, and David needed to feel engaged with others. So most of her motherly appeals were directed at Mark, but addressed to all three. Mark invariably led the charge.

The laughter returned upstairs as she dragged her feet back to the kitchen with a sigh.

In their bedroom, the boys flung clothes across the room at each other. Mark grabbed a wadded pair of dirty socks from the floor and tossed it at David. It bounced off his head, and the game was on. Each T-shirt, pair of underwear, and pair of socks was now rolled, tied, or wadded into an expertly shaped laundry baseball. Dirty-laundry baseballs were lobbed back and forth like projectiles from outer space, each boy ducking from or swinging at them. The pillows became bats and bases as the game evolved. The laughter built to a crescendo, and just as the bases were loaded, and the boys could hear the roar of the crowd, the bedroom door slammed open and the "stadium" disintegrated into a cluttered bedroom. The boys stood paralyzed.

As their mother surveyed the room, her face turned as red as a fire engine. She gripped the doorknob so tight, her knuckles became white. The boys, frozen in place, said nothing.

"Boys, untie—all—this—laundry, and bring it to me—*immediately*!" She spoke through clenched teeth, and her low voice sounded menacing, but she didn't scream at them. She glared at each of them. "If your father was here …" The boys understood her meaning. Mark cringed at the memory of his father's past punishments.

The waiting room was filled with weary mothers, frail old people, crying babies, frightened children, assorted *Life* and *Look* magazines, and a menagerie of overused stuffed animals. Exhausted anticipation covered each face as the door to the exam rooms opened and the nurse called the next patient's name.

"Mark Grayson." Mark looked up from his magazine, alarm gripping him. His father sighed with apparent gratitude. As they walked through the door to the dreaded torture chamber beyond, Mark's small body stiffened with fear, Dad's relaxed, and the rest of the parents slumped back into place. Mark felt like he'd been coming to the doctor every week his whole life, yet it'd only been a year. But, when you are seven years old, a year seems like a lifetime.

The nurse led them to the exam room. Mark sat on the cold, wooden table in silence as his father took his place in a nearby chair. Conversation was stunted, existing mostly of Mark's verbal desire to "be at home playing baseball with the guys." His father grunted his agreement, but said little.

When Dr. Moreno entered, his attitude filled the exam room like fresh air. His smile was made to order for putting patients and families at ease. He reached his hand out to Mark's father. "Good to see you, Mr. Grayson."

"You too," he said.

The doctor turned his attention to Mark. "Hey, Mark. How are you? Are you ready for your shot?"

"Yeah, I guess." Mark shrugged his shoulders.

Mark received shots on a weekly basis to boost his immune system. He hated them, but there wasn't much he could do about it. Each week he would clench his teeth, turn his head, and endure the needle in his arm.

Time seemed to slow down as the doctor prepared the syringe. Mark's stomach began to rumble and bubble. "I have to go to the bathroom."

Dr. Moreno's smile never faded. "Sure, Mark, go ahead."

"He can wait," his father said, before Mark could hop off the table.

Dr. Moreno turned casually to Mark's father. "No reason for him to be uncomfortable."

His father fixed steely cold eyes on Mark. "He can wait."

Dr. Moreno's smile remained in place, but some of its luster faded. He opened his mouth to say something, when Mark gave a small sob. He turned to look at Mark. He had broken out in a cold sweat, his face felt on fire. He had soiled himself.

His father almost leaped from his chair, shaking his head wildly. His face was deep red. He whacked Mark on the side of his head. "Go to the lavatory and clean up." He followed Mark in and helped him out of his trousers.

"I told you to wait, Mark. What's wrong with you, anyway? Can't you control yourself at all?" His angry voice scratched the air like sandpaper, and shame scraped Mark's heart with each word.

When they emerged from the lavatory, Mark was minus his trousers. His T-shirt hung to his thighs, his wet, soiled undershorts hidden beneath.

Dr. Moreno reached for the syringe to give Mark a shot. The room was quiet and tense. The doctor was extra gentle with Mark. When he finished, he ruffled Mark's hair and gave him a compassionate smile. "See you next week, Buddy."

Mark jumped off the table and reached for the trousers in his father's hand.

Dad pulled them away. "They're dirty." He did not even look at Mark.

"But, I can't go out there in my underwear." His breathing increased as his fists clenched and unclenched.

"I checked. No one's out there." He still avoided looking at Mark.

The air in the room evaporated as Mark stared at his dad in terror. He darted a look at Dr. Moreno, and his bulging eyes revealed full well that was not true. The waiting room was packed. His dad ignored the horror on both their faces and marched Mark out of the exam room and through the packed waiting room—leaving little puddles of humiliation along the way as Mark's self-esteem melted into the floor.

Chapter Four

Stella, Myra's Mom,

January 1956

The trees outside the window lifted their bare branches toward the gray sky. They had long since been robbed of their garment of leaves, and fresh whispered snowfall now dusted each branch with a thin layer of virgin snowflakes. The sweet, unspoiled snow covered yesterday's slush and mud and glistened in the sun with glorious newness. No yellow snow, no random footprints, no tire tracks in the street remained to spoil the picture-perfect "Currier and Ives" scene.

Stella peered out the window with swollen, red eyes. The house sat quiet. John had packed up the boys and gone to church while Stella stayed home. Alone. In silence.

Beneath her bathrobe, her swollen belly belied her denials of pregnancy. She tried to hide it under loose fitting dresses, but as time pushed forward toward the truth, her body betrayed her. She'd felt tremendous relief that morning when excused from squeezing her fat feet into high heels and donning lipstick for the obligatory church attendance. She never intended to return to church. The only reason she went was to please John. She sat next to him, but didn't experience any emotional or spiritual connection to what she heard. The yet-to-be announced pregnancy was as good as any reason to stay home.

She had heard them downstairs preparing to leave.

"Where's mommy?" Billy's loud voice carried up the stairs. "We all have our coats and boots on."

"Mommy's not feeling well," John said.

"She sick?" Billy sounded concerned.

"She's not going to church this Sunday."

In her room, Stella sat on her bed awash with anxiety and nodded in agreement. *Or any other Sunday, for that matter.* She had better things to do than to sit in church and pretend it meant something to her. The memory stung like a bee.

"Stella, I hear your mother just had another baby," Father Rodolfo said, stepping in front of her as she left Mass.

She slowed to a halt in front of him. "Yes, my *step*mother just had another baby, and I need to get home to take care of him."

"I have a little gift for him. Please come with me to the rectory, and I will give it to you to take home." He flashed a serpentine smile at her, then turned and headed toward the rectory with quick, deliberate strides.

Stella fell into step behind him, almost running to keep up. She was in a hurry to get home, so she didn't object to his speed.

As they entered the rectory, Father Rodolfo spoke over his shoulder. "Come to my office. The gift is in there."

Without a word, Stella followed the priest. Their staccato footsteps echoed in the large, ornate corridor. The priest stopped at a door, opened it, and went in, holding the door for Stella. She entered, and he closed the door in one quick motion. Stella turned to look at the closed door and the priest standing beside it. She stared at him a moment. What was so private about a gift to a baby that required the office door to be closed? She continued to stare, wary, but dismissed it and turned away. *He's just a strange duck.*

"Father, I really need to hurry. My stepmother gets very angry when I make her wait."

Stella took a step toward the desk, thinking the gift must be there. She wanted to hasten this visit along so she could get home to her brother and avoid facing the granite woman's disapproving disposition.

She felt his sweaty hand wrap around hers like a vice grip. Confused, she whirled around and opened her mouth to speak.

"You are so beautiful, Stella. I long every day to be alone with you, to touch you, to feel you close." He put her hand to his lips and kissed it.

Horror filled her throat, and she yanked her hand away. She swung her fist at him, and made direct contact with his face.

"You pig!" Her scream increased her rage, and it flared up like hot, burning coals, scorching the very air in the room.

He tried to grab her, but her foot was faster than his hands, and it struck the priest's shin with unbridled force. He jerked back with a screech, grabbed his leg and toppled over, landing in a heap on the floor. With uncontrolled wrath she stalked toward the door, then turned and spat on the floor next to him.

Stella pointed to his neck and screeched. "You are a dog in a white collar. You phony. Stay away from me, you worthless pig!" She whirled around and left. The door's slam echoed down the hall as she made her way out of the building and up the street. She did not slow down, and she did not look back. With clenched teeth and tightened fists, she forged ahead, creating distance between them.

When she could see her father's house, she slowed, looked around, and stopped. She hadn't noticed she was shaking. Stella took a deep breath, and blew it out. She tried to relax, but anger coursed through her veins like a runaway train.

How would she ever explain this to her father? He would never believe the truth. He would blame her, and the pig would go unpunished. Tears welled up in her eyes, and she swiped them away with resolve and continued home. She would never go back to church. She would simply tell her father she would stay home to care for the baby. He and his wife were free to attend Mass together.

Hot, bitter tears stung Stella's eyes and rolled down her face. She could never forget that day. For a long time, she sat and stared out the window at the snow. Any beauty eluded her. All she saw was a cold, lifeless winter morning. The silence in her heart had become deafening.

Chapter Five

John, Myra's Dad

February 1956

John arrived home from work and entered through the back door. Coming in this way allowed him to step into the kitchen and greet his dinner's aromas that filled the room with promise. It was where he met his wife with a kiss and a "hmmmm, that smells good" greeting.

Today no tantalizing smells met him, and no wife greeted him. The kitchen was empty, except for laughter filtering down through the heating vent. The boys were in their room, and it was apparent they were having a very good time.

Irritated with the lack of sensory stimulation, John removed his jacket. "Stella. Stella, where are you?"

A stampede of feet herded down the stairs. The sound struck a nerve in John's heart and took him aback. The irritation vanished beneath years of suppressed memories. He stood frozen.

Abigail Grayson flew into the kitchen. "Boys, quick! Your father's home. Get to the cellar. Now."

"But, Mama, our dinner …" John said.

"Take the bread with you, John. Go. All of you."

John grabbed the warm loaf of bread his mother had baked and ran out the back screen door with his three older brothers, straight to the cellar. Opening the doors, John's oldest brother, Gerald, held the door as his three younger brothers descended the five stairs. He entered the cellar himself and lowered the cellar door with silent stealth, burying them in darkness. The sound of him sliding a broom through protruding door handles gave him comfort. Gerald didn't need to see the task; he'd done this many times before.

The boys sat on the chilly cellar floor, shivering with cold and shaking with fear. John clutched the warm loaf of bread to himself like a mother protecting her infant. None of the four spoke a word. Above their shallow breathing, they heard the front door screen open and slam shut. Then, the inevitable shout. "Abigail!" John could hear his mother's quick steps skitter through the kitchen and fade as they entered the parlor.

"Where are those worthless boys?" their father shouted, his speech slurred.

No detectable answer filtered through the floor, but an unmistakable scream did.

"I said, 'where are the boys?'" he growled in a low, guttural tone. Still no answer seeped through the floorboards to the cellar below.

A loud crash, a bang, and their mother's shriek cut through the floorboards like a hunting knife. John's small body stiffened, and hot tears ran down his cheek. Still, neither John nor his brothers made a sound.

The sickening sound of fists hitting flesh seemed to echo in John's head, and an eternity passed before silence fell on the floorboards. No doubt his father finally passed out in his favorite armchair beside his precious Victrola, as he always did.

The boys never attempted to leave the cellar. John absent-mindedly picked bread crumbs off the loaf while he waited for his mother to rescue them. He and his brothers knew their father probably sat splayed in the easy chair, head bent, mouth distorted and open, drooling spittle, and reeking of booze.

They listened to the familiar sound of their mother's quick footsteps. First toward the sink for a wash rag to clean the blood from her face, then over to the ice box to chip off a chunk of ice to reduce a swollen lip or eye. Then a pause—probably to take a deep breath and smooth her skirt down.

The footsteps rushed out of the back door, and there were three gentle taps on the cellar door. John heard his brother, Gerald, slide the broom handle out, put it against the wall, and the four boys emerged, shaken but untouched.

"To bed, boys. Don't wake your father. He's asleep."

Even as a child, John wondered about her choice of words. "He's asleep" was mother-talk for "in a drunken stupor."

His father had not always been a monster. There were happier days, but the depression of 1920 put his father out of work. His father blamed the end of the Great War. There were too many returning soldiers seeking work. Mr. Grayson lost his well-paying, respectable job and was now forced to do whatever menial task would pay him a few dollars.

Since then, his personality had turned dark. He became a mean drunk and took his frustrations out on his family. After he beat the boys the first time, Abigail became vigilant about protecting them. She stood at the window every evening and waited for him to get home. She glanced at the floor clock, then out the window, then back to the clock. When she spied his staggering figure in the dark, she corralled the boys into the cellar. He then redirected his anger toward her. To John, she was a hero. He never knew a lady as strong or as beautiful.

The next morning, John tarried in his room until his father left to search for work. Then he went to his mother, who sat in her armchair, straight-backed and proper, and knelt before her. Her lips curved into a peaceful smile. He placed his head in her lap, and without a word, she stroked his hair with soft fingers. He felt safe for now. The evening would bring its own worries.

"Hey, Dad," the boys chimed in unison.

Startled back to the moment, John looked into the impish face of each boy.

"Hi, boys," he said, craning his neck to see past them. "Where's your mom?"

"Sleeping on the sofa in the parlor," Mark said. "Where's dinner? Can we have pizza?"

"Go upstairs, boys," John said as he left the kitchen.

The boys were just a memory as they whizzed by him and flew up the stairs.

"Stella," John said. "Stella," John increased his volume.

His wife stirred from her slumber.

"Where's dinner, Stella?" John stood with his arms folded tightly across his chest.

"I don't feel good, John. Take the boys out for pizza."

"I don't want pizza, Stella. I want decent food," he said, moving across the floor to shorten the gap between them.

"Well, I don't feel good, John. If you want decent food, make it yourself." She rose from her resting position, marched past him as stiff and straight as a soldier, and headed toward the bedroom.

John burned with anger. When was that woman going to tell him about her condition?

"Stella, are you …"

His wife whirled around with an abruptness that startled John. "No, John, I am *not* pregnant." Her angry eyes bored into him with electric heat. He stepped back a few inches. She walked away without another word.

Chapter Six

March 1956

Stella ascended the stairs, dragging each foot up to the next step. Exhausted, but not sleepy, she felt confident that once she put her head on the pillow, sleep would come. She entered the room without snapping on the light. It was cave dark as she inched her way across the room.

John had gone to bed several hours ago, but she stayed up to watch *Tonight Starring Steve Allen.* Just last week the moon shone through the curtains bright enough to light her way to the bed. Tonight, no glow illuminated the room. She peeked through the curtains. Just a sliver of the moon hung in the sky. Not even a shadow of its former self. *Funny, that's how I feel.*

She reached over to pull her side of the bed down, when an abrupt tightening in her abdomen bent her over with such force she expelled a gasp. When the pain eased, Stella stood up and inched her way back to the door and left the room. She made her way down the stairs and back to the parlor. No point in turning on the TV, the stations had already signed off for the night. Stella sighed. She headed toward her knitting, and again her abdomen tightened, forcing her down. When she stood, her eyes brimmed with tears. It wasn't the pain of labor which frightened her. Labor pain was familiar. She'd experienced it with boys already. It was the unknown beyond that caused her distress.

"Mrs. Grayson, I really don't understand why you're not getting pregnant. You're in perfect health." The doctor eyed Stella with a puzzled look. "Maybe you're trying too hard. Often, that can reduce your chances."

Stella's face warmed. She turned away from the doctor's inquiring face. "What can I do, Dr. Moreno?" Her voice was almost inaudible.

The doctor hesitated a moment. "I know this young, unmarried girl with a baby. She lives with her father, but her life is miserable. Her father is forcing her to work to support the child, but refuses to care for the baby while she's at work. The baby is severely neglected."

Stella moved her head back as if slapped. "You mean *adopt*?"

"Sure, why not? You want a baby, and he needs a loving home."

Six months later, Stella and John were parents of an eighteen-month-old baby, and Stella was pregnant with her first child.

Stella was no expert, but even she could see signs of neglect in this precious baby. At eighteen months, David could barely sit up and he made no attempt to talk. He didn't even make happy baby sounds and only cried when in pain. Dirty diapers and hunger didn't stir him to tears, like other babies.

But he *was* smart. He watched everything and everyone with a keen eye and he was beautiful. He had Stella's dark curly hair and soulful, brown eyes. A beautiful baby and one on the way. Stella's dream had become a reality—she thought.

The dark hours dragged by in agonizing pain. Or was it being alone with her despair that was so agonizing? Stella wasn't sure. The pain pressed in on her abdomen with each step across the floor. One step after another, leading her nowhere, except over the same linoleum covered path she just walked.

One thing was certain; she would not go to the hospital. She would not move from this house. Whatever happened would take place here. *I am not pregnant.* A contraction knocked the wind and the resolve out of her. Her eyes brimmed, and her teeth clenched to keep from crying out.

John stood at the bottom of the stairs. "How far apart are the pains?"

She hadn't heard him coming. "It's all one big pain." Her voice trembled.

John disappeared without a word. Barely able to put thoughts into complete ideas, Stella continued her hike across the linoleum. John passed her with Billy, wrapped in a blanket. Her mind rambled. *Going to the neighbors …* He came back, went upstairs. She could hear his barely audible voice as he spoke with someone. *The boys …*

The hall light snapped on, rousing Mark slightly from his deep sleep.

"Boys."

Mark thought he heard his father's voice.

David and Danny stirred. "Huhhhh," they managed to mumble.

"Boys," his dad's voice again, more persistent.

Mark rose up on his elbow, Danny and David followed suit.

"Yeah, Dad," Mark croaked.

"I'm taking your mom to the hospital. Be good."

"Yeah, Dad, sure," the trio said.

The hall lights snapped off. Slumber once again eased back behind their eyelids.

The morning cold penetrated every inch of John's winter clothes, making him shiver. Thick ice covered the windshield, like frosting on a birthday cake. He scraped it with sharp, quick movements, as the ice flew in every direction. His breath curled in puffs before him, coming in rapid fire as he moved through the frigid night.

"Come on, Stella. Let's go. Get in the car." John's voice remained calm and controlled when he returned to the parlor.

"I'm not pregnant." Stella stood with her hands on her hips, belly protruding.

John stepped over to her and wrapped his fingers firmly around her upper arm. "Get in the car, Stella. You can 'not-be-pregnant' at the hospital."

The trip to the hospital was like riding with Barney Oldfield at the Indianapolis 500. John never drove so fast or with such focus. *Barney would be proud.*

While John pulled up in front of the hospital like an experienced ambulance driver, Stella gasped as another contraction ripped through her.

A nurse pushed Stella in the wheelchair to the elevator, and John went to park the car. A bemused Dr. Moreno, shaking his head, met them on the fourth floor. His nurse, Doreen stood beside him like an obedient soldier.

"Well, Mrs. Grayson, what a surprise to hear from your husband this morning. I haven't seen you in a couple of years. I had no idea you were …"

"I'm not pregnant," Stella snapped before he could finish.

His eyebrows shot up, and he glanced over to his nurse with an amused expression.

"Then, let's prepare the OR, shall we? We'll remove that growth causing you so much discomfort." His words were light, his attitude joking. He smiled and put his hand on her shoulder. She jerked her shoulder away, but said nothing.

His smile did not fade. He took the wheelchair and pushed it forward toward the delivery room with the speed of … *Oh brother, is everyone competing for the best Barney Oldfield imitation?*

Stella said nothing else as they entered the delivery room. Dr. Moreno and his nurse, Doreen, began to prepare for this birth with as much speed as possible. With Stella in position, Dr. Moreno announced, "I see the head."

Stella growled between contractions, "I'm not pregnant."

"Push, that's it. Push. Good," he encouraged, ignoring her denials. "One more time. A big one. Push!"

A loud, lusty cry from the baby filled the room, followed immediately by a mournful howl from Stella.

"Mrs. Grayson, you have a beautiful, baby girl."

"Noooooooooo! No, no, no."

"She's a beauty," Doreen encouraged.

"NO!" Stella's eyes bore into Doreen. "No. I don't want that baby. I never wanted another baby. Get it away from me."

Dr. Moreno attempted to calm Stella down. "Mrs. Grayson, look at her. She's a lovely baby."

"I *don't* care. Put her up for adoption." Stella's demands grew louder with every syllable.

"Mrs. Grayson … Stella … You know I can't do that without your husband's signature. You know he'd never agree."

Stella was adamant. "I don't care. I don't want it. I don't care what you do with it. I won't take it home."

Dr. Moreno bent his head and shook it slowly. His nurse stood beside him immovable. The baby continued to cry her lusty presence. He handed the baby to his nurse with a somber expression etched into his face. "Take her to the morgue, Doreen."

Chapter Seven

March 1956

The bare trees and light poles stood in eerie silence, like sentries that guarded the intersection of reality and foreboding. John made his way to the hospital entrance.

A shiver crept up John's spine. He shook it away and hurried forward. It was a bitter cold winter, but a surprise of warmth grew within the confines of John's heart. Despite the months of tension between Stella and himself, he had a refreshing sense of approaching summer blooming inside him. After four boys, he hoped he could finally add a daughter to his brood. A little girl … Ever since the secret of his two sisters' deaths were uttered, John held an unspoken longing to be the father of a sweet baby girl.

"Quiet, John. You'll wake Father."

"But—" John whispered.

"Shhhh," came the commanding chorus from his older brothers.

"But, I don't understand." John looked from one brother to the next. "We don't have any sisters. Why do the three of you talk about sisters like that?" John mimicked his older brother's words. " 'They're so lucky, because they don't have to hide from the monster.'"

The older boys exchanged glances.

"We used to have two sisters," his oldest brother, Gerald, said. "One was born after William." He pointed at the second oldest. "And, one was born after Jack." He pointed to the third born.

"What happened to them?" John's voice hushed with wonder.

"Lily, the oldest, died mysteriously after Jack was born." Gerald's voice had an edge to it.

"Yeah," William said, "and Emma was born after Jack, but died without warning six years ago, just after you were born."

"Whaaaaaaat happened?" John's voice croaked.

The younger brothers all deferred the answer to the oldest. He leaned in as if sharing a ghost story around a campfire.

"We were told they were sick and died in their sleep. But, they weren't sick. They were just babies, see? They each died at two years old after a new boy was born." Gerald paused, and looked John straight in the eye. "People say that Father never wanted girls, so, he killed them. Smothered 'em with a pillow, see?"

Terror flooded John's body. "That true, Gerald?" His voice came out in a hoarse whisper, and tears were collecting in the corner of his eyes.

Gerald looked straight into John's eyes, took a breath, and hung his head. "Yes, it's true. No one knows I know. But I saw it."

"Saw w-w-what?" A shiver ran down John's spine as he tried to steady himself in front of three brothers.

"Lily was crying that night. Father went in her room, real sneaky like. The cries got all muffled. Then, nothin'. Mother cried for days after that."

John's jaw gaped open, and his mouth went dry. "You didn't tell no one?" His voice cracked.

Gerald shook his head. "Who would believe me, John? The doctor said she had weak lungs."

"And, the other sister too?" John said, his voice raising an octave higher.

A grim expression covered Gerald's face like a thick cloud of Midwestern dust. "I didn't see him do it that time. But, he did it. I just know it. We got the same report from the doctor; mother had baby girls with weak lungs." Gerald paused. "How could two healthy babies just die from weak lungs?"

John sat in stunned silence. His brothers didn't say a word. They had already roasted these thoughts over the open fire of their brains, but it had done no good. The thoughts just burned, smoldered, and stank. John had thought his father's mean streak was related to the lack of money. But, both babies died before the money problems even started. *Why would a man kill his own babies just because they were girls*?

The elevator to the fourth floor opened, and John stepped out and headed toward the father's waiting room. He suspected his wait would be short since Stella lingered so long at home.

He walked into a small, empty room. *Slow night for babies*. John grabbed a magazine and settled into a chair. He sighed as he opened the publication and stared across the sparsely furnished room. Alone with his thoughts, he considered the possibility that he might get a girl this time. It was a fifty-fifty chance. He looked back across the room and was startled to see Dr. Moreno standing in the doorway. An icy chill gripped John's heart. He'd never seen *that* expression on the doctor's face before.

"Hey, Doc. Rough night?" John's casual manner belied his concern.

The doctor approached John as though on a mission and sat next to him. "Mr. Grayson, I'm so sorry," he said in a deep, anguished voice. "I tried everything I could, but your baby girl didn't make it. Her lungs were just not strong enough."

John heard "girl," and for one lightning quick moment, a thrill ran through him like electricity. Then the reality of the doctor's words hit him like a tsunami. He opened his mouth to say something, but nothing came out. He could no longer hear the doctor. The doctor's mouth was moving, but all John heard was buzzing in his ears.

He had to get out of that room. Without a word, John stood and moved toward the door to escape. The buzzing started to fade, but as John headed for the elevator, he sensed Dr. Moreno following him.

"Jaw, Jaw, ah yaw ah rah?" was all John heard as he absently stepped into the elevator.

My girl, my little girl. Gone. Gone. Gone …

The elevator door opened. John got off, head down, tears flowing freely.

The house seemed colder than usual as John entered through the back door and switched on the kitchen light. He walked the length of the room with leaden feet and battered heart. He dragged himself up the stairs—each step a monumental effort. He slowly went into his sons' room and snapped on the light. The boys stirred with slight movements.

"Boys." John could barely speak above a whisper. "Boys," he repeated with effort.

Mark rolled over toward the sound. "Yeah, Dad," Mark said with a sleepy voice.

"Your baby sister died," he said as he hung his head and left the room.

Chapter Eight

Marsha, Surgical Nurse

March 1956

The morgue's cold air forced itself against the door like a predator on its quarry. The door was helpless to stop its progression, and it slunk beneath and slid out into the hall. Marsha pushed the morgue's door open, swirling the air around her feet. She shivered slightly as she scanned the room. The chill almost made her forget why she came in, and she turned to leave. Then, she remembered and stepped forward.

An eerie atmosphere permeated the room. It felt bleak and hard and uninviting. The stainless steel tables lined up in a neat row like soldiers in formation. Some wore an enticing shine, as if waiting for the next occupant. Others were covered with people-shaped, white, linen mounds. It was those linen covered tables that gave purpose to this frigid, oppressive room.

Marsha moved further into the room and stepped past one of the covered tables. She stopped short with a gasp when she saw linen draped over a tiny infant shape. She reached out to steady herself, heart pounding. With her other hand, she covered her mouth to stifle a sob as tears formed in her eyes and spilled over the rims. She felt the blood drain from her face. No doubt it paled to match her dress and cap.

She would never get used to the sight of a dead infant. Unable to tear her eyes from the small figure, she just stood there—immobile. Wait, had the tiny form moved? She paused, and held her breath. *It did move.*

She grasped the sheet and pulled it down. The infant was moving in slow motion, struggling for life.

"Oh, dear Lord, thank you for bringing me here at this very moment in time. This baby is alive."

She grabbed the infant and wrapped her snugly in the sheet. Marsha made her way out of the morgue to the elevator, abandoning her original mission.

This is a miracle. This is really a miracle. Some dear mother upstairs is going to rejoice!

A dark shroud descended with insidious tenacity around Dr. Moreno. He sat motionless in front of his chart, like a Greek statue, pen in hand. The nurses' station became cold, freezing his racing thoughts to solid ice. A biting rawness touched every nerve, inch by frigid inch, making its way to his anguished heart. It pounded in his chest as he stared straight ahead. Remorse clung to him like a foul odor. He was in danger of stumbling into despair.

The usual hubbub of activity at shift change resumed. Each night nurse reported to the day nurse how her night went: how many mothers gave birth, the status of the baby, the condition of the mother, vitals taken, and medications given. Questions were asked, notes taken, gossip shared. Still, the doctor's eyes were riveted straight ahead. Bodies started to whiz by him, stirring the air that captured his full attention. He turned to follow their journey. When the sound of the approaching nurse's voice met his ears, he felt the color in his face dissolve.

"It's a miracle! This baby is alive. I found her in the morgue," the excited nurse said. Her voice emanated through the hall like a baseball announcer through a stadium.

Bile crept up the doctor's throat, and he hurried over to the nurse. "What's going on here?" The doctor's inquiry sounded stiff with courtesy. He hoped no one noticed his ghastly appearance or the slight tremor in his hands.

"Doctor, it's a miracle. I found this infant in the morgue. She's alive. Isn't that wonderful? Her mother is going to be so excited. What a blessing. She …"

Dr. Moreno reached over and took the baby in his arms, cradling her with a gentle touch. He glanced around in a casual manner, until his gaze fell on his nurse, Doreen. She stood against the wall, apart from the other nurses that had gathered. Her complexion had paled, and her eyes narrowed.

Dr. Moreno gave a dull smile to the nurse and read her nametag. "Thank you, Marsha. Good job."

As he turned to leave, Marsha reached over and put her hand on the infant with tender reverence. "God bless you, child," she said in a near whisper. "God bless you and all whose lives you touch. May joy be your constant companion in life, may it overshadow your pain, causing it to flee and hide in fear."

The doctor swallowed hard. His breath caught in his throat. Though the blessing was meant for the child, the doctor's hardened heart began to soften. Dr. Moreno stepped over to his nurse, Doreen. They exchanged knowing looks of relief. The doctor paused before handing the infant to her. He closed his eyes for a moment and exhaled.

"Nurse, take the infant to the nursery. Assess her, and monitor the vitals every fifteen minutes. When she's stable, I'll order some tests to be sure she's okay."

"Yes, Doctor. Right away, Doctor." Doreen hastened her way to the nursery, infant in arms.

Dr. Moreno turned towards Stella's room. He took a deep breath to steel himself against the impending onslaught of emotional bombs he knew she would throw. He started down the hall past the group of nurses chattering. He could hear the "nurse–hero," Marsha, still sharing her extraordinary story and the privilege at being a part of the miracle.

Stella sat in the bed, eyes closed, muscles relaxed. She hadn't felt this composed in months, and now breathing easily, she considered her life from this point forward. Now that she didn't have to worry about one more child, she could return to life unhindered. She sighed. Calmness spread over her like sunshine.

The sound of a cough caused her to frown. Someone had invaded her sanctuary. Her eyes opened, and she glared at the stoic features of Dr. Moreno. She'd never seen him so pale.

"A nurse from another floor found your baby," he began without preamble. "She carried her up here announcing the miracle to all who would listen. Then, when I took the baby from the nurse to have her checked out, the nurse pronounced a blessing on your baby that would rival Abraham in the Old Testament. Your baby is currently being assessed in the nursery. I am going to call your husband with the news of the miracle." He paused for a heartbeat. "Get some rest, Stella." Without waiting for her reaction, he turned and made an abrupt exit.

Large, salty tears brimmed in Stella's eyes. She closed them, trying to block out the fearful truth of what just happened. The tears spilled over and burned her cheeks with hot lava pain.

Chapter Nine

March 1956

The darkness outside the bedroom window began to dissipate, but inside John's heart, the shadows deepened with ferocious speed. John lay fully dressed on his bed, staring into the void. His mind couldn't comprehend what had happened. One minute he stood, rejoicing on a mountaintop, the next, he had plummeted down the side of a cliff, somersaulting over the jagged edges of life. How could this happen? *Oh, God, why did You let this happen*?

He should have gone in to see Stella, to give her support in her time of grieving, but he couldn't face her. Somehow, he felt this was his fault, or hers, or God's. He didn't know who to blame.

He just knew he couldn't face his wife's grief while he carried such a heavy burden of sorrow himself. There was a ringing in his head, in his ears, in the room, in the house. What was it? Where was it coming from? *The telephone!* He dashed down the stairs and into the hall to grab the call. It was probably Stella. *The least I can do is try to comfort her over the phone.*

"Hello?" John braced himself for the onslaught of grief and tears that Stella would pour out.

"Mr. Grayson? John? This is Dr. Moreno. I have some extraordinary news. You are not going to believe this …"

Blissful slumber embraced Mark as the night grew closer to dawn. His dream had wrapped him in sheer joy—his hand covered in the most exquisite baseball glove, ever. He lifted it to his face and touched it to his cheek to feel its smoothness. He inhaled deeply to smell its glorious aroma. *A new glove for my birthday.* His thoughts floated like a bird soaring through the sky. *Me and the guys will never bug Mom again. We'll stay outside and play baseball forever and ever …*

"Boys!"

Startled awake, Mark sat up squinting against the intrusive light. He said nothing, but waited, jaw tight, for his dad to give a reason for rudely interrupting the most wondrous dream ever. *My glove, my glove. It's gone—back into my head, forever.*

"Boys." Dad's voice rattled. "Boys, your baby sister *is alive*."

Did Dad just giggle? Mark scowled. Still, he said nothing.

His dad reached over and took Mark's arm, and gave it an excited shake, then pushed him down on his pillow and covered him up.

"Get some rest boys. We got us a little girl." His dad almost skipped out of the room, and his footsteps echoed down the stairs like gunshots in a canyon on a cheap Saturday morning TV western.

Mark stared into the dark. "You hear that, guys? Or am I having a weird dream?"

"If you are," David said, "we're with you in that weird dream."

"Yeah, right there," Danny said.

No other words were spoken as the guys resumed sleeping. Mark closed his eyes with a heavy sigh, determined to recapture the baseball glove dream once more.

John moved like fluid through the once deserted parking lot toward the hospital. The morning sun replaced shadows from the evening before, and the eerie night silence was replaced by the sound of distant traffic and scattered conversations. He marveled at the doctors with the clean, white coats, and sleek, black stethoscopes that hung like Olympic gold medals around their necks. John admired the nurses, clad in their white shoes and hose, perky white aprons, and simple paper hats. With swift purposeful strides, he advanced like a running-back with his eyes on the endzone.

As John moved toward the elevator, lightness in his spirit rose. His dark night was behind him. The elevator door opened and he stepped into his future.

John's face glowed in his reflection as he gazed through the nursery window at his brand-new baby girl. His smile was, no doubt, clownish, but his joy was evident.

Dr. Moreno joined him, but John didn't say anything for the longest time, as his eyes remained fixed on the infant lying in the ominous incubator. Finally, he turned to the doctor. "She's a beauty, huh, Doc?"

Dr. Moreno smiled at John. "That she is."

Dr. Moreno put his hand on John's shoulder. "Would you like to see your wife?"

John nodded, but his eyes remained riveted on his baby.

"She's this way," the doctor said, as he took a step away.

John looked at the doctor briefly, then back to his baby. He seemed hesitant to move, but after a moment, took a step toward the doctor. As the two men moved down the hall in silence, Dr. Moreno mulled over his thoughts. He considered John's reaction and concluded that he was correct in his assessment about him. John was thrilled about this child, and he never would have signed adoption papers.

Dr. Moreno dreaded Stella's reaction as they entered the room. It was apparent Stella was distraught. Her eyes were red and swollen, and she looked away when John approached with his bright, shining grin. Stella didn't utter a word to him. John looked around momentarily at the unoccupied beds in the room. He glanced towards Dr. Moreno, his expression heavy with question. Dr. Moreno gave a slight nod towards Stella to encourage John's interaction with her. John's smile returned, and he reached for Stella's hand.

"She's a beauty, Stella."

No reply.

"I stopped by to see her. She looks good. All pink and plump. You can hardly tell she's been through an ordeal."

No reply.

John lifted Stella's hand to his lips and kissed it softly. "I'll let you rest. You must be exhausted. I'll be back later after you've gotten some rest."

No reply.

John slowly placed her hand back on the bed and turned to leave. The question mark returned to his face. The two men left the room in silence.

As they walked down the corridor together, Dr. Moreno addressed John's unspoken concerns.

"She's had a rough night, John. We didn't think it prudent to give her any roommates. Give her a little time. She'll feel better after she rests."

Chapter Ten

March 1956

Mark sat on his bed thinking about the day ahead. It had been a long week without his mom. Dad did his best, but in the end, his mothering skills were not very good.

The guys lumbered into the room and collapsed on Mark's bed in succession.

"Mark, c'mon. Let's do something. We're bored. Don't just sit there."

Mark mulled the words over for a moment. "Whatcha wanna do, guys?"

There was a shrug all around.

Mark became somber. "Today's my birthday. Do you think Mom and Dad will remember? All Dad talks about is that baby. He said he went to get Mom from the hospital today. Do you think they'll stop and get me the baseball glove on the way home?"

"Sure, why not?" said Danny, his face beaming.

"Prob'ly not," David said. His lips remained a straight line across his face.

"Dad says he's bringing a surprise home for my birthday."

"Maybe cake and ice cream." Danny's eyes lit up like headlights on a truck.

"Maybe not," David said.

"Sure would like to have a new baseball glove." Mark's voice became dreamy and far away. "A new glove …"

A car door slammed in the distance, then another. The guys' eyes brightened as they heard the back door open.

Mark jumped up. "It's them. My new glove. Let's go. C'mon guys. Mom and Dad are home."

The three moved as one down the stairs, Billy pulling up the rear, as he took the stairs one at a time. They made an abrupt stop in front of their parents, and Billy toddled his way over to join his brothers.

"Hey, Mom. Hey, Dad." Mark's smile broadened. He stood tall and leaned forward.

"Hey, Mark," his dad said back. "We brought you a surprise for your birthday."

Mark's face warmed with anticipation. He couldn't stop smiling, and he laughed as he reached out for his surprise.

His father gazed at the bundle in his arms. It was wrapped tightly in a little blanket. He leaned over and opened the blanket a little and revealed its contents to Mark.

Mark peered into the face of a baby. He'd forgotten all about that baby. He looked up into his father's face. "I'd rather have a baseball glove."

Dad chuckled slightly and reached his hand toward Mark. He flinched slightly, as his father reached over and mussed his hair. The other boys drew closer to the birthday surprise. Mark stepped back, disappointed.

His mother remained silent. Mark glanced at her expectantly, but she looked distracted and tired and turned her head in the opposite direction. She headed for the stairs without a word to anyone. The guys fussed over his surprise, and Mark wondered what kind of birthday celebration this was that didn't include a "happy birthday" wish and a gift. What a terrible way to greet a new age. Being ten stinks. No cake, no ice cream, no glove. As Mark slunk toward the stairs and began his climb, he could still hear the guys.

"She's so little."

"She's so cute."

"Her fingernails are so tiny."

Crazy birthday gift.

The weekend came to an abrupt close with a disappointing thud in Mark's heart. The guys spent the weekend lolling around Dad and the baby. They oohed and ahhed and laughed and argued over who would hold her next, or stand at the end of the basket to watch her head-on instead of from the side. Dad sat watching the drama unfold with a permanent goofy smile plastered on his face. And Mom spent the majority of the weekend in her room. No one brought up Mark's birthday again.

The familiar sound of cattle stampeding down the stairs broke the empty silence in the kitchen where Stella poured four bowls of cornflakes. Although she spent most of the weekend alone in her room, she was exhausted. Her movements were slow and took great effort. She dreaded Monday morning, when John went back to work, and the boys went back to school.

She needed a plan—and thought about it all weekend. John was so thrilled about the baby, so Stella hadn't done a thing all weekend. John took it upon himself to make bottles, feed her, burp her, change her, and keep the boys thoroughly entertained. She hadn't touched the baby once. Not at the hospital, and not at home. Her only contact with it had been on the drive home. She held it in her lap, but she never even glanced down at it.

John had gotten up earlier than normal—fed and changed the baby. Then, coming into the bedroom, he patted Stella's back. "She's all yours, Stella. I'll see you this evening. You and Myra have a good day."

While the boys ate their cornflakes, Stella went next door to arrange for the neighbor to watch Billy.

The neighbor was thrilled. "He's such a good boy. No problem at all. Leave him here as long as you need to, Stella. You need time to get to know your new baby, dear."

She brought Billy next door with a grocery sack of clothes and toys and thanked her neighbor for her help. As Stella stepped back inside the house, the boys were scrambling for their jackets and hats.

"Danny, David, you boys go on to school. I need to speak with Mark." Her voice was humorless, and the boys complied without an argument.

Mark looked around, nervously. He started to fidget while he waited for his mom. Was he in trouble for something he did or said? He wanted to walk to school with the guys and not stay home and get bawled out for something he didn't remember doing.

The guys made their usual noisy exit with pushing, shoving, and laughing, and Mark longed to be in the middle of the commotion.

"Take your jacket off, Mark. I need to talk to you." His mother's eyes were flat and lifeless, matching her tone exactly.

Oh boy, this is going to be a long talk. Mark's jaw tensed, but he said nothing as he removed his jacket.

"I'm going to show you how to do some things." She spoke in matter-of-fact tones, as if to a group of strangers. "Pay attention. I don't want to say any of this more than once." She walked to the stove, got a pan, and filled it with water. Then she began to collect objects and set them on the table—glass baby bottles, nipples, evaporated milk, and other things he didn't recognize.

"We'll start with how to make a bottle, while your sister is asleep. She should be waking up pretty soon, and then I'll show you how to feed her and diaper her." Her voice sounded strange and unnatural.

But Mark didn't dare question why she chose now to show him all of this, when she had all weekend, or why she didn't wait until after school. *Man, I'm going to be late for the Pledge of Allegiance, and then I'll be in big trouble with my teacher.*

Stella walked him through the bottle making process, step-by-step. Mark listened closely, absorbing it all. As she finished up her instructions on how to wash the bottles and set them aside to be sterilized, there was a tiny whimper from the other room, then a small cry, and then a loud shriek as Myra made her presence known.

"Okay, grab the bottle. Let's go. I'll show you how to feed her. Then, I'll show you how to diaper her."

Mark followed without a word.

When all the lessons were done, Mark was thoroughly versed on infant care. He could demonstrate proper feeding, burping, diapering, dressing, and rocking techniques. Patting, rubbing, and soothing words were thrown in for good measure.

Stella headed toward the stairs and Mark followed, thinking she would write a note to his teacher explaining his tardiness. She reached the first step and faced him. "Go take care of your sister, Mark," she said in a frost-bitten voice. "I'm going to my room. And, Mark, you don't need to tell your father about this. Do you understand me?"

Clearly. "Yes, Mom. But, I …"

Stella turned and hiked up the stairs, leaving Mark alone and confused.

Chapter Eleven

March 1956

By the end of the week, Mark was exhausted and thoroughly disillusioned with his birthday surprise. All Myra did was eat, sleep, poop, pee, and cry. She was no fun at all—a whole week of school missed for nothing. He never thought he'd ever feel this way, but he couldn't wait to get back. He just didn't know when that would be. The guys probably thought he was sick. After the second day, he didn't even get dressed for school.

Every day was the same as the day before. The guys got up and ate their cornflakes. Then, they grabbed their brown lunch bags and left in a rush. His brown bag stayed in the fridge, for later consumption. Mom would head upstairs, and Mark would be left alone to care for his baby sister.

Occasionally, Mom stepped out of her bedroom—but looking like a fright with mussed hair and red eyes. She rarely said anything. The only bright spot in Mark's day was when Myra took a nap just before the guys got home, and he watched *The Linkletter Show*, from 2:30 p.m. to 3:00 p.m.

On Friday, Mark became so bored, he began looking for things to occupy his time and thoughts. He meandered from room to room, opening drawers and cupboards. In the kitchen, Mark surveyed the pantry, eyes scanning all the canned goods. *Myra must be bored with all that nasty evaporated milk I've been giving her. I'll make her some peas for lunch.*

Mark removed a small saucepan from the cupboard and set it on the burner. With nimble fingers he attached the can opener to the top of the can and twisted the key. He turned with determination, proud of his own clever idea, until the can opener clicked and the top had been sufficiently sliced. He dumped the whole thing in the pan and turned the knob on the stove. Fwop—the flames hit the bottom of the saucepan. Mark turned the flame to low and headed off to get Myra. It was the first time all week he looked forward to feeding her. *She'll love the peas. I'll smash them down so they fit in her little mouth better.*

In the end, Mark was disappointed when Myra refused to eat the peas. She moved her tiny tongue around until they all fell out of her mouth. Then she started to fuss as her hunger grew. He laid her down on the couch and went to the kitchen to whip up another batch of that boring milk before she started to squall.

As Mark was pouring the evaporated milk, he heard something behind him and turned to see his mom standing there watching him. He stared at her for a moment, but before he could say anything, she glanced over at the stove, which still held the pot of peas with the empty can beside it.

"What's that?" She kept her eyes fixed on the can. Mark followed her gaze.

"Oh," he said, chuckling at his own failing. "I thought Myra might be bored with milk, so I gave her some peas, but she …"

Stella's face went from emotionless to frantic in a heartbeat. Her eyes were wild as she turned them back on Mark.

"Peas? You gave that baby peas? Are you trying to choke her?" Stella ran down the hall and grabbed the phone. She shouted into the phone as her panic grew.

Mark stood frozen for a moment. *Holy cow, she's gonna have me arrested.*

"Work—peas—baby—"

"Mrs. Grayson, Stella ... Take a deep breath and calm down. Now, tell me what happened." Dr. Moreno waited as Stella took a breath. She began again, with a little more clarity.

"Mark fed peas to the baby. I was napping, and he fed peas to the baby." Her voice began to raise an octave.

He needed to calm Stella down before hysteria resumed. "Is that baby all right?"

"I don't know," Stella said, panic rising in her voice.

Dr. Moreno sighed and tried to assess the situation. "Mrs. Grayson, is Mark there now?"

"Yes."

"Where's the baby?"

"On the couch, in the parlor."

"Is she breathing?"

Stella burst into tears. "I don't know."

"Mrs. Grayson, put Mark on the phone, and check your baby."

"Mark, come to the phone."

The receiver clanged loudly in the doctor's ear as it collided with the floor. A frightened voice came on the line. "Hello?"

"Mark? This is Dr. Moreno. How are you, buddy?"

"Fine." His voice was small and shallow. He sounded frightened to Dr. Moreno.

"You didn't go to school today?"

"No."

"Are you sick, Mark? Are you feeling run down? You didn't come in for your shot last week."

"I'm okay. Mom kept me home to help with the baby."

"Oh, that's great, Mark. I'm sure you've been a big help. What have you been helping her with?"

"Stuff. You know, like feeding the baby, burping her, and changing her dirty diapers."

There was a pause while Dr. Moreno processed that information. "Your mom has been watching to make sure you are doing everything correctly, hasn't she?"

"Nah, she showed me how to do the stuff, and I've been doing it ever since."

A light went on in Dr. Moreno's head. *Ever since*? "Ever since when, Mark?"

"Monday."

Alarm bells began to ring in the doctor's head.

"What has your mom been doing while you have been helping out?"

"She's been in her room, crying, mostly. She comes out before Dad gets home, to make dinner."

The alarm bells were blaring now, and red lights were flashing like a patrol car. "Mark, where is your mom now? What is she doing?"

Mark glanced down the hall into the living room. "She's sitting on the couch, with the baby in her lap, patting her back, and staring into space."

"Thanks, Mark. You've done a good job helping your mom this week. Go be nice to her, buddy."

Dr. Moreno hung up. He may only be a family doctor, but he stayed current on healthcare issues. As he had originally thought, Mrs. Grayson was manifesting symptoms of a depressive reaction. There had to be a chemical imbalance going on. Her actions warranted further investigation.

He pulled Stella's file and did a quick search. Finding what he was looking for, he picked up the phone. *I need to make John aware of his wife's condition. Depression can be devastating if it goes untreated.*

Who would be calling him at the factory in the middle of the day? John arrived at the phone, not knowing if he was more annoyed at being interrupted off the assembly line, or concerned that something may be wrong with his new baby girl.

"This is John Grayson."

"John, it's Dr. Moreno. I'm sorry to bother you at work. There is something I need to tell you, and I didn't want to wait until you got home."

Dr. Moreno told John about how Stella had kept Mark home all week to take care of the baby, the incident with the peas, and Stella's reaction. "John, I'm concerned about Stella's mental condition. I think she's depressed and you should seek professional help for her. There's a new medication on the market that has had some limited success in treating depression. I could help you find a qualified doctor."

John cut him off before he could go further. He wasn't interested in this doctor mumbo jumbo. He would see to it that Stella's behavior was nipped in the bud right away. "Thanks for the call, Doc. I can take care of it from here."

The doctor paused a moment. "Okay, John, call me if I can do anything to help."

John left work early and arrived at home to find Stella sitting on the couch, baby across her lap, staring forward as Mark attempted to make small talk.

Mark looked up, his eyes full of fear. "Hi, Dad," he said with a trembling voice.

"Mark, put Myra in her basket, then go outside and play." John's jaw clenched tight like a bear trap.

Mark reached for the baby and saw the raw terror on his mother's face as she turned to look at his father. Mark placed Myra in her basket and brushed past his father. He thought he would get a spanking from his dad for giving Myra peas, but his dad hadn't mentioned anything about them. His stony expression frightened Mark, and he grabbed his jacket and hat and was out the door before his dad could change his mind.

The bleak and gray sky reached down to join the piles of cold, grimy snow. The afternoon reflected layers of gloom that covered Mark's thoughts like blankets on a cold night. The frozen air cut through Mark's jacket as a knife through a down pillow. His feelings were piling up inside of him faster than he could push them away. Fear and confusion fought for control in his head. He wanted to make sense of everything that had happened. What were his parents talking about inside? His punishment for giving Myra peas? How did his dad even find out about his mistake? He wished he'd never seen that stupid can of peas.

Mark stopped short and stood frozen as a thought crept into his mind. *Oh, man, I bet Dr. Moreno called Dad. Rats, I'll never get that baseball glove now.*

Kids up the block were walking toward him. David and Danny wouldn't be far behind. He ran to a place in the alley where he couldn't be seen, but could watch them enter the house.

David and Danny got home, and they roared into the house like a miniature riot. Mark stepped out of hiding and opened the door in time to hear them rocketing up the stairs, shouting greetings to their parents. They never even noticed that Dad was home earlier than usual. They never noticed anything.

Reluctantly, Mark stepped in the house and began to peel off his jacket. His father breezed past him without a word about the peas and headed up the stairs.

Halfway up the stairs, his dad stopped. "Look up the number for Angelo's pizza, Mark. I'm going to take a shower now. When I'm done, bring Myra to me."

"Uh, sure, Dad."

Mark headed down the hall toward the phone to get that number out of the telephone book. His discomfort level rose. Why had Dad come home early if it wasn't to spank him for the peas?

With the telephone number tucked inside his pocket, he went to the parlor to get Myra. His mother still sat on the couch, her face turned away. She didn't say anything as he reached into the basket for Myra.

"Mom, I'm sorry about the peas," he blurted, his guilt overwhelming him. "I didn't know she wouldn't like them."

Stella turned her head slowly, deliberately, and stared at Mark, her piercing eyes boring into him like a hot drill.

Mark stared at her in horror. One side of her face was swollen, her eye had puffed up, and her bottom lip was split and bleeding. She said nothing.

Mark felt the blood drain from his face as the realization of what happened roared over him like a monstrous wave. *Holy cow, she thinks I called Dad and told him about our secret.*

Chapter Twelve

July 1958

The summer sun baked the city like a hot pizza oven, causing heat waves to rise from the sidewalk as if emancipated spirits. Mark, the guys, Myra and mom were headed home after an afternoon's swim at the city's public pool.

Myra had been thoroughly delighted and entertained by both the wading pool and Mark, while Stella sat in her lawn chair in the shade. The other boys were at the bigger pool where the lifeguard watched them. But at the wading pool, there was no lifeguard, just the watchful eyes of mothers, and for Myra, Mark.

Mark usually enjoyed his time with Myra. She was a happy baby who made Mark laugh. But today, he really wanted to be in the big pool with the guys. He looked over at his mom sitting in the shade, staring off in the opposite direction. Mark watched her for a long time, hoping to catch her eye so he could make a plea to go to the big pool. She never once looked over at them. He turned his attention back to Myra. At least she was having fun at her first pool adventure. Mark had a strong bond with his little sister, since that week a little over two years ago, when he took care of her. That week changed everything.

His mother never spoke of the incident. She never asked if he called his dad at work, never verbally accused him. But she had treated him like an outcast ever since, trusting him only to take care of Myra and to babysit when the need arose. She spoke to him only when necessary. She made his meals, did the laundry, and all the chores a mother does, but without the warmth and affection that she showed the guys.

"Mark, change your sister's diaper."

"Mark, wash your sister's hands."

"Mark, check on your sister, she's too quiet."

He wondered what his mom did with Myra during the school year when he wasn't home all day to do that stuff for her. Yet, Mark was thankful that Myra was so easy to take care of, easy to amuse, and easy to love.

"Mark, get your sister. Let's go. We have to get home so I can start dinner." His mother folded the lawn chair and headed to the big pool to gather the other boys.

"C'mon, Myra. We have to go home now." Mark reached his hand out to take hers.

Myra snatched her hand back and clasped it against herself. "No. Stay," she said, a pout firmly in place on her chubby face.

"Myra, we have to go." He reached for her hand, again.

"No. Stay." She was not going to go easy.

Mark reached over, took her wrist, and gently pulled her up. She began to cry as he led her to the edge of the pool. She pulled against him and tried to sit back down in the water.

"Stay," she said. "Stay." Her face scrunched up and she began to wail.

"No, Myra. We have to go. Mom needs to get home." Mark pulled her to her towel and wrapped it around her shaking form.

"Stay, Mar'. Stay."

Mark sat down and slipped her little sneakers on her feet.

"P'ease, stay. Stay."

Mark took her hand, and half pulling, half begging, led her out of the gate, toward Mom and the guys.

Billy, Danny, and David strolled ahead, towels draped like superheroes around their shoulders, trunks still dripping with pool water, sneakers squishing softly.

Mom followed at an even pace, encumbered by her lawn chair and her mirthless expression.

Trailing them, Mark had a wailing Myra in tow. He was unsuccessful in his attempts to calm her down. She pulled and tugged and cried and pleaded. "Stay, p'ease, stay."

"Mark, put your sister down for a nap. I'm going to start dinner." His mom brushed by Mark and headed for the kitchen.

He took Myra's hand and led her up the stairs, whimpering all the way to the bedroom. Mark picked her up and set her on his mother's bed, her eyes glassy and red from tears. She reached her chubby arms out to her brother and started to cry softly, spent from her loud, dramatic journey home. "Mar', swim."

Mark wrapped his arms around her. "I know, Myra. You loved the pool. We can go back another day, okay?"

"K." Myra snuggled her face into her brother's shoulder. "Mar', stay."

"Okay, but just for a little while." Mark lay down beside Myra on the bed, rubbing her back gently, humming softly. Myra sniffed a couple of times and fell asleep with a sweet smile.

Mark lingered for a few moments, rubbing Myra's back. He smiled. He liked Myra. She brought a new atmosphere to the family. She was happy and full of spirit. *Like a fresh-baked slice of joy-pie.*

If Myra was in the room, Dad wouldn't hit any of the guys for anything—no matter how angry he got.

Mark rose from the bed and gave Myra a final pat. *You're better than a baseball glove, Myra.*

The marinara sauce bubbled like hot lava on the stove, filling the kitchen with the savory aroma of tomatoes and oregano. Coupled with the garlic bread, it created a sensory banquet of imposing proportions.

Stella inhaled deeply. *So much pleasure with so little effort.* That's why she loved making spaghetti for dinner. She turned the heat down to simmer the sauce slowly and went to check on the kids. As she ascended the stairs, she could hear the boys' decibel level rising and darting out of their room like a racehorse out of the starting gate. She sighed. *Nothing ever changes.*

She entered her room to find the bedspread ruffled, but the bed empty. "Mark!" Stella shouted over the din. "Where's your sister?"

The noise stopped momentarily as Mark popped his head out of the door and yelled back, "Asleep on your bed, Mom."

Stella was already looking around—on the floor, in the closet, down the hall, and in the baby's room. "She's not with you?" her voice returned, annoyed.

"No, Mom. I put her down for a nap, like you said. She fell right to sleep."

Back down the hall Stella bounded, right up to Mark. "She's *not* here."

The edge in her voice must have set Mark in motion. "She's gotta be." He started to search in earnest. "Guys!" Mark shouted over his shoulder. "Help me find Myra!"

The house buzzed as each boy ransacked every nook and cranny in search of Myra.

Stella broke into a cold sweat thinking of what John would do when he got home.

Chapter Thirteen

July 1958

The three boys were scouring the neighborhood looking for their sister. John was on his way home, after Stella scraped up enough courage to call and tell him about the situation. His response froze the telephone wires and gave her ear frostbite. She paced the floor, wringing her hands; her heart was racing like a frenzied rush of wild Mustangs. Billy sat in the middle of the room playing with his trucks. Stella almost paced over the top of him.

"Billy, take your toys up to your room."

He gathered up his trucks and headed for the stairs. At the bottom of the stairs he hesitated a moment, then he started up the stairs, but stopped halfway. "Myra's okay, Mom."

Stella stared after him. She almost smiled at his effort to comfort her.

The front door opened, and John flew in like a storm. His eyes darted back and forth, and seeing Stella in the living room, headed toward her. The determination on his face as he came closer frightened her, and her tears erupted with volcanic force. He halted, and his angry face softened as he walked over to Stella and wrapped his arms around her.

"What happened?"

With great heaving sobs, she explained. "The boys are out looking for her."

The phone rang, startling them both. They glanced nervously at each other.

John quickly picked up the receiver. "Hello?"

"Hey, John, it's Peter Hale."

Peter Hale was on his bowling league. Why was he calling? "I won't be able to make it tonight, Peter. Something's come up."

"No, John. I'm not calling about tonight's game. I'm over here at work. You know, I'm the groundskeeper at the State hospital."

"I really can't talk right now, Peter." John started to pace. "My little girl's missing …"

"That's why I'm calling."

John held his breath.

"I believe I have your little girl here. I was working near the doctor's residences, and I saw her sitting in the sandbox on our little playground. I wouldn't have thought anything of it, except there was no adult with her. So, I went over to investigate. I recognized her from all the photos you shared, John. It pays to be a proud papa!"

"How did she get in?" It didn't make sense! John couldn't fathom what Peter was telling him. "There's a wrought iron fence around the entire property."

Peter chuckled. "The fence is meant to keep mentally ill patients in, not two-year-olds out. She slipped right through the bars."

"Still," John said, "how did she get to the State hospital? It's a half a mile from here. She'd have to cross a busy street."

When Stella heard "State hospital," realization flickered behind her eyes. She gave a little gasp.

"Hold on, Peter." John focused on his wife. "What?"

"We went to the city pool today. Myra didn't want to leave. She cried all the way home. She must have snuck out of the house to go back. We had to pass the State hospital to get there, so when she was passing it, she probably got sidetracked by the little playground inside the fence."

"I'll be right there, Peter." John eyed Stella, but spoke into the phone. "Thanks for calling. We're grateful." He hung up. "Wait here for the boys to get home. I'll get Myra and be right back. Then we'll talk."

Chapter Fourteen

October 1961

Stella pushed open the wooden screen door with her back, and headed toward the clothesline in the backyard with fresh laundry. Despite the unseasonably warm weather, there was mounting evidence that winter was lurking just behind autumn's beauty.

But for now, the maple trees stood in full Fall array with shades of vibrant red, radiant yellow, and golden orange. Every tree was adorned with a palette of colors that danced and swayed as the gentle morning breeze tickled each leaf.

Now that all the children were in school, Stella fell into a daily routine. It seemed her days blended together like cream into coffee. She could have enjoyed her time alone in the city, walking leisurely to the butcher for some nice pork chops or to the bakery for a fresh, warm loaf of bread. She could have spent time with a friend chatting over a cup of coffee. A stroll to the five-and-dime would be a welcome break in her day. But, she couldn't do any of those things here.

Here in this suburban "paradise," where she had to be driven to a grocery store, and where she didn't know most of her neighbors. Where every house on the block looked like every other house on the block, and the only thing that made them unique were the colors the homeowners painted them. Houses of yellow, pink, blue, green, red—whoever heard of such a thing? Rainbow-colored houses separated by driveways, not alleys—and big, sprawling backyards with metal chain-link fences that offered no privacy whatsoever. *What nonsense!*

Stella sighed as she reached into her wicker laundry basket. She pulled out a towel and fastened its corner down on the clothesline with the clothespin. She wished John would buy her a clothes dryer, but she knew he wouldn't. It was only a few months ago she talked him into buying a new washer. Before that she was still using that old washing machine with the wringer attached. She reached for another clothes pin. Her back began to ache.

The last three years had been so lonely, always having to depend on John to take her places. She had no friends and no activities to keep her occupied.

"It's a better neighborhood to raise kids in, Stella," John had insisted. "Especially, Myra. We can't have her wandering off into city traffic like that again."

Stella had given a resigned nod, and with that, she and John went house hunting in the suburbs. Now they lived far away from all she ever knew, all that was familiar and comfortable.

She picked up the last towel, flung it over the clothesline and shoved the clothespin down on it with force. The move had been good for everyone, except her. Tedium impelled her into a wearisome rut. Some days she could barely drag herself out of bed to get the younger kids ready for school. Stella had been both surprised and relieved that Myra wanted to go to school almost as much as Stella wanted her to.

Myra had a puzzled look on her face as she looked at the people around her. Stella noticed her concern, but didn't say anything. This was Myra's first day at school and most of the children had been escorted by their mothers. As they released their children into the care of the teacher, many of the young mothers had tears glistening in their eyes. One mother was openly weeping as she hugged her child close. *How foolish. Let the kid grow up.* Stella had walked Myra as far as she was going to and was ready to turn and walk home.

Myra peered up at Stella. "Why are some of the moms crying?"

Stella sighed. "Because they don't want their children to grow up. They want their children to stay babies forever. So the moms cry when they have to leave them."

"But why?" Myra scrunched up her nose.

"I don't know. It doesn't make sense to me."

"Me neither," Myra said, nodding her head. "I've been waiting my whole life to go to school. I'm glad you're not sad I'm growing up."

Stella's heart stopped for a moment, but she recovered quickly.

It was evident by the spark in her eyes that Myra's spirit of adventure had kicked in. As Myra gazed around the room, Stella could see that eagerness to play shining from her like a beacon.

Myra wrapped her arms around Stella's middle. "Thanks for walking me to school. Gotta go now. I love you, Mom." She dashed across the room to investigate her new surroundings.

Stella left the large, brick building and headed home, befuddled at her own inner conflict. The unwelcome tears brimmed at the corner of her eyes, but she wiped them away before they could spill over and reveal her heart to any prying eyes around her.

As the car made its way down the road, autumn leaves danced and jumped in the evening breeze as if in celebration. John drove in silence while his carpool buddies chattered away about the day's events. Since moving to the suburbs, everything remained the same—the car, the men, the destination—all except the direction he drove.

Hopefully, the move would help improve Stella's attitude. She had an attractive new house with a large yard, and she no longer had to worry about Myra wandering off into the city streets. Cars didn't fly down the streets in the suburbs. The streets were filled with kids—playing kickball, dodgeball, or hide-and-seek—whose parents also found it prudent to move from the city.

The car stopped in front of a house, and one of the passengers got out.

"See you tomorrow," he said. The remaining passengers called their good-byes and John drove on.

"Hey John, heard your boy tried out for the soccer team at school."

John nodded. "Yeah."

"Hope he makes it."

"Yeah." John hoped having Mark on the team and away from home more would dispel some of the strain between Mark and his mom. The mounting tension affected the entire family. But, John was at a loss for why Stella was still edgy with *him*. After all, wasn't he a good husband who worked hard and brought his paycheck home every week? He bought her a new house and was meeting her needs by providing for the family.

She wasn't meeting his needs, though. At night she acted like a guard dog behind a fence, growling and ready to snap at him if he dared reach out to her. John sighed. He was willing to try whatever he could to improve his wife's attitude. *I wish she'd meet me half way.*

Chapter Fifteen

September 1962

The horror of the memory stung Mark like an angry wasp disturbed from its nest. He closed his eyes as the burning spread through him slowly. The textbook before him yielded to the past.

"You're not my real mother," fourteen year old David said, with his arms crossed across his chest and his jaw jutting.

Startled into silence around the dinner table, everyone stared at David in shock. Mom's face blanched in horror.

Dad groped for words but before he could find them, David continued with his well-rehearsed speech. "Mrs. Rojek told me being adopted means you're not my real mother. My real mother would buy me anything I wanted."

Mom found her words "I've fed you and diapered you, clothed you and loved you, David. I can't be any more a real mother than that."

Mark looked at David for his reaction. David's eyes didn't even blink at Mom's obvious pain. He had, no doubt, planned this attack for some time. It had been at least a week since David visited Michael Rojek's house.

"You're not my real mother. We don't even look alike. You can't tell me what to do anymore." David stood, pushing the chair with such force that it toppled backwards to the floor. He stepped past it with slow deliberate steps, almost daring someone to stop him. No one did. After that, David began to get into serious trouble on a regular basis, until he was finally and permanently removed from the home, and the family he staunchly maintained wasn't his "real family," and placed in a facility.

The "guys" were officially reduced by one, leaving Mark and Danny to face the remainder of their teenage years without him.

Mark sat in his room and stared at the page for a long time, trying to separate the words into sentences, but the words blended together like watercolors. The haze held with tenacious vigor and began to spread. It moved over the pages of the textbook to the surface of the desk, continued to the edge, and slid down and across the floor until it consumed the entire room. Mark sat still as the fog surrounded him, unaware of its presence, while he listened to the drone of voices downstairs. The louder the voices, the deeper the blur became, until the voices were angry shouts, and the fog threatened to engulf him into the quicksand of oblivion.

The bedroom door opened, and the foggy mist was swept out of the room like a river over the edge of a waterfall. Mark looked up; Danny stood there, staring. He felt the sudden need to gasp for air, as if he had held his breath in the fog.

"Hey, Mark. How long have they been going at it?"

"I don't know. Pretty much since I came up here to study. Where's Myra?"

"I think she's at her friend's house. But she should be home any minute. It's almost dark. Want me to go get her?"

"Uh, I … Yeah that would be great, Danny. Bring her up here. Tell her I have a new song I want to sing to her." Mark was regaining his focus. Danny left, and the arguing downstairs continued. Upstairs, the churning in Mark's gut grew more intense with each angry word.

A few short minutes later, Mark heard Danny and Myra coming through the back door. Myra was all a flutter about the new song, jabbering loud and nonstop. At the sound of her voice, there was a brief pause in the arguing, one last angry slam of the door, and the shouting ceased. Mark took a deep breath, relief spreading over him like candle wax.

Myra burst in. “Is it Johnny Mathis? Is it, Mark? Sing it for me.”

Mark smiled at her, in spite of his churning emotions. “Yeah, it’s Johnny Mathis. Of course, it is,” he said laughing. “It’s called *Gina*.”

Mark began to sing to Myra, and her infectious smile spread sunshine through the once blurry bedroom. As he sang, he pondered the collapse of his family. *Whenc had everything fallen apart?* Had Myra been the cause of all this family turmoil, or a welcome relief from it?

Mom and Dad’s fights, the tension between him and his parents, and David’s permanent removal from the home had all taken its toll on everyone but Myra. Even Danny and he—the remaining “guys”—had suffered their share of petty arguments. His life would almost be normal if he could just filter it through the guileless eyes of his little sister. Myra, alone, seemed unaffected by the strain that regularly surged through the house like billowing ocean waves.

“Mark,” Myra said, clasping her hands in front of her, “that was really a great song. I loved it. Teach it to me.”

So, line by line, Mark took her through the lyrics. Myra, content to have his attention, shined in her brother’s presence. Before the lesson was complete their mother shouted up the stairs, “Myra, come down and set the table for dinner.”

Myra stood up to leave. “We’ll finish later, Mark. I have to set the table for Mom.” Her glow never diminished, and as she headed for the stairs, she left a trail of sparkles shimmering behind her. Mark couldn’t help but smile after her. Her joy was contagious.

Mark’s steps were light and carefree as he made his way home from school Friday. The slight autumn chill was refreshing and welcome after sitting in classes all day. When the bell had finally rung, he dashed to the locker room to check if his name was on the list posted. There he was. His name was on the list. He made the team! Practice started on Monday after school—five days a week. It was going to be great, and he couldn't wait to tell everyone at home.

At dinner, Mark waited until there was a slight lull in the conversation. "I made the soccer team!" he blurted out his good news. "I start practice on Monday after school." He waited for the verbal applause.

His father gave him a slight nod and a half smile.

Danny gave his arm a slight punch. "I knew you would make it, Mark."

Billy said nothing at all.

His mom's expression never changed. She remained unmoved and remote. "Guess that means you won't be home for dinner," she said in a distant tone. "I'll put the leftovers on the stove. You can eat them when you get home."

Myra, however, sat her fork down, her eyes widened, and her contagious smile spread across her face. "Wow, Mark. That's really neat. Wow. Cool. You're going to be on the soccer team." Enthusiasm dripped off her, like ice cream down a cone on a hot August afternoon. "Wow, Mark." Her smile remained fixed as she paused a moment. "Mark, what's soccer?"

Chapter Sixteen

October 1962

The autumn wind swirled around Mark's head, kissing his sweat-soaked skin, cooling it with an unfamiliar tenderness. He made his way toward home with building reluctance. Soccer practice was hard, exhausting work, and Mark was so thankful to be a part of it. It gave him sweet relief from his strained existence at home. His footsteps slowed to delay his arrival and survey the neighborhood. He was content to live here. Overall, the move from the city to the suburbs had been good. Many new friends were made, although Mark still missed a handful of friends from his city-dwelling days. Mark wished he could go see them. Maybe after his driver's license arrived.

Turning up his driveway, Mark approached the back door. He heard his dad's angry voice inside. *Now what? Who's getting berated this time?*

Reluctantly, Mark entered the back door, his heart about to pound out of his chest, and stood watching the scene at the kitchen table unfold.

"Read the sentence, Billy." His dad's impatient voice blared through the house like a foghorn.

Billy stared at the words on the page, his face awash with fear.

"Read-the-sentence." Dad repeated with punctuated anger.

Exasperation filled Billy's voice. "I can't."

"I said, read it." Dad's voice was clipped and irritated. Without warning, he slapped Billy's face and tears welled in Billy's eyes. Shame and embarrassment spreading across his face like a plague.

Mark burst into the room. "Oh, that's great, Dad. Slap his face—that'll help him read the words better."

His dad's eyes darted to Mark with manic speed. "Mind your own business, Mark," he spat out.

"I *am* minding my business. You can't just bully someone into learning. Billy has trouble understanding the letters, and beating him isn't going to help. What's next, Dad? You gonna beat Myra for reciting nursery rhymes wrong?"

Dad flew out of his chair with such force, it went crashing into the wall behind him. Mark bolted up the stairs like lightning and stood just out of sight on the landing. His father wouldn't attempt to climb the stairs. It would aggravate the pain in his knees. Mark heard his father walk back to the table, slam the textbook shut, and say, "Go, get ready for bed."

As Billy hiked up the stairs, Mark slipped quietly into his and Danny's bedroom and shut the door part way. Billy walked into his room and closed the door. Mark could hear him crying for a long time. It was the last time Billy cried. After that, his usual sweet nature became sullen, and eventually, rebellious.

The house was quiet and still. The kids were in school, and Stella finished all of the chores she intended to do.

The laundry was washed and hung out to dry in the sun. When Mark got home, he could take them down and fold them. It was about time he taught Myra how to do that job. He'd already taught Myra how to dust the furniture and dry the silverware and put them away. Mark dried the dishes and glasses, because Myra wasn't tall enough to reach the cupboards they went in. Everything Myra needed to learn, Mark was capable of teaching her, and Stella let him. Myra loved all her brothers, but she had a special connection with Mark right from the beginning.

Myra hadn't been as difficult as Stella imagined. She was easy to please, and mostly obedient. Stella reached for her coffee, struggling with her thoughts—Yes, Myra was fun.

She carried the coffee to the living room and set it on the end table. *Maybe I'll see what's on TV.* She turned it on, and stood there a minute while the TV warmed up, memories of Myra drifted through Stella's mind like a wispy vapor. She lit on thoughts like a butterfly on blossoms.

Stella remembered Myra as a baby, then as a toddler, and the funny things she'd said or done, and times she made everyone laugh with her quirky personality. More and more recollections came to her until they became a thick fog of barely recognizable nostalgia. The sound of the TV caught her attention, and she set her thoughts aside like a discarded old novel on a dusty bookshelf.

With the house straightened and dinner on the stove, she picked up her knitting, sat down in her chair, and put her feet up. She divided her attention between the game show on TV, and the gentle clicking of the knitting needles as her fingers moved in sharp, even gestures. She glanced at her watch. Myra would be home from school in an hour, then Billy, and then the older boys. She had a little time to relax before the flurry began.

The day's activities were catching up with her. The drone of the TV and the clicking of the knitting needles blended in a rhythmic cadence. Stella's eyes narrowed in the lazy afternoon lull, and the clicking stopped as her hands rested motionless in her lap. Only the TV remained alive—a dull buzz of laughter, applause, and commercial jingles. She remained motionless until the wooden screen door slammed and jarred her awake.

Myra's home. Time to get moving. She can set the table.

Billy walked in, startling her.

"Where's Myra?" Stella said as she rubbed her eyes.

"Dunno," Billy said walking passed her.

Stella jerked her arm up to inspect her watch. "She should have been home an hour ago. Isn't she with you?"

"No." He kept walking.

Stella bolted from her chair and dashed down the hall toward Myra's bedroom.

"Myra!" Her bed was sloppily made, and toys and clothes were strewn around in their usual disarray. For the first time, the mess didn't bother Stella—only her daughter's absence.

"Did you see her at school?" Stella called to Billy as he climbed the stairs.

He didn't turn or slow down. "No."

Frantic, Stella dashed to the phone and made a couple of calls to see if Myra was at a neighbor's house. After Stella yelled at her the other day for slamming the screen door and startling her awake from her late afternoon doze, Myra may have slipped in, and seeing Stella asleep, left so she wouldn't disturb her. *Or, maybe someone kidnapped her. You hear about that on the news all the time.*

Stella anxiously searched her address book for the name of someone who may know where Myra was.

The screen door banged shut, and Danny and Mark entered the house, engrossed in a conversation and laughing about an incident at school. They stopped short when they saw her sitting at the table, address book before her, crying.

Danny rushed to her. "Mom, what's wrong? What happened?"

"Myra isn't home from school yet." Mark glanced at the clock. "It's two hours past the time she normally gets home, and Dad will be here in less than an hour."

Danny wrapped his arms around his mom. "Don't worry, Mom. We'll find her. Won't we, Mark?"

Mark nodded, and out the door they flew like the Hardy Boys on a mystery adventure.

The chorus of birds sang from their telephone-wire choir loft. The spring breeze carried their melody and gently filled the air with sweet music. It swelled in Myra's heart like the Vienna Boys Choir, filling her with peaceful joy, just like in the movie she saw.

A smile spread across her face at the beauty of new life that appeared after the cold winter melted into spring. Everything seemed so new and clean and fresh and worthy to enjoy with wonder. She hummed with the birds, content to be alive. She had a good day. Her friend Cheryl had invited her to a Brownie meeting last week and she looked forward to the adventure all day. It was more fun than she had thought it would be. When she got home, she would ask her mom if she could join the Brownies.

She spotted Mark running toward her, and she dashed in excitement to meet him and tell him all about her Brownie adventure, the bird choir, and her wonderful day. It was a rare occasion she could share such pleasant news with someone on her way home. She didn't know where to begin—the Vienna Boy's bird choir, or the Brownie meeting.

She approached her brother, happy and out of breath. "Mark, Mark, guess what? I went to Brownies with Cheryl—and we—"

"Where've you been, Myra?" His face was frozen in place.

Myra was puzzled for a moment. "I just said I was at Brownies. Cheryl invited—"

"Mom is pretty worried."

Confused, Myra stated, "I told Mom last week Cheryl invited me to—"

"She probably forgot. She's really worried. She sent me and Danny out to find you before Dad got home."

"But, Mark. I told Mom." Myra held up her hands as if pleading.

"She forgot. Let's go home," he said with a soft voice soft and a slight smile.

The delight in Myra's heart burst, sending fragments of disappointment tumbling into her belly and filling her with panic. "But Mark … I *told* Mom."

Mark gave a knowing nod and put his hand on the back of her head to lead her home. "You probably did, Myra. Let's go."

Tears brimmed around the rims of Myra's eyes and spilled over, running down her cheeks and washing away the pleasure of her adventure with them.

"Where have you been?" Her mother's voice was at least loud enough for half the block to hear. The other half would hear about it from someone else.

"I went to the—"

"Why didn't you call me?"

"I told you last—"

"I've been worried sick."

"I thought you—"

"What were you thinking going off like that?" Her mother's voice shook.

"Mom, I told you last week about the Brownies," Myra cried out, exasperated at her mother's interruptions. "You said I could go." Hot tears were flowing down Myra's face.

Her mom paused for a moment. "Was that today? Why didn't you remind me? Go to your room." Her hard words weighed heavy on Myra's heart.

Myra turned and walked away. Looking behind her, she saw her mom rubbing her temples. "Sorry, Mom. I didn't mean to worry you."

Stella glared at her, and headed toward the kitchen.

Myra went to her room and cried whisper-soft tears so she wouldn't make her mom's headache worse. Her dream of joining the Brownies soaked into her pillow, leaving behind damp, salty stains.

Chapter Seventeen

April 1963

Exhilarated, Mark made his way downtown to see his old friends in his brand-new used car. For months he had saved a large portion of his paycheck from his part-time job at the restaurant. When the woman across the street put a "For Sale" sign on her 1960 red Corvair, he spoke with her. They haggled for a while, and in the end he paid more than he wanted, but the car was his. His car!

Mark had seen his buddies on a couple of occasions when Mom and Dad went to the city to visit their old friends, and a couple of times at sporting events, when their schools competed. But now he was alone, in his own car, and he was *cool.*

He parked half a block from the diner where they were meeting. For the first time in months, he was free from the oppression at home. Mark took a deep breath and blew it out, releasing all the tension, stress, and worry that had followed him for months—for years. It felt liberating. He walked toward his destination with each step lighter than the previous one, as if dropping the chains of his past along the way. He even wore a smile.

As he approached the entrance to the diner, he looked in and saw a group of his buddies sitting at a booth. He started to raise a hand of greeting when he heard his name called. He looked toward the voice and saw Dr. Moreno.

"Mark Grayson—I thought that was you. How are you?" The doctor offered his hand, and Mark slowly reached for it.

"Hello, Dr. Moreno" he said, in his most polite voice. "I'm well, thank you." *I'm terrific, now that I have that cool car.*

"How is your family, Mark? I haven't seen them since you moved to the suburbs. What has it been now, five, six years?" The doctor took no breath and left no time for Mark to reply. "How is your mom doing? Is your dad well?"

With the patience of Job, Mark waited for his chance to speak. His smile remained fixed.

"How is your family doing?" Dr. Moreno repeated the question, slowing his pace for Mark.

My mom is distant and cold and suffers from migraine headaches regularly. She hasn't looked at me with anything like love since I spoke to you on that day I gave Myra peas to eat. My dad is frustrated with sleeping in separate beds and is angry all the time. Half the time he takes his anger out on me and the guys—unless Myra's there. Thank God for Myra.

And Myra's a pretty spunky kid for someone whose mom didn't want to take care of her when she came home from the hospital. She's happy and loving and hardly notices her mom's cold heart, or her inattentiveness, or her short temper. She laughs and sings and says the funniest things. She's like an Oreo cookie filled with joy.

"Fine." Mark smiled politely at Dr. Moreno.

At Mark's answer, Dr. Moreno hesitated, and smiled. "Well, I'm glad it all worked out. I always hated doing that type of abortion. I'm glad the nurse found her crying in the morgue that morning. It all turned out for the best."

With an abruptness that slapped him off-balance, the air became thin and difficult to breathe, like the atmosphere on Mount Everest. He attempted to process the doctor's words through his limited understanding of the night Myra was born. His face became hot—then cold. He reached up to feel it. *Am I still smiling? I can't tell.*

The doctor's confession whirled around in Mark's head like an unexpected ocean squall. Torrents of unspoken words washed over him in an emotional melee, threatening to drown him. Mark dropped his hand from his face, determined to remain nonchalant. He forced a contrived smile across his face and started to move away from the doctor. *I should say something …*

"Um, yeah, uh good to see you, again. Um, thanks … Yeah. I, uh …" He cleared his throat to give his thoughts time to catch up with his mouth. "Did you, uh, call Dad at work the day Mom called you about the peas?"

"Oh, sure. I felt he should know what was going on. I told him your mom was suffering from depression and needed more support than you could offer her by staying home from school to help with the baby."

Mark gave a slight nod, and he turned toward his car and walked away, dragging the storm's destruction and rubble with him.

March 1964

The auditorium buzzed like a swarm of frenzied bees returning to the hive. Myra sat with anticipation, her enthusiasm unabated. Flanked on either side by her parents, she was in a world all her own. It was the first time she was in the auditorium of the high school where all the big kids went to school. Her eyes darted around, taking in every detail. She didn't want to miss a thing. Red velvet fold-down chairs—like at the movies—and a red velvet curtain on the stage. The high ceiling, slanted floor, and noisy auditorium contributed to her wonder and excitement. With every new sight she took in, she sighed, gasped, or pointed it out to her mom and dad.

"Myra, sit still," her mother said.

"Okay." Myra craned her head around to look behind her. "Mom, look at the—"

"Myra, sit still." Her mom put her hand on Myra's shoulder to tug her down.

People coming in from the side of the auditorium were all dressed in black, and they headed toward the very front of the stage.

Myra pondered their entrance. "They'll have to move the chairs around if they want to see." She was concerned for their viewing pleasure. "Look, most of the chairs are facing each other."

"Shhhhh." Her mom glared at her.

"That's the orchestra," her dad said.

"Ohhhh." Myra nodded her understanding. She spied a gentleman in a fancy, black suit with a shiny, wide belt and ruffled shirt. "Oh, I like that man's blouse," she blurted.

Her mother scowled as those around her chuckled.

The lights in the auditorium went out, leaving only the orchestra lights on. The man in the ruffled blouse stood on a box and tapped a stick on the bookstand in front of him. As he raised his hands to his side, the orchestra picked up their instruments. The man on the box moved his arms, and the orchestra began.

As the notes mixed together and blended into a beautiful song, it transported Myra to an unfamiliar, emotional place. She had often *heard* music, but Myra had never *seen* music, and she was enraptured by its ability to move her.

The music ended, the big red velvet curtain opened, and the scene began. Myra's heart raced like a wild stallion across a meadow as she sat enthralled with the action, waiting for her brothers to appear on stage.

Nothing escaped her attention. She loved the colorful costumes, the hairstyles, even the makeup the boys wore. She was captivated by the way everyone stood on stage and spoke with loud, clear voices. She wasn't just watching a musical, she was experiencing an event. When the auditorium filled with laughter, she was delighted. When the audience clapped, she was thrilled. And when her brothers walked out on stage, she squealed with glee.

At the end of the musical, all the actors appeared on stage one or two at a time, while the audience clapped and clapped. When the last two actors came out—the ones with the most lines—the audience clapped louder, then stood up, and clapped even longer.

Myra looked around at the faces of everyone she could. They were so happy, smiling, and clapping. The thrill of it spread through Myra like hot chocolate on a cold winter morning.

She nodded her head at her own inner determination. *I want to do that when I get to high school. I want to make people laugh and clap when I stand on stage and act and sing. I want to make people this happy. I want people to like me this much.*

Chapter Eighteen

August 1964

Stillness settled over the house like dust on an abandoned swing set. Stella cherished the silence. Myra had been in bed for several hours. Her rhythmic breathing was like a far-off melody to Stella. It was not loud enough to disturb the quiet, but just loud enough to soothe her weary soul, and she relaxed with her knitting in front of the barely audible TV. She looked forward to her time with Johnny Carson. While the family slept, *The Tonight Show* became Stella's nightly escape from the day's clamor. She luxuriated in the solitude. Alone. Peaceful.

Laughter from Myra's room startled Stella.

What was that girl doing in there? She should be asleep. *She's going to wake her father with all that ruckus. I'm going to box her ears.*

With one swift movement, Stella set her knitting needles aside and sprang to her feet. She strode to the bedroom and stood at the entrance of Myra's room, listening to her laugh. With a quick, angry motion, Stella flipped on the hall light.

The light fell across the bedding and beamed on Myra, illuminating her mirthful face. Her eyes were closed, and her sprawled body appeared relaxed—Myra was asleep.

Stella, her mouth open, watched her daughter for a moment. Laughter bubbled out of Myra like fresh, sweet water from a mountain spring.

Good grief, that child has so much happiness, it spills out of her even while she's asleep. Stella shook her head, bemused, and walked away, leaving Myra laughing in the dark.

The sweet scent of lilacs drifted through the window, filling the room with its delicate fragrance. Each gentle breeze caressed Myra like a soothing embrace. She sat motionless by the window, watching the birds pick at the chunks of stale breadcrumbs tossed there by her mom. Her mother did that every few days after she gathered the loaves' discarded end pieces. The birds waited with unwavering patience until she walked away, then they swooped down and enjoyed the feast. Most days Myra enjoyed their antics, but today she longed to sprout wings and fly away like the little sparrows.

Things were changing. Mark was getting ready to leave for college, Danny was starting his last year of high school, and Billy didn't seem to like her anymore. Being eight years old is hard work. Myra sighed. *Nobody really needs me here. I could probably fly away with those birds and no one would ever miss me.*

She got up to go to Brenda's house and dashed passed her mom. "See ya, Mom. I'm going to Brenda's house."

Myra bounced down the street past all the colorful houses—red, yellow, blue, green. She loved them. They were prettier than the gray houses in the city. She greeted each neighbor she saw.

"Hi, Mrs. Crandall. Pretty flowers."

"Hello, Mrs. Fox—nice day, huh?"

"Hey, Mrs. McNiece—how's your new puppy?"

"Good morning, Mrs. Lauranzano. How's Sofia? Tell her "hi" for me."

Down the block and around the corner she flew like a summer breeze through a wind chime, putting her blue mood behind her for the promise of laughter and merriment.

The fusty scent of hay hung heavy in the air. Mark tried to ignore the smell, but it was tenacious in its ability to interrupt his requisite slumber. He rolled over in an attempt to avoid it, but was unsuccessful. The odor permeated the entire barn with such intensity, Mark bolted upward. He lingered a moment in his thoughts.

He should be sleeping in a dorm room with his buddies, not in this smelly barn. But once again, his plans had been waylaid by his dad. Mark's anger still burned at yesterday's memory.

"Mark, you need to get a job this summer to save money for college," his dad had told him.

"Sure, Dad." Mark had already planned on seeing a restaurant manager about a busboy position that afternoon. "And when you find a job, bring me your paycheck, and I'll give you some spending money."

Mark had agreed, believing his money would be put aside for school in the fall, and he'd still have a few bucks in his pocket for gas and dates.

Mark worked hard five days a week, the entire summer. In the fall, he was ready for college, both mentally and financially. According to his calculations, he'd saved enough money to last the entire semester. He thought he might get a part time job at school to help pay for the second semester.

He went to his dad. "Okay, I'm ready for my college money."

"What money?" Dad said.

"The money you've been saving for me for college, Dad."

"I wasn't saving that money for you, Mark. That was your room and board. I gave you $20 a week to save for school."

Heat rushed into Mark's face. "You're joking!"

"No, I'm not," his father responded coldly.

A thousand thoughts ran through Mark's mind, but none of them found their way to his mouth. The intense anger choked the words in his throat before they ever made it to his tongue.

He glared at his father, then stomped up the stairs, went to his room, and grabbed his suitcase from the closet. He flung some clothes in it, collected all the money he had—$15.28—and went back down. His mother stood at the bottom and looked from his angry expression to the suitcase. The color faded from her face.

"Mark, don't leave like this." She pulled his arm as he walked away.

"I'm leaving for college, Mom."

She followed him to the door. "We'll work something out."

He stopped abruptly and turned to look at her. "I *thought* I had worked something out at the beginning of summer when I took that job. Looks like I was wrong—again!"

Mom opened her mouth, but nothing came out. A single tear escaped from the corner of her eye and ran down her cheek. "I'll talk to your dad," she said, her voice tight and choked.

"It's too late for that, Mom. Way too late." He turned to leave.

Desperately, she reached out for him. "Wait, what about Myra?"

Mark took in a slow, controlled breath. "What about her?"

"Aren't you going to say good-bye to your sister?"

"I'll see her before I go," he said as he went out the wood-framed screen door, letting it slam in his mother's face.

Mom let out a single sob.

Mark never looked back.

Mark brushed the hay from his clothes, now. He'd driven most of the day and was tired when he arrived at this small farming community at dusk. The college was not much farther up the road, but he was exhausted. He'd seen the barn close to the road and stopped. He was pretty sure whatever animals inhabited that barn wouldn't mind having an overnight guest. He slept fitfully and woke even more exhausted, but he needed to get to college. He also needed to find a job.

He promised Myra a letter as soon as he arrived. He'd have to find time for that too. He sighed. *Myra*. Mark felt like he abandoned her. He'd found her walking home from her friend's house, and their conversation hadn't been easy.

"Hey, Mark, where ya goin'?" she said, stepping over to his car when he pulled up.

"Get in, Myra. I need to talk to you."

Instantly thrilled to be invited into Mark's cool car, Myra opened the door and jumped in.

"I'm leaving for college, Myra."

"I know," she said with a giggle.

"No, I mean, *now*."

Myra's face registered her confusion and alarm. "Now? Why? Mark you can't leave now."

"I have to, Myra."

"But why, Mark?"

Mark was reluctant to burden his little sister with the details. She wouldn't understand anyway. She has never really seen their parents in the same light as he has. Never seen their father beat them, or belittle them or shame them. She is a gift that God sent to ease the ever-present tension in the home. When Myra was around, the family dynamics were completely different-almost bearable.

"I need a job before the semester starts."

"But, Mark," she said, "We planned a going away party for you. All our cousins and your friends will be there, and Danny will barbecue, and Mom will make her Jell-O gelatin with fruit cocktail in her pretty glasses with the stem—just like Christmas time—and I'm …" She considered her role in the party. "I'm going to sing a song for you."

Mark smiled at her offer. "Sorry, Myra. I really can't stay."

A shadow crossed Myra's face. "But, Mark, I'll miss you."

"I'll miss you too. But, you'll still have Danny and Billy at home."

She gave a slight nod, as tears stung her eyes.

"Billy doesn't talk to me much. Danny's busy with his last year at the big school."

Mark nodded his understanding. He hadn't meant to make her sad. "But Myra, Danny's got the four Bobbys." She looked puzzled for a moment, and Mark reminded her of Danny's favorite singers. Myra brightened. "Yeah, Mark. I can sing with all the Bobbys." She lifted her hand as she ticked off each name for Mark's benefit. "Bobby Daren, Bobby Vee, Bobby Rydel, and Bobby Vinton. He'll let me listen to his records, won't he, Mark?"

"Sure he will, Myra."

"Good morning. Did my cows behave themselves last night?"

Mark whirled around and saw a farmer standing in the doorway of the barn.

Chapter Nineteen

September 1964

Perspiration beaded up on Mark's face like condensation on a glass of iced tea. He felt the color change on his face, although he wasn't sure if he was pale with fear, or red with embarrassment. His mouth gaped open, wordless, like an ever-growing sinkhole.

The farmer wore an amused smile.

"You a college student, son?"

Mark nodded. Good guess.

"You need a place to stay and a job?"

Confused, Mark nodded. Very good guess.

The farmer chuckled. "That your beat-up, old Corvair on the side of the road?"

Mark was offended by the terms "beat-up" and "old" used in reference to his cool car, but decided not to press the issue. Besides, as of yet, no words found their way out of his brain to trickle down to his mouth. He gave a third mute nod.

The farmer stepped forward and offered his hand to Mark. "Name's Tennyson Acre. My friends call me Tenn. This is my place, The Tenn Acre Farm."

Mark's processing ability slowed down considerably, with all the words backing up in his head with no escape route. He shook the farmers hand without a word.

"Been looking for some part-time help with some simple chores, since the Mrs. got injured last week."

Mark raised a questioning eyebrow in response.

"Cow got spooked. Kicked Marjorie square in the face while she was milkin' her. Never saw a cow move so fast. The impact knocked my wife off her stool and injured her neck and shoulder. First time in forty years of marriage Marjorie's been unable to do her chores."

The words were piling up behind Mark's tongue like rush hour traffic behind a fender bender.

The farmer continued as if he were being interviewed by some big city journalist. "I met her in college. Graduated from the same college you're goin' to."

Mark's thoughts were pushing themselves forward in slow-motion. *A degree in farming?*

"I know what you're thinkin'. I didn't go to college to learn farmin'. Everything I needed to know about farmin', I learned from my father. I went to school to learn business. Farmin' is big business—not like in my father's day. This old barn belonged to him. It's Marjorie's now."

He gestured around the barn like a tour guide at the Smithsonian. "Her cow for milkin', and her chickens for eggs. Got a goat for cheese and a pig for … I don't know what, cause she won't never make that pig into a ham. Yeah, this is all Marjorie's. I call it Marjorie's "Play Farm Barn." She's even got a garden patch for vegetables and fruit. Naw, this isn't my farm, the real farmin' goes on elsewhere. That farm is sizeable. I have a number of employees, but can't spare them for Marjorie's Play Farm."

The farmer's words warmed Mark inside, and his impacted words began to melt and flow past the bottleneck. "Mark Grayson," he said, reaching his hand to Tenn.

The farmer grinned, grabbed Mark's hand, and shook it vigorously. "Good to meet ya, Mark."

Mark cleared his throat to remove any lingering word backlogs. "So, you need help?"

Tenn chuckled. "Yes, yes, I do." He slapped Mark on the back. "Come on, let's go meet Marjorie. She can still cook up a mean breakfast."

October 1966

The war in Vietnam meant nothing to Myra, because she didn't watch the news. At ten years old, she preferred to watch *That Girl*, or *The Monkees*. Even watching her mom's favorite show with her—*The Ed Sullivan Show*—was better than watching the boring news. Sometimes while waiting for real TV shows to begin, she sat in front of the news with her mom, but eventually her eyes frosted over like a couple of glazed doughnuts.

Her parents never spoke of the war. Her friends and she never had a reason to discuss it, and no one she knew was in the war. Until now.

Danny was in college now, but Mark had dropped out after his second year. He got tired of trying to study and keep a paying job at the same time. He felt he could learn more in the Air Force.

"I'll write to you all the time, Mark," Myra said, sadness tugging at the corners of her smile. "I'll see you when you get back from the war." Her eyes stung with tears as she hugged his neck, not wanting to let go.

"Be good," Mark whispered in her ear. "I'll miss you."

Myra watched through the terminal window as Mark's plane taxied down the runway. Then it slowly rose into the air and out of sight. Myra's heart ached.

October 1968

Myra stood at the entrance of the school library, gawking at the rows of books. *I had no idea there were so many books in the world.* She was no longer a little girl, she was practically an adult. She didn't go to the elementary school down the block anymore. She was now a seventh-grader in junior high school and she was beginning to see life in a different way. *I really miss the elementary school. It was easier.*

She didn't live in blissful seclusion any longer, now she was getting an education on what lay beyond her small corner of life. Most of what she learned didn't set well inside her delicate heart. Already this year she'd learned about stuff like demonstrations, rallies, protests, assassinations and the need for peace talks. The world was an ugly place, and the year wasn't even over.

Every morning she walked the one-mile journey to the junior high school with her best friend, Brenda. Sometimes they talked about current events, but most of the time they discussed the cute boys in their classes.

"I got a letter from Mark yesterday," Myra said.

"Oh, good. I know you were worried 'cause you haven't heard from him in a while. Is he okay?"

"Yeah, he said he was in Vietnam for several months. Then, he went back to his base in the Philippines. He says he'll be going back and forth between the two locations as long as they need him." Myra paused for a moment, watching her feet move automatically from one spot on the sidewalk to the next. "Danny's leaving college. He's joining the army." Myra's voice was stiff as a new pair of penny loafers. Brenda looked at Myra with a stunned expression. "My mom is pretty upset," Myra added. That was a poor description of her mother's emotions, but she knew Brenda understood her unspoken words as well as anything she could have verbalized.

Brenda nodded. She was the only person Myra shared her personal stuff with. Together they shared secrets, disappointments, victories, crushes, dreams, and gossip. No one at home understood Myra or had time for her. Her mother was too busy worrying about the boys, her father was too busy coaching his soccer teams, and her brother Billy was too busy avoiding everyone.

Mark was her buddy, but he was in the Air Force. Danny always treated her with love and respect, but he was leaving her for the army. *I'm glad Brenda's my friend and is willing to listen to me when stuff bothers me.*

A flood of disturbing memories filled Myra's head, diverting her attention from her conversation with Brenda and her journey to school. One painful incident she remembered had happened while she was at Brenda's house.

Brenda's mom cracked open the door to Brenda's bedroom. "Myra, your mom is on the phone."

At the mention of her mom, Myra's heart went cold with fear. She gasped and looked at Brenda.

"What?" Brenda said with alarm.

"I forgot my mom told me to watch the pot of sauce on the stove. I only came over here to get that book from you and …" They'd gotten caught up talking about the cute boys in their class.

The two of them went to the phone.

"Hello?" Myra's voice trembled with fear.

Her mom's voice blared through the phone with uncensored harshness. "I asked you one simple thing—watch and stir the meatballs and sauce so they don't burn while I rest my eyes. And you run over to your friend's house the first chance you get. You never think of anyone but yourself, Myra. You never think of me or how I feel. You are thoughtless and selfish. The meatballs are burnt to the bottom of the pot. Get home right now."

Myra was ready to hang up and run home immediately, but she couldn't hang up on her mother, who continued to rant, belittling and berating her until tears formed in her eyes. Her mother finally stopped spewing hurtful words and hung up. Myra's vision blurred from the tears she couldn't hold back.

"Wow. That was a little harsh for burning the sauce." Brenda had probably heard every word.

"No, Brenda. I told my mom I would watch dinner while she tried to get rid of one of her sick headaches. Then I came over here for that book and forgot. It's my fault. I completely deserve it." With shoulders slumped, Myra turned to leave for home to face her consequences.

November 1969

Myra discovered poetry. It crept up on her without warning and batted her into submission like a kitten with a ball of yarn.

She yielded herself to the utter ecstasy of the words. She loved the way she could put thoughts on a page that expressed her innermost feelings. It had a healing effect. The words grew wings and took flight, soaring and gliding and taking on a life of their own. They lit her up like the sky on the Fourth of July.

Her English teacher, Mr. Ingram, encouraged her to write. Sometimes she stayed after school to chat with him about poetry.

"I want to be a poet when I grow up," Myra said.

Mr. Ingram smiled. "It's hard to make a living writing poetry, Myra. You should have a backup plan."

Mr. Ingram held out a manila envelope to Myra. "Here are your anthologies. Thank you for allowing me to read them. I enjoyed them very much. I also enclosed a list of magazines you might consider submitting them to. Try all of them. Expect rejection, but keep on trying, because eventually you may succeed."

Myra reached for the envelope. "Thanks, Mr. Ingram. I'll do that when I get home."

She held her anthologies close to her as she left the building. Each one was hand-typed on her fifty-year-old typewriter. Each anthology had covers, a dedication page, a table of contents, and numbered pages. And each contained slices of her heart, carefully arranged on the page to resemble a poem or a short story.

They weren't just a part of her life, they *were* her life—her fears and insecurities, her crying out to the world, her need to be acknowledged and affirmed. All her deepest desires and dreams, all neatly wrapped in a few pages stapled together and disguised as her "anthologies"—a word synonymous for Myra's heart, which for *now* was *only* bruised and tender.

Chapter Twenty

March 8, 1970

The birthday card from Danny came right on time. It wasn't the usual funny card that made her laugh. The front was covered with roses and it said "To my Sister, with Love." Myra smiled as she opened it. The verse inside was the usual Hallmark fare—but a thrill went through her when she saw the handwritten note from Danny inside.

> *Dear Myra,*
>
> *You're 14 now. I know that you understand the difference between a good girl and a bad girl. I'll always love you because you are my sister, but I don't always have to like you. Respect needs to be earned. If you ever need an example of a good woman, look to Mom. I love you, Myra. Happy 14th Birthday.*
>
> *Love, Danny*

Myra closed her eyes and held the card to her heart. She was old enough to understand what Danny was saying about good girls and bad girls. At school they used other terminology for "bad" girls, but Myra knew it was not in Danny to be vulgar. She smiled. At this point she had no worries about being "bad." Boys just weren't interested in her ugly mug. She hugged the card tighter; she would never throw it away.

The arguing continued. The words were obscured, but the tone was unmistakable. Mom was yelling at Mark, again. Ever since he got out of the service, the tension in the air was thick and heavy like a wet, woolen blanket. Myra didn't understand any of it. She was thrilled Mark was back, but disappointed because life didn't return to normal as she had hoped. He wasn't the same. He'd changed during his four years in the service and was now someone she didn't recognize. She didn't understand why he changed, but he seemed mad at everyone. He yelled at Mom, and he yelled at Dad. He said mean things to her that sliced through her with razor precision.

Once, when she'd finished washing the dishes and announced the dishes were all done—clean and sterile—he'd informed her she didn't know the meaning of sterile. When she mentioned she was praying for peace, he scoffed at her prayers and raged that she didn't even know what peace was. And, once he overheard her gossiping on the phone about one of the "bad" girls and told her she was a prude. Myra was offended by his accusation and had snapped back that she wasn't a prude—he was just a pig. The glint in his eyes told her the game was on. He seemed to delight in offending Myra with his worldly-wise views.

"Girls in Vietnam are having babies at fourteen," he said. His smirk irritated her, but she was pretty sure he knew that.

"I don't care," Myra said, her volume increasing with each word. "I don't live in Vietnam, I live in America." Anger pressed out of every pore in Myra's body like potatoes through a ricer. Heat radiated from her face, and she ran from the house in confusion to get away from Mark. She hopped on her bicycle and tore off down the street, tears stinging her eyes.

"Prude!" Mark shouted after her.

Who is this guy tormenting me? She swallowed the painful lump. "Pig!" she screamed back.

His evil cackle followed her as she turned the corner.

March 29, 1970

Easter came early while the dirty snow still clung to the lawn in frozen patches. Myra woke from a dark dream about Danny that left her uneasy. She tried to shake it off. It was just a dream, after all. He'd been on her mind non-stop since he left for Vietnam. That's why her dreams of him were filled with sadness and death. *It's just a dream!*

She placed her bare feet on the cold, hardwood floor that sent a chill directly to her bones. What dress should she wear today? Myra reached for the knob on her closet door and heard knocking down the hall. She grimaced. Who on earth was knocking on the front door on Easter Sunday? Friends always used the side door. The front door was for salesmen and strangers. Who could that be? She opened her bedroom door and listened to the voices.

"Mr. Grayson?"

"Yes." It was Dad's voice, shaky and thin.

"Do you have a son named Daniel A. Grayson?"

Myra stepped out of the room to get closer to the conversation, her heart beating wildly. Could Danny be coming home soon? Excited, she almost ran down the hall to hear the good news for herself. She held her breath. *Is the war over?* She took a few tenuous steps.

There was a slight pause. "I'm sorry, sir."

Why would they be sorry that the war is over, or that Danny was coming home early? Myra emerged from the hall and looked toward the front door where two enormous men in army uniforms stood towering over her father. His head was bent as he read a piece of paper. No one said anything, and Myra felt her heart might cease beating from the tension. Tears welled in her father's eyes, but he didn't say a word, he only nodded.

"Danny? Not my Danny. Oh, God. Not *my* Danny!" Her mother sobbed, shoulders shuddering with grief.

The scene unfolded in slow motion before her, and Myra stood fixed in one spot, trying to make sense of what she was seeing and hearing.

Her father enfolded his arms around her mother as she continued to sob. From upstairs, Billy came down hurling curses across the room at the men in uniform. He reached the landing and headed towards them, but Dad grabbed him to stop the onslaught, nodding with embarrassment at the men that it was okay for them to leave. Myra stood like an island surrounded by a sea of confusion. She thought Danny was being sent home early. She thought the men delivered good news.

Billy spewed his anger and burst into loud, hot tears. Her mom sobbed into her hands. Myra was attempting to put the pieces to this confusing puzzle together in her mind.

Her mom continued to cry, while Dad tried to console her. "Danny, my son. Danny, my son. Dead, my son is *dead*."

With sudden awareness, the reality of the scene slapped Myra's face with such velocity, it almost knocked her off her feet. She looked around one more time. Mom sobbing uncontrollably, and Dad weeping as he attempted to calm Billy and console Mom. Myra's gut clenched tight, like a fist. She turned with slow deliberate steps and walked back to her room, shutting the door behind her.

When Myra emerged from her room, the kitchen was filled with neighbors and relatives. Mark had taken charge. Billy sat sullen in the corner, while Dad, unusually quiet, stared with dry, but vacant, red-rimmed eyes. People surrounded Mom, patting her arm, hugging her, and stroking her hand. It looked like she had not stopped sobbing since the fatal pronouncement. Myra needed to get out of the house.

"Would you drive me to church?" she whispered to a neighbor. "I don't have time to walk."

The neighbor looked surprised, but nodded her assent. They started to move away from the kitchen table.

Her mom stopped sobbing. "What does Myra want?" she barked.

"She wants to go to church," the neighbor replied with a tentative tone.

Her mom stared, silent for a moment, then lowering her head, she began to cry again. She waved her hand to indicate she didn't really care what Myra did.

Myra sat in her usual spot near the front, listening to the priest speaking, but not hearing a single word he said. She watched his every movement as tears silently slipped down her cheeks unimpeded. She couldn't stand being in that house another minute. Here she could be alone in this crowd.

She remembered her birthday card and the words Danny had written inside. "I will always love you, but I don't always have to like you. Respect needs to be earned."

All the music of the "four Bobbys" filled her head like an orchestra in a ballroom. The music vibrated from one end of her mind to the other like a basketball's journey during a heated game. She thought she saw the priest lift the basketball to make a bank shot off the backboard, but when she blinked to clear the tears, he was raising a chalice.

Respect needs to be earned.

Respect needs to be earned.

The wind whipped her face with bitter gusts as she walked the almost two miles home in silence. The coldness of her soul far surpassed the chilly afternoon air.

Everyone was still gathered in the kitchen as Myra slipped in and crept to her room. If anyone noticed her, they didn't acknowledge it.

She sat on the floor, with the door ajar, listening to the voices down the hall.

There were many awkward pauses, broken by empty comments.

"He's in a better place now."

Long silence.

"At least he didn't suffer. The shot came quickly."

More silence.

"And you know where he is. At least he's not M.I.A. That would be torture."

Silence.

"Four years of my life wasted ..." Danny's girlfriend said, voicing her feelings for the first time.

Myra's head jerked up. *What?*

More silence.

Is no one going to say anything to her about that thoughtless, ignorant remark? Myra shook her head, stupefied by the garbage people say to comfort the grieving. Her heart made an exodus, and she closed her bedroom door in an effort to remain separated from the nonsense and sobbing. The grief seemed determined to swallow her whole as she sat there alone in her sorrow.

She lay on the floor and pulled her knees to her chest. A bleak shadow spread over her like a winter night. To ward off the chill, she folded her arms around herself, but the cold pain continued its fierce onslaught, and she began to tremble. She rubbed her arms to warm them, but terrible, gnawing grief twisted in her like a Midwestern tornado. Her trembling increased and yielded to waves of quaking sobs that shook her young body like an earthquake without mercy.

The minutes slipped into hours as she agonized alone. She was weak and exhausted when the tears eventually subsided. Without moving, her eyes searched her room for a safe harbor to rest her weary mind. Her eyes lit on the crucifix on the wall. *Oh, God, what do I do with all this overwhelming pain?*

Chapter Twenty-One

April 1971

Ninth Grade

"Are you going to the party after the show?" Brenda raised her eyebrows and smiled.

Myra sighed. "I guess so."

"Freshman Ball is coming up," Brenda said.

"I know. It's just another event to remind me that I'm a loser." Myra became silent. She felt so lonely sometimes.

"Hey," Brenda's smile widened. "You're friends with Charlotte and her brother, Andy."

"Yeah, so?

"Maybe he would be willing to take you as a friend."

Myra's laughter was more of a mocking cackle.

Brenda scowled. "It won't hurt to ask, and he might go for the idea."

He's a junior, Brenda. Why would he take a freshman to the Freshman Ball at the junior high? He goes to the high school, for Pete's sake."

"But you're all friends. You should ask Charlotte what she thinks."

The rehearsals didn't prepare Myra for the tightness she felt in her gut as she stood backstage waiting for her entrance cue. People called it butterflies or stage fright, but Myra called it terror. She practiced this song for weeks. The Freshman Variety Show was the highlight of the year—a sort of farewell show as freshman were promoted to the senior high school the following fall. They went from "big man on campus," to "lowly sophomore."

Myra was quite apprehensive about the move. She managed to make her fair share of friends at the junior high school. They were all going to the senior high school, but there were so many more students there. The idea of "the big school" overwhelmed her. She hadn't been there since she saw Mark and Danny in the musical in 1964.

The memory of Danny sent wisps of sadness through her like dandelion seeds in the wind. She struggled everyday with his death. Myra wrestled with her own sorrow and her mother's overwhelming grief. *I really don't think I want to go to the high school.*

The previous act finished and she stepped out on stage and took her microphone. Her hands shook as the music started. Her knees shook like maracas in a Latin band, her voice wavered as she began the song. Each line gave strength to the next. She closed her eyes for a moment, remembering the first time she heard Sammy Davis Jr. sing the song.

Then with all she was worth, she belted out the last line of the song. "I've gotta be me!"

The applause surprised and delighted her. Rehearsals didn't prepare her for the audience's unexpected response. She placed the microphone back in its stand and floated towards stage right. The applause thundered in her ears like ocean waves slapping the shore. Standing still backstage, she listened. Even after the applause ended, she could still hear it echo in her memory.

"I told you he would take you. Nobody has to know that Andy is just a friend. You're here with a *junior*, Myra."

Myra gave Brenda a sheepish smile. She never really thought Andy would take her, but Charlotte and Andy thought it would be really fun for him to go.

"He'll make it really fun for you, Myra." Charlotte had said.

Myra looked around the gym, waiting for Andy to get her a glass of punch. Streamers were everywhere, and a glass ball hung in the middle of the room, reflecting the minimal light present. Myra had never been on a date with a boy before. She didn't know how to act. But then, this wasn't a date. He was a friend—the brother of a friend, really. *Just a friend.* Still, Myra was stunned when Andy gave her a corsage.

"Oh, it's pretty." Myra had felt her face blush. "Thank you."

"It *is* the Freshman Ball, you know." He winked at her. "That's what dates do. They give corsages."

After the initial awkwardness, Myra and Andy defaulted to their usual relationship, laughing and joking. She needed to remind herself it was just a big crowd of friends having a good time. *Relax, Myra.*

The local band attempted to imitate popular music. Most of the songs were loud imitations of Creedence Clearwater Revival, including "Travelin' Band," "Up and Around the Bend," and "Lookin' Out My Back Door." They attempted Chicago with "25 or 6 to 4," and the latest slow dance song, "Color My World." Three Dog Night and BJ Thomas were thrown in to keep it interesting and loud. But when the band attempted The Hollies', "He Ain't Heavy, He's My Brother," Myra excused herself to use the lavatory. She'd played that song every night following her brother's wake. Well, until her mother yelled at her, asking how Myra could play music with her brother dead. Myra never understood the question, but the song provoked feelings of melancholy that she chose to express in the bathroom instead of the gymnasium.

Andy walked Myra to her side door at the end of the evening. She'd had a pretty decent time, but she wasn't at all prepared for the kiss he planted on her mouth. His parted lips moved fast and were accompanied by … *Oh, my gosh. What's he doing*? Myra had never been kissed by a boy before. She thought it only entailed their lips touching—*not the tongue.* She was stunned when the kiss was over, and she had the distinct desire to throw up. Her mouth had been violated.

But Andy was her friend, so she smiled. "Thank you for taking me to the Freshman Ball, Andy," she said, her voice polite, but tense. "It was nice of you. I had a good time."

He looked amused by her reaction to his kiss. "See ya 'round, Myra."

She stepped into the house and closed the door without looking back. The nausea continued for days. She never wanted to endure that again. *Yuk!* Could people tell what happened just by looking at her? Myra dreaded the last few days of school. Maybe when she graduated from high school, she'd join a convent and become a nun.

Chapter Twenty-Two

November 1971

Each time John looked at his son's army portrait on the corner shelf, his eyes misted. He kissed the picture when no one was looking.

The emptiness gnawed at him. Stella had become increasingly distant, leaving him unfulfilled and frustrated. He spent five nights a week away from the house, coaching the local soccer teams. At least he felt needed there. The boys may not like his personality or his coaching style, but most clamored to be on his team because he had the most wins of any other coach.

The locker room had a combined odor of sweat from the boys that came to gather their equipment and chlorine from the pool just beyond the showers. After yelling at the boys for their sloppy plays, John headed for his car. His heart ached. He didn't want to go home and face Stella. She was an ever present reminder of all he'd lost.

Myra would no doubt be at some school activity, and Billy—who knew where he hung out? He'd put on his black boots and leather jacket and go out with other boys with dark personalities and leather jackets. Sadness overwhelmed John as he entered the house. He sighed, not knowing what to do with the heaviness in his heart.

"Hi, is Myra, home?"

"Not yet," Stella said. Her eyes remained riveted on the TV.

"Well, I'm going to get ready for bed."

Stella didn't respond.

Alone in front of the television again, Stella's bitterness rose with little effort and spilled out with hot tears.

She hadn't stopped asking "why" since that Sunday morning over a year ago when she found out about Danny's death in Vietnam. She had not stopped crying. Her sweet son was dead. Mark moved out of state and got married. Billy's anger had pulled him away from everyone. And, Myra didn't seem to care one way or the other. She was the classic social butterfly involved in every possible school activity. It seemed like she was always running somewhere: Brenda's house, auditions, Student Exchange Club, choir rehearsal, riding her bike, going to the mall, babysitting, and on it went.

She rarely came home for dinner. When did she ever have time for homework? But, when all was said and done, it didn't matter how well she did in school. After all, Myra was a girl. It wasn't like she'd be going to college.

The screen door slammed and jolted Stella. Myra came into the house and strode into the living room.

"Hi, Mom. How's it going? What did you have for dinner tonight?"

"Hamburger Helper," Stella said. She glanced at Myra and noticed her cringe. Stella didn't care. Why should she prepare fancy meals for an absent family who didn't appreciate the food she served. The simple meals became a permanent part of the weekly menu. Stella also noticed that Myra had lost some weight.

"Have a baloney sandwich," Stella said. Her eyes returned to TV screen.

"Thanks, Mom." Myra skipped out of the room toward the kitchen.

Even with people home, Stella felt alone. The loneliness grew like bubble bath suds under running water.

Myra bounded back into the room with a piece of bologna between two slices of Wonder Bread. "The school play was so cool tonight, Mom. You should've seen it. I'm gonna try out for the school musical next month. Rehearsals start right after Christmas vacation. The musical is in March, and I can't wait. I hope I get chosen to be in it."

Stella nodded. More lonely nights sitting in front of the TV while everyone goes on with their lives. Had everyone forgotten her? *Has everyone forgotten Danny?*

The stationery was pretty, with little pink roses in the corner that ran down the side of the page. It matched the envelope. Mark stared at the letter until the words flowed together like a stream through a flower garden. He'd already read it three times; it wasn't very long. The letter from Myra updated him and Elyse on her life in three simple paragraphs.

> *Dear Mark,*
>
> *Sorry I haven't written in a long time. I've been super busy since my last letter.*
>
> *I'm in the spring musical. We're doing Hello Dolly, this year. I got the part of Minnie Fay. She's the third largest female speaking part. I was so excited to get the part. I'm having a lot of fun doing a show. We have rehearsals five nights a week, so I have been too busy to write before this.*
>
> *The musical will be held on March 8, 9, and 10. I wish you could be here to see me, but I will write you all about it when it's over.*
>
> *Love, Myra*

There was no mention of Mom, Dad, or Billy. There was no mention of how she'd been doing since Danny's death. Myra seemed to be getting on with her life pretty well. No complaints about the family, no struggles of her own. Mark wished it were that way with him. Moving to another state helped him enormously. After Danny died, Mark just disappeared in his mother's head. Any good that Mark had ever done was now attributed to his brother—like his mother giving Danny credit for visiting him at college, when it had actually been Mark who had driven to see Danny.

Mark focused back on the letter and made a mental note of the show dates. How appropriate that opening night was Myra's sixteenth birthday. *At least Mom won't have to come up with an excuse for not having a birthday party for her.*

Chapter Twenty-Three

March 8, 1972

Myra ran into the house, the door banging shut behind her, and headed straight to her mom.

Stella frowned and opened her mouth to yell at Myra for slamming the door after she'd been told not to.

"I gotta be at school early, Mom," Myra said, jumping in with large gulping breaths before Stella could utter a word. "It's opening night. Aren't you excited?" Myra giggled and headed toward her room.

"Didn't you see the box?"

"Huh?"

"Right there on the couch."

Myra leaned over the long, white box and drew in a breath. With eyes wide, she turned to her mother. "What is it?"

"There's a card on top." Stella smiled at Myra's reaction. She'd never seen her daughter so excited about a gift.

Myra pulled the card out of its envelope and read it out loud. "Break a leg tonight. Wish we could be there to celebrate with you. Love, Mark and Elyse." Myra threw open the box with shaking hands. Three dozen assorted blooms smiled up at her. "Oooooh, how beautiful! Flowers, Mom. From Mark and Elyse. See?" Myra shoved the card at her mother. "They told me to break a leg tonight.

That means 'good luck' in theater talk, but saying 'good luck' is bad luck, so people just say 'break a leg.'"

Stella chuckled at Myra's rambling. "Go get ready, Myra. I'll put these in water for you."

"Thanks, Mom." Myra gave her mom a quick kiss on the cheek and headed for her room to unload her books and get changed for the big night.

Myra would do well. After all, she was a natural on stage, just like her brothers.

"Everyone, gather in the choir room. We need to go over notes from last night's dress rehearsal," the stage manager said, his voice already raspy from constant yelling to gain everyone's attention.

The electricity in the air crackled and sparked, charging each person with energy. They all glowed with excitement. Myra could barely sit still when Brenda attempted to apply the pancake to her face.

"Sit still, Myra."

"I can't, Brenda. I'm excited and nervous. What if I forget a line?"

"You'll be great, Myra. You're a natural."

"Yeah," the senior girl beside her said. "You *are* perfect for that part. I auditioned for it and was really mad when I didn't get it. But, you *are* that character." The girl tilted her head one way and then the other as she stared into a large mirror, checking her makeup. "You're lucky, you know. He never gives lines to sophomores. And, Minnie Fay is the third female lead. He always gives the leads to seniors because it's their last year. Guess he realized you were perfect despite the fact that you're *only* a sophomore." She took a quick breath. "Break a leg, Myra. Knock 'em dead."

Myra watched as the senior walked away. She'd no idea there was some hierarchy involved with casting a high school musical. It was her first time, and she was just riding the wave of excitement to the shores of opening night.

"Come on," Brenda said, pulling Myra's arm. "Let's get you to the choir room for notes."

Myra entered the crowded room. No chair to sit in. No surprise—the room had about sixty chairs for choir members to sit during class. The room was now packed like a cattle car with actors, singers, stagehands—just about everyone involved. Myra stood by the piano in the center of the room and tried to focus on what was being said, but the excitement wreaked havoc with her ability to concentrate. She played with her hair, cracked her knuckles, and swayed back and forth from one foot to another. Her biggest concern was messing up and disappointing everyone. She just didn't want to let anyone down. Maybe, if she did everything right, she wouldn't end up being a loser.

"Donna, during the second scene, don't go too far down stage. We can't see your face. Stay in the light," the director said, pointing to the ceiling as if there were a spotlight shining down on her.

Donna nodded.

"Choir, remember to smile. Waiters, don't look at your feet, and one last thing ..." The director glanced toward the door. "Ready?"

Myra looked up to hear the last stage note, and the entire room broke into "Happy Birthday." She smiled and started to sing, then leaned over to the girl next to her and said, "How cool. It's somebody's birthday on opening night."

Her friend, Sandra, carried a large round cake across the room. Myra waited to see who she stopped in front of. Sandra paused directly in front of her. Myra looked down and read the inscription on the cake: *Happy 16th Birthday, Minnie Fay*. Then gasping, her hands flew to her mouth. "Oh, I forgot today is *my* birthday."

The room erupted in laughter and applause, and Myra stood shocked by this enormous display of affection. Tears welled up in her eyes and she swiped at quickly. She'd have to go back to Brenda to have her makeup fixed.

Myra was living her dream on that stage. The orchestra, the choir, the smell of the grease paint, the fancy costumes—it was all a dream she didn't want to wake up from. It was true; the part was tailor-made for her. The role combined a little singing, a little footwork (not quite dancing), and numerous opportunities to make the audience laugh. Each outburst of laughter filled Myra with an inexplicable feeling of satisfaction. But, she was terrified she would wake up from this glorious dream and find she was everything she'd always thought—just another nobody pretending to be somebody.

Her initial stage fright melted like hot candle wax the minute she opened her mouth to say her first line. All those months of rehearsal culminated in one extraordinary night. How many times since she watched Mark and Danny on stage ten years earlier, had she envisioned a moment like this? It was exactly the way she dreamed it would be.

The stage manager gathered every one for the curtain call. "Come on everyone," he said, his voice a gravely whisper. "Get in line–choir, get behind the curtain, then the small parts go out, then the bigger parts–here Myra, stand here–then the leads go out. If the audience loved the show, they'll give a standing ovation *after* Dolly's curtain call."

Myra made a mental note—more theater etiquette to remember. Lead last, standing ovation, everyone bows together.

The closing music began. The applause started as the curtain opened, revealing the choir. Then each character stepped out on stage. Myra was told to meet Barry, the third male lead, in the center, bow, and step back. After that, the second lead and then the stars would come out. Myra's breathing had become shallow, her hands were cold. What if the audience stopped clapping when she came out? *What if I get booed?*

Her musical cue started, and the stage manager gave her a little tap. "Go, Myra."

Myra bounded onstage. The applause kicked up a notch; there were whistles and whooping. Her breathing quickened, and warmth spread across her face dragging a smile with it. She glanced toward her stage partner, Barry. She widened her grin. When they turned to the audience to bow, the entire crowd stood to its feet in one swift motion.

Myra could hardly breathe, her head was spinning. She stood there, stunned and overwhelmed by the audience's response. The stage manager's words regarding standing ovations rang through her head. *So much for theatrical etiquette.* Myra was thrilled to share this reaction with Barry. They'd been quite a team onstage. She closed her eyes for a split second. She would remember this moment for the rest of her life.

Backstage, Myra was removing her costume when the "director of theatrical etiquette" approached her.

"I've never seen an audience stand before the lead comes out," she stated in an accusatory tone.

Myra didn't know how to appropriately respond to her remark, so she said nothing.

"If I'd been the lead, I'd have been mad."

Again, Myra remained silent, hoping to glean some information on how to handle the situation. But, she had nothing to feel guilty about. It's not like she and Barry campaigned in the audience prior to the show to get people to give them a standing ovation. It just happened. It took her as much by surprise—and delight—as anyone else in the show.

But the girl was done putting Myra in her place. "See you at the cast party," she said, and left the room without further theatrical insights.

It was Myra's first cast party, held at a cast member's house. Everyone who had anything to do with the show was there. Myra soaked in everything—the people, the punch, the snacks, the noise, and the compliments. Everywhere she turned, she got a pat on the back, a hug, a kiss, or an encouraging word about her performance.

The lead, Angie, gave her a big hug. "You were amazing, Myra, you deserved that ovation." Myra hugged her back. Angie was far more gracious than the "director of theatrical etiquette."

Myra began to feel less like a loser each minute. Even people she didn't know had a good word for her. After receiving more praise, more love, and more encouragement on this one night than she had her entire life, Myra determined in her heart that this was the life for her.

The house felt hot and stuffy, so she stepped outside to get a breath of fresh air. Just outside the door stood her stage partner, Barry, and his girlfriend. Kate attended a different school, but Myra had seen her and Barry together after rehearsals a few times.

"Hi, Kate." Myra hoped her greeting would be returned, since she'd never spoken to Kate before.

"Oh, Myra, you were fantastic tonight. The audience just loved you. Every time you stepped out on stage, they laughed. You had them eating out of your hands. Myra you're a natural."

Myra smiled slowly, humbled by the compliment. She'd never received such kind words for anything before. And tonight she wasn't sure how to react.

"Thank you, Kate," was all she could manage.

Barry bristled, but said nothing.

"Hey, Myra, you're not here alone, are you? Where is your boyfriend?" Kate's question was innocent, but it stung Myra's heart.

She cleared her throat to get past the discomfort she suddenly felt. "I don't have a boyfriend," she said in a hoarse whisper.

"You don't? Why not?" Kate seemed oblivious to Myra's discomfort.

Barry jumped right in and cackled, "Because she's short, fat, and ugly, Kate. That's why."

Kate gave a slight giggle and slapped Barry's forearm gently. "Barry, don't be mean."

There was a massive lurch as the earth stopped rotating. Like a statue in a storm, Myra stood stunned as the evening's delight dissolved away, a mere chalk drawing on the sidewalk during a summer rain. Her mind whirled in the furious storm. She couldn't think of anything to say, and her eyes stung with the effort not to cry. She had only been fooling herself.

Chapter Twenty-Four

July 1973

The water shot from the sprinkler with a refreshing ease. Each drop jumped into the air in synchronized time, reached its pinnacle, and fell to the ground like a well-rehearsed acrobat. The droplets of water clung to the blades of grass, shimmering like diamonds under the sun's careful scrutiny. In the mist, a tiny rainbow formed an inverted smile.

Myra stared into the mist for a long time, enthralled by its simple beauty, until she spotted the mailman coming up the driveway with a handful of mail.

"Hi, George," she called.

"Good morning, Ms. Grayson," he said with a broad smile. "How are you?"

"I might be better if you brought me a letter," she said, cocking her head to one side and winking. Myra loved getting letters in the mail, and she always looked for one from her brother, her cousin, her pen pal—or anyone, really. She kept a drawer full of beautiful stationery that she pulled out and used as often as she could. Although her paper collection included pink and blue shades, her favorite had roses printed down the side.

"Well, let's see, we got, hmmm, bills, bills, an advertisement …" George said flipping through the stack. "Okay, look, a letter for Myra Grayson. And, a fat one at that." He handed it to her.

She looked at the unfamiliar return address, eager to open the envelope. "Thanks, George. I'll give the rest to my mom."

"Enjoy, Myra. I hope the sender is someone you've been waiting to hear from." George headed toward the next mailbox, and Myra stepped inside her house.

Myra sat at her desk and carefully opened the letter. It was fat, but it didn't feel as though it were filled with layers of stationery. It felt squishy. She finally got the envelope opened and stared at the contents she pulled out. *What on earth? Tree bark*?

She unfolded the bark carefully; there was writing on the inside of it.

Dear Myra,

I hope you are having a great summer. I am a counselor at a boy's camp this year It's a lot of fun. We hike and swim and play games. I hope your summer musical rehearsals are going well. I will call you long distance soon.

Love, Nick.

Myra held the letter in her hands for a long moment. She didn't move, and she didn't speak. She focused on trying to sort out her feelings. Her fingers clenched the letter as she reread the words once more. Was she more annoyed or flattered that he had nudged his way back into her thoughts?

As Myra stared intently at the tree bark letter, her thoughts rolled back over the last few months.

"Myra, you know that boy on the stage crew who's been flirting with you?"

"What? No, he's not flirting with me. We're just friends." Myra scanned the corridor to be sure no one had overheard Brenda's accusation.

Brenda sighed and shook her head. "He's flirting with you, Myra, even if you don't see it."

"What about him?" Myra was getting as impatient with this dialogue as Brenda sounded. "I overheard him talking to his best friend Kevin, about how he wanted to spend time with you at the cast party."

Myra's heart skipped a beat, but she neither smiled nor winced. "So?"

"So, he likes you, Myra." Brenda's exasperation spilled over like a toppled glass of lemonade. She smiled and grabbed Myra's shoulders. "He *likes* you Myra. You are a likable person." She winked at Myra. "He likes *you*. Wait and see."

Myra remained still for a moment as she considered Brenda's words. "We'll see."

"Hey, great performance." Nick sat on the chair beside her. The house was full of cast and crew members from the evening's performance. Talking and laughter mingled with the aroma of freshly delivered pizza.

Myra's head shot up at the sound of his voice.

"Oh, thanks," she said, scrambling to smile at him. Were those her only words? Is "Oh, thanks" the best she could do? Or had other words escaped her startled brain?

A long awkward moment nestled between them. "So, you like doing the musicals?"

Myra exhaled with relief at his words. *Thank goodness. I wasn't sure what to say next.*

"Oh, yeah, I love them. They're really fun. I meet a lot of great people. This is my third musical. I was in last year's school musical, and the summer musical with the school district's summer theater group." Did all that come out of her mouth at once? She winced at her inability to keep from yak, yak, yakking. *Does he think I talk too much or I'm too flirty, or too pushy or too needy*?

Nick grinned. "That's great. Did you have a part or were you in the chorus?"

Myra relaxed into the conversation. Someone had turned up the stereo and it was infringing on their ability to hear each other.

"Let's take a walk outside where we don't have to shout." He reached his hand toward her.

She hesitated, then reached up and took it. He led her out of the house and down the driveway. Myra walked beside Nick, aware that he still held her hand. She gazed up at the stars. Were they smiling down at her? *Is this moment really happening*? Myra glanced over at Nick, his dark curls hanging casually around his face. His voice was smooth and sweet, like a bowl of rich, chocolate pudding. She could get lost in that voice, and in fact she did.

"May I sit with you at lunch tomorrow?"

She quickly regrouped from her chocolate reverie. "Sure." Her eager attitude was beginning to get on her own nerves.

They stopped under a streetlight, and bathed in its glow, she caught Nick's impish smile. His eyes sparkled with pleasure, even in the shadows. He took a cautious step closer to her, leaned over, and placed his lips on hers with a surprising gentleness. Her last kiss had been a little more … ambitious. She almost pulled back at the memory, but instead, allowed this kiss to remain a moment longer. His lips were soft and warm and enchanting, drawing her in deeper. They were giving lips, not taking—not rushing to grab anything. They were relaxed and natural, Myra thought. The kiss ended and they each lingered in the moment without a word.

Then he whispered, "I'll meet you in the cafeteria."

"Okay," she said, her tone matching his.

For two months Nick sat with Myra at lunch, and he walked her home every day. Occasionally, he came by her house in the early evening bearing gifts of ice cream from Dairy Queen or a candy bar from the drugstore. They would sit on the porch, or watch a little TV. They didn't go places together, and they didn't discuss the intricacies of their relationship. They just enjoyed each other's company. Myra was thrilled to have a boyfriend.

One day, Nick didn't show up to walk her home, so she left without him, thinking he must have gotten held up.

The next day at lunch, Myra smiled when he sat down beside her. "Hi, missed you after school yesterday."

His smile pulled to one side, and he moved his eyes away from her gaze. "I hope you didn't wait long."

"No, I just figured something important came up."

He nodded and nothing else was spoken on the subject. When the bell rang, Nick stopped Myra as she stood up. "I'm going to come by your house tonight, okay?"

"Sure." She gave him a gentle smile. "I'll be home. Come on by."

At nine o'clock Myra headed for her bedroom, shoulders slumped. Nick had neither come by, nor called. She went to bed sad, but not surprised. She didn't really expect the relationship to last once he'd gotten to know her.

On the way to school, Myra and Brenda considered the situation between Nick and Myra.

"You're too available, Myra," Brenda said. "When he says he's coming over, try not to be there."

"That's rude, Brenda. He said he was coming over, I said 'okay.' Why would I lie? Besides, where else would I go?"

"I'm telling you, don't be so available. You have to play hard to get if you want a boyfriend."

Myra's forehead furrowed. Her eyes narrowed. "I don't want to play hard to get."

"You have to play games, Myra. It's a fact of life in high school."

Myra scowled. "I want a boyfriend, Brenda. I like Nick, a lot. But, I'm not going to play silly high school games. It's so ridiculous."

Four long, tedious days went by as Nick managed to avoid Myra between classes and after school. Her heart ached. Had he finally figured out what a loser she was? At the end of the fourth day, she searched for Nick at the school entrance on the other side of the building. She was determined to get some answers. She needed to face the truth. He was leaving with his best friend, Kevin.

"Hi, guys." Myra was surprised at her own sincere smile and even tone.

Kevin seemed genuinely glad to see her, but Nick's startled expression almost made Myra laugh. But she didn't. *You can't avoid me forever, Nick.*

"Nick, please come by my house this evening. I'd like to talk to you."

Nick blinked and cleared his throat. "Uh, sure." The tension was thicker than humidity at a beach resort.

Myra smiled and with a wave of her hand said, "Okay, I'll see you tonight."

That evening, Myra and Nick sat in the backyard on the yellow webbed aluminum folding lawn chairs. Something was on Nick's mind, so why wasn't he saying anything?

"You wanted to talk to me?" A nervous tremor in Nick's voice belied his confident stance.

"Yes." She inhaled a deep breath and sat tall. This was the moment of truth, now or never, full speed ahead. "Nick, if people didn't know you were my boyfriend already, they'd never know it by what's been going on between us the last few days." Her steady voice fell calmly into the space between them.

Nick's face took on a new shade of crimson while he studied his hands.

Myra sat in silence, anticipating his answer. A heaviness pressed down on her like an iron on a wrinkled cotton dress shirt. She feared he would call her names, accuse her of something, or admit he was tired of having a loser for a girlfriend.

He didn't say anything for a long time. His dull eyes just stared at his hands. Then, Nick's face lit up, and a smirk spread across his face. "My best friend's girlfriend is always accepting invitations for them to go places without asking him. She only wants to do what *she* wants to do and never what *he* wants to do." His smug expression lingered after his words evaporated into the silence.

Myra stared at Nick for a moment, grasping for clues that would help her make sense of his explanation.

"Yeah, and she always …"

Myra considered where his creative explanation was taking him. She interrupted him. "Nick, have *I* ever done that? Have I ever done *anything* like that?"

"No, but …"

"Then, why are you bringing it up? Are you afraid I might start acting like Kevin's girlfriend?"

When no answer came, Myra stood and said in a gentle, controlled voice, "I really enjoyed our time together, Nick. But, it's apparent you are ready to move on, and you're using Kevin's girlfriend as an excuse to break up. You don't have to do that. We can break up without the drama. No hard feelings, okay?"

Nick's jaw dropped, his stunned face registered both unbelief and relief. He stumbled over his tongue, trying to say something.

Myra felt sorry for him. She refused to play high school games to have a boyfriend, but it was obvious that the rules were pretty widely known by the other players. She wanted so much to hug him and get one last gentle kiss from him. Could she? But decided not to give him the chance to reject her, again. She reached over and put her hand on his arm. "Thanks for coming over to talk to me. I'll see you at school sometime."

She headed toward the side door and went inside, never looking back. She knew that relationship was too good to be true. There are no fairy tale endings here. Face it. You're a loser. Once inside her room, sadness welled up inside of her and found its exit through short, stifled sobs.

Chapter Twenty-Five

August 1973

Myra had not spoken to Nick since their breakup. There was no reason to. He was no longer her boyfriend. He'd probably moved on to someone else. Some pretty, thin, tall girl with shiny hair and a perfect set of teeth. Occasionally, she would pass him in the corridor at school and they would nod and smile. By the end of the school year, she was ready to embrace summer, forget about Nick and enjoy carefree afternoons and the welcome diversion of evening rehearsals. Now, a week before opening night, this huge distraction arrives in the mail.

Myra set the tree bark letter down. "I'll call you long distance soon," she repeated the last line he'd written. In answer, she said, "If you call in the evening, after the rates go down, I'll be at rehearsal, Nick. Thanks for the bark, though."

"Myra, phone." Stella set the receiver down on the counter and started down the hall toward her daughter's room to be sure Myra heard her call.

Myra flew out of her room and down the hall, pausing to catch her breath. "Who is it, Mom?"

"I don't know. Some boy."

Myra frowned. Stella went back to her chores, but kept an ear on Myra's conversation.

"Hello?"

A pause.

"Oh, hi. How are you?"

Silence.

"Yes, I got your letter. Very creative."

Quiet.

"Oh, um, opening night is August eighth, and it runs four nights."

Dead air.

"Yeah, so how's camp?"

A pause.

"Uh huh, yeah."

Laughter.

"No, no I understand. Long distance rates are pretty high in the afternoon. Thanks for calling."

Silence.

"Thanks."

More laughter.

"I'll try to break a leg."

Even more laughter.

"Okay, bye."

Myra hung the receiver in its cradle.

Stella sauntered back into the room with an air of nonchalance as Myra turned to leave.

"Who was it?"

"Nick. He called from camp to wish me well on opening night and told me to break a leg."

Stella nodded. "Will he be at any of the performances?"

"No, he won't be home from camp until after the show closes."

Stella nodded again, this time with a slight sigh of relief. Myra had been upset when they broke up, and Stella didn't want her daughter hurt again. She just didn't know what to say to her about boys, as she had no experience to draw from. Stella had a difficult time with teaching Myra anything of importance about being a teenager. At Myra's age, Stella was working in a factory and giving her pay envelope to her father. She didn't really understand the challenges or emotions her daughter faced.

"Good. He won't be missed." Stella was sure Myra agreed.

Myra fidgeted and paced most of the afternoon. Opening night always brought an indescribable excitement with it, and for the summer musicals, the excitement started the moment the sun peeked through the drapes and fell across her face.

"Myra, go do something. You're making me nervous with all this pointless activity."

"Sorry, Mom. It's just harder in the summer on opening night, because I don't have school to keep my thoughts occupied all day.

"Go write some poetry or something," her mom said. "You're driving me crazy."

Myra sat at her desk and wrote nonsense for about thirty minutes, but she couldn't concentrate. A knock at the front door sent a chill down her spine. The last time she heard that sound was on Easter Sunday morning three years ago when soldiers came to tell them about Danny. She rose from her chair as if under water and headed toward the bedroom door. Did she really want to know who was at the front door? Friends and neighbors go to the side door … *strangers go …*

"Myra, you just got a package," her mom's voice called down the hall.

Energized by that announcement, Myra's nerves shifted back into low gear as she swung the bedroom door open and bolted down the hall. Her mom stood at the end of the hall like an emcee at an awards ceremony, long white box in hand, waiting to give her the prize. *And the award for best living room entrance goes to Myra Grayson—yea, applause.*

Myra took the box from her mom with the care of a new mother receiving her infant from the delivery room nurse. She looked at her mom, her heart fluttering wildly with anticipation. She opened the card. It read: *Break a leg. Love, Nick.*

"Who's it from?" Stella asked, trying to read the card over Myra's shoulder.

Myra looked at her mother and paused a moment to reflect on her answer. "Nick."

She set the card down and slowly removed the top of the white box. Her breath caught in her throat. Ten long stemmed yellow roses arranged in perfect order.

"Oh, my gosh," she said, her voice barely audible.

Her mother peered over her shoulder. "Pretty."

Stunned silent by this unsettling gesture on Nick's part, Myra reached with trembling hands into the box and lifted the roses out, as if they might somehow explode in her face.

What kind of game was Nick playing? Was this a sincere gift, or was he messing with her mind? Myra set her jaw and decided to forget it for now. This was opening night, and the show must go on.

I'll think about you when school starts in September.

Chapter Twenty-Six

September 1973

September always started out warm and sunny with just a baby's breath measure of chill in the early evening. Leaves were still green, and the robins hadn't yet disappeared for the winter. Myra basked in the quiet morning as she made her way to Brenda's house so they could walk to school together.

The lull between the summer musical and the first week of school had given them a little more time together. So, they'd seen the new movie, *American Graffiti,* and really enjoyed it. There were an awful lot of "unknowns" in it, so she felt it probably wouldn't do well at the box office, but at least it was worth the price of admission.

They'd also managed to buy a couple of new 45s with their babysitting money. "Yesterday Once More" by The Carpenters made its way into their growing collection of singles. During their sleepovers and between gossip sessions, they also found time to enjoy reruns of their favorite TV shows. Myra loved *The Mary Tyler Moore Show*— Mary Richards had the best wardrobe on earth.

Now Myra was headed back to school on the first day of her last year in high school. Her usual bounce was somewhat stiff by the increasing heaviness surrounding her life. She was the only child at home now. David had disappeared into the world after his release from prison—a fact that lay heavy on her mom's heart. Mark lived in another state with his young family, and Billy graduated two years before and moved out. For the last three years, Danny had lived only in her heart. Her own loss was increased exponentially by her mom's increasing indifference to her, and her father's baffling distance. She still cried over her brother's absence, but not nearly as often as she wanted to.

Her personal disappointments seemed to be piling up. She wasn't good enough to get the parts she tried out for. She had all but stopped going to school dances because no one ever asked her to dance. And the face in the mirror was a constant disappointment to her. Is there anything worse than being a loser at seventeen? She wanted to push all the bad thoughts away, but they kept coming back. Would her senior year be better than her junior year? Looking back, she doubted it.

Myra peered up at the clock on the wall and sighed. She'd been sitting in the small waiting area for ten minutes. She glanced over at the receptionist behind the small boxlike desk. Her face held no expression, but her boredom was evident.

The plaque on the door read "Guidance Counselor." What did guidance counselors really do? Did they help students with personal problems like some sort of school psychologist? Myra chuckled softly. Good thing she was there about *school*-related issues. She doubted even a trained counselor could help make *her* life normal.

But Brenda had urged her to go to the guidance counselor after their conversation comparing their English classes.

"It's the same old stuff as last year." Myra frowned, tossing her English book aside.

"Myra, you should talk to your guidance counselor to see if you can transfer from regular English to honors English. We do a lot of creative writing. I think you would be happier in my class. Your writing talent is wasted in yours."

Brenda's class did sound more interesting than hers. And Myra loved to write. She enjoyed giving wings to words and watching them soar across the page.

The inner office door opened and a student appeared with a satisfied smile. Myra's eyes followed him out of the waiting room. When she looked back, a man stood in the door, ramrod straight.

"Myra." His only word seemed to be sucked into the dry office air.

Myra entered the dull, windowless office and stood before the desk.

"Have a seat," the counselor said, turning toward his desk. He sat down and clasped his hands together in front of him over a file folder. He didn't smile: he didn't exchange any pleasantries. "What can I do for you?" His voice was practiced and mechanical.

Myra wanted to run out of the room screaming. Instead, she sat on the edge of the hard wooden chair that had been placed in front of his desk. She cleared her throat as she decided what to do first—make her request, or give an explanation? She wished she hadn't come.

"I'd like to transfer into the honors English class."

"Why is that?" He cocked his head slightly to one side, as if seeing her from a different angle would help him understand her request better.

"They're doing more creative writing stuff, and I'm interested in that." She took a large breath.

The guidance counselor gazed at her for a moment, then looked down at the file folder. He opened it with slow deliberate movements, turning pages and lifting reports. He studied the report for an extended moment, his eyes not scanning, his head not moving, then looked up at Myra and stared.

"You got a "C" on your sophomore final exam. What makes you think you can compete with honors students in your junior year?"

The air evacuated from Myra's lungs, carrying her words with it. Apparently, it wasn't just written words that could take a flight. She inhaled to remain conscious.

She cleared her throat again. She needed to think, and breathe, think and breathe, think and breathe. She fidgeted in her chair, looked down at her hands, and said in a soft controlled voice, "I didn't realize it was a competition."

The guidance counselor's eyebrows shot up. His retort shot back, some explanation regarding average grades and teacher's expectations. But Myra had stopped listening. Her ears were ringing, and her face felt hot. What a stupid move to come here. Of course she couldn't get into honors English. What was she thinking? It didn't matter that she maintained an "A" average all year. This "C" on her final exam had been proof that she wasn't worthy of a second look, a second thought, or a second chance. She must have been crazy to even think of stepping out of her place. Myra closed her eyes. Being painfully average was a burden, and she wanted to unload it. But she had no idea where to put it.

Brenda was waiting for Myra in the corridor when she finished the counselor appointment. "How'd it go?"

"He said no."

Brenda's voice rose as her face turned deep pink. "But, why?"

"He said I was stupid."

"What?" Her voice screeched.

"He said I couldn't compete with honor students because I got a "C" on my final exam last year."

"But, you had an "A" average all year. Didn't you tell him that?"

Myra closed her eyes. Her lips quivered slightly as she attempted to form the words. "It's okay, Brenda. I'll just stay where I am. I can write stuff without being in that class. He's right, anyway. I can't compete with honor students."

Brenda sighed and touched Myra's arm lightly. "Oh, Myra, I'm so sorry he said that. You're way smarter than you think."

Myra closed her eyes tight, turned her head away, and sobbed. Brenda knew that the counselor's words would haunt Myra for a long time.

When Myra arrived at Brenda's house, she knocked on the side door.

Brenda's mom answered with her usual smile and unique greeting. "Hi, Myra, what do you know that you shouldn't?"

"Not a thing. Not a darn thing," she said, laughter bubbling in her throat.

Brenda grabbed her lunch and the two of them took off down the street.

Brenda looked Myra over. She was wearing a simple yellow dress with an empire waist and wide bell sleeves. "That a new dress?"

"Yeah, my mom just finished it. She said she was done making dresses for me now that I've taken sewing in Home Economics."

"Too bad. You always had a terrific wardrobe."

"Not as good as Mary Richards."

"That's true."

Brenda peered down the street with a far-away look in her eyes. "This is our last year, Myra. We're seniors now."

Myra considered her words. She doubted being a senior would transform her into anyone other than who she'd always been—a lonely, insecure girl. She almost laughed at her own self-analysis. If her "friends" at school knew she considered herself alone and lacking confidence, they'd say she was crazy. She had tons of friends, they'd say, and everyone knew her from the shows she'd performed in. She was happy and funny and fun to be around. *I wish I knew this girl that everyone thinks I am.*

She climbed the steps at the high school entrance and wondered what pain, what humiliation, what disappointment awaited her in her last year of high school.

"Not a single class together," Myra said to Brenda bitterly as they compared schedules. "Not even Home Economics, for Pete's sake."

A collective sigh rose between them like an escaped carnival balloon.

"Have you seen Nick, yet?" Brenda said, raising her eyebrows.

Myra scanned the crowded corridor as she shook her head. "No, I haven't. Have you?"

"No, but I'll let you know if I do."

"Okay. We better get going, or we'll be late for our first class. See you after school."

Brenda nodded and the two headed in opposite directions—Brenda to her French class and Myra to her Home Economics Class—Marriage and Family Living.

The class just before lunch was by far Myra's favorite—choir. She could put the stick shift of her brain in neutral, coast, and enjoy the ride. As she approached the choir room, her heart did a little flutter as she saw Nick coming toward her. He carried his books by his side as he made his way through the crowd like a zombie. She smiled and was about to say *hi* when he spotted someone beyond her and gave a boisterous and animated greeting and passed her without a word.

Maybe he didn't see me. She watched him walk away down the corridor. She gave a momentary sigh, then turned and entered the room minutes before the bell rang. She surveyed the crowd and made a mental census.

"Friends, Romans, choir members, lend me your ears," she said, misquoting her favorite line.

Everyone looked her way, and the room erupted with laughter and greetings. It kissed her ears like a symphonic melody.

"I have returned to the scene of the crime," she said, raising her finger in the air like a statue.

She scanned the room for an empty chair, bounded over to the soprano section, and sat next to a pretty redhead. She was obviously a sophomore, because Myra hadn't seen her in choir before.

"Hi, I'm Myra Grayson," she announced to the girl, as she heaved herself in the chair like a sack of flour.

"Ria James." Her wide smile glowed with confidence.

"Sophomore?"

Ria gave a hint of a nod, as if embarrassed to admit such an indiscretion.

Myra laughed. "Don't worry, Ria. There is no class distinction in choir, just voice distinctions. Are you a soprano?"

"Yes, but I can sing any part," Ria said.

"Ahh, ambidextrous." There was a slight teasing inflection to Myra's voice.

Ria's face contorted. "Huh?"

Myra laughed again. "You know … You can sing with the right hand …" she waived her right hand toward the sopranos, "and you can sing with the left hand." She waved her left hand in the direction of the altos.

They laughed together.

"And, I play the piano," Ria said.

"And, you're bilingual. You know the language of voice *and* piano."

They shared a hearty guffaw until the teacher came in and called for their attention. Myra felt like she'd made a new friend. Ria seemed nice, she made Myra feel … comfortable. She turned her attention away as the teacher explained the musical plans for the year. But, Myra could feel Ria looking at her. *Is she sizing me up? Has she already figured out what a nobody I am*?

Chapter Twenty-Seven

September 1973

The kids' enthusiasm swelled through the corridors between classes, building with each greeting like a shaken bottle of soda pop ready to explode. Teachers attempted to corral the frenzied conversations to start class, without much success. Everywhere Ria turned, conversations buzzed like bees around her head. She sat in frozen silence through most of her morning classes, summing up her new surroundings like a building inspector looking for problems. She felt small and insignificant in the crowd. It was not like last year, in junior high school, where she was the big, cool freshman.

Her eyes darted around looking for a familiar face, but she came up empty. No smiles, no greetings, only teeming hordes of upperclassman everywhere she looked. She was lost in a sea of unfamiliar faces. Had she any idea that moving from the junior high as a freshman to the senior high would leave her in such murky, unfamiliar waters, she would have opted to remain the bright star in her freshman class. But, remaining behind was not an option, so Ria found herself in sophomore limbo. *How long will it take to be cool again?*

It didn't help that she fell on her butt twice during cheerleader tryouts. Her complexion brightened and burned as the varsity squad's laughter bombarded her. Didn't they realize she was captain of the freshman cheerleading squad? But, in the time it took for her to jump in the air, slip, and land flat on her self-centered bottom, she went from popularity to certain obscurity. And, cheerleading ceased being an option. Where else would she have such a wide variety of boys to flirt with?

She sighed and looked out the window as the room filled with students. Her father's words played over in her head like a cassette recording.

"You have other gifts, Ria. There are other ways to be *cool* for the Lord. Try Honor Choir. God has a plan for you, and maybe He can use you there."

She flinched at the memory. If she tried out for Honor Choir and didn't make it, she'd spend the year in the Girls Chorus. What punishment! Imagine being banished to the Girls Chorus for the year. That was unacceptable to the blossoming flirt in her.

A loud, comical voice pulled Ria out of her thoughts.

"Friends, Romans, choir members, lend me your ears," the voice said. It was followed by a barrage of laughter and greetings.

"I have returned to the scene of the crime," the voice said. Ria's tension went down a notch. As she watched, the voice strode through the room, greeting everyone and stopping occasionally to give a hug.

Ria's eyes followed her journey and watched her alight on the chair next to her. Her colorful entrance intrigued Ria. *Who is this social butterfly?*

The voice turned to Ria with her radiant smile and said, "Hi, I'm Myra Grayson."

Ria watched Myra intently, eyes never leaving her face as she spoke. *She commanded a room, this girl with the spicy sense of humor and confident demeanor.* Ria listened and laughed, and even when the teacher interrupted them to start class, Ria's eyes didn't move from Myra.

She was a force to be reckoned with. Ria wanted to be this girl's friend so she could learn from her personality. God must have planned this meeting for her benefit. She'd been drowning all day, and He'd thrown her a life preserver. *Thanks, God.*

The silence stretched out before them like a highway through a desert. It wasn't the awkward silence between two people ensnared in a misunderstanding, but a thoughtful silence between two people who understood the heart of the other. The silence of *knowing.*

Brenda contemplated Myra's mood carefully.

"Did you see Nick?"

"Yeah, he walked right by me in the hall."

"Did he see you?"

"Probably not."

"Are you over him?"

"Yeah. Finally." *Although I'll never know why he sent those yellow roses, at least I'll always have one dried rose preserved for future memories of the boy I thought might have not seen me as a loser.*

The journey home continued as the silence once more slipped comfortably between them like a reassuring hug. Brenda reached over and gave Myra's arm a gentle squeeze.

Myra nodded and smiled toward the desert ahead.

"How was Honor Choir?" Ria's dad asked at dinner.

"Great. I love it. I met a girl, Myra, and we hit it right off. We have the same zany personality. I like her." Ria's voice bubbled like sparkling water.

Her dad smiled and nodded his head. After a moment's contemplation, he continued, "How did you meet?"

"Oh, it was like an answer to prayer, Dad. I was feeling all alone in that choir room and in walked Myra, bigger than life, and she just took over the room. Then she headed toward me, sat down, and introduced herself. And bingo! A kindred spirit was born." Ria laughed. "She made me feel so comfortable."

Once more, her dad offered a knowing smile.

Ria reached for the salt, "She's lots of fun and she's someone I can look up to. You know, someone to—you know—emulate."

Her dad put his fork down, smiling with his signature sparkle in his eye, and spoke with unnerving evenness. "So you know this girl well enough to set your sights on being more like her?"

His directness flustered Ria. "Well … you know … She's nice, she's funny. And, friendly and, you know, outgoing. I like her."

His warm smile never faded. "And, you believe God brought her into your life to teach you something?"

"Sure, why not?"

"Okay." He chuckled. "Let's see what Myra can teach you. Invite her to dinner sometime. We'll pray about it and see what God has planned." He picked up his fork and continued to eat, the glint in his eye never losing its luster.

Chapter Twenty-Eight

October 1973

The words echoed in the room as if in a canyon, bouncing from one wall to another, never stopping, increasing in speed until they whirled around the room like a tornado, consuming

Stella's every thought.

She closed her eyes to fend off the attack. But the words kept coming at her, like a Doberman Pinscher, snarling and snapping and threatening to tear her apart. Stella took a deep breath, as the stale air pushed heavy against her chest. She felt someone take her hand. She was in a haze; who was touching her? Someone spoke her name, blurry, distorted as if underwater.

"Stella, are you okay?" It was John speaking.

Stella reached for her head. *It's John. John is here.*

"Stella …"

She raised her head in slow-motion, opened her eyes, and stared into John's face. Her lips stuck together when she attempted to speak. "Jah … Jah … John."

She surrendered to the blackness that beckoned.

John looked down as Stella opened her eyes again and stared up at him.

"Are you okay, Stella?" His voice quivered.

"What hap … Where am …" Her eyes closed slowly, and she reached for her head. "What happened?"

"You passed out in the doctor's office." He touched her cheek with his fingertips. "Are you okay?"

She glanced around the room, and turned back to John, tears glistening in her eyes. "I'm okay." Her voice was mechanical, flat. She squeezed her eyes tight, forcing the tears to overflow, coursing down her temples into her hair.

John squeezed her hand tighter, willing his strength into her. He didn't know what to say; his own emotions were still uncertain.

Her eyes remained clamped shut as a hoarse whisper escaped her trembling lips: "breast cancer."

Brenda sat silently waiting for Myra to find the words to speak.

"My mom has breast cancer," Myra said. A sob caught in her throat as she looked over at Brenda.

The tears streamed down Myra's face like raindrops cascading down a windowpane. Brenda sat beside her, quiet. There wasn't much she could say to change the circumstances, so she didn't say anything. Her presence was all the comfort she could offer her best friend, and she suspected it was all Myra needed at this point. Brenda put her arm around Myra's shoulder, and Myra buried herself deep into Brenda's waiting arms. Her sobbing filled the room with the fragrance of heartbreak.

Brenda glanced at the clock. Myra needed to go. It was a school night, and Myra's mom would have a cow if she got home late. Or would she? Surely she would understand that Myra was upset after hearing the diagnosis. Brenda shook her head; *better not risk it.*

"Myra, let me walk you home. I don't want you to walk alone like this."

Myra nodded. Her eyes were swollen and reddened from the caustic tears. She sniffed and gulped, but the heaving sobs had subsided. As they slipped out of the back door, Brenda turned to see her mom watching. She didn't say a word. She gave a nod to Brenda to indicate she saw them leave, concern etched on her face.

They ambled in silence for half a block.

"I'm afraid, Brenda." Myra's gentle whisper betrayed her inner pain. "I'm afraid of losing my mom. I love her so much."

"I know, Myra," Brenda said. "I know."

"She had me late in life, Brenda. She's not young, like your mom. I've been a handful—an active teenage daughter when she should have been enjoying her grandchildren."

Brenda puzzled over Myra's words. She always took responsibility for everything. Pretty soon she'd take responsibility for the war in Vietnam and the Watergate scandal.

"She's had a hard life, Brenda. She deserves better," Myra said.

Brenda listened with a compassionate ear and silent lips.

"She has to have surgery to remove both of her breasts. She's a good woman. She deserves better. She deserves better, Brenda." Myra stared straight ahead.

For the remainder of the walk home, Myra rambled on, pouring out her heart to Brenda, who listened attentively and said little.

They reached Myra's back door, and she turned to Brenda. "Thanks."

"You're welcome."

Brenda could see that Myra was reluctant to go inside, so they lingered for a few minutes outside the door, chatting in quiet tones. Myra was finally calm, her voice steady, and her face softened.

The back door opened and Myra's mom appeared behind the screen door. "Are you going to stand out there yakking all night, Myra?" Her words snapped in the quiet darkness like a bullwhip. "Get in the house. It's late."

Chapter Twenty-Nine

October 1973

Ria soon found her place in choir and began to feel like her old self. Her dad was right. She didn't need cheerleading to be cool. She fell into a happy routine at school getting involved with activities and making friends. Still, her favorite class was Honor Choir, and Myra was one of her favorite people.

As Ria entered the choir room, she saw Myra in her usual seat, looking over the music. Ria glanced around the room to see if anyone else noticed Myra sitting there quietly. Several groups of people were involved in conversations, but no one seemed to notice Myra. How did she slip in without being noticed? Ria headed toward Myra and sat down beside her.

"Hey, you," Ria said.

Myra looked up at Ria with a slight smile." Hey, Ree. How are you?"

"What's wrong, Myra?" Ria had never seen Myra so subdued.

Myra sighed. "Aw, nothing." Another shadow of a smile crossed her lips.

The teacher walked in, and the bell was about to ring. Not a good time to push Myra. "Let's talk after school."

Myra nodded and squeezed Ria's arm.

"What's going on Myra?" Ria's voice was gentle.

Myra hesitated for a second, looked around, and whispered, "My mom has breast cancer."

"Oh, Myra, I'm sorry." Ria wanted to say something to make things better, but she couldn't find the words.

"I don't know what to do." Myra hung her head.

Nor did Ria. She saw so much sadness in her friend that she was unable to take away.

"I can tell my mom is worried. I am, too," Myra said. "I love my mom. I'm afraid of losing her." She paused. "I try to be good, so she has one less thing to worry about. But, I don't think she's worried about me at all. She's worried about the cancer. And, she's still mourning my brother's death."

Ria raised her eyebrows and moved closer.

"Yeah, my brother was killed in Vietnam three years ago."

Ria's lips separated slightly, but no words came out.

"It's hard on all of us. My brother, Mark, left the state. My brother, Billy, became real angry, my dad has become quiet and distant, and my mom cries all the time." Myra's words began to pile on top of each other, gathering momentum until they broke the dam and started rushing down river, flooding the moment with dark emotion.

Myra's darkness was overwhelming. Ria grappled for some words of comfort. She couldn't find any. She felt drawn to Myra because she was such a happy, in-control person. But, Ria could see that Myra hid a lot of grief over her family in her heart that she didn't share. She started to reach over to put her arm around Myra, but stopped herself. She'd never been a situation that required comforting someone before. She'd never seen Myra cry before. What should she say? Was there even a way for her to make a difference in Myra's life*? Lord, this is very uncomfortable. What do I do with all Myra's sadness?*

"Hey, think your mom will let you come to dinner Friday night?

Myra nodded.

Ria smiled. "Good. I'll let my mom know you're coming." *My dad will know how to cheer you up.*

Myra asked her dad if she could use the car, since Ria's house was about a mile away and she didn't want to ride her bicycle at night. He was pretty good about allowing her to use the vehicle when he didn't need it.

When Myra arrived at Ria's house, her parents welcomed her like an old family friend. During dinner, Mrs. James put Myra at ease by making small talk and asking questions to get to know her. Myra felt as if they may just like her, somehow. Not very many people made such an effort to get to know her. Ria and her father had the same sassy, silly sense of humor. He made Myra laugh through most of the meal the same way Ria made her laugh through class.

Mrs. James started clearing the table. "Tell us about your family, Myra. Do you have any brothers and sisters?"

Myra smiled. "I have four older brothers. I'm the only girl." She paused. "Actually, I only have three brothers left. One was killed in Vietnam three years ago."

"Oh, I'm sorry," Mrs. James said as her smile faded. "That must have been hard for you."

Myra pressed her lips together and nodded. "Mostly for my mom. Danny was her favorite." Myra looked up and smiled. "I'm the only child left at home now. So, I've had the best of both worlds. Before, part of a big loving family, and now—a small, close family."

"Oh, that's wonderful, Myra. Ria, sweetheart, please help me with the dessert."

Ria got up to help her mom.

"Be right back, Myra," she said.

Myra watched Ria closely—her smile, her reactions, the way she spoke to her parents, and the way they spoke to her. Myra was recording it all on her mental clipboard. She felt a huge puzzlement inside of her that she couldn't figure out. A piece was missing. There was something different about this family. There was real warmth here that was unfamiliar to Myra. *Laughter and warmth …*

"Come back again, Myra," Mr. James said at the end of the evening. "We'll share some more laughter."

"Definitely," Myra said, her smile spreading across her face.

"Soon," Ria called after her with a wave.

Myra waved back. She had every intention of returning—as often as they would let her. There was something so good about being there. Again that puzzle nagged her thoughts. *Why are they so nice to me?*

Myra looked around the examination room. She had only been to see this doctor a couple of times. Nothing super serious. Today she'd come with a small skin infection on her leg that seemed to be getting bigger.

"Mom, I really don't need you to come in the exam room with me. I'm not eight years old anymore," Myra said, trying to convince her mom. The effort proved useless.

"I need to speak with the doctor, Myra." End of discussion.

The nurse entered the room with a chart in her hand. "Hi Myra, I'm Marsha. How're you today?"

"Fine."

"What brings you in to see us?"

"A small infection on my leg."

Her mother gave a humph.

Myra ignored it and focused her attention on Nurse Marsha.

"Okay, let's get a blood pressure." Marsha made a note in Myra's chart. She stopped writing for a minute and stared hard at something in the chart. Then slowly looked over at Myra and smiled.

Myra smiled back at the nurse and took her warmth as an invitation to make small talk. “So, are you new here? You weren't the nurse the last time I was here.”

Marsha blinked. “Oh, yes, I am new. I worked at the hospital for eighteen years, but decided I needed a less strenuous job. So, when this position with Dr. Young became available, I took it.”

Myra nodded. It seemed the work *would* be easier and not as distasteful. “Do you like it?”

“It's *very* rewarding,” Marsha said.

Myra considered her words for a moment. Being a nurse didn't sound like much fun. It sounded like a lot of work with a bunch of sick people and stuff she would probably find *icky.* She smiled at her own word choice.

Marsha headed to the door. “I'll let Dr. Young know you're here.”

Marsha sprinted down the hall and almost collided with Dr. Young as he stepped out from an examination room.

“Oh, Doctor, you startled me.” She was out of breath.

“What is it, Marsha? Is everything okay?”

“Yes, yes. Fine. Everything is fine. Myra Grayson is ready to see you. I wondered …”

Dr. Young paused a moment. “Wondered what?”

“It's just that, do you know anything about Myra Grayson?”

He reached for Myra's chart, took it from Marsha, and opened it. “I know she had five stitches in her right arm when she was eight, but other than that, she's been a pretty healthy girl.”

“Do you know what hospital she was born in?”

“I'm not sure. Her family moved to the suburbs when she was a child. Possibly Downtown General Hospital. I know they used to live near there.”

Marsha's heart rate increased, and she squeezed her hands together in an effort to calm herself.

"Why, Marsha? What's wrong?"

"Nothing's wrong, Doctor," she said. Then, with a rush of energy, she added, "When I was a young nurse at Downtown General, I found—I had an encounter with an infant that touched my heart. I think it may have been Myra. Could you ask her mother if Myra was in an incubator for a few days after she was born?"

Dr. Young hesitated. "I guess I could ask. Why does it matter?"

Marsha took a deep breath. "I witnessed a miracle the morning of March 8, 1956, when a child was sent to the morgue, dead. But, she wasn't dead. I found her alive when I went in there. I took her back up to the postpartum floor and gave her to Dr. Jesse Moreno. I've thought of her and prayed for her many, many times. I never knew the child's name. I was just wondering if it could be Myra."

Dr. Young smiled at her story. "Well, let's go find out."

Dr. Young entered the exam room, followed by Marsha. "How are you Mrs. Grayson? Myra?"

Mrs. Grayson glanced at Dr. Young. "Fine. Thanks."

"Terrific," Myra said, her face all aglow.

"Well, ladies, before I examine Myra, I just need a little history for my records. Okay?"

There were no objections.

"Any allergies that you know of?"

Mrs. Grayson shook her head. "None that I know of."

"Any hospitalizations?"

"No."

"Any complications at birth?"

Mrs. Grayson shifted her weight in the chair.

Marsha held her breath with anticipation.

"I had weak lungs, so they put me in an incubator for a few days," Myra said with a triumphant grin.

Dr. Young pressed on without comment. "And that was at Downtown General, correct?"

"Yes," Mrs. Grayson said.

Marsha's excitement burst out of her. "I worked there in 1956. Was your doctor Jesse Moreno?"

Mrs. Grayson nodded. She was visibly uncomfortable.

"There was a story of an infant and a miracle that people talked about for weeks. Incredible story, really. I heard it many times. Is Myra that child?"

Mrs. Grayson stared at Marsha. "Maybe, I don't know."

"It had to be, Mrs. Grayson. It's too much of a coincidence not to be."

"I guess it could be …"

Dr. Young interrupted the conversation. "Well, then, that's all my questions. Let's take a look at that leg, Myra."

Marsha watched the doctor assess the infection for a moment and then picked up her stethoscope.

"I'll go prepare your next patient, Doctor."

"Thanks, Marsha."

She headed down the hall and slipped into an empty exam room, closed the door with one swift movement, and leaned against the door. She closed her eyes and inhaled deeply.

"Father, You are amazing. You've allowed me to meet that child again, after all these years. Thank You for reminding me of that awesome miracle seventeen years ago. Please continue to bless her—Myra—and her family. Keep your hand of protection around her heart, Lord. May she know You and the knowledge of Your love through Jesus Christ."

Chapter Thirty

November 1973

Excitement radiated throughout the air in the auditorium. Myra felt it to her very core. The night she'd planned, worked for, and dreamed of for weeks was finally here! Now, she sat in the front of the auditorium, her hands sweating and heart pounding.

It was the first time since she'd gotten involved with shows that she wasn't on stage. Myra held the prestigious position of student director for her last school play. Shocked when chosen, she thought surely there was someone more qualified and knowledgeable about such things. She was so excited she could have burst like an overfull water balloon.

Shortly into the rehearsal schedule, the faculty director was called to jury duty, leaving Myra with the bulk of the directing. And, she'd done it. Mr. Ames returned a few days before opening night to find the play ready to go.

This was Myra's baby, and she was about to birth her opening night. If her anxiety level over the cast's performance was her only issue, she'd have been fine. Opening-night jitters were nothing new to Myra. But her mother's ugly words earlier that evening had blighted Myra's happy anticipation of the play's success.

The house lights dimmed as the curtain opened on scene one.

The warm water soothed Myra's body as it rained down on her–over her hair and down her back. She began to relax.

She poured herbal shampoo in her hand, then swirled the creamy liquid into her long, wet hair. It foamed into rich, white bubbles on her head. Mmmmm it smelled delicious. The shower felt relaxing. Her day had been good. The play would be good. Myra felt lavished in "good." She sighed heavily. Good. *Real good.*

The phone rang. Myra chuckled. She was usually the first person to answer the phone. Heavens, she'd never want to miss a call. But, she was not about to dash out of the shower.

The ringing continued. Eight, nine, ten rings. *Isn't anyone going to answer the phone?* Frustrated, Myra climbed out of the shower, wrapped a towel around her, and dashed out of the bathroom, leaving a trail of water behind. "Is anyone going to answer the phone?" Her mom's shout startled Myra.

"I'm getting it!" Myra's heart galloped like a racehorse as she headed toward the phone. She rushed around the corner into the kitchen and almost collided with her mother, who had dashed up the stairs from the basement.

Her mother jumped back at Myra's sudden appearance. "Why am I the only one who can answer the phone in this house?" she barked.

"I was in the shower!" Cold and annoyed that she was interrupted, Myra's heart was still pumping.

The phone stopped ringing. They both looked over at the sudden silence.

"Probably your father calling to tell me what time he's picking me up for the wake tonight," her mother said, her volume increasing.

Myra was aware her mother's step-mother had died. Her mother had gone to the wake the past two nights. Was she really going again?

"But tonight is opening night."

Her mom peered back, her face an immovable concrete slab. "So?"

"So you've been to her wake two nights in a row. I'm your daughter, and tonight's important to me. It's not like you've had any kind of relationship with her for seventeen years. I never even met her."

"She's the only mother I ever knew." Tears filled her mother's eyes with the fierceness of a breaking dam.

"I've heard the stories, Mom. She treated you like a slave and lied about you until your father beat you. Why is she more important to you dead than I am alive?"

Her mom's face reddened, and she lifted her hand and swung with angry force.

Myra stepped back as her mother's hand whizzed by her face.

"I hope your lousy play flops!" Her mother's voice cracked with her scream.

The words echoed in Myra's head, bouncing from one side of her skull to the other, shaking her brain like gelatin.

Her mother marched off, descending the stairs with loud, even steps.

Myra continued to drip in the kitchen, creating a puddle on the floor, like a pool of unshed tears beneath her feet.

The curtain closed on the final scene and the players began to emerge from backstage for curtain call. First bit parts, then speaking parts, and finally the leads. Wait, where was Cindy, the lead? All the actors were bowing and Cindy wasn't among them. The audience was clapping, but they didn't give a standing ovation as Myra had hoped.

Where's Cindy?

Eventually, the stage emptied, the house lights came up, and Myra sat stunned at the explanation to why Cindy missed curtain call. She had waited in the dressing-room, and no one came to tell her it was time. It was a simple oversight. But, Myra had known from the beginning she wouldn't be able to pull this off. Why did she ever believe she could direct a successful play? Her empty heart echoed "loser" as her mother's words flooded her thoughts … *I hope your lousy play flops.* Myra's defeat loomed over her like dark, angry clouds.

January 1974

Myra ran her finger down the list posted on the stage door. *Wait, do it again.* There's the character she wanted, but her name wasn't next to it. She didn't get the part. She bowed her head and pressed her lips together to keep them from trembling. Her shoulders slumped as she looked at the name of the leading man playing opposite the part she wanted. She knew who he was. He was tall—very tall. Myra swallowed hard to stifle the tears. She didn't get the part. Mr. Ames had given it to someone he felt could do it better. But, he'd probably just tell her she wasn't the right height to play against this leading man.

A deep sigh escaped her lips. She followed her finger further down the list of names to the chorus. There. Placed under the soprano section.

Her name at the bottom of the page caught her eye. Understudy? A flash of heat moved from her toes to her head. Myra wiped the sweat from her forehead. Understudy? She'd never heard of such a thing. Mr. Ames had never used understudies in any of the musicals or plays he directed while she attended this high school. Understudy? Was this a joke? What was he trying to say? Whatever it was, she didn't like it. She reached up to feel her cheek. It stung—like she'd just been slapped.

She jostled through the gathering crowd toward Brenda.

"Well?" Brenda's impatience spilled out of her mouth.

"Understudy. He made me an understudy." Her voice sounded lifeless even to her own ears.

Brenda reached out to touch Myra's arm. But Myra looked beyond Brenda and shuffled past her.

"Wait, Myra." She grabbed Myra's arm. "I didn't know they used understudies."

"I've never seen them before." Her voice trailed off. "But what do *I* know ...?"

Myra's slow trek down the corridor ended at the doors where she merged into the crowd and exited the building.

February 1974

As she watched the scene unfold during rehearsal, Ria kept her eye on Myra instead of the director. *She's so funny.* Her antics during the scene had everyone laughing. Myra was a star. She commanded a room—or in this case, the stage—even when it was full of other people. *How did she do that?*

"You always manage to make people laugh when you're up there, Myra," Ria said as she met Myra after rehearsal.

Myra inhaled slowly and gave Ria a small, forced smile. "I love being up there, Ree. Big parts, little parts, chorus, walk-ons—anything that puts me on the stage. I love it all."

"And you're so good at it, My."

"Thanks." Myra's smile broadened.

"How are you finding time to learn all the music for the chorus and memorize all the lines for your understudy responsibility?"

"I'm not," Myra said pointedly.

Ria pursed her lips and cocked her head. She waited for Myra to explain her short answer.

Myra's lips pressed tightly together, and she stared at the floor. Myra didn't say anything for a moment. She sighed. "I consider it a slap in the face to be made understudy. This isn't Broadway, Ree. Chances are I will never play that part. We're only doing four shows. They've never had understudies before. It feels like … like they're throwing crumbs to a dog. Was that supposed to make me happy?"

Ria flinched. How could her friend be so upset? It would be an honor to be chosen for understudy, but obviously Myra didn't agree. *Was Myra just feeling sorry for herself?*

"I'm not learning the lines because they don't need me. And, I don't need sympathy from them because they didn't give me the part I wanted. I would be perfectly happy in the chorus. But giving me some bogus responsibility is an insult. They've never worked with me, rehearsed with me, or even asked if I *had* the lines memorized. So really, what good would I be if the lead got sick? It's a joke."

Myra drew in a breath and raked her hand across both eyes to remove the tears. "No one needs to tell me what a loser I am, Ree. I'm mediocre at best. Mediocre grades, mediocre talent. I have no boyfriend because what boy in his right mind would want me as a girlfriend? I ran for class president and lost. I wanted to be a cheerleader, a sorority sister …" Myra's voice broke. "I don't need anyone to remind me I'm not good enough, or tall enough, or pretty enough." She swiped the tears again. "I already know that," she whispered.

Ria's jaw fell open. Myra had shared some sadness in her life before, but this was different. *This* was something Ria had not realized existed in Myra Grayson. Ria hung her head, her face grew hot. She'd completely missed the hopeless despair that squeezed Myra's heart. *Oh, Lord, I'm sorry, I was wrong.*

Chapter Thirty One

February 1974

Ria opened her eyes and glanced around the dinner table. Warmth spread with slow determination over her soul like maple syrup over pancakes. It was the sweet spirit of gratitude.

Her father's prayers before meals revealed his thankfulness and created a sense of peace in their home Ria had never thought about before. She smiled and reached for the potatoes.

"You haven't invited Myra over lately, Ria." Her father winked at her and accepted the potatoes.

"Musical rehearsals keep us pretty busy, so I figured it was best to wait until after the show is over." She picked up the green beans and spooned some on her plate.

"How is she?" Her mom said as she passed the plate of pork chops.

"Fine." Ria looked at her dad and he smiled at her. He always smiled at her. She was blessed to have such a wonderful family. They loved her, prayed for her, and respected her. She'd taken it all for granted until faced with the reality of Myra's longing soul. While Ria was worried about getting on the cheerleading squad, what boys she could flirt with, and how she could maintain her coolness, she never once thought of anyone but herself. She'd made friends with Myra because she was funny and seemed to have it all together. Ria befriended her for selfish purposes—to emulate her. All the while, Myra's heart was searching for the very thing Ria had to offer.

"Dad, remember when I met Myra and told you she was an answer to prayer? I thought I knew the reason God had brought her into my life."

Her father's smile encouraged her to continue.

"I was wrong, Dad. He didn't bring her into my life so I could be like her. " She took a deep breath before continuing. "He brought *me* into her life so I could help *her*."

Her dad closed his eyes and nodded gently.

"It wasn't about me, Dad. It was never about me. It's always been about Myra. God just revealed that to me. He wants me to be Myra's friend so I can share Jesus with her."

"I knew you'd get it," he said as mirth bubbled from his throat and filled the room with laughter.

"God gave Myra an ability to laugh and love and sing. She's a force to be reckoned with. But, she's got a huge void in her life that stands in the way of real joy. She's made me realize how much I have to be thankful for. God put her in my path, and I need to do my part to point her in the right direction."

"I'll pray God opens your mouth and fills it with life-giving words, Ria. He will guide you in sharing the truth of Jesus's love with Myra." He reached over and gripped Ria's small hand with his big strong one.

Monday could not come fast enough for Ria. She'd been praying for Myra all weekend. She prayed that God would allow her to be a good friend to Myra.

Ria searched for Myra, but the corridors seemed more crowded than usual. She made a mental note of each time they passed in the hall. They exchanged a big smile and a wave at each sighting. Myra's bright, cheerful smile radiated genuine delight at seeing Ria.

At rehearsal that evening, Ria sat beside Myra. They giggled softly at everything and nothing. Ria's heart was ready to reach out to Myra, but she was prepared to take it slow.

"I'm so glad we've become friends, My. You are such a gift from God to me."

Myra's smile softened. She stared into Ria's eyes for a long moment. "I feel the same way, Ree. I'm glad we're friends."

"Jesus loves you, My."

Myra lifted one eyebrow, and a barely discernible grimace crossed her lips. "And Jesus loves *you*, Ree." Myra smirked as she said the words.

Only one week before opening night. The days were flying by like an express train through Chicago. Myra's heart was heavy. Just a few short months until graduation. Most of her friends were going to college. But, not her. She had no immediate plans for the months following graduation. When she asked her mom to fill out an application to help her get financial aid for college, her mother made it clear it wasn't going to happen.

"It's nobody's business how much money is in my savings account," she told Myra, jaw firmly set, eyes piercing Myra's soul.

Myra resigned herself to not attending college in the fall. Besides, she wasn't smart enough, and her father was adamant that girls didn't need more than a high school diploma. A college degree wasn't required to get married and raise a family.

Not that it mattered. Who would marry *her*? It's not like guys were beating a path to her door. She didn't even have a date for the prom. Shoot, she didn't even have a prospect. Oh sure, she had dozens of friends—many of the male persuasion, but none of those friends were interested in dating her. No matter. Maybe she would just be a nun and live in a convent. Maybe she could dedicate her life to the church and do some kind of good. So far she had proven to be of little use to anyone.

Myra had almost forgotten Ria's ridiculous statement *Jesus loves you, My* when she passed Ria again and she waved and called out to Myra, "Jesus loves you, My." It made Myra cringe.

Why on earth would Jesus love *her*? Does Jesus love losers? She wasn't smart enough for college, not pretty enough for a boyfriend, or tall enough for the part in the musical she wanted. She had no outstanding talents. She couldn't read music, she was bad at math, and she couldn't swim to save her life. So why would Jesus love her? Almost every time Ria passed her, it was the same thing.

Even if she was a loser, Myra considered herself a good person. She went to church every Sunday. She just couldn't remember anything that was said, that's all. She stared at the head in front of her, counted how many people wore green, recited song lyrics in her mind, and wondered what her mom and dad got out of the sermon.

She believed in God, and she wanted to make Him happy. So, she went to church out of respect for her parents and fear of God. What did love have to do with religion, anyway? As Ria passed her in the corridor, Myra put her hand up, palm forward, cheesy grin in place, and repeated, "Jesus loves you, too, Ree."

Jesus probably did love Ria. At least *she* was lovable.

The Monday after the musical, Myra and Brenda discussed the show's success on the way to school.

"Even if you didn't get the part you wanted, you were still funnier than heck in that one scene." Brenda was a straight shooter, she never minced words. She never pretended. That's why Myra loved her so much. Myra would miss Brenda terribly when she left for college.

"Yeah, it was a pretty fun show. I had a good time. Wonder what Mr. Ames would say if he knew I never memorized a single line as the understudy?" Myra smiled at Brenda.

"He probably knew," Brenda said.

"Yeah, probably."

Spring was attempting to poke its way through the frozen winter landscape. Tiny green buds appeared on the trees' barren branches. Lawns were reduced to scattered patches of dirty snow "islands." The tulips and daffodils were pushing up miniature green knife-shaped sprouts through the hardened soil. Myra loved the new life emerging in spring because it held the promise of better days ahead—warm, sunshiny days. If only her life held such promise.

"Greg asked me to the prom," Brenda said. Her announcement held no surprise to Myra. She knew that was coming when Greg and Brenda started dating.

Myra wanted to go to the prom, but she wasn't going alone.

"You know, maybe that guy you met during the musical will ask you to the prom," Brenda said.

"What guy?"

"The one you like." She turned her head and waved her hand in the air as if he was right in front of them.

"I doubt it."

"*Maybe* he will."

"I'm not counting on it."

"Well, maybe he will."

Myra laughed at Brenda's persistence. "Okay, maybe he will. And maybe I'll wake up a fairy princess tomorrow."

"Maybe you *will*."

Chapter Thirty-Two

May 1974

A sea of graduates filed into the auditorium like soldiers in a parade, creating an ocean of blue gowns and mortar boards at the front of the room. The somber air mixed with the thrill of anticipation, and the graduates' elation could barely be contained as they took their seats.

Myra twisted in her chair to look behind her. The ceremony had not even started, and she could already see mothers with red, swollen eyes dabbing tears with their tissues, and fathers boasting proud satisfied grins. Myra was glad to see her own parents sitting somewhere in the middle of the auditorium. Was that pride she saw on their face? She considered that for a moment, then dismissed it.

Myra faced forward again. She inhaled a long, slow breath and held it for a moment. Then she let it out with a quick burst of air.

Graduation closed the book on life as she had known it. What would she do now? Certainly not college. Myra could still hear the sound of the door slamming on her chance at a higher education.

The principal welcomed the audience to the graduation ceremony of the Class of 1974. "It has been an auspicious year ..."

Myra's thoughts slipped back over the *auspicious year*. Her senior year had slipped through her fingers with regrettable speed. *So, this is how it ends.* Was this tedious graduation ceremony to be her swansong? She'd endured a disappointing play, an anti-climactic musical, and then there was the underwhelming Senior Prom …

Myra couldn't wait to tell Brenda that Franklin had asked her to the prom. With her big cheesy grin firmly in place, Brenda's even tone hid her own excitement. "See, I told you."

Myra watched the couples dancing. Would Franklin ask her to dance before the night was over? He'd barely spoken to her all evening. The laughter they'd shared during the musical was long forgotten, and they sat at the table like strangers on a downtown bus.

Myra endured the long evening with patience. When Franklin walked her to her door, he shuffled his feet and looked down at his fingernails. She waited with anticipation, her heart racing, for him to lean in to kiss her good night.

"Thank you," she said, hoping to move things along.

Franklin cleared his throat several times. "Uh, thanks for, uh, going with me." An awkward moment splashed over them like a wave over a rowboat. With a languid smile, Franklin reached for Myra's hand and gave it a lethargic squeeze that matched his weak smile. Myra felt her color drain from her face and her hands were suddenly clammy. Was he shaking her hand goodnight like this was some sort of business deal? Her throat constricted and she could barely breathe.

Myra returned his unenthusiastic gesture with an equally meaningful nod and choked, "Okay, I guess I'll see you at graduation."

She turned toward the door and climbed the three concrete stairs. She opened the door and entered the house, never looking back.

"We'd like to congratulate our scholarship winners, and now we'll hear from our class valedictorian."

Myra clapped her hands together twice, then stared at them clasped and lying in her lap. Surely the entire year wasn't a bust. There was the camping trip with Ria's church youth group on Memorial Day weekend. That was a bright spot.

Myra reclined in the grass beside the bonfire, knees bent to the sky, arms resting beneath her head. Every star in the sky seemed to glitter a little brighter there. A quiet contentment settled over her. As the fire crackled and snapped, the dancing flames managed to mesmerize the small gathering.

Someone started to sing, and another camper joined in. Myra listened to the unfamiliar tunes as their voices flowed from one song into the next. The words seemed to captivate her soul until the lyrics of one song reached out and seized her attention.

Myra bolted up and turned to Ria. "This song says you know you're going to heaven. How could you possibly know that? No one knows that until they face God on Judgment Day, and He weighs your life and decides if you're good enough."

Ria smiled and leaned closer to Myra. "No one is *good enough*, My. The Bible says we are *all* sinners."

One by one, Ria's friends moved closer like a crowd at a rock concert.

Ria took Myra's hand. "But God loves us so much that He sent His Son to die on the cross for *our* sins."

Someone beyond the firelight chimed in. "All you need to do is ask Jesus to forgive your sins and come into your heart. That's how we *know* we're going to heaven."

Myra's eyes moved from one voice to another, trying desperately to follow their meaning. The barrage of words went on for a few minutes, until Myra jumped to her feet. Confusion churned and bubbled in her like hot molten lava.

"Stop," she shouted and shook her head. "Stop." She started to back away from the gathering. She heaved a sigh and looked down at Ria's imploring face. "Ree, if what you're telling me is true …" She turned and walked into the darkness.

The principal was back in front of the podium.

"Every year, one outstanding student is presented the Principal's Service Award. This student has consistently shown …"

Myra slumped in her seat. She closed her eyes. Maybe that would speed up this graduation ceremony. Her stomach growled.

"This student has proven …"

Myra shifted in her seat and bristled. Couldn't he just announce the cheerleader, jock, senior class officer, or Honor Society member who won this award and get on to the diplomas? Some people have parties to go to. Not me … but some people.

Stars hung in the sky as if they had been tossed like confetti at a celestial wedding. Myra leaned against the tree, knees bent, head tilted upward. Engaged in a heated debate with God, she was clearly the underdog. Myra placed her forehead on her knees, tears spilling from her eyes. She sensed the presence beside her, but didn't lift her head.

"Every year the youth group from my son's church comes to my farm for a weekend camp out and every year, I meet someone who is struggling with some unanswered questions." Mr. Meehan paused. "Would you like to talk, Myra?"

She nodded her head slightly, but remained silent.

"What's on your mind, Myra?"

She squeezed her eyes tight. "If what Ria says is true, I could have died yesterday and gone to hell. How come I never knew this stuff before?"

Mr. Meehan nodded. "Myra, we're all like apples. God picks us when we're ripe. You've probably had several opportunities to come to Christ in the past few months, but you just weren't ready to hear the good news."

Myra lifted her head and sat up straight. "Brenda and I went to the Billy Graham movie, *Time to Run.* I went forward to tell the lady I was very religious. I didn't want to just walk out on Jesus, you know?"

"See, there?" Mr. Meehan said, his voice rising slightly. "You weren't ripe yet. But, I think you may be now, Myra. What do you think?"

She nodded. Mr. Meehan reached out and took Myra's hand and led her in a simple prayer. Myra asked Jesus into her heart that day.

"This year's winner of the Principal's Service Award is Myra Grayson."

Myra's head snapped up. She looked around the auditorium as it thundered with applause. The sound of the applause rolled over her like a wave in a storm, washing away her thoughts. But, it was for her and she thrilled at the sound.

"Myra, you won. Go get your award." The girl beside her gave Myra a little shove.

Myra had not heard a single word the principal said. She had no idea what she'd done to deserve the award. Whatever accolades the principal shared with the audience were lost to her forever. She bounded toward the stage as the applause continued. Did everyone know she wasn't listening to a word the principal said? As she approached, he put out his hand and Myra took it.

"Thank you," she said, and followed it with a large smile, hoping it relayed her gratefulness.

"You deserve it, Myra." He handed her a plaque. She read it carefully, then turned to the audience and lifted the plaque like an

Olympic medal winner. Once again the applause sounded through the auditorium. It was like a healing balm to her grieving heart. This would be her last journey across this stage.

With her head held high and her smile firmly in place, Myra walked to the edge of the stage and descended the stairs. *How typical. On my last day of school—facing an uncertain future, I receive an award, and I'm completely in the dark as to why. Good grief.*

At the conclusion, the crowd headed toward the exit in the back of the auditorium, but Myra headed toward the stage. The crowd was thick and moved like ketchup from a new bottle. She'd have some time to say good-bye before she met her mom and dad in the parking lot.

For the last time, Myra climbed the stairs to the stage and slipped behind the curtain. Backstage was as she remembered it—would always remember it. She closed her eyes and breathed in scenes of shows she performed in. The spotlight warmed her face like an August sun. The applause tickled her ears like a baby's first giggle. She could smell the greasepaint, the spirit gum, the hairspray—it filled her with the thrill of opening night. The excitement, the butterflies, even the momentary stage fright just before an entrance. Scripts, costumes, upstage, downstage, house lights, orchestra pit, curtain calls—she was snatching each memory as fast as she could. She would lock all her memories away in her heart.

Myra peeked through the curtain and stole a glance at her auditorium one last time. It was emptying fast now. She needed to go face her uncertain future.

"What took you so long?" Her mother's scowl rebuked Myra as much is her words.

"I had to say good-bye," Myra said, looking back one last time.

"Congratulations on your award," her father said, reaching for the plaque.

"Thanks." Myra handed it to him. She looked around and started toward their car.

"We've made arrangements for you to go to college," her mother said, the words smacking Myra on the back of her head.

"Huh?"

"Yeah, I called a friend of mine. She lives near a community college, and she said you could stay with her family and go to school."

Confused, Myra turned slowly to face her mother. What friends did her mother have outside the few ladies in the neighborhood? "Who is it?"

"Oh, you don't know her. She was in my wedding."

"You're sending me away to a school I've never heard of, to live with people I've never met?"

"You said you wanted to go to college. So go."

Chapter Thirty-Three

November 1974

Raindrops hit the puddle with a splash that spread into tiny rings. A heavenly water ballet, the pitter-patter on the roof was the background orchestration. Every drop had a part in the show, entering on cue to fulfill its theatrical destiny. The diamond-like drops rushed eagerly toward Myra, covering her with wet kisses, thanking her for joining them in their spectacular display.

People rushed by, attempting to avoid the rain. Myra studied each face with longing. None of them were familiar. She heaved a sigh. After a whole semester at this college, she'd not met one person she wanted to befriend.

Each day she went to classes, attempted to smile at strangers, and went back to live with a family of strangers. None more strange than mother's friend whose house she lived in. Her critical spirit weighed heavy on Myra. But, it was almost over. This was the last day of the semester. She'd finished her last exam. By tomorrow at this time, she would be with her mom and dad again.

Good-bye cranky ol' woman.

Myra headed toward her bicycle with gratitude.

It was Myra's bicycle the woman had targeted the most.

"You can't continue riding that bicycle to college. The rainy season is coming. You'll have to start riding the bus," she'd said.

"Your father should have bought you a used car." Her retort zinged at Myra, like sharp razor blades flying through the air straight for her. She almost ducked to avoid being sliced. She picked up the five letters from the table addressed to her and headed to the room where she stayed.

"Yeah, don't forget your fan mail. You have to stop living in the past, My-Rah." Her words splintered into pieces against the door as Myra shut it.

After several days of badgering, Myra could no longer endure the sound of the woman's voice. She bought the bus ticket, hoping it would put an end to the constant criticism.

Myra dashed to the bus, lungs burning. *Why couldn't I just ride my bike and leave when I wanted instead of trying to be on time to catch this stupid bus?*

She resented being pushed into taking the bus because it *might rain*. As she fumbled for the bus pass in her bag, panic swept over her. What if she lost it? The allowance her father sent would not be enough to purchase another.

Her fingers felt the pass at the bottom and she snatched it up, almost disappointed. If she'd lost it, she could have ridden her bicycle. But then, she'd have wasted all that money. She scowled at the ticket as she shoved it into the machine.

Each day she dragged her floral canvas bag of textbooks onto the bus. The sun blazed bright and warm as if stuck in the wrong season. Apparently, no one had told the sun the rainy season was here. Each sunny day made sitting on the bus more difficult for Myra to endure.

Every time she walked by that woman, she was tempted to say, "Another warm, dry day my bicycle sat in your garage unused, while I wasted my allowance on that crazy bus." Oh, she really wanted to. But she didn't out of respect for her mom.

Myra stared out the window as the neighborhood rolled by like scenery in a play. After enduring the bus all week, Myra barely noticed the "set changes" anymore. As she dropped her eyes and slumped back in the seat, a man sat beside her. She didn't turn to acknowledge him. Why bother?

"Good morning," he said, his charismatic voice breezing through the stale air.

Myra turned slightly to see who the stranger was addressing. His blue eyes stared back. She gave a polite nod, noting his white shirt collar glaring out from beneath his red sweater vest, then turned her face to the window.

"Are you a student?"

"Yeah."

"On your way to class?"

Myra narrowed her eyes, and she turned back to face him. She wanted to tell him it was none of his business, but her eyes fell on his smile. His big, eager smile. She pressed her lips together for a moment to rein in her biting words.

"Yes."

"That's great," the stranger said, bursting with energy. "I went to that college too. About fifteen years ago. Did my general ed. and transferred to the university to get my master's degree."

Myra sighed, forced into politeness. "A master's in what?" Her jaw muscles stiffened.

"Oh man, it was hard. I never spent more time working on anything. Studied day and night to make decent grades. But it was worth it. Landed me a great job. High profile, you know? Pays well ..."

On and on he chatted, from one topic to the next. Myra listened, and soon his easy-going attitude and sharp sense of humor pulled her in and she began to smile. It wasn't until she got off the bus that she realized he'd never answered her question about his master's degree.

Three days in a row the stranger sat beside her, regaling her with stories from his past and poking fun at current events. It was the only time she laughed during the day, and she looked forward to it like a much longed-for dessert.

On Friday, he asked her out to dinner. "I know a nice restaurant on the top floor of a bank building downtown. It has a great view."

Myra longed to get out of that woman's house. A chance to sit in a nice restaurant with her new friend and talk quietly about her day would be a wonderful change from her host's constant criticism at the dinner table.

"Sure, but can we make it an early night? I have a paper due on Monday, and I haven't started it yet."

A satisfied smile spread across his face, as once again Myra noted his sweater vest. This was the fourth one he'd worn. His wardrobe was stuck in the '60s, but Myra brushed the thought aside. He was a nice man who is taking her to dinner. Who cared about his sweater vests?

The lights of the city twinkled through the night as Myra admired the view. Her date's conversation bubbled over like Root Beer over ice cream, and she listened with her head resting back against the booth. Myra glanced around the restaurant and smiled. She was having a good time. She'd almost forgotten what that was like.

He paused to take a breath, and Myra took the opportunity to inquire about him. He'd carefully and skillfully avoided conversation that would indicate who he was and what he did. He was just a guy with a master's degree who owned a lot of sweater vests.

"So, tell me about your job." Myra smiled and glanced at him. Warmth radiated from her face and body, as though she were glowing inside.

Without a pause, he set his fork down, his head nodding eagerly. He leaned forward as his words rushed out like a speeding train. "Hey, I have a terrific idea. Why don't we go on a picnic Sunday morning? I know this beautiful place in the Valley—only an hour from here. I'll pick you up early, and we'll take a leisurely drive.

Maybe stop at some roadside fruit stands. How 'bout it? It'll be great."

Myra blinked once and stared across the table, attempting to process his abrupt disregard of her question. She cleared her throat and attempted to smile. "Thank you. I can't. I have church on Sunday morning, and I'm in the choir. We're doing a special song. Would you like to come hear it?"

A thundercloud of darkness crossed face. His jaw tightened, and his radiant smile vanished. "I don't need church. I'm perfectly fine without church. Church goers could learn a thing or two from me. I'm perfect. Perfectly perfect." He paused. "I'm perfect," he whispered, almost to himself. He turned to stare out the window, and his jaw began to relax.

Myra's mouth fell open. She sat rigid for a moment, dazed. Her hands felt clammy, and she reached under the table for the napkin in her lap. She wiped her hands on it, and brought it to her lips and patted them. She inhaled slightly. "Well, this was lovely. Thank you. I really need to be getting back. I told everyone I'd be in early to work on that paper."

He stared at her as if he wasn't sure who she was. Awkward silence filled the space between them. "Oh, sure," he said, as though suddenly recognizing her.

He signaled the waitress for the check. Nothing else was spoken until they reached the car. He opened the door for her and she slid in. Sitting quietly in the passenger seat, Myra looked around. She had no idea where they were. The parking lot was in the middle of downtown, and she wasn't familiar with the area. There was no pay phone in sight.

Why hadn't she noticed his car before? Was she blinded by anticipation of the date when she first got in? It was an old import with a broken dash, cracked windshield, torn upholstery, and a hole rusted through the floorboard on the driver's side. How did she not see that in the light of the day when it was blatantly visible to her in the dim light of the streetlight overhead? How did she not smell the sweat and cigarettes?

My gosh, the ashtray overflowed with crushed butts. Myra closed her eyes and shuddered. *What was I thinking? How did I miss this earlier? Didn't I see the signs?* A guy with a master's degree and a high profile job who rides the bus, makes small talk with teenagers, and wears a different sweater vest every day. Myra shook her head in disgust with herself. *Myra, you're such a loser.*

He got in the car, dug a single key out of his pocket, and reached toward the ignition.

Myra stared, mouth open. What on earth … a single key? No keychain? No house key, office key, key to the men's washroom, nothing …

Just before the key was slipped into the ignition, he dropped it. It clanked on the floorboard. He cursed. Myra cringed.

Myra stopped breathing. Her thoughts began to run amok. Would she be tomorrow morning's headline? *College Student Found Dead in Ditch.* She cleared her throat and willed herself to be calm.

"Here, let me help." Her voice was strained and her hand was trembling as she reached toward the floorboard.

His hand grabbed her wrist with startling force.

"I was just trying to help." Her quivering voice was barely audible.

Shadows fell across his face, and even in the dimly lit night, Myra saw his countenance change, again. His eyes darkened and blazed with rage.

"I don't need your help." His jaw tightened, and he bared his teeth like a mad dog. "I don't need anyone's help," his deep, guttural voice growled.

Myra's blood froze in her veins like water in pipes on a Chicago winter morning.

He stared at her for a moment. Could he see the sweat that had trickled down her temple? Without another word, he threw her wrist back at her with such force that her own hand slapped her.

Myra's lip trembled. With a sheer force of will, she remained as calm as possible. Her eyes stung at the effort it took not to cry.

He reached to the floorboard and muttered, "Don't need help. I'm perfect …" His hand patted around the floorboard, he swore again, then with a quick snap of his hand, he raised the key into the air like the Holy Grail. His face relaxed as his smile broadened across his face like a clown.

"Here it is!" His voice was suddenly full of childish delight. "I found it." He chuckled.

Myra's eyebrows shot up. She moved a little closer to the door, and her knees began to tremble. She clasped her hands tightly on them to stop the shaking but failed.

Her date, giddy like a child with a new toy, started the car and took off. The image of the next morning's headline kept appearing in Myra's mind. When he pulled up to the house, she pushed open the door and was out of the car before he could say another word.

"Thank you for dinner. It was a nice restaurant," Myra managed to spit out as she flung the door shut. She strode up the driveway without a backward glance.

She was so thankful to get back to the woman's house, she almost cried. Myra paused just inside the door to take a deep breath, and she hoped the woman didn't ask her about her date. She stood resolute for a moment. *One thing is for sure. I'll never get on that bus again. My bike is perfectly good transportation to get me where I need to go. Let the rainy season begin.*

"There's a letter from your mother on the table." The woman didn't look up from her book, but her voice crackled through the room like static.

Myra picked it up and stared down at her mother's perfect penmanship. A deep longing filled her heart. Only a few weeks left before the holidays, and Myra couldn't wait to fly home for Christmas to be with her mom and dad. She hated living here with her mother's friend. She hated this city, this state, this life. Tomorrow morning she would call her mom and tell her she wanted to come home to stay. She missed her friends and everything familiar she treasured. This was not what she expected college to be.

She sat on the bed and opened the letter. Her eyes moved across the brief note, and a hot tear slid mockingly down her cheek.

Dear Myra,

Dad and I are sick of these cold winters. Your dad is getting too old to shovel snow from the driveway and sidewalk. We sold the house, and we are moving to be closer to Mark and his family. It will be good to see the grandchildren again. See you in a few weeks, after your semester ends.

Mom

Chapter Thirty-Four

October 1985

After the phone call unsettled her, Myra paced around her little house, trying to busy herself like a squirrel preparing for winter. But the morning dishes were half done, the laundry was gathering wrinkles in the dryer, and the beds were unmade. She needed to get a hold of herself.

Myra stood in the cramped living room and stared out the window. All this pointless activity was getting her nowhere, so she forced herself to sit down on the well-worn couch. She took a generous breath and exhaled slowly, waiting for her heart rate to slow.

Ever since Myra got married and had kids, her mom called almost every morning. They would chat for three or four minutes, and then she would tell Myra, "I'll let you go so you can get your house clean."

Myra always managed to sound chipper, even when her mom assumed her house was a mess.

This morning when she answered, it wasn't her mother's voice that greeted her. "Myra, I took your mom to the hospital late last night. She's in ICU."

Is it possible to freeze-dry someone's heart with just a few words strung together like pearls?

Myra knew she could only stay in the hospital room for fifteen minutes while her mom was in ICU, but she wanted to see her anyway. Her husband, Steve could watch the kids later, after he got home from work.

"I'll come after dinner, Dad."

"See you then." He hung up.

Myra had been wringing her hands ever since. Would Steve get home in time for her to see her mom? She willed herself to stay calm. She should get a book and read. *Yes, yes, a book.* Where was that book she started months ago?

She found it and headed to the living room. Myra curled up on the couch with the book without the usual guilt. Housework could wait. She opened the paperback and began to read.

Chapter 3 Portia had never intended to be a thief. It just worked out that way …

It's good to relax. The boys would probably nap another hour. Rosalie wouldn't be home from school until two o'clock. When Steve got home, she could share her heart with him and tell him how worried she was about her mom.

Myra was thrilled when her mother's cancer had gone into remission after her first round of chemo. She'd been able to share the joy of her children with her mom. She loved her so much and wished her cancer hadn't come back. And, now her heart ached at the thought of her mom in the ICU.

The room was far more quiet than she was used to. She usually had the radio on in the morning. A little encouraging music on the Christian radio station helped hem her day so it was less likely to unravel around her. She sighed again. *Just read.*

Chapter 3 Portia had never intended to be a thief. It just worked out that way …

Steve was a far better husband than she deserved. She smiled as she thought about their working together at the donut shop where they met. Even now the aroma of freshly made doughnuts filled her senses with delight.

"Hey, Steve, breakfast is on me. What will it be-glazed, cake, fritter, or jelly?"

"No thanks. I make these things all night and the last thing I want to do is eat them in the morning." He turned back to the fryer and flipped the latest batch with his sticks.

"My, my, aren't you the fussy one. I'd never marry a guy like you. You're too finicky. What *would* you eat for breakfast?"

"Eggs and grits."

Myra laughed. "Yes, that does sound good."

Myra closed her eyes tightly and shook her head to clear the thoughts from her mind. *C'mon, concentrate on the words.* But the words on the novel's page blurred.

Chapter 3 Portia had never intended to be a thief. It just worked out that way …

Since her parents had moved here and purchased a small condo, Myra had only one other date. He'd never called her again after that. So, when Steve asked her to join him for a double date with his sister and her boyfriend, she was glad for the opportunity. They dated for six months. Usually they went to a local park or back to her parents' place to watch TV. Her mom and dad really liked Steve and welcomed him into their home.

At that time, Steve wasn't a Christian, a fact that caused Myra a great deal of anguish. She loved him, but knew in her heart it could never work out between them. He flat refused to enter church—any church—with her.

The way he saw it, Christians were all hypocrites. They left church every Sunday, stopped by the shop for a dozen doughnuts, then headed next door to the liquor store for a six-pack of beer and a pack of cigarettes.

Myra had encouraged him to not judge all Christians by the actions of a few. Not able to convince Steve that he was mistaken, and knowing if they couldn't relate spiritually, there would always be a part of her heart missing, she'd broken up with him.

Afterward, she had cried every night for a month, but continued to pray for him. *Lord, I love Steve. If it's Your will for us to be together, let him find Jesus before the end of the month.*

It was a long thirty days for Myra. On the evening of the last day of the month, the phone rang. Steve wanted to talk …

Chapter 3 Portia had never intended to be a thief. It just worked out that way …

Once again, Myra shook her head to clear the memories. She glanced at the little round clock on the wall. She'd been reading the first few lines of the same chapter for twenty minutes.

She got up and walked down the hall and peeked in at Danny and Jeremiah. Still snoozing like a couple of fuzzy bear cubs in hibernation. She went back to the couch and picked up the book, hoping once again to lose herself in the story. But three lines later, her thoughts drifted back to her wedding day …

Chapter 3 Portia had never intended to be a thief. It just worked out that way …

From the back of her tiny church, Myra could see her brothers, Billy and Mark and Mark's wife, Elyse standing beside her mom. There were a few friends from choir and a handful of her parents' friends from the condo.

Myra's heart had surged with emotion. She blinked back tears and swallowed hard several times to remove the lump in her throat. Steve's phone call on the last day in October was a gift from God. She could hardly believe He'd answered her lowly prayer. Why would He bother over her silly tears in the night? He had the whole world to take care of. Why was her prayer for a husband worthy of His precious time? But, He'd answered. Myra was mystified but thankful.

Her dad stood beside her in a dark suit. She'd never seen him dressed up in a suit before. Nor had she'd ever seen her mom in such an elegant dress. Myra's heart swelled like an ocean wave.

The wedding music began. Myra and her dad started down the aisle. Her friends had smiled, her brothers nodded, her mother sobbed.

Good grief, Mom, this is my wedding not my funeral. Myra had smiled at her mom as she walked by, but her mom looked away. Myra's smile had never faded.

Chapter 3 Portia had never intended to be thief. It just worked out that way …

Myra set the book aside. So much for enjoying a little light reading to take her mind off her worries. She crossed the tiny room and stared into the unkempt backyard. Toys were strewn everywhere. No landscaping needed here, Fisher-Price had taken over the yard.

She closed her eyes and the tiny clock on the old brick fireplace gave an anemic bong at the top of the hour. It reminded her of an elevator opening to the second floor at the hospital and one of the most important days of her life …

"Her water broke." There was excitement in Steve's voice. From the moment Myra called him at his sister's to tell him, he'd remained unruffled. He was always calm. Never panicked. His relaxed demeanor melded into happy anticipation. His smile and placid attitude helped Myra quell her own rising fear of what she was about to face. Steve remained with her through the entire delivery, encouraging her to breathe, relax, breathe, don't push, breathe, and push.

Myra burst into tears when the nurse handed her a baby girl. "Are you okay, Mrs. Collins?" The nurse touched Myra's shoulder "Why are you crying?"

Myra nodded her head. "Yes. Fine. I'm just so overwhelmed with the joy of it all. I'm crying for every woman who ever missed out on this miracle because she chose not to have her baby.You must have the happiest job on earth-watching all these babies born."

The nurse patted Myra's shoulder as if placating a weepy child.

When her parents arrived later, Myra was sitting in her bed with the tiny bundle, swaddled in a hospital receiving blanket.

Her dad beamed like a lighthouse. "What did you name her?"

Myra didn't remember him ever shining like that before. "Rosalie."

Her dad nodded. "She's a beauty, Myra."

She gazed down at her baby. Her soft skin was blotchy, tiny eyes swollen, misshapen head barely covered by the blanket. "Yes, she is!"

Her mom had her hands on her hips and with a stern expression, glared into Myra's eyes.

"Now-you-know."

When Myra's second baby arrived a couple of years later, her mother's response was equally confusing.

"What's his name?" she asked.

"Jeremiah."

"Ewww, I would never want to be called Jeremiah."

Myra blinked, but didn't miss a beat. "Well then, Mom, I promise never to call you Jeremiah."

Hardest of all for Myra, was telling her mom that she and Steve had named their third baby after her brother.

"What did you name him?" her dad asked after taking a huge visual gulp of his new grandson. His glow had brightened the dark hospital room immensely.

Myra looked at Steve, who nodded his encouragement.

"Daniel John Collins, after Danny and you, Dad.

Her mom's eyes welled with tears that spilled down her face. She put her hand to her mouth.

Her dad's beam dimmed a little as he reached for her mother's arms and pulled her to the farthest corner of the hospital room. In a stage whisper that could be heard across the corridor, he admonished her.

"Why are you acting like that, Stella? It's a lovely thing that Myra has done, naming her baby after Danny."

Her mom's nod was barely discernible. "I just have to get used to it, that's all."

Myra sighed at the memory and though she returned to her book, her thoughts drifted elsewhere …

Chapter 3 Portia had never intended to be a thief. It just worked out that way …

The clock on the living room wall gave another anemic gong. A tear slipped out of Myra's eye. After her mother's surgery to remove her breasts, and the ensuing chemotherapy, the cancer went into remission. A couple of years ago, Myra noticed her mother begin to change. She watched her mom closely as her weight dropped, energy ebbed, words came in short breaths, and her telephone calls became even more brief. But her mother never spoke of the illness to Myra.

One Saturday, while visiting her mom, a neighbor called and asked Myra to come by to pick up some soup she'd made for her mom.

She handed Myra a full Tupperware container and shook her head. "It's a shame your mom's cancer has returned."

Myra had seen its progress, but to hear the word *cancer* spoken out loud hit her like a glacier, tearing her chest open and exposing her wounded heart. *My mom is going to die.* Her eyes filled with tears.

The neighbor's face blanched. "Oh, Myra, I'm so sorry. I thought you knew."

Chapter 3 Portia had never intended to be a thief. It just worked out that way ...

Again, the tired gong split the silence in her living room and brought Myra back to the present. She'd lost another hour. Rosalie would be home soon. Myra looked around the house; it was still a mess, and she hadn't managed to relax with her book at all. She should wake the boys. She shivered.

Myra walked down the short hall to the boys' room and covered them, then pulled on a sweater and went back to her reading. Her mom would have had her own house clean by now. But Myra was unable to function. She tried to whisper a prayer, but was incapable of forming an intelligent thought.

Lord, thank You for hearing my heart, as I have no words.

Chapter 3 Portia had never intended to be a thief. It just worked out that way ...

After Myra's encounter with the neighbor, her mother had been in and out of the hospital on numerous occasions. Each admission came closer to the previous. Myra tried to visit when she could get away from her responsibilities.

One afternoon she quietly entered her mother's hospital room so as not to wake her. Myra sat in the plastic chair at the end of her mom's bed and watched her sleep. She seemed peaceful. Myra thought of her mom's struggles in life. She was a tough lady, but she'd also been a great mom—always there for Myra.

She bent her head and tears fell from her eyes into her lap like raindrops. Then she'd looked up to see her mom's half-opened eyes.

Her mother's eyes had darkened, and she asked why Myra was crying.

Myra cleared her throat and explained that she wished she could be half the mom to her children that her mother had been to her.

Her mom had scowled. Then she lifted her hand from under the blanket as if to brush Myra aside and told Myra to stop the silly crying.

Instead, Myra had bent over her, kissed her cheek, and told her mother that she loved her.

Chapter 3 Portia had never intended to be a thief. It just worked out that way …

The phone on the wall screamed and interrupted Myra's thoughts.

Her throat tightened into a knot. "Hello."

"Myra, it's Dad. You don't need to come to the hospital, sweetheart. Your mom just died."

Chapter Thirty-Five

August 1987

A sweet aroma wafted through the grocery store, spilling into each aisle, enticing the shoppers toward the bakery.

Susan filled her lungs. It was better than a fresh spring morning, a floral shop, and any expensive perfume. It was a sensory banquet for the nose like no other. Fresh, hot baked cinnamon rolls.

She surrendered to the aromatic pleasure and headed to the source. Done with other shopping, she could purchase her items and leave the store with warm pastries. Myra's kids would love them. They rarely got such delightful treats, now that Steve had been unemployed for so long.

Since the recession's peak in December, 1982, Steve had been out of work more than he had been employed. Myra and Steve had been struggling financially for so long it had become a normal lifestyle. It was especially difficult for Steve, trying desperately to find work that would support his family. His physical restrictions were a handicap. He'd had several back and neck surgeries, and employers were reluctant to hire someone so limited.

Susan looked down at the groceries she'd purchased for them. Sadly, this month Steve hadn't made enough to pay the rent. The landlord had evicted them. Before they moved out, Susan wanted to be sure they had enough food for a few days.

She and Myra had become close over the past couple of years. Susan and her husband were new at the church, and Myra seemed to be a one-woman welcoming committee. It wasn't long before they were attending a small group Bible study together. Susan enjoyed Myra. She had a joyful countenance even in the tough times.

Susan rang the doorbell and waited. Myra answered the door, her swollen, red eyes lighting on Susan's face. A smile burst from her face like a fireworks display.

"Oh, Susan, it's so good to see you." She reached over to draw her friend into a hug. "Please come in. I was just packing everything into boxes."

"Myra, I have some groceries in the car for your family. Let's get those first."

Myra's tears started up again. She raised her hands, pressed her fingers to her lips, and nodded at Susan. "Thank you, Susan," she whispered, her voice thick and soft. She reached out to Susan and took her hand and squeezed it hard as the tears fell. She opened her mouth to speak again, but nothing came out. She nodded and mouthed *thank you*.

"Hey, come on," Susan said, nodding toward the door. "Let's get this stuff in the house before something spoils."

Myra gave a little-girl laugh and bounded toward the car with her friend.

"It's not much, just a little something to take with you." Susan handed her two plastic bags and picked up the last two. Do you know where you're going?"

Myra hesitated a moment and swallowed hard.

"Everything is going into storage except some clothes, some food, and essentials. I'm glad it's summer. Kids are out of school for a few more weeks. Steve knows a little campground about twenty minutes out of town at the base of the foothills." She sighed and hung her head. "Right now the kids think this is a grand adventure. But it will get old soon enough." Myra began to cry large, heavy tears.

Susan waited for Myra to continue. She knew her friend's heart was heavy and she wanted to be a compassionate, understanding friend.

"Oh, Susan, I'm such a terrible mother."

Susan's eyes widened. Her mouth parted slightly. This was not what she expected Myra to say. She thought finances and homelessness burdened Myra's heart. Or, she might worry how long they would be unemployed, homeless, and penniless. But, a bad mother?

"Why would you say that?" Susan asked spreading her hands wide.

"Because I yell at the kids all the time. I'm short tempered, cranky, and critical with them. And, now I'm dragging them out of their home."

Shaking her head, Susan recalled her own parenting past, when her children were small. She opened her mouth to tell Myra that young children had a way of bringing that out in a mother. And, that children were resilient and would survive this trial.

"Oh, Susan, I'm a failure as a Christian. My faith is so small. I struggle with understanding why God has allowed all this to happen to us."

They set the grocery bags on the kitchen counter and there was a slight pause in the conversation as Susan grabbed Myra's hand and gave it a gentle yank. "Myra, you are not a failure in your faith, or a terrible mother. You're not struggling with trusting God. You're struggling with making sense of your circumstances. Don't look at your life and wonder what God is doing. Look at God and know that He is in control, and there is a purpose for everything—even the bad things. Myra, make an appointment with Pastor and tell him about your struggles. He can help guide you through some of these dark days."

Myra poured out her heart to Pastor Edward. When she was done, he leaned forward, put his arms on his desk, and looked into Myra's eyes. Fear and confusion permeated Myra's spirit.

"Myra, I want to explain what is happening to you in a way that makes sense. To assure you that God isn't punishing you, but creating something beautiful."

He paused and Myra scooted to the edge of her seat. She didn't want to miss a word.

"Myra, have you ever seen a tapestry?"

She nodded.

Pastor Edward smiled. "The front is beautiful. The work of a craftsman."

Myra nodded again.

"The front makes sense. The weaver works on the design he sees and makes it beautiful. But the back is a tangled mess of strings and knots. It doesn't make sense, and it is most often not a pretty sight."

She made no comment, but her eyebrows rose in expectation.

"Our heavenly Father is weaving our lives like a tapestry. He can see the beauty from His perspective above. But when we look up from our earthly position, we only see the strings and knots crisscrossing the fabric. We must believe that He's making something beautiful of our lives."

Myra closed her eyes and considered the strings of her life. She felt tangled up in them. Her life was imploding like the demolition of a long-abandoned building. A tear escaped its captivity and ran down her cheek. She opened her eyes and looked at Pastor Edward. She hesitated while she tried to make sense of it.

"I guess it's like the song the Gaithers sang about making something beautiful of all the awful things in my life. My castles have crumbled and God will make my life beautiful. Maybe, not in spite of my trials but because of them?"

Pastor Edward encouraged Myra with a broad smile.

I must be getting it.

"Myra, look, God is working in your life. Sometimes we need a little help, a little counsel. I know a wonderful counselor, a dear Christian lady, who you can talk to and help you work out your frustrations. The church will pay for six sessions for you. Sometimes it helps just to talk through the crumbling castles."

Another tear escaped Myra's eye. She nodded, her lips said *thank you*, but her voice remained captive in her throat.

In Lisa's eyes, Myra seemed to be a contradiction. She had all the joy of a new puppy romping through the house, but with a small, barely discernible shadow crossing her. After three sessions listening to Myra, Lisa began to unravel that shadow.

"You seem depressed, Myra."

Myra scowled and shook her head. "I'm not depressed. I'm a very happy person."

Denial. Lisa dropped the subject, for now. "Tell me about your mom."

"I had a great mom. She's gone now, but she was a terrific lady. She was generous and kind to people. She was a good mom. Considering all she'd been through, she was a really good mom."

"What had she been through?"

"She lost her mom in the 1917 flu pandemic. Her dad put her in an orphanage when she was about two, while he went to find himself a new wife. Then when she was about nine, he came and got her, and she had to endure the evil stepmother treating her like a slave. She only went to school through the eighth grade because she had to get a job to help the family out financially. She gave her pay envelope to her dad every week. Even when she was an adult. She married my dad when she was twenty-seven years old and still went over to do her stepmother's laundry. Well, until my dad found out. He put a stop to that." She smiled at Lisa.

"Did you and your mother get along?"

"Oh, sure. I loved my mom. We had a few arguments in my teen years, but she was a great mom. I usually got what I deserved when I was punished."

Lisa nodded, and jotted some notes on her paper.

Myra smiled. "I wish I could be as good a mom as she was."

Lisa wrote some more notes. Myra was genuinely convinced she was happy, genuinely convinced she wasn't a good mom, and genuinely convinced her mother was just next door to perfect.

After their last session, Lisa said, "This is the last session your church has paid for."

"Yes, I know. I'd like to continue talking to you, but Steve and I don't have the money."

"I know your family is homeless right now, but I'd like to keep seeing you. Would you be able to keep coming to my office once a week, if I didn't charge you anything?"

Myra's face lit up like a casino marquee. "Absolutely. That would be great. I love talking to you. Thank you *so* much."

"Good. In time, I think I can help you sort through all your struggles."

Myra's expression was a reflection of puzzlement and doubt for a moment. She stood and smiled. "Okay, but I'm not sure there's anything that can be done for me. I believe God is trying to teach me something, and I'm just not getting it. I'm afraid my family will have to suffer until I grasp what God wants me to learn."

"We'll work on it together, Myra."

She managed a weak smile and left the office.

Lisa's musing followed Myra out the door and Lisa prayed they would stick with her.

Chapter Thirty-Six

January 1987

The shouting started after dinner. Myra sat on the bed with the only book she'd brought to the shelter. She couldn't concentrate on the words. The voices were escalating. Myra could hear a child crying, and when she heard something hit the wall and the child's scream, she couldn't take it any longer. She marched across the room, past her husband and children and reached for the door.

"Where are you going?" Steve asked.

"Downstairs, to report this abuse."

"Be careful, Myra."

They'd been given one of two end rooms. She stepped outside theirs and faced a giant-sized woman in front of the next door. The woman glowered down at Myra, daring her to say or do anything to intervene with the beating behind the door. No words were exchanged as Myra walked casually down the large, high ceilinged corridor to the lavatory. She entered a stall and slammed the door shut. But the child's screaming followed her and swirled around her head with the ferocity of a hurricane. Her heart raced as she sat down, covered her face with her hands and wept.

What a coward. You didn't even have the guts to go downstairs to report that abuse.

Eventually, the screaming subsided and Myra heard the door down the hall open and slam shut. The echo reverberated through the hall and exploded in Myra's heart.

She got up and left the ladies' room. The gorilla-woman was no longer doing sentry duty. Myra slipped down the stairs and into the office. The man behind the desk was writing furiously in a notebook.

"The woman in the room next to me just beat the living daylights out of her kid. She posted her larger-than-life sister in front of the door to stand guard in case someone tried to interrupt the beating."

"I know," the man said, without lifting his head. "She won't be here long. We found drugs in her room. She'll be gone in the morning."

Myra let his statement soak into her brain for a moment. His words were like stale, sour milk being absorbed into a sponge. Apparently the man misunderstood her. She didn't ask when they were leaving, she was reporting a beating.

"She just beat that little boy to a pulp. Aren't you going to do something?"

He looked up for the first time. "It's not my job. Besides, it's your word against hers. She'll be gone in the morning for breaking the 'no drugs' rule." He went back to his notes with a dismissive air.

Myra headed back toward the stairs, shoulders slumped, eyes downcast. She sighed. He wouldn't have stopped the beating even if she'd arrived while it was happening.

As she ascended the stairs, she took note of the noise in the corridor above. When she exited the stairwell, people were milling about in the hall, talking and laughing once more. The noise echoed down the corridor, against the walls, off the ceiling and settled on Myra like ash from a volcano. *Where was everyone ten minutes ago?*

Myra entered her room, sat on the bed, and picked up her book.

Steve looked over at her. "Well?"

"He says they'll be gone tomorrow, but he wasn't willing to do anything about the beating. My word against hers, he said."

They'd arrived at this shelter a couple of weeks ago. Dinner had just been served while Steve and Myra were being processed in. Myra was filling out some forms when there was a knock on the office door behind her and she heard a pleasant male voice.

"How many?"

"Five," the director answered.

Then the voice was gone. Myra glanced at the director and he smiled.

"The cook is holding dinner for you."

Myra looked at Steve, then over at her children.

"Thanks." Her smile was weak, but the gratitude was sincere.

When they entered the small dining hall, there were still a couple of families sitting at tables. Myra surveyed the room. There were four tables left to choose from.

"Welcome," said the same friendly voice Myra heard in the office.

She looked toward the source and was met with a warm smile.

"C'mon now. Get those youngsters over here so we can feed them," he said with a chuckle. "I've been waiting to serve you this gourmet meal since you arrived." He laughed, apparently amused at his own words.

Myra gathered her children in mother duck fashion and led them to the counter. They each took a tray, and the man beamed over the serving table as he handed the paper plate with the "gourmet meal" on it. Myra reached for the plate. Two hot dogs—no buns—and a side of pork 'n' beans.

She closed her eyes briefly to suppress any guilty tears that might escape. While they were living in the tent, she received several bags of food from the church's food bank. There were probably fifteen cans of pork 'n' beans. They ate them for several nights in a row, until the children began to whine about them. She promised that when they got their own home, they'd never have to eat pork 'n' beans again.

She placed the plate of hot dogs and beans on Rosalie's tray. Rosalie looked at them a long time but never said a word. Nor did the boys.

Myra looked up and smiled gratefully at the man serving. "Thank you very much. We appreciate you holding dinner for us."

"My pleasure," he said. "I'm Clark, the cook at this fine establishment."

Myra chuckled. "Well, I'm Myra. This is my husband, Steve. These are our three kids."

"Glad to have you," Clark said. "Breakfast is served at 8:00 a.m."

"Thanks, Clark."

"Let me know if I can help you in any way," Clark said.

Myra forced a small smile and nodded. *Our own home would be nice.*

Each morning after breakfast they were required to leave The Family Refuge Center for the day. So Myra got up early to get the children dressed for school. Then she would trek down the corridor to the large lavatory. Most of the eight sinks were being used by women washing up.

Myra had a job, and she refused to leave without a shower. She turned into the adjoining shower room and set her towel and clothes on the long wooden bench at the end of the room. Large high windows allowed light to filter in. The six showers created a steamy atmosphere. But even the steam didn't provide privacy in this locker-room-style shower. There were no partitions or shower curtains. Myra put her robe next to her clothes and walked to the shower at the end—past five women and two children also showering. No words were spoken except an occasional maternal encouragement to "rinse off so we can go eat."

Myra attempted to look nonchalant. It was like one of those nightmares where you are totally naked while singing in the choir, but no one seems to notice but you. Only this wasn't a dream, and everyone else was naked too. Though a chill permeated the air, Myra's face burned. It was all she could do to shower with an audience.

After breakfast, Myra gathered their valuables and headed toward the exit. None of the rooms had locks on the doors, and even though all residents were required to be out by 9:00 a.m., things managed to disappear.

"Okay, let's go Danny." Myra took Danny's hand and led him to the preschool around the back of the old building.

"Good morning, Kimiko," Myra said.

Kimiko's eyes glistened even in the dim light of the room. The corners of her lips turned up, revealing a brilliant smile. She turned her attention to Danny. "Good morning, Danny. How are you this morning?"

"Fine."

"We're so happy to see you this morning. Are you happy to be here?"

"I guess." Danny shrugged, then slipped away to be with the other kids.

"He's really a delight, Mrs. Collins. So many of the children from the shelter have behavioral problems. But Danny is so pleasant and humorous. He says the funniest things sometimes."

Myra felt a swell in gratitude for her funny, well-behaved son.

"Thanks, Kimiko. I appreciate this service The Refuge provides. And you're so good with the kids. Danny really likes you."

Kimiko was distracted by the shouting across the room. "Oh, gotta go play referee," she said, waving good-bye.

"Have a good day, Kimiko," Myra said, waving back.

Steve dropped Rosalie and Jeremiah off at school and then drove Myra to the hotel where she was a housekeeper. The rest of the day was his to look for a job.

Myra hated the work, but was thankful for a job, and it did give her the opportunity to be alone as she cleaned the rooms.

The vacuum roared to life, and Myra pulled it back and forth across the carpet while she backed out of the room with it. When she was completely out of the room, she turned the large vacuum off, pulled the plug from the wall, and heaved the machine onto her cart. She reached up and rubbed her shoulder. *Lord, thanks for this job. Help me make it through this day.*

"Myra, the boss wants to see you."

Startled, Myra turned to see another housekeeper coming toward her.

"Am I in trouble?"

"I don't know," she said and shrugged. Then she looked at Myra's face and reached out and touched her arm. "I don't think so, Myra. It's not like you've done anything wrong. If anything, he might want to tell you how much he appreciates your good attitude."

Myra swallowed hard. Although difficult to remain cheerful some days, she didn't want to bring personal problems to work.

"Thanks," Myra said as she began to shove the cart toward the linen room.

She knocked on the hospitality director's door. A knot the size of a grapefruit formed in her stomach.

"Oh, Myra, come in, please. Your daughter's school would like you to call."

Alarm shot through Myra with electric intensity.

"Is everything okay? Is she hurt?" Her shrill voice shot across the room with the speed of a bullet.

"Oh, I'm sure everything is fine. The caller didn't indicate there was an emergency. Just asked that you call them back. Here, use my phone. The number is on the paper next to it. I'll just step out a moment to give you some privacy." He started to leave the office.

"No, no, you don't have to leave your office. I'll only be a minute."

As her boss sat down, Myra reached for the phone and dialed the school's office number.

"Hi, this is Mrs. Collins. I'm returning your call about my daughter, Rosalie."

"Yes, Mrs. Collins. Rosalie needs to be picked up. She's been vomiting. She's in the nurse's office."

"Um, I can't. I, um, have no way to get there. I'm at work."

"She needs to be at home, Mrs. Collins."

Myra noted the woman's stern tone and took in a long slow breath before replying. "I realize that, but I have no way to get there. We only have one car and ..."

"Then you need to call your husband to come for her."

Myra felt her frustration rise. "I'm sorry. I can't do that either. I have no way of getting in touch with him."

"Can't you leave him a message at work?"

Myra swallowed hard and noted her boss was writing something in his calendar and looking very uncomfortable. Now she wished she'd let him leave his office, or she'd gone to the payphone in the employee's lounge. She turned slightly as tears came into her eyes without warning.

"He has no job. He's out looking for one. That's why I can't get in touch with him. I have no way to get to the school and no way to call my husband."

There was an angry *tsk* on the other end. "Well, can't you call someone else to come and get her?"

Fear rose in Myra's throat.

"No, I really don't know anyone who could. My husband and I are ..."

"Very well. She'll be in the nurse's office when you get here. I'll let the nurse *and* the principal know." The unmistakable sound of the receiver slamming down assaulted Myra, causing her ear to ring. She set the receiver down in its cradle and turned away to leave.

Please don't ask any questions. Please.

"Myra, are you okay?"

Myra lowered her head and shook it slowly. Her heart was beating like a base drum in a rock band. She turned to look at her boss as acid tears burned down her cheeks.

"Myra, sit down. What's going on?" Her boss's voice dripped with concern.

He probably thinks I won't be able to work now. He's going to fire me.

Chapter Thirty-Seven

March 1987

Myra sunk into the chair in front of her boss's desk. She kept her eyes on the trembling hands in her lap.

"What's going on, Myra?"

Myra shrugged, as if it were no big deal. "My husband hurt his back while we were moving into a smaller, cheaper home and lost his job. We haven't been able to find an affordable place to live since."

Her boss sighed as he nodded his head.

"I'm so sorry, Myra. What can we do? Do you have enough food for the kids?"

Myra looked up, eyes wide. She opened her mouth to speak, but was overwhelmed with his concern. Tears began to trickle down her face. She nodded and cleared her throat.

"Um, yes. We're currently staying at The Refuge. We get breakfast and dinner there. The children get a hot lunch at school, and I get a free lunch here. My husband doesn't eat lunch while he's looking for work. He's really trying to find a job." Myra began to sob. "He's trying so hard."

"Let us help you, Myra. I'll call Human Resources to see if they can come up with any community resources that can help."

Myra nodded her thanks.

"Stop by my office at the end of your shift. I'll see what we can do."

With great effort, Myra dragged herself to her feet and looked her boss in the eyes. "Thank you. Even if there's nothing you can do, thank you for not firing me."

Billowing white clouds filled the sky with a strange luminescence. Birds flew with graceful ease, their flowing performance beautiful choreography in the sky. They moved with the fluidity of a waterfall. Flying in perfect synchronization to the musical sounds of spring, they crisscrossed in air toward the shining clouds, and plummeted toward the earth together.

The sight mesmerized Lisa as she sat at her desk and gazed with pure longing out the window. A car driving into the parking lot caught her eye. It was Myra. Her old, green station wagon had seen better days. Lisa smiled, remembering how Myra told her about the car.

Some friends gave it to us when our car died. It's not much to look at, but we're so thankful to have it. Well, Steve and I are thankful. The kids are embarrassed to be seen in it. They make me drop them off a block away from school so no one sees them getting out of it. Myra had chuckled. *I imagine they'll understand my gratitude over that 'ugly, stupid' car someday.*

Lisa stepped to the door and cracked it open. "Annette, when Myra gets here, please send her in, okay?"

"You got it, Lisa."

Lisa went back to the window and watched Myra exit the car. She shook her head slightly at the sight of Myra's clothes. They're all wrong. They weren't Myra. *I've only known Myra a few months, and I may not know her taste in clothes, but these hand-me-downs do not match her personality at all. Perhaps instead of that lifeless sweater, she could find a cute jacket with shoulder pads.* But Myra always wore her clothes—if not with pride—at least with gratitude. Lisa recalled Myra told her she often got hand-me-downs from her friend, Susan.

She volunteers at a home for women in crisis. You know—abused, homeless, or pregnant and unwed. It's a wonderful ministry, really. They receive a ton of donations—food, clothes, and such. Some they can't use, so Susan redirects it to other people and places. Sometimes she gives stuff to me. You'd be surprised at some of the really cute clothes people give away.

Lisa had to agree, some of the outfits were very cute. However, even though Myra never complained, Lisa couldn't help but think Myra was dressing for someone else's personality and not her own.

The outer office door opened, and Lisa heard Annette direct Myra to go inside. Lisa turned to see Myra enter with a bright smile on her face and dressed in a drab, brown sweater covering an old T-shirt with a frog printed on it.

"Hi, Lisa," Myra said, crossing the small office.

"Good to see you, Myra. It's been a while, hasn't it? Have a seat." Lisa indicated a cozy, stuffed chair.

"Yeah, too long. I'm glad I had the time to see you today."

Myra's attitude was always that of a friend speaking to a friend, as if she was starved for someone to share her heart with. She never looked for help, asked for advice, or expected that speaking with Lisa would change anything in her life. She seemed glad just to talk and share what was going on.

Occasionally she would cry over her circumstances, but she always left Lisa's office with a smile for the privilege of unburdening her soul. A couple of times Lisa suggested she was depressed, but Myra got indignant at the mere mention of the word.

Myra would insist that she wasn't depressed, despite being homeless. She admitted to crying, worrying about the kids, and not liking the circumstances of her life. But she remained grateful and clung onto believing that God had a purpose in it all.

How could Lisa argue with that?

Friends had started to avoid Myra. She just needed someone to talk to who wouldn't judge her or think she was looking for a handout.

Lisa situated herself in one of the overstuffed chairs and looked squarely into Myra's eyes. "So where are you now? Last time we spoke you were staying with Steve's brother."

"Oh, yeah, there were eleven of us in that small, three-bedroom apartment. Our family of five, Steve's older brother, his wife, and their four grandchildren all crammed together. We were so grateful they allowed us to stay there, but you know it's hard to blend two families—especially with kids. We needed to give them their lives back and move on. So we went back to the shelter."

Lisa nodded and wrote some notes.

"Where will you go from there when your thirty days are up?"

"We have a few friends who said we could stay a couple of weeks with them. So, the next several weeks are covered while Steve continues to look for work."

"How are things at The Refuge?"

Myra stared with empty eyes out the window, but didn't say anything for a long, awkward moment. Her eyes remained fixed on an unknown object outside.

"Last week a bunch of police cars came barreling up to The Refuge, and policemen barged into the lobby. They went over to this gal who just had a baby and grabbed her child. The girl started screaming and swearing, and she attacked one of the cops. They handcuffed her right there in front of everybody in the lobby and took her and the baby away." Myra turned her eyes on Lisa. "It scared me *so* bad. I grabbed my kids and headed up to our room. I was shaking and crying. I was so afraid they would come back and take my kids away too. I feel like a terrible mom because my children don't have a home."

"Do you know why the police came and took the girl's baby?"

"I don't really know. I heard some gossip about a drug test done in the hospital. After her baby tested positive at birth, they took the newborn away. Apparently, she managed to find a way to get the infant out of the hospital without being seen." Myra's breaths were coming in quick, uneven gasps. "But when it happened, I was sure my children would be next. I was so frightened. *So* frightened." Her voice trailed off.

Chapter Thirty-Eight

May 1991

"Where have you been, Myra?" Lisa was delighted to see Myra again after a year had passed with no word.

Myra laughed. "Everywhere."

"Well, fill me in. I've been praying for you." Lisa pointed to the chair for Myra to sit.

"Oh, thank you. I appreciate all the prayers I can get."

As Myra relayed what had transpired, Lisa couldn't help but notice her appearance. *Still wearing the same, used wardrobe. And she's gained some weight as well.*

"Let's see, we've lived with several friends. Then Steve got a job with a temp agency. We found a cute condo to live in, but the owner had to sell it because she was behind on her payments. Then more friends, then an apartment by the college, then some more friends ..." Myra sighed. "Sometimes the timeline gets mixed up in my head, but we've moved a lot. We had to change schools for the children several times. Most of the time we just left the majority of our stuff in storage." She smiled.

Lisa was astounded. After all that, how could Myra still manage to smile?

Myra sat forward in her seat. "I've learned a lot, Lisa. I've been praying for God to reveal why we're going through all these trials."

"What insight has He given you?"

"I think maybe He's teaching me compassion. I've noticed a lot of people want to help, but I can tell who's helping out of compassion and who's helping out of guilt or a sense of obligation—or even for how they could benefit from helping us."

Lisa made some notes on her yellow legal pad. "Give me some examples."

"Sometimes the smallest kindness is the best. Someone pays the electric bill or gives us a gift certificate for dinner out. But sometimes people do big things to help, and you can tell they regret it later. One couple allowed us to live in their rental, but decided Steve wasn't doing enough to find a job, then insisted we pay the rent weekly. After a few weeks I received a telephone call telling me we had to move because they sold the rental. It was two weeks before Christmas, and they wanted us out by January first. It was a difficult Christmas."

Lisa made more notes.

"That time we'd taken all of our stuff out of storage, so I spent the holidays packing and dragging everything back to the storage unit. We actually rented three different places where the landlord asked us to leave because they sold the place. In-between we stayed with friends, or in cockroach infested motels or other shelters, and once with my brother, Mark."

Lisa listened intently. She was astonished at Myra's account. "How did it go at your brother's house?"

"It was just me and the kids at that time. Steve lived with some guy close to the trade school he was attending. He studied how to use computers." Myra's eyes sparkled as she recounted the story. "We didn't stay very long. Only a couple of months. We left and went to another friend's house. It was really a strain on the relationship. Everywhere we've gone—whether to friends or family, we've damaged relationships.

"So much talk about the high rate of unemployment, and yet just about everyone we stayed with felt Steve wasn't trying hard enough to find a decent-paying job. I managed to stay employed with some minimum-wage job or another, but you can't support a family on twenty hours a week at a fast food restaurant. A couple of times Steve got jobs with a temp agency. Once he got a very good job, but two weeks later the company had a massive layoff. The economy has made it so difficult. That's why I'm so excited that Steve went to the special training school to learn computers. It's a good thing to know now. I think we'll finally be able to find a decent place to live on our own when he gets a job."

Lisa set her pen and notebook down.

"How are you feeling, Myra? This has to be taking a toll on you."

"I live day by day, Lisa. Every day I ask God, 'what do you want me to learn from this?' People often ask '*why me?*' when they go through trials. But, the way I see it, why *not* me? It's not like my life is so great that I deserve to be blessed in some special way. Why *shouldn't* I struggle or have hard times?"

"Do you think you deserve these challenges? Do you feel you're being punished for something?"

"Maybe." Myra sat silent.

"Why would you think God is punishing you? Why don't you deserve blessings?"

Myra stared at her hands. Her face turned red in the silence. Lisa waited for her to say something. Myra cleared her throat several times attempting to speak. She kept her eyes averted from Lisa.

"Myra, why do you feel unworthy?"

Myra pinched her lips together in a tight line. She pulled a deep breath in through her nose and blurted, "Someone hurt my Rosalie. Someone hurt her when she was seven, and I just found out. Her sweet spirit has been crushed." She moaned. "I didn't protect her. I should have protected her. I wasn't there for her. I didn't know. My daughter …"

Myra dropped her head, covered her face, and sobbed into her hands.

Lisa waited in silence while Myra continued to cry. After several minutes, she got up and walked over to Myra, and gently laid her hand on Myra's shoulder. Myra continued sobbing.

Myra's pain infiltrated the room like smoke, penetrating every corner, seeping into every tiny space until its pervasive presence filled Lisa's heart as well. Still, she waited quietly for Myra's tears to be spent. When Myra's quaking shoulders became still, and her heaving lungs became silent, Lisa reached for a tissue from the small side table and pushed it into Myra's hands still covering her face. She took the tissue and wiped the tears away. Her eyes were red and swollen, her face blotchy. She said nothing.

Lisa walked across the office to her desk and opened a drawer. She pulled out a small, wrapped box. She returned and crouched in front of Myra.

"Myra, I want you to have this. It's a little reminder of how much God loves you."

Her sad eyes looked at Lisa, then down at the box. She reached over and took it. She opened it and held up a colorful coffee mug. On it were the words "God danced the day you were born." Myra turned the cup reading the words several times. Her brows furrowed, and more tears escaped her swollen eyes.

She held the cup out toward Lisa and said with a choked voice, "Why?"

Lisa put her hands over Myra's hand and the cup and gently pushed them into Myra's lap. Lisa smiled. "Because I want you to have it."

Myra shook her head, tossing her hair from side to side. "No. Why would God dance on the day *I* was born?"

Chapter Thirty-Nine

August 1991

Outside the window, the sounds of the day's activities raced by relentlessly. Children in the courtyard laughed and screamed with delight, the neighbor's TV blared sounds of *The Guiding Light*, and a car horn blasted as a vehicle sped past the apartment building Steve and Myra had just moved into. Across their cramped apartment living room the radio was tuned to K-LOVE. The music played in the background of Myra's consciousness as she sat on the edge of her bed with the cup in her hand. She stared at the words, reading them over and over. *God danced the day you were born.*

Her eyes burned with the effort not to cry as she gritted her teeth with determination to remain in control. *God danced the day you were born. Why? Why? I just don't understand.*

Words from the song on the radio drifted in. They slowly filtered through her bedroom, encircling Myra's head, tickling her ears. She paused, then sat straight and listened. She stood and went to the living room to turn up the radio. Michael W. Smith's "Place in This World" was streaming through the speakers. Myra's mouth fell open.

That's how I feel. I'm looking for a place, a reason. But I'm afraid I'm just not good enough. Lord. Why would You dance the day I was born? Why would You care about a loser like me? I need to find a place where I belong. I'm so confused with all these thoughts that fill my mind all the time.

She glanced around the room. She was so thankful they'd finally found a place of their own to live, however small and cramped. But, surely there was more to life than not being homeless.

What can I do to make my life better? How did I become such a loser, and how do I stop?

September 1992

Myra stepped into the doctor's office and looked around. The waiting room had six chairs against the wall and a table spread with *People* magazines. A nurse sat at a desk. She must've been seventy years old. She wore a white dress, a white nurse's cap, white hose, and white shoes. Myra smiled. *She looks like a nurse straight out of a 1960s TV drama.*

When she'd shared with Susan how tired she was of being overweight, Susan had recommended a doctor she'd heard about. Myra was apprehensive about spending money on anything that was unnecessary, but when she'd mentioned it to Steve, he was supportive. Now that he was working again, he told her they could afford the co-payments. Myra took a seat in the small waiting room.

The nurse addressed her with a pleasant voice, and within the hour Myra had been examined, siphoned for blood, imposed upon to give a urine sample, and registered to see The Diet Doctor. Excitement about this new endeavor began to stir within. Maybe now she could lose some of the extra weight she'd been hauling around with her. She could stop being a loser one pound at a time.

Every day Myra went out of her way to check in at the doctor's office. The 1960s nurse monitored her progress and kept all the records. The weeks slipped by as her weight made its steady descent toward the next smaller size. Myra had put aside a few of the smaller clothes that Susan had given her. She hoped she would eventually fit into them. Her perseverance was paying off. A whole different size of hand-me-downs was just on the horizon. But in her heart, she still felt fat.

October 1992

The choir filed out and stood in front of the congregation, poised expectantly before the director. He was new to the church. He was hired last year when the previous director retired. He was very accomplished, very talented. Myra liked his easy-going personality.

She glanced at the ever-growing congregation. She'd been in this choir since before she and Steve were married. She loved being a part of it. Even when she was homeless, she managed to make it to choir rehearsal on Thursday evenings and to Sunday morning worship. It gave her more pleasure and got her through more trials than anything else.

Myra smiled at the congregation as the small orchestra began, and she looked toward the director. The anthem began. Joy poured over Myra like warm caramel on a baked apple. It burst out in song, stretched across her face as a smile, slid out of her eyes and down her cheek. The words flowed out, refreshing her like a spring of pure water. At the song's conclusion, Myra felt radiant.

Susan approached her after the service and encircled her with a big hug. "Oh, Myra, it's always so good to see your smiling face in the choir. I love to watch you worship God. It's as if it's just you and Him. The rest of us seem to disappear for you."

"Thank you, Susan. I just love singing to the Lord. Sometimes the enemy wears me down, telling me God can't use me in this choir. I feel like quitting then. But just when I'm about to, God sends somebody to remind me that my singing in choir is not about my voice. It's about my worship and praise to the Lord. I guess that's how God is using me in this choir. As a worship leader, not a singer."

Susan put her hands on Myra's cheeks and gave them a little squeeze. "And, He's using you big time, Myra. You are a blessing to me."

Myra lowered her eyes. "Thank you."

"Okay, see you at Bible study on Tuesday. I have a bag of clothes for you."

On the drive home, Myra was more quiet than usual.

Steve drove into the 7-Eleven parking lot. "Do you want something to drink?"

She smiled at him. "No thanks. Not today."

He turned to the kids. "What kind of drinks do you want?"

"Orange."

"Grape."

"Root beer."

Myra smiled at their answers. Always the same. The Sunday 7-Eleven tradition lived on. She was so glad they could once again afford this one small treat for the children. They always looked forward to it after church each Sunday. Her heart feared they may be homeless again if Steve's new job didn't work out. She closed her eyes to block out the pervasive thought.

Steve returned with three drinks and one big cup filled with cola. As they drank, the kids remained uncharacteristically quiet.

Steve's brows furrowed as he glanced over at Myra. "Why so quiet, Myra?"

"Just thinking about something Susan said to me this morning."

"What's that?"

"Well, I've been thinking of quitting choir. The new director has his favorite soloists and I'm not one of them. I asked his secretary several weeks ago if I could sing a special song. She scheduled me for the evening service and that was okay, but then she told me Stan only uses his best soloists for the morning services. Her remark really stung, and I felt second-rate after that. So, for a few weeks I've been toying with the idea of quitting."

"But Myra, you love choir. You live for choir. You wouldn't be happy if you quit, and the congregation would miss you up there."

"Yeah. I think I needed to be reminded about my place in that ministry. God sent Susan this morning to tell me how much she loved to watch me. Not to *hear* me singing. To *watch* me singing. My place in the choir is to be seen and not heard." She chuckled at her own words. "I may not like it, but it's where God wants me to be right now."

"I like to hear you when you sing around the house." Steve reached over and squeezed her hand.

"Thanks, Steve. I appreciate that." She glanced over at him and smiled. Ever the encourager, that was her Steve.

Susan's words padded around in Myra's head for the remainder of the drive home. *I love to watch you worship. God is using you big time. You are a blessing …*

When Myra got home she went to her room to change out of her Sunday clothes. Her eyes fell on the cup on her bedside table. *God danced the day you were born*. Myra picked up the cup and stared at it. She tried to picture God dancing, and the image made her grin.

Even if I'm not good enough to sing solos in the morning service, Lord, I'll stay in the choir. If my gift is mainly worship and not singing, then I'll be content to lift my hands in praise. At least I know You can hear me, if no one else does.

She set the cup down. *Are you still dancing, Lord? I can't hear the music with all the noise in my head.*

Chapter Forty

February 1993

Myra mentally checked off the remaining duties she needed to perform before going home. Penni, one of the bakery clerks from the day shift was usually in a hurry to leave, but she still lingered.

"I spoke with the assistant store manager about you this evening," Penni said. "I asked him if I could stay and give you some training. The bakery manager is planning to complain to the boss tomorrow about your performance. She's not very happy with your closings."

Myra squeezed her eyebrows together and tilted her head. She hadn't realized Misty wasn't satisfied with her work. "I don't understand. I do all the work they leave for me. I bag the bread, package the cookies, and put out all the pies after they've cooled."

"Yes, and you do that well. But no one ever gave you any formal training in this job, so you really don't know what's expected of you. I know they needed a person to close, so when you came along they tossed you in here without actually teaching you what you needed to get done to close the bakery every night."

Myra's face grew warm. Why didn't someone come to her sooner and tell her? Her probationary period was up in less than a week. She thought her work was satisfactory since no one told her otherwise. When would she ever do anything right?

Penni put a reassuring hand on her shoulder. "Look, I like you. You're really a good employee—willing to work hard. You're good with the customers, and you learn fast. I told the assistant manager the situation, and he agreed to let me stay on my own time and tell you what needs to be done. I'd hate to see them let you go because of that complaining bakery manager. She's crabby all the time. She just doesn't like you because everyone else does. She's jealous of your happy personality. You smile too much for her. She doesn't even use your name when she gossips about you. She calls you Pollyanna."

Myra felt as if she'd been struck in the face. There was a sudden tightness in her stomach that made it hard to breathe. How could someone not like a friendly, happy person? She glanced around the bakery as if she could locate an answer to the question darting through her mind.

Penni shook her arm. "Hey, it's going to be all right. I'll stay a couple of hours and help you. I'll show you what needs to be done and make a list for you to follow from now on. She can't complain if everything is done right."

The rain coursed down the windshield as the wipers tried furiously to propel it aside. They were in a losing battle. As she drove home, Myra's tears competed with the rain, and she tried relentlessly to swipe them from her eyes. Night seemed to be closing in on her, and fear was climbing up her throat like a phone repairman up a telephone pole.

I need this job, Lord. Please don't let me get fired. I don't want to be homeless again. Please don't let me lose this job.

Myra hoped Penni was right—that no one could complain about Myra's work after she was trained properly. But as she drove home, the knot in the pit of her stomach didn't loosen. It only became tighter. Nausea crept in, threatening to overtake her. She begged God to not let her get fired. She stopped at a red light, and an unfamiliar feeling spread over her. A strange moving in her spirit.

Love your enemies by praying for them.

"Huh?"

Myra, remember Matthew 5:44. Pray blessings on her. I will take care of you.

Myra swallowed hard. "Lord?" There was no reply, just an insistence in her spirit that wouldn't let up. She inhaled sharply and blew out slowly. What should she do?

"I, uh, I don't want to pray for Misty. I don't like it. This woman is trying to get me fired. She doesn't like me and gossips about me." She thought for a moment. "But, I'll do it if that's what You want me to do. It doesn't seem fair." She paused, considered her limited options, then sighed. "Please bless Misty, Lord. Bless her in a real big way. Pour blessings out on her until they overflow. Give her the desires of her heart, Lord."

The peace that hit Myra's heart shocked her. The fear vanished, and her tears dried up. For the remainder of the drive home, Myra's spirit was unexplainably light.

Myra arrived to work a little early the following afternoon. She greeted the day shift with a cheerful countenance and went to the back room and put her apron on. She passed Penni coming out of the storage room with a load of French bread bags in her arms.

"Myra, you're here early. I have some good news."

The good news had to be that she wasn't getting fired. Myra scanned the back room to be sure no one overheard her. "Where is *she*?"

"Hey, that's it. First thing this morning the boss came into the bakery and looked around. Then he asked me to send Misty to his office. When she got back, she announced that effective tomorrow, she had been promoted to the new store across town. It has a much bigger bakery. The store manager hired a new employee to take her place. He starts tomorrow. Misty forgot all about you. She came back bragging about how pleased he'd been at how good the bakery looked this morning."

Myra's mouth fell open. She laughed out loud and whispered, "Praise God. Thank You, Lord."

Penni cocked her head. "What? What'd you say?"

Myra reached over and hugged her. "I said 'praise God,' Penni. God answered my prayer."

"I told you that you wouldn't get fired."

"No, not *that* prayer. I prayed God would bless Misty. And He did. And in turn, I was also blessed. Thank you so much for your help, Penni."

"Okay, sure." Penni laughed. "You're funny, Myra. You prayed for *Misty*? Well, at least it all worked out." She walked away with the French bread bags, shaking her head.

When Myra walked through her apartment door that evening, she was walking on air. Her evening had gone well and she was so happy.

"Hey, I'm home," she called out.

Steve rushed out of the bedroom, anxiety splashed across his face like paint stains. "Myra, did Rosalie say she was going to a friend's after school? She's not home yet."

Myra looked at her watch. She felt the blood rush from her face. It was after 10:00 p.m. That morning she'd dropped Rosalie off at the school bus stop a little earlier than usual. It was still slightly dark. She pressed her eyes closed.

Dear God, what have I done?

Chapter Forty-One

October 1993

The silence hung in the small office like a Scottish mist, cool and heavy. Myra sat across from Lisa, head hung low, staring at her hands clasped tightly in her lap.

Lisa hadn't moved, spoken, or even cleared her throat. She waited for Myra's answer.

Myra squeezed her hands even tighter, turning her knuckles white, and making her joints ache. Her teeth, clenched like a vice, caused her jaw to ache and her head to throb. She felt as though she would explode like a faulty pressure cooker. Nervous perspiration snaked its way down her neck, soaking her collar. Say something, say something, *say something.*

"I ..." Her voice cracked. She choked and then coughed violently.

Once the fissure in her stoic facade began, it didn't stop. The coughing gave way to burning tears. She covered her eyes with her left hand in an attempt to hide them, but the dam had been broken. The weeping yielded to sobbing, shaking her shoulders with intensity. She covered her face with both hands, leaned forward in her chair with her chin on her knees and wept as her pain burst into the silence like an explosion, replacing it with loud anguished moans.

Everything disappeared for Myra. She was alone. Lisa disappeared, the furniture disappeared, the room disappeared. Myra had no idea how long she remained under this blanket of dark despair. There were no thoughts, no ideas, no words dashing around inside her head. Only tears and pain.

When the room became silent again, Lisa was leaning over Myra, hand resting on her back. "Are you ready to share this with me?" Her voice was barely a whisper.

Myra looked up and gave a slight nod.

Lisa reached for the box of tissues, removed one, and pushed it into Myra's hand.

Myra wiped her face before sitting up. "We called all the hospitals in the area that night, but she wasn't at any of them. We called her friends, but none of them knew where she was. We waited until morning and went to the school to see if anyone knew anything. We were shocked to find out she was there. The principal brought her from class to the office. She acted like nothing had happened. She said she was no longer living with us. She'd moved in with … with some dirt bag guy and *his* family.

"This is the way it's been going. She comes home, stays for a while, follows the rules, then leaves without notice. My sweet little Rosalie has changed. We've tried to get her help, without success. She's been like this ever since she …" Her voice trailed off. "When I think of how much she's been damaged, I get so angry, Lisa. I swear if I saw the guy on the street who hurt her, I'd drive up on the sidewalk to run him down. I'd never use my brake."

Lisa listened without comment, her face held no expression.

"My life has been a roller coaster. I never know what Rosalie is going to do. It's causing unrest with my family. I spend so much time worrying about her, I end up ignoring the boys. I go to work every evening and cry on the way home every night. I cry and eat. And I've gained all my weight back plus some. What kind of mother am I?

"I don't know what else to do for Rosalie. Or my boys. Or Steve. Oh, my gosh, I'm such a failure." She gritted her teeth and stared straight into Lisa's eyes. "I would rip that dirt-bag's heart out in a second if given half the chance." Her words spewed out and swirled through the room, settling on them like a thick layer of dirty brown dust.

Lisa gave a little nod in response to Myra's verbal explosion. "Are you looking for help, Myra? Or are you happy carrying around all this anger and bitterness?"

"I have a right to be angry." Her words snapped like a whip.

"No doubt. But, are you *happy* carrying this anger and bitterness?" Lisa's voice was even, but insistent.

"What am I supposed to do? Just forget what happened to my daughter?"

"I don't think you ever could. But, are you *happy* carrying the anger and bitterness? You said it's affecting your other relationships. It's probably affecting your job performance, and it's definitely affecting you physically. Are you trying to bury your anger beneath all this weight?"

Myra looked down at herself with disgust. She'd spent months dieting and exercising to get to a decent weight, and in a few short weeks had ballooned up to an even larger size. She couldn't wear cute clothes—just old polyester pants with elastic waist bands. What a loser.

"Have you buried your faith as well?"

"No, no," Myra said earnestly. "I haven't stopped believing."

"But you have stopped obeying." Lisa's gentle voice crossed the room, but was met with confusion.

Myra tilted her head, waiting for further explanation from Lisa. She'd not disobeyed God. She was a decent woman. She read her Bible, went to church, and helped others when possible.

Lisa smiled. "Myra, the load of anger and resentment you're carrying is too heavy for you. The bitterness has begun to squeeze your heart. It's causing you pain, and you must let it go."

"I don't know how." Myra's voice trembled

Lisa's eyes remained fixed on Myra's. Her soft voice drifted to Myra like a feather in a gentle breeze. "Yes, Myra, you do. It's called forgiveness."

Myra snapped to attention in her chair. "He does *not* deserve to be forgiven."

"I agree. But that's not our call. God doesn't tell us to forgive only people who deserve it. He tells us to forgive. Period. When we pray, we ask God to forgive us as we have forgiven other people. Do you want God to forgive you the same way you have forgiven this person who hurt Rosalie?" She didn't wait for Myra's response. "Myra, God has never suggested we forgive people who hurt us. He has *commanded* it. It isn't optional, it's mandatory."

Myra opened her mouth to protest, but Lisa kept speaking.

"Forgiveness is a gift you give yourself, Myra. Unforgiveness makes you physically ill. It affects your blood pressure, your heart rate, your sleep patterns, and your eating habits. Unforgiveness will kill *you*, but it won't do anything to your offenders. They'll go on living their lives as usual while you continue to die inside a little each day. Unforgiveness is like putting a gun to your head, pulling the trigger, and expecting the other person to die."

"So I'm just supposed to go to him and say, 'It's okay you hurt my daughter. I forgive you. Let's be friends.'"

Lisa shook her head in slow motion. "No, not at all. You don't need to have a warm fuzzy feeling toward that person. You don't have to say 'it's all right,' because it's not! You're allowed to be honest. Tell him what he's done is despicable, and it makes you sick. He's hurt your daughter and stolen something precious from her. You can't stand the sight of him, but in obedience to God, because *His* word commands it, you will forgive him. You will not allow what he's done to destroy your life. You forgive him. He will not have power over you any longer. Say 'I forgive you.'"

Myra was quiet as she processed these words.

"What if *he* never asks for forgiveness?"

"That's not your problem. That's between him and God. It's none of your business. God will deal with *his* heart. But what is between *you* and God is forgiveness. You are still commanded to forgive him. Free your heart, Myra. Be obedient to God. Lay your unforgiveness at His throne and regain the joy in your life."

Myra sat in silence for a moment while she mulled over Lisa's words. Then she hung her head in shame and nodded.

"Myra," Lisa whispered. "God has already forgiven *you.* Forgive that man, forgive yourself, and Myra, forgive your daughter. It's going to be a long, hard journey of forgiveness. Continue to forgive as needed. Every day. Every hour. Every minute if necessary. *Live* in that forgiveness. Don't let the darkness of unforgiveness swallow your heart."

Myra stared at Lisa. What did she mean *live in forgiveness*?

Chapter Forty-Two

December 1993

Myra sat on the bench at the mall and watched people sprint past her carrying packages, faces intent on completing their appointed mission. The store windows were adorned in splendid finery. Red, green, silver, gold, and deep purple decorations filled each display. Ribbons and trees, child-sized Nutcracker soldiers, old-fashioned St. Nicholas statues, angels and kings, elves and reindeer. Each danced before her eyes, awakening a smile, and creating delight in her heart. She never grew weary of Christmas. Maybe this year they would be able to afford to buy the kids a gift or two.

She loved each aroma that took her back to her childhood. The savory, warm smell of roasting turkey; the sweet, tempting smell of vanilla, cinnamon, and brown sugar. The crisp, sensual smell of the pine trees. The rich enticing aroma of chocolate chip cookies, clove-studded oranges in hot spiced cider, and fresh rosemary. She closed her eyes and remembered the cookies her mom used to make. Oatmeal raisin, chocolate chip, peanut butter … She was lost in the joy of memories.

A baby howled across the mall. Myra opened her eyes and looked toward the little North Pole village where children and parents were lined up waiting their turn to see the jolly fat man in red. The baby sitting on Santa's lap was clearly unhappy with the bearded gentleman.

Myra grinned at a memory of a Christmas when her children were younger. She'd always taught the children Santa was make-believe, like a cartoon character. She wanted them to know the real reason for the season was the birth of Jesus. One day while sitting in the food court, an elderly gentleman began to pass their table, but stopped when he saw the kids.

"Are you going to stop by and see Santa Claus?" The old man's eyes shimmered with mirth. The kids were taken by surprise at the stranger's words and said nothing. The old man's spirit was not deterred. "Merry Christmas," he offered and walked on.

When the man was out of earshot, four-year-old Danny's eyes lit up with shock. "Mom, that old guy believes in Santa Claus."

Myra laughed out loud at the memory. A few people sitting on nearby benches looked over at her. Her smile never faded as she rose from the bench and meandered away, passing all the beautifully decorated displays. As she strolled by a particularly festive window, she paused to gaze at the decorations and caught sight of her reflection in the window. Her shapeless form and rounded face stared back at her. She darted out of the mall, raced to her car, and drove home.

Myra unlocked the door and flew across the empty apartment to the phone on the wall. She grabbed the little black phone book on the small table nearby and located the number she wanted and dialed. She waited for someone to pick up. One ring, two rings, three, four, and finally someone answered. Myra, still out of breath from dashing from the carport, puffed out her response.

"Hi, this is Myra Collins. I'd like to make an appointment, please."

"Myra, it's good to see you. How are you?"

Myra shrugged, her eyes barely making contact. "Fine." She shifted her bulk uncomfortably. "I'm anxious to get going again."

The 1960s nurse led Myra to the exam room.

"You're a brave woman to start a diet in December, Myra."

"I'm tired of being fat. I want to start the New Year weighing less. Maybe 1994 will be better. Maybe I'll stop hiding behind this fat and do something with my life."

"Good for you, Myra."

The nurse chattered happily as she gathered all the data, drew Myra's blood, and gave her a specimen cup. Myra listened politely.

"Are you still working at the supermarket? I heard on the radio that the up-and-coming career of the '90s is physician's assistant. There's a two-year program at the community college. You should look into it. You don't want to work at the grocery store forever, do you?"

"Not really. But, it pays pretty well because it's union. I admit it's not terribly challenging, but the people are fun. It *is* the same stuff every day, though." Myra vacillated back and forth between why she liked her job and why she didn't.

The nurse smiled. "You should look into going back to school. It doesn't cost anything to check it out. If you go back to school, the store will probably work around your class schedule because they're union."

That caught Myra's attention.

"Yeah, but I'm not all that smart. I wouldn't do well in college." Myra fidgeted with her hands.

The nurse scowled at her. "Give yourself some credit, Myra. Look at all the things you've done right so far. You're smarter than you think. Go to the college and get a catalog. They're free, for Pete's sake."

Myra's mind whirred. She couldn't imagine going back to school in her thirties. Who was she kidding? College was for young people just out of high school. Not for old, fat women with children.

The nurse picked up the vials of blood and started to walk out of the exam room, then turned back. "I need a urine sample before you leave. The doctor will be right in."

She gave Myra of piercing look and with a smile, pointed a finger at her. "Go to the college, Myra."

The chili simmered on the stove, infusing the apartment with a wonderful robust aroma. The sound of sniffing filled the apartment as the boys rushed in from school and headed toward the kitchen.

"Hey, Mom, what's for dinner?"

"Chili and cornbread."

The phone rang and both boys raced to answer it.

Myra stepped to it first.

"*I'll* answer it, guys."

The boys retreated to their room as Myra put the receiver to her ear.

"Hello?"

"Myra, it's your brother, Mark."

Myra was delighted to hear from Mark. They didn't have many opportunities to talk anymore since Mark and his family moved two states away. "Hey, Mark. How's it going?"

"Fine. You know Dad moved in with us just before his stroke, right?

"Yeah." Myra's voice sounded tentative, waiting for unwanted news.

"Well, he's better now, but he wants to move back there. Says he hates the weather here. Will you pick him up at the airport?"

"Sure, when?"

"Thursday."

"Okay. Where's he staying? I thought he sold his condo."

"Yeah, he did. I guess he wants to stay with you until he finds a place of his own."

A moment of silence filtered between them.

"Oh, um, okay. I'll work something out, I guess."

The conversation ended with airline and flight arrival time information. Myra reached over to replace the receiver on the hook and the tiny kitchen suddenly became even smaller. She looked across the apartment. It was maybe twenty steps to the front door, but it appeared to be directly in front of her. The walls started to move in closer to each other. As the people's steps in the apartment above hers became louder, the cramped quarters threatened to engulf her.

This is a two-bedroom apartment with five people in it. One room is divided by a sheet to give some semblance of privacy to Rosalie when she's here. *And now, my dad's moving in.* She plopped heavily onto the kitchen chair and stared at the pot on the stove. *How will we afford to feed one more person?*

Chapter Forty-Three

November 1994

Myra trekked down the driveway toward her mailbox near the street. With each step she took, a grateful awareness washed over her like a wave on the sand. She marveled that she no longer needed a key to get into the apartment mailbox, and her car was in the driveway, not a carport. She looked back at the house they were renting and smiled.

That tiny apartment they'd lived in seemed to shrink when her dad moved in. It didn't take long before they all realized they needed a bigger place if her dad was going to stay for any length of time. Myra felt certain her father would be with them permanently, and she was glad to have him.

"I'll pay part of the rent," her dad said. "I'll pay room and board."

Even with Dad's financial help, they barely made ends meet. Add to that, the extra time Steve took every day driving him to and from the senior centers across town.

"Dad, why don't you go to the senior center in this neighborhood? There's a very nice one near the park. Then Steve wouldn't have to drive fifteen miles there and back twice a day. It's taking a toll on his back."

"I don't know anyone there." His answer was flat, with no indication he'd heard the part about the miles Steve was driving, or the pain he suffered.

Steve would never think to complain about such things. But still there was the gasoline for the daily sixty miles, the extra cost of heating the house because Dad was cold all the time, and the special food he requested. Dad rarely ate the simple meals she could afford to cook for her family.

"I can't chew that stuff, Myra. Give me mashed potatoes."

"You can't live on mashed potatoes, Dad," Myra would gently remind him.

"Then get me frozen dinners. The soft ones."

In the mornings, he insisted on instant oatmeal packets. "I don't want to bother anyone to cook oatmeal. Just buy the packets so I can add water."

"It's no bother, Dad. It only takes three minutes. And it's *much* cheaper."

"I like the packets better."

One day her dad asked her to go to the store and buy him a large bottle of aspirin. He reached to his back pocket and yanked out his wallet. He pulled out a dollar and handed it to her.

She looked at it for a second, wondering if he'd realized what he'd given her. Her voice became soft. "I think it might cost more than one dollar, Dad."

He looked a little confused, but said nothing. He pulled out another dollar and handed it over.

Myra nodded slowly. Ever since the stroke, he'd been acting differently. Forgetful. Even somewhat selfish.

A frustrated sigh escaped Myra's lips at the memory. Still, she was glad to get out of that tiny, cockroach-infested apartment. And the kids, especially the boys, enjoyed their grandfather's company.

Myra reached into the mailbox and pulled out a handful of envelopes. She flipped through them — plenty of junk mail. She liked that. She could throw them away, but the bills she had to contend with. She headed back to the empty house. Steve had taken Dad to one of the senior centers, and the kids were in school. She enjoyed these few blissful moments of silence every morning. It helped her gain perspective before she had to leave for classes in the evening.

She sat down at the kitchen table to take a closer look at the pile of envelopes she'd retrieved from the mailbox. The return address on one of them caught her eye. Why would City College be sending her a letter? She hadn't taken finals yet, so it wasn't grades, and her classes were paid for upfront, so it wasn't a bill. Filled with curiosity, she set the remainder of the letters aside to open this one first.

Her eyes darted back and forth across the page as the words jumped off the paper and slapped her face. Tears welled in her eyes and spilled over. She reached the end of the letter and put her forehead on the table as sobs erupted from her throat.

The front door opened, but she didn't look up.

"Myra!" Steve was beside her in an instant. "What's wrong? Why are you crying?" He crouched beside her and wrapped his arms around her. "Myra, what's going on?" he whispered.

He turned her chair to face him and took her face in his hands, but Myra's eyes remained tightly shut. She couldn't even look at him.

"Myra, what's wrong. Did someone get hurt? Are the kids okay?"

Myra opened her eyes to look at Steve and shook her head, then nodded, then frustrated with all the head bobbing, thrust the letter toward him and continued to cry.

He took the letter and read the contents, his smile spreading like sunshine. He looked up, eyes glowing. "Myra, this is wonderful news. Honey, why are you crying? It says your English instructor recommended you to be a charter member in the Phi Theta Kappa chapter at your college. Myra, how exciting to be asked to join this Honor Society." He shook his head. "Why are you crying?"

Myra couldn't even form the words. How could she explain to Steve how she felt, having spent her entire life believing she was a stupid loser and would never amount to anything? But somehow, since attending City College, she had managed to get "A"s in all of her classes.

She'd marveled at the first couple, thinking they were flukes, fully expecting to get "C"s again after that. But her grades remained high, and the work became fun as she looked forward to assignments for the sole purpose of seeing the "A" at the top of the page. She'd been tempted to put them on the refrigerator like a mother might do for her elementary school student, but she resisted. She inwardly glowed with each exceptional grade she received.

None of her teachers had any idea what those grades meant to her. Did they think she was just another student who glided through high school with all "As" on her report card? Perhaps she was one of those compulsive types who whined if they got a 92 percent instead of 98 or 100 percent. If they only knew. She had no idea what she'd been capable of. She was just an average, stupid student taking college classes, but all the while waiting to flunk out. That letter dispelled her previous false notion and ripped her reality in half like the veil in the temple. She looked up at Steve, searching desperately for a way to explain her turmoil.

As tears coursed down her cheeks, she opened her mouth to explain, but the words refused to exit.

She choked and ground her teeth together and tried again. Words, heavy with regret, squeezed past her lips. "Wasted years believing a lie," was all she could manage before the tears began again.

Chapter Forty-Four

April 1999

The car seemed to be driving itself. Myra acquiesced to its leading. She parked as close to the hospital entrance as possible, and as she emerged from the car she looked up. The building disappeared on the horizon. How did the parking lot move so far away from the building?

She trudged toward the building. As she dragged each foot in front of the other, her shoes felt like they were made of lead. The cars around her disappeared one by one as she found herself crossing a dry riverbed of asphalt.

The hospital doors loomed before her as she approached. They slid open just in time. Myra entered the foreboding lobby. People milled about like Greek statues. No one looked her way as she stood motionless for hours. With great effort, she headed down the long corridor. She couldn't see the end. It disappeared into a pinpoint miles beyond.

The air was thick and hot and difficult to breath. Her nose twitched from the faint smell of disinfectant snaking up her nostrils.

Still, the elevator lay beyond the corridor's horizon. She'd been walking for days. Where was the elevator?

Finally it came into view. She approached it with hesitant footsteps, gathered strength to reach over and pressed the button.

She could barely see the numbers above the elevator door, and her head was too heavy to maneuver it upwards. Her eyelids were too weak to look up any higher. She could sleep for a week waiting for the elevator to arrive.

The door opened in slow motion. Three hundred people piled off. Myra stepped in and the doors moved together like lips on an alien, swallowing her inside. She leaned against the wall to steady herself. She knew it would be a long slow ascent to the third floor. She could hear her slow rhythmic breathing. Was she asleep? The alien jarred to a stop, and the mouth opened and spit her out. She stared down the hall and sighed. Her destination was at least on the other end of town.

When she finally arrived in front of the locked door with a sign that read ICU, she read the garbled instructions on the wall and pressed the intercom button.

"Yes?" someone's voice snapped out of the static.

"I'm Myra Collins. I'm here to see …"

"Yes, come in."

A loud buzz startled Myra as the doors clicked open. She stepped in. Hot fear churned deep in her gut, boiling and rising up her throat.

The nurse's station loomed ahead like a tollbooth on an interstate. A large nurse in wrinkled scrubs with an unpleasant face lumbered forward like a gorilla and towered over her.

"You here to see John Grayson?" She smirked, revealing a crooked smile.

"Yes. My dad."

"This way." She put her hand behind Myra's back to guide her and shoved her foreword. Myra stumbled.

"Be careful. You don't want to fall." The nursed kept walking until she reached a room with a sliding glass door front.

All around her alarms shrieked and monitors beeped incessantly. Myra put her hands to her ears and squeezed her eyes shut, clamping down on the scream that threatened to escape.

The nursed turned, her eyebrows furrowed.

"The doctor will be here soon to talk to you. Your father is a DNR, so the doctor will tell you what's going to happen. Go in and sit down."

Myra took a faltering step forward and sat down on the chair next to the bed.

She remained there for about a year without moving. Then she reached over and took her father's hand, squeezing it softly.

Her voice was hoarse, and the words could barely make it past the tight ball of tears in her throat. "This is not a good time to choose to have another stroke, Dad. Not now." Her jaw was tight as she scanned the little room. *If he's a "Do Not Resuscitate," why is he on that machine?*

Myra remembered how his eyes glowed with pleasure when she told him Rosalie and Jeffrey were going to have a baby. He was so happy to be a great-granddaddy.

Who knew this massive stroke would undo their surprise that the baby would be his namesake?

But when Myra had expressed concern about his health, her father had assured her the doctor said he was fine. Still concerned, she'd encouraged him to attend the senior center one less day a week so he'd have a chance to rest. But he'd insisted she leave him alone—he could rest on the weekends.

Myra gazed out the glass window into the ICU's nursing station as a flurry of activity blew past. She heard *code red* from somewhere, and suddenly the ICU filled with hospital personnel. She looked back at her dad.

"Don't worry, Dad. That's not for you."

She was thankful for the time he'd stayed with her family. Thankful he'd gotten to know her kids better. Thankful he'd even had a chance to meet Rosalie's husband, Jeffrey.

But what about Jeremiah and Danny, Dad? They'll have girlfriends and weddings too. You won't be there for them. She looked at his bruised, swollen face. Sadness swept over her like a sandstorm, chafing her heart in its wake. She wished her brother, Mark, could be there with her now. But the earliest flight out had him arriving tomorrow evening.

She sighed. This never would have happened if her father hadn't insisted on moving into his own place last year. Someone would have heard him fall—or even noticed something strange about him before he fell and called 911. She bit the inside of her cheek remembering the argument with her dad.

"Dad, why do you want to move out? We moved you into this big house so you could have your own room. Steve takes you wherever you want to go. I buy the food you like, and do your laundry. The boys enjoy your company. They play cards with you, watch movies with you. Why do you want to move?"

"The boys are disrespectful to their father."

"What? They don't disrespect him, Dad. They tease him. They enjoy each other's teasing. Steve teases them back. Danny and Jeremiah love their father, Dad."

"I can't stand seeing Steve in so much pain."

Then stop expecting him to drive you to all the different senior centers across town five days a week. "Dad, pain is a way of life for Steve. After eight back surgeries, it's not going to get better. He's learned to manage."

"Myra, if you don't take me to find my own place, I'll take the bus."

"Dad, if you move out, Steve and I will not be able to stay in this house. We'll have to take the kids and move back to an apartment like the last one."

"Myra, you're so selfish. And, I'm leaving to get my own place."

After her dad moved out, she and Steve prayed that God would supply what they needed to stay in the house. To their relief, their money managed to stretch to cover the bills each month. God had answered their prayers before they were even spoken. Their grocery bill went way down, the cost of gasoline was cut in half, and the water, heating and electric bills fell. They were *barely* making it—but they *were* making it!

Her dad had moved into an adult community complex and found himself involved with every activity possible. Movies, cards, game night, dances. He never went hungry either, as he befriended some neighbors who had him over for dinner almost nightly. Still, Myra wished he hadn't moved. Since his stroke, he often became confused. He left water boiling on the stove, forgot his medicine, and he couldn't remember what day it was sometimes. He wasn't safe to live alone.

Behind her, Myra heard a small cough. She turned slightly and saw a doctor standing in the doorway. She leapt to her feet and faced him.

"Mrs. Collins? I'm Dr. Milligan." He put his hand out and Myra reached for it. His hand swallowed hers in a firm handshake. "Your father was brought in early this morning. Apparently a neighbor found him on his kitchen floor where he'd been all night. He's had a massive cerebral hemorrhage.

"There would be no quality of life if your father lived. He bled into his brain, causing severe damage. There is no brain activity. Your dad is a DNR. He's on life support, but now that all the tests have been done, we'll be taking him off." Dr. Milligan looked wary, almost as if he expected an argument for Myra.

"Those were my father's wishes, Doctor. My brothers and I will respect them. I know he didn't want to be hooked up to tubes for the remainder of his life."

The doctor nodded, and what looked like a relieved smile pulled at his lips.

"I'm going to disconnect everything."

"How long before he … slips away?"

"I imagine it won't take long."

The doctor stepped to the machine and began to disconnect it.

"My father was always my biggest fan, Doctor. May I sing him one last song?"

"Sure."

The monitor beeped his heart rate out as Myra took her father's hand. Then she closed her eyes and lifted her voice, singing "In the Garden" as she'd never sung before. She loved the image of walking and talking to Jesus in the garden.

She sang the last word, opened her eyes and looked at her dad, then glanced up at the cardiac monitor. His heart rate became erratic, then flat-lined across the screen.

"Bye, Daddy. Go be with Jesus."

She turned to leave just as the large nurse in the wrinkled scrubs came in. A single tear slid down Myra's cheek. The nurse approached her and placed her hand on Myra's arm and gave a tiny squeeze.

"Are you okay, Mrs. Collins? Can I get anything for you?" Her smooth and calm voice flowed over Myra's heart like a healing ointment. Myra looked into her gentle brown eyes.

"No, thank you."

"Would you like to go somewhere to be alone? We have a lovely chapel here."

"Yes, I'd like that."

She touched Myra's elbow with a feather-light tenderness as she led her toward the door. "When you're ready to talk to the doctor, come back. Take all the time you need. The chapel is on the first floor. Turn right off the elevator. You can't miss it."

Myra left and walked a few yards to the elevator. As the doors opened, she stepped in and hit the button for the first floor. It descended and she got off and walked the short distance to the chapel.

There were no other people there, and a sense of peace pervaded the little sanctuary as Myra stepped to the chair and sat down. She took a deep breath, inhaling the peace and exhaling the stress.

"Father, we need to talk. You start. I'll listen."

Chapter Forty-Five

June 2000

The morning air smelled like freshly washed herbs. A slight chill lingered in the air. Myra knew it would burn off as the sun made its way across the sky. She strolled down the path toward the college's nursing program department with a manila envelope clutched in her fist. She was enjoying the morning quiet and her own inner musings. The application for the nursing program was due today. After she dropped it off, she planned to enjoy her first day off in weeks. Most days were a flurry of activity, and with so much on her mind, she wondered how she contained it all in the confines of one small human skull.

She'd experienced her share of stress—both good and bad—this past year, but she managed to survive. Her father's death was a bittersweet memory. His absence had left a hole in her heart. How sad Dad will never meet his great-grandson, his namesake—John Philip Gordon. This sweet-natured baby with the enormous blue eyes managed to fill that small aching hole in her heart. She was truly blessed.

Myra entered the office and glanced around for someone to take her application but saw no one. Myra sat in the lone chair to wait.

This last semester had been a long, hard struggle. In the end, she'd made an appointment with Lisa to let off some steam and verbalize her disappointments. She and Lisa had a wonderful history together, and Myra was thankful for a counselor who was always willing to fit her in whenever she needed to talk.

"I was doing great until this last class, Lisa."

"Did you fail the class?"

"I got a stupid "C.""

"A stupid "C"? Interesting term."

Myra remained silent. She'd expected Lisa to say she was sorry for the poor grade, but her response was speeding down a different avenue.

Lisa arched one eyebrow. "What are you implying, Myra?"

"I'm just so stupid for getting that "C," that's all."

Lisa's eyebrow arched higher, matching Myra's anxiety.

"Myra." Lisa plopped her hands into her lap. "Stop that. You're not stupid. Stop demeaning yourself. You are *not* stupid. You're smart."

Myra's face grew warm. Lisa had never spoken to her that way before—with an unmistakable edge to her voice.

"What did you get in English, Myra?"

"A."

"In history?"

"A."

"In health and speech and cultural studies? In math, chemistry, and biology?"

Myra hung her head. "A."

"What would you say to anyone else *on the face of the earth* who got those grades?"

"They're smart?"

"Yes, and you are too. Didn't you tell me you were inducted into the Honor Society?"

"But I got a "C.""

"Forget this "C." Don't let it define you. Don't let it derail you. There may have been mitigating circumstances like distractions, time constraints, and family issues pulling at your attention. Cut yourself some slack, Myra. Microbiology is a difficult class. You told me you struggled—praying you would pass. Think of all the other classes you struggled in and got an "A." Each circumstance is different. Think about it for a moment, Myra. Heck, you could've had a lousy teacher."

Myra's head jerked up. Could a teacher be partly responsible for a poor grade? Her mind flew back to each of the last three classes she struggled with—all prerequisites to the nursing program.

When Myra shared with her Nutrition instructor that she was struggling with the material, her instructor took the time to go over the information in class and gave Myra extra time after class as needed to help her understand the lesson on metabolism. Myra went from a "C" to an "A." The same was true with her Anatomy and Physiology instructor. When Myra's final lab exam brought her grade below an acceptable level, her teacher gave her a "private" lab exam during her free hour, allowing Myra the extra time she needed to identify all the parts on the kidney's model. Once again, with the extra help she received, Myra got an "A."

However, the instructor that taught Microbiology didn't want to spare the time or the effort to help Myra do well. When she went to him and explained her struggles, he dismissed her as a product of a generation that never properly learned how to study. He reminded her that she was responsible for all the material in the textbook and suggested she find a tutor. The tutor did little more that recite the teacher's words back to her. Her final grade was a "C"-just high enough the make it into the nursing program.

Lisa was right. She was smart. Smart enough to know that caring, encouraging teachers who take the time to teach students will make all the difference.

Myra's eye caught the secretary's as she came out of a back room. Myra walked to the counter.

"May I help you?" the secretary asked.

"I have my application for the nursing program."

The woman reached over and took the manila envelope. She pulled the top page out and glanced at it.

"Okay, Myra. It looks in order. We'll review all the applications this summer and *if* you've been accepted, you'll receive a letter in the mail sometime in August."

Chapter Forty-Six

September 2001

All classes on campus were canceled and students and faculty were sent home. Myra sat frozen in front of the television—her hands clammy and her heart racing so fast, she thought she'd pass out. As much as she tried to make sense of the attack on the World Trade Center, she still couldn't comprehend the devastation or why anyone would do such a heinous act. Thoughts ricocheted from one end of her brain to the other. Her eyes burned from her tears as if drenched in acid. She felt as if she might vomit.

Since her son, Danny, joined the army right out of high school, she'd been on edge emotionally. The very idea that her "baby" was learning how to be a soldier in boot camp didn't really sit well with her. She considered the implications of the attack. Was this the work of a few individuals, or a nation bent on destroying the United States? Would they be going to war as the country did after Pearl Harbor? Could she bear losing her son in a war? How had her mom survived the years following her brother, Danny's death in Vietnam?

Myra's heart pounded in her chest with such ferocity she sat down. For the first time since Danny was born, she regretted naming him after her brother. *Don't be ridiculous, Myra. The attack isn't related to Danny. This would have happened even if you'd named your son something else.* She starred at the television as shocking images flashed by and the reporter droned on.

Was she a stronger woman than her mother? Myra recalled some of the trials her mother had been through—losing her mother at an early age, being raised in an orphanage, having an abusive father, losing her son in the war, battling cancer and losing. They all flashed through Myra's mind in a split second. Her mother was strong at the very end, there was no doubt. But knowing Jesus would have eased the strain of a lifetime of trials.

Would I continue to trust God, if He chose to take my son? She considered that sorrow. Could Myra stand on her faith? Yes, she could. It would hurt, but God would walk with her through that dark night. Oh, that her mom had embraced that same comfort when she lost her son. For the first time in several years, Myra acknowledged the pain she still carried in her heart for the loss of her brother. *Dear God, protect my son, please.*

Breathe, Myra, breathe. She was alone and afraid. Why didn't they send Steve home from work? The doorbell pierced the silence. After she scraped her heart off the ceiling and looked through the peephole, she pressed her head against the door and sighed. *Oh, thank You, Jesus.* Family members.

Myra opened the door and Jeremiah, his new wife, and their baby came in, followed by Rosalie and Johnny and their new baby girl. Since Myra had started nursing school, Jeremiah had married his high school sweetheart, Pearla, and they had a baby girl. Jeffrey and Rosalie had their second child, also a girl. And Danny had joined the army.

"Have you heard from Danny?" Rosalie's anxious voice cracked. She rushed in and gave her mom a hug.

"No, I called the recruiting office and spoke with the sergeant who recruited Danny. He said all communications have stopped since the bombings. He assured me Danny is safe while at boot camp." Myra's tears flowed freely. "I never should have let him join the army right out of high school."

Jeremiah hugged her. "You didn't *let* him, Mom. It was something he wanted to do. He's proud to serve his country. He'll be fine."

"Yeah," Myra whispered. "Rosalie, where's Jeffrey?"

"He left for work early, Mom. I wish they'd send him home."

Myra nodded. She bent her head and ran her hands through her hair. She paused a moment and a guttural sound escaped her throat. All those people. *All* those people. They'd gotten up this morning, gotten ready for work, and before they could eat lunch, they were gone. All those lives—all those families. Tears flowed like a river down Myra's face.

"Come on, we need to pray. We need to pray for your brother, for those families, for our country." Myra dropped onto the sofa, put her hands to her face and moaned. "Oh, God. We need You. God, we need You *now*."

Myra wept as each of the kids prayed.

Classes reconvened as scheduled the following week. Concentration was difficult with so many distractions slinging her thoughts around in her head like a paddleball. *Breathe deep. Breathe deep and focus, Myra.*

Her thoughts kept turning to Danny. When would a letter ever come? Each day the knot in the pit of her stomach tightened like a noose, squeezing her appetite into oblivion. If her brain had been a water balloon, it would have popped, soaking her to the core. She was thankful for whatever gray matter still functioned.

Finally, after a long, grueling week and a half, a letter arrived. *Oh, thank You, God. Thank You.* Her hands shook as she tore the letter open and scanned the pages. Not a word about the attack. She checked the date and her shoulders slumped. The letter was written two days before it happened. Probably got held up when the planes were grounded. Frustrated tears pushed themselves over the rims of her eyes and down her face.

This waiting for Danny to be in touch was far more difficult for Myra than waiting to hear if she'd been accepted to nursing school. But as great a gift as it was to be chosen for the program, a letter from Danny would be greater still. *Write your mom a letter, Danny. A postcard. Anything. Please just write.*

December 2001

Sundays were a glorious reprieve from the usual weekday stress. As the church service let out, Myra turned to see her friend, Susan rushing to catch up to her.

"How is your son in the army?" Susan asked.

"Well, I think he's okay. I get letters occasionally and sometimes he calls. When he's having trouble learning something, or he's got a test, or he's going to be doing something dangerous, he calls and asks me to pray for him."

Susan's eyes widened and her face brightened. "Good."

"And, each time I've prayed, God has kept him safe or helped him master his new skill. I just wish he could see that God has answered my prayers. I suspect he thinks it some sort of coincidence."

"It's great that he requests the prayers. We'll just have to continue to keep him in our prayers and ask God to open his eyes to see the connection."

Myra nodded as she squeezed Susan's arm.

"Oh, hey, how's nursing school?"

"It's a challenge, but I'm really enjoying it. So far, I've gotten great instructors. The clinicals have been fun, and I *love* working with the patients."

"I'm sure they love you as well, Myra. You are made for this. You have a caring, compassionate heart. I think you've found your niche, my friend."

"I know God wants me to be a nurse, Susan. He's opened all the doors—even ones that were firmly bolted shut."

"Steve must be so proud."

"He's amazing. He cleans the house, does the laundry, and makes all the meals so I have time to study. I just sit by the hour and read textbooks and do case studies."

"You're an inspiration, Myra."

"It's God, Susan. I'm just along for the ride."

"Take a little bit of the credit, my friend. God opened the door for you. But, *you* walked through it. *You've* put in the time studying, testing, working with patients."

Myra paused a moment and nodded. "I guess."

"But, keep trusting Him. I suspect that each semester will get a little more challenging for you."

Chapter Forty-Seven

April, 2003

The room seemed blurry, like seeing through heat waves. The distinct odor of perspiration hung in the air, foul and stale. Myra clenched her fists tight in her lap. *Focus, Myra.*

Myra kept her eyes on the moving lips across from her. What were they saying? *Focus, Myra, focus.*

Her heart rate had increased to the speed of sound. Sound—all she could hear was a loud ringing in her ears. The words were warbled, like spoken underwater. *Myra! Focus!*

She drew in a long, slow breath and held it, then let it slip slowly out of her nose. *Okay, okay, I can hear.*

"…and the nurses on the third floor tell me you aren't paying attention, and you're causing them extra work. Don't make me have to write you up again, Myra. Your clinical skills are lacking. Frankly, I don't think you have what it takes to be a nurse."

The woman's harsh eyes bore through Myra like a hot poker. The remnants of Myra's lunch pushed their way up. She swallowed hard. Throwing up on a clinical instructor was definitely grounds for dismissal.

The teacher cocked her head and raised her eyebrow. "You've got a week to improve your performance, or I'll release you from the program."

Release? You mean kick me out.

"Do I make myself clear, Myra?"

"Yes, ma'am."

"Go home and think about that."

You mean obsess about that. You just threatened to kick me out of nursing school four weeks before graduation. What'd you think I was going to do? Forget this conversation ever happened?

"Yes, ma'am."

Myra gathered her belongings and left the room. She headed up to the third floor to get her sweater and purse from the break room locker. *What nurses complained? Complained about what? Yes, I've made mistakes, but I've owned them and listened to the nurses and done what's expected of me. Oh, my gosh. How can I do better if I don't know what to improve? The nurses have been nice. Why didn't they just speak to me if there was a problem? Why go to her?*

Myra slipped off the elevator and headed for the break room. Coming toward her was one of the three nurses she worked with.

Myra approached her and cleared her throat. "May I speak with you for a moment?"

"Sure, Myra. What's up?"

"I want to apologize."

The nurse narrowed her eyes, but kept the smile. A small nervous laugh escaped her lips. "What for?"

"My clinical instructor tells me I've been making extra work for the nurses I'm assigned to, by not paying attention. She says they've all complained. So I want to tell you I'm sorry I've made your job harder and I'll try …"

"What?" she said, cocking her head and shaking it. She crossed her arms. "No, no that never happened. I would never complain to *her*. You are doing a fine job, Myra. The patients love you. If I had a problem with you, I'd tell you. She never spoke to me about you. There's no need to apologize."

Myra's breath caught in her throat. She gave a slight cough to clear the sob away. "Thanks."

The nurse nodded and touched Myra's shoulder, then continued toward the elevator. Myra headed to the break room. Her face was warm, again. *What was that? Who's telling the truth?* Myra entered the break room and saw Cathy and Terry, the other two nurses she had been assigned to.

"Hey, Myra. Time to leave? Have a good weekend." Terry said.

"May I speak to both of you for a minute?"

"Sure," they said in unison.

"I want to apologize to you for my poor performance. I know I've been making your job more difficult and I'm sorry. I'll be better next week."

The nurses exchanged looks and turned back to Myra.

"What are you talking about, Myra?" Cathy asked.

"Well, I was told the nurses I work with were upset that I don't pay atten—"

Terry gasped. "Did your instructor tell you that stuff?"

Myra nodded, shame rising inside. She blinked several times, cleared her throat, and croaked, "Yeah."

"It's a lie," Cathy shouted.

"Myra, sit down," Terry said calmly.

Myra sat.

"She never came up here. We never said that trash. You're not making our job harder. You're a student. You're doing a good job. You've made a couple of mistakes, big deal—everyone does. That's how we learn. No one died."

Myra shifted in the chair. Again her heart was pounding. *She lied? She made it up? Is she trying to get rid of me—setting me up?*

"Listen Myra, this is what she does. She chooses a student every semester and rides them until they quit. Apparently, you're her choice this semester. I had her for my clinical instructor four years ago, so I know."

"Should I quit?"

"No. Absolutely not. I'll tell you what to do. Go to her and tell her you want to improve your skills as a nurse and ask if you may follow her around for an entire shift sometime. She works here per diem in the evening. She won't flunk you when she sees you going above and beyond what is expected of you."

"Really?"

"Trust me. *I* did it." Terry said, nodding.

A tear slid down Myra's cheek. "Thanks."

"You're welcome. Go home, have a good weekend. Call her Monday."

The weekend seemed to last for months. Myra's heart rate never slowed down.

Pray, Myra, pray.

"Lord, I know You want me to be a nurse. Please let this teacher see something in me worthy of graduating."

Pray without ceasing, Myra.

"Lord, give me what I need to face the next few weeks. Help me be the kind of nurse You want me to be."

Pray, pray … That's it! Myra's eyes almost popped out at the thought.

She ran to her computer and printed "pray" in several different fonts—in the largest size she could. She printed several pages of them. She headed toward her sewing box and pulled out a pair of scissors. She cut out each "pray" and proceeded to tape them all over the house. On the bathroom mirror, on the microwave, refrigerator, TV, cupboards, doors, walls—everywhere her eyes fell, "pray" went up. In her car, on her notebooks, textbooks, and on the back of her ID badge. Any surface that she could tape one on, she did.

God wants me to be a nurse, and I will trust Him for that. I will pray without ceasing and trust Him until I'm holding that diploma in my hot little hand.

She crossed her arms and scanned her surroundings. Myra couldn't look anywhere without seeing a reminder to pray.

"Okay, God. Let's do this. Let's dispense with the lies and start living in truth."

Chapter Forty-Eight

May 2006

Myra trudged into the house at nearly midnight. She tossed herself on the couch like a sack of potatoes and stared into the darkness. There was no point going to bed. Sleep wouldn't come tonight. Myra was still in wonder that her clinical instructor had allowed her to shadow her for the entire shift at the hospital that evening.

They were in and out of patients' rooms all night. Her instructor seemed to relish having an audience of one. Myra realized every room her instructor went into was like a short stage play. There was no real instruction, just a little floorshow to demonstrate her fine nursing skills. Yet, Myra was grateful to be there. At the end of the shift, her instructor stood before her, hands on hips, with an expression that seemed to say, "And that's how it's done."

"Any questions, Myra?"

"No. But thank you for allowing me to shadow you tonight. I learned a great deal from this experience." The immense smile on Myra's face was only secondary to the beaming smile she felt in her spirit. *I even learned a little about nursing.*

"Myra, I want to see you in my office after lecture."

The muscles in Myra's jaw tensed. Thank goodness she was allowed to tape the lectures, she doubted she'd be able to focus on this one.

Standing in the office, hands to her side, Myra waited for whatever sentence her instructor would pronounce.

She glared up at Myra with sharp, mirthless features. All the instructor was missing was a black robe and a gavel. Judgment was hers alone. There was no jury present.

"Myra, you told me that you and your husband got a loan to pay for nursing school. And you would find it difficult to pay your bills on your current income. I feel sorry for you, Myra. So, against my better judgment, I'm going to let you graduate."

A thrill shot through Myra's heart like lightning at the thought of being able to graduate. Almost immediately she felt a pang in her heart as well.

Lord, this is not exactly what I was looking for, but I'll take it gratefully. Thank You that I'll be graduating. I had hoped she would see something worthy in me to graduate, but perhaps this is the best she could do. Thank You, Lord.

Myra cleared her throat and managed to croak a hoarse sounding, "Thank you."

"I'm glad you want to work in labor and delivery, Myra. You really don't have the skills to work on a med./surg. floor."

Myra had committed herself to doing the best she could in nursing school and leaving the rest to God. She knew He wouldn't let her down. With that conviction firmly planted in her heart, she'd walked through the entire semester as if she already knew graduation was guaranteed. The fact her instructor told her she would graduate didn't alter her determination to finish strong. And she knew other circumstances needed addressing. Her list of prayers had grown lengthy.

Praying had made her stronger and given her hope. She was more certain now than ever that God wanted her to be a nurse.

"I'm disappointed we only get five tickets for the pinning ceremony," Myra said to a fellow nursing student. "This is a large graduating class, so why didn't they find a bigger auditorium?"

Most of the other student nurses were just as disappointed at the number of tickets they received. Myra needed seven. One for her husband, Steve, and one each for Jeremiah and Pearla. One for Rosalie—Jeffrey had volunteered to watch the grandkids so everyone else could go to the ceremony. One for her friend, Susan, and one for her brother, Mark, who phoned he'd fly out to see her graduate. And of course, one for Danny in the army. There was no word as to whether his CO would give him leave, but Myra stood firm in her faith. She'd told Danny she knew he would be at graduation because she had gone over his CO's head. She smiled remembering the panic in his voice thinking she'd called the general. "No. Higher. I went right to the top. I prayed." she'd said. Myra knew he'd be there. She even requested he wear his uniform because she had a surprise for him at the pinning ceremony.

Two days later, Danny received word that his leave had been approved.

Her friend beside her nodded in agreement. "Yeah, I know. I'm not even inviting anyone to the pinning ceremony because I have too many family members. They'll all go to the college's graduation at the stadium."

Myra's ears perked up. "Really? Do you have any of your five tickets left?"

"Yeah, one. You want it?"

"I'd love to have it." Myra felt a thrill tingle on her skin. She only needed one more ticket. No sooner had Myra thanked her classmate, when she overheard the woman behind her say that she and her husband were flying to Europe to celebrate her graduation. She wasn't going to be at the pinning.

Myra whirled around. "Do you have an extra ticket? I'll buy it from you."

The woman's eyes twinkle. "Really? How much?"

"I'll give you ten dollars."

"Twenty."

"Okay."

"Thirty."

"Okay."

The woman's laughter blared through the classroom. "Just kidding, Myra. You can have it."

Myra's hands flew to her mouth as she squealed like a delighted kindergartner. *Seating covered, prayer answered.* Her heart leapt from its resting place and nearly exited her chest.

Myra's clinical group sat at a table in the hospital cafeteria. Half sat on one side, the other sat facing them.

The atmosphere was tense, and the conversation was stilted. Fingers drummed the table, palms were slid along white scrub pants, and eyes darted from face to face. The final evaluations were ready.

Nausea flared in Myra's stomach like fire from hot coals. She clutched at her abdomen in a vain effort to squelch the burning.

The instructor called them one at a time to her table across the room. They could see her severe expression from where they all huddled, but they couldn't hear her speak. Each of them sat rigid, wordless, occasionally glancing toward her as she went over a student's paperwork and final evaluations.

Myra's head was swimming. She was afraid when she got up her shaking knees might give way. The current victim stood and left the judgment seat. Her stone features sent a chill down Myra's spine. She walked straight to their table and without making eye contact said, "She wants Myra next."

Look casual. Look relaxed. She told you she's graduating you. Look confident. Look focused. It doesn't matter what she says. Look sharp. Look interested. It only matters what God has said. Look calm. Look professional.

Myra sat across from her. The teacher's eyes bored into her.

"This is the worst evaluation I've ever written," she said.

The words hit Myra like a blast of Arctic wind. Her face stung.

Look impassive.

"I'm going to hide this evaluation from the program director. She'll want to know why I'm graduating someone who's done so poorly in her clinical rotation."

Don't cry. Just listen.

Her instructor went through the six-page evaluation in detail, cutting Myra's heart out and slicing it into tiny pieces. When it was laid out on the table, shredded and bloody, the instructor smirked. "I guess you'll be glad to get out of this program. I'm sure you hate me."

The words forced Myra back in her chair like an explosion.

"No, that's not true!" Myra leaned forward. "I don't hate you at all. You can ask any of the other girls in the group. I said on many occasions that under other circumstances you and I could have been friends—you make me laugh. But you rode me like a horse this semester."

Myra didn't pause or take a breath. She just pushed on with her thoughts. "One thing I know for sure, God brought you into my life for a reason—perhaps to teach me nothing more than to pray without ceasing. I know He brought me into your life as well, but that's between you and God. I don't hate you at all. You forced me to work hard and trust God."

Her instructor's mouth fell open, but no words came out for a few moments. When she regained her composure, she looked down at the evaluation papers in front of her.

"Well, I'll give you this much. You were an ethical nurse, and you worked two hundred percent."

The words filtered through Myra's exhausted brain, and her shoulders relaxed as the anxiety evaporated off of them like dew from flowers. A single tear ran down her cheek and fell from her chin. A smile tugged at the corner of her cracked lips.

Oh, thank You, Jesus. That's all I wanted to hear—that she saw something in me worthy of graduating.

The auditorium was packed like a snack box full of raisins. As the nursing students filed down the dimly lit aisle, Myra's smile led the way.

She marveled that her heart could be so full and yet so feather-light. She looked down at her feet to be sure they were actually touching the floor.

Once on stage, the students took their seats. Myra and three other women stood and walked to the front of the stage. *This is for you, Danny.*

A man's voice boomed through the speakers. "Please stand out of respect, as Myra, LaTonya, Dolores, and Lucy pay tribute to our nation and our men and women in uniform."

"Oh, say, can you see …"

The four-part harmony blended with warm smoothness, as the a cappella voices sailed through the room like a sailboat on the wind.

Myra thrilled at the chance to sing before this crowd. The invitation to sing at graduation had been extended to the entire class, but only three other women volunteered to join her. It was no coincidence they each sang a different part. *This was orchestrated by God, no other instruments were needed.*

From where she stood on the stage, Myra could see her family. Her heart swelled. There were seven of them sharing this moment with her.

"…For the land of the free, and the home of the brave."

The audience erupted like a volcano. Myra was stunned by their response. Her glassy eyes turned to her family, she smiled, put her fingers to her lips and blew them a kiss.

The mistress of ceremonies took her place at the podium. "Our nursing students have worked hard to get here. They've earned the right to be called registered nurses. We're proud of them and want to honor them today. Each student has written a thank you to those people who supported them and encouraged them. I will call each student, and as they approach, I will read their words for you."

She called each student by name in alphabetical order, reading their words of gratitude. Myra sat still for a moment with head bowed and eyes closed. There was dancing in her feet and laughter in her throat that needed to be quelled for the sake of decorum. *Lord, how can I ever thank You enough for this moment? Nursing school has strengthened my faith and brought me closer to You like I've never dreamed possible. You are an awesome God.*

"Myra Collins."

Myra looked up from her prayer and stood to make the short journey across the stage as her words of gratitude were read for all to hear.

"Lord Jesus, thank You for this incredible miracle today. Thank You for blessing me with my loving husband, Steve, and my extraordinary family—Danny, Jeremiah, Pearla, Rosalie, and Jeffrey."

She reached her destination, and Myra bowed her head as the ribbon holding her nursing pin was slipped over her head.

Incredible. I made it through nursing school. Incredible. Myra, The Loser, made it through nursing school. She paused. *Maybe I'm not such a loser after all.*

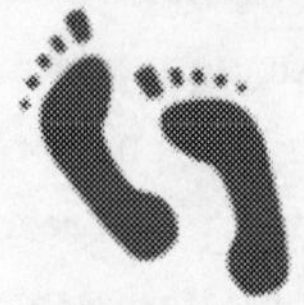

Chapter Forty-Nine

August 2007

Myra walked through the house with wide eyes. It wasn't the newest or the biggest house she and Steve had looked at, but she liked it. She liked the long thin windows on each side of the fireplace. She liked the large bathroom in the master bedroom. She liked the small kitchen.

She followed Steve and the realtor, Brian, out the side door into the backyard. Oh my, it was like stepping into a page of *Better Homes and Gardens*. The landscaping around the pool was truly artistic.

Steve caught her eye and Myra nodded. He gave a slight nod of approval back. They'd agreed earlier that no matter how much one of them loved a house, no offer would be made unless they *both* loved it. This was the twentieth house they looked at, and it was the last one on the realtor's list. God had saved the best for last.

"Okay, Steve and Myra, would you like to go grab some lunch and talk about which house you liked best?"

Over burgers and fries at Dairy Queen, Brian, Steve, and Myra filtered through a ship-wreck's worth of paperwork strewn across the table.

Myra's insides were tense and jittery as they covered all the details of making an offer on a house. *A house.* After years of rental-living and homelessness, God had led them to this. A house.

"Are we doing the right thing?" Myra whispered. "I'm a little scared. This is huge. It's not like we can take it back if we're not happy with our purchase."

When the paperwork was completed, Brian assured them he would add their offer to the one already on the table for that house and call them with any news. When they arrived home, there was a message waiting for them on their answering machine.

"Hi, it's Brian. The homeowners raised the price of the house because there were two offers. Call me and let me know how you want me to proceed."

Myra looked at Steve. "Do you think this is God's way of telling us not to buy this house?"

Steve looked as befuddled as Myra felt. He shrugged. "I honestly don't know, Myra."

"I'm going to call Susan and ask her to pray for us."

"Good idea, Myra."

"I don't know what to think or believe, Susan. Am I crazy for trying to buy a house? Steve worked so hard pinching pennies to get all our bills current, and it's scary to jump back into debt like this. Maybe God is trying to tell me something with the homeowners raising the asking price."

"Myra, if you want a specific answer from God, you must pray a specific prayer. Decide what you want from God and ask Him for that."

Myra felt a little silly. Was it as easy as that? The answer was so obvious. Why didn't she think of it? She laughed at herself.

"Wise counsel, Susan. Thanks. It's time for Steve and me to pray."

"Lord, if you want us to buy this house, the other offer on the table will disappear. Then, the homeowner will return to their original asking price. If all that happens and the owners are willing to pay half the closing cost, we'll accept that as final proof that You want us to have the house. Amen." At the end of their prayer, Myra and Steve felt at peace with their specific requests.

Myra called Brian and gave him their parameters.

"It needs to be in that order, Brian. I need to know God is in this."

"You got it, Myra. I'll be in touch with you after I speak with the sellers.

Myra and Steve pulled up in front of the house just behind Brian's car. They exited their vehicle and strode over to the driver's window.

Brian beamed at them as he handed Myra a set of keys.

"Congratulations, you two. You're homeowners."

Myra's insides were dancing the mambo. She moved back and forth from one foot to another as she reached for the keys with a giggle. Then she looked at Brian and became serious.

"Brian, thank you for making our first home buying experience a positive one."

"Are you kidding? I've never seen an escrow go so smoothly—without a hitch. It was definitely meant to be."

Myra leaned in closer to the window.

"That's because God wanted us to have this house, Brian. I knew it when you called and told us that the other couple's financing fell through and the sellers reinstated the original asking price. Then when they were willing to pay half the closing costs, my faith was confirmed. I knew the house was ours. Thanks, Brian, for all your hard work."

"Enjoy your new house, folks." Brian winked at them and started his car.

In the house, Myra sauntered through each room, mentally furnishing them. Tears slid down her cheeks and stopped at her smile. She passed a mirror and saw in the reflection that her face glowed like a candle in the night. She sighed and closed her eyes. Something was different inside of her, but she couldn't put her finger on it.

She was overwhelmed by the mystery of how she felt. Tears continued to slip from her eyes.

Steve smiled and enfolded her in his arms and kissed the top of her head.

"We are blessed, Myra."

Yes, that's it. Blessed.

September 2007

One month after moving into their new home, the phone jarred Myra awake.

"Hello?"

"Myra, this is Margot Wright."

Myra sat up in bed. Why was her boss calling her on her day off?

"Myra, you don't need to come in tomorrow ..."

"Are you firing me?"

"No, not firing. This is what the ninety-day probationary period is for—to see if things work out. We each can choose to end our relationship without penalty. I just don't think this is a good fit for you. Would you please stop by today and bring me your badge?"

Chapter Fifty

August 2008

The trees stood like towers, erect and proud. Their branches reached across to each other, as if friends in the forest. Blue sky peeked through the lace canopy of tree limbs spreading above the well-worn path. The shade they provided created a temporary shelter from the sun's harshest rays.

Myra smiled and continued down the narrow trail. She could hear a mountain stream not far away, bubbling over and around obstacles in its way. The percolating water combined with a lively choir of birds soothed her with their gentle strains, at once relaxing and invigorating her.

She came to the stream, sat on a large rock, and watched the water dancing between rocks and over fallen trees. She looked up to feel the warm sun kiss her face and smiled. When had she felt such contentment? When had she been so relaxed?

Not since before Steve and she purchased their new home. A warm flash of gratitude ran through her. This new home was everything she'd ever dreamed. Simply put, it wasn't a rental, and as long as they paid the mortgage, she couldn't be evicted. *Thank You, Lord, for the house. I'm so thankful for it. And, I can paint the walls any color I want.* She giggled.

Her only regret was leaving the church she'd attended more than thirty years. Steve's back pain would not allow such a long Sunday morning commute.

But the church God led them to was perfect. The people greeted them with warm smiles and the preaching was scripturally sound.

"And as a bonus," Myra had shared with Lisa in one of her sessions, "it has a choir."

"Will you be joining?"

"I'm going to wait until God makes it clear He wants me to join. I can worship God in the congregation just as easily as I can in the choir."

Lisa had agreed.

"And," Myra added, "I need to concentrate on my new job. There's a lot to learn, and I don't want to divide my attention between learning new work skills and learning new music."

That was almost a year ago.

Myra reached down and picked up a small stone and tossed it into the stream. It kerplunked and sank to the bottom.

Lord, You've been so good to Steve and me. I don't want to run out in front of You. Thank You for the ladies in Sunday school who encouraged me to come to this weekend retreat. I needed to get away and be alone with You. When You're ready, open a door if You want me to join choir or get more involved.

Myra glanced at her watch. It was almost time for dinner. Better get back to the lodge.

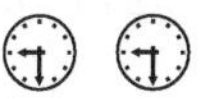

"Ladies, I hope you enjoyed your dinner. We have a real treat for you tonight. I think you'll really enjoy our speaker, Ronda."

Maribel, the women's ministry director, introduced their speaker. An energetic woman stood, smiled broadly at her audience, and thanked Maribel for her kind words.

Myra sat back, prepared to be blessed.

"Let's get to know each other better," Ronda said. "And, through that, we'll also get to know ourselves better. Break up into groups of four, and in the notepad you've been provided, number from one to ten down the page."

She paused as the ladies complied.

Myra was in a group of ladies whose faces were familiar, but she only knew two by name.

"Introduce yourself to the ladies in your group you don't know yet."

Myra added the names she didn't know to her ever-growing list of new people she met at church each Sunday. She only knew half of the thirty women at the retreat. Her goal was to know them all.

"Now, I want each of you to take no more than five minutes to share something about yourself—maybe how you came to Christ, or how you met your husband, or even how you came to be here this weekend. We'll take about twenty minutes to do this, and I'll ring a bell when our time is up."

The room immediately filled with chatter and laughter.

The pastor's wife, a familiar choir member, and a new woman who Myra had just met sat at her table. Each of them shared a short story, then turned to Myra.

"Glenda and Winnie invited me to come." She nodded her head toward a group across the room. "It's been a very long time since I've been at a women's retreat, and I was hesitant to commit at first. But, now I'm glad I did. It's good to get out and meet new friends. I've been so focused on school and my new job, I almost became a hermit."

The pastor's wife laughed. "I can't picture you as a hermit, Myra. You're far too outgoing for that."

Ronda's bell rang and the chattering slowed down and eventually stopped.

"Get the notepads you numbered one to ten." Ronda's cheerful voice salted the room with joyful energy, and its flavor seasoned her audience.

Myra suspected Ronda would have the women write ten things they remembered their group members had shared.

"Now, as fast as you can and without dwelling on your answers, I want you to write ten things that are wonderful about you."

Myra was stunned at this assignment and a little disappointed, because she'd made a huge effort to pay attention to each woman and remember what they'd told her. But she was determined to do as Ronda instructed, so without another thought, she wrote ten things that were wonderful about herself.

1. I smile a lot.
2. I love to sing to and about Jesus.
3. I am mostly happy.
4. I love Jesus.
5. I'm kind of fun.
6. I love to laugh.
7. I'm somewhat unpredictable.
8. I desire that my life bring glory and honor to God.
9. I want to touch other's lives in a positive way.
10. I'm able to cry with/for others.

She put her pen down, heaved a sigh, and sat back. She hadn't given herself a single moment to think of one solitary negative thought. While her companions continued to grapple with their list, Myra reread her words.

Did I write that?

Myra stared at the list for a moment. Amazement filled the crevices of her battle worn self-esteem.

I actually found ten wonderful things about myself.

Ronda's bell rang.

"Was this a hard assignment?" Ronda asked.

Heads nodded all around.

Really? All these wonderful ladies had trouble with this? Goodness, I could easily have written ten wonderful things about each of the ladies I'm acquainted with.

Myra closed her eyes. The women in the room disappeared as Myra's breath came in quick succession and her skin began to tingle. She placed her hands over her heart to slow the racing beats and the blood rushing through her ears.

The adrenaline rushing through her body warmed Myra to the bone. Her mind slipped to the past as she replayed the hurdles life had thrown at her. She could feel the grin spreading wide across her face as a tear slipped from her eye and made a slow descent down her cheek. She opened her eyes and once more read her list. *This is not the list of a loser.*

"Ladies, welcome back." Ronda's sparkling voice filled the room. "This morning I want to be more of a moderator than a speaker. I want us to consider joy. We hear a lot about it, but what is it? Do we have joy, what gives us joy, and how could we obtain more joy? What would need to happen in your life for you to have joy?"

Myra surveyed the room for the women's reactions. They were seriously considering the question.

"Take out your notepads, and on one page write what you would need to obtain more joy. On another page, write what joy means to you in *your* perfect world."

Myra bit her bottom lip and glanced around the room again. Everyone's hands were moving furiously. She swept her hair back and stared at the empty page. Swallowing hard, she lifted her pen, and with reluctant effort put it to the paper. A doodle formed beneath the pen's point.

What gives me joy? Or more joy? What would I need to increase my joy?

The doodle increased in size.

The silence in the room became louder. Myra rolled her neck as her thoughts raced through a series of possibilities. She set the notepad down and headed to the restroom.

On her way back, Ronda met her in the hall and smiled.

"Is everything okay?"

Myra nodded. "Um, yeah. Everything's fine."

"Want to talk?"

Myra tilted her head to the side and stared at Ronda for the briefest moment. Then a tentative smile grew across her face. "Sure, why not? I'm having trouble with your questions about what I would need in order to feel joy."

"I know you are."

Myra's eyebrows shot up. "You do? How?"

"I've been watching you. You're having trouble with the question because you 'get it.' Write what's on your heart, Myra. Write what you know. Then share it with these ladies, because they need to hear what's in your heart."

Myra's mouth slid open as Ronda put her hand on her shoulder, squeezed it, and walked away. Myra contemplated those words for a minute.

Back with her notepad, Myra picked up her pen. Words flowed from her heart, down her arm, and through her pen in a steady stream as God flooded the page with words.

"Okay, ladies, let's share our thoughts." Ronda glanced around the room. "Who wants to go first?"

Myra listened intently as the women shared their hearts. She was getting to know them better with each story. She was beginning to feel a kinship with these ladies. She could hear in their words and voices their happiness and pain.

Each lady shared, some briefly, some at length.

"My family gives me joy."

"I get joy from my job."

"I'd have more joy if my children knew Jesus."

"If my husband was more loving …"

"…if I could lose fifty pounds."

But, Myra sat silent with her thoughts. To her, it seemed as if the joy her new friends were seeking was somehow conditional on their life's circumstances. *If I received joy from my family or job, and lost either, my joy would be gone. Or if I waited until I lost weight or bought a new car for joy, I may never feel joy.*

She looked down at her notepad. She wouldn't share what she wrote. Myra didn't want others to think she thought she was better or more spiritual somehow. Their stories touched her life, and that was good enough for now.

Ronda's voice pulled Myra out of her reverie.

"I've been watching one lady here who exudes joy. Anyone here know who I'm talking about?"

A chorus of voices shouted Myra's name. Her eyes widened, and she looked around confused.

"Myra's been struggling with this assignment. I asked her to write her heart because I believe she 'gets it.' She understands what joy really is. Myra, would you share your thoughts on what gives you joy and how to obtain more?"

Myra hesitated.

Ronda stepped forward and reached a hand out to her.

"Come on, Myra, please read what you've written. I think you should share your insights."

Myra stood and faced the ladies. She looked over the small crowd and began to read.

"My life is full of joy because I believe that everything that happens to me is filtered through the Master's plan. My house makes me happy, but if I lost the house, my joy would remain because it isn't dependent on the house. I love my family—my husband, children, and grandchildren, and if I lost them through separation or death, I'd be very sad. But my joy would remain, because it isn't dependent on them. It isn't dependent on friends or things. My joy isn't dependent on how I feel about life and what happens around me. It's not even dependent on how I feel about myself. My joy comes from within—deep within. My joy comes from knowing that Jesus is in control, and He is my life. I don't need a better life to obtain joy. I already have it."

Myra didn't glance up from her notes to look at the other women. She was afraid to see the possible smirk or scowl she so often anticipated from others. She forged ahead with her narrative, remembering the words Ronda had tossed at her, "because they need to hear what's in your heart."

"*My* perfect world—for which I continually strive, would be a place where I don't need to take time to work through the circumstances of life. I could just press through without becoming rattled, even for a moment. In my perfect world, I would be able to express myself understandably to others, how and why the smell of honeysuckle wafting through my window can bring me to tears. Or why the dragonfly dive-bombing into the pool for a drink makes me smile, or how the size of a hummingbird egg can fill me with incredible wonder. In my perfect world, the joy God has filled me with would be so infectious that people God brings into my life would catch it."

She took a breath and looked over at Ronda's beaming face. She was nodding.

The women in the room burst into applause.

Myra's head began to swim and she sat down.

"She 'gets it', doesn't she?" Ronda's eyes twinkled.

A ripple of agreement flowed over the room like a gentle wave.

Myra's ears began to ring. She felt her face flush.

"Myra, you should write a book," Ronda said. "If you wrote it, I would read it."

Laughter and talking filled the dining hall, mingling with the enticing savory aroma of the Saturday afternoon lunch.

Myra sat at the table with Winnie, her friend from Bible study.

"Myra, good to see you here. Are you having a good time?"

"Oh, yes. It's good to get away for a while and relax."

"Good. Then I'm glad I invited you. What are your plans for the free time after lunch? Are you planning to go into town?"

"I hear someone brought a karaoke machine. I thought that might be fun. Maybe sing a few show tunes, or oldies from the '60s and '70s."

"Sounds like fun. We're going into town. There's a really cute craft boutique there, and I love to shop."

"Don't we all?" Myra said, laughing.

"Whatcha got?" Myra asked, reaching for the song list. She scanned the list for familiar tunes. "Hmm, 'Some Enchanted Evening.' Oooh, 'I Gotta Be Me.' I love that song. Lots of Barry Manilow—I liked him."

Myra caught the look the other three ladies gave her.

"C'mon, no one ever admits they liked Barry Manilow. Well, I'm not ashamed. His songs were fun to sing. 'I wrote the songs that make the whole world sing … '" Myra sang off key.

They all laughed.

"Oh, here's one by Johnny Mathis." Myra's voice melted into the atmosphere with a dreamy wistfulness.

The women laughed.

"I was more into The Doors, Moody Blues, Three Dog Night—that sort of thing," one of the women offered.

Myra smiled as memories surfaced. "Yes, I remember them well. I was more into Simon and Garfunkel, the Carpenters, Diana Ross. I could sing to their music. It's hard to sing to Led Zeppelin or Kiss."

Everyone nodded and laughed.

"Not if you want your voice to sound good," the same woman said.

"Here, put on 'The Twelfth of Never,' by Johnny Mathis."

The sweet sounds of the guitar began and Myra started to sing, "You ask how much I love you …"

Something stirred in her heart as she sang. Memories, wonderful memories of her childhood with Mark and Danny and Billy. The laughter and the joy she felt growing up.

"Until the twelfth of never, I'll …"

A few women came into the room and stood in the back listening. Myra wasn't deterred as she sang and her heart relived her wonderful childhood memories.

"…Still be lovin' you."

The small crowd clapped, and the woman from the previous night's small group stepped forward.

"I've been watching you worship God in the congregation for months, and you have been such a blessing to us in choir. When I heard music in the hall, I had to come in and see who was singing like an angel."

Myra's face grew warm, and she smiled slightly. "Thank you," she said, barely above a whisper.

Gloria looked directly at Myra. "Why aren't you in choir?"

Myra cleared her throat. "I've been waiting for God's leading and His timing," she stammered.

"Well, I think it's time," Gloria said with a wide grin. She came over and gave Myra a big bear hug. "We rehearse on Thursday evenings. Join us. You have a beautiful voice."

"Thank you," Myra whispered, not just to Gloria, but to God.

Chapter Fifty-One

August 2009

As Myra sat at a red light, she watched the birds on the electrical wire. There were hundreds of them lined up like tiny soldiers protecting their little corner of the sky.

It was the little things in life that made her smile and filled her heart with an irrepressible desire to sing or laugh or even jump and dance. Birds in flight, giggling babies, mischievous puppies—these were the ingredients of a worthwhile day. *Should this be what I write a book about? The stuff that gives me such joy?* Ronda's words whispered repeatedly in her mind." If you write it, I'll read it." Myra had put her writing on hold long before she married Steve and started a family. How many times in those years had she considered a storyline in her head, or thought a situation she was in would make a great novel? She remembered with longing the poems and stories she wrote when she was a teen. Ronda's statement had rekindled her desire to make words come alive. To sing into a reader's heart or dance gracefully across a page with ease. The idea of writing again brought an irrepressible smile to her face.

Going from patient to patient—house to house—in her job as a home health nurse was the reason to get out of bed. She loved every minute of it. The chance to touch lives in a positive manner, to make an ill person smile, to teach them one thing that might make them feel better or stay out of the hospital—Myra loved it all. *Or should I write a book about this? Nursing, the stuff that touches other's lives.*

Even on bad days when she met with a particularly crabby patient or someone so sick their next step was hospice, Myra found she could still make a difference with her prayers. Her car was her office and her prayer closet. *What about a book on prayer?*

She pulled up to her patient's house and went to the door and knocked.

"Oh, Myra, I'm so glad you're here. I need you to look at my wound. I think it's infected."

"Sure," Myra said, stepping through the door. *That's what I do. A book about infection? Well, maybe not. But, what then?*

Loretta, the choir director, handed Myra a piece of music before rehearsal started. "Would you take a look at this, Myra? I'd like you and Jane to sing this as a duet the first Sunday in October."

A thrill ran through Myra. Although she'd been asked to sing several solos since joining the choir, it never lost the excitement. Being able to sing for God gave Myra more enjoyment than she could calculate.

"Be glad to, Loretta. I like this," she said as she scanned the lyrics. "Very worshipful."

Loretta nodded. "Yes, it's a great song. I think it's perfect for you and Jane. Can you stay a few minutes after rehearsal to go over it with Michelle? She's already agreed to stay a little longer this evening and accompany you on the piano."

"Absolutely." Myra glanced at Michelle who had been watching her reaction. Michelle flashed an encouraging "thumbs up."

Myra rushed home that evening to finish planning the barbeque pool party scheduled for the end of the month. She kept pretty busy with her church activities, and she enjoyed the time spent planning and preparing. Last year she'd joined the women's ministry team, and now she was in charge of the secret pal ministry. She also signed up to be a group leader for the Women of Faith conference at the arena. She was pleased that all of the tickets had sold. And of course, she was back in choir. She loved that more than anything.

At work, she was on the patient satisfaction committee. She rarely had an evening off, but was happy for now. She had increased her list of people she knew by name and had befriended many more women than she anticipated. All the while she had not forgotten Ronda's words, "if you write a book, I'll read it." *I could write about staying connected through church activities. I could write about forgiveness—like I learned from Lisa.*

The telephone rang ending her contemplations.

"Hello?"

"Hey!" the voice called with a shriek and a giggle. "It's a blast from your past."

The voice slammed into Myra like a storm soaking her in a torrent of memories. She began to laugh with manic delight. "Brenda, how *are* you? Oh, my goodness, woman, it's so good to hear from you."

"Did you hear about our high school?"

"No, what happened?" Myra's voice sobered.

"Nothing happened. Next year it will be fifty years old. They're planning a huge anniversary celebration, a kind of reunion for all the classes since the beginning."

"Oh, man, you're kidding! What a blast."

"Can you come, Myra? I'd love to see you and catch up."

"Wow, I'd love to go. Let me discuss it with Steve and see what he thinks. Holy cow, this is great. Who else is going?"

"You can follow it online. Go to the website—um—well, I'll e-mail it to you. It has a list of everyone from each class who's coming, starting with the first graduating class in 1960."

"Great! I'll check it out, and I'll talk to Steve and let you know if it's possible."

"Myra, you go and have fun. I won't know a soul. I'll just be sitting there alone while you flit all over the room talking and laughing with your friends."

Myra's shoulders slumped. Steve hugged her.

"You'll have more fun without me, Myra."

"But, I didn't want to go alone."

"Call your brother, Mark, and ask him to go."

Myra pulled away from Steve. "That's a good idea, Steve. A *real* good idea." She shot to the phone like a rocket and dialed. "Hey, Mark, it's Myra."

December 2009

Myra slumped on the sofa and let out a long sigh. She felt like she could sleep for a month.

If I close my eyes right now, I won't wake up until after the holidays. Better not give into the exhaustion or I'll miss Christmas.

She scanned the living room. Satisfaction replaced exhaustion. Myra started a mental checklist of what she'd accomplished so far. Decorations up—check. All Santa figurines, all angel figurines.

Christmas cards received taped to entry hall closet door—check. She loved to watch the door fill up as Christmas drew closer.

Christmas letters written and sent out—check. She loved connecting with old friends, even if it was only once a year.

Christmas cookie ingredients purchased—check. The girls at work loved Steve's Christmas cookies, and the grandkids loved to come and help Papa make them.

Christmas pageant costume finished—check. Well, all but the hat. Susan was making that. It was a turn-of-the-century Christmas story. Myra adored the costumes.

All applications for secret pals received—check. This was just a fun ministry.

Gifts for all the kids and grandkiddos purchased—check.

Wrapping paper purchased so Steve could wrap all the gifts—check. He loved to put the tiniest gifts in the biggest boxes. Their kids already had their dad figured out, but the grandkids could still be surprised.

Christmas dinner planned—check. Everyone had at least one favorite food on the menu.

All pie ingredients purchased—check. Steve made everyone's favorite pie.

All Christmas record albums, cassette tapes, and CDs pulled down from the closet—check. It wouldn't be Christmas without music.

Porcelain bisque nativity set up on table—check. It was one of her most prized Christmas decorations. She had collected the entire set from Avon over a period of about ten years. She had the entire set. And it was beautiful.

The only task left was decorating the tree. Steve would wrestle with the lights until they were perfect, each flashing in sync, evenly spaced to perfection. Then they'd pile on all the antique bulbs received from her mother and all the decorations collected over the years. Each of her children had several ornaments with their names engraved, a couple with their pictures, and a few handmade ornaments. Each represented a memory that Myra cherished. Every year when the tree was done, she stood in front of it and stared in silent wonder.

Steve would watch her amused. "I don't know which glows brighter—you or the tree."

The memories of all her Christmases past enveloped her like a warm blanket and she smiled. She remembered all the joy and laughter of her childhood Christmases and all the fun she had creating memorable Christmases for her own children. At times it had been a struggle, especially when they were homeless, but she was always grateful they remained together as a family. After all, that was the most important thing. Even with the few shadows that hovered around the periphery of her mind, Myra's heart was filled with joy.

She loved Christmas—check.

Even when it exhausted her to celebrate it.

Hey, I could write a book about that.

Chapter Fifty-Two

April 2010

"It's your little sister."

"Oh, hey, Myra. We have reservations at the Convention Center Hotel. I got a suite. It's in my name, so just get a key and go up when you get there. Elyse and I will meet you."

"Fabulous, Mark. I'm so excited you decided to go."

"You don't sound excited."

"Just tired. Super tired. But, I'm as excited as my exhausted body will allow."

"Okay, I'll take your word for it." Mark laughed.

As she hung up, Myra sat on the sofa and stared out her window. The spring flowers had already painted the yard with brilliant color. Tulips, daffodils, and lilies swayed like graceful dancers in the breeze. The jasmine and honeysuckle would soon fill the yard with their fragrant perfumes beckoning the bees to nuzzle their blossoms.

She loved this haven of beauty that Steve had created behind their house. Myra could spend hours watching the dragonflies, butterflies, finches, hummingbirds, and the doves going about their business. And the squirrels made her laugh out loud with their clownish antics.

If only she had more time to enjoy their splendor.

"Lord, am I doing what You want me to do? Between all my ministries and work obligations, I hardly have time for Steve, or You, or me. What would You like me to do, Lord? Subtract ministries? Change some? Add some?"

Her eyes glanced at the coffee table and fell on the novel she'd started reading two months before. She picked it up and grinned. John Grisham was always a good read. When she had time. Which was never. She set the book down, and a thought flashed through her brain like lightning.

"And, if You want me to write a book, Lord, I'll need a story."

She went to the back room and picked up a book on fasting she'd recently read and reviewed its pages.

"Okay, Lord, I'll pray and fast for direction, and I'll wait on You for the answer."

Fourteen days later, at the end of her fast, Myra placed the book back on the shelf where she got it.

"Lord, I know Your timing is different from mine. So, we'll go by Your calendar. I shouldn't have been expecting a heavenly text message anyway."

Myra hauled out the luggage from the closet and started to pack for her trip. Little butterflies flurried around inside, and she kept pausing to refocus on her task.

She was anxious to see her brother, Mark—it's been a couple of years. They planned to pop in on their brother, Billy, while in town for the reunion. Old friends would be at the gathering too. How many years had it been since Myra had seen Brenda? And Ria, who loved Myra enough to share Jesus with her. And—and—oh my, this trip would be fun!

In their suite, after the reunion, Mark and Myra sat on the beds discussing the night's frivolity.

"What did you like best, Mark?"

"I haven't been back here since 1970. It was great just to see old friends."

"Yeah, seeing old friends was great. Ria, Brenda, Marie, Laurie—the whole gang. It was fun. The music was great too. Fifty years of music in one night. The planning committee did a great job. Funny slideshow too. Good memories. Brought me back to my childhood. Warm, wonderful memories." Myra fell back across the bed with a sigh, then sat straight up again.

"I had a great childhood, Mark. I've been pretty blessed, don't you think?"

She closed her eyes, smiling. Then opening her eyes, she leapt off the bed and began to tell him a story about an incident in high school between her and their mom. Her arms waved around with animated zeal as she recounted the events. Her laughter filled the room like hand packed ice cream—dense and sweet.

"There I was, wrapped in a towel, dripping water all over the kitchen. Mom was so mad I didn't answer the phone, I don't even think she saw the towel or the puddle I was making." She shook her head and laughed again. Then she plopped back down on the bed and sat quietly for a moment.

"I really miss Mom."

Mark shifted his weight. He cleared his throat.

"Myra, do you know what happened the morning you were born?"

She knit her brows together and nodded her head. She gave him a half smile. "Sure, Mark. I've heard the story a hundred times."

"Tell me."

"Well, I know Mom was forty-one when I was born. She had you guys—active little boys. She was overworked, probably tired. She didn't tell anyone she was pregnant."

Myra felt herself rambling, but she didn't slow down.

"The night she went into labor, she paced the floor non-stop, not wanting to wake Dad. When he woke up and saw her in labor, he rushed her to the hospital. I was born while he parked the car. I had some lung problems and spent a week in an incubator. We came home on your tenth birthday."

Her brother listened intently, his head cocked to one side. He scooted to the edge of the bed.

"Mark, I know Mom probably didn't want another baby. Who would at forty-one? But, I'll tell you something. Even though I knew she didn't want me, I never felt unloved a single day in my life." Myra flashed a grin.

A slow smile spread on Mark's face. He pressed his hand to his chest and said, "I'm so glad you felt loved, Myra. There's a little more to the story, though."

"Well, fill me in, brother. I'm up for one of your good stories."

She adjusted herself to be comfortable, anticipating one of Mark's funny tales. Her brother always left her laughing, reduced to hysterical tears. She'd had a good day filled with hilarity and was ready to finish her day with even more.

"You're right, Mom didn't want another child."

Myra nodded.

"But she never intended to go to the hospital. She *denied* being pregnant for nine months."

Myra's nodding stopped.

"Dad forced her to go. And, yes, you were born while he parked the car."

Her nodding resumed.

"But, you didn't have any lung problems."

The nodding ceased.

"After you were born, Mom made it clear to the doctor that she didn't want another baby. She told him she didn't care what he did with you, she wasn't taking you home."

Myra was as still as a statue.

Mark cleared his throat one more time.

"The doctor tried to talk Mom into at least holding you, or looking at you. But she refused. She told the doctor to give you up for adoption."

Myra leaned forward, eyebrows raised, waiting to hear the doctor's response.

"He told Mom that would never work. Dad would never sign the adoption papers."

Myra attempted to swallow, but her throat wouldn't allow passage. Besides, she was unable to muster any moisture out of her desert-dry mouth.

"So, the doctor handed you to his nurse and told her to take you to the morgue."

The words hit Myra like a runaway semi crashing into a wall. She could barely inhale from the impact. This wasn't the amusing story Myra had anticipated. And she knew absolutely by Mark's grave expression that he was *not* kidding.

"You mean the doctor sent a perfectly healthy baby to the morgue to die?"

Mark nodded hesitantly.

Myra's silence filled the room like a foul odor. Her mind scrambled to make sense of this story. "But, how did I, how come I didn't …"

"Some nurse came in and found you. Took you back to the maternity floor."

Myra's thoughts were whirling in her head like a tornado.

Some nurse found me …

"Yeah, but Mom wasn't happy. She kept me home from school for a week taking care of you while she cried in her bedroom."

Mom didn't want me …

Some nurse found me …

A nurse happened to be in the morgue …

The wind swirling in her head began to settle.

Lord, You saved me the morning I was born.

"So, Mom never loved me?"

"Of course she loved you. I mean—look at you. You just grew on her …" Mark attempted to make light of the story.

But Lord, You loved me from the day I was born. You saved me. And if You saved me, I must have a purpose. You have a plan for me. I'm not a loser. I'm a winner. You gave me my life back. I'm not-a-loser.

Myra stood up. Emotion overwhelmed her. She put her hand to her mouth.

God has a purpose for my life. God loves me. Myra! He loved me and saved my life on the day I was born then protected me all these years—from these facts, from my mother's behavior, from any bitterness. He gave me joy through the storms of life.

Tears started to stream down Myra's face. Her smile could not be quenched—even by the tears threatening to overtake it.

Seeing her tears, Mark came over to her and wrapped his arms around her.

"I'm so sorry, Myra. I've been carrying this burden around all these years. I've never shared it with anyone. I'm so sorry. I just thought it was time you knew the whole story. I never meant to hurt you."

Myra choked.

"No, no. I'm glad you shared it. You don't understand, Mark. God saved me on the day I was born. He loves me. I never realized how much until you told me this story."

The crying was getting in the way of her words. She could no longer express herself verbally. She sat down on the bed, again. She put her hands to her face, bent over her lap, and sobbed with an overwhelming sense of gratitude.

Eventually, Mark was able to complete the story with all the details that he knew. Myra sat with rapt attention as he regaled her with the finishing touches. In his unique way, he even managed to draw laughter from some of the grimmest details.

In the end, Myra sat back feeling oddly complete. A veil hindering her vision had been lifted. She could see her childhood clearly. And she was grateful for it. Grateful for what God had done.

Grateful for her mother's love *and* how much she loved her mom.

When she got into bed and turned off the light she thought of that nurse in the morgue.

I'll never know who that nurse was, Lord. But I pray a blessing over her. I pray that You'll always answer her sweet prayers.

Staring into the night, a revelation pierced her thoughts.

Oh, my goodness. The fast … God has answered my prayers. He's given me a story. My story.

A giggle bubbled up from the deepest part of her spirit. It burst out like a celebration as Myra lay there laughing in the dark.

Chapter Fifty-Three

Present Day

Myra paused and smiled at her audience.

"For the first time in my life I felt like I had a purpose. I was completely overwhelmed by God's love. To think He saved my life on the morning I was born! I knew the moment I heard those words God had an extraordinary plan for my life. I spent most of my life believing the lies whispered by the enemy of my soul—that I wasn't good enough. But now, I know I am good enough for God to love. And, He loves me just the way I am because He designed me."

Again, Myra paused and scanned the audience.

"Ladies, we must stop believing the lies of Satan and start believing God, the lover of our souls, our Creator, our heavenly Father."

She picked up a Bible from the podium.

"Discover the truth—how God really feels about you. Instead of looking in a mirror and judging your reflection against everyone around you, look into the Word of God and let His love reflect back on you."

Myra's voice became softer, and she set the Bible back on the podium.

"Did you know that God made you in His image? Genesis 1:27 tells us that. Would He do that if He didn't love you?"

All eyes were on Myra. She took a second to make eye contact with several women.

"Zephaniah 3:17 tells us that God rejoices over us with singing. You know, like a mother sings over her infant child. He sings over us with joy, ladies."

She caught the eyes of several more women.

"The New Living Testament says in Isaiah 41:9 that 'God has chosen me and will not throw me away.' I am not garbage to be tossed aside. And in John 3:16 it says He loves me so much that He sacrificed His Son Jesus, to die for my sins, so that I will not perish, but by believing in Him, I could be called a child of God. I can live forever with Him.

"God loves you. Jesus died for you. You are worthy to be called His child. The truth of His love will set you free from the bondage of lies the enemy wants you to believe. You *are* good enough for God's love, and Jesus makes you worthy of that love. He has a plan for your life.

"He made you, sings for joy over you, chose you, and sent Jesus to save you. That makes you good enough. That makes you *better* than good enough. It makes you valuable and deserving. Worthy. *You* are worthy!"

The early evening air felt refreshing on Myra's face as she headed toward her car, Bible in hand. She opened the passenger door, set the Bible on the seat, and bent to remove her tight shoes.

"Excuse me," a voice carried across the parking lot.

Myra stood and turned toward the voice.

An elderly lady with a walker assisted by a young woman, crossed the parking lot toward Myra. "Hi," the young woman began. "My name is Chrissy, and this is my grandma, Marsha."

"It's great to meet you ladies," Myra said, putting her hand out to the older woman.

"We've met before," the older woman said in a weak voice.

Myra bit her lower lip and gave a slight shake of her head. "We have? Have you been one of my patients?"

Marsha raised her eyebrows as she gave a soft chuckle.

"No, in fact you were one of my patients," the woman's voice warbled.

"Grandma is a retired nurse. She graduated from nursing school in 1955. She worked on the medical floor at the hospital where you were born."

"I was fresh from nursing school." Marsha's words came in slow arduous phrases. "An elderly patient of mine died in her room while I was assisting another patient across the hall." Marsha paused to take a breath. "I was devastated. I felt like a failure." She stopped to rest a moment. "During my break, I stole away to be alone and pray. I don't know why I chose to go to the basement, but I did. When I saw the morgue, I slipped inside. I prayed to God for peace and understanding of what had happened. I thought, 'why did I even become a nurse?'"

The woman leaned on her walker with both hands as her granddaughter held her steady. Chrissy's face offered encouragement to her grandmother.

"I turned to leave the morgue and noticed movement on a table. There was a baby moving in slow motion. It was a true miracle. A miracle that I was there, a miracle the baby was even alive in that cold morgue, and a miracle that God had answered my prayer at that very moment."

Myra's pulse quickened as her breaths became shallow.

"I wrapped the infant in a sheet and raced up to the postpartum floor. I exited the elevator shouting 'it's a miracle!' I remember the doctor's face when he approached me. He looked like he'd just swallowed a squirrel. He thanked me and reached for the infant, but I wouldn't release her until I imparted this blessing on her. On *you*, Myra. 'God bless you, child. God bless you and all those whose lives you touch. May joy be your constant companion in this life, may it overshadow your pain, causing it to flee and hide in fear.'" She inhaled sharply. "Every March 8, I pray for you."

Myra swallowed hard. Her breath caught in her throat. Could this be true?

"Many years later, I met you again at Dr. Young's office when you were a teenager. Your mother was with you."

Myra's eyebrows shot up, and her mouth went dry.

"I was so thankful to see you that day. You seemed healthy and happy. I thank God He's brought us together again. It has affirmed my prayers. I've continued to pray for you through the years. I prayed blessings—abundant blessings for you. I asked God to show me His handiwork one last time. My granddaughter insisted I come this evening …" She stopped to gather her strength.

Chrissy turned to Myra. "I wanted to get Grandma out of the assisted living facility. My church was having this ladies dinner today, and I felt Grandma should come. I just wanted to get her out of her room to have fun. She argued with me, and for once I didn't back down. I think Grandma was as surprised by my stubbornness as I was. But, obviously God had a plan."

Myra nodded, unable to speak.

Marsha reached over and placed her hand on Myra's arm. Her touch sent a strangely familiar sensation through Myra.

Marsha took a breath, and with a valiant effort continued. "I had asked God to show me why I became a nurse, and He orchestrated a symphony of reasons for me. I'm no longer able to follow that calling, but God has shown me through the years that I am still able to pray. This evening, He answered one of my most heartfelt prayers by reuniting me with you."

Tears welled in Myra's eyes, and she stepped over to the frail woman and wrapped her arms around her with tenderness. She held her close for a moment and whispered in her ear, "Thank you, my sweet guardian angel. Thank you for being there for me my whole life. Thank you for being sensitive to the Holy Spirit all these years.

You'll never know what a difference your prayers have made in my life."

Marsha gave her a strong squeeze, kissed her cheek, and slumped in Myra's arms.

Alarm rang through Myra's nerves. "Call 911," she blurted to Chrissy.

Chrissy's shoulders drooped, and her chin began to tremble. She reached for her cell phone and began to dial.

"I'll call 911, but I'm fairly certain it's too late. Just before we followed you out here, Grandma told me she could die happy this evening now that God has answered her prayers for you."

Myra assisted Marsha to the ground and sat holding her in her lap. A couple of fingers to her neck and Myra was sure what Chrissy said was true. Marsha had completed her purpose and had gone home to be with her Savior.

A peace flowed through Myra like a cool spring.

"Father, I am Your worthy servant. May I finish Your work *this* well."

Authors Note

This story is a fictionalized memoir. My purpose in changing the names of people in this story was not to protect the innocent — or the guilty — but to offer a neutral platform for my readers to relate with the people and events.

When I speak at events and share my story, I'm surprised at how many women tell me they can relate to one or more of the characters. Something similar has happened to them or their mother or grandmother or someone they know. The real point of the story was not to highlight what any of my characters did or didn't do. These characters are no different from me or you or anyone else on the planet. We are flawed, frail humans. Imperfect. We are all sinners in need of a Savior.

The one abiding truth of this story is what God has done in my life. His part in this story isn't fiction. It's fact. He snatched me from the grip of death as an infant and protected my heart as child. He redeemed my soul through His son, Jesus, and He allowed the struggles through my adult years to teach me the truth of His everlasting love.

As we make our journey through life, we will be faced with uphill battles, struggles, pain, disappointments, betrayal, bullying, and fear. People will lie to us, hurt us, use us, gossip about us, and disappoint us. We may *feel* abandoned but we are *not.* God uses every struggle to mold us, to shape us, and to use us for our good and His glory. Long before I heard the truth of my story, God used my circumstances to teach me the joy of forgiveness, grace, and love.

Take a fresh look at the circumstances God has allowed in your life. They have a purpose. Remember God loves you, even when you don't feel it or understand it.

The following pages contain some "food for thought" questions. You can use them in your quiet time, or in your journaling. They can be used as a personal or group Bible study, or even as a means to get started writing your own story. It may be a difficult story, but let God be your "happily – ever – after" theme.

Personal Reflections for the Reader

1. Make a list of ten *things* you are thankful for.
2. Now list five difficult circumstances you've struggled through. Through which of these fifteen items did you *grow* most? The things? Or the circumstances? Why?
3. What bad habit, bad attitude, or bad life style choices have you learned from your parents? Where did they learn them? Do you have children? Have they made the same choices? How can you break this cycle of bondage?
4. Who has God placed in your life that's been there for you in the bad times? How did they help? Why do you remember their names? Can you do the same for someone else?
5. Make a list of all the people you can remember who have hurt you, lied to you, betrayed you, gossiped about you, cheated you, or made you angry. Do you think they deserve to be forgiven? Why or why not?
6. List all the people you have hurt, lied to, betrayed, gossiped about, cheated or made angry. Do you feel you deserve to be forgiven? Why or why not?
7. What's your first reaction to a personal crisis? Do you ride the roller coaster of happy and sad through life's ups and downs, or do you remain steadily joyful like a commuter train through rush-hour traffic? What does it take to make it through life's difficulties?

8. "I'm not good enough" is a blatant lie of the enemy of our soul. What are the lies that he has been whispering into your heart? You're not tall enough? Pretty enough? Thin enough? Smart enough, talented, rich, professional, or cultured enough? The truth is you *are* enough for God. He created you like that and He loves you the way you are. Fill in the blank and then say it out loud often. I am_______ (pretty, thin, tall, smart, good) enough for God.
9. The Bible says that God loves the whole world, and that everyone has sinned. (John 3:16, and Romans 3:23) The Bible also says that if we admit our sins, and ask for His forgiveness, He is faithful to forgive us. (I John 1:9) Have you accepted this truth? Do you want to? Jesus is only a prayer away.

To get information about booking Mary for a speaking engagement or ordering more copies of

Crying in the Morgue, Laughing in the Dark
Visit Mary's Web site- My Bountiful Journey- at
www.MaryAAllen.com
or on her Facebook fan page
https://www.facebook.com/pages/Mary-A-Allen/248165518641389

Books can also be ordered at:

Inspiringvoices.com

Table 2.2 Coverage Rate of Water Supply, by Country Income and Urbanization Status
(percent)

Population weighted	Household piped water	Public standpost	Well or borehole	Surface water	Vendors
By country income					
Middle	44	22	13	18	1
Low	11	14	40	32	2
By urbanization level					
Low	7	16	36	39	1
Medium	17	12	35	33	0
High	21	15	40	19	4

Source: Banerjee, Wodon, and others 2008.
Note: Urbanization level: low (0–30 percent), medium (30–40 percent), and high (> 40 percent).

Figure 2.2 Extent of Access to Piped Water through Household Connection, by GDP and Urbanization Rate

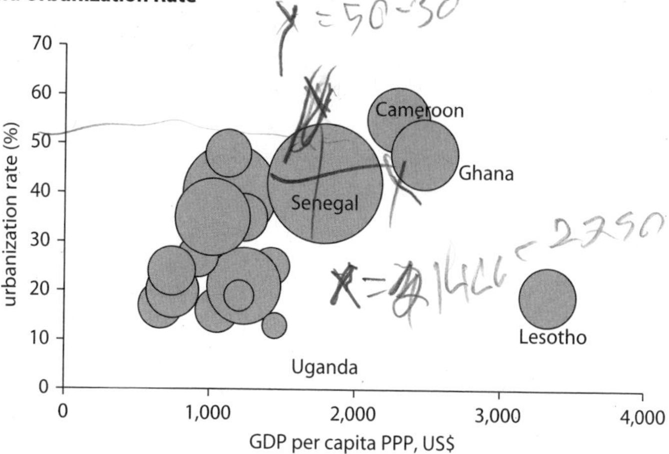

Source: Banerjee, Wodon, and others 2008.
Note: PPP = purchasing power parity.

piped-water coverage relative to peers. Benin, a strong performer on piped-water access, provides a good contrast with Nigeria. Zambia, too, performs reasonably well on access to piped water, relative to its per capita national income and rate of urbanization.

Low Access to Piped Water. . . for Various Reasons

Access to piped water is low in most of Africa and has not expanded substantially in recent years. The main reasons are rapid population growth and shrinking household size (box 2.1), two trends that continually increase the size of the unserved population and challenge the capacities of weak and underfunded utilities to expand connections to growing numbers of households.

Box 2.1

The Problem of Shrinking Households

As incomes rise, African households are getting smaller. Urbanization, lower fertility, and greater economic resources all allow nuclear families to disengage from extended households because they no longer need the economies of scale provided by larger households. In Benin, for example, the average household size decreased from 6.0 in 1996 to 5.2 in 2001.

Shrinking household size exerts a strong effect on the need for new water-supply connections, sometimes canceling out the effect of slower population growth. For that reason, the new-connection needs of richer countries may equal or outstrip those of poorer countries.

There is a wide cross-country dispersion in the relative growth rates of population versus the number of households. For the AICD sample as a whole, however, the average rate of population growth is 2.5 percent, and the average increase in the number of households is 3.2 percent, so the trend toward smaller household sizes represents almost one-third (0.7 percent) of the new connections needed to keep access rates constant (Diallo and Wodon 2007).

In a few countries, by contrast, household size has increased. Typically this occurs during hard times, as households join forces to cope with deterioration in their living conditions.

Rates of Change in Number of Households and Population, Selected Countries

Difference between annual household growth and population growth	*Countries*
Higher than 2 percent	Benin, Namibia, Zimbabwe
Between 1 and 2 percent	Cameroon, Guinea, Mali, Nigeria
Between 0 and 1 percent	Burkina Faso, Côte d'Ivoire, Kenya, Madagascar, Malawi, Niger, Rwanda, Senegal, Tanzania, Zambia
Less than 0 percent	Chad, Ethiopia, Ghana, Mozambique, Uganda

Source: Banerjee, Wodon, and others 2008.

The challenge of reaching universal access to safe sources of water is typically understood as a supply-side problem of rolling out infrastructure networks to increasingly far-flung populations, entailing major investments. However, even in densely populated urban areas, where infrastructure is already present or easy to expand, service coverage is by no means universal. Part of the access problem therefore appears to be related to demand-side barriers that prevent households from hooking up to available services. In addition to high connection charges that make hookups unaffordable, demand-side barriers include illegal land tenure, which disqualifies households from connecting, and a variety of other social and economic factors that may deter households from becoming utility clients.

Household surveys can be used to explore the reasons why a household might elect not to connect to the water-supply network. Samples are based on geographic clusters that *at least for urban areas* are physically small, amounting to no more than a few city blocks. It is therefore possible, at least in urban areas, to study the extent to which people who lack access to infrastructure live in clusters where infrastructure is available (as indicated by the fact that some of their immediate neighbors are connected). The resulting analysis gives us a sense of the degree to which low access to services is driven by supply-side issues (infrastructure networks not reaching the areas where people live) or by demand-side issues (people not connecting to available infrastructure networks). The building blocks of the analysis are presented in box 2.2.

The novelty of this approach is that we break down the traditional measure of household *coverage* into two components (using the method of Foster and Araujo 2004 and Komives and others 2005). The first component, which we call *access*, is the percentage of the population that lives in a cluster where at least one household has service coverage, indicating that the infrastructure is physically proximate and that households probably have an opportunity to connect. The second component, which we call *hookup*, is the percentage of the population living in clusters where the opportunity to connect to the service is available. Using these two concepts, we can estimate the percentage of the unserved population that constitutes a supply-side deficit (meaning that they are too far from the network to make a connection until the network is expanded to reach them) versus a demand-side deficit (meaning that something other than distance from the network is preventing them from taking up the service).

The optimal policy response to the two conditions is very different—hence the importance of making the distinction. The solution to a supply-side deficit is to make further investments to extend the geographic reach

Box 2.2

Coverage, Access, and Hookup Rates: Relationships and Definitions

Coverage rate = number of households using the service / total number of households

Access rate = number of households living in communities or clusters where service is available / total number of households

Hookup rate = number of households using the service / number of households living in communities where service is available

Coverage = access rate x hookup rate

Unserved population = 100 – coverage rate
Pure demand-side gap = access rate – coverage rate
Supply-side gap = unserved population – pure demand-side gap
Pure supply-side gap = supply-side gap x hookup rate
Mixed demand and supply-side gap = supply-side gap x (100 – hookup rate)

Proportion of deficit attributable to demand-side factors only = pure demand-side gap / unserved population
Proportion of deficit attributable to supply-side factors only = pure supply-side gap / unserved population
Proportion of deficit attributable to both demand- and supply-side factors only = mixed demand and supply-side gap / unserved population

Source: Foster and Araujo 2004.

of the network. The solution to a demand-side deficit is to make policy changes that address barriers to service take-up, such as high connection charges or illegal tenure.

For various reasons, it could be questioned whether everyone in a given geographic cluster really has the opportunity to connect. First, even in a small cluster, some residents may live too far from the network to connect. Second, the network may not have the carrying capacity required to service all residents in a particular geographic cluster without further investment and upgrade. Third, even if a household is physically close to a network with adequate carrying capacity, it may choose not to connect because it has an acceptable alternative (such as a borehole).

Diallo and Wodon (2007) use a statistical approach to correct for these problems. They simulate the maximum connection rate obtainable in any primary sampling unit based on that of the richest households in that area. If less than 100 percent of the richest households (which are assumed to be able to play) are connected, something other than demand-side barriers is probably at work. The methodology is less applicable to rural areas because the clusters tend to be larger and population densities much lower.

Rates of access to piped water in urban areas of Africa exceed coverage rates by 30 to 40 percentage points (table 2.3). Indeed, access rates are as high as 70 to 90 percent, which means that the vast majority of the urban population, even in low-income countries, lives in relatively close proximity to existing water networks. Hookup rates are another story: They are significantly higher in middle-income than in low-income countries. The proportion of the coverage deficit that is attributable to demand-side factors, adjusted using the method of Diallo and Wodon (2007), is 14 percent in the low-income countries (meaning that one in seven urban residents elects not to connect to the available service) and 36 percent in the middle-income countries. Without the adjustment, the share of the coverage deficit attributable to demand-side factors appears much larger.

When coverage is examined by country, one sees a very strong relationship between the level of access (that is, the share of the population living in areas where piped-water service is available) and the size of the demand-side deficit (figure 2.3). That relationship is intuitively satisfying because, as rates of access rise with expansion of infrastructure network,

Table 2.3 Water-Service Coverage in Urban Africa and Share of Coverage Deficit Attributable to Demand-Side Factors
(percentage of urban households)

	Decomposition of coverage			*Proportion of coverage deficit attributable to demand-side factors*	
	(1)	*(2)*	*(1) x (2)*		
	Access	*Hookup*	*Coverage*	*Unadjusted*	*Adjusted*
Country income					
Low	68	42	31	58	14
Middle	91	74	69	61	36
Urbanization level					
Low	76	42	33	65	20
Medium	76	56	46	63	8
High	71	49	34	55	45

Source: Banerjee, Wodon, and others 2008.

Figure 2.3 Country Scatter Plot of Current Access Rates for Piped Water and Demand-Side Factors in Coverage Deficit

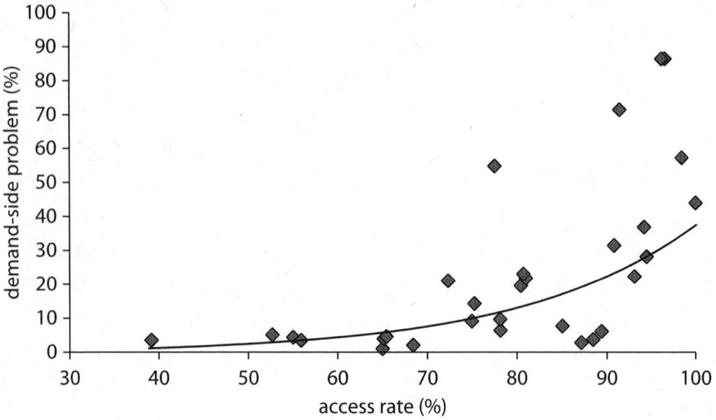

Source: Banerjee , Wodon, and others 2008.

demand-side factors come to assume a greater role in the remaining coverage deficit. One also observes, however, substantial variation across countries in the size of the adjusted coverage deficit that is due to demand-side factors—from less than 5 percent in Burkina Faso, the Central African Republic, Chad, Ethiopia, Mozambique, Rwanda, Tanzania, and Uganda, to more than 50 percent in Côte d'Ivoire, the Republic of Congo, Gabon, Senegal, and Zambia.

We have already noted the importance of distinguishing between demand- and supply-side factors when making policies to increase access. The demand-side problems are comparatively more deep-rooted and are directly related to the consumer's income and ability to pay. The supply-side problems are related to the utilities' investments in its network and to expand its consumer base. The ability to do so depends on the strength of its revenue: If the volume of high-value industrial and residential consumers is low in the consumer mix, the utilities will find it difficult to generate adequate funds to invest in network expansion.

Multiple Players in the Urban Water Market

Our analysis of patterns of access to water in urban areas reveals three categories of countries (table 2.4). The first comprises countries in which a large share of the urban population obtains water through wells and

Table 2.4 Patterns of Urban Access to Water
(percent)

Dominant modality	*Range of prevalence*	*Average prevalence*	*Countries*
Piped water	28–93	57	Benin; Comoros; Congo, Dem. Rep.; Congo, Rep., Côte d'Ivoire; Ethiopia; Gabon; Kenya; Lesotho; Mauritania; Namibia; Senegal; South Africa; Togo; Zambia; Zimbabwe
Standposts	37–53	43	Burkina Faso, Cameroon, Central African Republic, Ghana, Guinea, Madagascar, Malawi, Mozambique, Niger, Rwanda, Tanzania, Uganda
Wells/ boreholes	33–48	39	Chad, Mali, Nigeria, Sudan

Source: Banerjee, Wodon, and others 2008.

boreholes, while other improved sources also provide substantial coverage. The second comprises countries where the majority of the urban population depends on public standposts. The third group comprises countries where the majority of the urban population has piped water from household connections.

Urban households that lack a piped-water connection have several alternative sources from which to choose: public standposts, water kiosks, vendors (or resellers) of water, rainwater harvesting, shallow wells, and surface water. Although the ability of these alternative suppliers to provide adequate service to the unconnected population is debated, their operations recently have come to be better understood (Collignon and Vézina 2000; Kariuki and others 2003; Kariuki and Schwartz 2005; Keener and Banerjee 2005). These providers have come to occupy an important place in urban Africa, particularly in dense periurban areas and in postconflict economies. In these areas, the formal sector's ability to deliver services is continually challenged, and an informal market has emerged to fill the gap.

Household connection rates are directly linked to the strength of the informal market. Not surprisingly, the percentage of unconnected households served by water tankers or water vendors is higher in countries where household connection rates are lower. In countries with very low rates (less than 30 percent) of household connection, 13 percent of the unconnected urban population, on average, relies on water trucks or water vendors. In countries with low to medium (30–60 percent) rates of household coverage, just 4 percent of the unconnected urban population relies on water trucks or vendors. For countries with medium to high (> 60 percent) rates of household coverage rates, only 2 percent of the unconnected urban population relies on water trucks or vendors.

In an analysis of data available from Africa's 24 largest cities from the AICD Water Supply and Sanitation (WSS) Survey, we found that public standposts are the principal source of water for unconnected households. Average standpost coverage in the cities studied was 28 percent, but standposts supply water to up to 53 percent of unconnected households (table 2.5).

The actual coverage of public standposts may be lower, however, than suggested by the foregoing figures, which are derived from official data reported by utilities and governments. Several independent sectoral surveys assessed the coverage provided by standposts and other alternative providers in a way that made it possible to compare the results with official statistics. In Maseru, the capital of Lesotho, for example, data from an official multiple-indicator cluster survey revealed that about half of the urban population lacked a piped-water connection and that the utility *assumed* that this segment was reliant on its free public standposts. But an earlier, more detailed sectoral survey undertaken in Maseru in 2002 showed that coverage by free public standposts was as low as 16 percent of the population, with the coverage among the unconnected falling from 100 percent to 24 percent (Hall and Cownie 2002).[2] It is unlikely that the three-year lag between surveys accounts for the stark differences in these numbers.

In fact, utility data deviate from household survey data in estimating standpost coverage. Most utilities calculate that coverage by multiplying the number of existing standposts by a "standard" number of users (usually 300 to 500).[3] The resulting estimates can be very inaccurate, however, because they do not take into account the factors that affect the real usage of standposts—such as their location relative to population, water pressure, operating hours, and even whether a given standpost is actually working. In Ouagadougou, for example, the number of people relying on standposts was often calculated using a multiplier of 700 people per standpost. After detailed field studies showed actual coverage to be much lower, the utility reduced its standard number of users from 700 to 300 people per standpost.[4]

About one out of five standposts in Africa is in poor working condition. In some places, the figures are much worse. In Kinshasa, for instance, only 21 percent of the standposts are in good working condition

Table 2.5 Water Supply in Africa's Largest Cities, by Source

Country	Largest city	Household connection (%)	Standpipes/ kiosks (%)	Water tankers (%)	Household resellers (Yes/No/%)	Water vendors (Yes/No)	Small piped networks (Yes/No)
Benin	Cotonou	31	—	n.a.	Yes	No	Yes
Burkina Faso	Ouagadougou	34	61	n.a.	No	5	No
Ethiopia	Addis Ababa	39	40	n.a.	Yes	Yes	No
Mozambique	Maputo	26	26	n.a.	26	Yes	12
Niger	Niamey	31	21	n.a.	No	10	No
Nigeria	Kaduna	48	2	—	Yes	Yes	No
Rwanda	Kigali	35	51	3.21	10	No	No
Senegal	Dakar	77	19	n.a.	Yes	No	No
South Africa	Johannesburg	88	12	0.24	No	No	No
Congo, Dem. Rep.	Kinshasa	36	—	n.a.	Yes	No	Yes
Ghana	Accra	56	—	—	Yes	Yes	No
Kenya	Nairobi	51	41	—	No	8	9
Lesotho	Maseru	33	16	1.00	31	5	No
Malawi	Blantyre	47	—	n.a.	Yes	No	No
Namibia	Windhoek	73	20	n.a.	No	No	No
Sudan	Greater Khartoum	27	0.11	0.43	Yes	60	No
Zambia	Lusaka	27	58	n.a.	Yes	Yes	No
Cape Verde	Praia	34	60	6.30	No	No	No
Chad	N'Djamena	22	—	—	Yes	Yes	Yes
Côte d'Ivoire	Abidjan	65	—	n.a.	Yes	No	Yes
Madagascar	Antananarivo	42	34	n.a.	Yes	8	Yes

(continued next page)

Table 2.5 *(continued)*

Country	*Largest city*	*Household connection (%)*	*Standpipes/ kiosks (%)*	*Water tankers (%)*	*Household resellers (Yes/No/%)*	*Water vendors (Yes/No)*	*Small piped networks (Yes/No)*
Tanzania	Dar es Salaam	29	4	2.00	35	2	Yes
Uganda	Kampala	30	5	—	Yes	Yes	Yes
	Average	43	28	2.20	—	—	—
	Median	35	21	2	—	—	—
	Minimum	22	0.11	0	10	2	6
	Maximum	88	61.0	6	35	60	12
	Number of countries with relevant presence	All	All	11/23 (48)	17/23 (74)	14/23 (61)	9/23 (39)

Source: Keener, Luengo, and Banerjee 2009.
Note: For the unconnected market, the data obtained from independent studies have been highlighted. The remaining data come from utility and government sources. n.a. = not applicable, — = not available.

(table 2.6). In many cities where standposts tend to be in poor working condition, vendors sell water door to door or from household connections. In such cases, although people may occasionally obtain their water directly from the standpost, they also get it from vendors who make it their business to transport water from operating standposts.

The growing role of household resellers is usually hidden in household surveys, because it is illegal to sell water in many countries, and households are unwilling to admit to engaging in proscribed activities. However, the results of the module of AICD's WSS Survey devoted to small-scale independent providers (module 5) reveal that household reselling is a common occurrence in 70 percent of the countries studied—despite being prohibited in 24 percent of the countries in which it is prevalent. In Maputo, for instance, one-third of the unconnected obtain their water from neighbors (Boyer 2006). Similarly, in Maseru, household resellers provide water to 31 percent of the population and to almost half of the unconnected (Hall and Cownie 2002).

Table 2.6 Working Status of Standposts in the Largest Cities in Africa
(percent)

Country	*Largest city*	*Population depending on standposts*	*Share in good working order*	*Share free of charge*
Sudan (HCI)	Greater Khartoum	0.11	100	0
Congo, Dem. Rep. (HCI)	Kinshasa	n.a.	21	—
Mozambique (MCI)	Maputo	26	58	0
Rwanda (MCI)	Kigali	51	75	0
Namibia (MCI)	Windhoek	20	100	100
Lesotho (LCI)	Maseru[a]	16	48	100
Kenya (LCI)	Nairobi	41	89	0
Nigeria (LCI)	Kaduna	2	55	96
Benin (LCI)	Cotonou	n.a.	100	0
Burkina Faso (LCI)	Ouagadougou	61	100	0
Cape Verde (LCI)	Praia	60	100	0
Niger (LCI)	Niamey	21	98	0
Zambia (LCI)	Lusaka	58	97	0
Malawi (LCI)	Blantyre	n.a.	90	0
Madagascar (LCI)	Antananarivo	34	82	40
	Average	32.40	81	24

Source: Keener, Luengo, and Banerjee 2009.
Note: Data obtained from independent studies have been highlighted. The remaining data come from utility and government sources. HCI = high conflict index, MCI = medium conflict index, LCI = low conflict index, n.a. = not applicable, — = not available.
a. A negligible percentage of the standpipe/kiosk coverage is paid.

Legalizing household resale of water could be beneficial in expanding access to safe water, as demonstrated in Côte d'Ivoire (box 2.3).

Other alternatives to piped water are offered by small-scale service providers who sell water from boreholes, wells, and other nonnetwork sources. In the past decade, water vendors, such as standpost operators, have gained some attention from the development community. Overall, vendors serve only 4 percent of urban Africa, but in some countries they play a prominent role. In Mauritania, 32 percent of urban residents depend on vendors. Vendors serve more than 5 percent of urban households in Burkina Faso, Chad, Niger, Nigeria, and Tanzania.

Water truckers tend to supply high- and middle-income households. They are especially visible in cities where the piped-water service is very poor in reach and reliability, such as Dar es Salaam, Kampala, and Nairobi. Truckers are present in half of the cities considered in this study, but their market share is limited (between 0.2 and 6.5 percent). In some cities, such as Accra and Luanda, water tankers not only supply directly to upper- and middle-income households but also play a key role in the

Box 2.3

Legalizing Household Resellers in Côte d'Ivoire

To make it easier for the poor to receive safe water, Côte d'Ivoire legalized household resellers in informal settlements. Legalization enabled the water utility, Société de Distribution d'Eau de Côte d'Ivoire (SODECI) to indirectly influence the price and quality of water sold in these areas. It issued about 1,000 licenses to water resellers, many of whom have invested in last-mile network extensions to cater to demand in poor neighborhoods. SODECI reduces the risk of nonpayment by charging a high deposit (about $300) and invoicing resellers monthly.

But the scheme faces implementation challenges. Household resellers pay SODECI twice—in the form of reseller payments and a price markup for network extensions. Furthermore, there is no special tariff for household resellers; they pay the high consumer tariff, so the incentive to become a household reseller is limited. An association of water resellers called AREQUAPCI that includes members licensed by SODECI has successfully worked out a deal to buy water at the same preferential rate as standpipe operators.

Source: Collignon and Vézina 2000.

supply chain. Because of the limited extent of the piped network, many kiosks depend on water supplied by tankers.

Small piped-water networks are relatively new in the urban landscape. In 40 percent of the largest cities, small, secondary water networks are operated by independent providers. These may be connected to the main city network (as in Abidjan, Cotonou, and Nairobi) or completely separated from the city network (as in Kampala, Maputo, and Nairobi). Even then, their coverage is marginal, at 12 percent in Maputo and 9 percent in Nairobi.

The Role of Wells, Boreholes, and Surface Water in the Rural Water Market

In most countries, wells and boreholes remain the most important source of water in rural Africa. Surface water is the second most important source, extending to more than 30 percent of the rural population in half of the sample countries. In no country in our sample does piped supply extend to more than 25 percent of the rural population. In fact, only in Namibia and South Africa does piped water reach more than 15 percent of the rural population, and in 7 out of 10 African countries it reaches less than 5 percent. Also, water collection imposes an enormous burden on households, primarily on women and children (box 2.4). Taking water closer to people promises enormous gains from health and time savings even if the opportunity cost of time is severely discounted.

Our analysis of access patterns at the rural level reveals three categories of countries (table 2.7). The first comprises those in which most of the rural population depends on surface water, the second those in which most rural dwellers obtain water through wells or boreholes, and the third group countries in which the rural population tends to rely on standposts.

The challenges in rural water supply management are many, but perhaps the most important is sustaining the service. Governments struggle to enhance access to safe water and to maintain existing facilities, but low capacity at the local level hobbles water supply management, because inadequate maintenance leads to frequent breakdowns and cuts the useful life of equipment obtained with scarce resources. The need for new or rehabilitated systems widens the gap between available funding and the funding needed to meet the water MDG.

In many countries, more than a third of rural water systems are not working at any given time (figure 2.4). Senegal, where 85 percent of rural water facilities are functioning, is the top performer, providing a stark

Box 2.4

The Opportunity Cost of a Distant Water Supply

Fetching water from outside the home is an activity dominated by women and girls. Blackden and Wodon (2006) compute that more than two-thirds of the 6 million hours that Ghanaians spent fetching water in 1992 were spent by women. If access to water were more convenient, those hours might be spent on education or other productive purposes. Providing African households with reasonable access to water would bring significant gains in productivity, health, and welfare.

On average, urban households that lack private water connections live about 500 meters from their water source, while in rural areas the average distance is closer to one kilometer. Some 20 percent of urban households and 30 percent of rural households live more than one kilometer from their water source.

Distance of Households from Water Source in Selected Countries
(Percentage of Households)

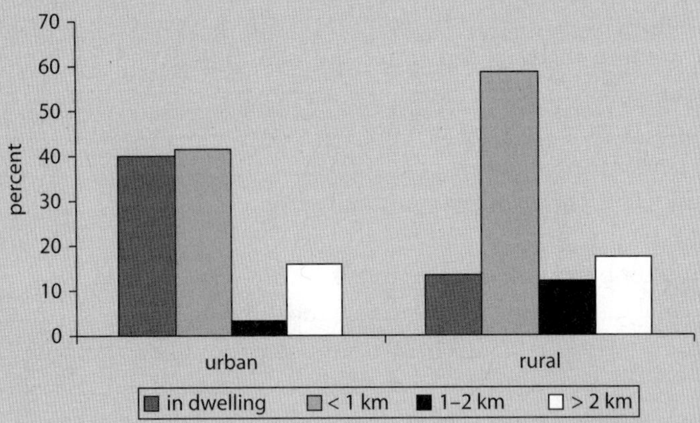

Patterns of access vary from country to country, but, on average, urban households have more convenient access to water than do rural households. For instance, 53 percent of rural households in Tanzania live more than two kilometers from their water source. At the other extreme are Madagascar, Nigeria, and South Africa, where less than 2 percent of rural households live more than two kilometers from their water. Even in urban areas, water can be far away. In urban Mauritania, for example, 66 percent of households live more than two kilometers away from their water source. In urban Ghana and Sierra Leone, the corresponding figure is 53 percent. In comparison, less than 5 percent of households in urban areas in the Democratic Republic of Congo, the Republic of Congo, Ethiopia, Morocco,

(continued next page)

Box 2.4 *(continued)*

Niger, Nigeria, South Africa, Uganda, and Zambia live more than two kilometers from their water source.

Household surveys allow us to measure changes in the time households spend fetching water. Since 1990, the average time spent fetching water for household consumption has remained virtually unchanged, at 45 to 50 minutes (round trip). In some countries, more time is spent at the task. Households in Ethiopia, Mozambique, Tanzania, and Uganda spend more than one hour each day fetching water for household consumption. In Ethiopia, Mozambique, Tanzania, and Uganda, moreover, the amount of time has increased over the years. These are also countries where more than 90 percent of households fetch water from outside their dwelling.

Source: Banerjee, Wodon, and others 2008.

Table 2.7 Patterns of Access across Countries in Rural Areas
(percent)

Dominant modality	*Range of prevalence*	*Average prevalence*	*Countries*
Standposts	28–93	57	Lesotho, South Africa
Wells/ boreholes	41–87	62	Benin, Burkina Faso, Cameroon, Central African Republic, Chad, Comoros, Côte d'Ivoire, Ghana, Guinea, Malawi, Mali, Mauritania, Mozambique, Namibia, Niger, Nigeria, Senegal, Sudan, Tanzania, Togo, Uganda, Zambia, Zimbabwe
Surface water	56–87	65	Congo, Dem. Rep.; Congo, Rep.; Ethiopia; Gabon; Kenya; Madagascar; Rwanda

Source: Banerjee, Wodon, and others 2008.

contrast with the Democratic Republic of Congo, where no more than 40 percent of rural water equipment is in working order. A significant number of rural water facilities are in need of rehabilitation at any given time—more than half in the Democratic Republic of Congo, Madagascar, and Malawi.

Evidence from Ethiopia suggests that mechanized boreholes are more likely to be nonfunctional than springs and hand pumps, probably for lack of a reliable supply chain of replacement parts (Water and Sanitation

Figure 2.4 Working Status of Rural Water Points

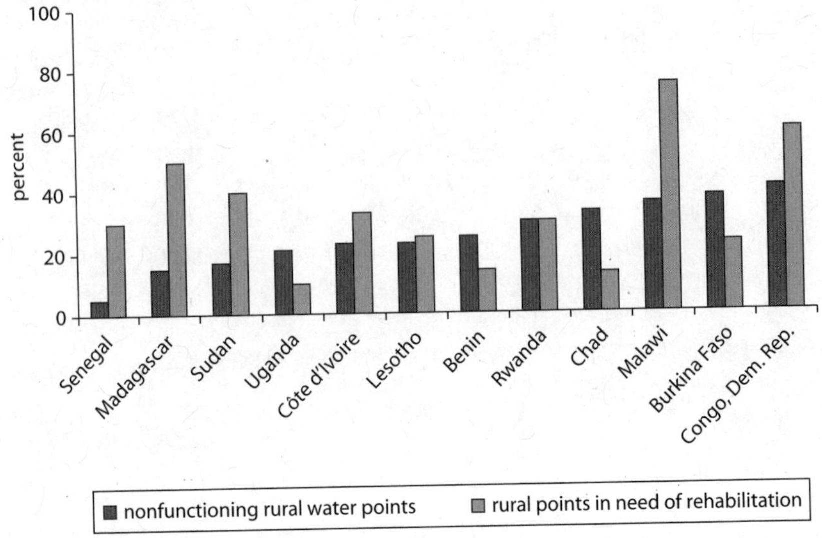

Source: Banerjee, Skilling, and others 2008.

Program 2006). Field research from Ghana, Kenya, Uganda, and Zambia reveals that the supply-chain problem also affects hand pumps, because of factors specific to the African rural water realm—among them the separation of pumps from other machines requiring spare parts, low pump density, poor choice of technology, restrictive maintenance systems, and relatively poor and immobile end users (Harvey and Reed 2006) Analysis of 25 studies across 15 countries in Africa has clarified the division of responsibility in the supply chain for spare parts. Governments and donors are responsible for managing the chain, but public and private sector entrepreneurs are important players as well. One thing is clear: Depending on the private sector alone to supply spare parts is unlikely to be sustainable because of the low population density and income level of many rural areas (Water and Sanitation Program 2006).

Steep Growth of Wells and Boreholes as Sources of Water

The dynamics of service expansion reveal a similar overall pattern in both urban and rural areas. Across the board, the use of wells and boreholes is expanding more rapidly than all the utility-based alternatives put together.

Water supply has evolved differently in Africa's urban areas than in its rural areas. Utilities have been unable to keep pace with the rising demand for water in urban areas, with the result that piped-water coverage has declined over the past decade. In the mid-1990s, 43 percent of urban African households received piped water; by the early 2000s, the figure had slipped to 39 percent (table 2.8). The situation with urban standposts is similar, with a decline from 29 percent to 24 percent over the past 15 years. The decline occurred because the combined growth rates of improved sources of water in urban areas (less than 1 percent a year) fell short of population growth (more than 4 percent a year). The decline in piped water has been matched by a rise in the prevalence of wells and boreholes, as well as slight increases in the use of surface water and water vendors in urban areas.

By contrast, the situation in rural areas has improved, though from a low baseline. More rural dwellers now have access to standposts, wells, and boreholes than they did in the early 1990s. Most important, dependence on surface water has declined substantially—from 50 percent to 42 percent in rural areas and from 41 percent to 33 percent overall.

To learn how households have moved from one source to another, we analyzed household surveys completed for the time periods 1995 to 2000 and 2001 to 2005. Our analysis used two indicators: annualized change in coverage (expressed as a percentage of the population) and absolute annual change in population coverage. The first indicator is defined as the number of people who gain coverage to each water source each year, divided by the population in the end year. The second indicator is the absolute number of people who move into or out of a specific source each year during the time period.

Each year during the decade from 1995 to 2005, about 400,000 people were added to the rolls of those who receive piped water (figures 2.5 and 2.6). In other words, the absolute number of people who gained piped water obtained through a household connection was that much higher than the number of those who lost it (or who were born into households without piped water). Most of the change came from network expansions in Ethiopia, Côte d'Ivoire, and Senegal—partially offset by contractions of coverage in Nigeria and Tanzania. Ethiopia annually moved about 300,000 people to piped-water service between 1995 and 2005, whereas Nigeria lost about 700,000 people from piped water in the same 10-year period.

Other sources—chiefly standposts, wells and boreholes, and surface water—recorded an increase in use. The rise in the number of people using surface water is primarily due to changes in the Democratic Republic of Congo, where more than 4 million people each year are added to the rolls of surface-water users.

Table 2.8 Evolution of Water-Supply Sources, 1990–2005
(percentage of population using source)

	Household connection to piped water			*Standposts*			*Wells and boreholes*			*Surface water*		
	Urban	*Rural*	*Overall*	*Urban*	*Rural*	*Overall*	*Urban*	*Rural*	*Overall*	*Urban*	*Rural*	*Overall*
1990–95	50	4	18	29	9	15	20	41	37	6	50	41
1995–2000	43	4	17	25	9	15	21	41	38	5	41	31
2001–05	39	4	17	24	11	16	24	43	41	7	42	33

Source: Banerjee, Wodon, and others 2008.

Figure 2.5 Annualized Change in Coverage of Various Water Sources, 1995–2005

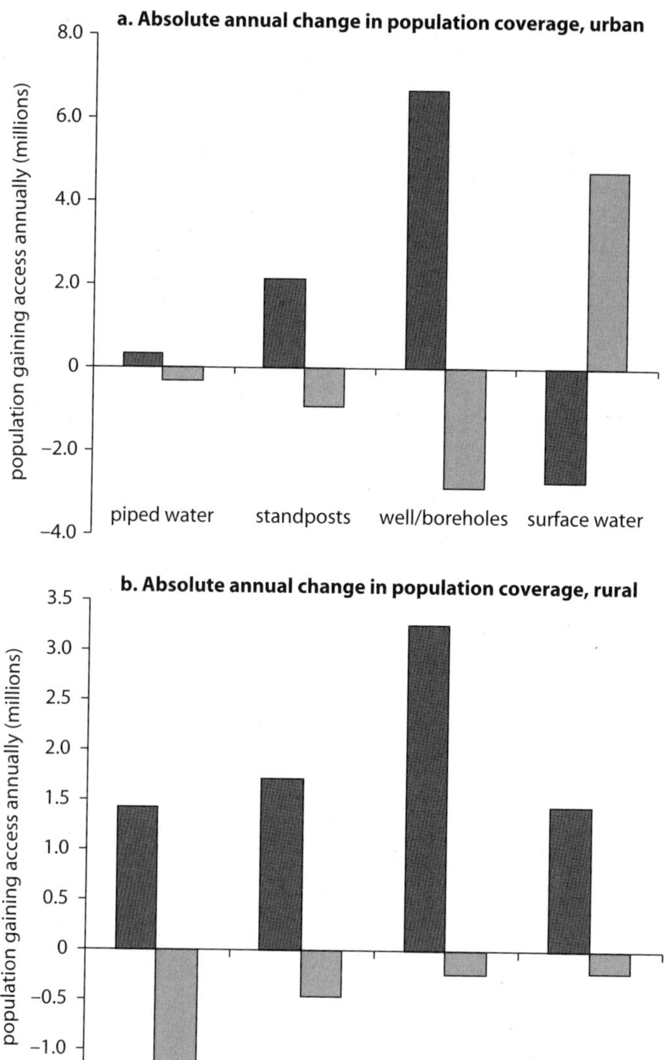

Source: Banerjee, Wodon, and others 2008.

A few outliers emerge as exceptions to the generally mediocre picture. Senegal stands out as having the largest average annual gain in piped-water coverage, adding almost 2 percent of its population each year, immediately followed by Benin (table 2.9). By contrast, the Democratic Republic of Congo, Malawi, Nigeria, Rwanda, Tanzania, and Zambia reduced their

Figure 2.6 Annualized Change in Coverage of Various Water Sources, 1995–2005

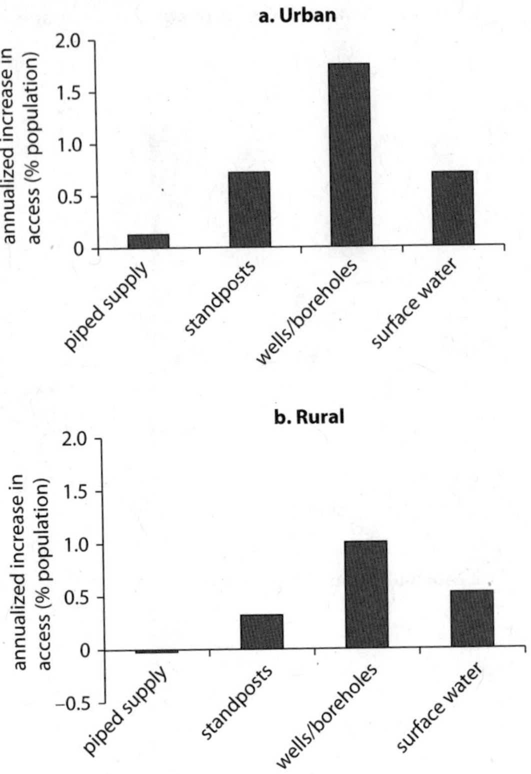

Source: Banerjee, Wodon, and others 2008.

coverage between the late 1990s and the early 2000s. In the case of public standposts, Mali has achieved the most accelerated expansion, followed by Benin. On the opposite side of the spectrum, Lesotho, Malawi, and Nigeria recorded reductions in access to standposts. Uganda was by far the leader in enhancing well and borehole coverage, adding almost 7 percent of its population each year.

Another way to assess national water-supply performance is to rank countries in terms of their success in reducing reliance on surface water. From this angle, the progress is far from dramatic. Uganda also stands out for moving almost 3 percent of its population away from surface water every year, immediately followed by Lesotho. In other countries, less than 2 percent of the population has moved away from surface water every year, although reliance on surface water has actually risen in the Democratic Republic of Congo, as noted, and in several other countries.

Table 2.9 Annualized Change in Coverage by Water Source and by Country, 1995–2005

(percentage of population accessing source)

Household piped water		*Standposts*		*Wells/boreholes*		*Surface water*	
Senegal	1.98	Mali	2.14	Uganda	6.53	Uganda	−2.75
Benin	1.78	Benin	1.88	Lesotho	3.75	Lesotho	−2.45
Zimbabwe	1.69	Burkina Faso	1.40	Nigeria	3.60	Mozambique	−1.81
Côte d'Ivoire	1.47	Tanzania	1.36	Mozambique	2.95	Namibia	−1.19
Namibia	1.43	Madagascar	1.18	Malawi	2.69	Cameroon	−0.99
Mali	0.83	Congo, Dem. Rep.	1.12	Rwanda	2.51	Ghana	−0.88
Burkina Faso	0.69	Ethiopia	1.09	Ghana	2.09	Côte d'Ivoire	−0.72
Cameroon	0.45	Côte d'Ivoire	0.94	Niger	1.55	Zimbabwe	−0.42
Ethiopia	0.44	Cameroon	0.81	Guinea	1.45	Benin	−0.40
Niger	0.27	Uganda	0.71	Cameroon	1.33	Nigeria	−0.39
Ghana	0.26	Namibia	0.57	Côte d'Ivoire	1.16	Ethiopia	−0.36
Chad	0.23	Niger	0.52	Namibia	1.06	Guinea	−0.16
Mozambique	0.16	Guinea	0.49	Zambia	0.95	Senegal	−0.07
Uganda	0.12	Senegal	0.44	Ethiopia	0.89	Niger	−0.02
Kenya	0.09	Rwanda	0.33	Tanzania	0.82	Mali	0.28
Guinea	0.08	Ghana	0.30	Chad	0.73	Tanzania	0.50
Madagascar	0.03	Mozambique	0.28	Zimbabwe	0.52	Madagascar	0.53
Lesotho	0.00	Chad	0.26	Kenya	0.40	Malawi	0.60
Malawi	−0.09	Kenya	0.20	Madagascar	0.25	Zambia	0.66
Zambia	−0.13	Zambia	0.19	Benin	−0.39	Kenya	0.86
Congo, Dem. Rep.	−0.16	Zimbabwe	−0.02	Mali	−0.57	Chad	1.20
Rwanda	−0.39	Malawi	−0.31	Burkina Faso	−0.77	Rwanda	1.81
Nigeria	−0.57	Lesotho	−0.47	Senegal	−0.99	Burkina Faso	2.31
Tanzania	−1.01	Nigeria	−0.66	Congo, Dem. Rep.	−4.75	Congo, Dem. Rep.	7.53

Source: Banerjee, Wodon, and others 2008.

Although most of Sub-Saharan Africa is not on track to reach the water MDG by 2015, a handful of countries have made remarkable progress in expanding access to improved sources of water, and at a rate that substantially exceeds their peers. This group includes Benin, Burkina Faso, Mali, and Senegal, which have moved a substantial share of their population to improved sources of piped-water connections or standposts. Lesotho, Nigeria, and Uganda have experienced the largest gains in expanding well and borehole coverage. The performance of four of those countries is tracked in figure 2.7.

Figure 2.7 Four Solid Performers in Expanding Access to Safe Water, 1995–2005

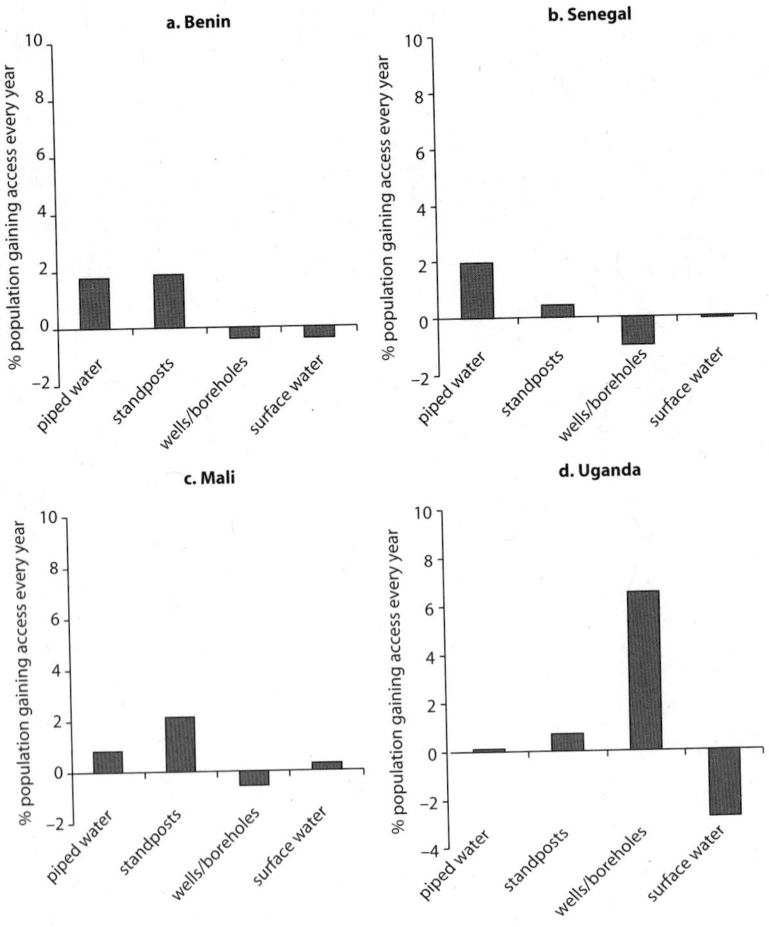

Source: Banerjee, Wodon, and others 2008.

When we analyze rural and urban spaces in isolation, other leaders emerge. Benin, Namibia, and Senegal each have managed to move more than 1 percent of their rural population to piped water supplied through household connections. Benin has also succeeded in raising standpost access in rural areas. Mali has provided standpost access to an additional 3 percent of its rural population each year. The biggest success story in well and borehole coverage is Uganda, where slightly more than 7 percent of the rural population has converted to this source of water each year. As noted, Uganda is also a major success story in reducing dependence on surface water.

In the urban water space, Ethiopia stands out as having achieved the largest average annual gain in household connections to piped water, adding almost 5 percent of its urban population each year, immediately followed by Côte d'Ivoire. By contrast, the Democratic Republic of Congo, Malawi, Nigeria, Rwanda, Tanzania, and Zambia slipped in their urban piped-water connections between the late 1990s and the early 2000s. In the case of public standposts, Uganda achieved the most accelerated expansion in urban areas, followed closely by Burkina Faso (which also did well with household connections). On the opposite side of the spectrum, Côte d'Ivoire, Lesotho, and Nigeria recorded urban dwellers' declining access to standposts. Nigeria, Malawi, and Rwanda were by far the leaders in enhancing well and borehole coverage, more than 4 percent of its urban population each year.

Notes

1. With a target date of 2015, MDG number 7 calls for ensuring environmental sustainability and—central to this analysis—reducing the number of people without sustainable access to safe drinking water by half.
2. These figures are likely to have changed. Since this study was completed, the water utility has undertaken, with apparent success, a new program focusing on token-run standposts.
3. For all the cities for which we could only rely on the utility's information, coverage was calculated this way.
4. Personal communication with Seydou Traore, Water and Sanitation Program, on September 25, 2007.

References

Banerjee, S., H. Skilling, V. Foster, C. Briceño-Garmendia, E. Morella, and T. Chfadi. 2008. "State of the Sector Review: Rural Water Supply." AICD Working Paper, World Bank, Washington, DC.

Banerjee, S., Q. Wodon, A. Diallo, N. Pushak, H. Uddin, C. Tsimpo, and V. Foster. 2008. "Access, Affordability and Alternatives: Modern Infrastructure Services in Sub-Saharan Africa." AICD Background Paper 2, World Bank, Washington, DC.

Blackden, C. M., and Q. Wodon, eds. 2006. *Gender, Time Use, and Poverty in Sub-Saharan Africa*. Washington, DC: World Bank.

Boyer, A. 2006. "Survey of Household Water Resale Activity in Peri-Urban Maputo: Preliminary Discussion of Findings." Water and Sanitation Program, Maputo, Mozambique.

Collignon, B., and M. Vézina. 2000. "Independent Water and Sanitation Providers in African Cities: Full Report of a Ten-Country Study." Water and Sanitation Program, Washington, DC.

Diallo, A., and Q. Wodon. 2005. "A Note on Access to Network-Based Infrastructure Services in Africa: Benefit and Marginal Incidence Analysis." Unpublished paper, Africa Poverty Department, World Bank, Washington, DC.

———. 2007. "Demographic Transition Towards Smaller Household Sizes and Basic Infrastructure Needs in Developing Countries." *Economics Bulletin* 15 (11): 1–11.

Foster, V., and M. C. Araujo. 2004. "Does Infrastructure Reform Work for the Poor? A Case Study from Guatemala." Policy Research Working Paper 3185, World Bank, Washington, DC.

Hall, D., and D. Cownie. 2002. "Ability and Willingness to Pay for Urban Water Supply: An Assessment of Connected and Unconnected Households in Maseru, Lesotho." Africa Urban and Water Department, World Bank, Washington, DC.

Harvey, P. A, and R. A. Reed. 2006. "Sustainable Supply Chains for Rural Water Supplies in Africa." *Engineering Sustainability* 159 (1): 31–39.

Kariuki, M., B. Collignon, B. Taisne, and B. Valfrey. 2003. "Better Water and Sanitation for the Urban Poor: Good Practice from Sub-Saharan Africa." Water Utility Partnership for Capacity Building, Abidjan.

Kariuki, M., and J. Schwartz. 2005. "Small-Scale Private Service Providers of Water and Electricity: A Review of Incidence, Structure, Pricing and Operating Characteristics." Policy Research Working Paper 3727, World Bank, Washington, DC.

Keener, S., and S. G. Banerjee. 2005. "Measuring Consumer Benefits from Utility Reform: An Exploration of Consumer Assessment Methodology in Sub-Saharan Africa." Africa Post-Conflict and Social Development Department, World Bank, Washington, DC.

Keener, S., M. Luengo, and S. G. Banerjee. 2009. "Provision of Water to the Poor in Africa: Experience with Water Standposts and the Informal Water Sector." AICD Working Paper 13, World Bank, Washington, DC.

Komives, K., V. Foster, J. Halpern, and Q. Wodon. 2005. "Water, Electricity, and the Poor: Who Benefits from Utility Subsidies?" Water and Sanitation Unit, World Bank, Washington, DC.

Water and Sanitation Program. 2006. "Spare Parts Supplies for Handpumps in Africa: Success Factors for Sustainability." Field Note 15, Africa Region, World Bank, Nairobi.

CHAPTER 3

Access to Safe Sanitation: The Millennium Challenge

To meet the sanitation target articulated in the Millennium Development Goals (MDGs), the number of people with proper sanitation in Africa needs to more than double—from 242 million in 2006 to 615 million in 2015. Some countries are closer to meeting the target than others. This chapter focuses on sanitation coverage trends in Africa with an analysis of progress made in the past decade. It then goes on to identify the countries that have managed to raise a substantial population up from the lower end of the sanitation ladder.

The Predominance of On-Site and Traditional Pit Latrines

Waterborne sewerage systems are rare in Africa. Only half of Africa's large cities have sewerage networks, and only Namibia, Senegal, and South Africa provide universal sewerage access. Sewerage networks that reach just about 10 percent of the population within the service area, such as those in Côte d'Ivoire, Kenya, Lesotho, Madagascar, Malawi, and Uganda, are more typical. Little more than half the households with piped water also have flush toilets, which are often connected to septic tanks rather than to sewers.

This is not surprising given that development of waterborne sewerage networks generally lags substantially behind the evolution of the piped-water networks on which they depend. In the low-income countries of

Africa, only 15 percent of the population enjoys private connections to piped-water networks, and this already places a low ceiling on the potential for waterborne sewerage (figure 3.1).

Sanitation is predominantly on-site and typically takes the form of traditional pit latrines. Half of the population uses traditional latrines, and the rate of use is approximately equal in both urban and rural areas. Overall, one-third of the population practices open defecation. Curiously, the number of improved latrines is not much greater than that of septic tanks, despite a significant cost difference between the two. An urban-rural divide emerges when access to improved sanitation is considered.

In rural areas, 41 percent of the population continues to practice open defecation, and improved sanitation modalities reach less than 10 percent. Conversely, in urban areas, 39 percent has access to improved modalities such as improved latrines or septic tanks, and less than 10 percent practices open defecation. Africa's low overall access rates to improved sanitation are partly due to negligible service coverage in rural areas, where most people still reside (table 3.1).

Traditional latrines are the most common sanitation option in Africa, but the health benefits they provide depend on how they are constructed and used. Even basic latrines can provide protection if they are covered and emptied in a timely fashion, and if people wash their hands after use. Conversely, improved latrines will not provide sanitary protection if people do not use them properly, or do not use them at all.

Figure 3.1 Population That Has Wastewater Connection in the Utility Service Area

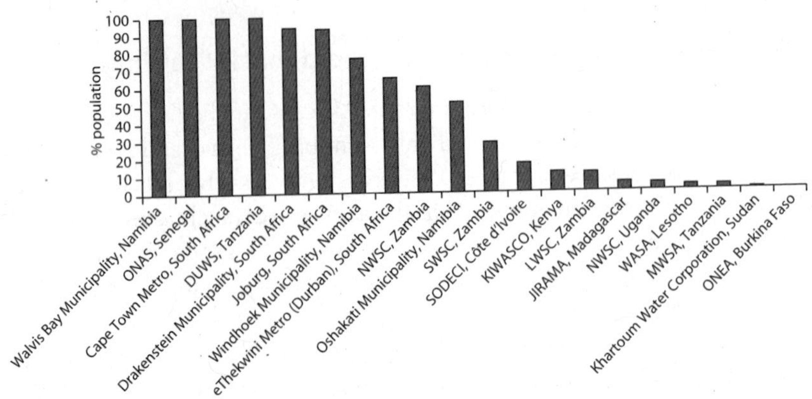

Source: Morella, Foster, and Banerjee 2008.

Table 3.1 Patterns of Access to Sanitation
(percent)

	Open defecation	*Traditional latrine*	*Improved latrine*	*Septic tank*
Urban	8	51	14	25
Rural	41	51	5	2
Overall	31	51	8	10

Source: Banerjee and others 2008.

Figure 3.2 Population Sharing Water and Toilet Facilities

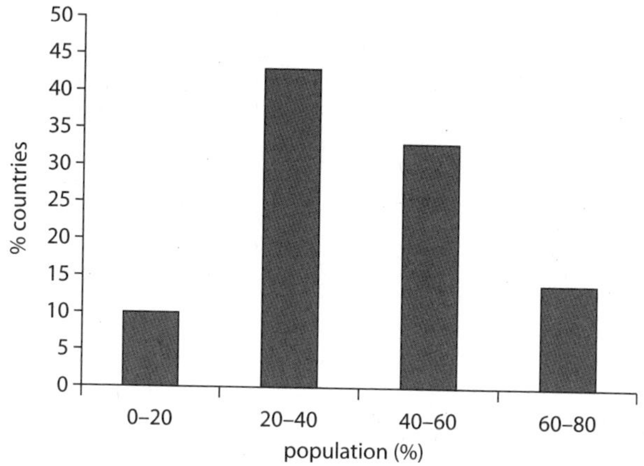

Source: Morella, Foster, and Banerjee 2008.

In urban areas, sanitation facilities are typically shared among multiple families. Household surveys focus only on formal service provision and do not take into account informal sharing between households. In urban areas, more than 40 percent of households report sharing toilet facilities with other households (figure 3.2). In Benin, Burkina Faso, the Democratic Republic of Congo, Ghana, Guinea, and Madagascar, more than half of households share toilet facilities. In Ghana—where compound housing is commonplace—as many as 80 percent of urban dwellers share water and sanitation facilities with other households. This practice suggests that people lose time waiting to access facilities and may also pay significant surcharges to the facility owners. Shared facilities are often poorly maintained, which poses health risks and may discourage use.

Figure 3.3 Access Patterns across Income Quintiles

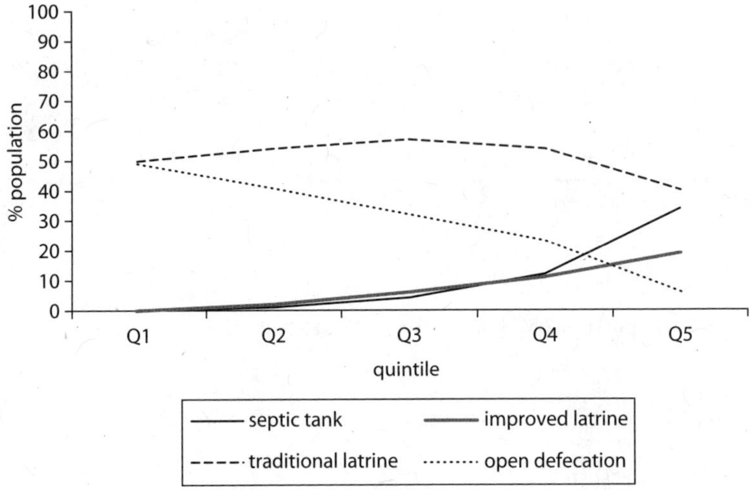

Source: Banerjee, Wodon, and others 2008.

Patterns of sanitation access vary dramatically across the socioeconomic spectrum. As might be expected, open defecation is more widely practiced by those in the lowest income groups, where it accounts for half of the population and declines steadily toward zero prevalence in the highest income groups. Conversely, the poorest half of the population has virtually no access to improved latrines and septic tanks; even among the richest strata, barely 20 to 30 percent of households have such access (figure 3.3). The figures indicate that although improved latrines cost less than septic tanks, they remain something of a luxury, even for the middle-income groups. As well, although high average rates might suggest comprehensive coverage, the numbers are somewhat misleading, because people in higher income groups are generally the ones benefiting from these sanitation improvements, and those in the more vulnerable populations are left without adequate coverage. Finally, traditional latrines are by far the most egalitarian form of sanitation, used in about 50 percent of households across all income ranges.

The Sanitation Challenge across Countries

In most countries, well below 10 percent of the population has septic tanks and less than 20 percent has improved latrines. The difference is made up, in varying degrees, by traditional pit latrines and/or open defecation.

Fifty-one percent of the population uses pit latrines, and this number remains remarkably constant between urban and rural areas and across the socioeconomic spectrum. In Malawi, Tanzania, and Uganda, as much as 80 percent of the population uses traditional pit latrines. These general patterns masks huge differences in access to different modalities of sanitation throughout the African countries (table 3.2).

In all countries, the patterns of access between urban and rural areas differ greatly. In Zimbabwe, 95 percent of urban residents use septic tanks, but rural coverage is less than 2 percent. In Namibia, Senegal, and South Africa more than 50 percent of the urban population has access to septic tanks; the numbers in rural areas range from 14 percent (Senegal) to 6 percent (South Africa). Burkina Faso has the best coverage of improved latrines in urban areas, where 70 percent of the population uses this type of facility. Yet, in rural areas, coverage is 10 times smaller, down

Table 3.2 Patterns of Access to Flush Toilets and Alternatives
(percentage of households, population-weighted average)

	Septic tank	Improved latrine	Traditional latrine	Open defecation
By time period (national)				
Early 1990s	9	6	50	46
Late 1990s	9	7	47	37
Early 2000s	10	9	52	34
By location				
Rural	2	5	52	41
Urban	28	14	49	8
By quintile				
First	0	0	50	49
Second	1	2	54	41
Third	4	6	57	32
Fourth	12	11	54	23
Fifth	34	19	40	6
By country income group				
Low	7	8	52	33
Middle	33	8	41	13
By subregion				
East Africa	4	4	56	35
West Africa	12	8	48	33
Southern Africa	23	11	36	28
Central Africa	3	13	65	18

Source: Banerjee, Wodon, and others 2008.
Note: The total on trend analysis (by time period) may not add to 100 because a balanced panel has been taken in the three time periods.

to 7 percent. In Zimbabwe, the unserved population in urban areas is close to zero, as opposed to more than 40 percent in rural areas. In all countries, urban sanitation coverage generally exceeds national averages. In many countries, most of the urban population enjoys septic tanks and improved latrines, while less than 20 percent practices open defecation. Conversely, most of the population in rural areas uses traditional latrines, and no more than 15 percent of the rural population has septic tanks. Open defecation remains common in rural areas, and more than 50 percent of the population in half the countries engages in this practice. In a few countries—Benin, Burkina Faso, Chad, Namibia, and Niger—nearly all the rural populations still practice open defecation.

Countries can be categorized in three ways, based on their urban sanitation coverage. The first group includes countries where most of the urban population—between 50 and 90 percent—rely on traditional latrines. This is the case of the Central African Republic, Chad, the Comoros, the Democratic Republic of Congo, the Republic of Congo, Ethiopia, Guinea, Lesotho, Malawi, Mali, Mauritania, Mozambique, Nigeria, Sudan, Tanzania, and Uganda. The second group comprises countries where most of the urban population—from one-third to one-half—use improved latrines, along with a significant percentage—20 to 40 percent—who use traditional latrines. This is the case of Benin, Burkina Faso, Cameroon, Ghana, Madagascar, Niger, and Rwanda. The third group includes countries where at least one-third and up to 95 percent of the urban populations have septic tanks, although in some countries up to 45 percent still use traditional latrines. This is the case of Côte d'Ivoire, Gabon, Kenya, Namibia, Senegal, South Africa, Zambia, and Zimbabwe.

Similarly, countries can be categorized based on coverage in rural areas, but a different group of countries emerge. The first category includes countries where more than 50 percent of the rural population still practices open defecation: This is the case of Benin, Burkina Faso, Chad, Côte d'Ivoire, Ethiopia, Mauritania, Mozambique, Namibia, Niger, and Sudan. The second category includes countries where most use traditional latrines. This is the largest group, including Cameroon, the Comoros, the Democratic Republic of Congo, the Republic of Congo, Gabon, Ghana, Guinea, Kenya, Malawi, Mali, Nigeria, South Africa, Tanzania, Uganda, and Zambia. In the third category, an increasing number of people use improved latrines, although many still use traditional latrines and practice open defecation. This is the case in the Central African Republic, Lesotho, Madagascar, Rwanda, Senegal, and Zimbabwe (table 3.3).

Table 3.3 Patterns of Access to Sanitation across Coun
(percent)

Dominant modality	*Range of prevalence*	*Average prevalence*	
Urban			
Flush toilet	30–95	58	Côte d'Ivoire, Senegal, Sou Zimbabwe
Improved latrine	29–67	50	Benin, Burkina Faso, Cameroon, Ghana, Madagascar, Niger, Rwanda
Traditional latrine	45–87	68	Central African Republic; Chad; Comoros; Congo, Dem. Rep.; Congo, Rep.; Ethiopia; Guinea; Lesotho; Malawi; Mali; Mauritania; Mozambique; Nigeria; Sudan; Tanzania; Uganda
Rural			
Improved latrine	11–44	25	Central African Republic, Lesotho, Madagascar, Rwanda, Senegal, Zimbabwe
Traditional latrine	50–83	71	Cameroon; Comoros; Congo, Dem. Rep.; Congo, Rep.; Gabon; Ghana; Guinea; Kenya; Malawi; Mali; Nigeria; South Africa; Tanzania; Uganda; Zambia
Open defecation	54–94	74	Benin, Burkina Faso, Chad, Côte d'Ivoire, Ethiopia, Mauritania, Mozambique, Namibia, Niger, Sudan

Source: Banerjee, Wodon, and others 2008.

Steep Increases in the Use of Traditional Pit Latrines

Not only are traditional latrines the most common form of sanitation in Sub-Saharan Africa, but they have also been by far the fastest growing one since 1995. Annualized reports show that an estimated 2.8 percent of the urban population and 1.8 percent of the rural population gains access to traditional latrines each year (figure 3.4). This is a much faster rate of growth than expansion of septic tanks and improved latrines together. Given that the MDG target focuses on the two higher-end improved sanitation options (septic tank, improved latrines), this rapid increase in the number of traditional latrines is not always fully recognized in policy discussions.

Expansion rates of improved latrines and septic tanks are four times faster in urban areas than in rural areas. Another piece of good news is that the prevalence of open defecation in Sub-Saharan Africa has finally begun to decline, albeit at a very modest pace. Approximately 0.3 percent

e 3.4 Annualized Growth in Coverage in Urban and Rural Areas, 1995–2005

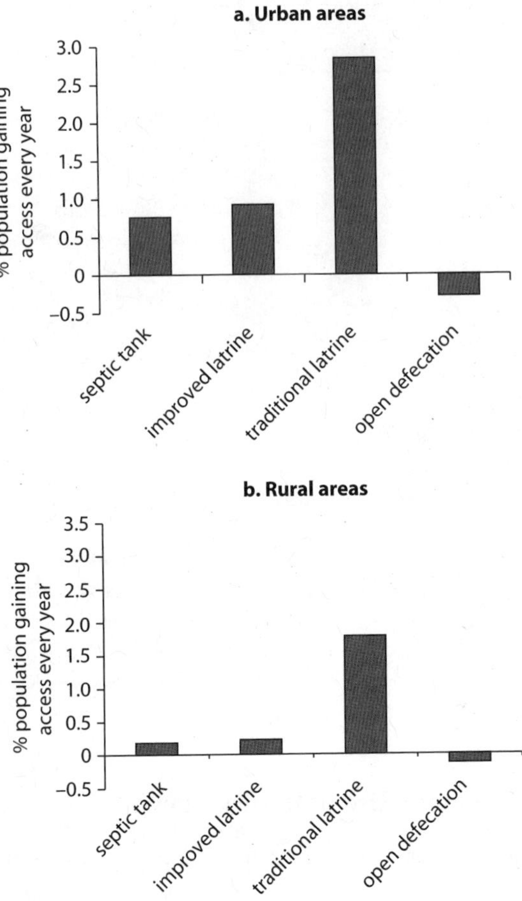

Source: Morella, Foster, and Banerjee 2008.

of the urban population has been moving away from open defecation each year into some form of sanitation service, and the corresponding figure for the rural population is 0.1 percent.

Expansion rates across income groups show that the poorest have little access to the best forms of sanitation. The expansion of septic tanks is concentrated in the middle- and upper-income quintiles, reaching a peak in the third quintile, well beyond the growth in the fifth quintile. Although people in all income groups have gained better access to improved latrines, those in the highest income groups have benefited the most. Those in all income groups have also gained more access to traditional latrines; however, this gain has been greatest for those in the lower-income groups. The number of people practicing open defecation decreases only in the second quintile of the distribution (figure 3.5).

The geographical distribution of improved sanitation modes shows the rates of development in various countries over the years. Nigeria and Senegal account for much of the increased septic tank coverage, 35 percent and 17 percent, respectively, mainly due to their sizes. Burkina Faso, Madagascar, and Rwanda account for much of the improved latrine growth. For traditional latrines, Nigeria and Ethiopia account for 51 percent of new users. Despite these improvements, the largest populations (70 million people) still practice open defecation in Ethiopia and Nigeria.

Good Progress in a Handful of Countries

A handful of African countries have been making impressive gains in sanitation since 1990. Although the improvements in these countries may still be too small and too late to meet the sanitation MDG, the successful cases could provide valuable lessons for other countries in the region.

The following analysis highlights countries that have had the greatest changes in access to different levels of sanitation. This list was dominated by some of the larger countries, such as Ethiopia and Nigeria, where, as a result of their sizes, even relatively modest percentage changes had major results. In this section, the focus is on countries that have achieved large percentage gains relative to the size of their populations. This signals successful experience, although in the case of the smaller countries this does not prove to be material at the regional level. Any country moving more than 2 percent of its population up any of the rungs of the sanitation ladder each year can be considered to be making noteworthy progress (table 3.4). Several solid performers emerge.

In the case of septic tanks, Senegal stands out as having by far the largest average annual gain, as more than 3 percent of its population gains access to septic tanks each year. As a result, the number of people using a septic tank in Senegal has increased from 9 percent to 36 percent from 1997 to 2005 (figure 3.6). By contrast, Lesotho, Madagascar, and Zambia show declining septic tank coverage from the late 1990s and the early 2000s.

Figure 3.5 Growth in Access by Mode and Quintile

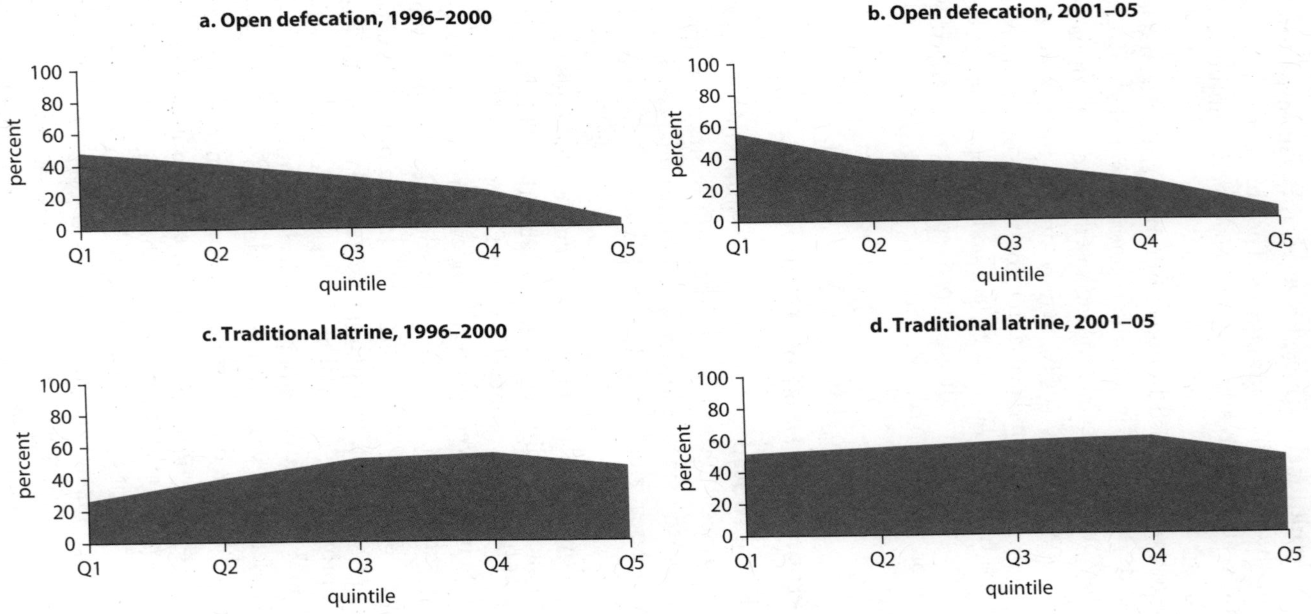
a. Open defecation, 1996–2000
b. Open defecation, 2001–05
c. Traditional latrine, 1996–2000
d. Traditional latrine, 2001–05
percent
100
80
60
40
20
0
Q1
Q2
Q3
Q4
Q5
quintile

Source: Morella, Foster, and Banerjee 2008.

Table 3.4 Annualized Change in Coverage, 1995–2005

(percentage of population per year)

Septic tank		*Improved latrine*		*Traditional latrine*		*Open defecation*	
Senegal	3.50	Madagascar	6.46	Côte d'Ivoire	4.10	Ethiopia	−2.30
Zimbabwe	1.51	Rwanda	4.59	Uganda	3.96	Zimbabwe	−1.37
Mali	1.02	Burkina Faso	4.43	Ethiopia	3.92	Mozambique	−1.25
Namibia	1.00	Benin	2.53	Congo, Dem. Rep.	3.63	Madagascar	−0.84
Ghana	0.70	Zimbabwe	1.13	Nigeria	2.84	Senegal	−0.84
Nigeria	0.63	Cameroon	0.95	Mozambique	2.79	Guinea	−0.55
Benin	0.48	Mali	0.81	Malawi	2.61	Mali	−0.43
Cameroon	0.38	Lesotho	0.64	Guinea	2.09	Cameroon	−0.29
Ethiopia	0.37	Ghana	0.61	Mali	1.36	Côte d'Ivoire	−0.14
Burkina Faso	0.34	Tanzania	0.57	Zambia	1.08	Congo, Dem. Rep.	−0.05
Tanzania	0.25	Kenya	0.48	Chad	0.90	Malawi	−0.04
Chad	0.23	Guinea	0.34	Ghana	0.79	Rwanda	0.20
Malawi	0.17	Niger	0.32	Kenya	0.77	Nigeria	0.34
Uganda	0.10	Namibia	0.30	Niger	0.63	Namibia	0.35
Côte d'Ivoire	0.08	Congo, Dem. Rep.	0.26	Cameroon	0.57	Uganda	0.38
Kenya	0.05	Zambia	0.20	Zimbabwe	0.52	Zambia	0.42
Guinea	0.04	Uganda	0.20	Tanzania	0.52	Ghana	0.61
Congo, Dem. Rep.	0.04	Mozambique	0.17	Namibia	0.15	Tanzania	0.63
Niger	0.00	Malawi	0.16	Senegal	0.03	Kenya	0.82
Rwanda	0.00	Ethiopia	0.12	Rwanda	−0.44	Benin	0.90
Mozambique	0.00	Chad	−0.52	Lesotho	−0.48	Burkina Faso	1.04
Madagascar	−0.01	Nigeria	−0.68	Benin	−1.08	Lesotho	1.05
Lesotho	−0.09	Côte d'Ivoire	−1.20	Burkina Faso	−2.25	Chad	1.60
Zambia	−0.12	Senegal	−1.29	Madagascar	−3.69	Niger	1.81

Source: Morella, Foster, and Banerjee 2008.

Figure 3.6 Successful Examples from Up and Down the Sanitation Ladder, 1995–2005

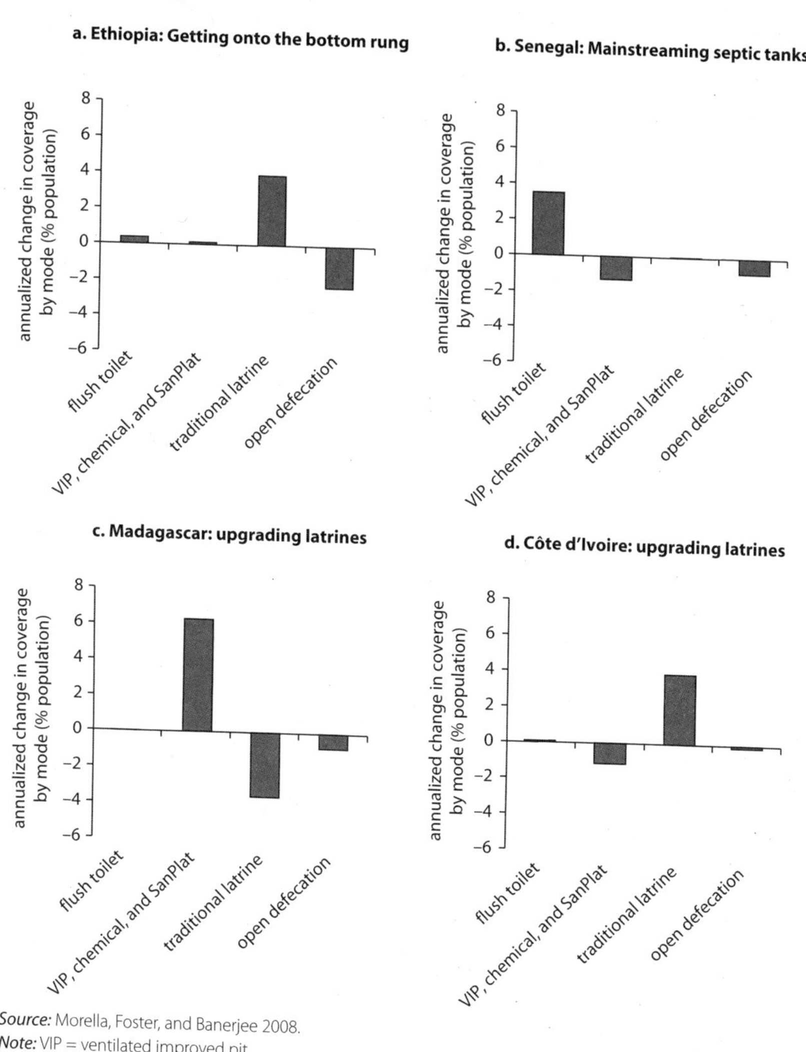

Source: Morella, Foster, and Banerjee 2008.
Note: VIP = ventilated improved pit.

In the case of improved latrines, Burkina Faso, Madagascar, and Rwanda stand out as having achieved accelerated expansion. In Madagascar, about 7 percent of the population has gained improved latrine coverage every year; in Burkina Faso and Rwanda, the corresponding figure exceeds 4 percent. In the Democratic Republic of Congo, Côte d'Ivoire, Ethiopia, and

Uganda, more than 3 percent of the population has gained access to traditional latrines every year.

Another way to quantify success is to identify the countries that have had the most rapid reductions in the number of people practicing open defecation. Ethiopia has had the biggest reduction: between 2000 and 2005, the share of the population without access to any form of sanitation dropped from 82 percent to 62 percent. Mozambique and Zimbabwe immediately follow: more than 1 percent of their populations have stopped the practice of open defecation every year. Nigeria, which has made impressive gains in many areas of sanitation improvement, has not had such rapid reduction in its open defecation rate. Conversely, Senegal continues showing a salient performance on septic tank coverage.

Individual countries are focused on different goals, based on their current levels of sanitation coverage, and the strategies they employ have distinct financial and health implications. In Ethiopia, for example, the main goal is to reduce the practice of open defecation by getting people onto the bottom rung of the sanitation ladder. Ethiopia therefore adopted a culturally appropriate formula rather than simply spending money on hardware, which yielded significant results (box 3.1).

Countries such as Burkina Faso and Madagascar are focused on upgrading services for people who are already engaged in some kind of basic sanitation practice. In Senegal, the aim is to move people from the middle to the top of the ladder by building more septic tanks.

A similar analysis of a country's performance can be conducted at the urban and rural levels. For example, Senegal appears to have made great strides in septic tank coverage when looking at figures for urban areas, but the increase in rural areas is much less remarkable. The same applies to Zimbabwe, where the noteworthy expansion in urban areas is offset by the decline in septic tank coverage in rural areas. Also, in Burkina Faso there has been little improvement in latrine access in large cities, and the results in rural areas are 10 times smaller. Conversely, Côte d'Ivoire and Uganda show similar progress in traditional latrine coverage across urban and rural areas, as does Ethiopia in reducing the practice of open defecation (table 3.5).

Box 3.1

Ethiopia's Success with a Community-Led Program

The southern region of Ethiopia—home to diverse cultures and scores of ethnic groups—has a population of 15 million, much larger than many African countries. Population density varies, peaking at 1,100 people per square kilometer in the Wanago district.

In early 2003, access to on-site sanitation was lower than 13 percent, below the national average of 15 percent (see figure). Traditional latrines were most prevalent but scarcely used, poorly maintained, smelly, and dangerous to children and animals. Meanwhile, population expansion, growing household densities, and deforestation were combining to reduce private options for open defecation.

Latrine Construction 2002/03 and 2005/06

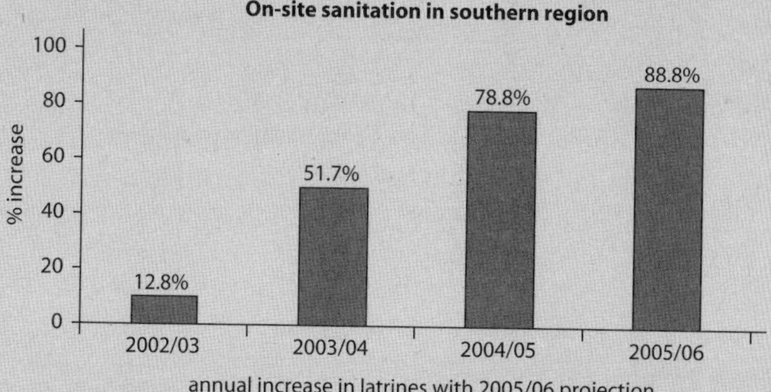

The Southern Regional Health Bureau, charged with promoting sanitation and hygiene by the national Ministry of Health, applied a community-led total sanitation approach, including zero subsidies but allowing the community to devise its own innovative and affordable models.

With a modest but dedicated sum of money, a mass communication campaign was launched using the slogan "Sanitation is everyone's problem and everyone's responsibility." It promoted sustainable and affordable sanitation by creating awareness and encouraging self-financing across all income quintiles. Close collaboration with all stakeholders created advocacy consensus building and capacity building, promotion (by community volunteers), and supportive supervision.

(continued next page)

Box 3.1 *(continued)*

At the household level, women were identified as the main drivers of latrine construction. At public consensus-building meetings, they complained about how open defecation directly affects their lives, highlighting the health risks of contact with feces in the banana plantations and in the fields where they collect fodder for cattle. They also complained of the bad smell and embarrassment of seeing people defecate in the open space. Featured stories cited shame as an important factor in consensus building and a strong motivator for latrine construction. Volunteer community health promoters went house to house across villages with health extension workers and members of the subdistrict health committee to persuade households to build latrines, and then they supervised construction.

Alongside other gains in public health, pit latrine ownership rose from less than 13 percent in September 2003 to more than 50 percent in August 2004. By August 2005, it had reached 78 percent, and a year later was on track to reach 88 percent.

Source: Reproduced from Water and Sanitation Program 2008.

Table 3.5 Annualized Change in Coverage by Modality and by Country, 1990–2005
(percent)

Septic tank		*Improved latrine*		*Traditional latrine*		*Open defecation*	
Urban							
Senegal	5.7	Burkina Faso	17.2	Nigeria	5.1	Malawi	1.0
Zimbabwe	3.0	Madagascar	8.5	Congo, Dem. Rep.	4.7	Rwanda	0.4
Mali	2.3	Rwanda	6.1	Côte d'Ivoire	4.5	Namibia	0.4
Namibia	1.8	Benin	5.3	Uganda	4.4	Tanzania	0.3
Burkina Faso	1.3	Ghana	2.0	Mozambique	4.2	Kenya	0.3
Ghana	1.2	Tanzania	1.8	Ethiopia	3.9	Benin	0.2
Benin	1.2	Mali	1.7	Chad	3.6	Chad	0.1
Ethiopia	1.2	Niger	1.4	Malawi	3.3	Cameroon	0.1
Tanzania	1.1	Cameroon	0.9	Guinea	2.3	Burkina Faso	0.1
Chad	0.9	Congo, Dem. Rep.	0.8	Rwanda	2.2	Uganda	0.1
Malawi	0.9	Uganda	0.7	Niger	2.0	Zambia	0.1
Uganda	0.5	Mozambique	0.6	Kenya	2.0	Zimbabwe	0.0
Nigeria	0.5	Kenya	0.6	Ghana	1.7	Guinea	0.0
Côte d'Ivoire	0.5	Lesotho	0.5	Cameroon	1.6	Ghana	−0.1
Rwanda	0.4	Guinea	0.5	Zambia	0.8	Lesotho	−0.1
Lesotho	0.3	Ethiopia	0.5	Mali	0.7	Senegal	−0.1
Cameroon	0.2	Malawi	0.4	Lesotho	0.6	Niger	−0.2
Madagascar	0.2	Zambia	0.3	Namibia	0.4	Nigeria	−0.2
Congo, Dem. Rep.	0.2	Zimbabwe	0.2	Tanzania	0.2	Mali	−0.4
Zambia	0.0	Namibia	0.2	Zimbabwe	0.0	Côte d'Ivoire	−0.5
Guinea	0.0	Senegal	−0.1	Benin	−3.2	Congo, Dem. Rep.	−0.5
Kenya	−0.1	Nigeria	−0.3	Senegal	−3.8	Mozambique	−0.9
Niger	−0.2	Côte d'Ivoire	−0.9	Madagascar	−5.3	Madagascar	−1.1
Mozambique	−0.4	Chad	−1.6	Burkina Faso	−13.1	Ethiopia	−2.2

(continued next page)

Table 3.5 *(continued)*

Septic tank		*Improved latrine*		*Traditional latrine*		*Open defecation*	
Rural							
Senegal	1.7	Madagascar	5.9	Ethiopia	4.3	Niger	2.5
Mali	0.6	Rwanda	4.6	Côte d'Ivoire	3.9	Burkina Faso	1.6
Namibia	0.5	Zimbabwe	1.8	Uganda	3.9	Chad	1.5
Nigeria	0.5	Burkina Faso	1.7	Congo, Dem. Rep.	3.1	Ghana	1.5
Ethiopia	0.3	Lesotho	1.1	Senegal	2.6	Kenya	1.0
Zambia	0.2	Benin	1.0	Malawi	2.5	Benin	0.9
Burkina Faso	0.1	Mali	0.6	Guinea	2.1	Tanzania	0.7
Guinea	0.1	Kenya	0.4	Mali	1.7	Lesotho	0.6
Benin	0.1	Namibia	0.4	Mozambique	1.7	Nigeria	0.5
Chad	0.1	Guinea	0.3	Nigeria	1.3	Namibia	0.5
Côte d'Ivoire	0.1	Tanzania	0.2	Zambia	1.1	Uganda	0.4
Malawi	0.0	Zambia	0.2	Zimbabwe	0.9	Zambia	0.3
Uganda	0.0	Uganda	0.1	Tanzania	0.6	Congo, Dem. Rep.	0.2
Niger	0.0	Malawi	0.1	Cameroon	0.6	Rwanda	0.1
Kenya	0.0	Ethiopia	0.1	Ghana	0.5	Malawi	−0.2
Mozambique	0.0	Congo, Dem. Rep.	0.0	Kenya	0.5	Cameroon	−0.2
Rwanda	0.0	Niger	−0.1	Chad	0.4	Côte d'Ivoire	−0.4
Tanzania	0.0	Chad	−0.1	Benin	0.4	Mozambique	−0.8
Congo, Dem. Rep.	0.0	Mozambique	−0.1	Niger	0.3	Mali	−0.8
Madagascar	0.0	Cameroon	−0.1	Namibia	0.1	Guinea	−0.9
Ghana	0.0	Ghana	−0.8	Burkina Faso	−0.3	Madagascar	−1.0
Zimbabwe	−0.1	Nigeria	−0.9	Lesotho	−0.5	Senegal	−1.0
Lesotho	−0.1	Côte d'Ivoire	−1.3	Rwanda	−1.3	Zimbabwe	−1.5
Cameroon	−0.1	Senegal	−2.1	Madagascar	−3.1	Ethiopia	−2.8

Source: Morella, Foster, and Banerjee 2008.

References

Banerjee, S., Q. Wodon, A. Diallo, N. Pushak, H. Uddin, C. Tsimpo, and V. Foster. 2008. "Access, Affordability and Alternatives: Modern Infrastructure Services in Sub-Saharan Africa." AICD Background Paper 2, World Bank, Washington, DC.

Morella, E., V. Foster, and S. Banerjee. 2008. "Climbing the Ladder: The State of Sanitation in Sub-Saharan Africa." AICD Background Paper 13, World Bank, Washington, DC.

Water and Sanitation Program. 2008. "Can Africa Afford to Miss the Sanitation MDG Target? A Review of the Sanitation and Hygiene Status in 32 Countries." World Bank, Washington, DC.

CHAPTER 4

Improving the Organization of the Water and Sanitation Sectors

Many African governments have reformed their water and sanitation systems to provide quality services for their citizens. The sector reforms are critical in creating the necessary institutional structure for improved service delivery, but, although costs are predominantly paid up front, it takes time to reap the benefits, and costs are sometimes not shared equitably among the various stakeholders.

Most African countries are taking gradual steps, cautiously weighing the benefits and costs based on their socioeconomic conditions. Governments have approached the reform process in various ways, but because most of the documentation of these processes is anecdotal rather than systematic, it is difficult to assess their impact or to replicate successful programs. Collecting this kind of data in Sub-Saharan Africa is challenging, and the situation is made worse by the relatively limited history of the monitoring and evaluation efforts related to the Millennium Development Goals (MDGs), as well as by the broader context of weak institutional capacity.

In this chapter, the sector organization and market structure are assessed in four distinct water and sanitation spaces with a focus on developing succinct indexes on the institutional development: urban piped water, standposts and other informal services in the unconnected market, rural water, and sanitation. The indexes are a standardized survey-based methodology that employs categorical values (0s and 1s), and the questions in the Africa Infrastructure Country Diagnostic (AICD) Water Supply and Sanitation (WSS) Survey (modules 1 and 3) require an implicit judgment of what is commonly accepted as good practice in other developing countries. The 1s are added to create a composite index for each country. These indexes from the questionnaire responses allow the ranking of institutional maturity and where the country stands at this point in time. It is important to note that a 100 percent score does not imply that there is no scope for improvement.

The Heterogeneity of the Urban Water Market

No consistent set of institutional arrangements is found across Sub-Saharan Africa. Institutional structures range from national-level utilities responsible for countrywide coverage to those with limited jurisdictions. Generally, the central government is responsible for managing the urban water sector, but several providers, including municipal agencies, public-private partnerships, and corporate utilities, also deliver services.

Some utilities are responsible for water, sanitation, and even energy, whereas others handle only water distribution. Generally, water utilities are dedicated to providing water and, in some cases, wastewater facilities. Half of the countries have utilities that jointly provide water and wastewater services (figure 4.1). Only ELECTRA in Cape Verde, Société Tchadienne d'Eau et d'Électricité (STEE) in Chad, Jiro sy Rano Malagasy

Figure 4.1 Range of Institutional Arrangements in Water Service Provision

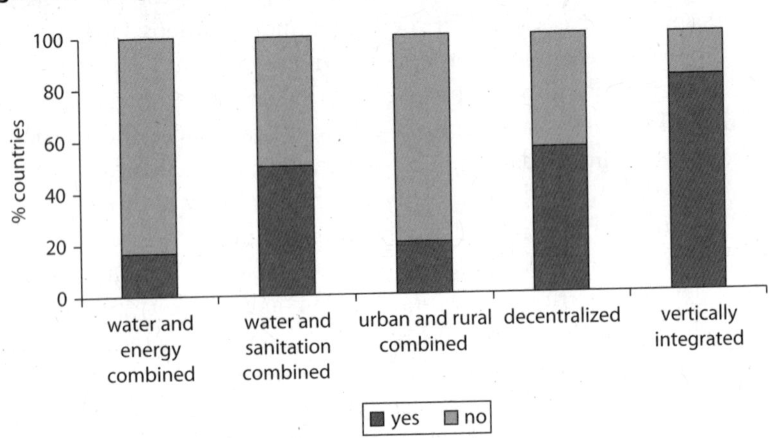

Source: Banerjee, Skilling, and others 2008a.

(JIRAMA) in Madagascar, and ELECTROGAZ in Rwanda provide both water and energy. Few countries in Africa have unbundled bulk water generation and distribution facilities. Most utilities primarily cover urban areas. In Benin, Kenya, Rwanda, South Africa, and Tanzania, utilities provide services to both urban and rural dwellers.

The urban water scorecard is a snapshot of three key institutional dimensions: broad sectoral policy reforms, amount and quality of regulation, and enterprise governance. It is composed of three indexes: the urban reform index, the regulation index, and the state-owned enterprise (SOE) governance index. Table 4.1 shows the components of these indexes. First, we define reform parameters as the implementation of sectoral legislation, restructuring of enterprises, and introduction of policy oversight and private sector participation. Second, autonomous, transparent, and accountable regulatory agencies and regulatory tools (tariff methodology) should be established to monitor quality. Third, to properly maintain facilities, SOEs should encourage shareholder participation, create greater board and management autonomy, and improve accounting and disclosure mechanisms. They should also consider various forms of management, including outsourcing to the private sector. Note that reform and regulation are country-level indicators, but governance is measured at the enterprise level.

Urban Water Reforms across Countries

The urban water sector reform was evaluated based on four attributes: legislation, restructuring, policy oversight, and private sector involvement (Vagliasindi and Nellis 2009). At the country level, each subindex is expressed as a percentage of positive responses to the binary questions to the total number of indicators. The urban reform index is an average of these four subindexes; each subindex carries the same weighting.

Most African countries have undertaken at least one key reform step. One way to establish a transparent framework for service provision is to outline a water policy that includes the government's sector goals and institutional commitments. In most countries, governments have recently begun the reform process; only eight countries have sector legislation more than five years old. Côte d'Ivoire passed a water law in 1973, but most countries implemented water legislation only in the past decade. As of 2005, all but five countries have established water policies, and two of those countries are in the process of drafting water policies.

The most common reform steps are corporatization and the passing of a private sector participation law. However, the passing of a law does not

Table 4.1 Urban Reform, Regulation, and the SOE Governance Index

Reform	*Internal governance*
Legislation	**Ownership and shareholder quality**
Existence of de jure reform	Concentration of ownership
Implementation of reform	Corporatization/limited liability
Restructuring	Rate of return and dividend policy
Unbundling/separation of business lines	**Managerial and board autonomy**
SOE corporatization	Autonomy in hiring/firing/wages/production/sales
Existence of regulatory body	Size of the board
Policy oversight	Presence of independence directors
Oversight of regulation monitoring outside the ministry	**Accounting, disclosure, and performance** monitoring
Dispute arbitration outside the ministry	Publication of annual report
Tariff approval outside the ministry	International Financial Reporting Standards/external audits/independent audit
Investment plan outside the ministry	Audit publication
Technical standard outside the ministry	Remuneration of noncommercial activity
Private sector involvement	Performance contracts/with incentives
Private de jure/de facto	Penalties for poor performance
Private sector management/investment ownership	Monitoring/third party monitoring
Absence of distressed/renegotiation/renationalization	External governance
Regulation	**Labor market discipline**
Autonomy	Restriction to dismiss employees
Formal autonomy on hiring/firing	Wages compared with private sector
Financial autonomy (partial/full)	Benefits compared with private sector
Managerial autonomy (partial/full)	**Capital market discipline**
Multisectoral agency/commissioners	No exemption from taxation
Transparency	Access to debt compared with private sector
Publication of decisions via report/Internet/public hearing	No state guarantees
Accountability	Public listing
Existence of appeal	**Outsourcing**
Independence of appeal (partial/full)	Billing and collection
Tools	Meter reading
Existence of tariff methodology/tariff indexation	Human resources
Existence of regulatory review	Information technology
Length of regulatory review	

Source: Vagliasindi and Nellis 2009.
Note: SOE = state-owned enterprise.

guarantee private sector participation. Although 83 percent of countries have legalized private participation, only 63 percent have been able to attract some kind of private participation in any of the three largest utilities in their respective countries. Private providers have entered into management contracts in only half of the countries and have invested in water sectors in only 5 percent of cases. Leases have been used widely, and management contracts are the second most common form of private participation.

The cancelation rate of private sector contracts for water supply has been much higher in countries in Africa than in other developing countries. Approximately 29 percent of private contracts for water supply have been prematurely terminated. As a result, just a handful of private operators are still active: one each in Cameroon, Cape Verde, Côte d'Ivoire, Gabon, Ghana, Mozambique, Niger, and Senegal, and four in South Africa.

The private sector is disproportionately more involved in the West African francophone countries (Côte d'Ivoire, Guinea, Niger, and Senegal), with some exceptions (Mozambique and Uganda). Senegal's successful private sector experience is presented in box 4.1. Another distinctive feature of the African experience has been the use of concessions for joint power and water utilities, as in Gabon and Mali. Only a single divestiture has occurred: the 1999 sale of 51 percent of equity in the water company in Cape Verde.

Policy oversight is relatively well defined in Africa. In at least half of the countries studied, functions such as tariff approval, investment plans, technical standards, regulation monitoring, and dispute arbitration are clearly allocated to bodies other than the line ministries, such as special entities within the ministries, interministerial committees, or regulators. Oversight of economic regulation and tariff setting by bodies other than the line ministries exists in 78 and 65 percent of the countries, respectively.

Progress in restructuring has been relatively slow. Only five countries—Burkina Faso, Namibia, Niger, South Africa, and Uganda—have separated bulk-water production from the distribution function. In the other countries, the functions are performed in tandem, by the same utility. Niger has made the most progress and reports a score of more than 80 percent on the restructuring subindex. In 2000, the water company Société Nationale des Eaux (SNE) in Niger was separated into the asset-holding company, Société de Patrimoine des Eaux du Niger (SPEN), and a private operator, Société de Exploitation des Eaux du Niger (SEEN), responsible for production, transmission, and distribution in the urban areas (World Bank 2007).

Box 4.1

Senegal's Successful Experience with Private Sector Participation

The Senegal experience under the *affermage* is characterized by two remarkable results: first, an impressive expansion of access, and second, a large increase in operational efficiency that mainly originated from a reduction of nonrevenue water (NRW).

The first result was mainly related to a massive subsidized connection program sponsored by donors and, in part, to the cash-flow surplus generated by the private operators. In particular, the social connection program, implemented with donor support, provided about 129,000 connections (75 percent of all new connections installed) benefiting poor households living in targeted neighborhoods. A portion of the new connections, however, ended up disconnected, despite tariffs declining in real terms up to 2006 and the social tariff corresponding to a consumption of six cubic meters per month—mostly applying to poor households.

The second result was strictly related to contract innovations geared toward increasing the operator's incentives to perform efficiently. In particular, the contract included targets for NRW reduction and bill collection backed by financial penalties for noncompliance. These targets were then applied to a notional sales volume based on the amount of water actually produced, which was used to determine the operator's remuneration in lieu of the actual water sold. Whenever the operator fell short of the NRW and bill collection targets, the notional sales volume would be lower than the actual sales, penalizing the operator.

Another innovation in Senegal's public-private partnership was the responsibility of the private operator to finance part of the network's rehabilitation using cash flow. This approach provided the operator with more flexibility to identify and reduce water losses, lessening its dependency on the public asset-holding company.

The impact of these innovations on efficiency has been remarkable, making Senegal's *affermage* a prominent example of private participation in Africa. Today, Senegal can report a level of NRW comparable to the best water utilities in Western Europe. These results also confirm that operational efficiency is perhaps the area in which a private operator can make the most positive and consistent impact.

Source: Adapted from Marin 2009.

Most countries have achieved 40 to 80 percent in the urban reform index. A majority of countries score well on certain subcomponents, but not on others. For instance, Benin scores very high on legislation and policy oversight but very low on restructuring and private sector involvement, whereas Rwanda scores high on restructuring and private sector involvement but low on policy oversight and legislation. Côte d'Ivoire, Kenya, Mozambique, Sudan, Tanzania, and Uganda scored more than 50 percent in each of the subindex scores, suggesting a balanced approach to the reform process (figure 4.2).

Two Distinct Approaches to Sector Regulation

The regulation index is created using four essential attributes of what is conventionally considered a good regulatory framework: autonomy, accountability, transparency, and tools (Vagliasindi and Nellis 2009). The index is an average of these four subindexes and presents a picture of the maturity and depth of the regulatory framework.

Anglophone and francophone countries have taken two distinct approaches to sector regulation. About half of the countries (mainly anglophone) have established regulatory agencies for the water sector, although a significant number of these do not have private sector participation. Conversely, several francophone countries with private participation have adopted regulatory frameworks without establishing an independent regulatory agency. These approaches appear to be equally effective; in both cases, the established regulatory frameworks typically meet only about half of the corresponding good practice criteria.

Line ministries (or subentities), such as ministries of finance/economy and health/environment, continue to play a strong role in the regulation of water services. Parliaments, state water corporations, or asset-holding companies also help to set tariffs or approve investment plans (table 4.2). In some cases, the allocation of regulatory responsibilities is efficient. For instance, monitoring water quality requires different skill sets than those needed to review tariff adjustment proposals. In other cases, the fragmentation might create inefficiencies in the sector and a lack of depth in regulatory capacity. The regulatory entities also have a designated responsibility for monitoring and enforcing the license/charter provisions as well as setting customer service regulations. The gaps in water regulation fall more within the area of customer service and quality standards.

Half of the countries studied have set up regulatory agencies to govern the sector and bring it in the purview of formal rules on tariff and service standards. In the 11 countries with distinct economic regulatory bodies,

Figure 4.2 Country Ranking and Prevalence of Key Reform Activities

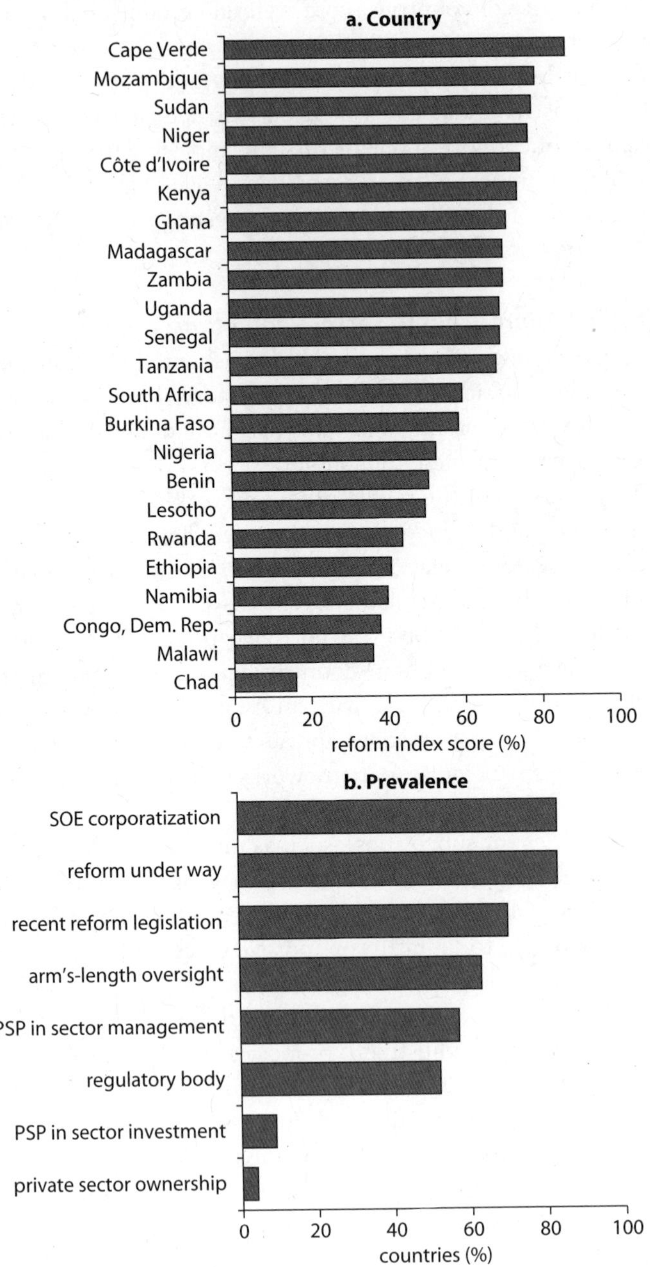

Source: Banerjee, Skilling, and others 2008a.
Note: PSP = private sector participation.

Table 4.2 Regulatory Roles in the Urban Water Sector
(percent)

Role	*Line ministry*	*Entity within ministry*	*Regulatory body*	*Interministerial committee*	*Other*	*Unregulated or nobody*
Granting licenses and/or assigning service obligations	57	22	13	9	0	0
Approving investment plans	52	13	13	4	17	0
Establishing technical standards and minimum service levels	40	24	20	8	4	4
Arbitrating in a dispute	36	12	20	12	16	4
Approving tariffs	35	13	22	0	30	0
Setting water quality standards	27	18	23	9	18	5
Monitoring and enforcing compliance with economic rregulation	26	17	30	9	13	4
Providing customer service regulations	26	13	26	9	17	9
Monitoring water quality	26	22	13	9	26	4
Proposing/advising on tariffs	13	25	13	17	33	0

Source: Banerjee, Skilling, and others 2008a.
Note: Rows may not add to 100 because roles may be performed by more than one institution.

10 were created between 1995 and 2003 (figure 4.3). In Côte d'Ivoire, the regulatory agency, Direction de l'Hydrolique was set up in 1973–74. Of the 11 stand-alone regulators, five have jurisdiction over multiple sectors, and the rest are responsible for only WSS activities. The nascent regulators face the challenge of establishing a track record of sound decision making and acquiring competent staff.

Most countries are adequately equipped with regulatory tools. Regulatory institutions in a majority of African countries appear to have established a tariff methodology to conduct periodic reviews. Madagascar is the only country that does not have an established set of regulatory tools to manage tariffs. The tariffs in Sub-Saharan Africa are largely regulated—to the degree that proposals are made and approved. It is sometimes unclear how tariff increases are determined and why they are increased. Most countries use the price cap methodology of adjusting tariffs as opposed to other forms, but some countries raised tariffs based on "reasonableness" or to reflect actual costs. Although some countries perform periodic tariff adjustments, few index tariffs on an annual basis. In the 12 countries with periodic tariff reviews, the time between reviews ranges from one to five years. The annual periodic reviews might, in fact, be more comparable to annual indexation.

The regulatory agencies are likely to be headed by boards. Only in Côte d'Ivoire and Lesotho are regulators headed by individuals. In all countries, except for Mozambique and Rwanda, the president or the line minister has the authority to appoint the head or commissioner of the regulatory agencies. Clearly, the president and the line ministry play strong roles in the governance of the regulator, and the judicial and legislative branches of government play more limited roles. The term limits

Figure 4.3 Year of Establishment of Regulatory Agencies

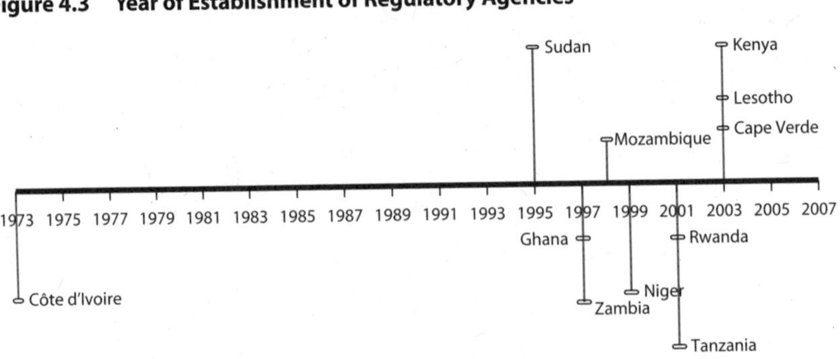

Source: Banerjee, Skilling, and others 2008a.

for the head or commissioner vary between three and six years, with an average of 3.3 years. The heads of these institutions can be reappointed, except in Niger, where they serve a single term.

Some regulatory agencies have achieved partial financial autonomy. The agencies are most commonly funded by sector levies or license fees, or by the central government. Cape Verde, Mozambique, Niger, and Rwanda use sector levies or license fees to fund the regulatory agencies. Côte d'Ivoire and Lesotho rely completely on the central government for funding, whereas donors play a substantial role in funding the regulators in Ghana, Tanzania, and, to a lesser extent, Sudan (figure 4.4).

Almost all countries use a standardized format to compile regulatory reports. Regulatory entities are less likely, however, to share their findings and decisions with the general public. In some cases, there is no mechanism to share decisions, but when decisions are made public, this usually occurs in the form of published reports (as in 81 percent of the countries studied). Public hearings are infrequent and held in only 50 percent of the countries. Similarly, hearings are rarely published on the Internet.

Consumer participation in the regulatory process is relatively limited. Where consumers have a role in the actual regulatory process, they are most often part of the appeals process rather than reviewers of regulatory proposals or board representatives. A social accountability index including four indicators[1] represents consumer influence in the regulatory process. Burkina Faso, Ghana, Malawi, Tanzania, and Zambia have the most socially accountable regulatory framework. In these countries, consumer

Figure 4.4 Understanding Performance in Regulatory Autonomy

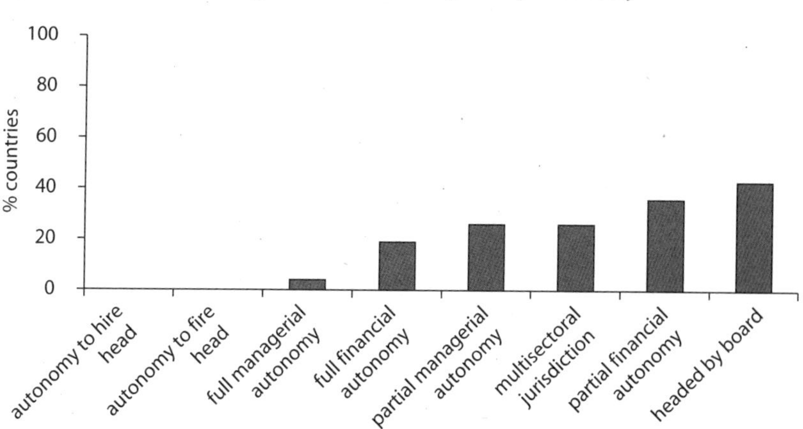

Source: Banerjee, Skilling, and others 2008a.

representation exists in the regulatory body; consumers have the right to comment on draft regulations, review tariff proposals, and appeal regulatory decisions. Consumer representation is even less frequent within the regulatory body itself. Only in Burkina Faso, Ghana, Namibia, Tanzania, and Zambia do consumers have representation within the regulatory agency (figure 4.5).

Only Cape Verde, Kenya, Niger, Senegal, Tanzania, and Uganda have scored higher than 60 percent on the regulation index. A majority of countries have poor regulatory independence across all sectors, demonstrating that the standard model has limited relevance in Africa. Regulatory attributes can be identified that very few countries have adopted, such as formal autonomy to hire and fire, full managerial autonomy, and full independence to appeal. The countries have neither the authority to hire or fire head commissioners, nor do they allow full independence to appeal regulatory decisions (figure 4.6).

Water Utilities: Halfway toward Good Practice Criteria for Enterprise Governance

The SOE governance index is used to determine whether SOEs are being governed using sufficiently commercial principles. Several aspects of SOE management are examined, including ownership and shareholder quality; managerial and board autonomy; accounting, disclosure, and performance monitoring; outsourcing; labor market discipline; and capital market discipline. Using this scoring system, we can see which utilities in Sub-Saharan Africa have adopted policies of good governance and commercial orientation.

The goal in governance reforms has been to move toward corporatization of SOEs, decentralize responsibilities to lower levels of government, and improve the governance of SOEs by adopting modern management methods. In 83 percent of the countries, at least one water utility has been corporatized, thereby laying the foundation for more commercial management. Close to half of the countries sampled have decentralized their water utilities over the past decade, thereby making local communities more responsible for utility management. Lesotho and Zambia began their decentralization processes in the early 1990s, and the rest of the countries decentralized in the past decade. All of the francophone countries studied still have centralized water utilities.[2]

About 52 percent of the sample utilities are corporatized entities, meaning that the public sector service provider functions as a private

Figure 4.5 Prevalence and Key Attributes of the Social Accountability Index

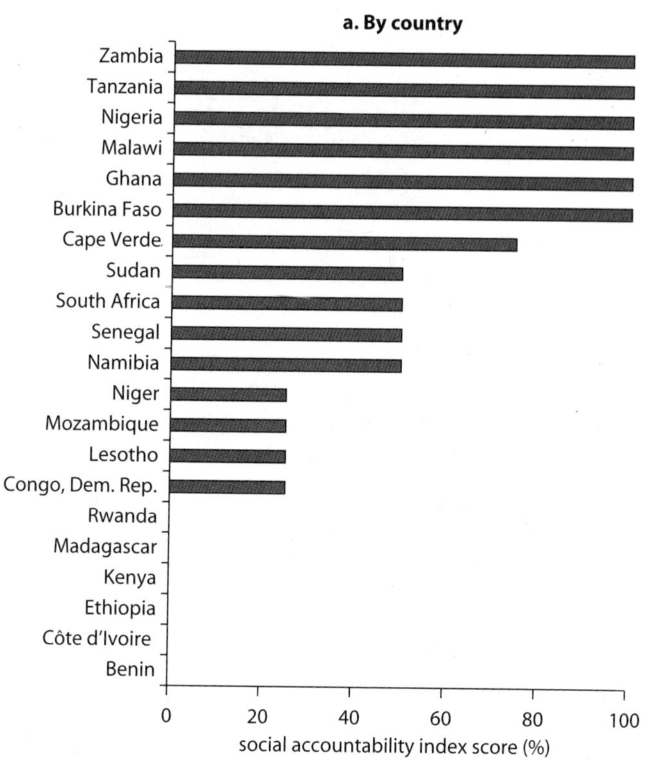

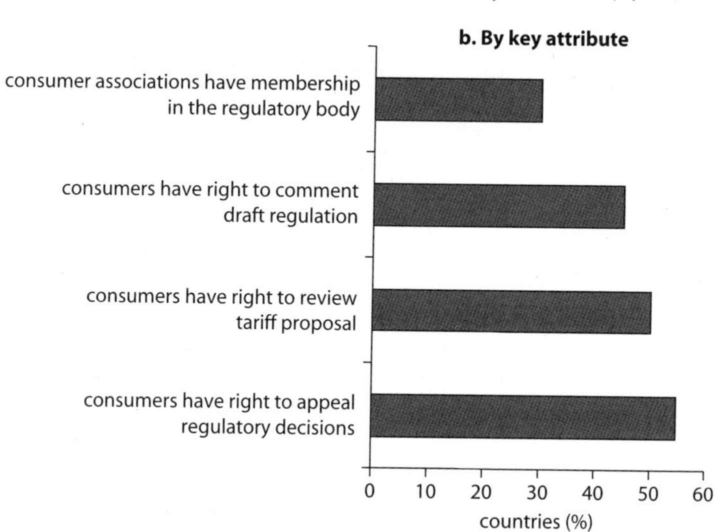

Source: Banerjee, Skilling, and others 2008a.

Figure 4.6 Country Ranking and Prevalence of Key Attributes of Regulation

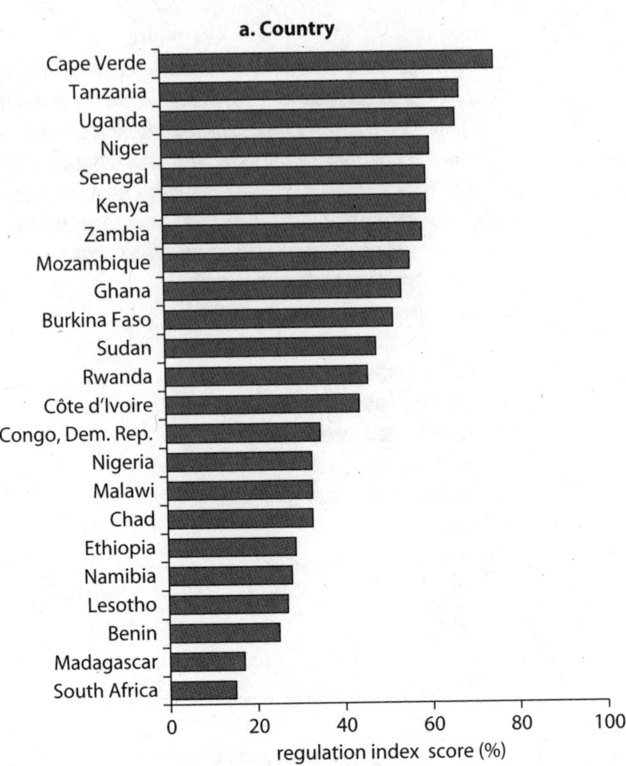

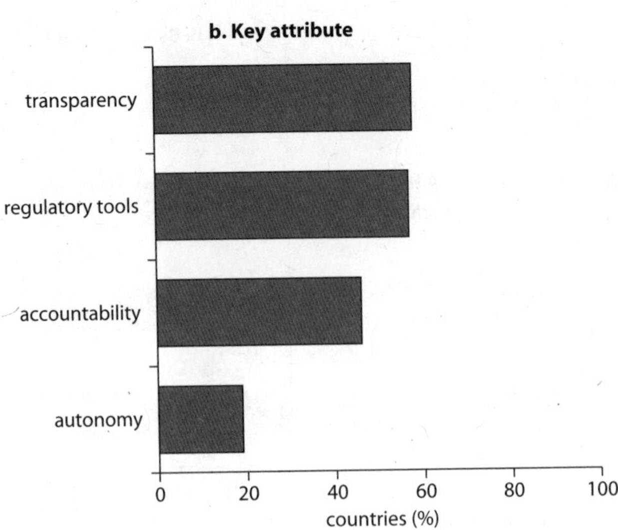

Source: Banerjee, Skilling, and others 2008a.

company in terms of efficiency, productivity, and financial sustainability (figure 4.7, panel a). The public sector provider does this through implementing some or all of a series of changes, including establishment of a distinct legal identity; segregation of the company's assets, finances, and operations from other government operations; and development of a commercial orientation and managerial independence, while remaining accountable to the government or electorate. Although other utilities are not corporatized, they could be better governed through the adoption of some or all of these corporate practices. The heart of corporate governance is to protect and enhance the long-term value of the company for shareholders (government and other) by increasing sales, controlling costs, and increasing revenue.

Nearly half of the African water utilities are SOEs, the majority owned by the central government; others are owned at the state or municipal level. Together, 92 percent are state owned, with ownership varying at different levels of government (figure 4.7, panel b). In a few countries, such as Kenya, Namibia, South Africa, and Zambia, where water service delivery has been decentralized to the local level, utilities are majority owned by municipalities. Namibia still provides service through municipal

Figure 4.7 Legal Status and Ownership Structure of Water Utilities

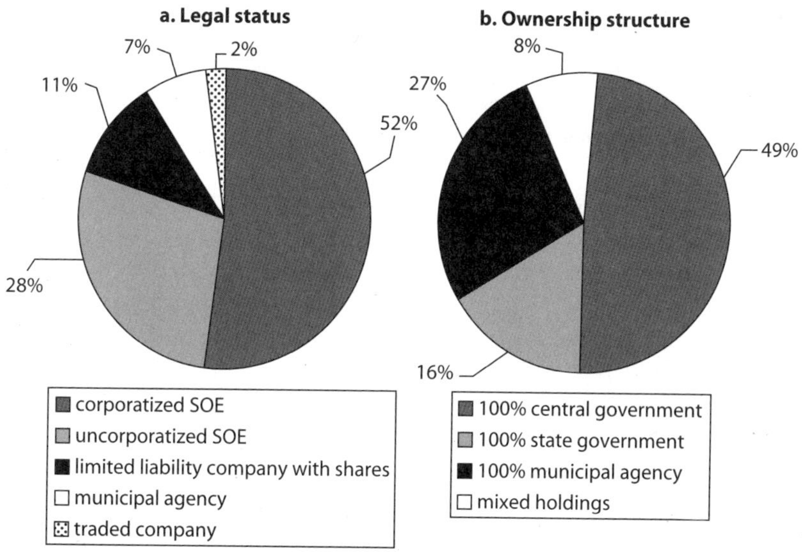

a. Legal status

Legal status	Share
corporatized SOE	52%
uncorporatized SOE	28%
limited liability company with shares	11%
municipal agency	7%
traded company	2%

b. Ownership structure

100% central government	49%
100% state government	16%
100% municipal agency	27%
mixed holdings	8%

Source: Banerjee, Skilling, and others 2008a.
Note: SOE = state-owned enterprise.

departments, and only the utilities engaged in active public private partnerships, as in Cape Verde, Côte d'Ivoire, Niger, and Senegal, have diversified shareholding.

The use of external financial and independent audits is common. Similarly, the management or board determines wages and bonuses in the majority of entities. Utilities perform poorly on indicators such as public listings, outsourcing functions, and dividend payments. Société de Distribution d'Eau de Côte d'Ivoire (SODECI) in Côte d'Ivoire is the only water utility that is listed on a stock exchange; its shares are publicly traded. Similarly, only 27 percent of the utilities are required to pay dividends to their shareholders.

About 84 percent of the entities have boards of directors, though few are well represented or benefit from the presence of independent directors. Only half the entities have a board with more than five members, and only 40 percent of the entities—notably in Kenya, Tanzania, Uganda, and Zambia—have at least one independent director on the board. Sixty percent have government-appointed boards (figure 4.8). Obviously, the owners' interests are well represented on the boards, and the managerial decision-making process is heavily influenced by politics. Only Société de Exploitation des Eaux du Niger (SEEN), in Niger, has a representative board appointed by shareholders, with independent directors. For instance, in the National Water and Sewerage Company (NWSC) in Uganda, the Ministry of Water, Lands, and Environment appoints the board of directors; in the Office Nationale des Eaux et d'Assainissement

Figure 4.8 Performance in Managerial Autonomy

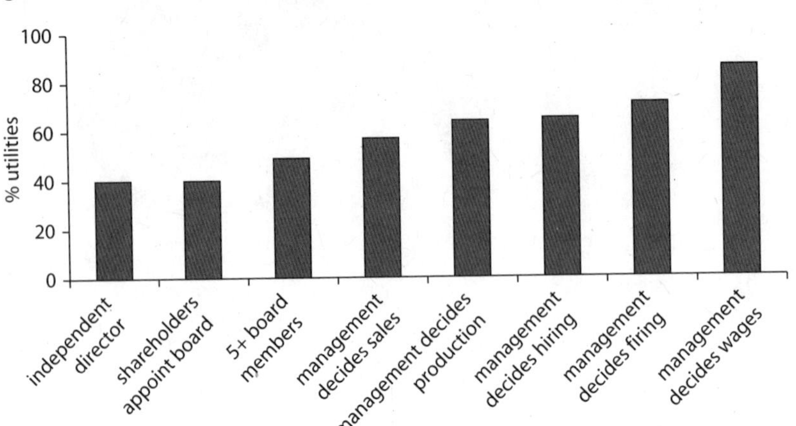

Source: Banerjee, Skilling, and others 2008a.

(ONEA), the board is appointed by the Council of Ministers (Baietti, Kingdom, and Van Ginneken 2006).

Half of the entities have performance contracts with defined and monitorable targets. Management through such contracts takes a systematic approach to performance improvement through an "ongoing process of establishing strategic performance objectives; measuring performance; collecting, analyzing, reviewing, and reporting performance data; and using that data to drive performance improvement" (PA Consulting 2007). All entities in South Africa, Tanzania, Uganda, and Zambia use these contracts. The NWSC uses annual and multiyear performance contracts (Baietti, Kingdom, and Van Ginneken 2006). Sixty-five percent of the firms use third-party monitoring, which demonstrates a commitment to enhancing external accountability for results. The extent to which these performance contracts are implemented depends on how the internal incentive mechanisms are established. More than half of the utilities have performance-based management systems, and 39 percent penalize for poor performance. In about 57 percent of the utilities, staff members are given periodic performance reviews (figure 4.9).

Outsourcing is relatively new and still not widespread. It allows an entity to focus on its core business and potentially lower costs. Utilities in Mozambique and Khartoum, Sudan, are the only utilities that report outsourcing billing and collection, meter reading, human resources, and information technology. In fact, 88 percent of the utilities score less than 40 percent on the outsourcing subindex. Outsourcing operating expenses can be quite expensive. For instance, outsourcing as a share of operating

Figure 4.9 Performance Monitoring

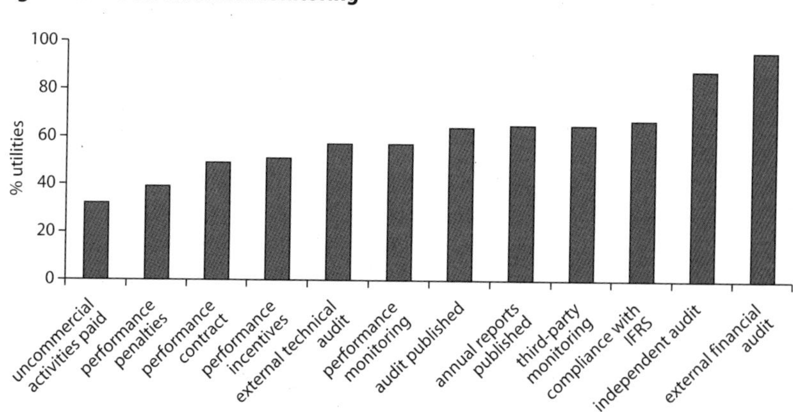

Source: Banerjee, Skilling, and others 2008a.
Note: IFRS = International Financial Reporting Standards.

expenses of the NWSC in Uganda is in the range of 30 to 40 percent (Baietti, Kingdom, and Van Ginneken 2006).

SODECI scores the highest on capital market discipline, which relates to the commercial nature of the utility. Águas de Moçambique (ADeM) in Maputo, SEEN in Niger, FCT in Nigeria, ELECTROGAZ in Rwanda, the South African utilities, and Lusaka Water and Sewerage Company (LWSC) in Zambia also score high on capital market discipline. About 25 percent of the utilities in Africa adhere to the highest levels of labor market discipline, which relates to the ability to hire and fire workers and to set wages and benefits with regard to the private sector.

A majority of the entities score between 40 and 80 percent on the SOE governance index. Africa's state-owned water utilities typically meet only about half the good practice criteria for enterprise governance. Firms do well on "capital market discipline" and "accounting, disclosure, and performance monitoring" subindexes, with more than 60 percent of the utilities scoring between 40 and 60 percent in each subindex. African water utilities rarely outsource. Most are a long way from achieving managerial and board autonomy; less than one-fourth score more than 80 percent on this subindex. Interestingly, the correlation between the SOE governance index and the earlier reform and regulation index is very low, which is to say that some countries do much better on SOE governance than on reform and regulation, and vice versa.

Countries have made more serious efforts to improve internal processes and corporate governance mechanisms during the past decade than in other infrastructure sectors. A growing number of utilities in countries such as Lesotho, Uganda, and Zambia are using performance contracts, though some do not incorporate the penalties, performance-based remuneration, and third-party monitoring that makes these mechanisms truly effective. The Mozambican and Zambian utilities have the highest scoring internal governance structures when it comes to meeting the needs of their consumers, regulators, governments, and other stakeholders. The LWSC in Zambia is the best-governed utility in Africa according to the criteria developed in this chapter, scoring 73 percent. Johannesburg, SEEN, and Sénégalaise des Eaux (SDE) have also made substantial progress in governance reforms (figure 4.10).

In summary, many African countries have initiated water sector reforms, and two major thrusts to this reform agenda have been seen: private participation and improvement of internal governance. Some countries, such as Burkina Faso, Kenya, Mozambique, Niger, Senegal, Tanzania, Uganda, and Zambia, are remarkable performers that have progressed at

Figure 4.10 Country Ranking and Prevalence of Key Attributes of the SOE Governance

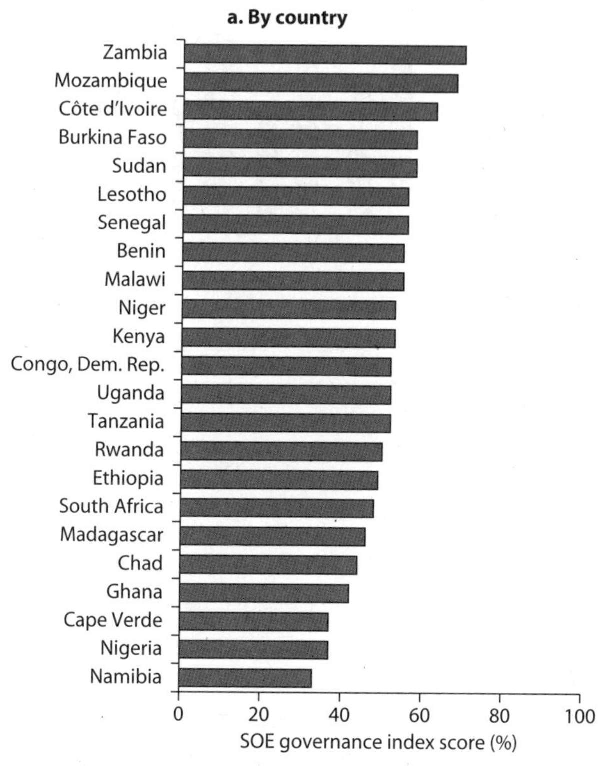

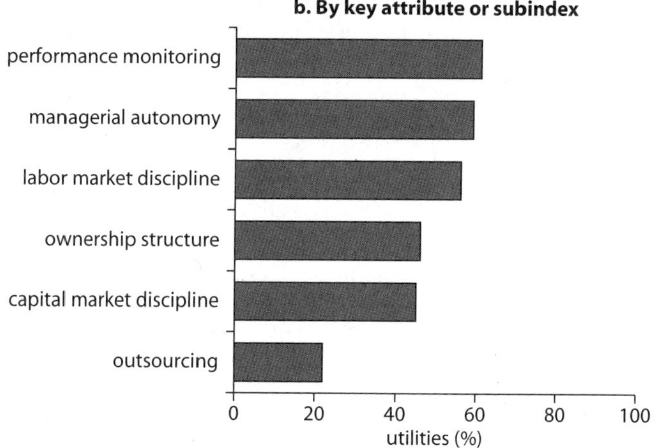

Source: Banerjee, Skilling, and others 2008a.
Note: SOE = state-owned enterprise.

Figure 4.11 Solid Country Performances

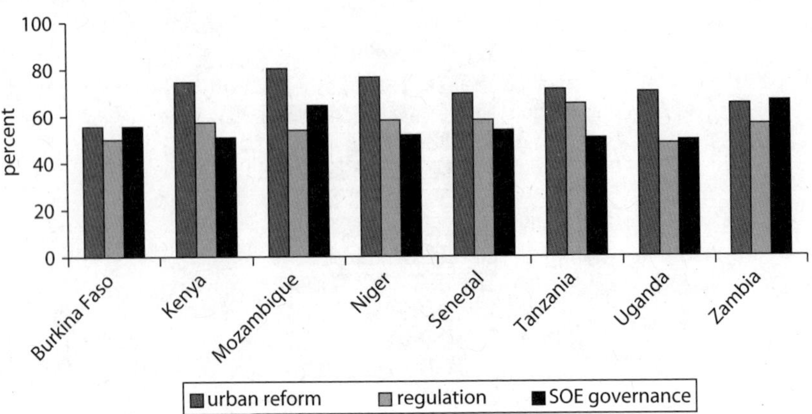

Source: Banerjee, Skilling, and others 2008a.
Note: SOE = state-owned enterprise.

a steady pace in different areas of urban sector reform (figure 4.11). These countries have developed a formal regulatory structure, a market-oriented and accountable internal governance mechanism, and wide-ranging urban sector reforms.

Varied Institutional Models for Nonpiped Services in the Urban Water Market

Because utilities and standpost operators do not keep track of the different types of customers they serve, raw coverage numbers conceal essential parts of the urban water picture. Breaking down consumers by type is very important, for example, when it comes to understanding the price structure of the market, because the standpost operator usually charges the direct consumer and the reseller differently. In periurban areas of Accra, although most water is sold through standposts, 20 percent is resold by cart operators (Sarpong and Ambrampah 2006). Likewise, standpost operators in Khartoum sell most of their water (80 percent) to cart operators, who then resell to households (Elamin and Gadir 2006). Similarly, in Ouagadougou, more than 80 percent of water sold at standposts is bought by cart operators and not by individuals (Collignon and Vézina 2000). In Luanda, Angola, most of the water delivered in periurban areas, where the majority of the population lives, is carried by water trucks that sell water obtained either from the piped-water system or directly from the main river. The water trucks sell to an estimated 10,000 nonmobile water vendors and households that have built water storage tanks; these households in turn sell water to the rest of the population. In periurban areas of Luanda, 70 percent of residents purchase their water from water vendors (Development Workshop 1995).

People in urban areas who do not have access to piped water get their water from a number of different sources. There are "formal" sources, such as standposts and boreholes, as well as an emergence of "informal" sources, such as water vendors and tankers, resellers, and small piped systems. The quality of the water from these suppliers is not monitored in the same way as piped water.

Public standpipes can be managed by a number of different parties that retain responsibility for payment, supervision, and maintenance. Two main systems are found: one in which the utility retains control, and the other, in which the utility delegates various functions to third parties and serves primarily as a bulk water supplier.[3] In a little more than one-quarter of the 24 largest cities studied in the module for small-scale independent providers of the AICD WSS survey, utility staff manages standpipes using one of three management models (free, prepayment, or managed by a paid utility staff member). In almost three-quarters of the cases, utilities had a contract with a third party (whether a private individual or a community organization), a support institution (local government, community-based organization [CBO], or nongovernmental organization [NGO]) to manage the standpipe (table 4.3).[4]

Direct Management by Utilities. In the past three decades, a shift has occurred so that standpipes that were once owned and provided to the population free of charge by utilities are now run by either private individuals or community groups (figure 4.12). The data indicate that many utilities viewed the free standpipes as a financial drain. As a result, only five of the sample cities still had free standpipes. With the exception of Madagascar, where less than half of the standpipes provide free water, free public standpipes in countries including Namibia, Lesotho, Nigeria, and South Africa were mostly concentrated within larger piped systems or in cities with sufficient levels of piped coverage to help subsidize the costs. Other cities, except for Kaduna, Nigeria, are moving toward paid standpipes or kiosks; Johannesburg, Maseru, and Windhoek are installing prepaid standpipes, and Antananarivo is installing kiosks.

The second model, in which the utility hires a salaried attendant, is an increasingly uncommon practice that is still used in a few countries. This

Table 4.3 Standpipe Management
(percent)

Ownership	*Country*	*City*	*free of charge*	*Management (by)*		
				Private	*Utility*	*Community*[a]
Utility	Cape Verde	Praia	0	0	100	0
	Lesotho	Maseru	100	0	97	3
	Madagascar	Antananarivo	40	60	0	40
	Namibia	Windhoek	100	0	100	0
	Nigeria	Kaduna	96	4	96	0
	South Africa	Johannesburg	100	0	100	0
	Sudan	Greater Khartoum	0	0	100	0
	Zambia	Lusaka	0	5	90	5
Private	Benin	Cotonou	0	100	0	0
	Burkina Faso	Ouagadougou	0	100	0	0
	Niger	Niamey	0	100	0	0
	Kenya	Nairobi	0	88	0	12
	Rwanda	Kigali	0	100	0	0
	Senegal	Dakar	0	85	0	15
Community	Ethiopia	Addis Ababa	0	0	0	100
	Malawi	Blantyre	0	—	—	70
	Mozambique	Maputo	0	44	0	56

Source: Keener, Luengo, and Banerjee 2009.
Note: — = not available.
a. In the community category, we merge the delegated management model with direct contracting with a community group and the delegated management model with institution support as discussed later in this section.

Figure 4.12 Utility Direct Management Models

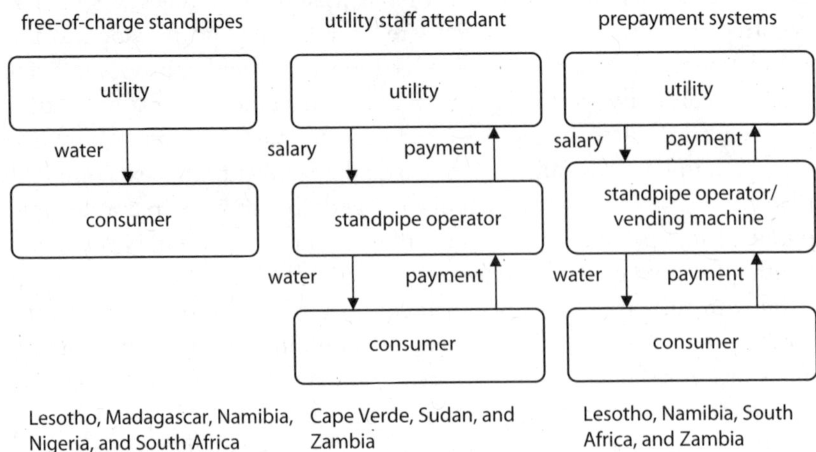

Source: Keener, Luengo, and Banerjee 2009.

model has been rejected in some countries because, typically, limited incentive exists for a wage-earning employee to ensure cost recovery. In Zambia, the utility has tried to improve this model by introducing water commissions.

A newer model, in which customers can pay for water at standpipes using electronic systems, is being introduced to reduce management costs and problems with nonpayment and to potentially provide more targeted subsidies as payment tokens can be distributed via existing systems. South Africa currently uses this model, and electronic prepayment cards and vending machines are also being introduced in Lesotho and Namibia. In Zambia, customers use tokens or monthly cards instead of vending machines. These systems allow for tariffs to be set at a unit rate that is lower than the smallest coin (Brocklehurst and Janssens 2004; Kariuki and others 2003) and may allow for lower prices, because they eliminate the middleman. In Lesotho, the water utility and retail outlets sell prepaid cards. In some instances, however, independent "operators" sell tokens, at a higher price, at the standpipes. Although this is more convenient for customers, it is important to have formal outlets to maintain set prices.

Delegated Management Model. In the increasingly common delegation model for public standpipes, utilities either sign a contract directly with a standpipe operator, who pays the standpipe bill (and in some cases maintains the standpipe), or sign a contract with a support institution. In the support institution model, local officials or members of a water committee then supervise operators. Under this system, the institution pays the utility for each standpipe, based on a bulk water price. Community groups or local officials typically select the standpipe operators, and the process is generally far from transparent and often influenced by local politics (figure 4.13).

Over the medium term, the delegation model has not always provided reliable service with timely bill payment to the utility and has been largely ineffective in providing a subsidized or "social" price to the end consumer. The most successful delegation models have been those that are heavily monitored by the utility, or another external body, which in turn has increased costs. Conversely, when utilities delegate most of their critical functions such as management, monitoring, maintenance, and oversight, this can result in higher consumer prices and more frequent breakdowns in service. There are exceptions, particularly in areas with high social capital.

Figure 4.13 Delegated Management Models

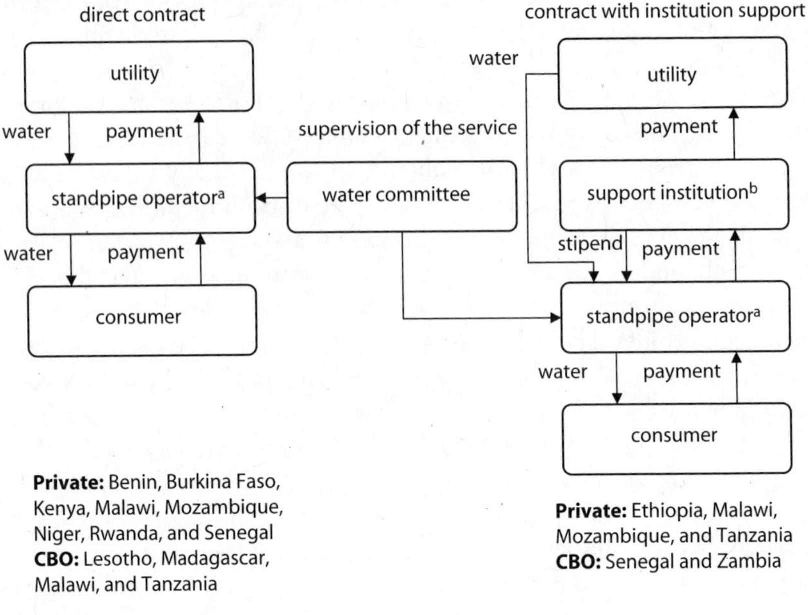

Source: Keener, Luengo, and Banerjee 2009.
Note: CBO = community-based organization.
a. Standpipe operator can be a private individual or a CBO.
b. Support institution: Local leaders, local authority administrators, or NGOs.

Community-Based Management (Local Leaders, Local Authority Administrators, NGOs, and CBOs). Community management works only where there is a true sense of community, and where there is personal security and accepted methods for dealing with those who do not follow regulations. Unlike rural areas, urban neighborhoods share a greater degree of heterogeneity.

Local leaders and community organizations play various roles in standpipe management and oversight; in some cases (in parts of Addis Ababa, Blantyre, Dar es Salaam, and Maputo), utilities have put local leaders in charge of operations and maintenance, with the assumption that these leaders will act in their constituents' best interest. In these cases, the performance of the standpost, in terms of pricing, maintenance, timely bill payment, and so forth, is largely dependent on the management skills and legitimacy of the local leader and the degree of oversight by an external party.

Several schemes have put community organizations in charge of management or oversight in an effort to make standpipe/kiosk operators more accountable to their customers. These projects have been somewhat more effective than schemes that simply delegate management to a local leader. This practice is still very limited in the urban and periurban areas of Sub-Saharan countries, and in places where there is not enough social cohesion or strong local power structures and no oversight from a supporting institution, the model can also lead to corruption and mismanagement. In Blantyre and Lilongwe, for instance, community-managed kiosks that had been developed with extensive community involvement were taken over by local elites as soon as the mediating NGO left.

The effectiveness of schemes involving community organizations varies and depends on the community's social cohesion and management capacity, as well as external monitoring. A Water and Sanitation Program report on the role of small- and medium-size organizations providing water in urban areas (Vézina 2002) stressed the limitations of community-based management models that lacked external monitoring and support: there is a tendency to minimize expenses by limiting the extension of the system, and although in principle these organizations are based on the voluntary participation of community members, to reduce operating and maintenance costs, actual management is often controlled by a small group that may monopolize control of the finances. With such arrangements, elite capture remains a problem that requires strong institutional controls and active monitoring.

Some more recent models for community involvement use sophisticated incentives and monitoring to mitigate corruption. In Blantyre, Malawi, the water users association controls as many as 70 water points each. The utility provides technical assistance, legally registers the association, and monitors operation of the standpost. The association employs both the kiosk attendants and meter inspectors. The latter check the meter readings; if there is a difference between the inspector's meter reading and the amount of revenue collected, it is subtracted from the attendant's salary. Although the price of this water is 25 percent higher than at other kiosks, residents prefer to use these kiosks because the quality of service is monitored and reliable. (This is not necessarily the case with other neighborhood kiosks.) In Dakar, Senegal, about 15 percent of the public standposts have been built via a partnership between the utility and an NGO, ENDA Tiers Monde. ENDA partners with communities and local neighborhood associations (for example, women's groups and self-help groups); the community groups pay 25 percent of the capital costs of a standpipe, which is then built by the utility. The community also selects a standpost operator who collects revenue for the utility, and ENDA helps to create a local water council.

Private Management. Although utilities contract out the operation of standpipes to private managers on the premise that this will promote efficiency and cost recovery, the results are not always positive. Many utilities in Sub-Saharan cities such as Blantyre, Cotonou, Dakar, Kigali, Nairobi, Niamey, Ouagadougou, and Quelimane have leased their installations and sold bulk water to private operators. The model has two particular weaknesses: (1) The selection process of standpipe operators, particularly when the municipality is involved, is rarely transparent, and (2) because a private manager is running the standpipe, the water utility is less involved in collecting water revenue, ensuring good quality service, and maintaining adequate tariff levels. The price and hours of operation are also crucial to the success of this model: In the 1990s in Quelimane, Mozambique, private standpipe operators were billed according to fixed estimates of water consumption, but the water supply was extremely limited and intermittent. Certain standpipe operators found it difficult to generate enough water revenue to pay back the water bill and did not have funds to adequately maintain the standpipes (SAWA 1997).

Household Resellers

Reselling of water by households with private connections is commonly believed to be illegal in Sub-Saharan cities (Boyer 2006; Collignon and Vézina 2000; Kariuki and others 2003), but only 4 out of 15 cities in the study with prevalence of household water resellers explicitly prohibit the resale of water by households (table 4.4). Only three cities have legalized household resale and require a permit for this business. Box 4.2 presents a case study of regulated water reselling in Abidjan. In the majority of cases, a confusing legal limbo prevails; household water resellers are neither prohibited nor legalized. Even if regulations are in place prohibiting household water resellers, they are not enforced, as in Dakar or Dar es Salaam. Utilities and government simply do not control and rarely contest this practice, and in the case of Kampala, the practice is encouraged in areas at the end of the network. Detailed case studies that highlight the importance of this source in allowing access where standposts or individual connections have not kept pace point to the serious impact that prohibition of this source would have on poor urban households.

Table 4.4 Regulation of Household Water Resellers

Country	*City*	*Prohibited*	*License*
Benin	Cotonou	No	No
Chad	N'Djamena	No	—
Congo, Dem. Rep.	Kinshasa	No	No
Côte d'Ivoire	Abidjan	No	Yes
Ethiopia	Addis Ababa	No	No
Ghana	Accra	No	No
Lesotho	Maseru	—	—
Madagascar	Antananarivo	No	No
Malawi	Blantyre	—	—
Mozambique	Maputo	No	No
Nigeria	Kaduna	Yes	n.a.
Rwanda	Kigali	No	Yes
Senegal	Dakar	Yes	Yes
Sudan	Greater Khartoum	Yes	No
Tanzania	Dar es Salaam	Yes	No
Uganda	Kampala	No	No
Zambia	Lusaka	No	No
	% yes	24	18

Source: Keener, Luengo, and Banerjee 2009.
Note: n.a. = not applicable, — = not available.

Box 4.2

Regulation in Water Reseller Market in Abidjan

Abidjan is one of the few cities with experience in attempting to regulate this sector, though they also focus on removing illegal connections. Although the results have been disappointing because of a lack of incentives, there is still potential to explore better mechanisms for using this source. In the early 1980s, the utility SODECI and the national government decided to address the increasing growth of household water resellers that tapped into illegal connections to the network. The authorities would provide permits to the household water resellers as long as they converted their connections into formal ones. The expected outcomes were an increase in sales among the poor, a reduction in illegal activity, and an improvement in revenue collection. The campaign did not provide any incentive to the resellers; they were billed as domestic customers and faced an increasing block tariff. Moreover, the water vendor was required to provide a title deed for the permit and to invest in an extension from the meter to the water point. As a result, only 1 percent of the total resale at the household level is currently conducted through legalized resellers.

Source: Kariuki and others 2003.

Table 4.5 Regulation of Water Tankers

Country	*City*	*Regulated*
Cape Verde	Praia	Yes
Chad	N'Djamena	Yes
Ethiopia	Addis Ababa	Yes
Ghana	Accra	No
Kenya	Nairobi	Yes
Nigeria	Kaduna	No
Rwanda	Kigali	No
South Africa	Johannesburg	No
Sudan	Greater Khartoum	Yes
Tanzania	Dar es Salaam	No
Uganda	Kampala	No

Source: Keener, Luengo, and Banerjee 2009.

Given the coverage gap and the ready distribution system that household resellers provide, a valid question is whether to explore methods to partner with private households to increase coverage.

Water Tankers

The utility emerges as a minor player in the operation of water tankers. The formal and informal private sectors are the main operators in four out of nine cities with water tanker supply (table 4.5).

Many Levels of Government Players in the Rural Water Market

Different levels of government play various roles in rural water provision. Box 4.3, for instance, presents the typical issues faced by Cross River State in Nigeria. In about one-third of the countries, the central government is responsible for rural water supply, and it shares this task with regional/state or local governments in another 27. In Cape Verde, Chad, Madagascar, South Africa, and Uganda, local governments are responsible for water supply.

The central government, local government, and NGOs play the greatest roles in most aspects of rural water service provision. Urban utilities and community service providers play the smallest roles, though community service providers are most involved in the direct provision of service. Although regional governments, rural agencies, and the private sector also contribute to water provision in certain countries, they are generally less involved across the range of countries and tasks (table 4.6).

Box 4.3

Issues Constraining Rural Water Supply in Cross River State, Nigeria

Cross River State, one of the 36 states in Nigeria, is located in the tropical rain forest belt of Nigeria. About 75 percent of its population, 3.25 million people, lives in rural areas and is engaged in subsistent farming, and more than 70 percent lives with less than $1 a day.

Cross River State is one of the states selected by the World Bank to carry out an assessment of the rural water supply based on public expenditure reviews. This is part of a substantial effort implemented by the World Bank to assess rural water sector performance in West Africa. The review, whose findings are reported here, covers the period from 2002 to 2007.

Water supply in the Cross River State is in crisis. Coverage stands at only 25 percent in urban areas and 31 percent in semiurban and rural areas. Rural water is mainly supplied through boreholes with hand pumps and wells, 65 percent of which are not functioning. Moreover, no water treatment is provided.

Meeting the MDG for water is estimated to require an additional 10,098 boreholes with hand pumps and 2,525 motorized boreholes to be built across the state by 2015, a daunting task given the current financial, institutional, and technical capacity.

Lack of adequate budgetary funding and low disbursement efficiency are major constraints. Rural water captures only 0.5 percent of the state capital budget, and execution ratios average less than 20 percent. Weak institutions and fragmented responsibilities translate to feeble leadership and rural water falling behind in the political agenda. The sector is under the responsibility of the State Rural Water Supply and Sanitation Agency (RUWATSSA), which remains a section of the Rural Development Agency. Differently from in other states, no dedicated ministry champions for reforms and allocations. More importantly, although a rural water policy does exist nationally, this is not necessarily reflected in state policies, and effective cooperation is not pursued between the national and state governments. Responsibilities are decentralized locally, but RUWATSSA continues to be characterized by a weak and poorly funded mandate and loose connections to the national water sector.

Maintenance and rehabilitation of rural water schemes are jeopardized by the lack of skilled staff and the substantial underdevelopment of a local private sector. Technical capacity for routine maintenance remains low; spare parts for boreholes are difficult to find and very expensive where available.

(continued next page)

Box 4.3 *(continued)*

Finally, no effective strategy to promote community participation has been put in place, with the result that involvement by local communities in rural water provision remains shallow at best. Absent any sense of ownership, rural communities do not take responsibility in preserving and repairing facilities, and they would not have the capacity to do so without adequate training.

Source: Iliyas, Eneh, and Oside 2009.

Table 4.6 Stakeholder Involvement in Rural Water Activities
(percent)

	Planning projects	*Preparing projects*	*Financing rural water*	*Providing services*	*Providing technical assistance*	*Ensuring water quality*
Central government	41	31	50	8	31	48
Regional government	14	17	13	8	11	16
Local government	24	24	18	24	14	10
Rural water agency	16	14	5	14	11	6
Utility	0	0	0	5	11	16
Community	3	7	8	24	3	3
Private sector	3	7	8	16	19	0

Source: Banerjee, Skilling, and others 2008b.
Note: Columns do not add to 100 percent because more than one agency can be responsible for performing the activities.

Rural water points are typically managed by the level of government closest to the communities themselves, and, in some cases, the government and community share the responsibility. In half of the countries, the community is primarily responsible for maintaining the rural water points (figure 4.14). The central government does not play a major role, except in Malawi, where it shares this responsibility with the local government, community, and private groups. The ministry in charge of water supply is by far the most important institution when it comes to collecting data and monitoring the rural water points, as in Cape Verde, where the

Figure 4.14 Responsibility for Maintenance and Monitoring of Rural Water Points

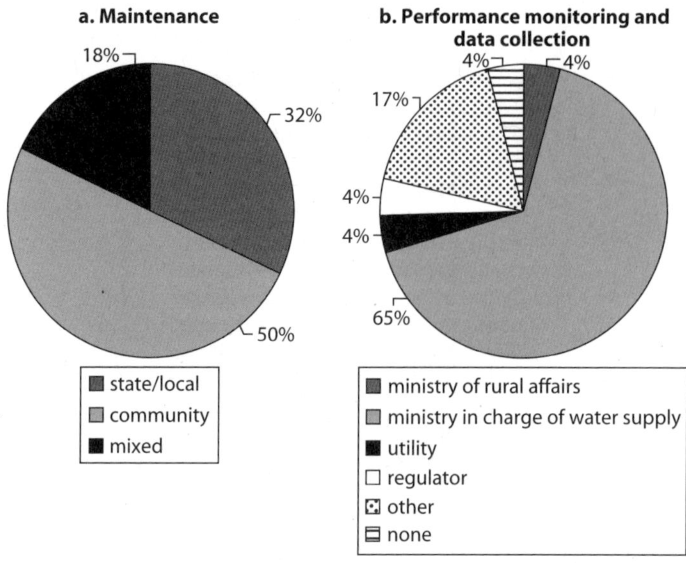

Source: Banerjee, Skilling, and others 2008b.
Note: Panel b total is 98 percent because of data unavailability for some countries.

Ministry of Rural Affairs performs this role. The regulator (Direction de l'Hydrolique) tracks data in Côte d'Ivoire, and the utilities are responsible for the same in Sudan.

About half of the countries reportedly have a rural water agency, but most countries at least have an established policy in place specifically for the rural water sector. A few countries, such as Benin, Burkina Faso, Côte d'Ivoire, Ghana, Lesotho, Mozambique, Namibia, Nigeria, Senegal, and Uganda, have both a rural water policy and a rural water agency to ensure service delivery to rural dwellers. The water points are dispersed across the rural space and are often mapped to monitor their functioning. Of these countries, only Benin, Burkina Faso, and Uganda have a rural water map as well.

The rural water index is used to measure each country's progress. This is done using five indicators: existence of a rural water agency, existence of a rural water policy, existence of a map of rural water points, existence of a dedicated budget or rural water fund, and existence of a cost-recovery policy (figure 4.15). Burkina Faso, Côte d'Ivoire, and Uganda score the highest and are the best-performing countries in creating wide-ranging reforms for the rural sector. Though we cannot evaluate the performance

Figure 4.15 Country Ranking and Prevalence of Key Attributes for the Rural Reform Index

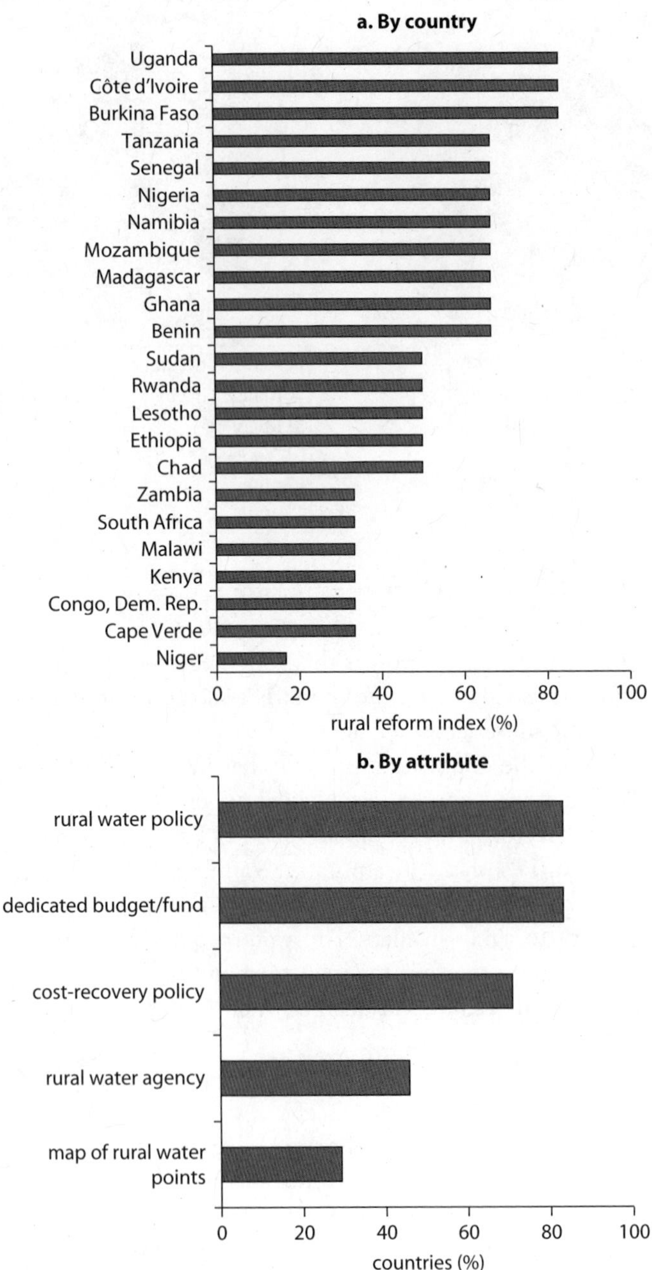

Source: Banerjee, Skilling, and others 2008b.

of rural facilities using the existing data, we find that the percentage of rural water points in need of rehabilitation and the rural water index are negatively correlated,[5] suggesting a positive association between rural reforms and functioning rural water facilities.

WSS services in small towns are often neglected and are often not taken into account in urban and rural water strategies. In many countries, particularly more populous ones, people are concentrated in small towns, and there is a need for an explicit strategy to provide infrastructure services. For instance, in Côte d'Ivoire, Benin, Madagascar, Nigeria, and Senegal, more than 30 percent of the population lives in small towns. Small towns range in size from 2,000 inhabitants in Benin, Ghana, Madagascar, and Niger to 160,000 in Nigeria. Small towns are covered under a rural or urban strategy in only five countries. Half of the countries surveyed have a specific policy or strategy for provision of small town water services. Even among these countries, only a few, such as Côte d'Ivoire, Ghana, Lesotho, and Uganda, have a specialized agency for small town water services.

Many Players with No Clear Accountability in the Sanitation Market

The sanitation sector is governed by a complicated institutional framework characterized by complexity, a multiplicity of actors, and lack of clear accountability for sector leadership. On-site sanitation operation requires financing, technical assistance, maintenance, emptying (or desludging) of facilities, and regulation. In most countries, central ministries, national and city-level utilities, local government agencies, households, NGOs, and other institutions share these responsibilities. In most countries, regulation is the only area where there is a clear delegation of responsibility to a single entity (figure 4.16).

Institutional arrangements tend to differ sharply across urban and rural environments. In rural areas, communities and households typically manage sanitation, with oversight from ministries of health. The central government is generally responsible for urban sanitation under the oversight of ministries of water, environment, housing, or public health. Municipal agencies or utilities are typically responsible for running and maintaining sanitation operations.

About 60 percent of water utilities operated sewerage networks, and a similar proportion had some responsibility for on-site sanitation as well (figure 4.17). Sanitation either can be treated as a separate business, with

Figure 4.16 Responsibilities for On-Site Sanitation Functions

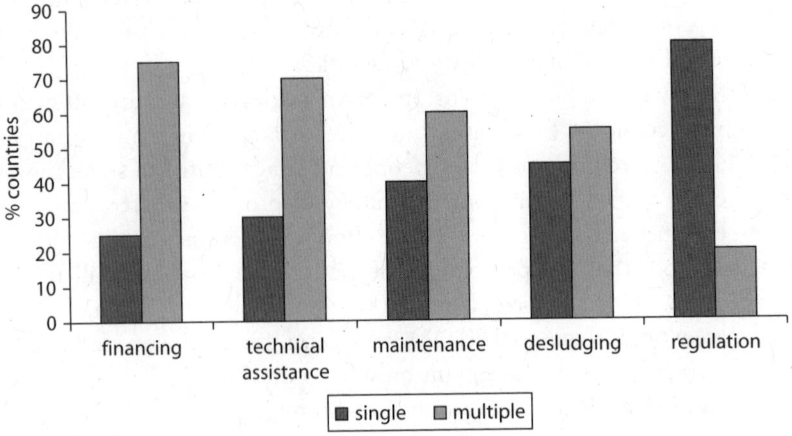

Source: Morella, Foster, and Banerjee 2008.

Figure 4.17 Urban Utilities' Responsibility over On-Site Sanitation and Wastewater Management

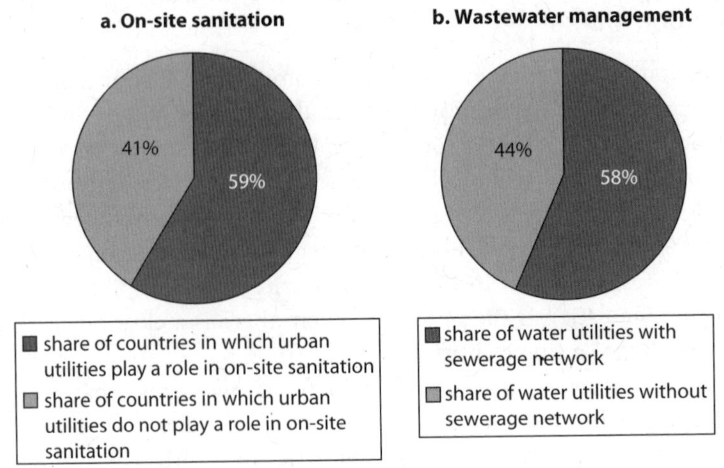

Source: Morella, Foster, and Banerjee 2008.

dedicated staff, organization, and management, or it can be operated jointly with water; both approaches are equally prevalent. Senegal is the only country with a specialized sanitation utility, Office National de l'Assainissement du Sénégal (ONAS), which reports to the Ministry of Sanitation, which was recently restructured as the Ministry of Urban

Affairs, Housing, Urban Water, Public Hygiene and Sanitation. In Burkina Faso, the water utility Office Nationale des Eaux et l'Assainissement (ONEA) has a separate department that is responsible for sanitation.

The devolution of provision of sanitation services to subnational governments has been the most significant reform of the past decade, affecting 80 percent of countries surveyed. Decentralization first began in large cities, where it had effectively been the practice because of the comprehensive role played by many water utilities. Utilities in rural areas are also being decentralized, with responsibilities transferred to small local authorities, many of which have been recently established, as in Benin, Burkina Faso, and Mali.

Reform progress can be evaluated using a simple scoring system, called the sanitation index. Countries have worked to establish a comprehensive sanitation framework to move more people away from open defecation. This reform index focuses on on-site sanitation, because a vast majority of Africans depend on this source, and the prevalence of piped sewerage is miniscule in comparison. The sanitation index includes six indicators: existence of a national sanitation policy, existence of a hygiene-promotion program, existence of an accepted definition of sanitation, existence of a specific fund for sanitation, involvement of utilities in on-site sanitation, and clear cost-recovery policies for on-site sanitation. The index is calculated by adding the values of the six indicators, and the countries with any missing data points are dropped to ensure consistency. Together, these six indicators provide a holistic measure of a country's sanitation agenda.

Most countries have worked to create an accepted definition of sanitation and a hygiene-promotion program to establish a strong sanitation framework. Fifteen countries have also established a national sanitation policy, and seven countries have developed operating cost-recovery policies, known to pay significant dividends. Only eight countries have set up a sanitation fund or a dedicated budget line; in Chad and Ethiopia, these are funded exclusively by donors or a combination of government, sector levies, and donors. Côte d'Ivoire is the only country with a fund financed entirely by sector levies. Burkina Faso, Chad, Kenya, Madagascar, and South Africa stand out for having scored 100 percent on the sanitation index. At the other extreme are countries such as the Democratic Republic of Congo, Lesotho, Nigeria, and Zambia, which are struggling to establish appropriate sanitation systems (figure 4.18).

The widespread use of on-site sanitation facilities brings up issues of construction, management, and maintenance of latrines. The AICD WSS survey provides an overview of the practice with respect to latrine

Figure 4.18 On-Site Sanitation Index

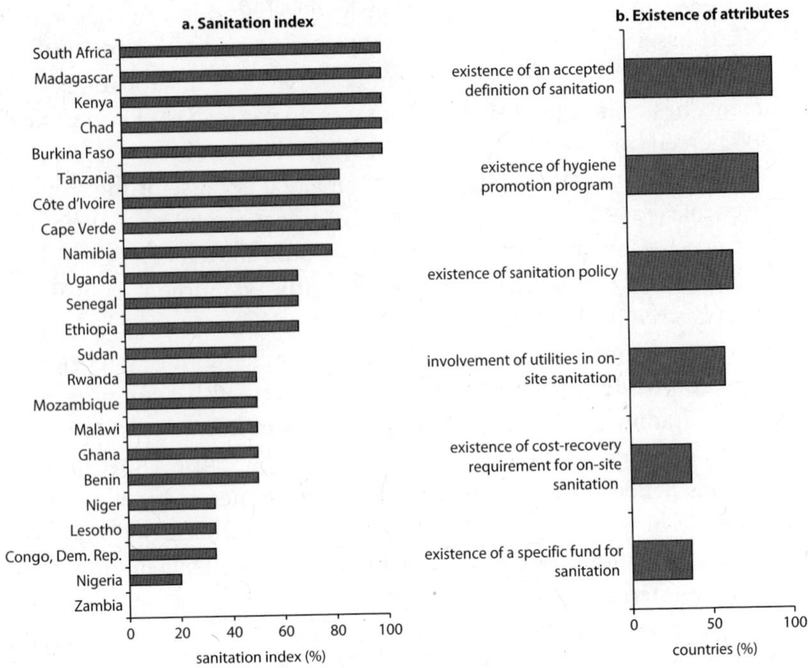

Source: Morella, Foster, and Banerjee 2008.

construction and operation. In most cases, the private sector, households, and/or NGO/CBOs are responsible for the construction of on-site sanitation. The government rarely finances the construction of sanitation facilities. Latrine emptying is predominantly a private sector function, although in a substantial number of cases the municipality and/or local utility takes primary responsibility. Only nine countries reported having formal regulatory oversight of latrines, and the majority of countries report concerns about proximity of unhygienic latrines to drilled holes, with the potential for cross-contamination (table 4.7).

Table 4.7 Management of Latrines

	Latrine construction	*Emptying of latrines*	*Regulation of latrines*	*Level of latrine regulation*	*Problem with groundwater contamination*
Benin	Households	Local private	No	n.a.	Yes
Burkina Faso	Government	Combination	No	n.a.	No
Cape Verde	NGO/CBO	Municipality	No	n.a.	
Chad	NGO/CBO				No
Congo, Dem. Rep.	Private sector	Local private	No	n.a.	No
Côte d'Ivoire	Government, households	Utility, combination	Yes	Utility	
Ethiopia	Private sector	Municipality	No	n.a.	Yes
Ghana					Yes
Kenya	NGO/CBO	Combination	Yes	Central government, utility	
Lesotho	Households	Utility	Yes	Central government	No
Madagascar	Households	Local private, combination	Yes	Municipality	No
Malawi	Government/NGO/ households	Municipality, local private, utility	Yes	Central government , municipality, community	Yes
Mozambique	Households/NGO	Other	No	n.a.	Yes
Namibia	Government/households	Municipality			Yes
Niger	Households	Local private	No	n.a.	Yes
Nigeria		Local private	No	n.a.	Yes
Rwanda	Households	Combination	No	n.a.	No
Senegal	Government/NGO/ households	Local private	Yes	Central government	Yes
South Africa	Government	Municipality	Yes	Municipality	Yes
Sudan	Households	Local private	Yes	Municipality	No
Tanzania	Households	Local private	No	n.a.	Yes
Uganda	Households	Combination	Yes	Municipality	Yes
Zambia	Households	Local private	No	n.a.	Yes

Source: Morella, Foster, and Banerjee 2008.
Note: CBO = community-based organization, n.a. = not applicable, NGO = nongovernmental organization.

Notes

1. Indicators include "consumer associations have membership," "consumer associations have a right to appeal regulatory decision," "consumers have a right to comment on draft regulations," and "consumers have a right to review tariff proposals."
2. There is centralized mode of service delivery in urban centers, but they might be decentralized for small towns and rural areas.
3. In the majority of Sub-Saharan cities, the utility follows one of these two models. Examples exist of kiosks that are both owned and operated by private individuals that use utility water, as in Nairobi and Blantyre (Chirwa and Junge 2007; Oenga and Kuria 2006), or that are owned and operated by community groups, as in Dakar (Brocklehurst and Janssens 2004). These are largely the exceptions, however.
4. In about half of the AICD sample cities, more than one management model was being used, either because one model is in the process of being replaced by another (Lesotho, for example) or because of heterogeneous areas demanding different management approaches.
5. The correlation coefficient between the percentage of rural water points in need of rehabilitation and the rural water index is –0.46.

References

Baietti, A., W. Kingdom, and M. van Ginneken. 2006. "Characteristics of Well-Performing Public Water Utilities." Water Supply and Sanitation Working Note 9, World Bank, Washington, DC.

Banerjee, S., H. Skilling, V. Foster, C. Briceño-Garmendia, E. Morella, and T. Chfadi. 2008a. "Ebbing Water, Surging Deficits: Urban Water Supply in Sub-Saharan Africa." AICD Background Paper 12, World Bank, Washington, DC.

———. 2008b. "State of the Sector Review." AICD Working Paper, World Bank, Washington, DC.

Boyer, A. 2006. "Survey of Household Water Resale Activity in Peri-Urban Maputo: Preliminary Discussion of Findings." Water and Sanitation Program, Maputo, Mozambique.

Brocklehurst, C., and J. G. Janssens. 2004. "Innovative Contracts, Sound Relationships: Urban Water Sector Reform in Senegal." Water Supply and Sanitation Sector Board Discussion Paper, World Bank, Washington, DC.

Chirwa, E., and N. Junge. 2007. "Poverty and Social Impact Analysis—Private Sector Participation in the Distribution and Management of Water Services in

Low-Income Areas in the Cities of Blantyre and Lilongwe: Republic of Malawi." Ministry of Economic Planning and Development, Ministry of Irrigation and Water Development, Malawi.

Collignon, B., and M. Vézina. 2000. "Independent Water and Sanitation Providers in African Cities: Full Report of a Ten-Country Study." Water and Sanitation Program, Washington, DC.

Development Workshop. 1995. "Water Supply and Sanitation in Luanda: Informal Sector Study and Beneficiary Assessment." Africa Urban and Water Department, World Bank, Luanda.

Elamin, M., and A. Gadir. 2006. "A Study of Small Water Enterprises in Khartoum." Water, Engineering and Development Centre, Loughborough University, Leicestershire, England.

Iliyas, M., D. Eneh, and I. Oside. 2009. "Public Expenditure Review in the Rural Water and Sanitation Sector for Cross River State, Nigeria." Africa Urban and Water Department, World Bank, Washington, DC.

Kariuki, M., B. Collignon, B. Taisne, and B. Valfrey. 2003. "Better Water and Sanitation for the Urban Poor: Good Practice from Sub-Saharan Africa." Water Utility Partnership for Capacity Building, Abidjan.

Keener, S., M. Luengo, and S. G. Banerjee. 2009. "Provision of Water to the Poor in Africa: Experience with Water Standposts and the Informal Water Sector." AICD Working Paper 13, World Bank, Washington, DC.

Marin, P. 2009. "Public Private Partnerships for Urban Water Utilities: A Review of Experiences in Developing Countries." Trends and Policy Options 8, Public-Private Infrastructure Advisory Facility and World Bank, Washington, DC.

Morella, E., V. Foster, and S. Banerjee. 2008. "Climbing the Ladder: The State of Sanitation in Sub-Saharan Africa." AICD Background Paper 13, World Bank, Washington, DC.

Oenga, I., and D. Kuria. 2006. "A Study of Small Water Enterprises in Nairobi." Water, Engineering, and Development Centre, Loughborough University, Leicestershire, England.

PA Consulting Group. 2007. "Corporatization of Bangladesh Power Development Board." Auckland.

Sarpong, K., and K. M. Abrampah. 2006. "A Study of Small Water Enterprises in Accra." Water, Engineering, and Development Centre, Loughborough University, Leicestershire, England.

SAWA (Strategic Alliance for Integrated Water Management Actions). 1997. "Beneficiary Assessment on Urban Water in Mozambique: Maputo and Quelimane." República de Moçambique, Ministério das Obras Públicas e Habitaçao. Direcçao Nacional de Águas, Maputo.

Vagliasindi, M., and J. Nellis 2009. "Evaluating Africa's Experience with Institutional Reforms for the Infrastructure Sectors." AICD Working Paper 23, World Bank, Washington, DC.

Vézina, M. 2002. "Water Services in Small Towns in Africa: The Role of Small and Medium-Sized Organizations." Water and Sanitation Program, World Bank, Washington, DC.

World Bank. 2007. Private Participation in Infrastructure Database. Washington, DC. http://ppi.worldbank.org.

CHAPTER 5

Urban Water Provision: The Story of African Utilities

Most countries in Sub-Saharan Africa cannot provide adequate water and other services for their citizens because of low coverage rates. People lack proper services because systems fail, often because not enough was invested to appropriately build and maintain them, and also because of the stress that urbanization places on this existing infrastructure. In the past decade, Africa's population grew at an annual average of 2.5 percent, and the urban and slum population grew at almost double that rate.

A well-performing utility provides service to customers who demand it, at a level that meets their needs and at a price that they are able and willing to pay (Tynan and Kingdom 2002). This chapter closely examines the performance of the individual utilities that form the core of service provision in African countries, drawing on the Africa Infrastructure Country Diagnostic (AICD) Water Supply and Sanitation (WSS) Survey. This chapter introduces a measure called "hidden cost," which comprehensively quantifies underperformance or inefficiencies and defines the economic burden. The relationship between hidden cost and institutional indicators demonstrates the contribution of institutional reforms to utility performance and service delivery.

Access to Utility Water

Utilities in Africa operate in service areas of varying sizes (annex 5.1). They can serve as few as 30,000 people, as in Oshakati, Namibia, or more than 15 million residents, as in the Democratic Republic of Congo, Ghana, and Lagos, Nigeria. The utility in Johannesburg has the highest number of residential water connections—more than 1 million. About 40 percent of the utilities in Africa have fewer than 20,000 residential water connections.

Although water access trends are typically analyzed based on national coverage statistics from household surveys (see chapter 2), it is also interesting to look at the trends that emerge directly from the utility data. These statistics focus solely on access within the utility service area and show how utility water is distributed to different segments of the population. Utility-based coverage statistics tend to differ from the figures found through household surveys. In general, coverage statistics based on household surveys tend to reveal higher access rates because they include informal and illegal connections.

With regard to piped-water service, comparing household survey access rates with utility data is complicated by the fact that some service areas fall outside the national or urban geographic spheres covered by household surveys. For the handful of countries where a reasonable match can be made between geographic areas, the population coverage rates reported by the household surveys are 4 to 16 percent higher than those in the utility coverage data. Moreover, the household surveys show an additional served population that represents 14 to 33 percent of the total population with access (table 5.1).

Utilities in some countries also provide service for "off-grid" consumers in addition to servicing formal clients when their service area is bigger than the network area. These off-grid provisions include off-grid boreholes with networks or water quality checks. In Lusaka and Dar es Salaam, community partnerships manage large off-grid systems.

About 98 percent of the population in the utility service areas in the middle-income countries receives utility water, whether through private piped connections, shared connections with neighbors, or standpost services. In the low-income countries, however, only 69 percent of residents in the service area are accessing utility water, leaving a sizeable minority that must rely on other sources, such as ground or surface water. The low-income, fragile countries have the maximum connection deficit—only 26 percent are covered by piped-water supply and 56 percent by some sort of utility water. These countries also have the highest

Table 5.1 Comparison of Coverage Statistics for Water, Based on Utility Data versus Household Surveys
(percent)

	Coverage rate derived from household surveys (A)	*Coverage rate derived from utility data (B)*	*Difference in coverage rates (A–B)*	*Potential rate of informality (A–B)/(A)*
SONEB (Benin)	29	25	4	14
SDE (Senegal)	77	66	11	15
ONEA (Burkina Faso)	33	25	8	25
JIRAMA (Madagascar)	17	13	4	25
ELECTROGAZ (Rwanda)	16	11	5	30
WASA (Lesotho)	50	34	16	33

Source: Banerjee, Skilling, and others 2008.
Note: JIRAMA = Jiro sy Rano Malagasy, ONEA = Office Nationale des Eaux et d'Assainissement, SDE = Sénégalaise des Eaux, SONEB = Société Nationale des Eaux du Benin, WASA = Water and Sanitation Authority.

proportion of people sharing taps with neighbors, confirming a degree of informality not witnessed in other countries.

The connection deficit varies drastically among income groups. The middle-income countries have piped-water coverage that is multiple times higher than that of other income groups—twice the low-income, three times the resource-rich, and more than three times the low-income, fragile countries. In middle-income countries, the vast majority of people who access utility water do so through private residential connections. In low-income, fragile countries, however, less than half of those who receive utility water do so via private piped connections; the rest share connections with neighbors or rely on communal modalities such as utility standposts. Few people in the middle-income countries informally share connections, but in the low-income countries, this practice is almost as common as the use of formal utility standposts, albeit with substantial regional variations. The East African Community (EAC) and Economic Community of West African States (ECOWAS) regional groups have the highest number of households dependent on a neighbor's connection (table 5.2).

The water-abundant countries have fewer utility-provided connections, and the water-scarce countries not only have more private water connections, but also have better coverage through standposts and from neighbors. Overall, the large utilities are better at providing some sort of

Table 5.2 Overview of Access Patterns in the Utility Service Area
(percent)

	Access by private residential piped-water connection	*Access by standpost*	*Access by sharing of neighbors' private connection*	*Access to utility water by some modality*
Sub-Saharan Africa	44.3	13.0	21.7	64.0
By income				
Low-income	42.2	23.2	22.5	68.6
Low-income, fragile	25.6	2.2	41.0	56.0
Resource-rich	30.3	15.8	7.4	48.8
Middle-income	88.0	9.7	0.3	97.8
By regional economic community				
ECOWAS	38.1	8.8	34.3	68.6
SADC	53.2	11.1	8.1	62.2
CEMAC	24.2	—	—	65.0
EAC	44.7	26.5	40.4	91.6
COMESA	26.0	18.2	23.7	54.7
By water availability[a]				
High water scarcity	56.4	16.3	15.2	68.8
Low water scarcity	32.5	8.9	19.6	57.1
By utility size[b]				
Small	47.0	15.5	20.7	68.6
Large	39.5	13.8	25.6	80.9

Sources: AICD WSS Database; Banerjee, Skilling, and others 2008.
Note: CEMAC = Central African Economic and Monetary Community, COMESA = Common Market for Eastern and Southern Africa, EAC = East African Community, ECOWAS = Economic Community of West African States, SADC = Southern African Development Community. — = not available.
a. Water abundance is defined as renewable internal freshwater resources per capita in excess of 3,000 cubic meters.
b. Large utilities are defined as those serving more than 100,000 connections.

utility water to consumers and manage to serve four out of five residents in their service area.

The Pace of Expansion of Utility Water Coverage

Although utilities might have substantially different access rates for private piped-water connections, a key issue is how quickly the coverage gap is being closed. This can be gauged by looking at the average annual growth rate of connections in recent years. It is currently 5 percent; however, that value differs from country to country (figure 5.1, panel a).

Figure 5.1 Expansion of Utility Water Coverage

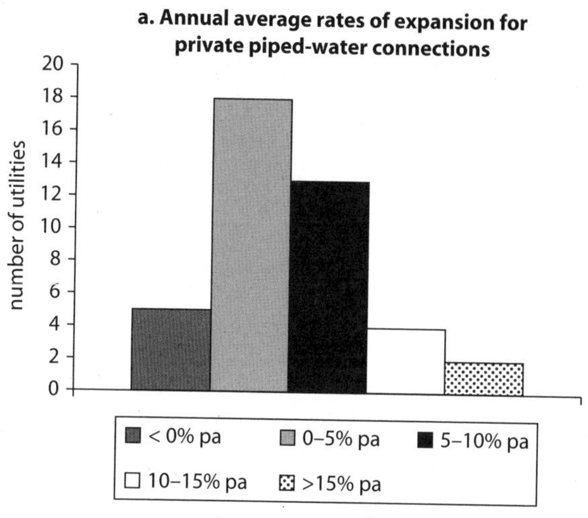

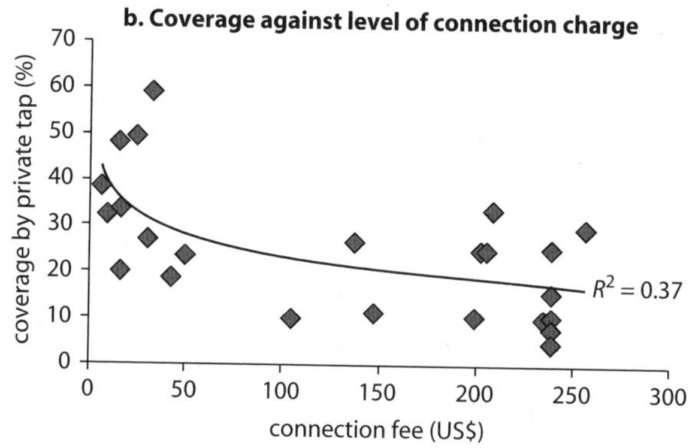

Source: Banerjee, Skilling, and others 2008.

Five utilities (in the Democratic Republic of Congo, Kenya, and Nigeria) actually report an absolute decline in the number of customers connected. In contrast, the 10 fastest-expanding utilities (in Benin, Cape Verde, Ethiopia, Malawi, Uganda, and Zambia) are growing at an average annual rate in excess of 7 percent, a pace that would allow the utilities to double the number of connections if it were sustained over a decade. In absolute terms, utilities are growing fastest in the largest cities; Cape Town, Johannesburg, and Lagos each add between 30,000 and 50,000 new connections each year. Given Sub-Saharan Africa's 3.5 percent urban demographic growth rate, however, more than one-third of the utilities in the region are simply not expanding rapidly enough to achieve proper coverage.

One factor that sometimes hampers growth of connections is cost. The average connection fee for piped-water service, among the 26 utilities able to supply this data point, is $265. In the low-income countries, significant negative correlation is seen between the connection charge and the coverage of private taps in the utility area (figure 5.1, panel b).

Water Production Capacity Varies from Country to Country

Utilities can expand coverage only if there is sufficient water production in the service area relative to the resident population. Water production varies widely across the country income groups. Middle-income countries produce around 209 liters per day for each resident in the service area, indicating that enough water would be available to adequately serve the entire population if the distribution networks were expanded.

By contrast, utilities in the low-income countries produce only 130 liters per capita per day, just enough for those customers who are already connected to the system. If these utilities were to connect their entire unserved populations to the network, the availability of water would drop to only 66 liters per capita per day, suggesting that these utilities need to invest in both water production capacity and water distribution networks to reach universal coverage. The low-income, fragile countries experience the lowest production, at only 77 liters per capita per day for their consumers, which falls to only 36 liters per capita per day if the water is spread to all the residents in the service area. Once again, there is a difference in water production between water-scarce and water-abundant countries, with the latter group serving 176 liters per capita per day compared with 125 liters per capita per day for the former (table 5.3). This reflects the higher ability of utilities to produce and serve more water in water-rich countries compared with utilities facing arid environments.

Two-Part Tariff Structures for Piped Water

Many countries in Africa have adopted a two-part tariff structure that incorporates both fixed and water-use charges. Two-part tariffs are designed so that the fixed part helps to cover production and administrative costs (such as billing and meter reading) and the water-use portion covers partial operations and maintenance (O&M) costs. Fixed charges can take two forms—a minimum consumption charge and a monthly

Table 5.3 Water Production per Capita in the Utility Service Area

	Water production per capita in the utility service area (liters per capita per day)	*Water production per capita served by utility in service area (liters per capita per day)*
Sub-Saharan Africa	116.4	162.9
By income		
Low-income	66.0	130.2
Low-income, fragile	35.7	76.5
Resource-rich	140.5	208.8
Middle-income	208.8	233.6
By regional economic community		
ECOWAS	42.3	96.8
SADC	132.5	184.4
CEMAC	107.4	229.5
EAC	71.3	118.9
COMESA	142.4	183.3
By water availability[a]		
High water scarcity	81.5	125.4
Low water scarcity	115.3	175.9
By utility size[b]		
Small	102.5	160.1
Large	106.2	189.4

Sources: AICD WSS Database; Banerjee, Skilling, and others 2008.
Note: CEMAC = Central African Economic and Monetary Community, COMESA = Common Market for Eastern and Southern Africa, EAC = East African Community, ECOWAS = Economic Community of West African States, SADC = Southern African Development Community.
a. Water abundance is defined as renewable internal freshwater resources per capita in excess of 3,000 cubic meters.
b. Large utilities are defined as those serving more than 100,000 connections.

fixed fee—and they also allow for the recovery of investment costs without distorting price signals. The volumetric tariff, which is based on water use, usually takes the form of increasing block tariffs (IBTs). The IBT has long been a common structure in developing countries, where unit prices in the lower brackets of consumption (in cubic meters per month) tend to be smaller than the prices in higher brackets.

Fourteen utilities have designed a two-part tariff, including 13 that enforce a "fixed charge plus IBT." Only the National Water and Sewerage Company (NWSC) in Uganda uses a "fixed charge plus linear tariff" structure. In addition to these utilities, seven have a "minimum consumption plus IBT" structure. The remaining 24 utilities use an interesting range of structures: 19 impose an IBT structure and three enforce a linear structure, which means that households pay the same price per unit of consumption. The remaining two utilities have different tariff structures: the Central Region Water Board (CRWB) in Malawi charges a flat fee or fixed charge for the first 32 units of consumption, and the Kisumu Water and Sewerage Company (KIWASCO) in Kenya has a U-shaped structure, in which tariffs decline after the first block and rise again after the third.

The block structure can add to the complexity of tariffs. It can range from one (linear) to seven, with the average being just above three blocks. The most common is a three-tiered block structure, used by 16 utilities. Ten water utilities in Africa use a four-block structure. At the high end are utilities such as Drakenstein, in South Africa, which has seven blocks. ELECTROGAZ in Rwanda, as well as in Johannesburg and Tygerberg in South Africa, has a six-block water tariff structure (figure 5.2).

Twenty-nine percent of the water utilities in Africa use a monthly fixed fee, which is usually based on pipe size. The lowest fees are for the typical residential pipe size of 15 to 20 millimeters. Fixed fees can also be determined based on consumption. This charge is meant to cover the fixed part of the O&M cost. Fifteen percent of the utilities levy this charge, and, in all cases, the fee includes consumption of, at most, 10 cubic meters (m^3).

The size of the first block varies. In most countries, the first block is usually below 10 m^3; only 20 percent have a first block higher than 10 m^3. Only 36 percent have a first block of less than 6 m^3 per month, which is considered almost subsistence consumption. At the other extreme are utilities with a large consumption spread in the first block. The size of the last block also reveals interesting patterns. The last block can start from 5 m^3, as it does in the Société Nationale des Eaux du Benin (SONEB) in Benin or the Dar es Salaam Water and Sewerage Company (DAWASCO) in Tanzania. It can also start at 1,000 m^3, as it does in Drakenstein, South Africa, or Katsina, Nigeria. In 64 percent of the utilities, the starting point of the last block is less than or equal to 50 m^3.

Developing countries have often used the price of a first block as a social tariff, or lifeline, so that the poor can get at least a minimum quantity of safe water at a subsidized price. In numerous countries with a minimum consumption charge, such as Côte d'Ivoire, Malawi (Blantyre Water Board), and Mozambique, the block structure begins from block two, and the price of block one is therefore zero. The price of the last block is often set with cost recovery and water conservation in mind. In about one-third of utilities, the tariffs are set higher than $0.8/$m^3$. The fixed charges, which are expected to be paid every month, irrespective of consumption, are usually less than $4. Of the 44 percent of the utilities

Figure 5.2 Variations in Tariff Structures

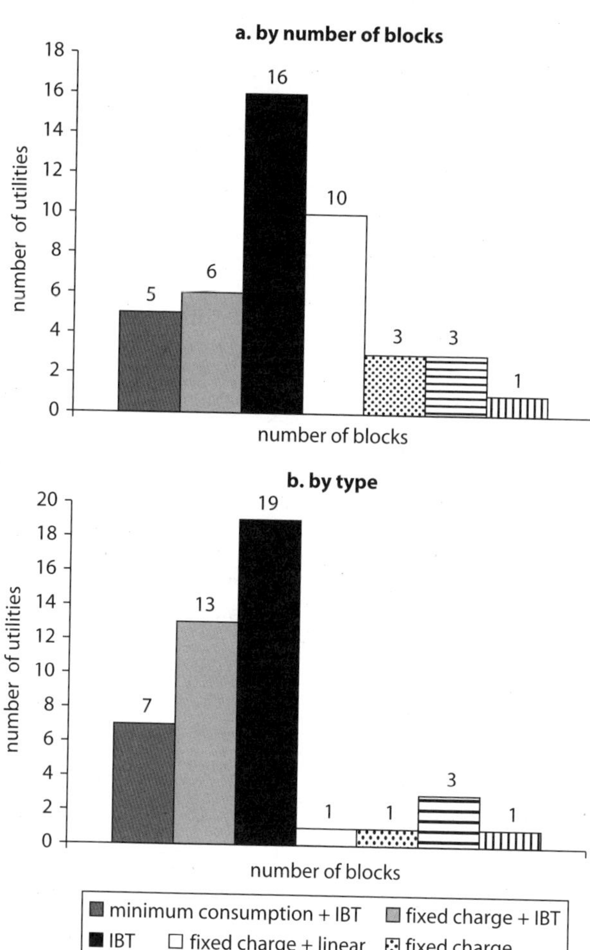

Source: Banerjee, Foster, and others 2008.
Note: IBT = increasing block tariff.

that enforce a fixed-fee or minimum-consumption charge, about half are set between $2 and $4 (figure 5.3).

Sewerage Charges Linked to Water Bills

Sewerage payment structures vary and can be calculated either as a surcharge percentage on the water bill or by using an independent block or fixed tariff structure. In more than half of utilities, the sanitation charge

Figure 5.3 Utility Prices and Charges

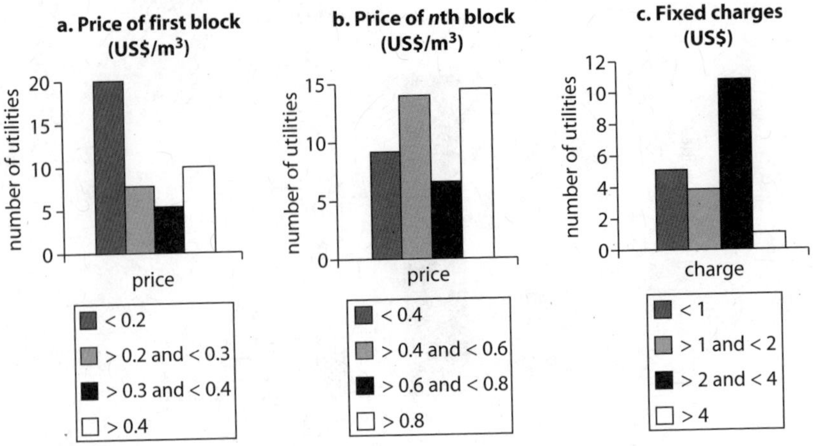

a. Price of first block (US$/m³)
number of utilities
price
< 0.2
> 0.2 and < 0.3
> 0.3 and < 0.4
> 0.4

b. Price of *n*th block (US$/m³)
number of utilities
price
< 0.4
> 0.4 and < 0.6
> 0.6 and < 0.8
> 0.8

c. Fixed charges (US$)
number of utilities
charge
< 1
> 1 and < 2
> 2 and < 4
> 4

Source: Banerjee, Foster, and others 2008.

is levied as part of the water bill. That charge ranges from 30 percent in Zambia to 85 percent in Lesotho, with an average of 53 percent. Six African utilities use the block-tariff structure for sewerage, with the blocks varying between one and five. Walvis Bay in Namibia stands out because of its use of a decreasing block tariff, in which prices decline with rising consumption. KIWASCO in Kenya is the only utility that reports levying a separate connection fee of $90 specifically for sewer service (table 5.4).

Burkina Faso has taken an innovative approach by levying a sanitation tax as a surcharge on the water bill, which is then used to subsidize access to on-site sanitation facilities in Ouagadougou (box 5.1).

Modest Water Consumption by End Users

Demand management can be reliably assessed only for those water utilities with good metering coverage, as they would therefore be expected to have relatively meaningful estimates of water consumption and nonrevenue water (NRW). There are four categories of sample utilities. The first category comprises 15 utilities that do not report meter coverage. The second category comprises 26 utilities (mainly in Ethiopia, Nigeria, and Zambia) with low meter coverage (less than 50 percent of residential connections), averaging 19 percent for the group. The third category comprises 11 utilities (mainly in South Africa and Tanzania) with moderate

Table 5.4 Structure and Level of Wastewater Tariffs

Utility	*Country*	*Type of tariff*	*Connection fee (US$)*	*Fixed charge (US$)*	*Number of blocks*	*Size of first block*	*Size of nth block*	*Price of first block (US$)*	*Price of nth block*
ONEA	Burkina Faso	Flat	0	0	1	0+		0.04	0.04
AWSA	Ethiopia	Flat	0	0	1	7.1+		0.07	0.07
NWASCO	Kenya	IBT	0	0	4	0–10	60+	0.13	0.21
KIWASCO	Kenya	1BT	90	0	5	0–10	60+	0.21	0.42
Walvis Bay	Namibia	DBT	0	2.69	4	0–15	85+	0.34	0.02
ONAS	Senegal	IBT	0	0	3	0–20	40+	0.02	0.13

Source: Banerjee, Foster, and others 2008.

Note: AWSA = Addis Ababa Water Services Authority, DBT = direct block tariff, IBT = increasing block tariff, KIWASCO = Kisumu Water and Sewerage Company, NWASCO = Nairobi Water and Sanitation Company, ONAS = Office National de l'Assainissement du Sénégal, ONEA = Office Nationale des Eaux et d'Assainissement.

Box 5.1

Burkina Faso's Sanitation Tax

The on-site sanitation problems in Ouagadougou are specifically addressed in the Sanitation Strategic Plan's implementation by the national public utility in charge of water supply and sanitation.

A sanitation marketing approach has enhanced construction services offered to households by small providers and stimulated household demand for improved sanitation facilities. Approximately 700 masons and social workers have been trained since the beginning of the program.

Burkina Faso's national utility offers to provide part of the material for free to households—equivalent to about a 30 percent subsidy with the rest financed by the households. The subsidy is financed by the utility through a small sanitation tax on the water bill.

This example shows that on-site sanitation corresponds to a strong demand from urban dwellers, with more than 60,000 pieces of sanitation equipment subsidized so far—latrines as well as gray-water-removal systems. It also demonstrates the importance of a local financing mechanism. Donors have contributed to the mechanism, but only modestly. Most of the funds come from the tax on the water bill.

Source: Reproduced from Water and Sanitation Program 2008.

meter coverage (50 to 70 percent of residential connections), averaging 58 percent for the group. The fourth and final category comprises an additional 32 utilities (mainly in Burkina Faso, Cape Verde, Côte d'Ivoire, Ethiopia, Mozambique, Lesotho, Namibia, Niger, Rwanda, Senegal, and Uganda)[1] with high meter coverage (greater than 70 percent of residential connections), averaging 95 percent for the group. This section focuses only on the last three groups.

Although water consumption measurements are not necessarily very accurate, evidence from the African utilities reviewed suggests that end-user water consumption is quite modest. The overall average consumption is 80 liters per capita per day, ranging from 189 liters per capita per day in the middle-income countries to 37 liters per capita per day in the low-income, fragile countries. Among the regional economic communities, consumption is particularly low in the EAC (at 42 liters per capita per day) compared with the Southern African Development Community (SADC) and ECOWAS (at 77 to 86 liters per capita per day). In some countries, the actual consumption per capita might be lower because of widespread reselling, particularly in periurban areas with intermittent supply.

Pricing is the main way that utilities can manage demand and requires a proper metering system to support volumetric charging and the application of metered tariffs to provide an adequate cost signal to customers. The overall reported rate of water metering in sample African countries whose utilities report medium to large metering ratios stands at 85 percent. Interestingly, the low-income, fragile countries report a 100 percent metering ratio compared with only 68 percent in the middle-income countries, suggesting that rebuilding after a conflict has involved a more formal release of connections with individual household meters. The average revenue per cubic meter of water billed ranges from around $0.40 in low-income countries to more than $1.10 in middle-income countries. The tariffs in water-abundant countries are two-thirds of those found in water-scarce countries. Within the regional economic communities, the ECOWAS has the highest average revenue, at $0.6 per cubic meter, compared with only $0.3 to $0.50 elsewhere in Africa. Many of the francophone countries of West Africa are in the CFA franc region, where prices tend to be systematically higher (table 5.5). Although this revenue is typically not sufficient to cover full capital costs, these costs are nonetheless quite high compared with those in other developing regions. Overall, evidence shows that significant price signals are getting through to a substantial share of the customer base.

A fairly strong negative correlation is found between metering levels and average residential water consumption in utilities with a metering level of about 50 percent of residential connections. Essentially, these utilities fall into two groups: Those with metering ratios of 50 to 70 percent tend to have average water consumption of about 188 liters per capita per day, and those with metering ratios of 90 to 100 percent tend to have average water consumption of about 50 liters per capita per day.

Surprisingly, consumption and price are positively correlated as tariff rates are near cost recovery at high consumption levels. Utility clients pay a substantially higher price per unit of consumption, particularly high-volume nonresidential consumers. Thus, no strong evidence is evident of wasteful overuse of water in Africa, and the relatively modest levels of consumption would not be further reduced by more aggressive use of demand management tools.

Table 5.5 Indicators of Demand Management Calculated across Utilities with Metering Ratios above 50 Percent

	Water consumption per capita served (liters per capita per day)	*Metering ratio (%)*	*Revenue per cubic meter of water consumed (US$/m³)*	*Nonrevenue water (%)*
Sub-Saharan Africa	79.5	85.4	0.5	30.1
By income				
Low-income	64.1	86.7	0.4	31.3
Low-income, fragile	36.9	100.0	0.6	24.8
Resource-rich	—	91.3	0.7	34.3
Middle-income	188.8	68.0	1.1	21.7
By regional economic community				
ECOWAS	77.0	101.4	0.6	22.1
SADC	85.8	82.1	0.5	30.0
CEMAC	—	—	—	—
EAC	41.6	78.9	0.3	28.8
COMESA	60.0	90.1	0.5	35.8
By water availability[a]				
High water scarcity	102.2	81.0	0.6	30.2
Low water scarcity	68.6	87.2	0.4	30.0
By utility size[b]				
Small	64.6	85.4	0.4	30.8
Large	133.6	85.5	0.8	27.0

Sources: AICD WSS Database; Banerjee, Skilling, and others 2008.
Note: CEMAC = Central African Economic and Monetary Community, COMESA = Common Market for Eastern and Southern Africa, EAC = East African Community, ECOWAS = Economic Community of West African States, SADC = Southern African Development Community. — = not available.
a. Water abundance is defined as renewable internal freshwater resources per capita in excess of 3,000 cubic meters.
b. Large utilities are defined as those serving more than 100,000 connections.

Substantial Water Losses in Distribution System

Although end-user water use is modest, a substantial volume of water is lost during the distribution process. The average level of NRW in the sample is close to 30 percent, well above good practice levels (below 23 percent) for developing countries (Tynan and Kingdom 2002) (figure 5.4). The middle-income countries have the lowest nonrevenue losses, followed by the low-income, fragile countries. This good performance can be attributed to different factors—in the middle-income countries, it is due to superior technical and management performance, and for the low-income, fragile countries, it is due to relatively new systems constructed as part of the

Figure 5.4 Frequency Distribution of Nonrevenue Water

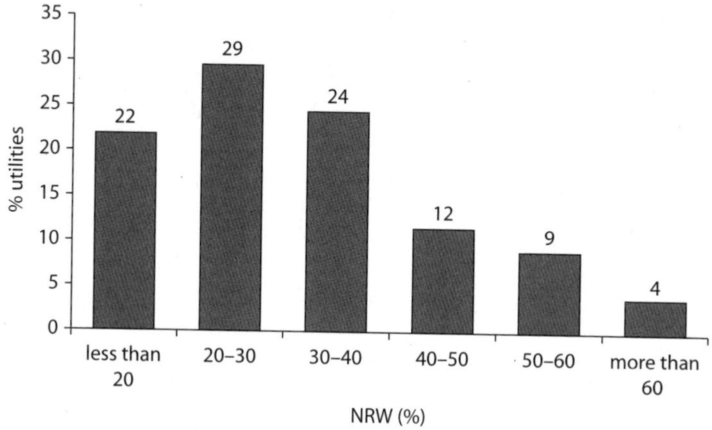

Sources: AICD WSS Database; Banerjee, Skilling, and others 2008.
Note: NRW = nonrevenue water.

Figure 5.5 Cross-Plots between NRW and Other Variables

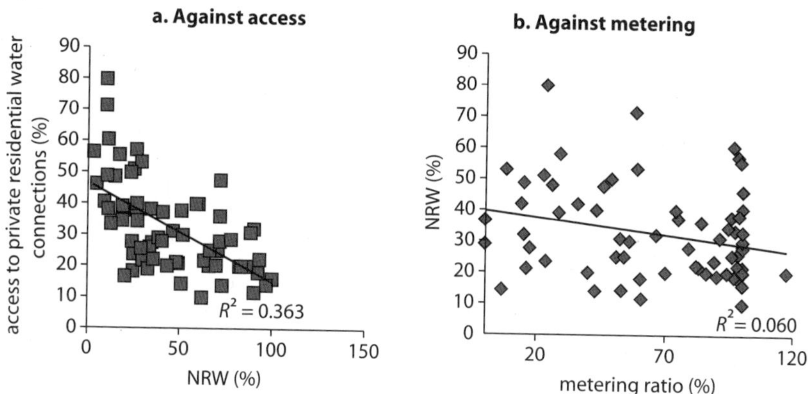

Sources: AICD WSS Database; Banerjee, Skilling, and others 2008.
Note: NRW = nonrevenue water.

rebuilding effort. Within the regional economic communities, the range is capped between 22 and 36 percent.

Nonrevenue water measures include both technical and nontechnical losses. Experience in Asia suggests that NRW tends to be inversely proportional to access rates, because lower rates of access invite higher rates of informal and clandestine use, by both households and small-scale providers (McIntosh 2003). This relationship clearly holds for the African utilities, where there is a negative correlation of close to 33 percent between access rates and NRW (figure 5.5).

In principle, higher metering rates should help to reduce NRW by enabling utilities to pinpoint the location of losses on the network, but no evidence of such a relationship was found in the sample of African utilities. In fact, among utilities claiming 100 percent meter coverage, the level of NRW ranges between 20 and 47 percent. Moreover, utilities reporting moderate levels of meter coverage have an almost identical range for NRW. This suggests that utilities are not using metering effectively to control NRW.

Difference in Quality of Service among Country Groups

It is difficult to properly evaluate some of the services provided by African utilities. The only way to evaluate water quality is to look at the percentage of samples, taken from a water treatment plant, that pass the chlorine test. This indicates the effectiveness of the treatment process but says nothing about the quality of water received at the tap. The scores show a substantial difference in performance between utilities in middle-income countries, which score close to 100 percent on this variable, and those in low-income, fragile countries, which score only 75 percent. Among the regional economic communities, the Central African Economic and Monetary Community (CEMAC) is at the lower end of this indicator, compared to the EAC and SADC, which report a more than 90 percent success rate.

On average, utilities for the sample group provide just under 20 hours of continuous service per day. However, low-income, fragile, and resource-rich countries provide, on average, five to six hours less service per day than middle-income countries. The countries with high water scarcity offer longer hours of service compared with water-abundant countries.

Finally, the "complaints lodged by customers" indicator provides somewhat nebulous information, because low levels of complaints could indicate either good service or a poor system for recording complaints. Overall, the indicators show much higher levels of complaints in low-income countries, where more than 200 complaints were lodged in the preceding year. The middle-income countries, on the other hand, recorded only 26 complaints per 1,000 connections. Among the regional economic communities, the number ranges from 50 to 183 complaints per 1,000 connections. The rate also varies widely among high- and low-water-scarcity countries, where the latter reported more than twice the number of complaints per 1,000 connections (table 5.6).

Table 5.6 Indicators of Service Quality

	Percentage of samples passing chlorine test (%)	*Continuous water service (hours per day)*	*Water and wastewater consumer complaints per connection (number per 1,000 residential connections)*
Sub-Saharan Africa	87.9	19.6	78.4
By income			
Low-income	92.8	19.0	211.0
Low-income, fragile	75.3	18.2	—
Resource-rich	78.1	18.4	41.9
Middle-income	97.2	24.0	25.6
By regional economic community			
ECOWAS	88.4	22.8	183.0
SADC	90.1	17.2	50.0
CEMAC	68.0	19.5	—
EAC	94.8	16.0	119.7
COMESA	85.5	15.5	69.5
By water availability[a]			
High water scarcity	86.5	22.2	27.0
Low water scarcity	88.9	17.8	60.7
By utility size[b]			
Small	89.4	17.6	94.4
Large	80.8	19.6	77.5

Sources: AICD WSS Database; Banerjee, Skilling, and others 2008.
Note: CEMAC = Central African Economic and Monetary Community, COMESA = Common Market for Eastern and Southern Africa, EAC = East African Community, ECOWAS = Economic Community of West African States, SADC = Southern African Development Community. — = not available.
a. Water abundance is defined as renewable internal freshwater resources per capita in excess of 3,000 cubic meters.
b. Large utilities are defined as those serving more than 100,000 connections.

Technical Efficiency and Effective Management of Operations

Labor productivity, pipe water breaks, and operating cost are the three indicators used to evaluate the technical operations of the utilities (table 5.7). State-owned enterprises (SOEs) can be social buffers to (very inefficiently) transfer rents or resources to the population. Labor productivity rates can be hard to compare because of differing reliance on contractors. Nevertheless, a frequently used international benchmark for labor productivity is 2 employees per 1,000 connections, which has been modified to 5 employees per 1,000 connections for developing countries (Tynan and Kingdom 2002). Overall, African utilities in the sample report an average

Table 5.7 Indicators of Operational Efficiency

	Employees per 1,000 water connections (number/1,000 connections)	*Water pipe breaks per year per km of water network (number per year/km)*	*Operating cost per cubic meter of water consumed (US$/m³)*
Sub-Saharan Africa	5.6	8.0	1.2
By income			
Low-income	9.1	6.6	0.7
Low-income, fragile	11.1	7.9	0.7
Resource-rich	10.0	14.1	0.3
Middle-income	2.9	7.2	1.5
By regional economic community			
ECOWAS	5.2	3.6	0.7
SADC	5.0	7.3	1.3
CEMAC	6.3	58.0	0.5
EAC	11.0	5.5	0.5
COMESA	14.7	9.7	0.5
By water availability[a]			
High water scarcity	4.3	5.7	1.3
Low water scarcity	7.1	9.3	0.5
By utility size[b]			
Small	14.0	7.5	0.6
Large	6.3	13.7	0.7

Sources: AICD WSS Database; Banerjee, Skilling, and others 2008.
Note: CEMAC = Central African Economic and Monetary Community, COMESA = Common Market for Eastern and Southern Africa, EAC = East African Community, ECOWAS = Economic Community of West African States, SADC = Southern African Development Community.
a. Water abundance is defined as renewable internal freshwater resources per capita in excess of 3,000 cubic meters.
b. Large utilities are defined as those serving more than 100,000 connections.

of about 5.6 employees per 1,000 connections, which is right around the developing country benchmark cited above. The variation among the income groups is wide, ranging from 11 employees per 1,000 connections in the low-income, fragile countries to just about 3 employees per 1,000 connections in the middle-income countries.

A commonly used international benchmark for average operating costs of water utilities is around $0.40 per cubic meter (Global Water Intelligence 2004). The costs reported by the African utilities are substantially higher, ranging from $0.30 per cubic meter in resource-rich countries to $1.50 per cubic meter in middle-income countries. The latter result is due to the high cost of water in Namibia and South Africa. Even within the regional economic communities, the average operating cost ranges from $1.30 per cubic meter in the SADC (which includes Namibia and South Africa) compared with $0.50 to $0.70 per cubic meter in other regional blocks. As operation costs depend largely on water availability, the difference in costs between water-scarce countries and water-abundant countries is stark: The former have average operating costs almost three times that of the latter.

The rate of bursts per kilometer of water main provides some indication of the condition of the underlying infrastructure, and hence the extent to which it is being adequately operated and maintained. The resource-rich countries report the highest rate of bursts, at 14 per year per kilometer, compared with only 6.6 in low-income countries. The utilities in the CEMAC regional community report a significantly higher number of bursts compared with the other regional blocks.[2]

Three indicators are used to evaluate the primary components of operating costs: labor costs, energy costs, and service contracts (table 5.8).

Table 5.8 Utility Cost Structures
(percent)

	Share of labor costs in operating expenses	*Share of energy costs in operating expenses*	*Share of service contracts in operating expenses*
Sub-Saharan Africa	21.4	12.0	11.3
By income			
Low-income	28.3	14.9	26.3
Low-income, fragile	24.5	11.8	4.0
Resource-rich	33.9	29.7	12.5
Middle-income	15.9	1.6	6.6
By regional economic community			
CEMAC	34.5	—	—
COMESA	34.9	20.8	4.4
EAC	32.9	14.0	10.5
ECOWAS	22.1	14.8	23.6
SADC	19.1	7.5	6.8
By water availability[a]			
High water scarcity	18.7	10.8	8.2
Low water scarcity	25.5	10.0	6.8
By utility size[b]			
Small	33.4	19.7	15.1
Large	29.1	16.2	20.6

Sources: AICD WSS Database; Banerjee, Skilling, and others 2008.
Note: CEMAC = Central African Economic and Monetary Community, COMESA = Common Market for Eastern and Southern Africa, EAC = East African Community, ECOWAS = Economic Community of West African States, SADC = Southern African Development Community. — = not available.
a. Water abundance is defined as renewable internal freshwater resources per capita in excess of 3,000 cubic meters.
b. Large utilities are defined as those serving more than 100,000 connections.

Overall, African utilities allocate just more than 21 percent of their operating expenses to labor and just about 12 percent to energy. The structure of operating expenses differs substantially across the different groups. The share of labor and energy is lowest in the middle-income countries. In particular, utilities in the low-income and resource-rich countries allocate almost twice as high a share of their operating expenses to labor and multiple times to energy compared to the middle-income countries. The share of service contracts is lowest in the low-income, fragile, and middle-income countries. One simple explanation for this is that in both Namibia and South Africa, water-distribution utilities are not involved in production, but instead purchase their water from bulk suppliers. So, although they spend a significant amount of operating expenses on bulk water purchase, their direct labor and energy costs are correspondingly reduced. Utilities in the ECOWAS allocate more than 23 percent of their operating costs on service contracts—more than utilities in the other regions. This may also explain why they have a correspondingly lower labor share than those in other regional blocks.

Financial Efficiency and the Alignment of Operations and Finances

Five indicators are used to evaluate the financial performance of the utilities: collection efficiency, operating cost ratio, debt-service ratio, value of gross fixed assets per connection, and average operating revenue (table 5.9). A well-performing utility is one that maintains its assets and uses them efficiently. This minimizes the need for new investments and reduces capital costs.

The average operating ratio of African utilities shows that operating costs are barely covered and fall short of what is needed to recoup capital expenditures. This ratio is below the benchmark level of 1.3 for developing countries identified by Tynan and Kingdom (2002). Paradoxically, the operating ratio reported for middle-income countries is below unity exhibited by low-income and resource-rich countries. One reason for this may be the exceptionally high operating costs (in excess of $1 per cubic meter) that are reported by utilities in middle-income countries. All the regional economic communities, except the SADC, which includes the middle-income countries of Namibia and South Africa, meet operational cost coverage. The economies of scale of large utilities are evident in the very high operating cost coverage at 3.4, which is three times that of the small utilities.

Table 5.9 Utility Financial Ratios

	Collection efficiency (%)	Operating cost coverage (ratio)	Debt-service ratio	Value of gross fixed assets per connection (US$)	Average operating revenue (US$/m³)
Sub-Saharan Africa	92.2	0.9	11.1	490.2	0.9
By income					
Low-income	95.7	1.0	11.4	999.4	0.5
Low-income, fragile	96.9	0.8	20.4	558.7	0.5
Resource-rich	72.4	1.0	157.4	752.4	0.3
Middle-income	99.8	0.8	3.6	358.3	1.2
By regional economic community					
ECOWAS	105.4	1.0	16.0	934.1	0.8
SADC	86.8	0.8	4.7	385.7	1.0
CEMAC	91.0	1.1	157.4	1,112.1	0.4
EAC	97.5	1.0	21.8	353.8	0.3
COMESA	76.6	1.0	14.3	388.6	0.4
By water availability[a]					
High water scarcity	83.9	0.9	7.4	372.9	1.1
Low water scarcity	76.3	0.9	8.2	426.5	0.5
By utility size[b]					
Small	87.1	1.1	36.7	930.1	0.5
Large	91.4	3.4	15.3	1491.0	0.6

Sources: AICD WSS Database; Banerjee, Skilling, and others 2008.
Note: CEMAC = Central African Economic and Monetary Community, COMESA = Common Market for Eastern and Southern Africa, EAC = East African Community, ECOWAS = Economic Community of West African States, SADC = Southern African Development Community.
a. Water abundance is defined as renewable internal freshwater resources per capita in excess of 3,000 cubic meters.
b. Large utilities are defined as those serving more than 100,000 connections.

More utilities are able to cover operating costs at extremely low or extremely high levels of consumption than at average levels. More than 50 percent of the utilities recoup the operating cost at consumption levels of 4 m^3 or 40 m^3. Capital cost recovery,[3] however, is close to impossible in the African context. The highest number of utilities accomplish capital cost recovery at a subsistence consumption level of 4 m^3, which has significant implications for equity. The degree of cost recovery is the lowest at an average consumption level of 10 m^3. Households at the low and high ends of consumption are contributing more to cost recovery than the average consumer (figure 5.6).

The average revenue per unit of water sold is $0.9, primarily because of relatively higher tariffs in the middle-income countries. The revenue in

Figure 5.6 Effective Tariffs at Various Consumption Levels

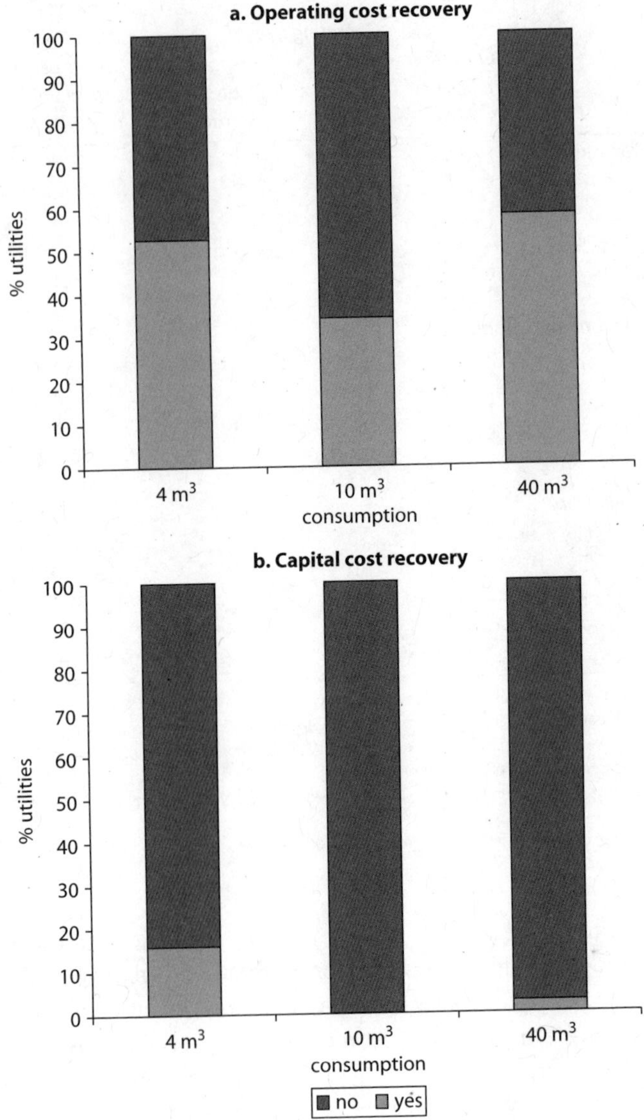

Source: Banerjee, Skilling, and others 2008.

the middle-income countries is three times that of the low-income and low-income, fragile countries, and four times that of the resource-rich countries. Among the regional economic communities, the SADC reports an average revenue of about $1, which is significantly higher than anywhere else on the continent. Water is priced higher in water-scarce countries than in water-abundant countries, suggesting that price signals are aligned with scarcity.

Because of inconsistent accounting standards, data on asset values can paint only a broad picture. Replacement cost accounting is not widely practiced, so reported values likely reflect historic costs of investment. The average value of gross fixed assets per water connection is $490. The low-income countries report an average gross fixed value that is three times higher than the value in middle-income countries, primarily because the latter group has a significantly higher number of connections.

We have few solid data points on utility debt. It appears that most utilities do not list long-term debt on their balance sheets. Most utilities are not creditworthy and do not carry their own debt. The central government borrows the money, and the utilities are simply the recipients of the capital grants. As a result, the derived debt-service ratios indicate that levels of debt are so minimal that utilities can easily cover them through their operating revenue.

The African utilities surveyed report collection ratios of more than 92 percent, on average. Resource-rich countries have the lowest levels of collection. In the regional economic communities, the collection ratio ranges from 76 percent in the Common Market for Eastern and Southern Africa (COMESA) to 105 percent in the ECOWAS, which may simply reflect a drive to collect arrears from earlier periods.

Government entities are some of the most important consumers for water utilities. For instance, 42 percent of the total billings for the Régie de Production et de Distribution d'Eau (REGIDESO), in the Democratic Republic of Congo, are for government entities. Government agencies are responsible for 20 to 30 percent of total billings for the Office Nationale des Eaux et d'Assainissement (ONEA), Société de Distribution d'Eau de Côte d'Ivoire (SODECI), Lilongwe Water Board, and Nikana Water and Sewerage Company (NWSC). These agencies, however, can be the worst offenders in paying bills as well. Though no direct data are available on government arrears, it is worth noting that the highest collection period—in REGIDESO—lasts about 2,000 days.

The collection-efficiency ratios reported by the utilities are very high, relative to their experience. We, therefore, carried out a number of cross-checks on the data. First, using household survey data it is possible to calculate the percentage of households with water service that do not report paying a utility bill. This provides a first-order estimate of the extent of undercollection from the residential sector, though the numbers will make the phenomenon seem greater than it really is

Figure 5.7 Reported versus Implicit Collection Ratios

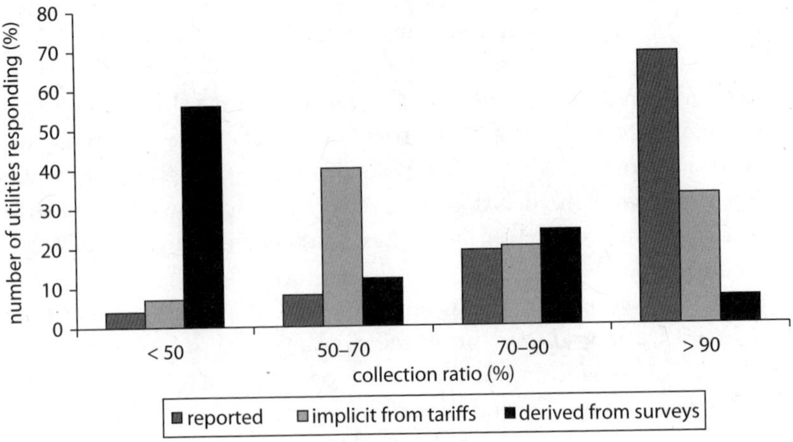

Sources: AICD WSS Database; Banerjee, Skilling, and others 2008.

because they do not distinguish between formal connections that do not pay for service and informal connections that are not billed. Second, it is possible to compare the average revenue that the utility collects per cubic meter with the average tariff charged based on the tariff schedule. This shows which revenue falls short of the tariffs that have been charged. Figure 5.7 compares the distribution for these three measures of collection efficiency. Whereas the vast majority of utilities report collection ratios above 90 percent, almost half of the utilities present implicit collection rates below 70 percent, and more than half of the utilities collect tariff revenue from fewer than 50 percent of their customers, according to household surveys.

The High Cost of Inefficiencies in Operations and Pricing

The inefficiency of the service providers and considerable mispricing in the water sector adversely affects optimal resource allocation and the financial sustainability of the sector. One way of presenting a global measure of utility inefficiency is to quantify the dollar cost of observable operational inefficiencies. This concept, the "hidden cost," is a measure of wastefulness and ineptitude. Hidden cost indicates the cost of inefficient production and partially quantifies opaque transfers from producers to consumers (Mackenzie and Stella 1996). Hidden cost also provides distorted incentives to the utilities and consumers, leading to overconsumption and wasting of scarce resources (Briceño-Garmendia, Smits, and Foster 2008). Even without explicitly revealing itself in the budget, it affects the macroeconomic stability and underreports the size of the public sector.

The hidden cost estimates the financial losses associated with four components—undercollected revenue, distribution losses, underpricing, and overstaffing—and expresses these losses as a percentage of the utilities' overall turnover. These inefficiencies can be quantified by comparing the revenue available to the utility with the revenue available to an ideal utility that is able to charge cost-recovery tariffs, collect all of its revenue, minimize distribution losses, and employ an ideal number of workers per connection (box 5.2).

Box 5.2

Methodology for Estimation of Hidden Cost

The current profile of the utilities on these four indicators is measured against the ideal scenario, which includes the following:

Nonrevenue water. An internationally accepted benchmark of 20 percent NRW is employed.

Cost-recovery tariff. A capital premium of $0.40/m^3 (Global Water Intelligence 2004) is added to the O&M cost (available from the AICD WSS Database) to arrive at the cost-recovery tariff.

The collection ratio. This is instituted as 100 percent.

Overstaffing. Two hundred connections per employee is an accepted benchmark. This estimate is taken from two sources:

(a) The estimate—averaging more than 302 utilities from developing countries, excluding Sub-Saharan Africa—taken from the database amassed by Gassner, Popov, and Pushak (2008, http://www.ppiaf.org/documents/trends_and_policy/PSP_water_electricity.pdf) is 230 connections per employee.

(b) An analysis of data from 246 water utilities (including 123 utilities from 44 developing countries) proposed a benchmarking target of 5 or fewer staff per 1,000 connections for developing-country water utilities (that is, 200 connections per employee). This target was based on the levels of productivity actually being achieved by the top quartile of developing-country utilities within the database. By contrast, many developing-country utilities reported more than 20 staff per 1,000 connections (Tynan and Kingdom 2002).

Source: Briceño-Garmendia, Smits, and Foster 2008.

The hidden costs constitute 145 percent of the total billings in water utilities in Africa. The utilities that report the lowest hidden cost (as a share of total billings) are Plateau in Nigeria and Togolaise des Eaux in Togo. The highest is Upper Nile Water Corporation in Sudan, which loses 1,700 percent of its revenue to operational and pricing inefficiencies (figure 5.8).

The hidden costs, comprising underpricing and operational inefficiencies, amount to 0.4 percent of gross domestic product (GDP) (table 5.10). On average, the contribution of the two components is similar. Underpricing costs Africa 0.2 percent of GDP or $1.5 billion annually. In other words, revising tariffs to make them equal to historic recovery unit average costs, which would enable all African water utilities to recover capital costs as well, would increase the potential for efficiency gains to $1.5 billion a year. In GDP terms, the countries that are most affected by the pricing inefficiency are low-income fragile states, where it accounts for 0.9 percent of their GDP (or $0.4 billion per year). On the other hand, under-recovery of tariffs weighs the least on GDP for utilities in resource-rich countries (0.1 percent of GDP or $0.2 billion per year).

Three types of operational inefficiencies account for 0.2 percent of GDP on average, or $1.3 billion per year: distributional losses, undercollection of bills, and overstaffing or labor inefficiencies. First, utilities incur substantial losses on their water distribution networks. Poor network maintenance (which leads to physical leakage) and poor network management (which leads to clandestine connections and various forms of theft) each partially explains these distribution losses. Distribution losses amount to $0.4 billion a year (0.07 percent of GDP). African water utilities typically lose 35 percent of their water in distribution losses, nearly twice the 20 percent benchmark. Second, water utilities face serious problems in collecting their bills: Undercollection of bills costs almost $0.5 billion a year (0.07 percent of GDP). African water utilities manage to collect about 90 percent of the bills owed to them by their customers, short of a best practice benchmark of close to 100 percent. Third, SOEs may retain more employees than are strictly necessary to discharge their functions, often because of political pressure to provide jobs for members of certain interest groups. Overstaffing is estimated to cost utilities at least $0.4 billion a year, or 0.06 percent of GDP. African water utilities have overstaffing ratios of 24 percent over developing-country benchmarks, and a typical utility has approximately 5.6 employees per

Figure 5.8 Utility Inefficiencies as Percentage of Total Utility Revenue

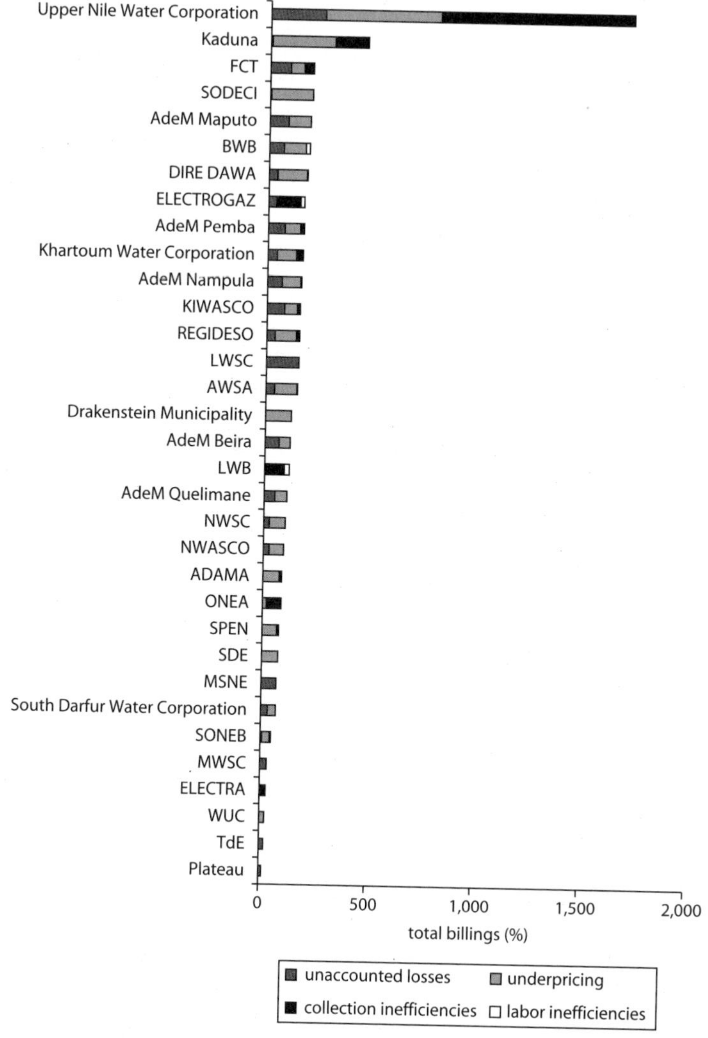

Source: AICD WSS Database; Banerjee, Skilling, and others 2008.

Note: ADAMA = Nazareth Water Company; AWSA = Addis Ababa Water Services Authority; BWB = Blantyre Water Board; FCT = Federal Capital Territory Water Board; KIWASCO = Kisumu Water and Sewerage Company; LWB = Lilongwe Water Board; LWSC = Lusaka Water and Sewerage Company; MSNE = Mauritania Société Nationale d'Eau et d'Electricité; MWSC = Mombasa Water and Sewerage Company; NWASCO = Nairobi Water and Sanitation Company; NWSC = National Water and Sewerage Company, Uganda; ONEA = Office Nationale des Eaux et d'Assainissement; REGIDESO = Régie de Production et de Distribution d'Eau; SDE = Sénégalaise des Eaux; SODECI = Société de Distribution d'Eau de Côte d'Ivoire; SONEB = Société Nationale des Eaux du Benin; SPEN = Société de Patrimoine des Eaux du Niger; TdE = Togolaise des Eaux; WUC = Water Utilities Corporation, Botswana.

Table 5.10 Hidden Cost of Inefficiencies

	GDP share (%)						US$ million per year					
	Operational inefficiencies						Operational inefficiencies					
	Labor inefficiencies	Losses	Undercollection	Total operational inefficiencies	Tariff cost recovery	Total	Labor inefficiencies	Losses	Undercollection	Total operational inefficiencies	Tariff cost recovery	Total
Sub-Saharan Africa	0.06	0.07	0.07	0.2	0.23	0.43	375	425	458	1,259	1,450	2,709
Low-income, fragile countries	0.04	0.17	0.06	0.28	0.93	1.21	17	65	25	106	358	464
Low-income, nonfragile countries	0.08	0.1	0.06	0.24	0.35	0.59	87	111	67	265	381	646
Middle-income countries	0.03	0.06	0.1	0.18	0.2	0.38	68	150	274	492	537	1,029
Resource-rich countries	—	0.05	0.03	0.08	0.1	0.18	—	103	69	172	214	386

Source: Briceño-Garmendia, Smits, and Foster 2008.
Note: — = not available.

1,000 connections though the developing-country benchmark is only 2 employees per 1,000 connections. In some cases, there are 42 employees per 1,000 connections. These results for labor inefficiencies underscore the importance of strengthening external governance mechanisms that can impose discipline on the behavior of SOEs. Overstaffing partially explains why in African countries with a publicly owned operator the share of spending allocated to capital spending frequently remains below 25 percent despite increasing spending needs. Utilities in low-income, nonfragile countries present the highest labor inefficiencies among the four-country group (0.08 percent of their GDP).

These inefficiencies can be attributable to the fact that African SOEs are characterized by low investment and high operating inefficiency. Water SOEs account for 40 percent of total public expenditures (central government and nonfinancial enterprises). Despite their large resource base, they invest comparatively little (on average) only 18 percent of the government water resource envelope. As a result, governments are typically required to step in to assume most SOE investment responsibilities, which are confined to undertaking daily O&M. Most SOEs operate at arm's length from the central government and fail in practice to meet criteria for sound commercial management. When these enterprises run into financial difficulties, the central government—as the main stakeholder—acts as the lender of last resort, absorbs debts, and assumes by default the financial, political, regulatory, and mismanagement risks. Lumpy capitalizations and debt swaps that cover the cumulative cost of operational inefficiencies are frequent events in the African utility sector, which have the potential to create a moral hazard that would perpetuate operational inefficiencies if proactive reforms are not undertaken.

Undermaintenance is another source of inefficiencies in African WSS utilities, although this has not been quantified given the scarce data for the sector. The underinvestment in O&M can greatly affect continuity of service, level of technical and commercial losses, and adequate capacity and functioning of treatment, transmission, and distribution systems. The lack of institutional capacity and regulation, the absence of fiscal discipline and availability of resources, and the persistence of civil conflict in Africa during the past two decades have left WSS facilities neglected by inadequate O&M, which eventually increases the spending needs for rehabilitation and construction of new assets.

Operating inefficiencies have been impeding expansion. Inefficiencies not only drain the public purse but also seriously undermine the performance of utilities. One casualty of insufficient revenue is maintenance.

The rate of bursts per kilometer of water mains reflects the condition of the underlying infrastructure, and the extent to which it is being adequately operated and maintained. Among African utilities, huge variation is seen between low- and middle-income countries, with bursts ranging from five per kilometer in the latter to just more than one per kilometer in the former. Utility managers often have to choose between paying salaries, buying fuel, or purchasing spare parts. Often they have to cannibalize parts from other working equipment. The investment program is another major casualty. Service expansion—measured as the percentage of residents in the utility service area that gains access to either piped water or standposts per year—is significantly higher for more efficient utilities. In particular, utilities with low hidden costs have an average annual increase in coverage of more than 3 percent, essentially twice as much as the annual increase of utilities with high hidden costs (figure 5.9). Overstaffing also seems to hinder expansion.

For similar reasons, more efficient utilities deliver better quality water. Utilities with lower rates of employees per connection manage to have on average 85 percent of water supplied with adequate chlorine, compared with 75 percent of the rest of the utilities. Conversely, utilities with higher hidden costs tend to deliver slightly higher quality water.

Figure 5.9 Utility Efficiency Affects Access Expansion and Water Quality

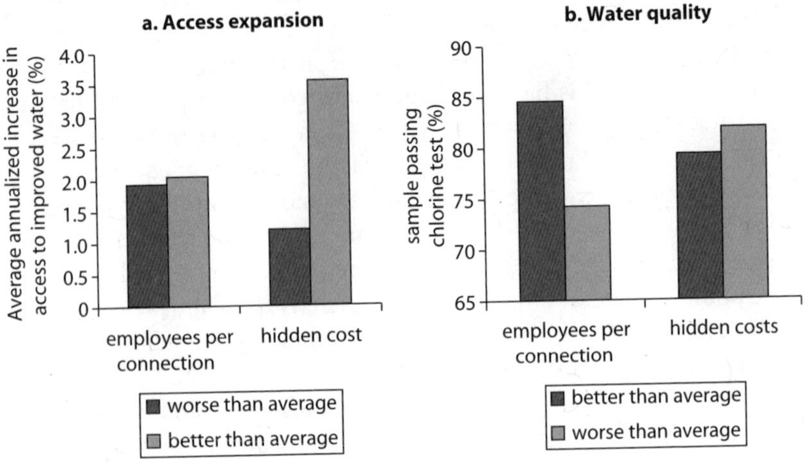

Source: Banerjee, Skilling, and others 2008.

The Role of Institutions in Improving Performance

Good institutional frameworks help to lower the inefficiency of utilities, and institutional reform is key to improving performance. Utilities that have decentralized or adopted private sector management have substantially lower hidden costs than those that have not. Unbundling also has a significant effect, but unbundling is rare in Africa and exclusively concentrated in middle-income countries, whose superior performance can be explained for many other reasons. Conversely, higher levels of regulation and governance, as well as corporatization, are associated with lower efficiency in the form of higher hidden costs (figure 5.10).

The reform agenda has had two major thrusts: increasing private participation and improving governance from within.

Private sector participation has helped to improve utility performance, with Senegal being particularly noteworthy. Management contracts, being relatively short-term instruments, have had a material effect on improving revenue collection and service continuity. However, they have not had much of an impact on more intractable issues, such as unaccounted for water and access. Lease contracts (and the associated public-funded investments) have drastically improved access and boosted operational

Figure 5.10 Hidden Costs and Institutions

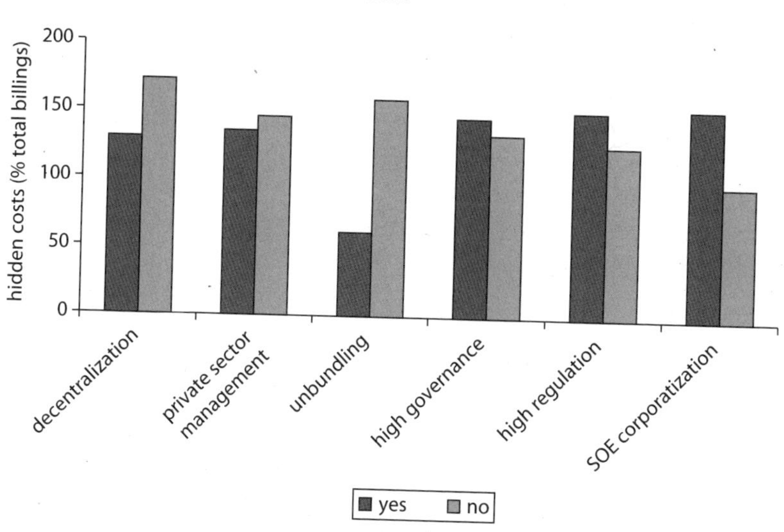

Source: Banerjee, Skilling, and others 2008.
Note: SOE = state-owned enterprise.

efficiency. With the exception of Côte d'Ivoire, however, the associated investments have been publicly financed. The lease contracts in Guinea and Maputo have been affected by a lack of coordination between the private contractor and the government, which has stalled progress in key areas, such as unaccounted-for water. Overall, private sector contracts accounted for almost 20 percent of the increase of household connections in the region, twice the amount that would be expected, given their market share of only 9 percent (table 5.11). However, half of these gains were made in Côte d'Ivoire alone (which has been adversely affected since the onset of civil war in 2002).

About half of the countries (mainly anglophone) have established distinct regulatory agencies for the water sector, although a significant number of these have not adopted private sector participation. Conversely, numerous francophone countries with private participation have adopted regulatory frameworks contractually, without establishing an independent regulatory agency. There does not appear to be any evidence supporting the superiority of any one of these two approaches. Even where explicit regulatory frameworks have been established, these typically meet only about half of the corresponding good practice criteria. However, evidence on the links between introducing an independent regulator and improving performance is negligible for the water sector. Similarly, no conclusive evidence is seen for the superiority of regulation by contract over the traditional form of regulation by agency (Vagliasindi and Nellis 2009).

Of governance reforms that appear to be the most important drivers of higher performance, two appear especially promising: performance contracts with incentives and independent external audits. Uganda has enjoyed success using a performance contract in its water company, providing the utility with incentives for good performance and producing greater accountability (box 5.3). The introduction of independent audits has also positively affected efficiency.

Table 5.11 Overview of Impact of Private Sector Participation on Utility Performance

	Contract	*Unit change in performance before and after private participation*					
		Household connections	*Improved water*	*Service continuity*	*Unaccounted-for water*	*Collection ratio*	*Labor productivity*
Gabon	Concession contract	+20			−8		
Mali		+15	+29		−14		
Côte d'Ivoire	Lease contract or *affermage*	+19	+22				+2.6
Guinea			+27		0		
Maputo			+2	+10	−1	+24	
Niger		+9	+3		−5		+3.2
Senegal		+18	+17		−15		+2.8
Johannesburg	Management contract				0	+10	
Kampala				+6	−2	+12	
Zambia				+5	−28	+19	

Source: Adapted from Marin 2009.

Note: Blank cells denote missing data; household connections and improved water are measured as additional percentage points of households with access; service continuity is measured as additional hours per day of service; unaccounted-for water is measured as reduced percentage points of losses; collection ratio is measured as additional percentage points of collection; and labor productivity is measured as additional thousands of connections served per employee.

Box 5.3

Uganda's Successful Case of State-Owned Enterprise Reform

The National Water and Sewerage Corporation (NWSC) is an autonomous public corporation, wholly owned by the government of Uganda, that is responsible for water and sanitation services in 23 towns with a population of 2.2 million, 75 percent of the population in Uganda's large urban centers.

Large inefficiencies before 1998, including poor service quality, very low staff productivity, and high operating expenses, with the collection rate at only 60 percent and a monthly cash deficit of $300,000, posed an urgent need to revamp operations.

Turnaround strategies culminated in establishing area performance contracts between a NWSC head office, which performs contract oversight and capital investment, as well as regulation of tariffs, rates, and charges, and the area managers, acting as operators and, therefore, responsible for management, operation and maintenance services, revenue collection, and rehabilitation and extension of networks. The objective was to enhance each area's performance by empowering managers and making them accountable for results. A comprehensive system of more focused and customer-oriented targets was designed. Typical performance indicators included working ratio, cash operating margin, nonrevenue water, collection efficiency, and connection ratio. Performance evaluation looked at both processes and outputs and was conducted through regular as well as unannounced visits. Incentives were both financial (including penalties for performances below targets) and nonfinancial (including trophies for best performing areas/departments and publication of monthly, quarterly, and annual best as well as worst performances).

In fiscal 2003–04, the Area Performance Contracts were changed into Internally Delegated Area Management Contracts (IDAMCs), aimed at giving more autonomy to operating teams and based on clearer roles, better incentive plans, and a larger risk apportioned to operating teams. The IDAMC framework was

(continued next page)

Box 5.3 *(continued)*

later consolidated by the use of competitive bidding as a basis for awarding contracts to the operating units.

A review of 10 years of NWSC operations shows that gains in operational and financial efficiency and service expansion have been substantial and impressive relative to the performance of the NWSC's peers in Africa.

NWSC Efficiency Gains

	Year	
Performance indicator	*1998*	*2008*
Service coverage	48%	72%
Total connections	50,826	202,559
New connections per year	3,317	25,000
Metered connections	37,217	201,839
Staff per 1,000 connections	36	7
Collection efficiency	60%	92%
NRW	60%	32.50%
Proportion of metered accounts	65%	99.60%
Annual turnover (billion U Sh)	21	84
Profit (after dep.) (billion U Sh)	−2.0	+3.8

Source: Muhairwe 2009.
Note: NRW = nonrevenue water, U Sh = Ugandan shilling.

Key success factors are indentified in the empowerment of staff, devolution of power from the center to regional operations, increased customer focus, as well as adoption of private sector–like management practices, including performance-based pay, the "customer pays for good service" principle, and so on. Also, the emphasis on planning, systematic oversight and monitoring, information sharing through benchmarking, and continuously challenging management teams with new and clear performance targets have created a strong system of checks and balances and powerfully triggered involvement, engagement, and a sense of pride on the side of the staff, beyond what simple financial incentives may obtain.

Sources: Adapted from Muhairwe 2009; National Water and Sewerage Corporation n.d.

Annex 5.1 Utilities in the AICD WSS Database

No.	Country	Utility	Population in service area	Coverage of service area	Sewerage network
1	Benin	SONEB	2,900,000	National	No
2	Burkina Faso	ONEA	2,779,875	National	Yes
3	Cameroon	SNEC	—		Yes
4	Cape Verde	ELECTRA	231,882	National	Yes
5	Chad	STEE	—	National	No
6	Congo, Dem. Rep.	REGIDESO	18,000,000	National	No
7	Côte d'Ivoire	SODECI	8,892,850	National	Yes
8	Ethiopia	ADAMA	218,111	Urban	No
9	Ethiopia	AWSA	2,887,000	Urban	Yes
10	Ethiopia	Dire Dawa	284,000	Urban	Yes
11	Ghana	GWC	17,199,942	National	Yes
12	Kenya	KIWASCO	465,613	Urban	Yes
13	Kenya	MWSC	826,000	Urban	No
14	Kenya	NWASCO	2,496,000	Urban	Yes
15	Lesotho	WASA	540,500	National	Yes
16	Madagascar	JIRAMA	4,885,250	National	Yes
17	Malawi	BWB	833,418	Urban	No
18	Malawi	CRWB	288,705	Urban	No
19	Malawi	LWB	634,447	Urban	Yes
20	Mozambique	AdeM Beira	580,258	Urban	No
21	Mozambique	AdeM Maputo	1,778,629	Urban	No
22	Mozambique	AdeM Nampula	385,809	Urban	No
23	Mozambique	AdeM Pemba	131,980	Urban	No
24	Mozambique	AdeM Quelimane	288,887	Urban	No
25	Namibia	Oshakati Municipality	31,432	Urban	Yes
26	Namibia	Walvis Bay Municipality	54,025	Urban	Yes
27	Namibia	Windhoek Municipality	300,000	Urban	Yes
28	Niger	SEEN/SPEN	2,240,689	National	Yes
29	Nigeria	Borno	—	Urban	No
30	Nigeria	FCT	6,000,000	Urban	No
31	Nigeria	Kaduna	3,126,000	Urban	No
32	Nigeria	Katsina	2,845,920	Urban	No
33	Nigeria	Lagos	15,367,417	Urban	No
34	Nigeria	Plateau	1,334,000	Urban	No
35	Rwanda	ELECTROGAZ	2,010,000	National	No
36	Senegal	SDE/ONAS	7,808,142	National	Yes
37	South Africa	Cape Town Metro	3,241,000	Urban	Yes
38	South Africa	Drakenstein Municipality	213,900	Urban	Yes
39	South Africa	eThekwini (Durban)	3,375,000	Urban	Yes

(continued next page)

No.	Country	Utility	Population in service area	Coverage of service area	Sewer network
40	South Africa	Johannesburg[a]	3,753,900	Urban	Yes
41	Sudan	Khartoum Water Corporation	7,602,000	Urban	Yes
42	Sudan	South Darfur Corporation	2,051,000	Urban	No
43	Sudan	Upper Nile Water Corporation	250,000	Urban	No
44	Tanzania	DAWASCO	—	Urban	Yes
45	Tanzania	DUWS	279,000	Urban	Yes
46	Tanzania	MWSA	458,493	Urban	Yes
47	Uganda	NWSC	2,284,000	National	Yes
48	Zambia	LWSC	1,564,986	Urban	Yes
49	Zambia	NWSC	990,806	Urban	Yes
50	Zambia	SWSC	294,000	Urban	Yes

Source: Banerjee, Skilling, and others 2008a.
Note: ADAMA = Nazareth Water Company; AWSA = Addis Ababa Water Services Authority; BWB = Blantyre Water Board; CRWB = Central Region Water Board; DAWASCO = Dar es Salaam Water and Sewerage Company; DUWS = Dodoma Urban Water and Sewerage Authority; FCT = Federal Capital Territory Water Board; GWC = Ghana Water Company, JIRAMA = Jiro sy Rano Malagasy; KIWASCO = Kisumu Water and Sewerage Company; LWB = Lilongwe Water Board; LWSC = Lusaka Water and Sewerage Company; MWSA = Mwanza Water and Sewerage Authority; MWSC = Mombasa Water and Sewerage Company; NWASCO = Nairobi Water and Sanitation Company; NWSC = National Water and Sewerage Company, Uganda; NWSC = National Water and Sewerage Company, Zambia; ONAS = Office National de l'Assainissement du Sénégal; ONEA = Office Nationale des Eaux et d'Assainissement; REGIDESO = Régie de Production et de Distribution d'Eau; SDE = Sénégalaise des Eaux; SEEN = Société de Exploitation des Eaux du Niger; SNEC = Société National des Eaux du Cameroon; SODECI = Société de Distribution d'Eau de Côte d'Ivoire; SONEB = Société Nationale des Eaux du Benin; SPEN = Société de Patrimoine des Eaux du Niger; STEE = Société Tchadienne d'Eau et d'Electricité; SWSC = Southern Water and Sewerage Company; WASA = Water and Sanitation Authority. — = data not available.

Notes

1. Francophone countries have a much stronger metering tradition, which reflects different traditions in France and England.
2. This number reflects the value for SNDE (Société Nationale de Distribution d'Eau, the Republic of Congo).
3. Capital cost = O&M cost + capital premium of $0.4/m^3$. The capital premium is based on internationally used benchmarks computed by Global Water Intelligence (2004).

References

Banerjee, S., V. Foster, Y. Ying, H. Skilling, and Q. Wodon. 2008. "Cost Recovery, Equity, and Efficiency in Water Tariffs: Evidence from African Utilities." AICD Working Paper 7, World Bank, Washington, DC.

Banerjee, S., H. Skilling, V. Foster, C. Briceño-Garmendia, E. Morella, and T. Chfadi. 2008. "Ebbing Water, Surging Deficits: Urban Water Supply in Sub-Saharan Africa." Background Paper 12, Africa Infrastructure Country Diagnostic, World Bank, Washington, DC.

Briceño-Garmendia, C., K. Smits, and V. Foster. 2008. "Financing Public Infrastructure in Sub-Saharan Africa: Patterns and Emerging Issues." AICD Background Paper 15, World Bank, Washington, DC.

Global Water Intelligence. 2004. "Tariffs: Half-Way There." Global Water Intelligence, Oxford, UK.

Mackenzie, G. A., and P. Stella. 1996. "Quasi-Fiscal Operations of Public Financial Institutions." Occasional Paper 142, International Monetary Fund, Washington, DC.

Marin, P. 2009. "Public-Private Partnerships for Urban Water Utilities: A Review of Experiences in Developing Countries." Trends and Policy Options 8. PPIAF and World Bank, Washington, DC.

McIntosh, A. C. 2003. "Asian Water Supply: Reaching the Poor." Asian Development Bank and International Water Association, Manila and London.

Muhairwe, W. T. 2009. "Fostering Improved Performance through Internal Contractualisation." Paper presented at World Bank Water Week, Washington, DC, February 17–20.

National Water and Sewerage Corporation. n.d. NWSC Corporate Plan 2006–09, Kampala, Uganda. http://www.nwsc.co.ug/affairs02.php?cat=corporate_plan.

Tynan, N., and W. Kingdom. 2002. "A Water Scorecard: Setting Performance Targets for Water Utilities." Public Policy for the Private Sector Note 242, World Bank, Washington, DC.

Vagliasindi, M., and J. Nellis 2009. "Evaluating Africa's Experience with Institutional Reforms for the Infrastructure Sectors." AICD Working Paper 23, World Bank, Washington, DC.

Water and Sanitation Program. 2008. "Can Africa Afford to Miss the Sanitation MDG Target? A Review of the Sanitation and Hygiene Status in 32 Countries." World Bank, Washington, DC.

CHAPTER 6

Cost Recovery, Affordability, and Subsidies

The need to provide Africans with safe drinking water is immense and immediate. As a poor continent, however, Africa lacks the level of household and government funds required to significantly expand water networks and improve service quality. In the best-case scenario, its governments could set tariffs at cost-recovery levels so that water service providers could justify investments in expanded networks, but a significant share of the existing and potential consumer base cannot afford to pay at that rate.

This chapter uses household survey data in the Africa Infrastructure Country Diagnostic (AICD) to examine Africa's ability to pay for water services and implement operating and capital cost-recovery tariffs. It evaluates the targeting and actual performance of existing tariffs' subsidy mechanisms and considers alternative systems with potentially better outcomes.

Average Monthly Spending on Water

Most African households live on very modest budgets. The average African household survives on not more than $180 per month; urban household budgets are about $100 per month higher than those of rural households. Household budgets range from $60 per month in the lowest

Figure 6.1 Spending on Water Services

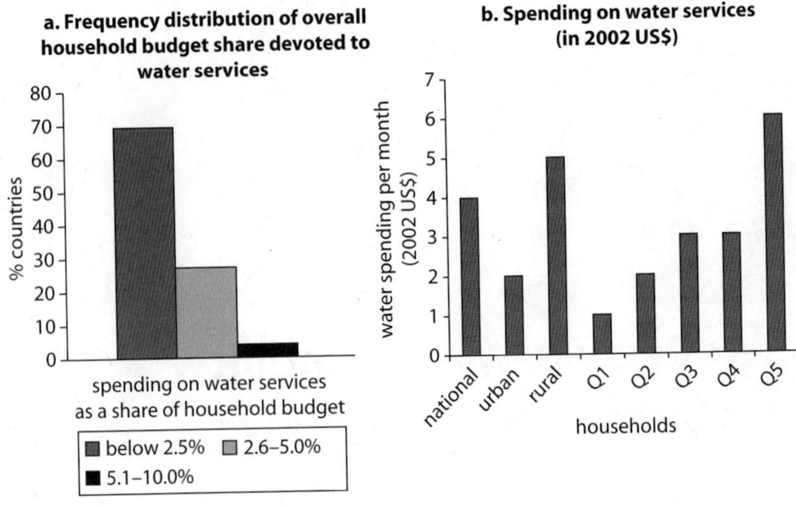

Source: Banerjee, Wodon, and others 2008.
Note: Q = quintile.

quintile to no more than $400 per month in the highest income quintile except in middle-income countries, where the richest quintile has a monthly budget of $200 to $1,300 (table 6.1).

On average, Africans spend more than half their household budget on food. Monthly spending on water averages $4, or 2 percent of household budgets, and rarely exceeds 3 percent. Only in Cameroon, Mauritania, and Rwanda are water expenses more than 5 percent of the household budget. Spending on water services increases with rising income levels: The top 20 percent of African households pay $6 per month (2 percent of income), primarily because they are disproportionately connected to formal water networks (figure 6.1).

Wide Price Variations among Service Providers in the Urban Water Market

The price of water in the unserved market is substantially higher than the price utilities charge for household connections. Utilities supply piped water delivered through public standposts in addition to piped connections to houses and yards. Prices at public standposts are usually subsidized so that low-income households in periurban areas can benefit from improved water supply. The important policy questions are whether this practice realizes the objective of providing affordable water to public standpost users and the extent of cross-subsidy between the low-volume

Table 6.1 Monthly Household Budget

	Total household budget (2002 US$)								*Food expenditure as a share of total household budget (%)*							
	National	*Rural*	*Urban*	*Q1*	*Q2*	*Q3*	*Q4*	*Q5*	*National*	*Rural*	*Urban*	*Q1*	*Q2*	*Q3*	*Q4*	*Q5*
Overall	177	130	241	59	97	128	169	340	55	61	48	63	64	63	60	48
Low-income countries	139	109	208	53	80	103	135	258	59	64	50	67	68	66	64	52
Middle-income countries	300	199	350	79	155	181	282	609	45	54	42	51	55	52	50	38

Source: Banerjee, Wodon, and others 2008.
Note: Q = quintile.

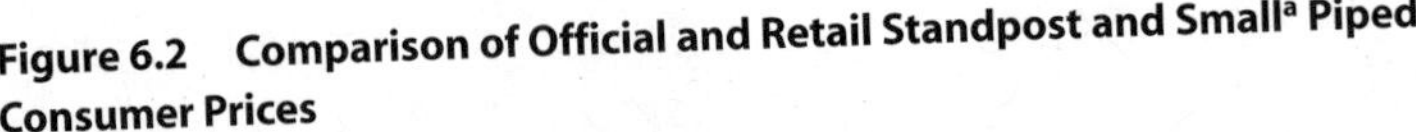

Figure 6.2 Comparison of Official and Retail Standpost and Small[a] Piped Consumer Prices

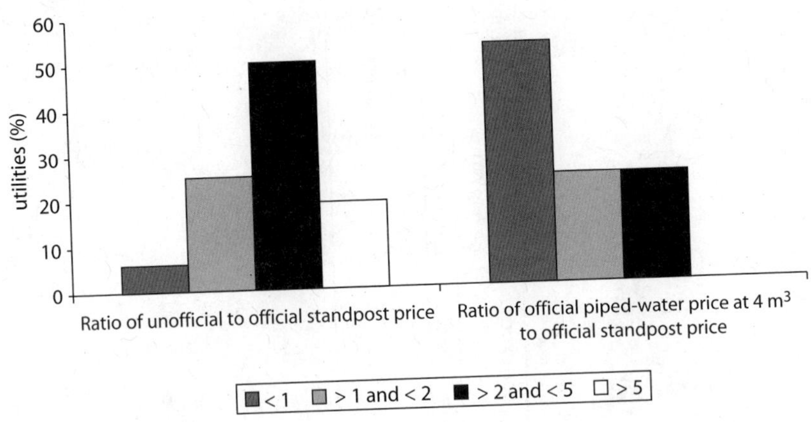

Source: Banerjee, Foster, and others 2008.
Note: The Democratic Republic of Congo is not included in the graph because the formal standpost price is almost negligible. Figure based on information available for 12 utilities.
a. Refers to minimum consumption level of 4 m^3.

consumers at public standposts and those who have household connections to piped water.

The average official price is \$0.63/cubic meter (m^3) at public standposts and \$0.55/m^3 for small consumers of household connections to piped water. Standpost consumers are paying more to approximately half the utilities. For the rest, the evidence suggests that consumers whose households are connected to piped water are cross-subsidizing standpost consumers at the same level of consumption (figure 6.2). This would be extremely inequitable if the standpost and low-volume piped-water consumers were in similar income strata.

The official standpost tariff may not, however, be what consumers really pay. Operators and middlemen come between the utility and consumers. The result is a highly dynamic market in which, except in Ouagadougou, informal retail prices are much higher than the official standpost tariffs. For half the utilities, the informal standpost price is between two and five times the formal standpost price. This is true of dense periurban areas with shortages of households connected to piped water and a significant dependence on public standposts (box 6.1). For instance, in Antananarivo, Lusaka, and Cotonou, retail prices are more than five times higher than official tariffs.

In the largest African cities, alternatives to piped water supply are priced from 1.3 times as high for small piped-water networks to 10 to 20

Box 6.1

Piped Water Delivered through Public Standposts in Kigali, Rwanda

The water production capacity of ELECTROGAZ, the main utility in Kigali, is inadequate to meet network demand. The lack of bulk supply causes rolling outages throughout the city and often forces residents with private connections to seek water at public sources, such as public standposts.

The financial stability of Kigali public standposts can be estimated from the tariff paid by standpost operators (RF 240, $0.42 per cubic meter), the total cost of production by ELECTROGAZ (RF 205), the rate of unaccounted-for water in distribution and selling (35 percent and 5 percent, respectively), and the volume and price of water sold at the public standposts. Three operators selling 100 jerricans each per day at RF 10, 20, and 30 per jerrican would earn estimated monthly net incomes of $314, $949, and $1,584 (the 2008 gross domestic product per capita was $370). The combination of a low tariff and a 35 percent rate of unaccounted-for water in distribution creates losses for the utility.

Of the roughly 240 public standposts in Kigali, an estimated 193 (80 percent) were operating in December 2008. Utility officials estimate that 60,000 people use piped water delivered through public standposts, though this figure includes consumers who use them only when their primary source is unavailable. Based on total water volume recorded at meters, public standposts could supply only 48,500 people with 20 liters daily. That figure is equal to the upper segment of the population that depends primarily on public standposts (about 6 percent of the city's population).

The utility's limited production capacity has affected both the level of peak demand at public standposts and the cost of production. Observations and interviews with consumers indicate that prices have often been higher in areas when and where water service has been cut—and lower after periods of precipitation that increase the availability of other supply options, such as rainwater and natural springs.

Source: Keener and others (forthcoming).

times as high for mobile distributors (table 6.2). The lower prices are paid by small utility consumers, and the higher prices are paid by unserved consumers of alternatives. They do not benefit from utility service and must pay significantly more. Moreover, the prices charged by each water provider in the informal sector also show a higher variation than those

Table 6.2 Prices by Alternate Water Service Provider

Country	Largest city	Household connection (US$/m³)	Small piped network (US$/m³)	Standpipe (US$/m³)	Household reseller (US$/m³)	Water tanker (US$/m³)	Water vendor (US$/m³)
Benin	Cotonou	0.41	n.a.	1.91	1.91	n.a.	n.a.
Burkina Faso	Ouagadougou	0.90	n.a.	0.48	n.a.	n.a.	1.67
Ethiopia	Addis Ababa	0.19	n.a.	0.87	1.44	3.85	—
Mozambique	Maputo	0.96	0.98	0.98	0.98	n.a.	—
Niger	Niamey	0.52	n.a.	0.48	n.a.	n.a.	1.79
Nigeria	Kaduna	0.17	n.a.	—	—	3.43	5.71
Rwanda	Kigali	0.44	n.a.	1.79	1.79	4.48	n.a.
Senegal	Dakar	0.37	n.a.	1.53	—	n.a.	2.29
South Africa	Johannesburg	0.05	n.a.	n.a.	n.a.	—	—
Congo, Dem. Rep.	Kinshasa	0.05	2.11	1.02	1.01	n.a.	n.a.
Ghana	Accra	0.52	n.a.	5.51	1.53	5.46	6.89
Kenya	Nairobi	0.18	0.60	1.73	n.a.	3.74	3.47
Lesotho	Maseru	0.40	n.a.	2.58	—	—	—
Malawi	Blantyre	0.12	n.a.	1.16	3.38	n.a.	n.a.
Namibia	Windhoek	1.45	n.a.	n.a.	n.a.	n.a.	n.a.
Sudan	Great Khartoum	0.37	n.a.	1.15	—	4.32	3.00
Zambia	Lusaka	0.56	n.a.	1.67	—	n.a.	3.00
Cape Verde	Praia	2.67	n.a.	9.44	n.a.	9.67	11.38
Chad	N'Djamena	0.22	—	—	—	n.a.	—
Côte d'Ivoire	Abidjan	0.04	—	0.93	1.82	n.a.	3.35
Madagascar	Antananarivo	0.11	0.47	1.24	—	n.a.	2.33
Tanzania	Dar es Salaam	0.39	—	0.87	0.98	2.40	2.56
Uganda	Kampala	0.25	n.a.	1.40	1.40	—	4.50
	Average	0.49	1.04	1.93	1.63	4.67	4.00
	Median	0.37	0.79	1.24	1.49	4.08	3.00
	Minimum	0.04	0.47	0.48	0.98	2.40	1.67
	Maximum	2.67	2.11	9.44	3.38	9.67	11.38

Source: Keener, Luengo, and Banerjee 2009.
Note: n.a = not applicable, — = not available.

offered by the utilities to connected households; this further underscores the volatility and inequity in the market structure.

Households with private connections or yard taps face water prices significantly lower than those dependent on piped water delivered through public standpipes and the informal market. The prices for each water provider in the informal sector also show higher variability than those offered by the utilities to connected households. This applies to alternative providers in different cities (the standard deviation of the prices for each informal water service is 1.3 to 5 times higher than for the household connection), as well as for different neighborhoods within the same city (figure 6.3). Cape Verde's prices for formal and informal water services are highest because of the specifications of its water production system.

When formal household connections to piped water are not available or the retail public standpipe price varies from the official price, utilities lose potential revenue from unserved or underserved customers. For the cities studied, the ratio between informal to formal standpipe prices goes from 0.9 in Ouagadougou, to 20.4 in Kinshasa, with a median ratio of 3. High retail prices and the size of the population coverage by standpipes

Figure 6.3 Price by Water Service Provider

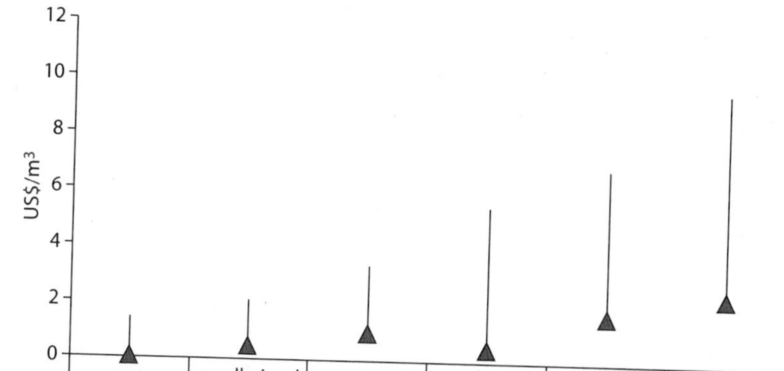

	HH connection	small piped network	HH reseller	standpipe or kiosk	water vendor	water tanker
average	0.39	1.04	1.63	1.52	3.38	4.67
max	1.45	2.11	3.38	5.51	6.89	9.67
▲min	0.04	0.47	0.98	0.48	1.67	2.40

Source: Keener, Luengo, and Banerjee 2009.
Note: The average prices are presented. Cape Verde is excluded from this graph because it is an outlier.
HH = household.

combine to create an economic environment in which estimates of the total gross profit[1] captured by standpipe operators ranged from $15,477 in Khartoum to almost $10 million in Lusaka.[2] These amounts can represent a significant percentage of formal utilities' revenue: in Maputo, 12 percent; Addis Ababa, 44 percent; and Lusaka, 120 percent. Thus, although standpipes are already heavily subsidized by utilities, none of this subsidy reaches the final consumers.

Two-Part Tariffs and the Small Consumer

The tariff at an average consumption level of 10 m^3 is about $0.49/m^3 in Africa. However, tariffs at ELECTRA, in Cape Verde, exceed $3 for that consumption level because of the expense of desalination, which raises the cost of water production. If Cape Verde is excluded from the continental figure, the average tariff is $0.43/m^3. The tariff levels in Africa are comparable to the average in Latin America and the Caribbean, which at $0.41/m^3 at an average consumption of 15 m^3 is higher than other regions in the world, such as East Asia, Eastern Europe, and the Middle East. South Asian water tariffs are the world's lowest, with an observed average tariff of only $0.09/m^3 (table 6.3).

The implementation of the increasing block tariff (IBT) structure is based on the implicit assumption that small consumers are poor and large consumers will cross-subsidize the small ones. To investigate whether small consumers pay lower prices than large consumers, the water price

Table 6.3 Comparison of Water Tariffs in Africa and Other Global Regions at Various Levels of Consumption
($/m^3)

Consumption level	*4 m^3*	*10 m^3*	*15 m^3*	*40 m^3*
Average	0.55	0.49	0.52	0.65
Median	0.41	0.38	0.40	0.51
Comparable tariffs (average consumption = 15 m^3)				
Organisation for Economic Co-operation and Development			1.04	
Latin America and the Caribbean			0.41	
Middle East and North Africa			0.37	
East Asia and Pacific			0.25	
Europe and Central Asia			0.13	
South Asia			0.09	

Sources: Banerjee, Foster, and others 2008; Foster and Yepes 2006.

per cubic meter for three consumption levels—4, 10, and 40 m^3/month—is calculated. The effective price sharply declines at the average consumption of 10 m^3, and then rises again. The price at the subsistence consumption rate of 4 m^3 is roughly comparable to the price at 20 m^3 of consumption (figure 6.4).

The two-part IBT tariff structure can fail to favor small consumers for two reasons. First, the fixed-fee and minimum-consumption charges place an enormous burden on low-volume consumers. This is the part of the water bill the households cannot control regardless of their level of consumption. Komives and others (2005) compare the average price per m^3 of IBT, IBT with fixed-fee, and IBT with fixed-fee and minimum-consumption charges. They find that low-volume consumers under the two-tariff regimes bear the burden of higher prices. Small consumers pay the lowest prices in only a few countries in Africa. Among the 45 utilities in the sample, the effective price increases with rising consumption in 27 utilities. In the majority of utilities, high-end consumers pay more than low-end or average consumers. Inequity is more prevalent, however, at the lower end of consumption, among households consuming 4 to 10 m^3/month. In 16 utilities, the effective tariffs of small consumers are higher than those of average consumers. This difference is pronounced in the case of five utilities in Mozambique. Because these utilities have a minimum threshold of 10 m^3, the small consumer whose water intake is about 4 m^3 pays on average about $0.57 more than those consuming 10 m^3 and about $0.40 more than those consuming 40 m^3 (figure 6.5).

Figure 6.4 Average Water Tariffs for Africa at Different Consumption Levels

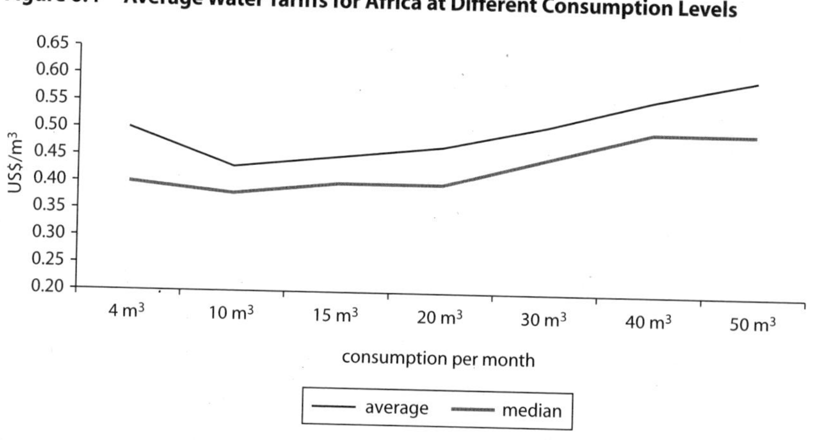

Source: Banerjee, Foster, and others 2008.
Note: Cape Verde is not included in this graph because it is an outlier.

Figure 6.5 Utilities Charging Higher Effective Prices to Small Consumers

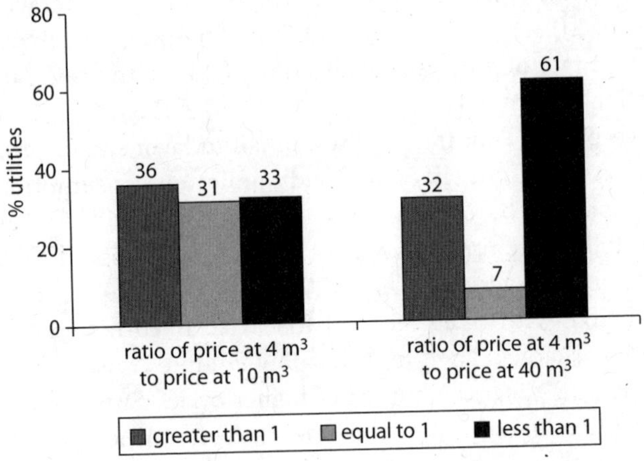

% utilities	greater than 1	equal to 1	less than 1
ratio of price at 4 m³ to price at 10 m³	36	31	33
ratio of price at 4 m³ to price at 40 m³	32	7	61

Source: Banerjee, Foster, and others 2008.

Second, the arrangement of the block's size and price is important, particularly that of the first block. If the first block is wide, it allows leakage of the implicit subsidy to the nonpoor and leads to a higher price per m^3 for the low-volume consumers in the band. Fixed and minimum consumption charges have a significant impact on the unit price paid by small consumers. With a fixed charge, small consumers usually have to pay a higher price per unit than large consumers. For utilities that impose a fixed-fee or minimum consumption charge, the average price at 4 m^3 is $0.64/$m^3$, as opposed to $0.47/$m^3$ for those who do not. The size of the first block can also impact the price paid by small consumers. Generally speaking, the larger the size of the first block in an IBT structure, the higher the probability that subsidies for the low price of the first block will leak to large consumers. Of the 45 utilities in the sample, only nine have a tariff design with a first block that rises above 10 m^3 (the rest have a flat or linear structure). This effect, though important, is overwhelmed by the fixed-fee and minimum consumption charges, which can erase the block-tariff structure's positive impact on small consumers.

The subsidy to the low block under the current IBT structure does not benefit small consumers (usually the poor) exclusively; instead, a large amount of the subsidy leaks to large consumers (usually the nonpoor). Further, the fixed and minimum consumption charges and the large size of the low blocks often cause small consumers to pay higher effective prices per unit than large consumers.

Paying for Water: How Common?

The discussion so far has focused on formal utility customers who report paying a utility bill. But to focus only on this category of users is to miss a substantial part of the African story. Household surveys provide unique insights into two other key categories of consumers. First, there are those who do not have their own household connection to piped water but nonetheless register expenditure because they are accessing the network through some secondary source, usually a neighbor's tap. Second, there are those who do have a household connection to piped water but do not register any expenditure, whether because they are in arrears or because the connection itself is clandestine.

About 61 percent of the African population is not connected to and does not pay for formal water services (figure 6.6). The traditional customers who connect and pay are actually a minority of those who use the service; the population that connects but does not pay is almost as large as the percentage that connects and pays. Moreover, for access to household connections to piped water, the population that is unconnected but nevertheless pays to obtain the service through secondary sources is slightly higher than the one that connects and pays for proprietary service.

Figure 6.6 Connection and Payment, by Consumer Categories

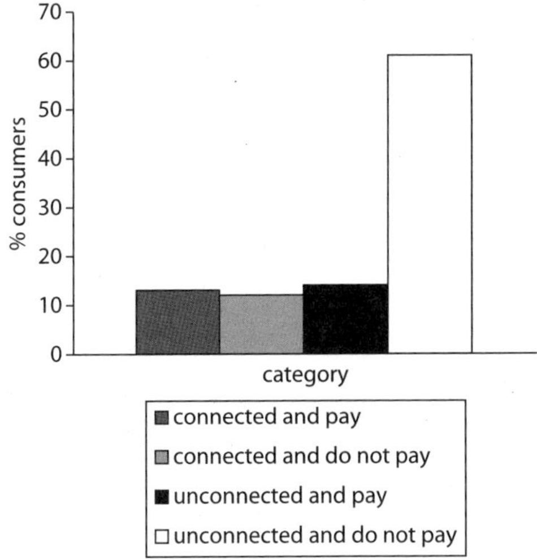

Source: Banerjee, Wodon, and others 2008.

Overall, an estimated 12 percent of those who have household connections to piped water do not appear to be paying for them in any given month. Nonpayment rates in excess of 65 percent can be found in 30 percent of customers with household connections to piped water (figure 6.7, panel a).

The extent to which nonpayment is higher among the poorest can be seen as an indicator that households are facing affordability problems. In the first quintile, the nonpayment ratio amounts to approximately 63 percent of households, and this ratio declines steadily to 26 percent of households in the fifth quintile (figure 6.7, panel b). This pattern indicates that nonpayment, to some extent, does represent an affordability issue, given the decline as household budgets rise across the distribution. Nevertheless, the existence of a significant nonpayment rate, even among

Figure 6.7 Nonpayment Rates of Water Services

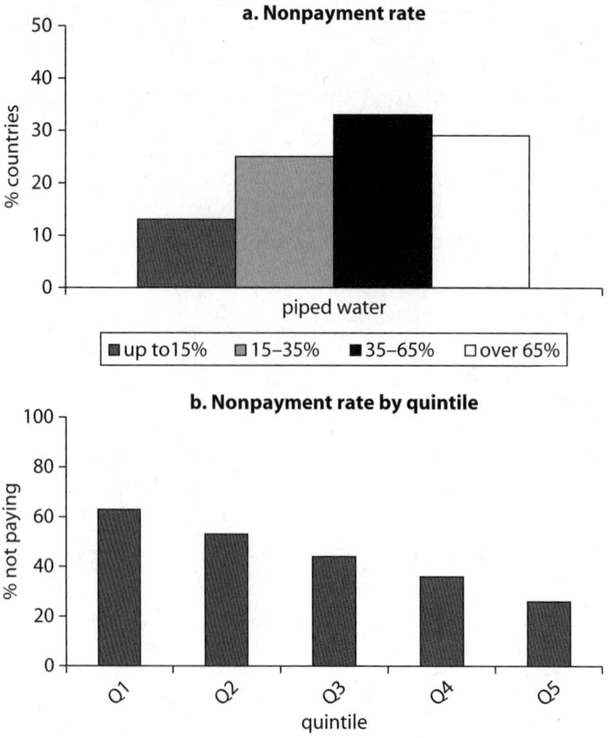

Source: Banerjee, Wodon, and others 2008.
Note: Q = quintile.

the richest quintiles, suggests that problems of payment culture also exist. Moreover, given that the majority of connected households are in the richer quintiles, in absolute terms the largest number of nonpaying customers also comes from the richer quintiles (even though the nonpayment ratio for this group is comparatively low).

Recovering Operating Costs: Affordable

As utilities move toward commercial entities, it becomes essential to establish demand for services. Affordability is typically measured by the share of infrastructure spending in the total household budget and whether it exceeds a set threshold (Fankhauser and Tepic 2005). There is no absolutely scientific basis for determining the value of such affordability thresholds; however, based on experience with actual household expenditure patterns and results of willingness to pay surveys, certain thresholds have come to be widely used by practitioners. The World Health Organization, for example, uses a 5 percent affordability threshold for water and sanitation services in developing countries. The evidence presented on current expenditure patterns earlier suggests that households spend 2 to 5 percent on water services. In the discussion that follows, 5 percent is used as a reference affordability threshold.

To estimate the percentage of African households likely to face affordability problems for modern infrastructure services, two elements are needed. First, indicative values of the true cost of infrastructure services are needed as a reference point. The absolute cost of the total monthly bill can be computed based on different assumptions about subsistence household consumption and the tariff applied. For piped-water service, subsistence consumption ranges between 4 m^3 per month (based on an absolute minimum consumption of 25 liters per capita per day for a family of five) and 10 m^3 per month (based on a somewhat more comfortable but still modest level of 60 liters per capita per day for a family of five). The indicative tariff ranges from $0.40/$m^3$ to $0.80/$m^3$, depending on whether the goal is operating or full capital cost recovery. The lower-bound monthly bill is about $2, and the upper-bound monthly bill is about $8 for household connections to piped water (table 6.4).

Second, the survey data on budget expenditures are used to estimate what percentage of households would hit the 5 percent affordability thresholds at different levels of absolute expenditure. For example, a household with a monthly budget of $100 would hit the affordability threshold of 5 percent of income once any service cost more than $5 per month.

Table 6.4 Reference Points for the True Cost of Infrastructure Services

	Piped water	*Reference*
Lower bound	Subsistence household consumption	4 m^3
	Tariff (operating cost recovery) $/$m^3$	$0.40/$m^3$
	Total monthly bill ($)	$2
Upper bound	Subsistence household consumption	10 m^3
	Tariff (capital cost recovery) $/$m^3$	$0.80/$m^3$
	Total monthly bill ($)	$8

Source: Banerjee, Wodon, and others 2008.

By pooling all African households across countries and grouping them into a common set of quintiles based on purchasing power parity adjustments to their budgets, it is possible to report results for the continent as a whole. Figure 6.8 plots the share of budget required to meet increasing levels of spending on infrastructure services for the average household in each of the continental income quintiles.

The average household in the first quintile hits the 5 percent affordability threshold at close to $4 per month, which is more than enough to pay for the subsistence minimum consumption of piped water. The average household in the second quintile hits the 5 percent affordability threshold at close to $8 per month and would be able to pay for the upper bound of piped water. Households in the third, fourth, and fifth quintiles do not face any affordability constraints within the range of service baskets considered here.

Very modest consumption baskets priced at levels compatible with operating cost recovery appear to be affordable across the full range of household budgets in Africa. Nevertheless, an estimated 60 percent of the African population cannot afford to pay full cost-recovery tariffs or extend consumption beyond the absolute minimum subsistence level.

These continental results mask a great deal of variation across individual countries because almost all the households in the poorer countries may be in the bottom quintile for Africa as a whole, whereas almost all the households in the more affluent countries may be in the uppermost quintile for Africa as a whole. Table 6.5 provides a similar type of analysis at the country level to calculate the percentage of households in each country that would fall beyond the 5 percent affordability threshold at any particular absolute monthly cost of service.

The countries divide into three groups. At one extreme is group 1, in which a majority of urban households can afford a monthly expenditure of $8, and often considerably more. At the other extreme is group 3, in

Figure 6.8 Share of Average Urban Household Budget Required to Purchase Subsistence Amounts of Piped Water, by Continental Income Quintiles

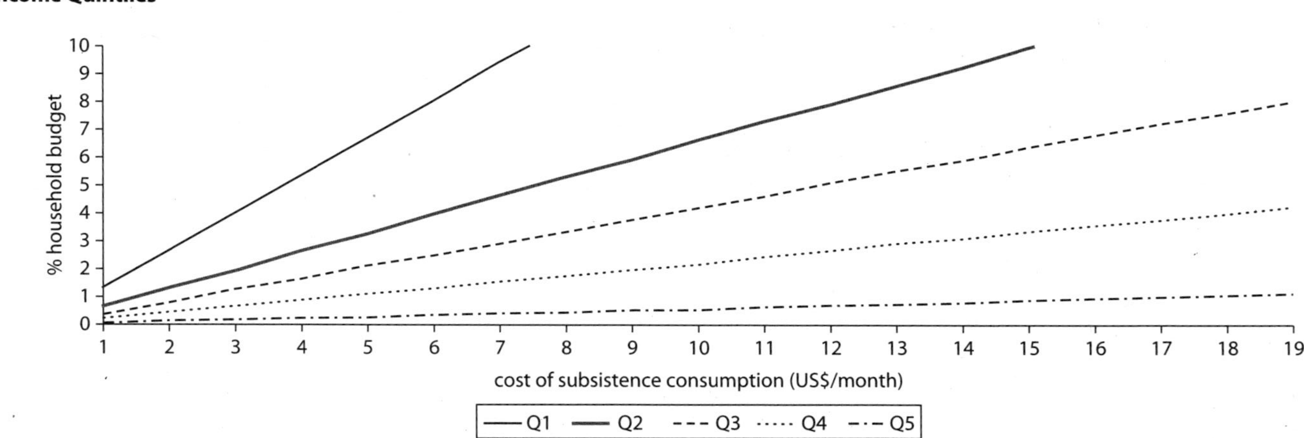

Source: Banerjee, Wodon, and others 2008.
Note: Q = quintile.

Table 6.5 Share of Urban Households Whose Utility Bill Would Exceed 5 Percent of the Monthly Household Budget at Various Prices

		Monthly bill ($)							
Group		*2*	*4*	*6*	*8*	*10*	*12*	*14*	*16*
1	Cape Verde	0	0	0	0	0	0	0	0
	Morocco	0	0	0	0	0	0	0	0
	Senegal	0	0	0	0	0	0	1	1
	South Africa	0	0	0	0	1	1	1	1
	Cameroon	0	0	0	0	1	2	7	17
	Côte d'Ivoire	0	0	1	2	3	5	7	10
	Congo, Rep.	0	0	3	5	12	21	28	35
2	Ghana	0	2	7	11	30	46	55	67
	Benin	0	2	4	12	33	45	60	71
	Kenya	0	0	5	20	36	62	72	78
	Sierra Leone	0	4	16	30	44	54	62	67
	São Tomé and Principe	0	2	13	29	46	64	77	81
	Burkina Faso	0	4	20	34	47	62	72	78
	Zambia	0	4	18	35	50	58	67	76
	Nigeria	3	10	23	35	57	78	89	95
	Madagascar	0	16	28	47	61	68	78	85
3	Niger	1	11	28	55	70	79	89	93
	Tanzania	1	8	25	55	75	89	96	98
	Guinea-Bissau	0	6	38	65	81	89	91	93
	Uganda	2	17	45	65	82	90	96	97
	Burundi	7	29	53	72	82	90	97	100
	Malawi	2	32	66	78	87	92	93	94
	Congo, Dem. Rep.	9	49	79	91	98	99	100	100
	Ethiopia	40	87	95	99	99	99	99	100
Summary	Low-income	5.0	18.4	32.4	44.5	59.5	72.3	79.7	84.3
	Middle-income	0.0	0.0	0.1	0.2	1.2	1.8	2.9	4.7
	All	3.7	13.7	24.2	33.2	44.7	54.3	60.2	64.1

Source: Banerjee, Wodon, and others 2008.

which at least 70 percent, and in some cases more than 90 percent, of urban households would be unable to afford a monthly expenditure of $8 for water. All the remaining countries fall into group 2, in which a substantial share of the urban population—between one- and two-thirds—would face difficulties covering an upper-bound monthly expenditure.

The High Cost of Connecting to Water and Sanitation Services

Network connection costs can prove to be a significant barrier to consumer access in Africa. The connection charges vary widely, from about

$6 in the Upper Nile in Sudan to more than $240 in Côte d'Ivoire, Mozambique, and Niger,[3] and more than $300 in Drakenstein, eThekwini, and Johannesburg, South Africa. Connection costs can vary even among water utilities in the same country. For instance, Addis Ababa Water Services Authority (AWSA), Nazareth Water Company (ADAMA), and Dire Dawa—three utilities in Ethiopia—charge connection costs of $14, $9, and $43, respectively. A comparison with the gross national income (GNI) per capita suggests that, in some countries, the connection charge is relatively expensive. On average across Africa, the connection charge is 28 percent of the GNI per capita. In middle-income countries such as South Africa and Namibia, though the connection cost is high, it is negligible compared with GNI per capita, but in countries such as Niger, the connection charge is more than 100 percent of the GNI per capita (figure 6.9).

Similarly, for sanitation, the capital costs associated with infrastructure facilities can be considered prohibitive when compared with the limited budgets. For instance, standardized unit costs drawn from the Senegal sanitation sector can be employed to estimate the percentage of households' monthly budget that would be absorbed by the upfront investment cost associated with different types of sanitation facilities (table 6.6). The results indicate that although traditional latrines look quite affordable across the income spectrum in Senegal, improved latrines represent more than a month of the household budget even for households in the highest income group. These findings are borne out by the patterns of access to sanitation already observed across the socioeconomic spectrum. Half of Sub-Saharan African households have invested in traditional latrines in

Figure 6.9 Formal Water Connection Cost

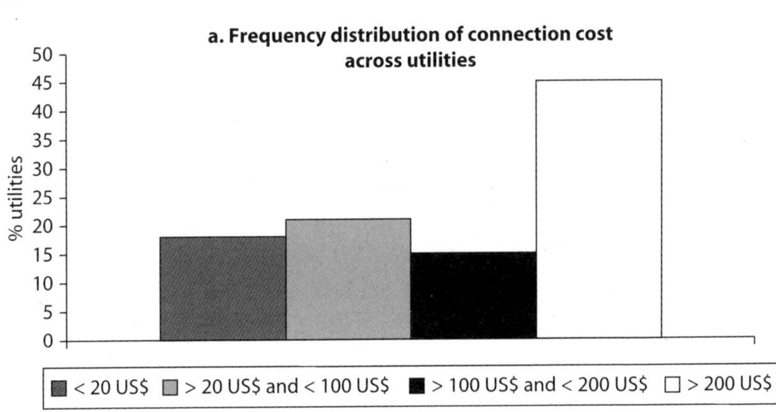

(continued next page)

Figure 6.9 *(continued)*

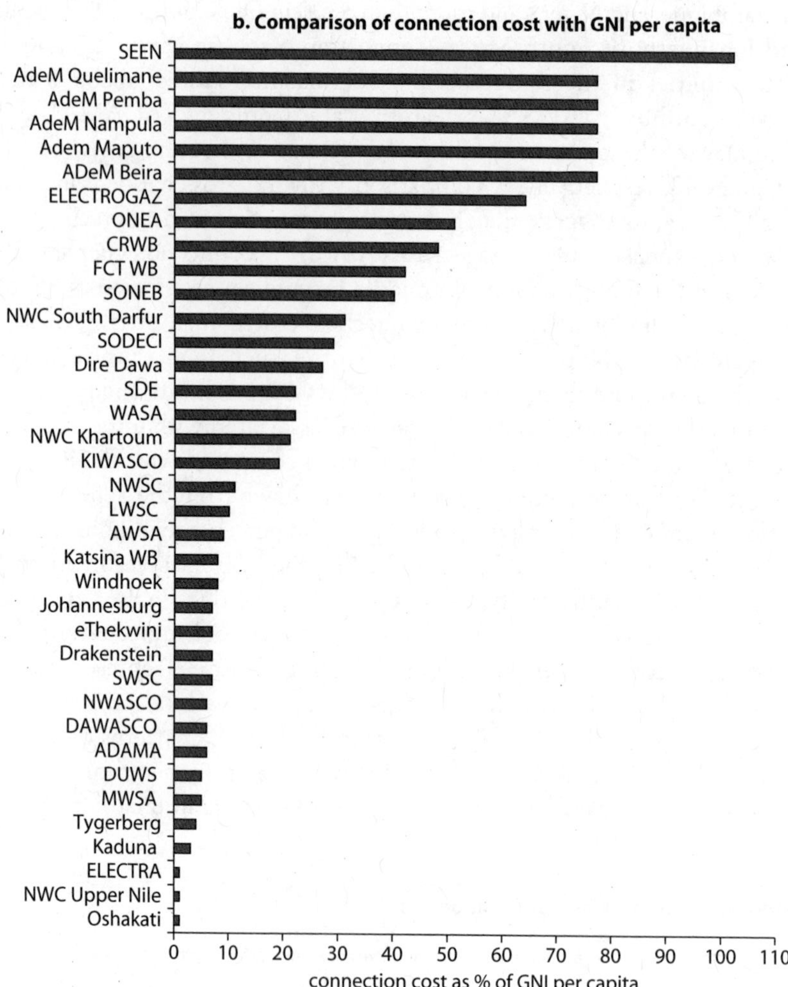

Source: Banerjee, Foster, and others 2008.
Note: ADAMA = Nazareth Water Company; AWSA = Addis Ababa Water Services Authority; CRWB = Central Region Water Board; DAWASCO = Dar es Salaam Water and Sewerage Company; DUWS = Dodoma Urban Water and Sewerage Authority; FCT WB = Federal Capital Territory Water Board; GNI = gross national income; KIWASCO = Kisumu Water and Sewerage Company; LWSC = Lusaka Water and Sewerage Company; MWSA = Mwanza Water and Sewerage Authority; NWASCO = Nairobi Water and Sanitation Company; NWC = National Water Company; NWSC = National Water and Sewerage Company, Uganda; ONEA = Office Nationale des Eaux et d'Assainissement; SDE = Sénégalaise des Eaux; SEEN = Société de Exploitation des Eaux du Niger; SODECI = Société de Distribution d'Eau de Côte d'Ivoire; SONEB = Société Nationale des Eaux du Benin; SWSC = Southern Water and Sewerage Company; WASA = Water and Sanitation Authority; WB = Water Board.

Table 6.6 Cost of Facility as Percentage of Monthly Household Budget in Senegal

	National	*Rural*	*Urban*	*Q1*	*Q2*	*Q3*	*Q4*	*Q5*
Total monthly household budget in Senegal (2002 US$)	227	154	315	102	134	166	225	394
Cost of facility as percentage of monthly household budget								
Septic tank	289	427	209	641	491	396	292	167
Improved latrine	194	286	140	430	330	266	196	112
Traditional latrine	22	32	16	48	37	30	22	13

Source: Morella, Foster, and Banerjee 2008.
Note: Q = quintile.

the absence of any far-reaching subsidization policy; this corroborates other evidence that investments of this size are affordable across the income spectrum. At the same time, the fact that improved latrines are confined to upper-income groups bears out the high budget shares that families would need to finance an improved latrine.

The Cost of Subsidizing Capital and Operating Expenses

The affordability of infrastructure services needs to be considered not only at the household level, but also at the level of the public finances of each country. To the extent that households cannot afford to pay cost-recovery tariffs, the move toward universal access will create burgeoning liabilities for the state, which must bridge the gap between the tariffs the public can afford to pay and the real cost of service provision. This analytical framework also can be used to estimate the aggregate value of these subsidies in each country, which helps to assess whether subsidizing services to reach universal coverage is an affordable strategy at the country level. Once again, no absolute scientific method can determine the affordability threshold at the country level; nevertheless, it is possible to get a sense of when costs reach a level that is manifestly unattainable.

A one-time, finite capital subsidy of $200 per unserved household, designed to cover the costs of connection of these households over a 10-year period, will cost approximately 1 percent of the annual African gross domestic product (GDP). An estimated 60 percent of the countries would face costs in excess of 1 percent of GDP. The cost would exceed 2 percent of GDP in Ethiopia, Malawi, the Democratic Republic of Congo, the Republic of Congo, and Sudan. The highest burden on fiscal

Figure 6.10 Subsidy Needed to Maintain Affordability of Water Services

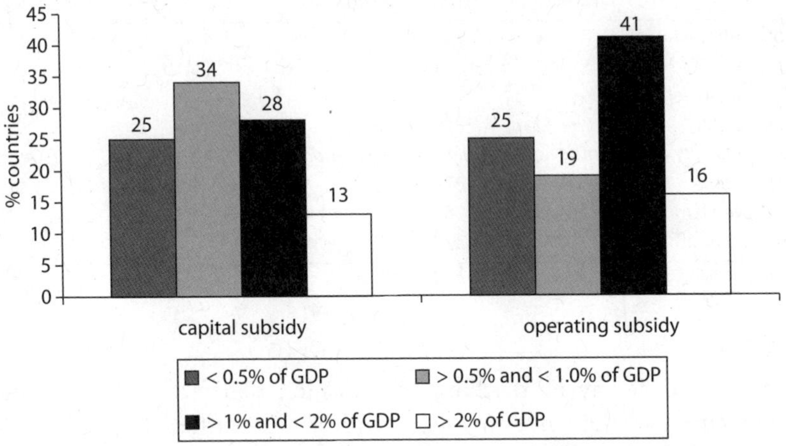

Source: Banerjee, Wodon, and others 2008.

resources would be for the Democratic Republic of Congo, which must spend a projected 18 percent of its GDP on household connections to piped water. In more affluent countries, such as Gabon, the cost of this policy would amount to no more than 0.02 percent of the GDP.

An indefinite, ongoing operating subsidy of \$2 per month to ensure that currently unserved customers can continue to afford service once connected places similar strains on the government budget. For 40 percent of the countries, providing a monthly subsidy of \$2 for water would amount to spending 1 to 2 percent of GDP. For 16 percent of the countries, it will be more than 2 percent of GDP. The highest burden would be on the Democratic Republic of Congo, followed by Ethiopia, Malawi, Niger, and Sudan, which would have to spend more than 2 percent to maintain a sustainable consumer base for water services. Like the capital subsidy, this operating subsidy would consume 1.1 percent of the African GDP (figure 6.10).

Poor Targeting of Utility Subsidies

Customers receive substantial subsidies in most African countries, because residential water tariffs tend to be below utility costs. The working assumption is that the price per m^3 in the highest bracket of consumption in the tariff schedule can be used as a first approximation of the cost of providing the service. (Actually, the estimates of targeting performance are not very sensitive to that assumption.) As shown by Komives and others (2005), a simple framework can be used not only to analyze the targeting performance of water subsidies in about 20 African countries for which data are available, but also to understand what affects targeting performance through so-called access (who uses water) and subsidy design factors (who benefits from subsidies and by how much among users).

The targeting performance indicator used in the analysis, denoted by Ω (omega), is simply the share of the subsidies received by the poor divided by the proportion of the population in poverty. In other words, a value of one for Ω implies that the subsidy distribution among the poor is proportional to their share in the overall population. If the poor account for 30 percent of the population, then a neutral targeting mechanism would allocate 30 percent of the subsidy to the poor. A value (lower) greater than one implies that the subsidy distribution is (regressive) progressive, since the share of benefits allocated to the poor is (lower) larger than their share in the total population. For instance, suppose that 30 percent of the population is poor and obtains 60 percent of the subsidy benefits. In such a case, Ω would equal two, meaning that the poor were receiving twice as much subsidy as the population on average.

Utility subsidies tend to be very poorly targeted. As shown in figure 6.11, in none of the countries is the targeting indicator superior to one; it is often well below one. Although comparability issues are found among countries, on average the poor are benefiting only from one-fourth to one-third of what a household randomly selected in the population would get.

The targeting performance indicator Ω can be deconstructed into "access" and "subsidy design" factors[4] to allow analysis of why subsidies are targeted as they are. Access factors are those related to the availability of water service in the area in which a household is located and to the household's decision to connect to the network when service is available. These access factors have a strong influence on targeting performance but are usually difficult to change in the short run. Policy design is more susceptible to subsidy factors, such as tariff structure changes that affect who is targeted to receive the subsidies. Policy design also is affected by rates of subsidization and the quantities of water consumed by the households that benefit from the subsidies. Investigations reveal that most water subsidy mechanisms are poorly targeted, essentially because most of the poor

Figure 6.11 Overall Targeting Performance (Ω) of Utility Subsidies

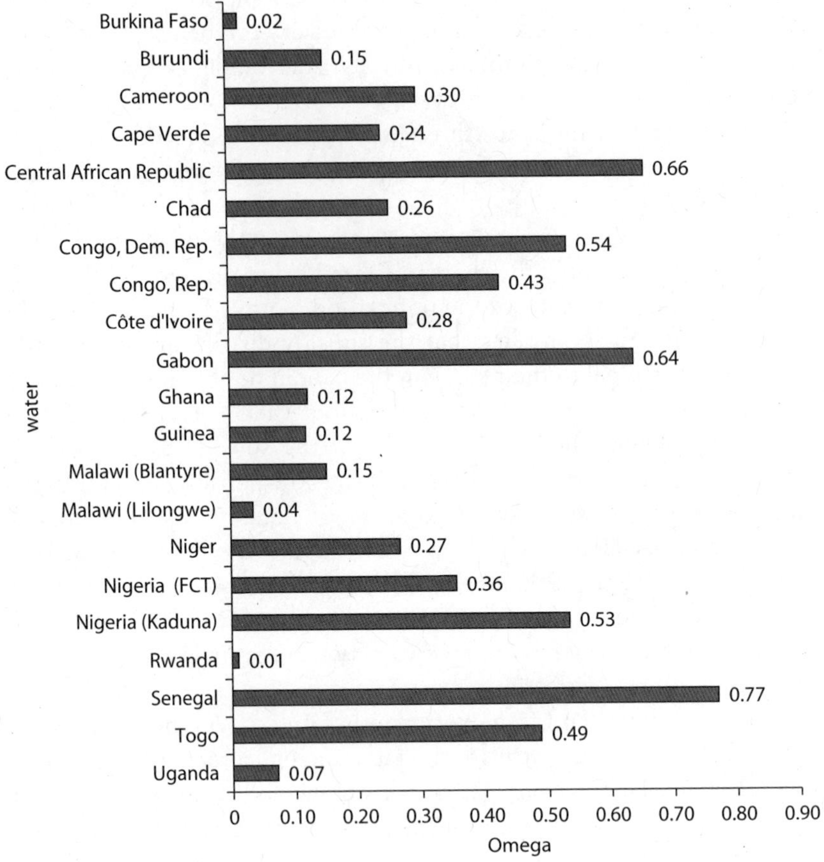

Source: Banerjee, Wodon, and others 2008.
Note: FCT = Federal Capital Territory.

lack access to the water network and, therefore, cannot benefit from water subsidies, but also because the existing tariff structures are not designed to target subsidies to the poor.

This can be seen clearly in figure 6.12, which deconstructs the value of the targeting indicator into access and subsidy design factors. The curves added to the graphs represent combinations of access and subsidy design factor values that result in the same value for Ω. The closer a country is located to the upper right of the graphs, the better the targeting performance, because again Ω is the product of the access and subsidy design factors.

Figure 6.12 Access Factors and Subsidy Design Factors Affecting Targeting Performance

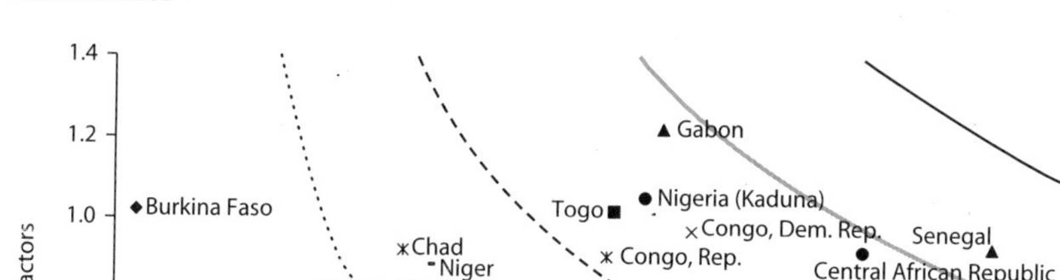
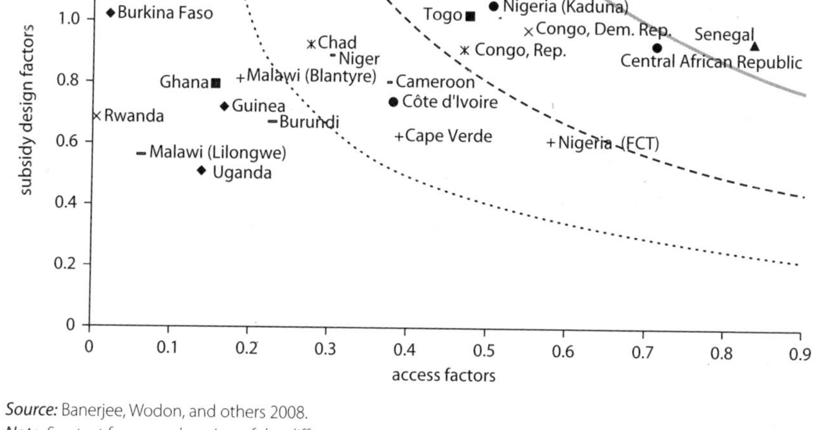

Source: Banerjee, Wodon, and others 2008.
Note: See text for an explanation of the different curves.

The two variables used to compute the access factors are, first, whether a household is located in an area served by the water network, and, second, whether a household in such an area is actually connected to and getting service from the network. The value of the access factors is simply the rate of connection to the network among the poor (which depends on access and uptake when there is access) divided by the rate of the connection in the population as a whole. As expected, the access factors are much lower than one for all countries, simply because on average the poor have much lower connection rates than the population as a whole.

Subsidy design factors, which take into account who benefits from subsidies among households connected to the network and how large the subsidies are, make up the second variable affecting the value of the targeting parameter. The subsidy design factor represents the ratio of the average benefit from the subsidy among all poor households that are connected to the network, divided by the average benefit among all households connected to the network, whether poor or nonpoor. Surprisingly, in many countries the subsidy design factors are also below unity, thereby limiting targeting performance. The main explanation is that although the rate of subsidization of the poor (that is, the discount versus the full cost of providing water for the utility) is often larger than for the population as a whole that is connected to the network, the quantities consumed by the population as a whole tend to be larger than those consumed by the poor, so that the overall subsidy received by the poor is lower on average than that received by the population as a whole.

Consumption subsidies for water appear to be poorly targeted in African countries for several reasons. Access factors are important in determining the potential beneficiaries of consumption subsidies. Poor households tend to live in areas without water service, and so it is impossible for them to benefit from the subsidies. Even when they live in an area that offers potential access to the network, many among the poor remain unconnected to the networks because they live too far from the water pipes or the cost of connecting to the network and purchasing the equipment required to use water is too high. Good subsidy design mechanisms would allow countries to compensate for the negative impact of access factors on targeting performance. Unfortunately, the traditional IBT structures that prevail in many countries tend to be poorly targeted. They spread subsidies to all households connected to the network; even those that consume high amounts of water benefit from a subsidy for the part of their consumption that belongs to the lower level blocks of the tariff structure. In addition, the lower blocks often are too high in terms of consumption to target the poor well. Finally, significant differences in unit prices may not be present among the various blocks.

Connection Subsidies as a Viable Alternative

One possible alternative is to provide connection rather than consumption subsidies, assuming that the generation or production capacity is sufficient to expand the network. Figure 6.13 provides the potential targeting performance of connection subsidies under the three scenarios.

First, we assume that connection subsidies will be distributed in the same way as existing connections. This is a pessimistic assumption from a distributional point of view because it tends to favor better-off households, but it could be realistic if access rates to the network are low. Second, we assume that new connections could be distributed randomly among households that currently are not connected but are located in a neighborhood where connections are available. Third, we assume that new connection subsidies could be randomly distributed among all households that do not currently have access. This is a very optimistic

Figure 6.13 Potential Targeting Performance of Connection Subsidies under Various Scenarios

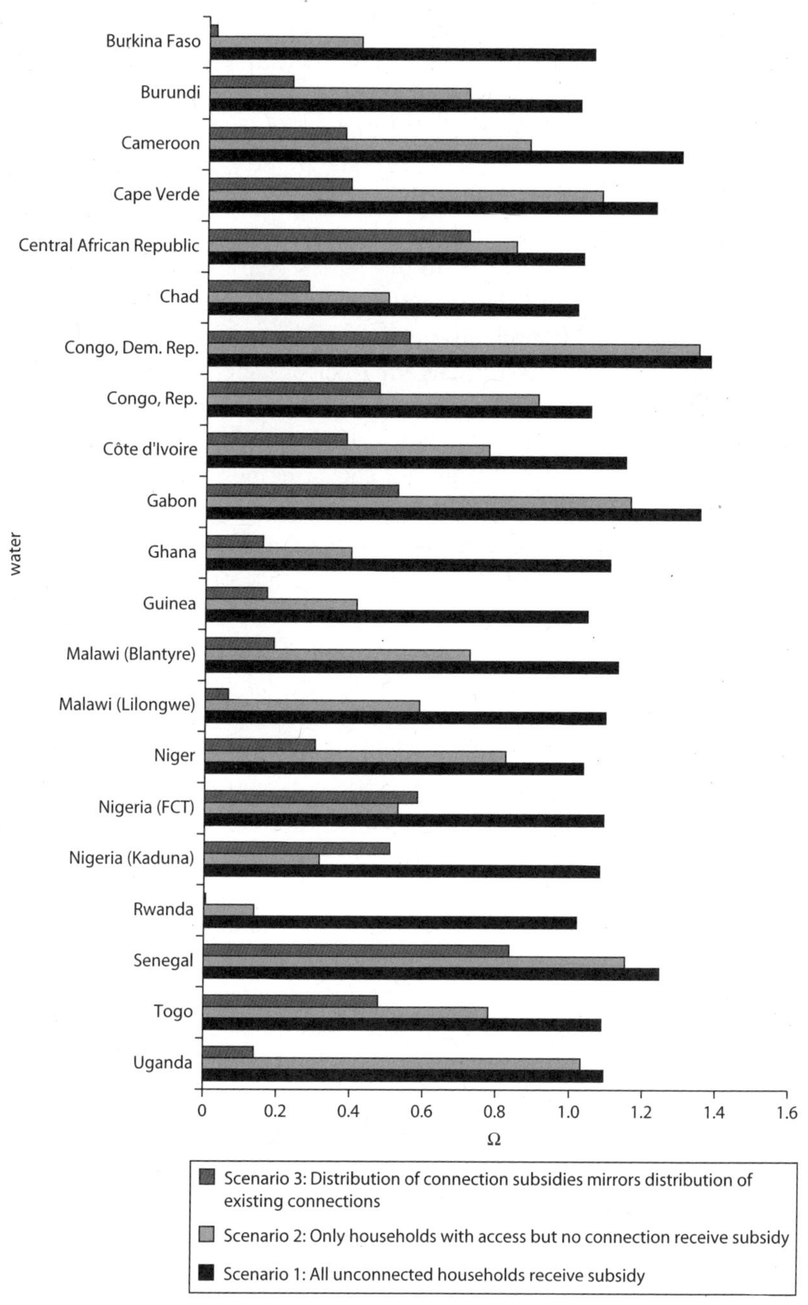

Source: Banerjee, Wodon, and others 2008.
Note: FCT = Federal Capital Territory.

assumption given that many of these households are not located in neighborhoods where access is available.

The value of Ω is largest under the assumption that new connections benefit households that are selected randomly from the population without access. In all countries, Ω is larger than one under this assumption. Yet, the assumption is not realistic. The second scenario assumes that households that benefit from new connections are selected from unserved households located in areas where there is already access to the network. The values of Ω, although often lower than one, are still much better than those for consumption subsidies. In the third scenario, targeting performance remains poor. Thus, if connection subsidies could be designed to reach the majority of households not connected today but living in areas where service is provided, the targeting performance of those subsidies would be better than that of consumption subsidies. In addition, connection subsidies help to reduce the cost of service for users (compared with street vendors for water, for example) and bring positive externalities in areas such as education and health.

Finally, it is often argued that any removal of utility subsidies would be detrimental. Again, the household survey evidence provides an opportunity to test this hypothesis. In most countries, water spending represents only a tiny fraction of total consumption for the population as a whole. Among households connected to the network and consuming water, the fraction is much higher, typically 3 to 5 percent. This, in turn, is directly related to the impact of a proportional increase in water tariffs on poverty. For simplicity, relative poverty measures can be used: The poverty line in each country is set at half the mean level of per capita consumption. In many countries, the impact of a 50 percent increase in tariffs or even of a doubling of the tariffs is truly marginal at the national level, with estimates of the shares of the population living in poverty changing by barely one-tenth of a percentage point. Among households with a connection to the network, the impact is larger, but still fairly limited. There is rarely an increase in the share of households in poverty larger than one or two percentage points, and because the households that benefit from a connection tend not to be poor compared with other households, the increase in poverty starts from a very low base.

Thus, in general, it can be said that the impact on poverty of an increase in tariffs is small in most cases. This does not mean that such a poverty impact does not have negative consequences on those hit by it. It does mean, however, that if subsidies were reduced, and the funds were used in a different, more pro-poor way, there would be a potentially substantial gain for poverty reduction.

Annex 6.1 Methodology for Estimating the Annual Gross Profit and the Annual Cross-Subsidy between Household Consumers and Standpipes Captured by Standpipe Operators in a City

The following figure shows the prices charged by the utility to the standpipe operators (formal or official standpipe price), to a household with a private connection, and by the standpipe operator to the consumers (informal standpipe tariff). We define *unitary standpipe operator gross profit, unitary cross-subsidy between consumers with a household connection* and *standpipe operators* in the following way:

Unitary standpipe operator gross profit (P_G) (\$/m^3) = informal standpipe price (\$/m^3) – formal standpipe price (\$/m^3)

Unitary cross-subsidy household (HH) connection-standpipe operator ($S_{HH\text{-}Stdp}$) (\$/m^3) = HH consumer price (\$/m^3) – formal standpipe price (\$/m^3).

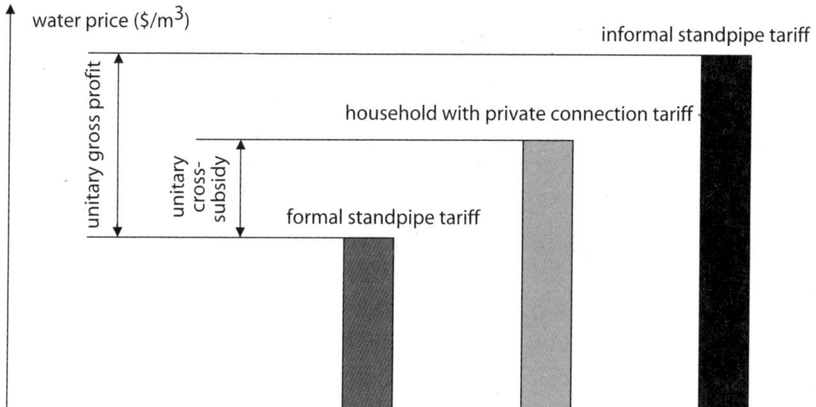

Source: Luengo, Keener, and Banerjee 2008..

Because households with private connections are assessed tariffs based on consumption levels, we have to define a common level of consumption to compare tariff structures across countries. The reference we use for this in an average consumption level of 60 liters per capita per day for people with a household private connection (Water Utility Partnership 2002). When analyzing the cross-subsidies between small and large consumers, one interesting finding is that the fixed-fee and minimum-consumption charge means an economic burden on low-volume consumers with a household connection. Although the increasing block tariff is commonplace in African countries, the two-part tariff structure can fail to lead to a price that favors small consumers (Banerjee, Wodon, and others 2008). Except in a few countries, among those who have a household connection, average consumers (60 liters per capita per day), not small consumers (25 liters per capita per day) pay the lowest price. In that sense, the 60 liters per capita per day reference can help us to define the lower boundary (and a better estimate) of the cross-subsidy between consumers with a household connection and standpipe operators.

To estimate the annual gross profit of the standpipe operators and the annual cross-subsidy between the consumer with a household connection and the standpipe operator, we use the following formulation:

Annual gross profit of standpipe operators (\$/year) = $P_G \times U \times 365$ (days/year) × 1,000 (liters/m^3) × $P \times$ C,

where

P_G (\$/m^3): Unitary standpipe operator gross profit

U (liters per capita per day): Standpipe unit consumption; based on the AICD data, it is fixed at 25 liters per capita per day

P (#): City population

C (%): Coverage of the water service by standpipes

Annual cross-subsidy between the consumer with a household connection and the standpipe operator (\$/year) = $S_{\text{HH-Stdp}} \times U \times 365$ (days/year) × 1,000 (liters/m^3) × $P \times$ C,

where

$S_{\text{HH-Stdp}}$ (\$/m^3): Unitary cross-subsidy between household consumer-standpipe operator

U (liters per capita per day): Standpipe unit consumption; based on the AICD data, it is fixed at 25 liters per capita per day

P (#): City population

C (%): Coverage of the water service by standpipes.

Notes

1. Gross profit = revenue from water sales – cost of water sales. This calculation does not include operation and maintenance costs, other overhead costs, taxes, and financial costs.
2. See annex 6.1 for the calculation methodology.
3. Based on 26 utilities for which information on connection charges were available.
4. Ω = (access factors) × (subsidy design factors).

References

Banerjee, S., V. Foster, Y. Ying, H. Skilling, and Q. Wodon. 2008. "Cost Recovery, Equity and Efficiency in Water Tariffs: Evidence from African Utilities." AICD Working Paper 7, World Bank, Washington, DC.

Banerjee, S., Q. Wodon, A. Diallo, N. Pushak, H. Uddin, C. Tsimpo, and V. Foster. 2008. "Access, Affordability and Alternatives: Modern Infrastructure Services in Sub-Saharan Africa." AICD Background Paper 2, World Bank, Washington, DC.

Foster, V., and T. Yepes. 2006. "Is Cost Recovery a Feasible Objective for Water and Electricity? The Latin American Experience." Policy Research Working Paper 3943, World Bank, Washington, DC.

Fankhauser, S., and S. Tepic. 2005. "Can Poor Consumers Pay for Energy and Water? An Affordability Analysis for Transition Countries." Working Paper 92, European Bank for Reconstruction and Development, London.

Keener, S., S. G. Banerjee, N. Junge, and G. Revell. Forthcoming. "Informal Water Service Providers and Public Stand Posts in Africa." Africa Post-Conflict and Social Development Department, World Bank, Washington, DC.

Keener, S., M. Luengo, and S. G. Banerjee. 2009. "Provision of Water to the Poor in Africa: Experience with Water Standposts and the Informal Water Sector." AICD Working Paper 13, World Bank, Washington, DC.

Komives, K., V. Foster, J. Halpern, and Q. Wodon. 2005. "Water, Electricity, and the Poor: Who Benefits from Utility Subsidies?" Water and Sanitation Unit, World Bank, Washington, DC.

Morella, E., V. Foster, and S. Banerjee. 2008. "Climbing the Ladder: The State of Sanitation in Sub-Saharan Africa." AICD Background Paper 13, World Bank, Washington, DC.

Water Utility Partnership. 2002. "Final Project Summary Report: Service Providers' Performance Indicators and Benchmarking Network Project." Abidjan.

CHAPTER 7

Spending Needed to Meet Goals in Water and Sanitation

The Millennium Development Goal (MDG) for sustainable access to safe drinking water and improved sanitation presents an enormous financing challenge, particularly to many low-income countries. This chapter focuses on the levels of investments required to meet the water and sanitation MDG, assuming that access patterns remain broadly the same during the period from 2006 to 2015. The analysis presented here takes into account population growth and estimates the investment needed to expand access, rehabilitate existing assets, and ensure adequate maintenance.

The Challenge of Expanding Coverage

The progress toward the MDG for sustainable access to safe drinking water and basic sanitation has been made mostly in the water space as of 2006. Twenty-six countries are on track to meet the water MDG. At one end stand Niger, Equatorial Guinea, Nigeria, Mozambique, Sierra Leone, and the Democratic Republic of Congo, which show coverage rates of more than 25 percentage points below the MDG targets (figure 7.1).

At the other end, five countries had already reached the target as of 2006. Among these, two are middle-income countries: Namibia and South Africa. The rest are low-income countries: Burkina Faso; Malawi,

Figure 7.1 Water MDG Gap, 2006

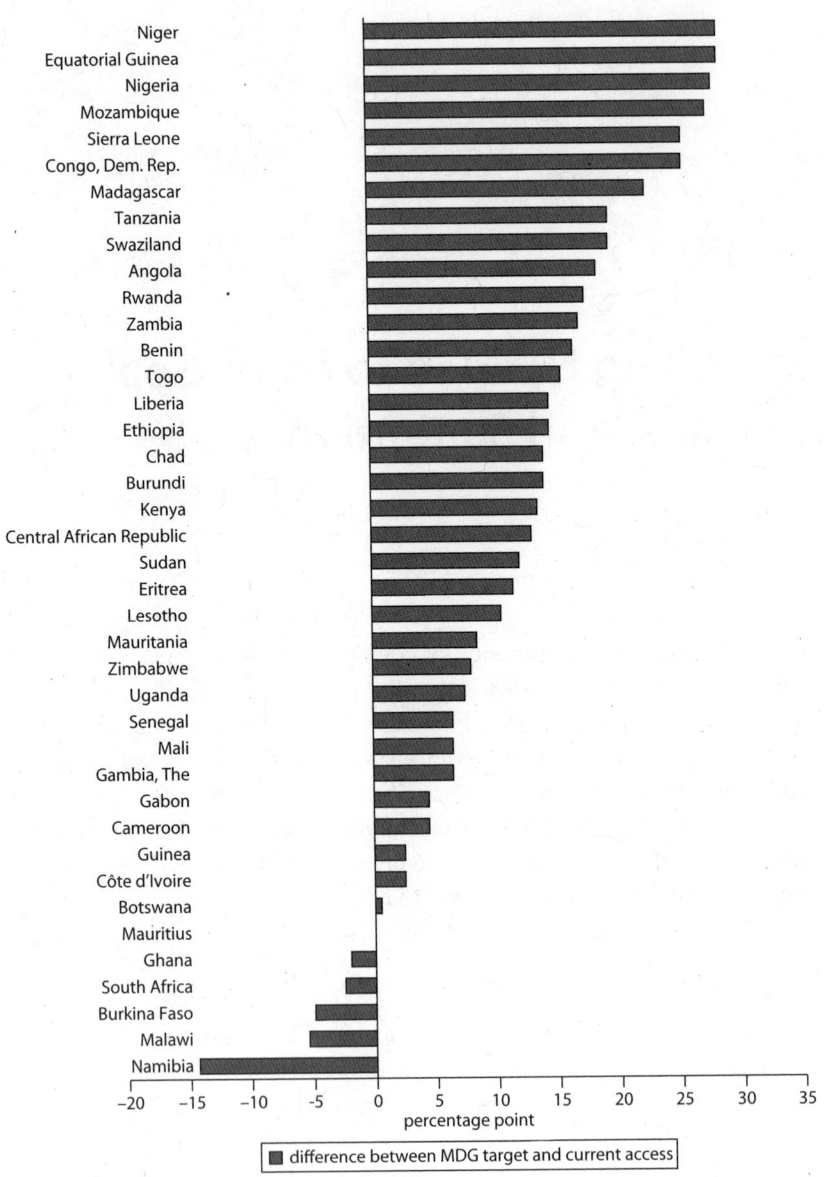

Source: JMP 2006.

where improved water coverage doubled from 1990 to 2006; and Ghana. In the middle, 17 countries are 10 to 25 percentage points away from the target. These include, in decreasing order, Madagascar, Tanzania, Swaziland, Angola, Rwanda, Zambia, Benin, Togo, Liberia, Ethiopia, Chad, Burundi, Kenya, the Central African Republic, Sudan, Eritrea, and Lesotho. Also, Botswana, Cameroon, Côte d'Ivoire, Gabon, The Gambia, Guinea, Mali, Mauritania, Senegal, Uganda, and Zimbabwe are less than 10 percentage points away from the target.

Progress is more modest in sanitation: in 29 countries, improved sanitation coverage will have to more than double for the MDG target to be reached. In the sanitation space, at one end stand Eritrea, Sierra Leone, Togo, Niger, Chad, Ghana, Madagascar, Rwanda, Ethiopia, and Burkina Faso, all more than 40 percentage points away from MDG targets. A second group—including Liberia, Guinea, Mauritania, Côte d'Ivoire, Senegal, Tanzania, Nigeria, Uganda, Sudan, Gabon, Burundi, Lesotho, Mozambique, Namibia, Kenya, the Democratic Republic of Congo, Zimbabwe, Benin, Swaziland, Equatorial Guinea, the Central African Republic, Mali, Botswana, and The Gambia—show coverage rates between 20 and 40 percentage points below targets. Only Zambia, South Africa, Cameroon, Malawi, Angola, and Mauritius report coverage rates less than 20 percentage points away from targets (figure 7.2).

For countries that have already reached the water MDG, the analysis presented here sets the bar a little higher, assuming that the number of people without access in 2006 (instead of 2000) is halved by 2015. Also, it is assumed that the water and sanitation MDG is reached equally in urban and rural areas. The challenge is particularly severe for rural areas, whereas in some countries urban access is already on or above target. In this case, current urban access is assumed to be maintained in 2015.

The water and sanitation MDG targets translate into 764 million water customers and 646 million sanitation customers by 2015 using demographic projections for urban and rural populations, and assuming urban and rural population growth rates are equal to the averages for the past decade. This means that improved water service will need to be extended to an additional 308 million Africans, equal to one-third of the overall population in 2006 (table 7.1). Almost 70 percent of the new customers will be located in rural areas. To reach the sanitation MDG, the population with improved sanitation will need to more than double. New customers stand at 409 million people, equal to more than half of the overall population in 2006. Again, almost 70 percent of new customers will be located in rural areas.

Figure 7.2 Sanitation MDG Gap, 2006

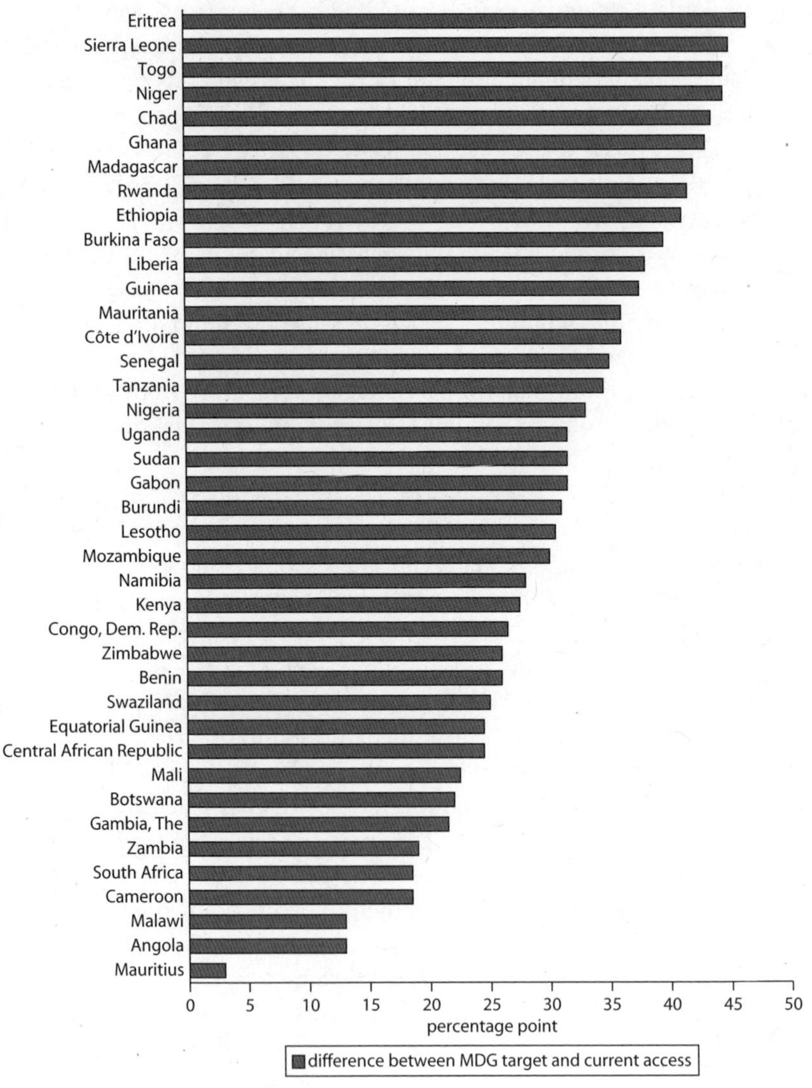

Source: JMP 2006.

Middle-income countries are better positioned with respect to the MDG challenge in both absolute and relative terms, given the typically higher starting levels of coverage. They will have to improve water service for 9 million Africans and improve sanitation for 16 million. Nonfragile, low-income countries will face the largest number of new

Table 7.1 Additional Population to Be Served by 2015
(millions of people)

	Water			*Sanitation*		
	National	*Urban*	*Rural*	*National*	*Urban*	*Rural*
Angola	7.0	4.3	2.7	5.3	3.6	1.6
Benin	3.7	1.4	2.4	3.8	0.9	3.0
Botswana	0.3	0.2	0.0	0.6	0.3	0.3
Burkina Faso	6.0	1.5	4.6	8.2	1.1	7.1
Burundi	4.0	0.5	3.5	4.5	0.6	3.9
Cameroon	4.2	3.6	0.6	6.5	4.0	2.5
Cape Verde	0.2	0.1	0.0	0.2	0.1	0.1
Central African Republic	1.1	0.3	0.8	1.4	0.4	1.0
Chad	3.8	1.1	2.8	6.6	1.6	5.0
Congo, Dem. Rep.	26.2	5.3	20.9	26.8	8.5	18.3
Congo, Rep.	1.2	0.6	0.6	2.0	1.3	0.7
Côte d'Ivoire	4.5	4.2	0.3	8.9	3.7	5.1
Equatorial Guinea	0.2	0.1	0.1	0.2	0.1	0.1
Eritrea	1.9	0.4	1.5	3.2	0.7	2.5
Ethiopia	23.3	5.6	17.8	42.5	6.2	36.3
Gabon	0.3	0.3	0.0	0.6	0.5	0.1
Gambia, The	0.6	0.5	0.2	0.8	0.6	0.2
Ghana	7.1	4.0	3.0	12.6	6.6	6.0
Guinea	1.5	0.9	0.6	4.4	1.3	3.1
Kenya	11.9	2.5	9.4	16.8	5.9	10.8
Lesotho	0.4	0.2	0.2	0.8	0.2	0.5
Liberia	1.5	0.9	0.5	2.2	1.1	1.1
Madagascar	8.0	1.7	6.3	10.9	3.2	7.7
Malawi	4.9	1.4	3.5	4.5	1.6	2.9
Mali	3.3	1.7	1.6	5.2	1.6	3.6
Mauritania	0.8	0.3	0.6	1.6	0.4	1.2
Mauritius	0.1	0.0	0.1	0.2	0.1	0.1
Mozambique	9.5	2.7	6.8	9.5	2.9	6.6
Namibia	0.4	0.2	0.1	0.8	0.2	0.6
Niger	7.5	0.8	6.7	8.7	1.0	7.7
Nigeria	69.7	29.0	40.7	72.0	37.7	34.4
Rwanda	4.3	1.3	3.1	6.0	1.5	4.6
Senegal	3.5	1.5	2.0	6.2	1.5	4.8
Sierra Leone	3.3	0.8	2.5	3.8	1.3	2.5
South Africa	7.7	5.9	1.8	13.4	7.8	5.6
Sudan	11.8	6.9	4.9	17.8	7.7	10.1
Swaziland	0.4	0.1	0.3	0.4	0.1	0.3

(continued next page)

Table 7.1 *(continued)*

	Water			*Sanitation*		
	National	*Urban*	*Rural*	*National*	*Urban*	*Rural*
Tanzania	15.4	3.5	11.9	20.4	6.5	13.9
Togo	15.9	1.4	14.5	20.7	2.1	18.6
Uganda	9.3	1.4	7.9	15.6	2.4	13.3
Zambia	3.6	0.7	2.9	3.7	1.2	2.5
Zimbabwe	2.0	1.0	1.0	4.2	1.1	3.0
Resource-rich	101.8	46.5	55.3	114.6	57.7	57.0
Middle-income	9.3	6.7	2.6	16.3	8.7	7.6
Low-income, fragile	62.5	16.2	6.3	81.0	21.5	59.4
Low-income, nonfragile	118.5	31.2	87.4	172.7	43.3	129.4
Sub-Saharan Africa	**307.7**	**92.4**	**215.3**	**408.7**	**130.0**	**278.7**

Sources: JMP 2006; World Development Indicators Database 2006 (http://data.worldbank.org/).

water customers in absolute terms: 120 million. Yet, in relative terms, they are better positioned than fragile, low-income countries, which will need to raise by more than 40 percent the number of people with access to improved water. Interestingly, even in relative terms, fragile, low-income countries score second to resource-rich countries, which will need to add more than 100 million Africans to water service, equal to 42 percent of their current population. In the sanitation space, nonfragile, low-income countries face the most difficult challenge: they will have to add more than 170 million customers, equal to more than half of their current population. Fragile, low-income countries follow closely in relative terms, although in absolute terms resource-rich countries will need to add a larger number of customers given their size.

The analysis assumes a *base scenario* in which the share of the population using high-quality or improved water and sanitation services relative to the overall served population will remain the same in 2015, although in absolute terms more people will enjoy high-quality services because of demographic growth (figure 7.3). As a result, in 2015 private water connections will account for no more than one-third of improved water coverage, standposts for another third, and wells and boreholes for the remaining 40 percent. Similarly, improved sanitation coverage will still be achieved predominantly through safe traditional latrines (around 60 percent); ventilated improved pit latrines will account for one-fifth of

Figure 7.3 Population Split across Water and Sanitation Modalities Given Current and Target Coverage by 2015 under the Base Scenario Assumptions

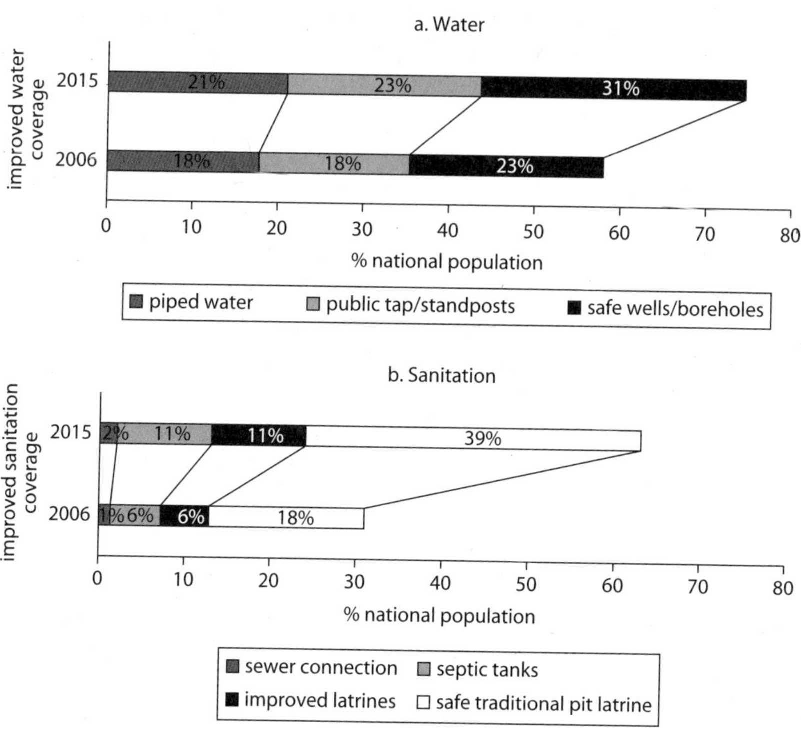

Source: Authors' compilation.

improved sanitation coverage, septic tanks for another fifth, and sewer connections for less than 5 percent.

The Unit Cost of Service Provision across Countries

The unit costs of infrastructure determine the level of spending on service expansion, rehabilitation, and operations and maintenance (O&M). Unit costs vary to a large extent across countries and within regions as a result of density, location, technological innovation, and level of local market development—factors that are almost all exogenous, at least in the short and medium terms.[1] Concentration largely reduces investment costs for water and sewerage networks in dense city centers, whereas great distances make it impractical to roll out connection lines into dispersed rural areas.

Poor capacity in the local construction sector, lack of skilled construction workers, shortage of materials, and scarce financing reduce the range of available on-site technologies and constrain the development of innovations that would ensure higher quality at more affordable prices. Efficiency considerations call for understanding of what level of service can be realistically provided to as many people as possible rather than channeling limited public resources into higher-quality services accessible by considerably fewer people. Therefore, the typology of country settings ultimately shapes the trade-off between political objectives and spending constraints.

Vast differences in costs are seen across countries and between urban and rural areas. The capital cost per capita of an urban residential water connection can range from $200 in countries where urbanization and concentration have taken off up to $1,000 in countries that are primarily rural. Similarly, the capital cost per capita of an urban standpost connection can range from $60 to $150. The price of a residential water connection in rural areas fluctuates even more across countries. It increases from $700 in countries where rural areas are more densely populated to a price 10 times higher in countries with mostly remote rural spaces. The capital cost per capita of a standpost installed in rural areas fluctuates less, with a range of $100 to $200.

Similar differences in network infrastructure prices can be found within countries between urban and rural areas. Table 7.2 reports capital costs per capita of water connections at different urban and rural locations. Locations span from megacities with populations of more than 3 million people and densities of about 5,000 people per square kilometer, to rural areas more than six hours of travel time away from the nearest urban center, whose typical densities barely reach 15 people per square kilometer. The capital cost per capita of a private connection increases exponentially from highly dense megacities to remote rural areas. The capital cost per capita of a standpost connection quadruples.

The considerable sensitivity to density makes infrastructure networks less affordable in Africa than elsewhere. Africa remains a predominantly rural continent and is therefore low-density. Sixty-six percent of Africans still live in rural areas, and of those 50 percent live in the rural hinterlands and up to 16 percent in remote villages. Also, one-third of the urban population—equal to 10 percent of the overall population—lives in peri-urban areas with fewer than 100 people per square kilometer, and a slightly larger share—13 percent of the overall population—lives in cities with a population of more than 1 million and densities of about 3,500 people per square kilometer.

Table 7.2 Unit Costs of Water Network Infrastructure Services by Location in the Median Country

	Large cities							
	> 3 million people	*2.0–2.99 million people*	*1.0–1.99 million people*	*0.5–0.99 million people*	*0.1–0.49 million people*	*Secondary cities*	*Rural hinterland*	*Deep rural area*
Median density (inhabitants/km^2)	5,009	4,083	2,855	2,712	1,373	1,282	38	13
$ per capita								
Private water connection	232	255	302	309	428	443	1,825	3,156
Standpost connection	66	72	85	87	119	123	268	273

Source: Authors' compilation.

Note: Cities are classified by population size with typologies spanning from secondary cities with populations of fewer than 100,000 people to megacities with more than 3 million inhabitants. Nonurban areas are classified by distance or travel time to the nearest city. In particular, "rural hinterland" indicates rural locations within six hours' travel time from the closest urban center, and deep rural areas are those more than six hours away. Urban and rural locations are assigned with the median of the densities estimated for each location in 42 Sub-Saharan African countries.

Unit costs of on-site facilities also vary across countries. The price of a borehole with hand pump is $20 to $90 per capita, and the price of a well with hand pump is $15 to $80 per capita (table 7.3). More advanced technologies, such as boreholes with hand or even electric pumps, are typically used in urban areas, whereas less-expensive technologies are more common in rural areas, where low densities require less capacity.

Unit costs of on-site sanitation services range from $39 for a traditional latrine to $60 for an improved latrine to $125 for a septic tank (table 7.4). Sanitation unit costs are adjusted by a construction index factor (box 7.1) to reflect differences across local construction markets and levels of technological innovation in the sanitation sector.

For sewerage networks, owing to their low prevalence in Africa, a median unit cost based on experience from World Bank operations has

Table 7.3 Unit Costs of Wells and Boreholes

	Borehole with hand pump ($ per capita)	*Well with hand pump ($ per capita)*
Benin	50	36
Burkina Faso	36	26
Cameroon	76	58
Cape Verde	50	36
Chad	50	36
Congo, Dem. Rep.	50	36
Côte d'Ivoire	50	36
Ethiopia	50	36
Ghana	22	20
Kenya	50	36
Lesotho	50	36
Madagascar	50	17
Malawi	50	36
Mozambique	50	36
Namibia	50	36
Niger	94	82
Nigeria	50	36
Rwanda	50	36
Senegal	50	36
South Africa	50	36
Sudan	50	36
Tanzania	50	36
Uganda	50	36
Zambia	50	36

Source: World Bank's public expenditures reviews for Cameroon, Côte d'Ivoire, and Niger.

Table 7.4 Unit Costs of On-Site Sanitation Services

	Septic tank	*Improved latrine*	*Traditional latrine*
$ per capita	125	57	39

Source: World Water Assessment Programme 2000, http://www.unesco.org/water/wwap/wwdr/indicators/.

Box 7.1

The Construction Index Factor

The construction index used in this analysis results from the Basket of Construction Components (BOCC) approach introduced in the 2003 to 2006 round of the International Comparison Program (ICP) to calculate comparable prices in the construction sector.

The ICP, the world's largest statistical initiative, produces internationally comparable price levels, economic aggregates in real terms, and purchasing power parity estimates. The ICP uses a series of statistical surveys to collect price data for a basket of goods and services. By using estimates of purchasing power parity as conversion factors, the resulting comparisons of gross domestic product allow for measuring the relative social and economic well-being of countries, monitoring the incidence of poverty, tracking progress toward the MDGs, and targeting programs effectively.

The launch of BOCC followed the conclusion that lack of comparability of capital goods in different countries had weakened the effectiveness of the past ICP round. In particular, BOCC resulted from the attempt to respond to the following issues: Given the nature of the construction sector and the inherent difficulties in construction price comparisons, what improvements can be made? What basis and level of comparison is appropriate for the sector? How can quality and level-of-service differences among countries be incorporated in these comparisons?

The BOCC measures relative prices at the level of the construction component, which can be thought of as an aggregation of several construction work items. These items include the material put in place, labor and equipment, and any consumables required. The price comparisons are performed using three baskets: residential, nonresidential, and civil works. Each basket is broken down into construction systems. Under each system a set of construction components is identified and defined. The approach was endorsed by the ICP Technical Advisory Group as a much simpler price comparison tool than the current practice, and it is expected to reduce resource and expertise requirements in the price collection process in the construction sector.

Source: Adapted from World Bank, "International Comparison Program 2011," http://www.worldbank.org/data/icp.

been estimated at $400. After adjusting for the construction index factor, the average cost per capita of a sewerage connection is estimated at $440.

To Close the MDG Coverage Gap

The total spending required for reaching the water and sanitation MDGs is valued at $22.6 billion per year or 3.5 percent of Africa's gross domestic product (GDP). Most of the needs come from the water sector, which is estimated to require allocations up to $17 billion per year or 2.7 percent of Africa's GDP (table 7.5).

The cost of new infrastructure appears to carry the heaviest weight and require allocations up to 1.5 percent of Africa's GDP every year, or 43 percent of overall spending. O&M needs immediately follow and stand at 1.1 percent of Africa's GDP, or 31 percent of overall costs. Rehabilitation of existing assets requires lower yet substantial allocations—up to 0.9 percent of Africa's GDP—which accounts for one-fourth of the overall needs. A similar composition can be observed for water spending needs, 42 percent of which are generated by investments in expansion, 25 percent by rehabilitation of existing assets, and 33 percent by O&M. The sanitation sector shows a different composition: investments in new infrastructure dominate spending needs and account for more than 40 percent, and rehabilitation and O&M each account for one-fourth.

A larger share of spending on water and sanitation is allocated to rural areas because of the large urban-rural divide in access to infrastructure services, quality of service, and asset conditions, which are estimated to account for 59 percent of overall requirements (figure 7.4). In particular, rural areas should absorb up to 63 percent of the overall investments in new infrastructure. Almost the same share of rehabilitation spending should be channeled to rural areas, owing to a much more severe obsolescence of rural infrastructure. O&M needs are almost evenly split between urban and rural areas.

These distribution patterns do not apply equally to water and sanitation. In the water space, more than 60 percent of spending needs originate from rural areas, whether they are investments in new infrastructure, rehabilitation of existing assets, or maintenance. In the sanitation space, 55 percent of overall spending needs originate from urban areas. O&M needs mainly concern urban sanitation assets, yet rural areas account for 57 percent of rehabilitation needs.

The composition of spending needs differs between middle- and low-income countries (table 7.6). Low-income countries, whether fragile or

Table 7.5 Overall Water and Sanitation Spending Needs

	Share of GDP (%)					*$ million/year*				
	CAPEX					*CAPEX*				
	Expansion	*Rehabilitation*	*Total CAPEX*	*O&M*	*Total Needs*	*Expansion*	*Rehabilitation*	*Total CAPEX*	*O&M*	*Total needs*
Water	1.13	0.68	1.80	0.89	2.69	7,225	4,327	11,553	5,686	17,239
Sanitation	0.41	0.21	0.62	0.22	0.84	2,617	1,352	3,969	1,432	5,401
Total	1.54	0.89	2.42	1.11	**3.53**	9,843	5,679	15,522	7,118	**22,640**

Source: Authors' calculations.

Note: CAPEX = capital expenditure, GDP = gross domestic product, O&M = operations and maintenance.

Figure 7.4 Urban-Rural Split of Spending Needs

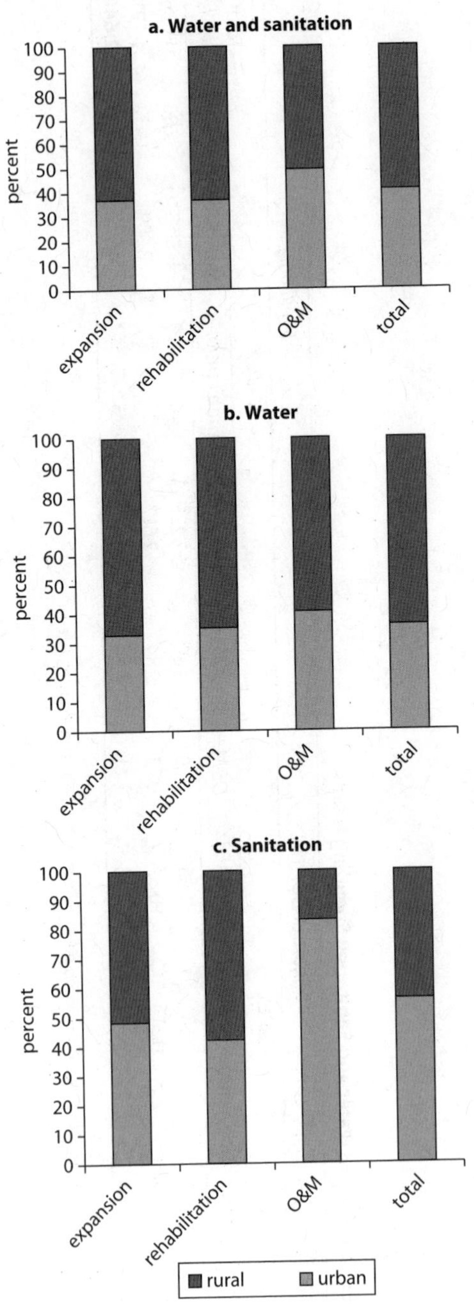

Source: Authors' compilation.

Table 7.6 Split of Spending Needs by Category

	Share of GDP (%)					*US$ million per year*				
	CAPEX					*CAPEX*				
	New investment	*Rehabilitation*	*Total CAPEX*	*O&M*	*Total spending needs*	*New investment*	*Rehabilitation*	*Total CAPEX*	*O&M*	*Total spending needs*
Sub-Saharan Africa	1.5	0.9	2.4	1.1	3.5	9,843	5,679	15,522	7,118	22,640
Resource-rich	1.3	0.8	2.1	0.8	2.9	2,864	1,741	4,605	1,759	6,364
Middle-income	0.4	0.4	0.7	0.7	1.5	1,034	951	1,985	1,991	3,976
Low-income, fragile	5.9	2.7	8.5	3.3	11.8	2,208	1,006	3,213	1,223	4,437
Low-income, nonfragile	3.4	1.8	5.1	1.9	7.1	3,714	1,968	5,682	2,128	7,810

Source: Authors' calculations based on access data as of 2006.

Note: CAPEX = capital expenditure, GDP = gross domestic product, O&M = operations and maintenance.

nonfragile, and resource-rich countries show much similarity, with costs divided almost equally among expansion and rehabilitation and maintenance. Conversely, middle-income countries focus more on maintenance, which accounts for half the overall needs, and the high coverage rates and relatively lower rehabilitation backlog make infrastructure expansion and rehabilitation less of a priority.

The total spending needs range from a maximum of $3.3 billion per year in the case of South Africa to a minimum of $19 million per year in the case of Equatorial Guinea, with a fair number of countries, including Nigeria, Sudan, Kenya, the Democratic Republic of Congo, Ethiopia, and Tanzania, that should spend between $1.0 and $2.3 billion per year to halve the gap of people without access to water and sanitation services by 2015 (figure 7.5). Middle-income countries together report the highest needs, almost $3 billion per year, followed by resource-rich countries, with $1.5 billion per year. Despite the lower size of their economies, low-income countries altogether account for a similar amount, owing to the larger service gap they have to make up for.

It should be noted, however, that for some countries, part of the information required to calculate specific spending components is not available. For these, estimates may be just lower bounds of the actual spending needs.

Normalizing needs by the size of the countries' economies reveals that most countries should allocate well over 3 percent of their GDP every year to water and sanitation.

As expected, the level of spending required by the MDG varies to a large extent across countries. Three country groups can be identified. The first group represents countries with large spending needs—more than 10 percent of the GDP per year. The second includes countries with medium spending needs—3 to 10 percent of the GDP per year. The third group consists of those with needs less than 3 percent of GDP per year. Among these, Equatorial Guinea stands at the bottom of the distribution, with overall needs below 0.3 percent of the GDP. On the opposite end, Togo, the Democratic Republic of Congo, and Liberia, show manifestly unaffordable needs that reach more than 20 percent of the GDP per year.

The affordability of the MDG challenge appears to correlate strongly to a country's income. Halving the population without access to water and sanitation services by 2015 is estimated to require only 1.5 percent of middle-income countries' GDP per year. Resource-rich countries should invest twice as much annually—3 percent of their

Figure 7.5 Africa's Water and Sanitation Needs by Country

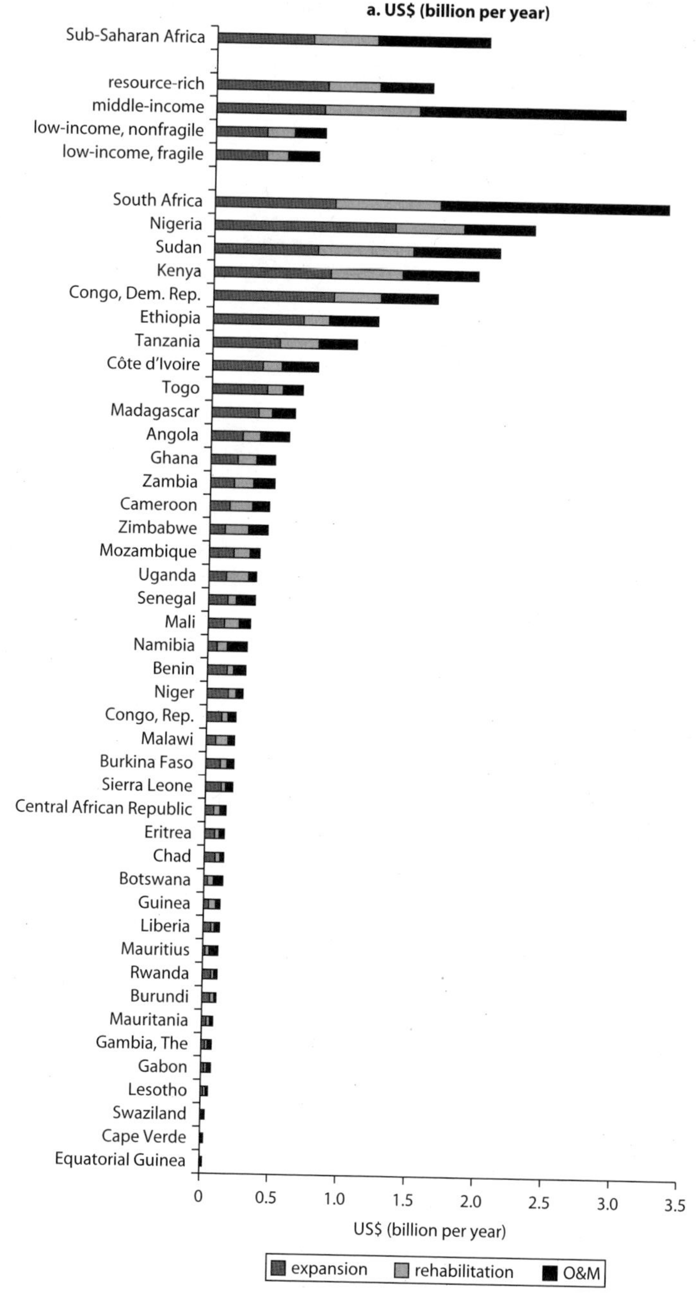

(continued next page)

Figure 7.5 *(continued)*

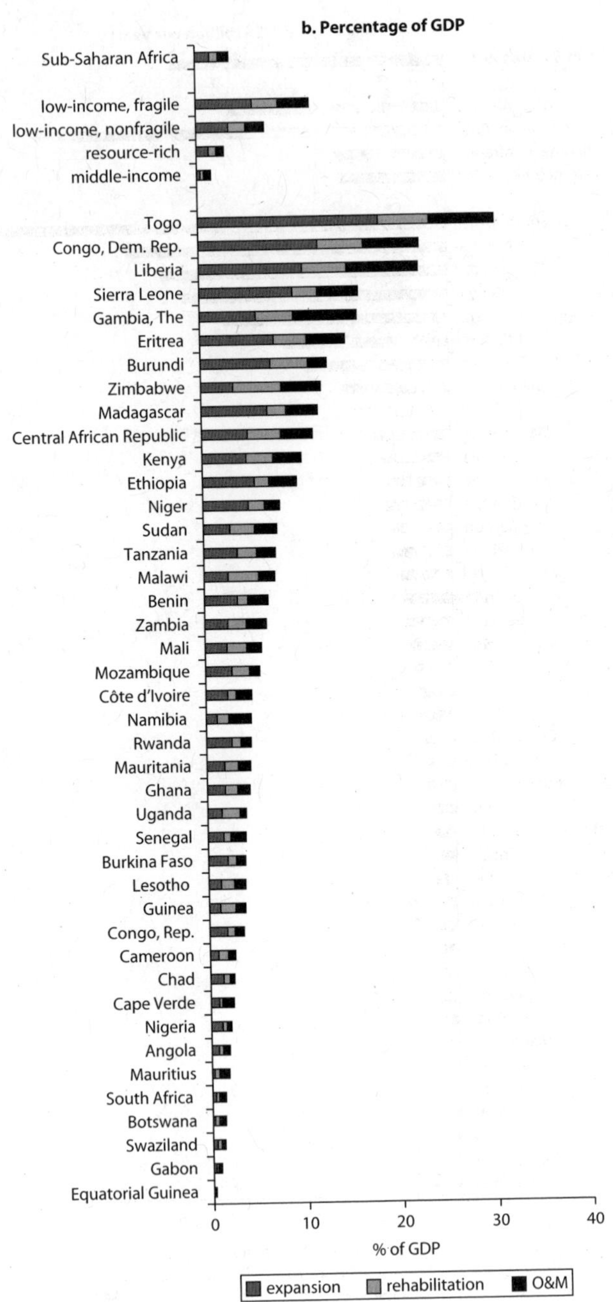

Source: Authors' compilation.

Note: O&M = operations and maintenance.

GDP. The bill becomes prohibitively expensive for low-income countries, which are required to allocate at least 7 percent of GDP annually to water and sanitation every year, and especially for fragile states, for which water and sanitation needs reach almost 12 percent of GDP per year.

Compared with existing spending on water and sanitation—a topic of discussion for the next chapter—delivering the additional financing needed to meet the water and sanitation MDGs looks comfortably manageable only for middle-income countries and barely manageable for resource-rich countries. Both might be able to afford service expansion in tandem with maintaining and even improving service standards. This is not the case for low-income countries, however, particularly fragile states. Realistically, these countries must either accommodate new customers with lower-cost technologies that substantially reduce investment needs and maintenance costs or postpone their achievement of the goals.

Annex 7.1 Unit Cost Matrix Model: A Methodology for Estimating Nonstandardized Unit Costs of Network Assets

The unit costs matrix model is designed specifically to estimate the capital cost per capita of expanding networks in all relevant infrastructure sectors, including water and sanitation, energy, information and communication technologies, and roads, as a function of density and location. The main value of this model is that it allows estimation of country-specific, as opposed to standardized, unit costs. As such, it provides a tool to assess the affordability and efficiency of networks given a country's typical geography, urbanization, and density patterns, and to explore the viability of lower-cost technological alternatives.

A prerequisite to the analysis is the definition of density-based city categories and rural regions, which ideally compose an urban-rural gradient. Cities are classified by population size using data from Henderson (2002)[2] so that typologies span from secondary cities with populations fewer than 100,000 people to megacities with more than 3 million inhabitants. Nonurban areas, including rural hinterlands and deep rural regions, are classified by distance or travel time to the nearest city. Densities are attributed to each typology (table 7.1A) using extent layers from the Global Rural-Urban Mapping Project (GRUMP). This makes it possible to convert the distribution of human population

Table 7.1A Population Density across Urban and Rural Typologies (Number of People per Square Kilometer)

	Large urban					*Secondary cities*	*Rural hinterland*	*Deep rural area*
	> 3 million people	*2.0–2.99 million people*	*1.0–1.99 million people*	*0.5–0.99 million people*	*0.1–0.49 million people*	*< 0.1 million people*	*Between 1 and 6 hours' travel time from nearest city*	*More than 6 hours' travel time from nearest city*
Benin				4,861	1,446	840	46	13
Burkina Faso			2,108		271	268	43	15
Cameroon			4,897		645	1,640	31	7
Cape Verde						1,248	102	40
Chad			2,854		1,373	200	23	4
Congo, Dem. Rep.			2,571	2,617		1,367	35	13
Côte d'Ivoire	4,743			2,306	1,430	1,142	34	13
Ethiopia		4,724			1,644	1,440	107	25
Ghana			3,159	3,199	413	690	71	29
Kenya		2,461		19,928	1,367	1,682	89	5
Lesotho					1,168	—	71	35
Madagascar			3,134		1,040	1,692	40	15
Malawi	—	—	—	—	—	—	114	12
Mozambique	5,008				2,318	1,601	26	9
Namibia					534	—	2	2
Niger				1,573	1,950	1,246	36	2
Nigeria	5,394		4,349	2,806	2,614	1,315	91	50
Rwanda					2,650	—	309	103
Senegal		8,630			1,903	1,383	33	7
South Africa		1,765	1,076		574	400	22	1
Sudan	—	—	—	—	—	807	22	6
Tanzania		4,083	5,406		2,032	1,672	36	16
Uganda			2,529			3,060	122	37
Zambia			1,307	1,105	850	582	14	8

Sources: Authors' compilation based on GRUMP data and Henderson 2002.
Note: Blank cells indicate no cities with that population size. — = not available.

from national or subnational spatial units (usually administrative units) to a series of geo-referenced quadrilateral grids. In urban areas, where multiple cities of a country fall in the same category, the median density of the category is calculated.

It should be noted that density figures are approximate at best owing to the limitations associated with input data. A particular limitation is posed by the paucity of data sets that observe city populations at the same point in time. Henderson (2002) is one of the few, but its data are no more recent than 2000.

The analysis disaggregates unit cost structures of network water services in subcomponents, such as water production and storage, distribution, and connection, and estimates them separately. Although water production, storage costs, and connection costs do not vary by density and location, distribution costs are a function of distance from the water source and concentration of connections.

Standard values for key inputs to the analysis, such as water production capacity per day, storage capacity per connection, and urban and rural water consumption by house and standpost connection, are derived from World Bank water programs in Africa.

In addition to these, a few assumptions are made regarding the number of people per standpost—no more than 200—and the normative walking distance to a standpost—1 kilometer maximum.

Unit prices of materials and technologies (such as the cost of a well with an electric pump or of a meter of water main and small diameter pipe) and connection costs are derived from a study undertaken as part of the Africa Infrastructure Country Diagnostic that collected evidence on unit costs from water and sanitation programs financed by donors in Africa between 2002 and 2006 (box 7.1A).

Box 7.1A

Unit Costs of Infrastructure Projects Study

The objective of the Unit Costs of Infrastructure Projects Study is to design, generate, and analyze a database of standardized unit costs for different types of commonly financed infrastructure investments in Sub-Saharan Africa over the past decade. Actual unit costs are gathered from recently completed projects by

(continued next page)

Box 7.1A *(continued)*

using documentation on procured contracts obtained from four development finance institutions.

The analysis spans relevant infrastructure sectors, including roads, water and sanitation, and energy. Although the objective was to compile a representative sample of projects, with a target of 150 contracts per sector, practical constraints limited the sample to 115 road contracts, 144 water contracts, and 58 electricity contracts over a shorter period of time—approximately 2002–06.

The study focuses on unit output costs—that is, the cost per unit of infrastructure (a water connection, for example) as opposed to the cost per unit of input (such as labor costs). Standardized output costs are especially useful for planning purposes and for estimating value for money. The spread of unit cost values is described using the median—not affected by outlier values—as the center point and the interquartile range to explain the distance from the center. Outlier values are excluded in the calculation of the range.

Three main challenges emerged from this study and are likely to affect similar exercises of this kind. First, the great variability among collected unit cost figures mainly reflects differences in project design. This is an issue because available information on project design does not easily allow standardizing the infrastructure outputs being compared. Where this information is available, it takes the form of technical specifications that run to hundreds of pages. The variability in the design of the outputs made it necessary to subdivide contracts into ever-smaller categories—something not conducive to making generalized conclusions. Second, many practical challenges are involved in parsing and compiling information. Not least of these is the difficulty of obtaining decentralized paper records of projects from donors. Even where electronic databases are maintained, locating and segregating the relevant data remains a complex and time-consuming exercise. Third, data collection difficulties normally occur, reducing the sample size and the significance of the comparisons being made.

As far as water and sanitation is concerned, the 144 sampled projects include 33 well contracts, 60 distribution main contracts, 14 reservoir contracts, 26 service connection contracts, and 11 public latrine contracts. Data are drawn from only one development institution, and the country coverage is highly skewed, with more than 80 percent of the contracts coming from just five countries: Mozambique, Namibia, Nigeria, Tanzania, and Zambia. The water and sanitation unit costs are summarized in the following table.

(continued next page)

Box 7.1A *(continued)*

Unit Costs for Water and Sanitation Projects, 2006 US$

Type	*Unit*	*Lower quartile*	*Median*	*Upper quartile*
Wells—no pump	*$/well*	*5,297*	*6,341*	*6,707*
Wells—electric pump	$/well	14,112	37,492	54,701
Wells—electric and hand pump	*$/well*	*11,288*	*13,959*	*14,896*
Pipe—small diameter	$/m	14	26	40
Pipe—midsize diameter	$/m	122	144	219
Pipe—mains	*$/m*	*358*	*457*	*633*
Reservoir construction—steel	$/kl	437	1,067	2,584
Service connection—yard	$/conn	13	24	74
Service connection—standpipe	*$/conn*	*177*	*282*	*363*
Latrines—public	$/conn	14,014	19,659	29,662

Source: Adapted from Africon 2008.
Note: Italicized rows denote sample sizes large enough to provide reliable unit cost predictions. conn = connection, kl = kiloliter, m = meter.

Annex 7.2 Methodology for Quantifying Rehabilitation and O&M Needs

Network infrastructure:

$$R_i = k \times \frac{UC_i}{30},$$

UC_i = Unit cost per capita of asset *I*,
k = coefficient that takes a value of 5 or 10 depending on country category.

Nonnetwork infrastructure:

$$R_i = a \times \frac{UC_i}{l},$$

UC_i = Unit cost per capita of asset *I*,
a = value of the components of asset i to be replaced expressed as percentage of the total cost of *I*,
l = life span of asset *I*.

Values for a and l:

	a (%)	l (years)
Water		
Urban areas	40	10
Rural areas	80	5
Sanitation		
Septic tank	12.5	10
Improved latrine	12.5	10
Traditional (safe) latrine	100	5

Per capita O&M:
$O\&M = p \times UC_i$,
UC_i = Unit cost per capita of asset I,
p = coefficient that takes a value of 3% for network assets and 1.5% for nonnetwork assets.

Notes

1. Based on unit cost matrix model (annex 7.1) designed for this analysis. It estimates the capital cost per capita of a network connection at varying levels of density in both urban and rural areas.
2. This is one of the few databases compiling city populations at the same point of time.

References

Africon. 2008. "Unit Costs of Infrastructure Projects in Sub-Saharan Africa." AICD Background Paper 11, World Bank, Washington, DC.

Henderson, J. Vernon. 2002. "World Cities Data." http://www.econ.brown.edu/faculty/henderson/worldcities.html.

JMP (Joint Monitoring Programme). 2006. "Meeting the MDG Drinking Water and Sanitation Target: The Urban and Rural Challenge of the Decade." World Health Organization, Geneva, and United Nations Children's Fund, New York.

CHAPTER 8

Bridging the Funding Gap

The price tag for many countries to accomplish the Millennium Development Goals (MDGs) for water supply and sanitation (WSS) is prohibitive when compared with current levels of spending. This chapter delves into the levels and composition of spending on WSS, evaluates how much more can be done within Africa's existing resource envelope by alleviating inefficiencies, and finally arrives at the annual funding gap. It further explores the potential for raising additional financing and policy adjustments to reduce the burden of the funding gap.

Current Spending on Water and Sanitation

Africa is spending a total of $7.9 billion a year to address its WSS needs, which is equivalent to 1.2 percent of Sub-Saharan Africa's gross domestic product (GDP). Existing spending on infrastructure in Africa is higher than previously thought when the calculation takes into account budget and off-budget spending—including state-owned enterprises (SOEs) and extrabudgetary funds—as well as external financing, a category that comprises official development assistance (ODA) from the member states of the Organisation for Economic Co-operation and Development (OECD), financiers from outside the OECD, self-household financing, and private participation in infrastructure. Overall, however, these numbers might be underestimated given the complexity of traced resources allocated to the sector, in particular those coming from nongovernmental organizations and allotted to sanitation or rural water programs, which are not always centrally recorded and hence could not be fully captured in this exercise.

In absolute terms, spending levels vary significantly across the country groups (table 8.1): Middle-income countries spend $2.6 billion, followed by low-income countries ($1.8 billion), and resource-rich countries ($1.7 billion); fragile states spend about $0.5 billion in capital investment and operations and maintenance (O&M). Expressed as a percentage of GDP, infrastructure spending fluctuates widely across different country groups; whereas low-income countries and fragile states spend 1.1 percent and 1.7 percent of their GDP, respectively, middle-income countries and resource-rich countries spend 1 percent or less of GDP (1.0 percent and 0.8 percent, respectively).

The composition of spending also varies substantially across country groups. Middle-income countries allocate 80 percent of WSS spending to maintenance, likely reflecting the fact that they have already built much of the infrastructure needed. By contrast, all the other country groups allocate at most 30 percent to this item. Therefore, resource-rich countries, low-income countries, and fragile states spend 70 to 90 percent of their budgets on capital investments. Although this reflects their need to build new WSS facilities, a danger exists of neglecting the maintenance needs of the limited network that is available.

Table 8.1 Spending by Functional Category, Annualized Average Flows, 2001–05

	GDP share (%)			*US$ (million per year)*		
	O&M	*Total CAPEX*	*Total spending*	*O&M*	*Total CAPEX*	*Total spending*
Sub-Saharan Africa	0.5	0.7	1.2	3,112	4,778	7,890
Low-income, fragile	0.3	0.8	1.1	128	313	441
Low-income, nonfragile	0.3	1.4	1.7	307	1,533	1,840
Middle-income	0.7	0.2	1.0	1,996	641	2,637
Resource-rich	0.1	0.7	0.8	188	1,564	1,753

Sources: Foster and Briceño-Garmendia 2009; Briceño-Garmendia, Smits, and Foster 2008 for public spending; PPIAF 2008 for private flows; Foster and others 2008 for non-OECD financiers.
Note: Aggregate public sector covers general government and nonfinancial enterprises. Figures are extrapolations based on the 24-country covered in AICD Phase 1. Total might not add up exactly because of scaling up among country groups and rounding error. CAPEX = capital expenditure, GDP = gross domestic product, O&M = operations and maintenance.

The explanations for this composition of spending are different in each case. For low-income fragile states, the problem is the limited flow of resources available; this fosters a preference for investing in expansion of access to new customers. Resource-rich countries, in contrast, have a limited propensity to spend on infrastructure.

The spending effort is relative to the size of the economy. The divergence in WSS spending across countries is also considerable; it ranges from 0.7 percent of GDP in Chad to 3.1 percent in Ethiopia. Particularly important differences are seen in the shares of spending in O&M and capital spending (figure 8.1). Namibia, Ethiopia, Botswana, and South Africa allocate the highest percentages of their GDP to O&M of the existing infrastructure, whereas Chad and Madagascar spend the least in this category. Surprisingly, Uganda and Senegal, some of the best performers in Sub-Saharan Africa, assign less than 0.05 percent of GDP to O&M. Ethiopia, Benin, Zambia, and Niger dedicate the highest percentages of GDP to capital investment, and South Africa the least, at 0.07 percent of its GDP.

Three key players are seen in WSS sector financing: the public sector, donors, and households (table 8.2). In Sub-Saharan Africa, households are important financiers of capital investment (0.3 percent of Sub-Saharan African GDP) and account for $2.1 billion, most of it dedicated to the construction of on-site sanitation facilities, such as latrines. The level of contributions from OECD donors is similar to that of domestic public resources (comprising tax revenue and user charges raised by SOEs), equivalent to 0.2 percent of Sub-Saharan African GDP. The contribution of non-OECD countries is only 0.03 percent of Sub-Saharan African GDP, and that of the private sector is almost nonexistent (close to 0 percent of Sub-Saharan African GDP).

Financing follows specialization patterns. Across country groups, households' contribution to rehabilitation and construction of new facilities ranges between 0.2 percent (middle-income countries) and 1.4 percent (low-income, nonfragile countries; figure 8.2). The role of ODA is particularly important to low-income, nonfragile countries because it represents on average 0.7 percent of GDP of countries with limited domestic resources but adequate institutional capacity. In resource-rich countries, the public sector plays a significant part in financing the WSS sector (0.3 percent of GDP), but its role in the fragile states and middle-income countries is very modest. Non-OECD finance has shown a preference for low-income countries (fragile and nonfragile) and resource-rich countries.

Figure 8.1 Water and Sanitation Spending from All Sources as a Percentage of GDP, Annual Averages by Functional Category, 2001–05

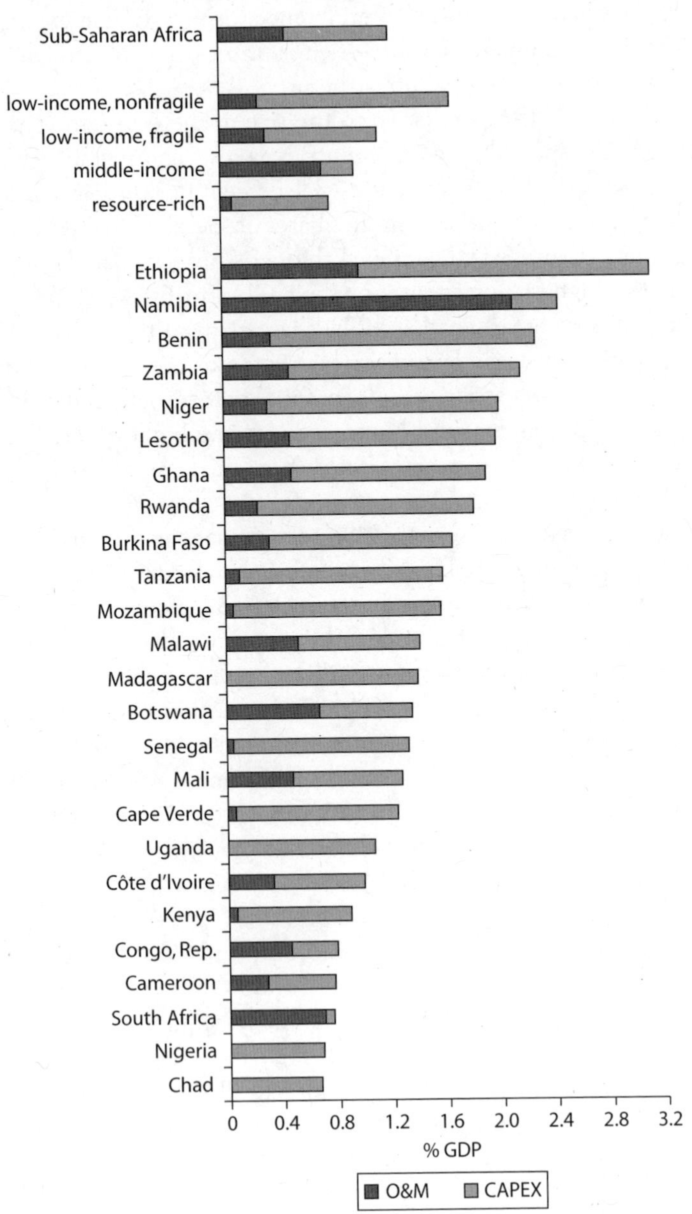

Source: Authors' calculations.
Note: CAPEX = capital expenditure, GDP = gross domestic product, O&M = operations and maintenance.

Table 8.2 Capital Investments of the Most Important Players, Annualized Average Flows, 2001–05

	GDP share (%)						US$ (million per year)					
	Public sector	*ODA*	*Non-OECD financiers*	*PPI*	*Household self-finance*	*Total CAPEX*	*Public sector*	*ODA*	*Non-OECD financiers*	*PPI*	*Household self-finance*	*Total CAPEX*
Sub-Saharan Africa	0.2	0.2	0.03	0.0	0.3	0.7	1,252	1,227	163	10	2,125	4,778
Low-income, fragile	0.1	0.3	0.05	0.0	0.4	0.8	30	105	20	0	165	313
Low-income, nonfragile	0.2	0.7	0.05	0.0	0.4	1.4	243	783	55	2	451	1,533
Middle-income	0.1	0.0	0.00	0.0	0.1	0.2	324	101	8	2	206	641
Resource-rich	0.3	0.1	0.04	0.0	0.2	0.7	717	238	80	7	522	1,564

Source: Foster and Briceño-Garmendia 2009; Briceño-Garmendia, Smits, and Foster 2008 for public spending; PPIAF 2008 for private flows; and Foster and others 2008 for non-OECD financiers.
Note: CAPEX = capital expenditure, GDP = gross domestic product, ODA = official development assistance, OECD = Organisation for Economic Co-operation and Development, PPI = private participation in infrastructure.

Figure 8.2 Water and Sanitation Capital Investment as a Percentage of GDP, by Funding Source, Annualized Averages for 2001–05

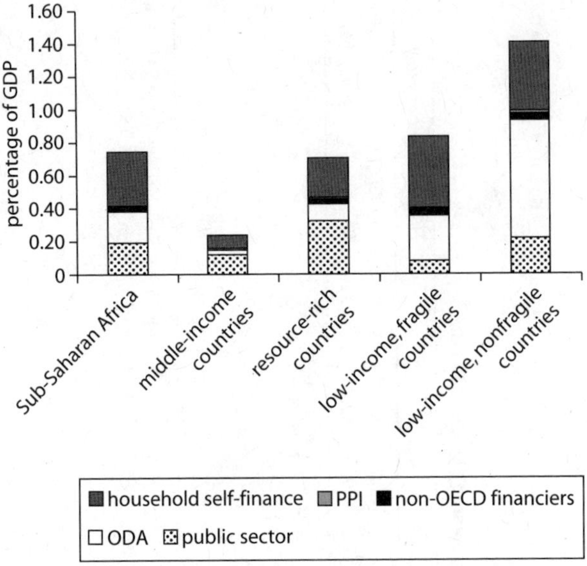

Source: Briceño-Garmendia, Smits, and Foster 2008; Foster and Briceño-Garmendia 2009.
Note: GDP = gross domestic product, ODA = official development assistance, OECD = Organisation for Economic Co-operation and Development, PPI = private participation in infrastructure.

Poor Budget Execution by the WSS Sector

African governments allocate 0.7 percent of their GDP to support the provision of WSS infrastructure from their central government budgets alone (table 8.3). For Africa, this effort translates to an estimated $180 million a year for an average country. For a perspective on this figure, an investment of $100 million can purchase about 100,000 new household connections to water and sewerage. It runs well short of covering the WSS spending needs presented in chapter 7 of this book.

As a percentage of GDP, budget spending on WSS infrastructure is comparable across resource-rich and low-income countries (fragile and nonfragile). In absolute terms, however, middle-income countries have a much larger infrastructure budget, with spending per capita several times higher than in low-income countries because of the much larger value of GDP (table 8.4). Overall, WSS spending is the second-largest infrastructure item in central government accounts, after spending on transport, particularly in the middle-income countries. It ranges from about half of all

Table 8.3 Annual Budgetary Flows, Annualized Averages, 2001–05

	Share of GDP (%)	*US$ (billion per year)*
Sub-Saharan Africa	0.7	4.4
Low-income, fragile	0.4	0.2
Low-income, nonfragile	0.5	0.5
Middle-income	0.9	2.5
Resource-rich	0.4	0.9

Sources: Foster and Briceño-Garmendia 2009; Briceño-Garmendia, Smits, and Foster 2008.
Note: Annualized averages for 2001–06 weighted by country GDP. Figures are extrapolations based on the 24-country sample covered in the AICD Phase 1.
GDP = gross domestic product.

central government spending on infrastructure in middle-income countries to 60 percent in low-income countries.

In Sub-Saharan Africa, about 40 percent of budgetary spending in water goes to O&M (table 8.1). In middle-income countries the percentage allocated to O&M is more than 75 percent of the public spending in WSS infrastructure. Resource-rich and low-income (nonfragile) countries spend most of their budgetary resources in capital investments; very little remains for O&M. In low-income countries (fragile), the public spending in O&M is close to 30 percent.

On average, in Sub-Saharan Africa governments finance 75 percent of the total budgetary spending, and the utilities contribute the remaining 25 percent (figure 8.3). The distribution of responsibilities among the central government and the utilities varies across the four typologies: In resource-rich countries, most of the public spending is financed by the central government (80 percent), whereas in low-income countries (fragile), 70 percent of the spending in the sector comes from nonfinancial public institutions (equivalent to 0.04 percent of their GDP).

In comparison with the central government, nonfinancial public institutions, such as utilities and other service providers, make little infrastructure investment (at most 20 percent of total capital investment) in both absolute and relative terms. This spending pattern reflects government control of some of the main sources of investment finance, be they royalty payments (in resource-rich countries) or external development funds (in fragile states and other low-income countries). It also reflects, to some extent, SOEs' limited capability to fund their capital investments through user fees.

Table 8.4 Public Infrastructure Spending by Institution in the WSS Sector, 2001–05

	Share of GDP (%)				*US$ (million per year)*			
	OPEX		*CAPEX*		*OPEX*		*CAPEX*	
	On-budget	*Off-budget*	*On-budget*	*Off-budget*	*On-budget*	*Off-budget*	*On-budget*	*Off-budget*
Sub-Saharan Africa	0.35	0.14	0.17	0.03	2,216	896	1,073	180
Low-Income, fragile	0.04	0.29	0.08	0.00	16	111	30	0
Low-Income, nonfragile	0.15	0.13	0.16	0.06	164	143	176	67
Middle-income	0.62	0.18	0.10	0.02	1,691	494	275	49
Resource-rich	0.03	0.05	0.30	0.02	68	121	663	54

Source: Authors' calculations.
Note: CAPEX = capital expenditure, GDP = gross domestic product, OPEX = operating expenditure.

Table 8.5 Average Budget Variation Ratios for Capital Spending

	Overall infrastructure	*Water supply and sanitation sector*
Sub-Saharan Africa	75	66
Low-income, fragile	—	—
Low-income, nonfragile	76	72
Middle-income	78	66
Resource-rich	65	43

Sources: Foster and Briceño-Garmendia 2009, adapted from Briceño-Garmendia, Smits, and Foster 2008.
Note: Budget variation ratio is defined as executed budget divided by allocated budget. Based on annualized averages for 2001–06. — = not available.

Figure 8.3 Split Investment Responsibilities between Governments and Public Enterprises

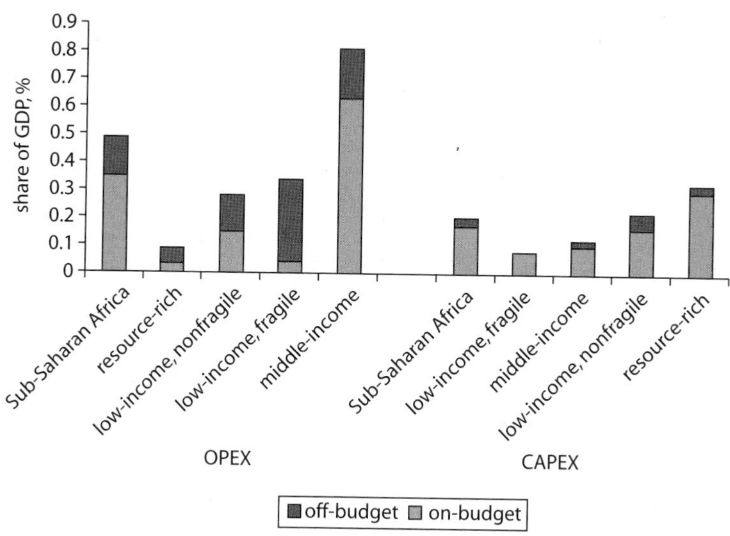

Sources: Briceño-Garmendia, Smits, and Foster 2008; Foster and Briceño-Garmendia 2009.
Note: Based on annualized averages for 2001–06. Averages weighted by country GDP.

In Sub-Saharan Africa, SOE spending (off-budget) in O&M accounts at most for 30 percent of total spending on this item. The SOEs are essentially asset administrators. Interestingly, in fragile states almost 90 percent of O&M expenses are financed by nonfinancial public institutions, whereas in middle-income countries, approximately 80 percent of the spending on O&M is in the budget.

Inefficiencies within the public expenditure management systems are particularly detrimental because central governments are such major players in capital investment and O&M relative to nonfinancial public institutions. A key issue is that central governments face significant problems in executing their infrastructure capital budgets. African countries are, on average, unable to spend more than one-quarter of their WSS capital budgets. In particular, resource-rich countries executed less than 45 percent of their budgets. The poor timing of project appraisals and late releases of budgeted funds because of procurement problems often prevent the use of resources within the budget cycle. Delays affecting in-year fund releases are also associated with poor project preparation, leading to changes in the terms agreed on with contractors in the original contract (deadlines, technical specifications, budgets, costs, and so on). In other cases, cash is reallocated to nondiscretionary spending driven by political or social pressures.

Compared with the other infrastructure sectors, the WSS sector is the worst offender of unused budget allocations, in particular in resource-rich countries, where governments are able to spend barely 66 percent of budget allocations (table 8.5).

Even after Efficiency Savings, a Persistent Funding Gap

Inefficiencies of various kinds total an estimated $2.9 billion a year (0.5 percent of GDP; table 8.6). In absolute terms, the gains can be maximized for higher-income countries so that they contribute about 0.4 percent of GDP. In relative terms, the low-income fragile countries can leverage the most from exploiting the efficiency gains, amounting to 1.2 percent of GDP.

Three opportunities can be identified for efficiency gains. First, raising user charges closer to cost-recovery levels would provide more efficient price signals and help capture lost revenue of about $1.5 billion per year. Second, reducing utilities' operating inefficiencies would prevent waste of significant resources, support healthier utilities, and improve service quality, leading to savings of about $1.3 billion per year. Third, improving budget-execution rates would increase the potential of fully using resources allocated to public investment by about $0.2 billion per year. If the bottlenecks in capital execution could be resolved, countries could, on average, increase their capital spending by 4 percent without any increase in current budget allocations. For middle-income countries, an additional potential efficiency gain comes from reallocating $0.3 billion of existing spending to those subsectors in greatest need. This tactic would generate the highest economic returns, which would increase the

Table 8.6 Potential Gains from Greater Efficiency

	GDP share (%)							US$ (million per year)						
	Operational inefficiencies							Operational inefficiencies						
	Labor inefficiencies	*Losses*	*Under-collection*	*Total operational inefficiencies*	*Capital execution*	*Tariff cost recovery*	*Total*	*Labor inefficiencies*	*Losses*	*Under-collection*	*Total operational inefficiencies*	*Capital execution*	*Tariff cost recovery*	*Total*
Sub-Saharan Africa	0.06	0.07	0.07	0.20	0.03	0.23	0.45	375	425	458	1,259	168	1,450	2,877
Low-income, fragile	0.04	0.17	0.06	0.28	0.02	0.93	1.23	17	65	25	106	6	358	471
Low-income, nonfragile	0.08	0.10	0.06	0.24	0.03	0.35	0.62	87	111	67	265	39	381	685
Middle-income	0.03	0.06	0.10	0.18	0.00	0.20	0.38	68	150	274	492	8	537	1,037
Resource-rich	—	0.05	0.03	0.08	0.06	0.10	0.23	—	103	69	172	137	214	522

Source: AICD, adapted from Briceño-Garmendia, Smits, and Foster 2008.

Note: Based on annualized averages for 2001–06. Averages weighted by country GDP. Figures are extrapolations based on the 24-country sample covered in AICD Phase 1, and they are lower bounds because inefficiencies might be higher as reported in the table due to data constraints. Totals may not add exactly because of rounding errors. — = not available, GDP = gross domestic product.

impact of the current budget envelope on covering needs and raise the value for money of public funds.

At the country level, Madagascar and Mali have the highest potential gains as a percentage of GDP (1.5 percent), results that would stem in particular from tackling the underpricing of tariffs (around 80 percent of the total gains; figure 8.4). Malawi is close to Madagascar and Mali in its level of inefficiencies (almost 0.9 percent of GDP), but the gains from resolving tariffs below cost-recovery levels account for around 40 percent of the total gains, whereas the operational inefficiencies account for about 50 percent of the potential gains. Nigeria has the lowest potential efficiency gains as a percentage of GDP (0.14 percent).

Even if all the efficiency gains are internalized, a funding gap remains. Existing spending and potential efficiency gains can be calculated from estimated spending needs to gauge the extent of the financial shortfall. Africa would still face an annual funding gap of $11.9 billion a year, or 1.8 percent of GDP, to meet the MDG for WSS (figure 8.5).

The smallest funding gap is found in middle-income countries where the highest inefficiencies are present. After tackling the inefficiencies, middle-income countries would have a negligible funding gap of $0.3 billion. In fact, for these countries, potential exists for reallocation of resources of $0.2 billion, which can be swung from O&M to capital expenditure or transferred to some other infrastructure sector. The largest funding gap remains in low-income countries (nonfragile), representing about half of the total funding gap for Sub-Saharan Africa ($5.3 billion; table 8.7).

The net annual funding gap represents 9.4 percent of the GDP of fragile states and less than 0.1 percent of the GDP of middle-income countries. The gap between the low-income (nonfragile) and resource-rich countries is 4.8 percent and 1.8 percent of GDP, respectively (table 8.8).

Although the infrastructure funding gap is primarily for capital investment ($8.6 billion), a shortfall of almost one-fourth also exists for O&M (table 8.8). In the aggregate, Africa needs to increase water infrastructure capital investment by 1.3 percent of GDP; low-income, nonfragile countries need to invest an additional 3.3 percent, and fragile states an additional 6.8 percent. The shares of GDP for middle-income countries and resource-rich countries are below the African share of GDP (0.1 percent and 1.2 percent, respectively). The remainder of the infrastructure funding gap ($3.2 billion) relates to O&M needs and is approximately evenly distributed across fragile states, low-income countries, and resource-rich countries. Middle-income countries do not face an O&M funding gap.

Figure 8.4 Potential Efficiency Gains from Different Sources

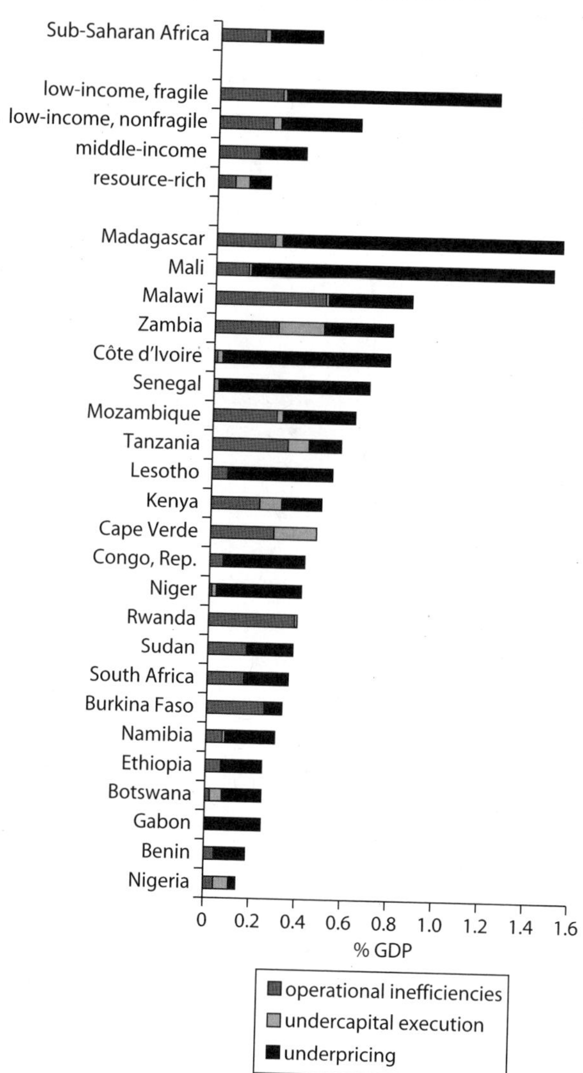

Source: Authors' compilation.
Note: GDP = gross domestic product.

Closing the $11.8 billion WSS infrastructure funding gap depends in part on raising additional funds, but it may also require taking more time to attain targets or using lower-cost technologies, such as standposts and traditional latrines.

Figure 8.5 Water Infrastructure Funding Gap

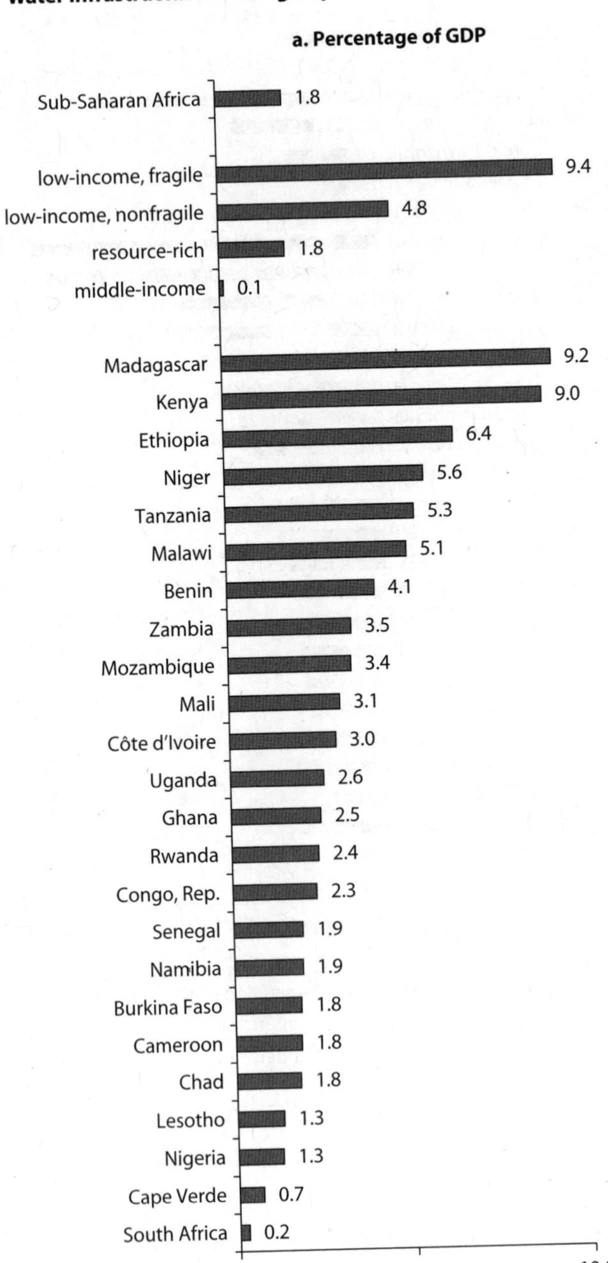

(continued next page)

Figure 8.5 *(continued)*

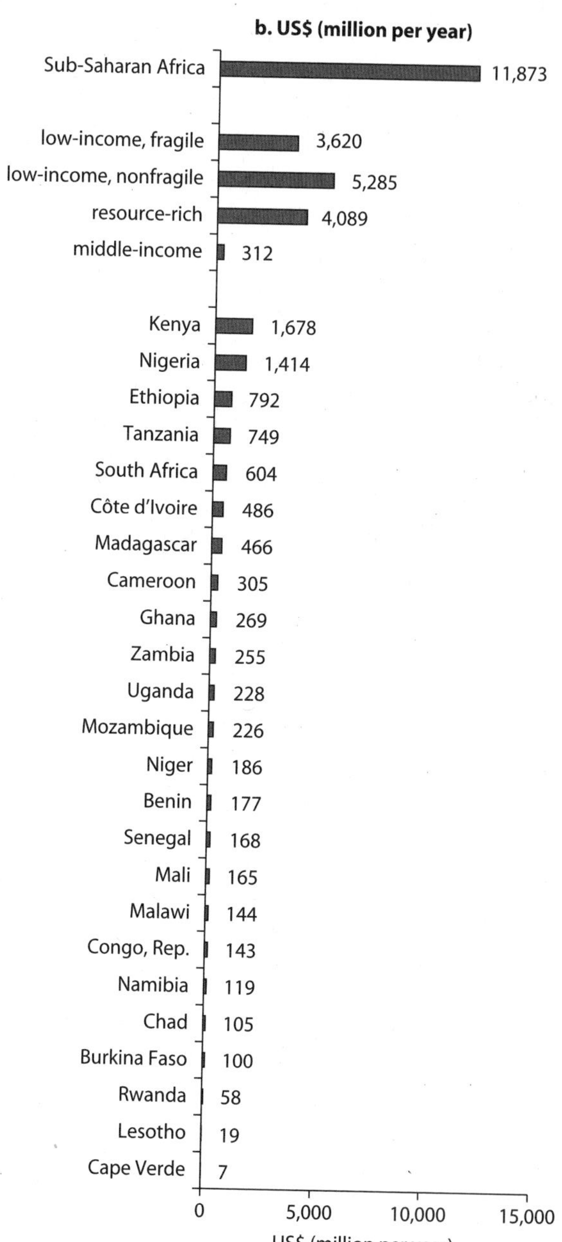

Source: Briceño-Garmendia, Smits, and Foster 2008.
Note: GDP = gross domestic product.

Table 8.7 Funding Gap
(US$ million per year)

	Total needs	Spending traced to needs	Gain from eliminating inefficiencies	Sources of inefficiency			Funding gap or surplus
				Underexecution of budget	Operating inefficiencies	Underpricing	
Sub-Saharan Africa	–22,640	7,890	2,877	168	1,259	1,450	–11,873
Low-income, fragile	–4,531	441	471	6	106	358	–3,620
Low-income, nonfragile	–7,810	1,840	685	39	265	381	–5,285
Middle-income	–3,987	2,637	1,037	8	492	537	–312
Resource-rich	–6,364	1,753	522	137	172	214	–4,089

Source: Briceño-Garmendia, Smits, and Foster 2008.

Table 8.8 Size and Composition of the Annual Funding Gap by O&M and Capital Expenditure

	Share of GDP (%)			*US$ (million per year)*		
	CAPEX gap	*O&M gap*	*Total funding gap*	*CAPEX gap*	*O&M gap*	*Total funding gap*
Sub-Saharan Africa	1.3	0.5	1.8	8,648	3,225	11,873
Low-income, fragile	6.8	2.6	9.4	2,627	993	3,620
Low-income, nonfragile	3.3	1.5	4.8	3,673	1,612	5,285
Middle-income	0.1	0	0.1	312	—	312
Resource-rich	1.2	0.6	1.8	2,696	1,393	4,089

Source: Briceño-Garmendia, Smits, and Foster 2008.
Note: CAPEX = capital expenditure.

Limited Scope for Raising Additional Finance

Limited financing sources are available, and the global financial crisis is likely to affect some of them adversely. Domestic public finance is one of the main sources of funding today, but it presents little scope for an increase, except possibly in countries that enjoy natural resource windfalls. Another point to consider is that household finance is one of the most important sources of funding today for capital investments in African infrastructure (0.3 percent of GDP; see table 8.2), mainly of sanitation facilities. It is very likely that this source will be affected by the financial crisis, but given that other forms of private participation have not been very important in the WSS sector, no concern is found on that score about the negative impacts of the downturn on global markets. In addition, ODA is an important player in financing capital investments in the sector (0.2 percent of GDP; see table 8.2). It has grown substantially in recent years, in line with political pledges, but this assistance could slow down if countercyclical assistance were put in place. Finally, local capital markets have so far contributed little to WSS sector finance outside South Africa, and there is not much expectation that they could eventually assume greater role in some of the region's larger economies.

Little Scope for Domestic Finance

A key question is the extent to which countries may be willing to allocate additional fiscal resources to the WSS sectors. In the run-up to the current financial crisis, the fiscal situation in Sub-Saharan Africa was favorable. Rapid economic growth averaged 4 percent a year from 2001 to 2005, which translated to increased domestic fiscal revenue of just over

3 percent of GDP on average. In resource-rich countries, burgeoning resource royalties added 7.7 percent of GDP to the public budget. In low-income countries, substantial debt relief increased external grants by almost 2 percent of GDP.

Surprisingly little additional resources were available during the recent growth surge allocated to infrastructure (table 8.9). The most extreme case is that of the resource-rich countries, particularly Nigeria. Huge debt repayments more than fully absorbed the fiscal windfalls in these countries. As a result, budgetary spending actually contracted by 3.7 percent of GDP. Infrastructure investment bore much of that contraction and fell by almost 1.5 percent of GDP. In middle-income countries, budgetary spending increased by almost 4.1 percent of GDP, but the effect on infrastructure spending was almost negligible and the additional resources went primarily to current social sector spending. Only in the low-income countries did the overall increases in budgetary expenditure have some effect on infrastructure spending. Even there, however, the effect was fairly modest and confined to capital spending. The low-income countries (nonfragile) have allocated 30 percent of the budgetary increase to infrastructure investments. The fragile states, despite seeing their overall budgetary expenditures increase by about 3.9 percent of GDP, have allocated only 6 percent of the increase to infrastructure.

Compared with other developing regions, public financing capabilities in Sub-Saharan Africa are characterized by weak tax revenue collection. Domestic revenue generation of around 23 percent of GDP trails averages for other developing countries and is lowest for low-income countries (less than 15 percent of GDP a year). Despite the high growth rates in the past decade, domestically raised revenue grew by less than 1.2 percent of GDP,

Table 8.9 Net Change in Central Government Budgets, by Economic Use
(% of GDP)

Use	Sub-Saharan Africa	Middle-income	Resource-rich	Low-income, nonfragile	Low-income, fragile
Net expenditure budget	1.89	4.08	−3.73	1.69	3.85
Current infrastructure spending as a share of expenditures	0	0.02	0.03	0	0.09
Capital infrastructure spending as a share of expenditures	−0.14	0.04	−1.46	0.54	0.22

Sources: Foster and Briceño-Garmendia, 2009, adapted from Briceño-Garmendia, Smits, and Foster 2008.
Note: Based on annualized averages for 2001–06. Averages weighted by country GDP. Totals are extrapolations based on the 24-country sample as covered in AICD Phase 1. GDP = gross domestic product.

suggesting increasing domestic revenue from current levels would require undertaking challenging institutional reforms to increase the effectiveness of revenue collection and broaden the tax base. Without such reforms, domestic revenue generation will remain weak.

The borrowing capacity from domestic and external sources is also limited. Domestic borrowing is often very expensive, with interest rates far exceeding those on concessional external loans. Particularly for the poorest countries, the scarcity of private domestic savings means that public domestic borrowing tends to precipitate sharp increases in interest rates, building a vicious circle. For many Sub-Saharan African countries, the share of debt service to GDP is more than 6 percent.

The global financial crisis can be expected to reduce fiscal receipts because of lower taxes, royalties, and user charge taxes—Africa is not exempt from its impact. Growth projections for the coming years have been revised downward from 5.1 percent to 3.5 percent, which will reduce tax revenue and likely depress the demand and willingness to pay for infrastructure services. Commodity prices have fallen to levels of the early 2000s. The effect on royalty revenue, however, will depend on the savings regime in each country. Various oil producers have been saving royalty revenue in excess of $60 a barrel, so the current downturn will affect savings accounts more than budgets. Overall, the adverse situation created by the global financial crisis will put substantial pressure on public sector budgets. In addition, many African countries are devaluing their currency, reducing the purchasing power of domestic resources.

According to recent global experience, fiscal adjustment episodes tend to fall disproportionately on public investment in general and WSS infrastructure in particular. Experience from earlier crises in East Asia and Latin America indicates that infrastructure spending is especially vulnerable to budget cutbacks during crisis periods. Based on averages for eight Latin American countries, cuts in infrastructure investment amounted to about 40 percent of the observed fiscal adjustment between the early 1980s and late 1990s (Calderón and Servén 2004). This reduction was remarkable because public infrastructure investment already represented less than 25 percent of overall public expenditure in Latin American countries. These infrastructure investment cuts were later identified as the underlying problem holding back economic growth in the whole region during the 2000s. Similar patterns were observed in East Asia during the financial crisis of the mid-1990s. For example, Indonesia's total public investment in infrastructure dropped from 6 to 7 percent of GDP during the period from 1995 to 1997 to 2 percent in 2000. Given recent spending patterns, there is every reason to expect that in Africa changes in the overall budget envelope will affect infrastructure investment in a similar pro-cyclical manner.

Self- or Household Finance

Self- or household finance has been the main source of external financing in the sanitation sector, representing almost half of the total spending in capital investment ($2.1 billion, or 0.3 percent of the African GDP; see table 8.2). These figures are largely driven by private investments at the household level in people's own sanitation facilities. Households in Africa's resource-rich countries and low-income countries (nonfragile) invest the largest volume of funds in absolute terms (almost half of the total household or self-finance for the region). Households in fragile states invest the least in absolute terms (less than $0.2 billion). Nigeria has the highest amount of the total household investment in sanitation (equivalent to $295 million), which accounts for 0.3 percent of its GDP. The financial crisis is likely to affect households' willingness to invest in new WSS facilities or improvements given the potential reductions in household income, although it is hard to make exact predictions.

Official Development Assistance

Commitments of ODA from OECD donors to water infrastructure in Sub-Saharan Africa have increased from $0.8 to $1.2 billion between 1995 and 2007. Across countries, The Gambia captures the highest level of ODA commitments as a percentage of GDP (1.5 percent of GDP), followed by Benin and Burundi (1.4 percent of GDP) (figure 8.6). In absolute terms, Tanzania and Nigeria receive the largest shares of ODA commitments in the region (around 20 percent of this source).

A significant lag occurs between ODA commitments and their disbursement, which suggests that disbursements should continue to increase in the coming years. The commitments just reported are significantly higher than the estimated ODA disbursements of $1.2 billion, or 0.2 percent of Sub-Saharan African GDP (see table 8.2). This gap reflects delays typically associated with project implementation. Because ODA is channeled through the government budget, the execution of funds faces some of the same problems affecting domestically financed public investment, including procurement delays and the capacity of low-income countries to execute funds. Divergences between donor and country financial systems, as well as unpredictability in the release of funds, may further hinder the disbursement of donor resources. Bearing this in mind, as long as all commitments up to 2007 are fully honored,

Figure 8.6 Aid Commitments for Water Supply and Sanitation as a Percentage of GDP, 2001–05

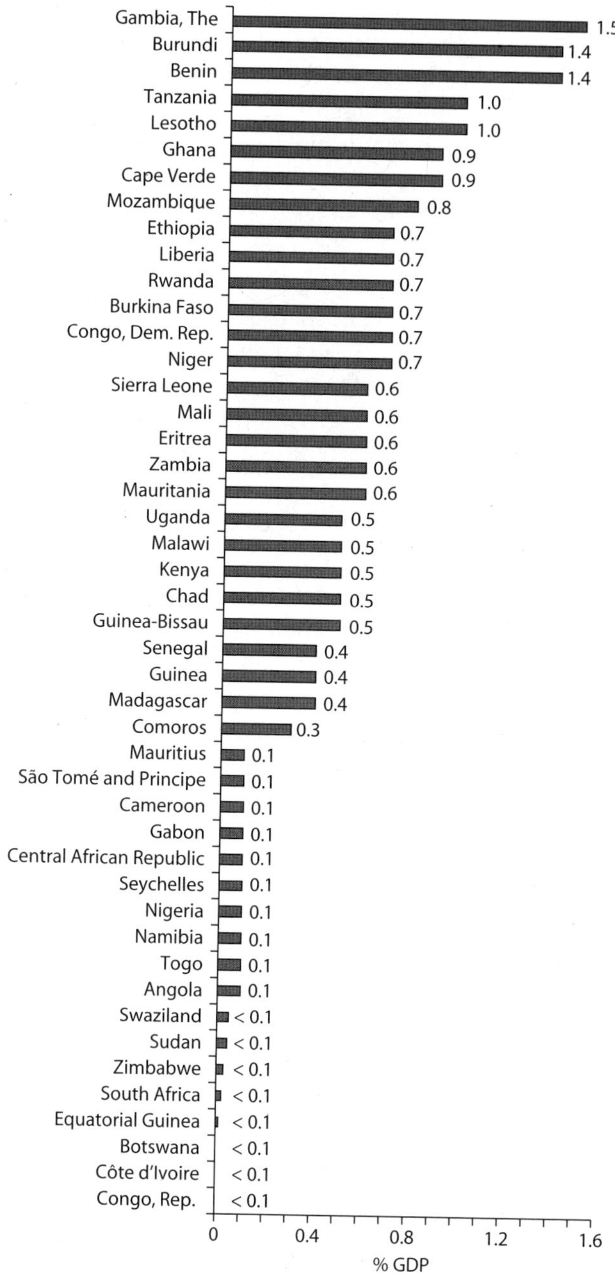

Source: Briceño-Garmendia, Smits, and Foster 2008.
Note: GDP = gross domestic product.

ODA disbursements could be expected to rise significantly over the next few years (IMF 2009; World Economic Outlook 2008).

ODA was set to increase further before the crisis, but prospects no longer look as promising. The three multilateral agencies—the African Development Bank, the European Commission, and the World Bank—secured record replenishments for their concessional funding windows for the three to four years beginning in 2008. In principle, funding allocations to African WSS sectors totaling $1.2 billion a year (see table 8.2) could come from the multilateral agencies alone in the near future. In practice, however, the crisis may divert multilateral resources from infrastructure projects toward emergency fiscal support. Bilateral support, based on annual budget determinations, may be more sensitive to the fiscal squeeze in the OECD countries, and some decline can be anticipated. Historical trends suggest that ODA has tended to be pro-cyclical rather than countercyclical (IMF 2009; ODI 2009; UBS Investment Research 2008; World Economic Outlook 2008; and references cited therein).

Other Financial Players: The Private Sector and Non-OECD Financiers

Most of the private investment commitments in the water sector ($10.7 million) come from foreign participation and predominantly target Sudan ($6.7 million, or 65 percent of the total). This number may be significantly underestimated, however, given the difficulty in capturing data on private investment coming through nongovernmental organizations and foundations when the resources do not enter the public treasuries.

Private capital flows, in particular, are likely to be affected by the global financial crisis. In the aftermath of the Asian financial crisis, private participation in developing countries fell by about one-half over a period of five years, following its peak in 1997. Existing transactions are also coming under stress as they encounter difficulties refinancing short- and medium-term debt. Given the very limited volume of private participation in the WSS sector in Africa, however, the downside risk is also limited.

Non-OECD countries financed less than $0.2 billion worth of African WSS infrastructure annually between 2001 and 2005 or 0.03 percent of GDP (see table 8.2). Non-OECD financiers have been active primarily in resource-rich countries, mainly oil-exporting countries (Angola, Nigeria, and Sudan), which receive half of the total resources coming from non-OECD financiers ($80 million). Just over one-third of the resources, or $55 million, has gone to low-income countries (nonfragile).

These financiers' contribution to middle-income countries is very small ($8 million per year).

China's official economic assistance for infrastructure project quadrupled between 2001 and 2005 and reached more than 35 Sub-Saharan African countries. Most of the inflows went to resource-rich countries; in some cases, they made use of barter arrangements under the "Angola mode."[1] The WSS sector accounts for a relatively small share of China's assistance (2 percent, or $0.14 billion) when compared with the commitments made to other sectors. Most of the projects are focused on meeting immediate social needs directly related to water supply, such as smaller dams in Cape Verde and Mozambique.

How the current economic downturn will affect non-OECD finance is difficult to predict because of the relatively recent nature of these capital inflows.

Local Sources of Finance

Local capital markets are a major source of WSS sector infrastructure finance in southern Africa and the resource-rich countries, but not yet elsewhere (table 8.10); they account for about $3 billion. Local infrastructure finance consists primarily of commercial bank lending, some

Table 8.10 Outstanding Financing Stock for Water and Sanitation Infrastructure, as of 2006

Outstanding financing for infrastructure	*Bank loans*	*Corporate bonds*	*Equity issues*	*Total*	*Share of total stock (%)*	*Share of total infrastructure stock (%)*
Resource-rich	1,119	—	2	1,121	37	43
Low-income, nonfragile	350	—	—	350	11	5
Low-income, fragile	69	—	11	80	3	17
Middle-income (excluding South Africa)	103	—	—	103	3	19
South Africa	1,264	—	130	1,393	46	2
Total	2,905	—	142	3,047	100	4
Share of total stock (%)	95	—	5	100		
Share of total infrastructure stock (%)	4	—	0	4		

Source: Adapted from Irving and Manroth 2009.
Note: Bank loans combine transport, communication, energy, and water for the Democratic Republic of Congo, Ghana, Lesotho, and Zambia. Bank loans combine electricity, water, and gas/public utilities for Benin, Burkina Faso, Cape Verde, Côte d'Ivoire, Ethiopia, Malawi, Namibia, Niger, Nigeria, Rwanda, Senegal, South Africa, Uganda, and Zambia. — = not available.

corporate bond and stock exchange issues, and a nascent entry of institutional investors. These markets remain underdeveloped, shallow, and small, in particular for financing the WSS sector in fragile states. Long-term financing with maturities commensurate with infrastructure projects is scarce.[2] The capacity of local banking systems remains too small and constrained by structural impediments to finance infrastructure. Most countries' banks have significant asset-liability maturity mismatches for infrastructure financing. Bank deposits and other liabilities still have largely short-term tenors. More potential may exist for syndicated lending with local bank participation, though the increase in new loans over the 2000–06 period occurred in a favorable external financing environment. The African banking system did not feel the effects of the global financial crisis at first, but the crisis slowly but surely affected financial systems around the region and added to the already enormous challenge of developing local financial markets.

Costs of Capital from Different Sources

The various sources of infrastructure finance differ greatly in their associated costs of capital (figure 8.7). For public funds, raising taxes is not a costless exercise. Each dollar raised and spent by a Sub-Saharan African government has a social value premium (or marginal cost of public funds) of almost 20 percent. That premium captures the incidence of that tax on

Figure 8.7 Costs of Capital by Funding Source, 2001–05

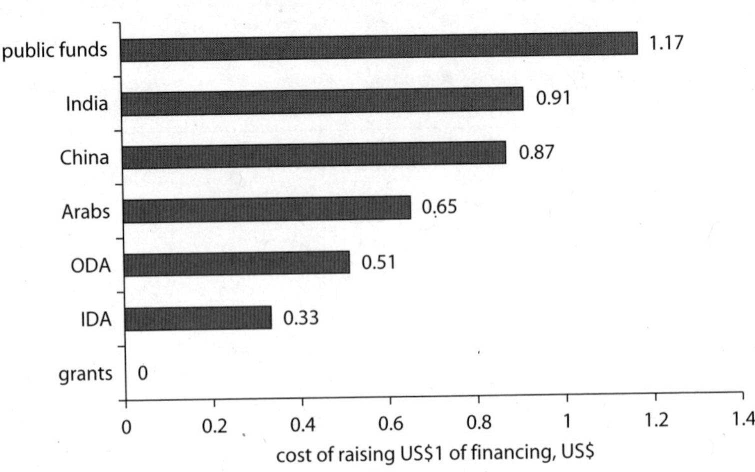

Sources: Average marginal cost of public funds as estimated by Warlters and Auriol 2005; cost of equity for private sector as in Estache and Pinglo 2004 and Sirtaine and others 2005; authors' calculations.
Note: IDA = International Development Association, ODA = official development assistance.

the society's welfare (caused by changes in consumption patterns and administrative costs, among other things).[3] To allow comparisons across financing sources, this study standardized the financial terms as the present value of a dollar raised through each of the different sources. In doing so, it recognized that all loans must ultimately be repaid with tax dollars, each of which attracts the 20 percent cost premium.

Wide variation exists in lending terms. The most concessional International Development Association (IDA) loans charge zero interest (0.75 percent service charge) with 10 years of grace. India, China, and the Gulf States and Arab funds charge 4 percent, 3.6 percent, and 1.5 percent interest, respectively, and grant four years of grace.

The cost of non-OECD finance is somewhere between that of public funds and ODA. The subsidy factor for Indian and Chinese funds is about 25 percent, and for the Arab funds, 50 percent. Official development assistance typically provides a subsidy factor of 60 percent, rising to 75 percent for IDA resources. In addition to the cost of capital, the different sources of finance differ in the transaction costs associated with their use, which may offset or accentuate some of the differences.

Promising Ways to Increase Funds

Given this setting, what are the best ways to increase availability of funds for water infrastructure development? The place to start is clearly to get the most from existing budget envelopes, which can provide up to $2.9 billion a year of additional resources internally if inefficiencies are tackled, equivalent to one-fourth of the total funding gap. For middle-income countries, reducing inefficiencies would imply not only completely closing the funding gap, but also achieving total positive net savings. In particular, for Botswana this would in and of itself be enough to close the funding gap. In the case of resource-rich and low-income countries (fragile and nonfragile), reducing inefficiencies would contribute to reducing the gap by more than 10 percent.

Beyond that, a substantial funding gap still remains. Before the financial crisis, the prospects for reducing—if not closing—this gap were reasonably good. Resource royalties were at record highs, and all sources of external finance were buoyant and promising further growth. With the onset of the global financial crisis, that situation has changed significantly and in ways that are not yet entirely foreseeable. The possibility exists across the board that all sources of WSS finance in Africa may fall rather than increase, further widening the funding gap. Only resource-rich countries have the potential to use natural resource savings accounts to provide a source of financing for infrastructure, but only if macroeconomic conditions allow. The international community's agreement on a major stimulus package for Africa, with a focus on infrastructure as part of the effort to rekindle economic growth and safeguard employment, is one of the few options for reversing the overall situation.

Other Ways to Reach the MDG

Except for middle-income countries, all other countries face a substantial funding gap even if all the existing sources of funds—including efficiency gains—are tapped. What other options do these countries have? Realistically, they need to either defer the attainment of the infrastructure targets proposed here or try to achieve them by using lower-cost technologies.

Taking More Time

Extending the time horizon for the achievement of these goals could make the targets more affordable. What if countries delay the upper bound of MDG attainment by 5 to 10 years without increasing existing resource envelopes?

One caveat to this analysis must be taken into account. The spending needs presented in chapter 7 are based on nonstandardized unit costs. Many of the variables are exogenous at least in the short run, which should guarantee that assumptions made on these variables remain valid if the analysis time horizon is not extended too long into the future, but this may not be the case for density. Africa is urbanizing rapidly and is expected to become predominantly urban by 2020. Although urban sprawl is more common in Africa than elsewhere, it is likely that 15 years from now average urban densities will be greater than those assumed here. More important, the density data set used in this analysis dates to 2000, because it is one of the very few available that observed city populations and densities at the same point in time. As density increases, network infrastructure unit costs decrease, as does the investment required on new infrastructure. Therefore, the results presented here should be taken as an upper bound of the overall spending needs that countries would face to reach the MDG by either 2020 or 2025.

As the time horizon to achieve the water and sanitation MDG is extended by five years, annual spending needs for Africa as a whole decrease from 3.5 percent to 3.2 percent of GDP per year (figure 8.8).

Figure 8.8 Spending Needs by Country Type under Different Time Horizons
(base scenario, % of GDP)

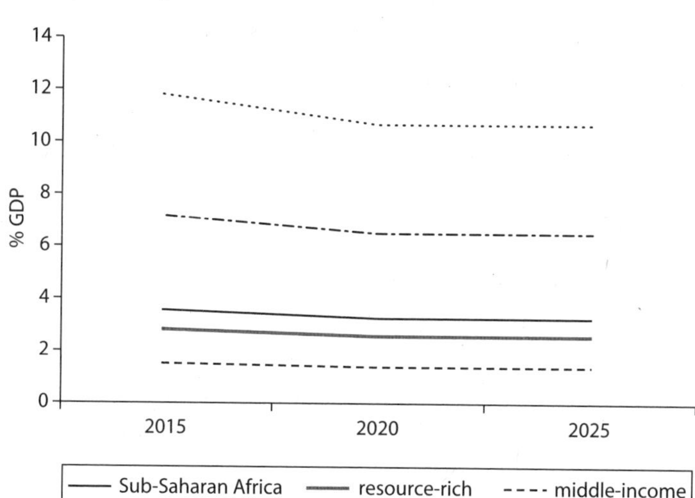

Source: Authors' calculations.
Note: GDP = gross domestic product.

The same trend is observed across all income groups. Savings are not outstanding—annual needs decrease by less than 10 percent—but are still beneficial, especially for low-income, fragile countries.

If the time horizon is extended by an additional five years, to 2025, the decreasing trend continues, but at a falling rate. The overall annual burden for Africa lessens only marginally, as does the burden for the resource-rich and low-income, nonfragile countries. Fragile countries would save the most, yet just 1 percent of GDP per year, with overall needs decreasing from 12 percent to 11 percent of GDP. Middle-income countries would also save if they could take 10 more years to reach targets, yet they would be better off by postponing the achievement of the water and sanitation MDG by 5 rather than 10 more years.

Zeroing in on the composition of needs reveals that if countries are allowed to take more time, the annual spending to be allocated to new infrastructure decreases (figure 8.9, panel a). Although the overall number of new customers to be served rises with time as the population grows, fewer new customers per year would need to be accommodated.

Similarly, as the time horizon is extended, annual rehabilitation costs decrease (figure 8.9, panel b). In fact, this analysis considers only the

Figure 8.9 Annual Spending Needs over Different Time Horizons, by Country Type

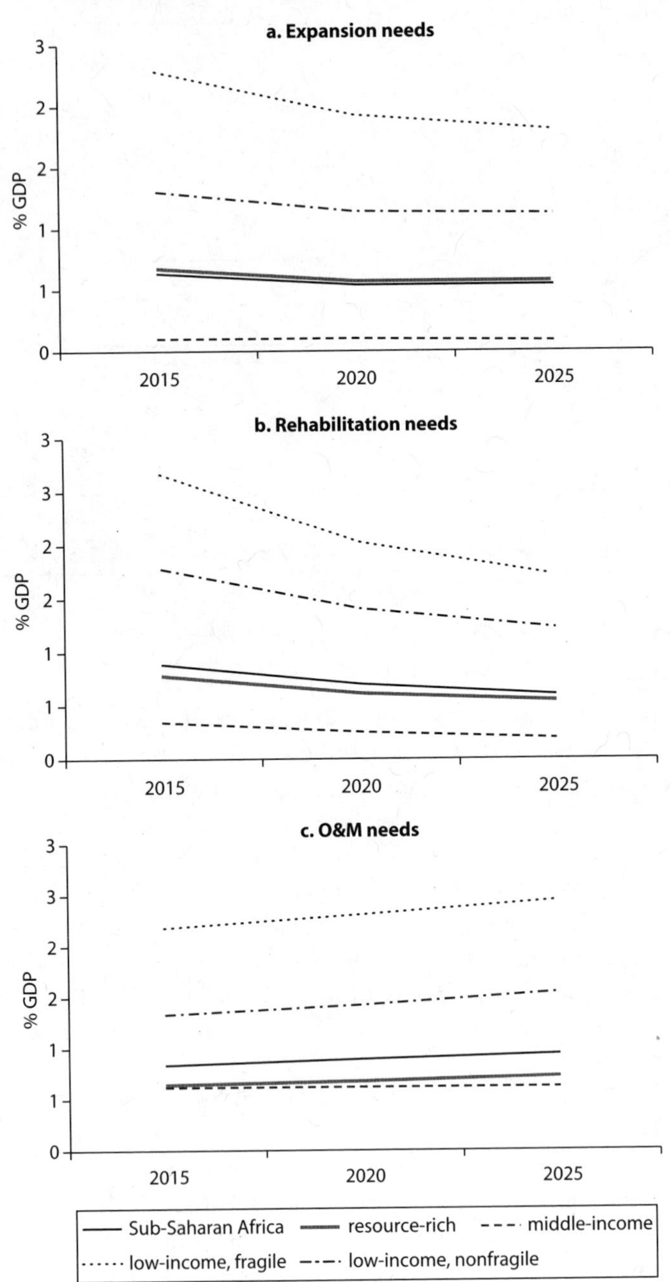

Source: Authors' calculations.

rehabilitation backlog related to existing assets and assumes that no significant rehabilitation will need to occur on new assets, supposing that these are adequately maintained. It may be argued that some on-site facilities' life span is less than 20 years, which implies that some rehabilitation should take place at some point between 2006 and 2025. The assumptions made here, however, mainly reflect the fact that the largest rehabilitation needs originate from assets—markedly network assets—with a life span more than 20 years.

Conversely, O&M needs increase as the time horizon is extended (figure 8.9, panel c). Overall, countries will need to add a larger number of new customers, and therefore, more assets will need to be maintained.

Sub-Saharan Africa would be able to reach the MDG by 2027 if it were to tackle its utilities inefficiencies given the current levels of spending. If resource-rich and low-income countries (nonfragile) spread the spending needs over 26 to 32 years rather than 10 years, they could achieve the proposed targets within the existing spending envelopes. Fragile states would need more than 57 years to achieve the MDG targets if currents levels of spending were not changed (table 8.11). Middle-income countries could achieve the MDG's target in 21 years given the current level of spending, but this conclusion assumes they have first fully captured efficiency gains. Without such efficiency gains, the targets could not be met even over 30 years without increasing spending above current levels.

Using Lower-Cost Technologies

Using alternative lower-cost technologies to provide water and sanitation services to new customers appears to respond to both affordability and efficiency considerations. A direct water connection is regarded as the modality at the top of the water ladder for safety and time-saving reasons; similarly, septic tanks are more likely to deliver health benefits than are improved or traditional latrines. For these reasons, higher-level services

Table 8.11 Time Needed to Meet the MDG Targets with Today's Budget Envelopes

Years to reach MDG target (counting from 2006)	*Sub-Saharan Africa*	*Middle-income*	*Resource-rich*	*Low-income, nonfragile*	*Low-income, fragile*
Existing spending plus efficiency gains	21	10	26	32	57
Existing spending only	33	28	94	69	104

Source: Authors' calculations.
Note: MDG = Millennium Development Goal.

attract the attention of policy makers, but they come at a substantially higher cost. Unit cost analysis reveals that the cost of network expansion is highly sensitive to density. This is especially detrimental to African locations, generally less dense than their counterparts in other regions. When the ultimate goal is expanding access and economies of scale are not possible, nonnetwork, lower-cost technological alternatives might offer a much more efficient solution. Moreover, in some cases—and markedly within the range of on-site sanitation alternatives once the basic level of sanitary protection is reached—higher costs are associated with diminishing returns in terms of safety and health.

This analysis assumes a pragmatic scenario (as opposed to the base scenario assumed in chapter 7) assuming that all new customers are served with lower-cost alternatives: standposts and improved latrines in urban areas and protected wells and boreholes and traditional latrines in rural areas. The overall spending needs in this scenario are presented in figure 8.10.

In 2015, the share of the population enjoying higher-quality services, such as a direct water connection, a sewer connection, or a septic tank, will be lower than it is today. Under this assumption, however, overall spending needs for Africa drop from 3.5 percent to 2.3 percent of GDP per year (table 8.12).

Under the pragmatic scenario, the bill looks substantially more manageable across all countries, with the majority of them required to allocate no more than 5 percent of GDP annually to water and sanitation. Equatorial Guinea, Gabon, Swaziland, South Africa, Botswana, Angola, Mauritius, Cape Verde, Nigeria, Democratic Republic of Congo, Cameroon, Chad, Senegal, Lesotho, and Burkina Faso report, in increasing order, needs below 3 percent. Zimbabwe, The Gambia, Liberia, and Togo still stand as outliers with spending needs over 10 percent of their GDP.

Overall spending needs would become substantially less prohibitive for low-income countries were the pragmatic scenario to be adopted. Compared with the base scenario, the use of lower-cost technologies makes needs drop considerably for fragile states, from 12 percent to 7 percent of GDP, and to a lower extent for low-income, nonfragile countries, from 7 percent to 4 percent of GDP. Nevertheless, the bill is still high, especially for fragile states, and largely in excess of current spending (figure 8.11). Conversely, under the pragmatic scenario, middle-income countries would need to allocate only 1 percent of their GDP to water and sanitation, and resource-rich countries, 2 percent.

Although a pragmatic scenario better matches the capacity of most low-income countries, a high-end scenario based on the use of top-quality

Figure 8.10 Spending Needs by Country under Different Level-of-Service Assumptions

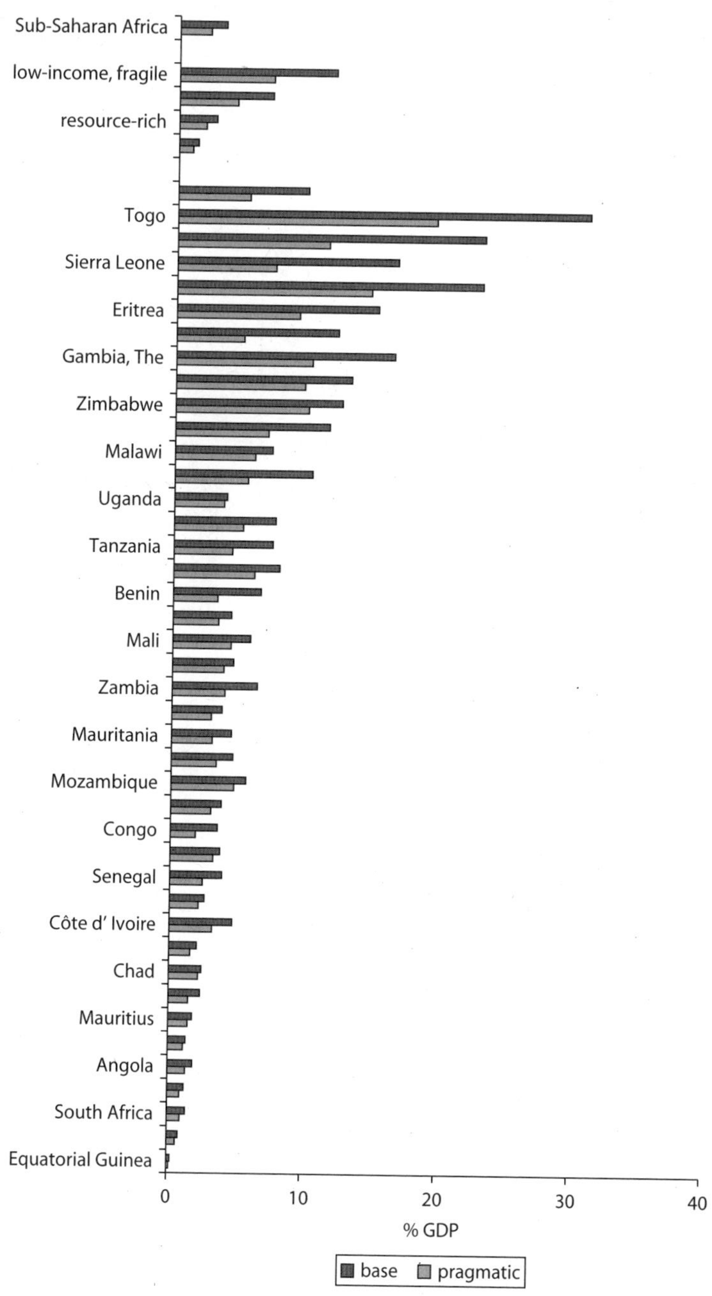

Source: Authors' calculations.

Table 8.12 Spending Needs to Meet the MDG Targets under Different Level-of-Service Scenarios

	Share of GDP (%)						*US$ (million per year)*					
	Pragmatic			*Base*			*Pragmatic*			*Base*		
	Water	*Sanitation*	*Total*	*Water*	*Sanitation*	*Total*	*Water*	*Sanitation*	*Total*	*Water*	*Sanitation*	*Total*
Sub-Saharan Africa	1.6	0.7	2.3	2.7	0.8	3.5	10,392	4,688	15,080	17,239	5,401	22,640
Resource-rich	1.3	0.7	2.1	2.1	0.7	2.9	2,963	1,636	4,599	4,718	1,646	6,364
Middle-income	0.7	0.3	1.1	1.0	0.5	1.5	2,023	862	2,885	2,733	1,243	3,976
Low-income, fragile	4.8	2.3	7.1	8.9	2.9	11.8	1,822	857	2,679	3,337	1,099	4,437
Low-income, nonfragile	3.2	1.2	4.4	5.8	1.3	7.1	3,560	1,322	4,881	6,410	1,400	7,810

Source: Authors' calculations.
Note: In the base scenario, it is assumed that the relative prevalence of WSS supply modalities will remain constant between 2006 and 2015. In the pragmatic scenario, access to new customers is granted using low-cost technologies, which provide improved safe drinking water and sanitation. GDP = gross domestic product, MDG = Millennium Development Goal.

Figure 8.11 Overall Spending Needs by Country Groups under Different Service Assumptions

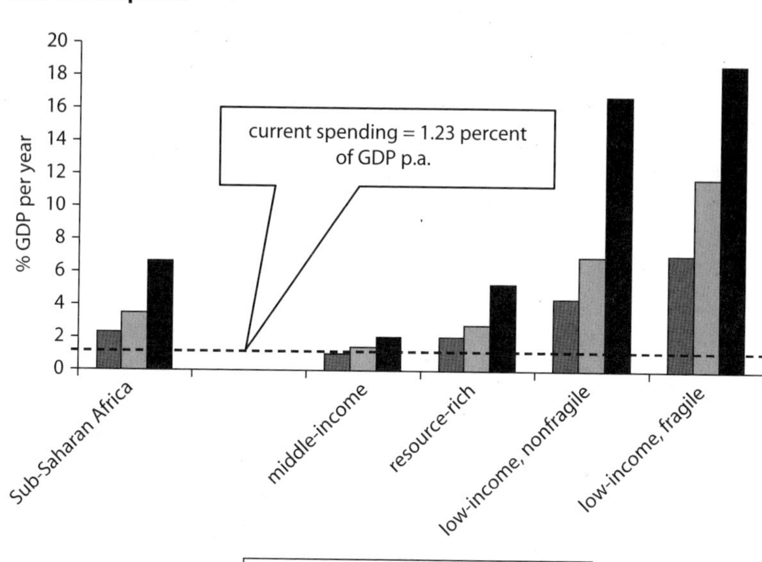

Source: Authors' calculations.
Note: GDP = gross domestic product, p.a. = per annum (every year).

technologies could be considered for middle-income and resource-rich countries. If a high-end scenario were to be adopted, the bill would remain below 3 percent of GDP not only for middle-income countries such as South Africa, Botswana, and Swaziland, but also for low-income countries such as Equatorial Guinea, Gabon, and Angola. Resource-rich countries, however, would end up allocating more than 5 percent of their GDP to water and sanitation. Also, the high-end scenario does not appear feasible for low-income countries, fragile and nonfragile alike, which would be required to allocate more than 15 percent of GDP annually to water and sanitation.

The availability of alternative lower-cost technologies has the potential to reduce the funding gap by more than 60 percent (table 8.13). This implies a reduced cost of meeting the MDG by almost 5 percent of GDP for fragile states, which represents reductions in the funding gap of more than 50 percent. Similarly, if the low-income countries (nonfragile) adopted a pragmatic scenario rather than a base scenario, savings would account for as much as 38 percent, or 2.7 percent of GDP, leading to

Table 8.13 Funding Gaps under Base and Pragmatic Scenarios

	Share of GDP (%)			*US$ (million per year)*			*Reduction of the funding gap (%)*
	Base scenario	*Pragmatic scenario*	*Savings*	*Base scenario*	*Pragmatic scenario*	*Savings*	
Sub-Saharan Africa	1.8	0.7	1.2	11,873	4,313	7,560	64
Resource-rich	1.8	1.0	0.8	4,089	2,324	1,765	43
Middle-income	0.1	−0.2	0.4	312	−779	1,091	350
Low-income, fragile	9.4	4.8	4.7	3,620	1,862	1,758	49
Low-income, nonfragile	4.8	2.1	2.7	5,285	2,356	2,929	55

Source: Authors' calculations.
Note: GDP = gross domestic product.

reductions in the funding gap of more than 55 percent compared with the base scenario. For the middle-income countries, the savings would be at 0.4 percent of GDP, chiefly because these countries have high rates of access to network services whose expansion has a reduced marginal cost, which would lead the funding gap to disappear.

Notes

1. Essentially, the Angola mode was devised to enable African nations to pay for infrastructure with natural resources. In a single transaction, China bundles development-type assistance with commercial-type trade finance. A Chinese resource company makes repayments in exchange for oil or mineral rights. The China Export-Import Bank acts as a broker, receives money for the sale, and pays the contractor for providing the infrastructure. This arrangement safeguards against currency inconvertibility, political instability, and expropriation.
2. Because South Africa's financial markets are so much more developed than those of the other 23 focus countries, this section excludes South Africa.
3. The marginal cost of public funds measures the "change in welfare associated with raising an additional unit of tax revenue" (Warlters and Auriol 2005, 2).

References

Briceño-Garmendia, C., K. Smits, and V. Foster. 2008. "Financing Public Infrastructure in Sub-Saharan Africa: Patterns and Emerging Issues." AICD Background Paper 15, World Bank, Washington, DC.

Calderón, César, and Luis Servén. 2004. "Trends in Infrastructure in Latin America, 1980-2001." Policy Research Working Paper 3401, World Bank, Washington, DC.

Estache, Antonio, and Maria Elena Pinglo. 2004. "Are Returns to Private Infrastructure in Developing Countries Consistent with Risks since the Asian Crisis?" Policy Research Working Paper 3373, World Bank, Washington, DC.

Foster, Vivien, and Cecilia Briceño-Garmendia, eds. 2009. *Africa's Infrastructure: A Time for Transformation*. Paris and Washington, DC: Agence Française de Développement and World Bank.

Foster, Vivien, William Butterfield, Chuan Chen, and Nataliya Pushak. 2008. "Building Bridges: China's Growing Role as Infrastructure Financier for Sub-Saharan Africa." Trends and Policy Options 5. Public-Private Infrastructure Advisory Facility, World Bank, Washington, DC.

IMF (International Monetary Fund). 2009. "The State of Public Finances: Outlook and Medium-Term Policies after the 2008 Crisis." IMF, Washington, DC.

Irving, Jacqueline, and Astrid Manroth. 2009. "Local Sources of Financing for Infrastructure in Africa: A Cross-Country Analysis." Policy Research Working Paper 4878, World Bank, Washington, DC.

ODI (Overseas Development Institute). 2009. *A Development Charter for the G-20*. London: ODI.

PPIAF (Public-Private Infrastructure Advisory Facility). 2008. Private Participation in Infrastructure Project Database. http://ppi.worldbank.org/.

Sirtaine, Sophie, Maria Elena Pinglo, J. Luis Guasch, and Vivien Foster. 2005. "How Profitable Are Infrastructure Concessions in Latin America? Empirical Evidence and Regulatory Implications." Trends and Policy Options 2, PPIAF, World Bank, Washington, DC.

Warlters, Michael, and Emmanuelle Auriol. 2005. "The Marginal Cost of Public Funds in Africa." Policy Research Working Paper 3679, World Bank, Washington, DC.

World Economic Outlook. 2008. "Estimating the Size of the European Stimulus Packages for 2009." International Monetary Fund, Washington, DC.

UBS Investment Research. 2008. "Global Economic Perspectives: The Global Impact of Fiscal Policy." UBS Investment Research, London.

CHAPTER 9

Policy Options for the Water and Sanitation Sectors

Policy Options for the Water Sector

The analyses of the water sector performed by the Africa Infrastructure Country Diagnostic reveal the following key areas for policy attention.

The institutional reform agenda remains as relevant as before, even if its focus has shifted toward a more pluralistic view of public and private sector roles. The reform agenda also needs to move beyond utilities to encompass relevant government agencies and the whole public expenditure framework that underpins, and too often hinders, sector investment programs. Room for improvement can be found in cost recovery so that scarce subsidy resources are redirected to provide access among the poorest.

For meeting the needs of the majority of people who do not enjoy access to household connections to piped water, greater thought needs to be given to making standposts effective sources of urban water supply and optimizing the use of small-scale independent providers. The burgeoning use of wells and boreholes for supply in urban areas demands policy makers' attention; they must improve their understanding of this trend to develop suitable regulatory tools.

However, Africa remains a predominantly rural continent with a population of approximately 400 million people excluded from any form of utility-provided water. This segment of the continent's population often depends on unsafe supply sources, such as surface water, in addition to wells and boreholes. The central challenge is to reduce reliance on surface water through a sustainable network of water access points, most typically boreholes.

Inadequate maintenance of rural water systems reflects both institutional weaknesses and inappropriate technology choices. In addition to weak institutional capacity, undermaintenance is worsened by inadequate attention to technology choices, low pump density, restrictive maintenance systems, and lack of a supply chain to adequately maintain complex machinery. This sector needs specialized attention through either improvements to the supply chain of spare parts for rural water points, development of community-designed and -maintained small systems, or better execution of rural water funds.

The Importance of Continued Institutional Reforms

Institutional reforms are key to improving water sector performance. Countries pursuing institutional reforms create more efficient and effective sector institutions and promote more rapid expansion of higher quality services. The potential dividend is large, because addressing utility inefficiencies alone could make a substantial contribution to closing the sector funding gap in many countries.

Although the majority of African countries have embarked on the sector reform agenda, few have completed it. The experience of those countries that are farthest ahead provides some guidance for the region.

A strong correlation is found between aggressive pursuit of institutional reforms and progress toward achieving the targets of the Millennium Development Goals. The countries that have been most successful in bringing the rural population out of surface water are, without exception, among the most aggressive reformers in Africa. Benin, Côte d'Ivoire, Mozambique, Namibia, Nigeria, Senegal, and Uganda are outstanding performers in reducing the share of population consuming surface water and rank highest in rural reform. Conversely, the Democratic Republic of Congo, Kenya, Malawi, Niger, and Zambia increasingly rely on surface water and score very low on the rural reform index. Burkina Faso and Tanzania perform poorly on access expansion, which is surprising given their strong track record on institutional reforms. For moderate reformers, the results can go either way.

The degree of reform also affects how adequately rural water points are maintained. The percentage of rural water points needing rehabilitation tends to be lower for countries with more advanced rural reform processes. Thus, Benin and Uganda score high on sector reform and in maintaining rural water points. The opposite is true for the Democratic Republic of Congo and Malawi.

In rural areas, a few critical interventions can make a difference. Establishing a clear sector policy, creating a strong central capability for sector financing and project implementation, moving to greater cost recovery, and developing a system to monitor the condition of rural water points are all measures that, when implemented as a package, can boost performance. The governments can also take a leading role in initial supply-chain management and donor coordination until the private sector is capable of taking over.

In urban areas, the story is more complex. The traditional reform agenda of the 1990s has not fully proven its complete relevance to the sector. In addition, unlike in rural areas, no clear evidence is seen in urban areas that regulation has made a positive contribution to sector performance across the board.

Certain types of institutional reforms hold the key to improving utility performance. Good institutional frameworks pay off in improving utilities' efficiency. Utilities that have decentralized or adopted private sector management reveal substantially lower hidden costs than those that have not. A large effect is also associated with unbundling; however, unbundling is uncommon in Africa and is concentrated exclusively in middle-income countries whose superior performance can be explained for many other reasons.

The new reform agenda for water retains a role for private participation. Private sector participation, although controversial in implementation, has in many cases been a useful tool for improving operational performance and efficiency. Expectations that the private sector would finance new infrastructure for water utilities have not been met; negligible private capital flows are dwarfed by public and donor finance. Despite this, the private sector has contributed to expanding access, though typically with public funding.

Lease contracts may be the form of private participation best suited to African water utilities. They have provided greater scope for operational improvements by transferring more responsibility to the private sector than in a management contract. In contrast to concessions, lease contracts are recognized explicitly as requiring publicly funded investments, even in cases in which the private sector can help execute them. A key lesson from Africa's experience with lease contracts is that it is difficult to achieve seamless coordination on investment plans between the contractor and the public holding company. Incorporating clear contractual incentives for efficiency improvements—for example, by basing the contractor's revenue on ideal rather than actual performance parameters—is important.

The new agenda places greater emphasis on broader reforms to governing state-owned enterprises. Given the limited scope of private participation, state-owned utilities remain center stage. Without addressing the typical deficiencies that afflict such enterprises—including numerous and conflicting objectives, political interference, and lack of transparency—it will be difficult for the sector to exit low-level equilibrium. Three key areas for attention are internal process improvements, increased managerial autonomy, and more stringent performance monitoring. It is essential to incorporate measures to streamline corporate processes such as procurement, financial management, and performance management to strengthen commercial principles and accountability mechanisms. Measures to broaden the board of directors, increase use of external audit and independent audit of accounts, and incorporate independent directors from beyond the public sector would help to depoliticize decision making and consolidate the arm's-length relationship. Adopting performance-based monitoring arrangements that mimic private sector contracts is also of interest, but only to the extent that they create credible incentives by incorporating meaningful rewards and penalties at the personal and corporate levels and are subject to third-party monitoring.

The Benefits of More Effective Public Expenditure

The bulk of investment in the water sector is made by relevant government agencies through the budgetary process, often with external support. The existing patterns of spending clearly show that although utilities are instrumental in delivering services, the general government—using either domestic or external capital—continues to make most of the investment decisions. For this reason, a solid public investment appraisal system and strong public spending management are prerequisites for improving both urban and rural water supply.

Major bottlenecks hold back the disbursement of public investment funds. Capital budget execution ratios for public investment in water are fairly low, 75 percent on average. In many instances, the binding constraint is not availability of budgetary resources, but rather the capacity to disburse them in a timely fashion. In Tanzania, there were steep increases in budget allocations to the sector following its identification as a priority in the country's poverty reduction strategy. Disbursements increased at a much slower pace, in contrast, and no immediately discernible impact on access is seen.

The budgeting process needs to move toward a medium-term framework and make stronger links between sector objectives and resource allocations. This needs to be underpinned by clear sector plans that detail specific activities and their associated costs. It is essential that maintenance needs be incorporated into medium-term sector planning tools to prevent asset rehabilitation. Administrative processes that delay the release of budgeted funds also need to be overhauled. At the same time, procedures for procurement, disbursement, financial management, and accountability should be modernized and streamlined.

Donor resources are best channeled programmatically as budgetary support or through sectorwide projects. Given the sector's high dependence on external funds, a solid public expenditure management system for African countries also requires that donors improve the predictability of their support and make progress on streamlining and harmonizing administrative procedures. In that sense, it is preferable to focus on multidonor initiatives that pool funds to provide general budgetary support for a sectorwide program of interventions.

Technical assistance to the sector should include support to relevant government agencies for project identification and appraisal. Technical assistance to the sector has traditionally been understood as improving management practices of utilities. However, an equally important role is available for technical assistance to support government agencies in improving the framework for identifying, appraising, prioritizing, planning, and procuring investment projects. Donors can support countries in the development of good project identification and appraisal tools that systematically consider the technological alternatives for expanding access and that weigh the importance of spending on maintenance and rehabilitation against new investment.

Institutional Models to Connect the Unconnected

The role of standposts in urban water supply has the potential to expand to serve safe water to a larger number of consumers. Most countries' governments and utilities continue to focus attention on expansion of piped-water connections, but rapid urbanization and the utilities' weak financial position make this a questionable strategy to pursue so single-mindedly. Standpost use is very limited in the African urban water scene, is expanding relatively slowly, and remains concentrated among the more affluent segments of the population. Simple simulations suggest that the rate of service expansion could double if utilities shifted their investment budgets from piped-water connections to standposts. As long as urban households are inconvenienced by higher payments and longer water collection times, however, standposts will not necessarily be a superior solution, even if they are a cheaper alternative to private piped-water connections. In low-income countries, resale of water by neighbors through informal standpost arrangements is almost as prevalent as formal standposts.

The explanation of this paradox may lie in the problematic institutional arrangements associated with standposts in African cities. Utilities charge little or nothing for standpost water, and standpost revenue constitutes a negligible portion of the revenue base. This means that utilities lack a financial incentive to expand the service. Standpost operators, where they exist, often charge substantial markups that make the service prohibitively expensive and may generate significant revenue that is never captured by the utility. Quality of service provided by standposts can be very low because of both high rates of malfunction and the large numbers of people expected to rely on each one.

The solution to this conundrum is not yet clear, but it will require intensive experimentation with alternative network designs and institutional setups. Standposts cover a wide range of communal arrangements or delegated management models, some of which may be less promising than others. One option would be to increase the density of standposts to increase competition, with immediate impact on water supply quality and price. Yard taps can provide communal access to four or five contiguous households; this option lowers costs but only partially addresses the problem of maintenance and management. Whatever the approach, an important component of the solution will be to ensure fairer distribution of revenue among utilities and standpost operators or other secondary water retailers. The experiences of the handful of low-income countries that have achieved more than 20 percent urban coverage of standposts—notably Côte d'Ivoire, Rwanda, and Senegal—deserve study.

The popularity of the household resale option could also be exploited by making it an explicit part of the utility's rollout strategy. Household resale of water through yard taps appears in wide use in many African cities. Survey evidence highlights a variety of reasons why residents may find this approach preferable to official standposts. Neighbors can offer more convenient opening hours, better water pressure levels, and more convenient proximity, which reduces the time needed to collect the water. In addition, they offer more flexible payment mechanisms than either public standposts or a private connection. It is therefore advisable to give increasing recognition to this water supply modality, to remove any legal barriers to its implementation, and to consider making these household-based water retail enterprises an integral component of the utilities' expansion plans.

Ultimately, investing in utility production and distribution of water is the best policy for maintaining low-cost alternatives. Within cities, the formal and informal water markets are strongly connected, which influences the final price offered to the consumer. The greater the disruption within the formal piped-water system, the higher the price in the informal sector relative to the formal one. Increasing water production capacity and improving the efficacy of the distribution network can have a significant impact on the welfare of the unconnected as well as the connected, because it drives down the premium on alternative sources of water supply.

Accompanying Cost Recovery with Careful Social Policies

Underpricing is debilitating the water sector and slowing coverage expansion without contributing much to equity objectives. Underpricing water is contributing to utilities' financial weakness, slowing access expansion, and restraining quality of service. Because utility customers are drawn from the upper end of the income distribution, the result is a highly regressive incidence of subsidies to the sector. A large (and generally poor) segment of the urban population is paying multiples of these prices to access utility water indirectly, and in many cases more than the utility cost-recovery price.

Countries need to make progress toward further cost recovery while considering the economic circumstances of their populations. Although African households' purchasing power is quite limited, analysis confirms that operating cost recovery is a perfectly feasible objective for just about all African countries. Tariffs that recover full capital costs also look to be affordable for the richest 40 percent of the population in low-income countries, of which 10 percent already has access to piped water. There is thus little economic justification for the subsidies that exist today. Countries would be better served by recovering full costs from their existing customer base and using the resulting cash flow to accelerate access expansion in poor neighborhoods. In the longer term, however, as access to piped water increases, low-income countries will need social tariffs that provide water priced at operating cost-recovery levels for a minimum level of consumption to the substantial share of their population that cannot afford full capital cost-recovery tariffs. The key is verifying water tariffs' affordability with reference to household budgets, rather than simply assuming that they will be unaffordable.

Government entities need to become better customers. Government entities can easily capture 20 to 30 percent of total billings. They can be the worst offenders in paying bills, as well, with a significant lag in payment time. Often, they repay a large chunk of arrears with little indication of future payment schedules. This hampers efforts to sustain a robust payment culture and to improve utilities' investment-planning base.

A need is also present to rethink the design of water utility tariff structures. Most African utilities are increasing block tariffs to make water tariffs more equitable, but in reality, half of the utilities using this strategy incorporate fixed charges or minimum consumption thresholds that inflate the costs of water for poor households with modest levels of consumption. Compounding this counterproductive result is the fact that a significant share of utilities with increasing block tariffs also have very high subsistence blocks (in excess of 10 cubic meters); as a result, they end up providing subsidized water to the vast majority of consumers, rather than a targeted group of low-volume users.

Connection charges should be kept as low as possible, and subsidies could be reoriented toward connections. The majority of African water utilities levy piped-water connection charges in excess of $100, an insurmountable barrier for low-income households. Utilities intent on achieving universal access should explore ways to radically reduce connection charges to levels that are more in line with household affordability. Several alternative means of recovering connection charges are available, including offering payment plans that spread them out over time or sharing connection costs across the whole customer base through the general tariff. Connection costs may also be more suited to public subsidy than water-usage tariffs. They have the advantage of being one-time payments linked to a concrete and monitorable action that addresses a real affordability constraint. Simulations suggest that connection subsidies can be much more pro-poor than general subsidies to the water tariff, particularly if simple targeting mechanisms are used.

Toward a Better Understanding of Groundwater in Urban Water Supply

Groundwater, sourced from water wells (boreholes and dug wells), now supplies one-fourth of urban dwellers and is by far the fastest-growing source of improved water supply in African cities. Although wells and boreholes have long been a dominant source of improved water in rural areas, they have also become an increasingly important source of water supply in almost all urban areas. This is true in more than just those cities (such as Abidjan and Lusaka) where groundwater has long been a major source of utility supply. With utility coverage rates falling in urban Africa, groundwater has essentially stepped into the breach, with the fairly rapid growth of boreholes showing the appetite for lower-cost solutions. Investments in boreholes provide the opportunity to reach a wider demographic with relatively modest resources. One in four urban Africans relies on wells and boreholes for improved supply, a figure that rises to one in two urban Africans in the low-income countries. In Burkina Faso, Malawi, Mali, Mozambique, Uganda, and Zimbabwe, the share rises as high as three in four. In Malawi, Nigeria, and Rwanda, reliance on urban wells and boreholes is increasing particularly rapidly; more than 3 percent of the population gains access to this water source each year.

Too little is known about the physical, institutional, and financial characteristics of groundwater use. Household surveys provide a good picture of overall reliance but leave many questions unanswered. The prevalence of simple, shallow, hand-dug wells relative to professionally drilled boreholes is unknown, and so then is the extent to which groundwater supplies are adequately protected from direct wellhead contamination. The institutional arrangements associated with groundwater supplies are also unclear, particularly in terms of the extent to which they constitute stopgap services provided by municipalities as opposed to private or communal self-supply initiatives. Depending on the conditions and arrangements, the capital costs of such wells could be anywhere between $5,000 and $25,000 (or $10 to $20 per capita).

Extensive decentralized and uncoordinated in situ groundwater use in the urban environment raises risks of contamination by in situ sanitation. In addition to growing groundwater reliance, African cities are characterized by heavy use of low-grade in situ sanitation, mainly in the form of traditional latrines. Deployment of latrine sanitation at excessive population densities or lack of proper latrine operation can lead to increasing groundwater contamination that can affect the entire urban aquifer providing the groundwater supplies.

Furthermore, extensive unregulated use of groundwater by private actors may prevent the most rational and efficient exploitation of the resource for public water supply. In particular, it prevents cities from reaching economies of scale in groundwater exploitation and from following the principle of conjunctive surface and groundwater use that allows groundwater to play its natural role as a backup supply in times of drought.

An urgent need exists to develop an improved understanding of the benefits and risks of groundwater use in fast-growing Africa cities and towns, as well as how this varies with the hydrogeological setting. This should begin with a city-level appraisal of the quantity and quality of available urban groundwater resources; the drivers, dynamics and patterns of usage; and an assessment of the vulnerability of urban aquifers to pollution from the land surface. Creating a groundwater-monitoring framework and the promulgation of appropriate construction and operation protocols for wells and in situ sanitation facilities (mainly latrines) would help to safeguard groundwater quality, but should be accompanied by guidelines for safe use of groundwater sources. Appropriate governance arrangements also need to be put in place, recognizing the broad reach of groundwater resources, and must involve water utilities, public health authorities, and municipal agencies. They should also provide a suitable channel for public consultation.

Policy Options for the Sanitation Sector

The analyses of the sanitation sector performed by the Africa Infrastructure Country Diagnostic reveal the following key areas for policy attention.

The ultimate objective should be to provide universal access by expanding service and reducing open defecation as much as possible. Policy makers are often tempted to concentrate infrastructure enhancement efforts on the higher rungs of the sanitation ladder, a strategy that often runs counter to the needs of the majority of the population. For example, officials may channel limited public resources into sewerage networks that serve only a few people and fail to address the more urgent need to significantly reduce the incidence of open defecation. Policy decisions and infrastructure programs achieve the greatest public health gains when they take local access patterns into account. Those programs then can be augmented with low-cost initiatives to leverage household spending for latrine construction. Public spending should target helping people on the lowest rungs to move up the ladder. More expensive options should be left to households with the resources to take them up.

Complexity, a multiplicity of actors, and lack of accountability for sector leadership are the three features of the institutional framework governing the sanitation sector emerging from an institutional survey of line ministries, sector institutions, and water utilities. Unlike water, many parts of the supply chain for sanitation—hygiene promotion, latrine construction, and latrine emptying, for example—are in the hands of different public and private players, which prevents one agency from championing the sector and contributes to sanitation's falling between the cracks. The recent trend toward government decentralization has complicated the capture of adequate public resources for sanitation and allocated responsibilities to entities that lack technical capacity. Fifteen countries have adopted formal national sanitation policies, and most countries have an accepted definition of sanitation and a hygiene promotion program. Only seven countries, however, have policies that include cost recovery, and only eight countries have a sanitation fund or a dedicated budget line (in some cases funded exclusively by donors, as in Chad and Ethiopia, or by a combination of the government, sector levies, and donors). Côte d'Ivoire has the only fund financed entirely by sector levies.

Sanitation challenges vary both across and within African countries, and solutions must be tailored to individual national or regional needs. Open defecation rates remain high in some African countries, especially in rural areas. Countries often pursue solutions such as construction of traditional latrines or septic tanks that reach a small share of the population, predominantly wealthier urban residents. The policy options for each issue are presented as separate cases in this summary, and countries may need to use different combinations of these approaches to meet their national and regional challenges. The first option is to stimulate demand for sanitation and behavior change where open defecation prevails. The second is to ensure adequate supply before addressing demand in settings dominated by traditional latrines. Finally, the third is to expand access to improved sanitation across larger shares of the population, which in high-density settlements requires making sewerage systems more affordable.

Stimulating Demand for Sanitation and Changing Behavior Where Open Defecation Prevails

Unlike other infrastructure services, demand for sanitation cannot be assumed. Populations accustomed to open defecation may require a substantial change in cultural values and behavior to use a fixed-point facility. Without such change, people may not use latrines or may use them in a way that undermines the potential health benefits. A study in South India showed that when a large public investment was made in latrine construction but neglected to address the need for accompanying hygiene education, only 37 percent of men used the facilities despite 100 percent coverage (WSP-SA 2002). Hygiene education is a critical component of addressing any sanitation challenge that a country faces. Safe disposal of feces and hand washing with soap protect health in all sanitation settings. Promoting hygiene can start a virtuous cycle that builds demand for better sanitation, raises awareness of the benefits of sanitation, and establishes codes of conduct and new life standards.

Incorrect use of latrines can dramatically reduce or even reverse their health benefits. A facility is sanitary and safe because of the technology and material used and because of good practices and behaviors, such as keeping the facility contained and clean. An improved latrine that is not used and emptied correctly still poses high risks of environmental contamination and disease. It thus makes little sense to roll out a physical investment program without an accompanying promotion of hygiene and adequate ways of emptying the latrines on a regular basis. Effective hygiene promotion alone may stimulate self-financed household investment in better facilities. Too often these "soft" aspects of sanitation are overlooked in favor of the "hard" aspects, such as installing and upgrading infrastructure.

Changing behavior requires sustained communication and public education at the community level. It is important to understand people's motivations with regard to hygiene and sanitation. Health is one, but not necessarily the first: Convenience, dignity, and social status may be regarded as more important. For communitywide involvement, it is essential to adapt hygiene and sanitation promotion programs to cultural and institutional norms and then market them in language that demonstrates awareness of and respect for those customs. A successful example is the Regional Health Bureau's Sanitation Advocacy Campaign launched in 2003 in southern Ethiopia, which increased latrine coverage from 13 percent of the population to 78 percent in just two years. Encouraging peer pressure can also help. Once a community recognizes certain behaviors as desirable, there is pressure to conform. Social institution and leaders then begin to contribute, and compliance with the new standards becomes tied to one's social status.

Ensuring Adequate Supply before Addressing Demand in Settings Dominated by Traditional Latrines

Where traditional latrines prevail, the problem becomes how to upgrade them to more hygienic facilities to achieve the full health benefits of fixed-point defecation. Countries in which traditional latrines are widely used have already overcome the behavioral challenge of moving people out of open defecation. The problem is rather of improving facilities.

The debate centers on whether the main impediment to upgrading latrines comes from the supply side or the demand side.

From the demand side, low coverage of improved latrines can be explained by low household incomes and high capital costs. In addition, poor dwellers in urban slum settings often do not own their land or house and so have fewer incentives to invest in improving their living conditions.

Although traditional latrines are more affordable across all income levels, improved latrines often remain a luxury. The fact that half of African households have invested in traditional latrines in the absence of any subsidy suggests that large investment costs are affordable across the income spectrum. Yet improved latrines are a luxury good limited to the wealthiest households.

To address the affordability problem, public policy will likely have to incorporate a public subsidy for incremental capital costs associated with building improved facilities. A subsidy may have drawbacks, however, including distorted demand and markets. Subsidies can reduce the demand of households with the ability to pay, and suggesting a standard facility may encourage poor households to feel entitled to such a facility regardless of whether it is the most appropriate for their circumstances and geographic location. Widespread adoption of a standard could also discourage innovations that may lower costs.

From the supply side, low incidence of improved latrines can be explained by poor knowledge in the construction sector about required designs, lack of skilled construction workers, and shortage of materials. Access patterns already provide some clues that supply-side issues are a real constraint in Africa. First, the prevalence of improved latrines is low, even in middle-income countries, except in a handful of cases. Second, traditional latrines are used by 40 to 50 percent of the population, even among the highest-income groups, who may be able to pay for more advanced facilities.

Supply bottlenecks should be tackled first. Otherwise, subsidy resources may be wasted on households that could have financed the facilities on their own. Allowing the local market to develop also provides space for innovation that can lower the cost of improved latrines. Technological innovation is needed to secure greater health benefits with cheaper variants that are tailored to a locality's circumstances. Thus, an important starting point is a more nuanced understanding of the facilities covered by the term *traditional latrine* and the best practices for their use and maintenance.

The supply problem is compounded by a weak private sector dominated by small entrepreneurs at the local level. Constructing latrines demands skills that are not widely available, and small enterprises often do not have the resources to develop new skills or adopt new technologies.

Policies need to address supply-side limitations. Government support is best channeled toward conducting research, developing products, marketing latrines, and opening supply channels for key inputs. Training small service providers and providing access to credit can also help. The National Sanitation Program in Lesotho, established 20 years ago, is dedicated to sanitation promotion and private sector training. Households directly employ private latrine builders trained under the program, which has increased national sanitation coverage from 20 percent of the population to 53 percent.

Making Sewerage More Affordable in High-Density Settlements

In much of Africa, on-site sanitation is the most cost-effective and only practical way to secure the health benefits of the hygienic disposal of feces. On-site sanitation also has its limits, however. Water consumption rises with urban population growth, which creates the challenge of safely returning large volumes of wastewater. In addition, increased urban population density constrains the use of latrines (particularly the simpler types), which require rotation of sites and, therefore, a greater area of land than may be available. At high population densities, sewerage systems are both more suitable and more cost effective.

It is critical to reduce the cost of sewerage networks through technological innovation. Although annual population growth in Africa averages 2.5 percent, the urban population is growing at 3.9 percent. By 2020, nearly 60 percent of the African population will be in urban areas, and within 20 years the population of most African cities will have doubled. Africa's burgeoning cities will need to develop more extensive sewerage networks to deal with this influx of people. The statistics on affordability suggest that waterborne sewerage is far beyond the reach of all but the most affluent households, and the public subsidies to support such sewerage networks are equally unaffordable.

Condominial sewerage systems, a lower-cost alternative developed in Latin America, could be explored in Africa. These low-cost secondary pipe networks are built upstream of the main sewerage networks at the residents' initiative. The public collection network just touches each housing block (or condominium) instead of surrounding it. Decentralized microsystems of collection, treatment, and disposal can also replace the conventional centralized treatment system. Construction costs are reduced by using small-diameter pipes, with work partially carried out by residents. Experiences in Latin America reveal savings of up to 65 percent. Pilot condominial systems are being implemented in several African countries, most notably in the periurban areas of Dakar, Senegal. The Dakar system was expected to furnish 60,000 households (270,000 people) with on-site sanitation and to support 160 condominial schemes serving 130,000 by 2009.

Addressing Several Common Challenges for All Countries

Several common challenges cut across all sanitation settings: securing fiscal space for sanitation expenditures, coordinating the numerous players in the sector, and developing a more refined approach to measuring progress.

Securing Fiscal Space. The unglamorous nature of sanitation puts it at a disadvantage in the competition for fiscal resources. Government decentralization and poor accounting for sector expenditures make it hard to understand the exact amount of public resources allocated. It is estimated that fewer than half of the countries reported any spending on sanitation, and those that did averaged no more than 0.23 percent of gross domestic product, including both investment and operation and maintenance.

At the 2008 African Conference on Sanitation and Hygiene in Durban, South Africa, governments committed to raising public expenditure on sanitation to 0.5 percent of gross domestic product by 2010. This would require spending close to the levels needed to reach the target spelled out in the Millennium Development Goals (MDGs), but reaching the target will still be difficult because of the need to make up for lagging past performance. Better accounting of public expenditure on sanitation will also be needed to monitor progress toward the target.

Although governments are called upon to provide more resources, innovative financing approaches that help providers and operators are also needed. Cost recovery has proven to be a limited incentive because the only tariffs in sanitation are on wastewater and apply only to the minority of the population served by waterborne sewerage. Moreover, most African utilities are responsible for providing wastewater services in addition to water supply, which makes it likely that water pays for sanitation. Burkina Faso has taken an innovative approach by levying a sanitation tax as a surcharge on the water bill; funds collected are then used to subsidize access to improved sanitation facilities in Ouagadougou.

Needed—A Champion for the Sanitation Sector. Given that on-site sanitation, as opposed to waterborne sewerage, will likely continue to dominate sanitation in Africa, households rather than government will remain center stage. Even so, the government's role in promoting demand and addressing supply bottlenecks remains. Even within the public sector, dispersion and duplication of sanitation functions too often prevent one entity from leading, and as a result sanitation issues fail to be addressed by any agency.

A key policy issue is therefore to identify and empower a clear sanitation champion within the public sector. Senegal demonstrates its decision to take sanitation seriously by creating a dedicated sanitation utility. Senegal was also the first country to establish a government body at the national level—the Ministry of Urban Affairs, Housing, Urban Water, Public Hygiene and Sanitation (originally the Ministry for Prevention, Public Hygiene and Sanitation)—to coordinate sector activity. Although it may not always be necessary to create a ministry in the central government, Senegal provides an important lesson in singling out one entity with a clear mandate to lead.

Measuring Progress. Although the Joint Monitoring Programme (JMP) has made strides in monitoring progress toward the MDG target for sanitation, a commensurate effort has not been made to create detailed and frequent country-level monitoring and evaluation systems critical to guiding policy interventions. Most countries have no evaluation system, and the countries that are developing such a system have found it is not possible to provide a clear picture of the sector. In any event, monitoring and evaluation systems rarely measure the impact of improved sanitation on health, which is clearly relevant to demonstrate the first-order benefits.

At the country level, better monitoring and evaluation systems could be built by ensuring more coordination at the ministerial level—for instance, between the ministry in charge of sanitation and the ministry in charge of health. A larger role should be played at the local level, especially by the decentralized technical departments, in collecting data and monitoring progress. This would require more capacity and resources from the central government.

A limitation of the JMP's framework is the classification of traditional latrines, which will continue to dominate African sanitation. Traditional latrines include a heterogeneous collection of installations, some of which can be regarded as improved sanitation. Unfortunately, the JMP's household survey instruments, which track progress toward achieving the MDG target, cannot distinguish among the differing quality of installations within the latrine category. As a result, the data on progress in sanitation in Africa are least clear precisely where most of the progress is taking place. The precision of household survey instruments should be improved in this respect. It may also be relevant to track the intermediate goal of increasing the share of households making use of some kind of sanitation facility, even if it is an unimproved latrine.

Reference

WSP-SA (Water and Sanitation Program–South Asia). 2002. "Strategic Sanitation Planning: Lessons from Bharatpur, Rajasthan." WSP-SA, New Delhi.

APPENDIX 1

Access to Water Supply and Sanitation Facilities

Table A1.1 Piped Water
(percentage of population)

Country	Time period (national)			Location		Expenditure quintile				
	Early 1990s	Late 1990s	Early 2000s	Rural	Urban	Q1	Q2	Q3	Q4	Q5
Benin	—	23.15	28.74	10.91	60.37	0.22	8.02	10.23	36.65	88.63
Burkina Faso	5.64	3.62	5.89	0.06	32.98	0.00	0.00	0.00	0.40	34.06
Cameroon	12.07	11.34	12.95	2.20	24.23	0.00	0.37	4.34	10.84	49.27
Central African Republic	2.65	—	—	0.00	6.24	0.00	0.00	0.00	0.00	13.26
Chad	—	3.36	4.45	0.00	21.71	0.00	0.00	0.00	0.02	22.27
Comoros	—	22.67	—	15.06	42.52	0.00	38.42	13.78	20.67	46.21
Congo, Dem. Rep.	21.00	—	15.03	0.35	40.45	0.00	0.00	0.00	6.88	58.84
Congo, Rep.	—	—	25.81	2.99	46.21	0.00	0.27	5.47	33.77	89.77
Côte d'Ivoire	23.98	27.93	—	6.73	64.58	0.00	1.73	2.62	38.23	97.63
Ethiopia	—	4.21	5.98	0.21	48.45	0.00	0.00	0.00	0.00	29.94
Gabon	—	43.03	—	8.84	55.06	0.07	6.90	30.08	78.44	99.76
Ghana	13.65	15.38	15.08	1.66	33.91	0.56	2.24	2.12	10.72	60.14
Guinea	—	9.62	9.13	1.22	28.06	0.00	0.00	0.44	1.56	43.77
Kenya	16.04	19.54	17.94	10.04	49.67	0.01	1.20	4.35	21.91	62.36
Lesotho	—	11.03	10.74	2.13	50.44	0.00	0.37	0.26	2.81	50.28
Madagascar	5.29	5.90	5.30	2.03	17.20	0.19	0.00	0.00	2.01	24.27
Malawi	6.11	7.74	6.49	1.68	32.04	0.00	0.81	0.42	1.12	30.14
Mali	—	5.66	9.06	1.86	29.25	0.24	1.27	1.25	4.48	38.34
Mauritania	—	—	17.41	9.84	27.51	0.00	0.00	5.31	25.29	56.57
Mozambique	—	6.55	6.86	0.33	19.72	0.00	0.00	0.00	0.04	34.43
Namibia	30.53	37.29	—	16.48	79.30	0.00	1.76	16.59	68.35	99.82
Niger	5.39	6.09	—	0.20	31.29	0.00	0.00	0.03	4.58	26.04
Nigeria	10.58	10.28	6.88	2.49	15.49	0.13	1.43	3.83	11.45	17.60

Rwanda	1.77	6.28	2.95	0.59	15.97	0.00	0.00	0.30	1.26	13.33
Senegal	26.60	31.10	43.36	17.68	76.76	0.92	9.08	36.24	74.59	96.48
South Africa	—	59.18	—	24.99	87.72	3.05	24.53	71.70	97.15	99.56
Sudan	—	21.12	—	9.73	37.44	0.02	0.22	5.39	44.57	77.45
Tanzania	10.23	13.78	7.36	2.86	21.87	0.00	0.00	0.20	6.92	29.72
Togo	—	17.75	—	3.11	51.30	0.99	2.22	4.98	17.28	63.35
Uganda	1.80	—	1.99	0.15	14.39	0.00	0.00	0.13	0.04	9.89
Zambia	31.41	21.03	18.32	2.73	46.43	0.00	0.12	0.28	14.67	76.75
Zimbabwe	26.68	32.75	—	4.43	93.04	0.00	11.42	6.64	49.01	98.57
Country typology										
Resourch-rich	14.65	15.10	12.01	3.18	23.52	0.08	1.02	3.95	17.34	35.39
Middle-income	63.26	56.46	52.07	22.90	87.00	2.80	22.64	66.60	92.24	97.63
Fragile states	27.01	24.30	26.09	2.85	46.56	0.05	2.08	1.65	17.28	67.45
Nonfragile, low-income	8.35	8.18	10.54	2.73	36.05	0.10	0.91	2.42	8.52	37.89
Level of urbanization										
High	24.24	22.91	21.84	7.01	38.76	0.69	5.83	17.18	31.99	49.01
Medium	24.56	23.41	21.77	3.75	41.28	0.05	1.60	2.64	20.12	64.39
Low	6.42	5.94	8.12	2.10	32.70	0.03	0.26	0.70	4.56	31.41
Level of water scarcity										
High	18.41	16.61	16.66	4.22	38.74	0.38	3.52	9.38	20.88	42.51
Low	15.95	16.63	16.37	3.24	37.81	0.08	0.90	3.08	13.60	52.44
Overall	17.60	16.62	16.57	3.92	38.39	0.28	2.65	7.28	18.46	45.81

Source: Banerjee, Wodon, and others 2008.
Note: Location and expenditure quintile data refer to latest available year. — = not available.

Table A1.2 Standposts
(percentage of population)

Country	Time period (national)			Location		Expenditure quintile				
	Early 1990s	*Late 1990s*	*Early 2000s*	*Rural*	*Urban*	*Q1*	*Q2*	*Q3*	*Q4*	*Q5*
Benin	—	5.49	14.12	18.74	5.94	13.36	18.07	20.17	16.18	2.83
Burkina Faso	10.16	8.29	12.74	4.03	53.21	0.00	0.00	4.76	16.92	46.85
Cameroon	22.34	23.39	26.01	9.56	43.26	0.00	17.03	28.44	49.15	35.50
Central African Republic	19.08	—	—	1.55	42.85	0.00	2.25	10.46	35.97	46.72
Chad	—	5.67	6.62	2.38	23.02	0.00	1.26	7.02	6.52	18.37
Comoros	—	26.66	—	25.31	30.19	69.10	7.95	25.62	15.37	6.75
Congo, Dem. Rep.	7.09	—	12.11	4.92	24.55	0.00	2.59	7.77	23.52	24.34
Congo, Rep.	—	—	23.49	5.34	39.71	3.86	11.29	45.58	50.46	6.20
Côte d'Ivoire	21.44	23.12	—	27.61	15.36	23.62	32.62	29.45	29.32	0.50
Ethiopia	—	11.62	15.82	12.42	40.86	0.00	4.24	17.72	20.07	37.27
Gabon	—	30.35	—	10.93	37.19	13.50	54.94	63.39	19.84	0.00
Ghana	18.65	21.18	20.48	7.89	38.14	2.48	21.59	17.06	34.99	26.99
Guinea	—	10.94	12.75	2.16	38.09	0.00	0.00	4.60	16.57	42.83
Kenya	11.15	9.41	9.44	6.70	20.45	3.08	5.16	10.21	15.26	13.53
Lesotho	—	51.68	48.04	50.15	38.35	55.03	42.97	56.23	54.95	31.16
Madagascar	11.71	11.21	17.95	10.11	46.51	0.00	0.46	5.57	33.90	49.89
Malawi	19.54	15.77	12.71	7.00	43.04	0.00	0.14	6.24	22.83	34.37
Mali	—	11.14	20.30	16.25	31.69	0.66	11.26	27.47	28.28	33.95
Mauritania	—	—	14.88	8.20	23.79	0.00	23.93	19.05	20.62	11.51
Mozambique	—	17.76	17.62	4.80	42.86	0.00	2.65	6.01	29.34	51.39
Namibia	19.21	20.80	—	21.85	18.68	13.48	29.86	38.16	22.51	0.15
Niger	11.31	12.58	—	6.76	37.48	0.00	0.00	0.00	32.26	31.00
Nigeria	13.12	13.52	9.38	5.56	16.91	3.66	6.71	8.76	13.05	14.77

Rwanda	20.92	29.40	24.71	21.83	40.60	0.00	3.45	50.51	22.74	47.55
Senegal	17.94	16.51	18.12	23.05	11.72	19.00	32.59	23.48	13.59	1.82
South Africa	—	19.25	—	30.16	10.15	30.74	47.69	17.36	0.42	0.00
Sudan	—	7.96	—	5.27	11.81	7.60	9.95	8.22	7.76	5.50
Tanzania	20.45	20.39	25.20	18.97	45.31	12.08	14.94	19.79	36.86	42.49
Togo	—	17.64	—	15.25	23.10	8.10	11.46	20.16	27.63	20.90
Uganda	4.17	—	7.23	1.24	47.49	0.38	0.20	0.85	2.68	32.34
Zambia	17.92	15.93	15.61	4.20	36.20	0.04	2.50	13.37	45.22	16.89
Zimbabwe	8.01	7.21	—	7.90	5.73	0.58	8.71	10.47	15.56	0.70
Country typology										
Resourch-rich	13.59	14.97	12.56	5.51	19.82	3.71	7.97	11.49	17.33	14.93
Middle-income	23.20	20.56	18.92	31.03	10.75	30.98	46.77	19.76	3.48	1.23
Fragile states	17.45	17.01	18.37	10.55	23.07	4.82	8.58	12.24	23.41	19.65
Nonfragile, low-income	13.11	12.62	16.17	10.76	36.23	3.11	7.57	14.27	23.13	33.66
Level of urbanization										
High	17.16	17.09	16.03	12.33	19.68	10.13	19.36	15.43	17.06	12.81
Medium	14.97	15.72	15.03	6.60	22.33	3.00	5.88	9.57	21.39	21.33
Low	12.19	11.55	15.59	10.71	38.87	2.65	5.15	14.04	21.95	34.90
Level of water scarcity										
High	14.12	13.45	14.00	9.30	20.16	5.33	10.42	11.94	14.51	19.97
Low	16.02	17.07	18.88	13.10	31.34	5.88	10.97	16.60	31.03	30.47
Overall	14.75	14.66	15.62	10.46	24.35	5.51	10.60	13.49	20.00	23.46

Source: Banerjee, Wodon, and others 2008.
Note: Location and expenditure quintile data refer to latest available year. — = not available.

Table A1.3 Wells/Boreholes
(percentage of population)

Country	*Time period (national)*			*Location*		*Expenditure quintile*				
	Early 1990s	*Late 1990s*	*Early 2000s*	*Rural*	*Urban*	*Q1*	*Q2*	*Q3*	*Q4*	*Q5*
Benin	—	54.71	44.93	54.40	28.15	49.70	60.09	62.41	44.20	8.23
Burkina Faso	78.58	82.30	67.66	79.45	12.89	65.35	83.06	84.16	77.14	18.61
Cameroon	28.14	26.68	32.13	48.15	15.34	46.57	55.87	33.57	19.61	5.02
Central African Republic	38.48	—	—	40.98	35.09	31.40	34.63	53.34	42.61	30.42
Chad	—	72.07	65.99	74.34	33.64	51.72	76.17	76.83	85.42	40.16
Comoros	—	46.10	—	54.50	24.19	19.09	49.72	57.46	62.13	46.00
Congo, Dem. Rep.	49.04	—	8.89	7.54	11.21	3.99	12.72	14.66	11.22	3.58
Congo, Rep.	—	—	15.35	25.46	6.31	17.75	27.05	21.40	8.45	2.09
Côte d'Ivoire	41.33	41.29	—	53.58	20.03	55.75	55.24	63.86	29.70	1.87
Ethiopia	—	6.07	9.88	10.96	1.97	5.46	13.53	11.97	10.89	7.55
Gabon	—	8.35	—	23.56	3.00	22.39	14.82	3.41	1.12	0.00
Ghana	32.51	35.33	42.10	57.41	20.61	51.25	55.55	49.40	46.18	7.95
Guinea	—	46.52	50.48	58.96	30.17	30.48	70.84	66.88	71.50	12.86
Kenya	24.96	21.98	21.64	23.54	14.04	11.78	24.99	29.60	25.52	16.48
Lesotho	—	14.97	33.33	38.40	9.97	43.52	42.64	31.93	33.42	15.00
Madagascar	15.67	23.06	21.72	22.42	19.18	18.98	17.90	18.65	28.44	24.63
Malawi	58.92	65.91	69.02	77.59	23.57	83.74	82.86	76.69	68.59	33.19
Mali	—	78.60	65.11	75.20	36.81	94.67	79.64	62.18	61.92	26.80
Mauritania	—	—	45.25	67.77	15.25	95.76	45.07	53.49	24.31	6.06
Mozambique	—	46.34	59.38	72.83	32.93	68.28	78.48	76.80	59.89	13.03
Namibia	27.26	31.57	—	47.14	0.13	66.50	51.99	34.72	4.41	0.03
Niger	75.17	71.95	—	86.85	8.18	99.00	95.15	92.01	52.15	20.31
Nigeria	31.64	44.17	53.71	56.77	47.71	59.03	57.79	52.13	48.35	51.24

Rwanda	1.53	9.77	20.21	20.68	17.65	6.16	37.13	17.96	25.34	14.96
Senegal	51.44	49.22	35.61	55.57	9.66	77.15	55.62	36.32	8.18	0.44
South Africa	—	4.07	—	8.55	0.33	8.92	7.26	3.17	0.93	0.06
Sudan	—	45.29	—	51.44	36.48	74.44	58.07	40.75	26.57	11.55
Tanzania	31.03	40.97	41.04	47.81	19.20	57.02	54.11	44.72	34.18	15.06
Togo	—	38.49	—	45.05	23.46	39.69	50.56	48.81	38.48	15.05
Uganda	40.48	—	68.23	73.25	34.52	65.55	68.72	72.30	82.22	52.11
Zambia	24.24	45.32	46.87	64.22	15.57	69.37	63.12	60.14	35.70	5.89
Zimbabwe	54.50	52.23	—	76.22	1.17	80.47	67.62	76.35	34.35	0.73
Country typology										
Resourch-rich	36.70	47.72	48.97	56.70	39.35	59.74	57.96	49.47	42.44	36.71
Middle-income	5.56	5.58	5.97	12.93	0.46	12.67	10.52	5.61	2.35	0.64
Fragile states	61.45	42.44	52.96	41.51	13.71	27.65	35.18	38.96	25.74	5.59
Nonfragile, low-income	34.37	33.55	38.33	43.36	18.14	42.68	46.63	43.21	37.69	17.20
Level of urbanization										
High	27.89	34.16	39.42	48.52	28.75	49.00	47.52	41.43	33.62	28.06
Medium	57.03	49.49	51.84	50.13	21.07	44.17	46.67	43.96	31.05	8.25
Low	33.28	32.04	36.81	40.92	16.75	38.02	43.76	40.98	38.37	20.28
Level of water scarcity										
High	34.97	36.31	41.12	44.33	28.17	44.09	46.22	42.57	37.18	25.25
Low	41.48	38.84	42.16	46.36	16.66	42.52	45.12	40.42	30.19	10.36
Overall	37.12	37.15	41.46	44.96	23.85	43.57	45.85	41.86	34.86	20.30

Source: Banerjee, Wodon, and others 2008.
Note: Location and expenditure quintile data refer to latest available year. — = not available.

Table A1.4 Surface Water
(percentage of population)

	Time period (national)			*Location*		*Expenditure quintile*				
Country	*Early 1990s*	*Late 1990s*	*Early 2000s*	*Rural*	*Urban*	*Q1*	*Q2*	*Q3*	*Q4*	*Q5*
Benin	—	16.51	12.13	15.87	5.50	36.60	13.82	7.04	2.90	0.28
Burkina Faso	3.91	4.87	13.42	16.21	0.50	34.63	16.51	10.75	5.33	0.04
Cameroon	35.05	37.14	27.65	39.96	14.75	53.22	26.74	33.03	18.63	6.53
Central African Republic	39.14	—	—	57.42	14.35	68.60	63.08	36.00	20.29	7.69
Chad	—	11.97	18.48	22.35	3.50	48.24	21.57	13.11	6.67	2.34
Comoros	—	2.88	—	3.49	1.27	9.72	1.33	1.34	0.40	0.47
Congo, Dem. Rep.	22.42	—	62.29	85.76	21.67	96.01	84.68	73.14	54.95	12.34
Congo, Rep.	—	—	30.28	59.11	4.52	75.88	54.68	16.78	3.76	0.13
Côte d'Ivoire	12.90	7.44	—	11.75	0.00	19.62	10.41	4.06	2.70	0.00
Ethiopia	—	78.03	67.94	76.11	7.88	94.49	81.62	69.96	68.68	24.71
Gabon	—	18.02	—	56.35	4.53	63.97	23.20	2.79	0.14	0.00
Ghana	34.37	27.35	20.12	32.36	2.95	45.35	19.96	29.72	3.96	0.60
Guinea	—	31.69	27.48	37.50	3.53	69.47	28.91	27.89	10.28	0.35
Kenya	44.66	47.00	46.35	56.34	6.20	84.21	64.54	51.83	29.15	1.66
Lesotho	—	20.44	7.67	9.15	0.87	1.37	13.73	11.39	8.42	3.46
Madagascar	65.27	59.25	55.02	65.44	17.07	80.83	81.63	75.78	35.63	1.17
Malawi	15.30	10.49	11.67	13.61	1.34	16.14	16.13	16.31	7.46	2.29
Mali	—	4.27	5.08	6.28	1.72	4.29	7.62	8.34	4.59	0.54
Mauritania	—	—	4.65	7.61	0.71	4.18	12.85	4.29	1.58	0.58
Mozambique	—	28.75	14.98	20.96	3.20	31.64	17.68	14.75	9.15	0.56
Namibia	21.00	8.30	—	12.42	0.00	17.11	14.42	7.06	2.89	0.00
Niger	3.28	2.60	—	3.16	0.19	1.00	2.86	4.66	3.16	1.54
Nigeria	42.02	27.77	23.18	30.76	8.28	33.39	29.96	28.19	16.14	8.15

Rwanda	75.41	54.07	51.43	56.29	24.58	93.72	58.60	29.86	50.19	23.42
Senegal	2.64	1.78	0.98	1.72	0.02	1.81	1.28	1.38	0.44	0.00
South Africa	—	14.40	—	31.30	0.29	53.31	14.48	3.95	0.23	0.00
Sudan	—	19.84	—	28.50	7.44	14.84	27.16	35.38	13.14	2.70
Tanzania	34.33	24.27	24.39	29.76	7.08	30.91	30.91	34.73	20.58	4.76
Togo	—	25.50	—	35.91	1.66	50.64	34.95	25.29	15.90	0.46
Uganda	53.08	—	21.59	24.47	2.19	33.70	30.41	25.28	14.35	4.07
Zambia	26.04	16.56	18.99	28.72	1.44	30.52	34.25	25.95	4.17	0.00
Zimbabwe	10.61	7.56	—	11.11	0.00	18.95	11.49	6.19	0.95	0.00
Country typology										
Resourch-rich	35.61	27.41	23.68	30.94	8.15	33.52	29.54	28.54	14.39	6.19
Middle-income	18.16	14.39	13.02	28.63	0.30	49.76	14.45	4.37	0.66	0.14
Fragile states	30.77	31.97	45.62	44.38	15.16	67.26	53.98	44.72	31.66	6.75
Nonfragile, low-income	51.41	34.55	37.42	42.17	5.66	53.87	43.78	38.65	28.36	7.93
Level of urbanization										
High	31.56	22.96	20.38	28.62	5.69	37.30	23.64	20.91	10.34	4.75
Medium	34.24	31.45	37.93	38.07	12.42	52.03	44.59	39.73	24.30	4.96
Low	53.87	37.05	41.25	45.33	7.07	59.11	49.87	43.06	33.22	9.52
Level of water scarcity										
High	45.14	31.65	32.56	39.84	5.78	48.35	36.98	32.04	22.15	7.69
Low	31.50	27.84	32.91	36.55	12.16	51.26	42.65	38.04	23.49	4.60
Overall	40.64	30.38	32.68	38.83	8.17	49.32	38.86	34.04	22.60	6.66

Source: Banerjee, Wodon, and others 2008.
Note: Location and expenditure quintile data refer to latest available year. — = not available.

Table A1.5 Septic Tank
(percentage of population)

Country	Time period (national)			Location		Expenditure quintile				
	Early 1990s	Late 1990s	Early 2000s	Rural	Urban	Q1	Q2	Q3	Q4	Q5
Benin	—	0.00	2.39	0.35	6.00	0.00	0.00	0.00	0.63	11.30
Burkina Faso	0.89	0.58	1.86	0.49	8.22	0.00	0.02	0.00	1.42	9.02
Cameroon	6.56	6.41	8.07	0.73	15.76	0.00	0.01	0.35	1.74	38.32
Central African Republic	1.11	—	—	0.11	2.48	0.00	0.00	0.00	0.31	5.26
Chad	—	0.24	1.83	0.46	7.13	0.00	0.00	0.00	1.19	7.97
Comoros	—	2.93	—	1.16	7.55	0.00	0.08	0.00	0.73	14.14
Congo, Dem. Rep.	1.56	—	1.42	0.02	3.83	0.00	0.00	0.00	0.00	6.07
Congo, Rep.	—	—	5.33	0.35	9.78	0.00	0.00	0.03	2.49	24.21
Côte d'Ivoire	14.03	12.45	—	2.26	30.07	0.00	0.00	0.00	2.15	60.26
Ethiopia	—	0.34	2.13	1.34	7.99	0.00	0.00	1.16	3.60	5.93
Gabon	—	24.50	—	4.45	31.56	0.09	0.91	4.51	21.69	95.49
Ghana	5.94	7.57	10.28	1.52	22.56	0.27	2.09	1.41	4.42	43.35
Guinea	—	2.65	2.62	0.58	7.51	0.00	0.00	0.00	1.11	12.04
Kenya	7.99	9.75	8.97	1.48	39.06	0.00	0.00	0.25	2.06	42.64
Lesotho	—	2.11	1.61	0.15	8.34	0.00	0.00	0.10	0.47	7.50
Madagascar	2.54	2.26	1.88	0.50	6.89	0.00	0.00	0.04	1.49	7.85
Malawi	2.62	3.30	3.58	0.89	17.87	0.00	0.81	0.08	0.67	16.37
Mali	—	1.12	6.05	3.01	14.56	0.00	0.03	6.86	5.54	17.93
Mauritania	—	—	1.77	0.05	4.06	0.00	0.00	0.00	0.44	8.41
Mozambique	—	3.22	2.88	0.21	8.12	0.00	0.00	0.00	0.02	14.42
Namibia	26.65	30.56	—	6.80	78.54	0.00	0.00	1.84	51.56	99.49
Niger	1.25	1.05	—	0.23	4.58	0.00	0.00	0.00	2.42	2.89
Nigeria	8.46	11.90	13.12	5.65	27.80	0.07	0.46	1.43	9.73	54.14

Rwanda	1.05	1.47	1.16	0.24	6.27	0.00	0.00	0.26	0.27	5.34
Senegal	10.62	9.07	36.04	14.15	64.51	1.10	7.46	37.24	56.93	77.81
South Africa	—	46.37	—	5.84	80.21	0.13	3.75	35.50	92.93	99.62
Sudan	—	6.42	—	1.12	14.02	0.21	0.12	1.42	6.59	31.30
Tanzania	1.41	1.66	2.75	0.47	10.12	0.00	0.00	0.00	0.93	12.84
Togo	—	0.00	—	0.00	0.00	0.00	0.00	0.00	0.00	0.00
Uganda	1.59	—	1.73	0.40	10.67	0.00	0.15	0.28	0.90	7.37
Zambia	27.13	20.69	18.09	2.11	46.92	0.00	0.12	1.07	13.65	75.85
Zimbabwe	26.25	31.45	—	1.54	95.12	0.00	11.32	5.92	42.64	99.21
Country typology										
Resourch-rich	8.94	12.41	11.18	4.08	23.63	0.08	0.32	1.25	8.32	47.82
Middle-income	49.37	44.02	40.78	5.51	79.18	0.12	3.44	32.71	87.57	95.99
Fragile states	7.13	7.21	6.65	0.85	14.48	0.00	1.43	0.75	5.87	27.15
Nonfragile, low-income	2.68	2.20	4.89	1.33	17.44	0.06	0.48	2.13	4.26	17.93
Level of urbanization										
High	17.16	17.53	18.77	5.07	38.09	0.14	1.44	8.89	24.80	60.81
Medium	7.42	9.27	6.42	0.80	14.26	0.04	0.95	0.88	6.57	26.57
Low	1.91	1.35	3.20	0.95	13.35	0.00	0.06	0.73	2.14	13.16
Level of water scarcity										
High	10.71	10.76	11.39	2.45	31.93	0.06	0.97	4.43	14.73	38.70
Low	5.53	6.59	6.49	1.64	14.45	0.06	0.42	2.52	5.36	24.75
Overall	9.00	9.37	9.77	2.20	25.37	0.06	0.78	3.80	11.61	34.06

Source: Banerjee, Wodon, and others 2008.
Note: Location and expenditure quintile data refer to latest available year. — = not available.

Table A1.6 Improved Latrine
(percentage of population)

	Time period (national)			Location		Expenditure quintile				
Country	*Early 1990s*	*Late 1990s*	*Early 2000s*	*Rural*	*Urban*	*Q1*	*Q2*	*Q3*	*Q4*	*Q5*
Benin	—	1.46	13.87	5.15	29.35	0.00	1.06	3.67	12.78	51.88
Burkina Faso	0.71	0.25	17.92	6.81	69.55	0.09	0.83	3.06	19.84	74.35
Cameroon	0.00	23.54	26.98	13.27	41.36	0.02	0.96	24.57	63.73	45.65
Central African Republic	13.28	—	—	18.43	6.31	16.06	27.59	13.42	6.73	2.61
Chad	—	7.51	2.74	0.23	12.46	0.00	0.00	0.00	0.45	13.26
Comoros	—	20.71	—	15.33	34.74	0.00	0.32	18.06	24.41	61.82
Congo, Dem. Rep.	10.77	—	9.77	0.35	26.07	0.00	0.00	0.00	1.81	40.42
Congo, Rep.	—	—	15.07	4.11	24.87	0.22	0.62	7.74	18.88	48.03
Côte d'Ivoire	22.48	13.30	—	7.73	22.92	0.00	1.21	10.59	28.38	26.92
Ethiopia	—	0.30	0.89	0.48	3.88	0.00	0.00	0.06	0.51	3.85
Gabon	—	22.09	—	8.40	26.91	1.89	12.71	38.22	53.28	4.27
Ghana	13.19	21.84	22.63	10.93	39.04	0.92	22.06	17.24	38.59	35.18
Guinea	—	0.00	2.06	1.65	3.02	0.00	0.55	3.77	2.23	3.77
Kenya	5.57	6.19	7.96	7.12	11.33	0.00	0.21	5.92	11.88	21.82
Lesotho	—	18.01	20.78	16.93	38.49	0.00	0.76	25.40	34.27	43.83
Madagascar	30.79	4.40	49.01	44.15	66.71	0.24	20.36	66.40	76.58	82.34
Malawi	0.67	0.64	1.20	0.96	2.44	0.00	0.00	0.07	0.01	5.90
Mali	—	7.77	10.79	7.08	21.18	0.04	0.62	7.80	17.32	28.30
Mauritania	—	—	3.82	0.25	8.59	0.00	0.00	0.30	3.27	15.57
Mozambique	—	0.88	1.81	0.07	5.26	0.00	0.00	0.00	0.02	9.09
Namibia	0.40	2.74	—	3.14	1.95	0.00	0.00	6.72	7.00	0.01
Niger	12.24	12.14	—	2.14	54.93	0.09	0.06	0.29	2.24	58.42
Nigeria	0.00	6.31	2.89	1.70	5.22	0.00	0.41	2.05	5.22	6.78

Rwanda	0.00	8.16	29.32	25.87	48.42	0.00	0.40	4.07	75.40	66.82
Senegal	21.97	23.08	10.10	10.78	9.21	6.48	16.32	10.02	10.23	7.43
South Africa	—	0.00	—	0.00	0.00	0.00	0.00	0.00	0.00	0.00
Sudan	—	0.00	—	0.00	0.00	0.00	0.00	0.00	0.00	0.00
Tanzania	1.32	0.93	3.69	1.06	12.17	0.00	0.00	0.09	1.25	17.11
Togo	—	18.01	—	11.55	32.82	0.00	3.94	6.72	31.79	47.69
Uganda	1.65	—	2.39	1.43	8.86	0.00	0.08	0.34	2.30	9.31
Zambia	1.39	0.38	1.56	1.25	2.12	0.00	0.25	1.19	4.43	1.93
Zimbabwe	21.18	24.96	—	35.73	2.03	6.54	23.27	57.63	36.06	0.36
Country typology										
Resourch-rich	1.63	6.63	6.39	2.26	8.04	0.02	0.44	3.71	9.35	9.62
Middle-income	0.94	0.93	1.43	1.36	0.58	0.00	0.03	1.28	1.64	1.73
Fragile states	20.28	17.07	16.23	10.34	22.22	1.38	4.36	10.33	12.43	28.80
Nonfragile, low-income	5.31	4.36	9.90	6.16	21.72	0.34	3.51	6.89	13.55	24.26
Level of urbanization										
High	4.23	9.05	8.39	3.96	11.53	0.41	3.17	5.76	13.41	12.86
Medium	10.80	9.82	10.89	5.88	14.21	0.88	2.72	5.81	5.94	19.27
Low	5.20	2.63	8.87	6.06	21.11	0.03	1.58	6.44	12.42	24.28
Level of water scarcity										
High	4.49	6.16	7.57	4.06	8.86	0.24	1.99	3.90	8.38	13.54
Low	9.73	8.12	12.45	8.38	23.38	0.64	3.36	10.33	17.01	29.49
Overall	6.22	6.81	9.19	5.38	14.31	0.37	2.44	6.04	11.24	18.84

Source: Banerjee, Wodon, and others 2008.
Note: Location and expenditure quintile data refer to latest available year. — = not available.

Table A1.7 Traditional Latrine
(percentage of population)

Country	Time period (national)			Location		Expenditure quintile				
	Early 1990s	Late 1990s	Early 2000s	Rural	Urban	Q1	Q2	Q3	Q4	Q5
Benin	—	24.07	15.25	9.16	26.04	0.30	2.29	9.21	37.11	27.35
Burkina Faso	26.13	22.13	10.03	9.18	13.96	0.16	0.20	12.33	25.27	10.34
Cameroon	45.21	59.89	57.61	73.20	41.27	84.44	84.10	70.54	33.53	15.36
Central African Republic	59.45	—	—	40.24	85.51	0.00	41.29	75.50	89.32	91.27
Chad	—	20.52	23.62	13.25	63.82	0.00	0.26	1.72	47.00	70.07
Comoros	—	75.07	—	82.30	56.23	99.75	96.53	80.67	72.63	24.04
Congo, Dem. Rep.	71.25	—	76.08	81.75	66.27	81.80	76.96	86.03	89.81	51.22
Congo, Rep.	—	—	69.76	78.41	62.03	79.99	80.23	87.10	74.40	26.93
Côte d'Ivoire	21.13	38.62	—	35.60	43.84	3.10	29.64	84.56	65.50	12.81
Ethiopia	—	16.90	34.70	29.00	76.55	0.00	12.07	55.72	32.81	73.47
Gabon	—	50.91	—	82.93	39.63	92.59	82.89	55.12	23.79	0.06
Ghana	47.22	40.82	40.53	50.40	26.69	88.07	52.26	25.75	24.96	11.33
Guinea	—	61.09	67.44	59.32	86.86	4.41	88.32	68.51	92.93	83.64
Kenya	67.74	67.61	64.32	69.33	44.21	86.73	81.20	59.62	61.48	32.40
Lesotho	—	36.16	32.85	30.13	45.44	0.00	13.27	48.62	55.55	47.39
Madagascar	5.63	32.78	2.54	1.53	6.21	0.00	0.01	0.38	3.85	8.47
Malawi	71.63	79.46	80.67	81.84	74.46	98.52	88.26	67.01	73.84	75.57
Mali	—	63.93	62.06	61.92	62.47	77.09	71.83	47.43	61.16	52.70
Mauritania	—	—	44.35	28.27	65.77	0.00	12.51	57.66	76.79	75.26
Mozambique	—	34.78	48.01	37.91	67.88	0.00	10.27	77.30	84.02	73.05
Namibia	7.42	7.50	—	8.97	4.54	0.06	0.12	22.48	14.61	0.28
Niger	3.77	6.92	—	3.58	21.23	0.00	0.02	0.55	9.92	24.38
Nigeria	61.61	53.97	59.40	60.05	58.13	75.18	75.03	61.96	60.98	23.59

Rwanda	92.95	87.22	66.13	70.40	42.50	100.00	97.34	87.83	20.05	25.21
Senegal	28.74	35.10	31.28	38.42	21.99	56.40	38.63	24.03	24.42	12.81
South Africa	—	34.08	—	63.87	9.20	47.60	72.02	47.11	3.60	0.00
Sudan	—	48.91	—	41.49	59.55	19.34	36.79	57.45	77.46	65.73
Tanzania	82.38	84.98	79.22	80.46	75.23	87.34	74.31	80.39	85.50	68.46
Togo	—	14.92	—	6.03	35.28	2.16	4.93	5.97	13.03	48.56
Uganda	78.74	—	80.25	80.60	77.89	86.46	83.07	67.65	82.85	81.14
Zambia	42.10	51.32	53.09	56.66	46.65	14.48	70.83	79.94	78.82	21.28
Zimbabwe	13.48	14.89	—	20.78	2.33	12.00	20.61	25.24	15.86	0.33
Country typology										
Resourch-rich	57.05	57.19	54.77	55.73	56.54	60.07	65.88	60.52	61.85	31.82
Middle-income	37.23	33.01	30.36	58.24	9.58	43.76	66.72	46.14	6.11	1.88
Fragile states	56.86	54.17	65.26	50.51	58.92	45.73	58.27	71.96	72.68	42.58
Nonfragile, low-income	44.46	40.27	50.10	47.60	50.17	45.72	42.97	51.13	48.97	50.87
Level of urbanization										
High	50.93	47.82	51.35	57.35	42.05	65.65	67.68	56.80	44.76	17.13
Medium	55.17	56.15	55.06	46.10	58.91	34.01	48.32	65.14	73.88	51.64
Low	44.98	40.51	51.81	48.04	57.12	44.91	44.57	51.84	49.50	55.38
Level of water scarcity										
High	47.48	40.38	47.88	48.31	46.80	49.14	52.45	51.29	46.32	38.33
Low	54.30	60.64	61.62	55.68	56.86	51.80	57.28	68.03	68.06	44.19
Overall	49.73	47.12	52.44	50.56	50.57	50.02	54.05	56.85	53.55	40.27

Source: Banerjee, Wodon, and others 2008.
Note: Location and expenditure quintile data refer to latest available year. — = not available.

Table A1.8 Open Defecation
(percentage of population)

	Time period (national)			Location		Expenditure quintile				
Country	*Early 1990s*	*Late 1990s*	*Early 2000s*	*Rural*	*Urban*	*Q1*	*Q2*	*Q3*	*Q4*	*Q5*
Benin	—	73.75	67.67	84.71	37.47	99.48	95.48	86.75	47.92	8.67
Burkina Faso	71.64	76.56	69.96	83.30	8.00	99.64	98.89	84.29	53.07	6.02
Cameroon	12.55	9.82	7.17	12.63	1.44	15.35	14.56	4.35	0.95	0.61
Central African Republic	25.91	—	—	41.13	5.26	83.90	30.97	10.97	3.21	0.39
Chad	—	71.48	71.61	85.83	16.47	99.89	99.55	98.00	51.36	8.23
Comoros	—	0.27	—	0.37	0.00	0.00	0.73	0.30	0.40	0.00
Congo, Dem. Rep.	16.41	—	12.24	17.40	3.29	17.74	22.30	13.53	8.32	1.54
Congo, Rep.	—	—	9.53	16.65	3.16	19.21	18.73	4.75	4.15	0.77
Côte d'Ivoire	42.10	35.41	—	54.21	2.92	96.90	68.55	4.85	3.51	0.00
Ethiopia	—	82.45	62.20	69.11	11.36	100.00	87.83	42.98	63.07	16.50
Gabon	—	2.09	—	3.75	1.51	5.11	2.77	1.78	0.72	0.07
Ghana	26.52	24.00	24.57	36.90	7.28	10.74	23.46	55.11	28.63	4.12
Guinea	—	34.39	27.60	38.14	2.40	95.58	10.99	26.64	3.64	0.51
Kenya	17.79	15.86	18.29	21.84	4.02	13.27	18.33	33.97	23.87	2.03
Lesotho	—	40.41	44.65	52.67	7.65	100.00	85.70	25.70	9.63	1.25
Madagascar	61.01	60.54	46.57	53.82	20.18	99.76	79.63	33.18	18.08	1.32
Malawi	24.98	16.52	14.46	16.23	5.06	1.48	10.94	32.79	25.21	2.02
Mali	—	26.70	20.92	27.73	1.79	22.77	27.28	37.38	15.96	1.04
Mauritania	—	—	49.30	70.44	21.13	99.94	86.54	41.28	17.82	0.40
Mozambique	—	60.27	46.73	61.34	17.98	100.00	88.82	21.53	15.50	3.04
Namibia	63.56	56.60	—	79.08	11.23	99.33	98.96	65.13	19.49	0.00
Niger	82.30	79.46	—	93.78	18.22	99.86	99.53	99.01	84.75	13.46
Nigeria	29.38	26.02	24.52	32.53	8.79	24.72	24.07	34.39	23.98	15.46

Rwanda	5.95	2.96	3.32	3.45	2.60	0.00	2.23	7.68	4.22	2.55
Senegal	38.39	32.44	22.01	36.12	3.67	35.43	37.26	28.47	7.50	1.19
South Africa	—	12.78	—	26.14	1.62	50.13	11.32	2.29	0.14	0.00
Sudan	—	42.65	—	55.92	23.63	78.42	60.50	38.78	14.05	2.13
Tanzania	13.98	12.38	14.29	17.96	2.44	12.54	25.63	19.51	12.31	1.56
Togo	—	64.09	—	79.12	29.68	94.81	86.07	85.05	51.83	2.54
Uganda	17.41	—	14.78	16.64	2.31	13.26	16.33	30.22	12.26	1.78
Zambia	29.11	27.01	27.04	39.94	3.78	85.52	28.75	17.64	3.07	0.13
Zimbabwe	38.71	28.41	—	41.61	0.32	81.46	44.46	10.64	5.00	0.00
Country typology										
Resourch-rich	33.25	31.72	27.56	37.67	11.11	39.44	32.86	33.98	20.10	10.51
Middle-income	17.71	15.79	14.25	31.17	1.95	54.14	17.89	5.82	1.31	0.05
Fragile states	51.61	42.71	38.56	37.74	3.87	52.49	35.12	16.44	8.64	0.99
Nonfragile, low-income	58.44	42.73	40.33	44.67	9.67	53.81	52.81	39.49	32.59	6.18
Level of urbanization										
High	26.50	23.25	21.44	32.86	6.05	33.36	25.34	25.75	16.00	8.55
Medium	57.13	49.19	42.36	46.50	11.43	64.36	46.83	27.11	12.80	1.89
Low	59.19	43.36	41.31	44.74	8.09	55.00	53.64	40.72	35.61	6.85
Level of water scarcity										
High	53.20	41.64	38.94	44.62	10.21	50.13	42.97	38.47	29.63	8.82
Low	32.58	28.48	24.58	34.06	4.91	47.30	38.53	18.75	9.35	1.25
Overall	46.39	37.26	34.18	41.39	8.22	49.19	41.50	31.92	22.89	6.30

Source: Banerjee, Wodon, and others 2008.
Note: Location and expenditure quintile data refer to latest available year. — = not available.

Table A1.9 Annualized Change in Water Access: National
(percentage of population)

	Technology			
Country	*Piped water*	*Standpost*	*Well/borehole*	*Surface water*
Benin	1.78	1.88	−0.39	−0.40
Burkina Faso	0.69	1.40	−0.77	2.31
Cameroon	0.45	0.81	1.33	−0.99
Chad	0.23	0.26	0.73	1.20
Congo, Dem. Rep.	−0.16	1.12	−4.75	7.53
Côte d'Ivoire	1.47	0.94	1.16	−0.72
Ethiopia	0.44	1.09	0.89	−0.36
Ghana	0.26	0.30	2.09	−0.88
Guinea	0.08	0.49	1.45	−0.16
Kenya	0.09	0.20	0.40	0.86
Lesotho	0.00	−0.47	3.75	−2.45
Madagascar	0.03	1.18	0.25	0.53
Malawi	−0.09	−0.31	2.69	0.60
Mali	0.83	2.14	−0.57	0.28
Mozambique	0.16	0.28	2.95	−1.81
Namibia	1.43	0.57	1.06	−1.19
Niger	0.27	0.52	1.55	−0.02
Nigeria	−0.57	−0.66	3.60	−0.39
Rwanda	−0.39	0.33	2.51	1.81
Senegal	1.98	0.44	−0.99	−0.07
Tanzania	−1.01	1.36	0.82	0.50
Uganda	0.12	0.71	6.53	−2.75
Zambia	−0.13	0.19	0.95	0.66
Zimbabwe	1.69	−0.02	0.52	−0.42
Country typology				
Resourch-rich	−0.40	−0.41	3.03	−0.28
Middle-income	0.75	0.07	2.34	−1.79
Fragile states	0.42	0.87	−2.32	4.15
Nonfragile, low-income	0.21	0.84	1.42	−0.15
Level of urbanization				
High	−0.06	−0.22	2.75	−0.50
Medium	0.28	0.76	−1.48	3.17
Low	0.08	0.88	1.41	0.08
Level of water scarcity				
High	0.05	0.18	2.34	−0.24
Low	0.12	0.98	−0.53	1.80
Overall	0.07	0.48	1.27	0.52

Source: Banerjee, Wodon, and others 2008.

Table A1.10 Annualized Change in Water Access: Urban
(percentage of population)

	Technology			
Country	*Piped water*	*Standpost*	*Well/borehole*	*Surface water*
Benin	3.58	0.80	−1.09	0.30
Burkina Faso	3.40	4.00	−1.01	0.13
Cameroon	−0.01	1.34	0.90	0.72
Chad	1.56	2.07	−0.34	0.27
Congo, Dem. Rep.	−0.31	2.56	−0.67	3.43
Côte d'Ivoire	3.81	−0.52	0.36	−0.04
Ethiopia	4.77	−0.27	−0.23	−1.08
Ghana	−0.18	0.60	2.65	−0.21
Guinea	0.47	2.10	0.10	0.16
Kenya	0.03	−0.12	1.49	0.35
Lesotho	2.69	−0.47	0.63	−0.66
Madagascar	0.39	2.03	0.33	−0.41
Malawi	−0.64	3.01	3.10	0.10
Mali	3.00	1.25	−0.37	0.28
Mozambique	−0.12	0.80	2.31	0.39
Namibia	1.75	1.15	−0.21	−0.08
Niger	1.49	0.93	0.28	−0.12
Nigeria	−1.37	−0.63	3.99	1.06
Rwanda	−0.66	3.67	3.03	3.15
Senegal	2.28	−0.42	−0.25	−0.03
Tanzania	−3.50	3.91	1.37	0.70
Uganda	0.85	4.67	2.01	−1.98
Zambia	−0.05	1.09	0.42	0.01
Zimbabwe	2.93	0.46	−0.19	0.00
Country typology				
Resourch-rich	−0.98	−0.17	3.19	0.91
Middle-income	2.19	0.38	0.19	−0.36
Fragile states	0.99	1.65	−0.33	1.99
Nonfragile, low-income	1.20	1.53	0.94	−0.20
Level of urbanization				
High	−0.44	−0.31	3.01	0.72
Medium	0.47	1.72	0.02	1.70
Low	1.32	1.77	0.76	−0.25
Level of water scarcity				
High	0.86	0.56	1.95	0.13
Low	0.01	1.87	0.40	1.08
Overall	0.54	1.05	1.37	0.49

Source: Banerjee, Wodon, and others 2008.

Table A1.11 Annualized Change in Water Access: Rural
(percentage of population)

	Technology			
Country	*Piped water*	*Standpost*	*Well/borehole*	*Surface water*
Benin	1.04	2.46	−0.16	−0.93
Burkina Faso	−0.01	0.63	−0.37	2.81
Cameroon	−0.10	−0.77	2.46	−1.40
Chad	−0.03	−0.17	0.74	1.34
Congo, Dem. Rep.	0.04	0.31	−7.09	9.89
Côte d'Ivoire	0.44	1.77	1.37	−1.28
Ethiopia	0.04	1.55	1.02	−0.76
Ghana	−0.20	−0.55	2.33	−0.80
Guinea	0.01	−0.10	1.93	−0.45
Kenya	0.05	0.26	0.14	1.05
Lesotho	0.04	−0.66	4.25	−3.19
Madagascar	0.01	1.14	0.20	0.50
Malawi	0.03	−0.93	2.58	0.69
Mali	0.25	2.77	−1.18	0.22
Mozambique	−0.07	−0.58	3.73	−2.38
Namibia	1.18	0.30	1.75	−1.69
Niger	−0.08	0.35	2.05	0.01
Nigeria	−0.30	−0.82	3.09	−1.24
Rwanda	−0.04	−0.18	2.35	1.10
Senegal	1.25	1.09	−1.07	−0.09
Tanzania	−0.18	0.59	0.60	0.41
Uganda	0.01	0.12	7.20	−2.86
Zambia	0.19	−0.11	0.85	0.83
Zimbabwe	0.27	−0.20	1.47	−0.49
Country typology				
Resourch-rich	−0.23	−0.73	2.74	−0.97
Middle-income	0.64	−0.16	2.94	−2.40
Fragile states	0.15	0.47	−3.47	5.38
Nonfragile, low-income	0.05	0.68	1.53	−0.29
Level of urbanization				
High	−0.11	−0.44	2.55	−1.14
Medium	0.15	0.18	−2.29	4.13
Low	0.00	0.76	1.46	−0.04
Level of water scarcity				
High	−0.08	0.05	2.29	−0.62
Low	0.11	0.53	−1.03	2.24
Overall	−0.01	0.23	1.05	0.45

Source: Banerjee, Wodon, and others 2008.

Table A1.12 Annualized Change in Sanitation Access: National
(percentage of population)

	Technology			
Country	*Septic tank*	*Improved latrine*	*Traditional latrine*	*Open defecation*
Benin	0.48	2.53	−1.08	0.90
Burkina Faso	0.34	4.43	−2.25	1.04
Cameroon	0.38	0.95	0.57	−0.29
Chad	0.23	−0.52	0.90	1.60
Congo, Dem. Rep.	0.04	0.26	3.63	−0.05
Côte d'Ivoire	0.08	−1.20	4.10	−0.14
Ethiopia	0.37	0.12	3.92	−2.30
Ghana	0.70	0.61	0.79	0.61
Guinea	0.04	0.34	2.09	−0.55
Kenya	0.05	0.48	0.77	0.82
Lesotho	−0.09	0.64	−0.48	1.05
Madagascar	−0.01	6.46	−3.69	−0.84
Malawi	0.17	0.16	2.61	−0.04
Mali	1.02	0.81	1.36	−0.43
Mozambique	0.00	0.17	2.79	−1.25
Namibia	1.00	0.30	0.15	0.35
Niger	0.00	0.32	0.63	1.81
Nigeria	0.63	−0.68	2.84	0.34
Rwanda	0.00	4.59	−0.44	0.20
Senegal	3.50	−1.29	0.03	−0.84
Tanzania	0.25	0.57	0.52	0.63
Uganda	0.10	0.20	3.96	0.38
Zambia	−0.12	0.20	1.08	0.42
Zimbabwe	1.51	1.13	0.52	−1.37
Country typology				
Resourch-rich	0.53	−0.45	2.39	0.35
Middle-income	0.48	0.46	−0.15	0.68
Fragile states	0.25	0.11	3.14	−0.29
Nonfragile, low-income .	0.38	0.99	1.47	−0.31
Level of urbanization				
High	0.73	−0.49	2.38	0.21
Medium	0.22	0.50	2.40	−0.31
Low	0.24	1.08	1.53	−0.25
Level of water scarcity				
High	0.44	0.25	2.24	−0.06
Low	0.34	0.71	1.59	−0.18
Overall	0.40	0.42	2.00	−0.11

Source: Banerjee, Wodon, and others 2008.
Note: VIP = ventilated improved pit.

Table A1.13 Annualized Change in Sanitation Access: Urban
(percentage of population)

	Technology			
Country	*Septic tank*	*Improved latrine*	*Traditional latrine*	*Open defecation*
Benin	1.20	5.30	−3.19	0.24
Burkina Faso	1.32	17.17	−13.07	0.15
Cameroon	0.24	0.92	1.62	0.15
Chad	0.90	−1.57	3.58	0.15
Congo, Dem. Rep.	0.15	0.76	4.70	−0.48
Côte d'Ivoire	0.48	−0.90	4.46	−0.48
Ethiopia	1.20	0.46	3.88	−2.23
Ghana	1.24	1.99	1.74	−0.09
Guinea	0.04	0.50	2.27	−0.03
Kenya	−0.07	0.60	1.97	0.27
Lesotho	0.28	0.53	0.64	−0.12
Madagascar	0.17	8.51	−5.30	−1.15
Malawi	0.87	0.41	3.27	0.98
Mali	2.32	1.69	0.66	−0.41
Mozambique	−0.43	0.62	4.22	−0.90
Namibia	1.75	0.19	0.36	0.37
Niger	−0.17	1.39	2.04	−0.19
Nigeria	0.53	−0.30	5.14	−0.20
Rwanda	0.39	6.15	2.24	0.40
Senegal	5.65	−0.05	−3.82	−0.14
Tanzania	1.12	1.82	0.17	0.28
Uganda	0.54	0.71	4.37	0.14
Zambia	0.04	0.29	0.81	0.07
Zimbabwe	2.99	0.24	0.00	−0.02
Country typology				
Resourch-rich	0.49	−0.21	4.41	−0.13
Middle-income	1.06	0.35	0.49	0.14
Fragile states	0.59	0.35	3.78	−0.37
Nonfragile, low-income	0.95	2.30	1.14	−0.53
Level of urbanization				
High	0.88	0.01	3.89	−0.18
Medium	0.45	0.91	2.93	−0.34
Low	0.81	2.31	1.29	−0.55
Level of water scarcity				
High	0.77	1.12	3.02	−0.42
Low	0.73	1.43	1.67	−0.31
Overall	0.76	1.24	2.52	−0.38

Source: Banerjee, Wodon, and others 2008.

Table A1.14 Annualized Change in Sanitation Access: Rural
(percentage of population)

	Technology			
Country	*Septic tank*	*Improved latrine*	*Traditional latrine*	*Open defecation*
Benin	0.07	0.98	0.37	0.93
Burkina Faso	0.11	1.68	−0.27	1.61
Cameroon	−0.09	−0.13	0.59	−0.24
Chad	0.07	−0.06	0.44	1.49
Congo, Dem. Rep.	−0.02	0.03	3.08	0.21
Côte d'Ivoire	0.06	−1.27	3.92	−0.40
Ethiopia	0.27	0.09	4.30	−2.76
Ghana	−0.04	−0.79	0.54	1.46
Guinea	0.07	0.28	2.11	−0.93
Kenya	0.02	0.45	0.50	0.97
Lesotho	−0.05	1.11	−0.53	0.60
Madagascar	−0.03	5.92	−3.13	−0.97
Malawi	0.04	0.11	2.47	−0.24
Mali	0.59	0.63	1.72	−0.81
Mozambique	0.01	−0.08	1.69	−0.80
Namibia	0.53	0.36	0.06	0.46
Niger	0.03	−0.06	0.28	2.46
Nigeria	0.52	−0.93	1.29	0.47
Rwanda	0.00	4.55	−1.35	0.14
Senegal	1.67	−2.08	2.64	−1.00
Tanzania	−0.01	0.19	0.64	0.71
Uganda	0.03	0.13	3.90	0.42
Zambia	0.17	0.15	1.15	0.32
Zimbabwe	−0.05	1.79	0.90	−1.55
Country typology				
Resourch-rich	0.41	−0.73	1.17	0.45
Middle-income	0.25	0.72	−0.22	0.52
Fragile states	0.00	0.05	2.85	−0.25
Nonfragile, low-income	0.16	0.57	1.66	−0.28
Level of urbanization				
High	0.43	−0.95	1.47	0.36
Medium	0.02	0.31	2.12	−0.17
Low	0.12	0.82	1.69	−0.32
Level of water scarcity				
High	0.25	−0.05	1.78	−0.01
Low	0.13	0.38	1.57	−0.14
Overall	0.20	0.11	1.70	−0.06

Source: Banerjee, Wodon, and others 2008.

Reference

Banerjee, S., Q. Wodon, A. Diallo, T. Pushak, H. Uddin, C. Tsimpo, and V. Foster. 2008. "Access, Affordability and Alternatives: Modern Infrastructure Services in Sub-Saharan Africa." AICD Background Paper 2, Africa Infrastructure Country Diagnostic, World Bank, Washington, D.C.

APPENDIX 2

Institutions in the Water and Sanitation Sector

Table A2.1 Specification of Urban Water Reform Index

Subindex	*Indicator*	*Definition*
Legislation	1. Existence of reform	0 = No reform of the water services delivery; 1 = reform of the water services delivery
	2. Legal reform	0 = No new sector legislation passed within the past 10 years; 1 = new sector legislation passed in the past 10 years
Restructuring	3. Unbundling	0 = Same entity responsible for bulk water production and distribution in urban areas; 1 = different entities responsible for bulk water production and distribution in urban areas
	4. Separation of business lines	0 = No separation of water and wastewater services from provision in urban area; 1 = separation of water and wastewater provisions in urban areas
	5. SOE corporatization	0 = No state-owned water utility corporatized in urban area; 1 = at least one state-owned water utility corporatized
	6. Existence of regulatory body	0 = No autonomous regulatory body; 1 = autonomous regulatory body
Policy oversight	7. Tariff approval oversight	0 = Oversight on tariff by line ministry; 1 = oversight on tariff by a special entity within the ministry, an interministerial committee, or the regulator
	8. Investment plan oversight	0 = Oversight on investment plan by line ministry; 1 = oversight on investment plan by a special entity within the ministry, an interministerial committee, or the regulator

	9. Technical standard oversight	0 = Oversight on technical standards by line ministry; 1 = oversight on technical standards by a special entity within the ministry, an interministerial committee, or the regulator
	10. Regulation monitoring oversight	0 = Oversight on compliance with economic regulation by line ministry; 1 = oversight on compliance with economic regulation by a special entity within the ministry, an interministerial committee, or the regulator
	11. Dispute arbitration oversight	0 = Oversight on dispute arbitration by line ministry; 1 = oversight on dispute arbitration by a special entity within the ministry, an interministerial committee, or the regulator
Private sector involvement	12. Private de jure	0 = Private participation forbidden by law; 1 = private participation allowed by law
	13. Private de facto	0 = No private participation in the three largest utilities; 1 = at least a form of private participation in the three largest utilities
	14. Private sector management	0 = No private sector involvement or service and works contracts only; 1 = management contract, *affermage*, lease, concession
	15. Private sector investment	0 = No private sector involvement, service and works contracts, management contract, *affermage*, lease; 1 = concession
	16. Absence of distressed private sector participation	0 = Canceled, distressed private sector participation; 1 = operational, concluded and not renewed private sector participation
	17. Absence of renationalization	0 = Canceled; 1 = distressed, operational, concluded and not renewed private sector participation
	18. Private ownership	0 = Concession, management, lease contract; 1 = greenfield/divestiture

Source: Banerjee, Wodon, and others 2008.
Note: SOE = state-owned enterprise.

Table A2.2 Urban Water Reform Index

Attribute	*Legislation*		*Restructuring*			
Country	*1. Existence of reform*	*2. Legal reform*	*3. Unbundling*	*4. Separation of business lines*	*5. SOE corporatization*	*6. Existence of regulatory body*
Benin	1	1	0	0	1	0
Burkina Faso	1	1	1	0	1	0
Cape Verde	1	1	0	0	1	1
Chad	0	0	0	0	1	0
Congo, Dem. Rep.	0	0	0	1	0	1
Côte d'Ivoire	1	0	0	1	1	1
Ethiopia	1	1	0	0	0	0
Ghana	1	1	0	1	1	1
Kenya	1	1	0	0	1	1
Lesotho	1	0	0	0	1	1
Madagascar	1	1	0	1	0	0
Malawi	1	0	0	1	1	0
Mozambique	1	1	0	1	1	1
Namibia	1	1	1	0	0	0
Niger	1	1	1	1	1	1
Nigeria	0	0	0	1	1	0
Rwanda	0	0	0	1	1	1
Senegal	1	1	0	1	1	0
South Africa	1	1	1	0	1	0
Sudan	1	1	0	1	1	1
Tanzania	1	1	0	1	1	1
Uganda	1	1	1	0	1	0
Zambia	1	1	0	0	1	1
Subindex	Legislation			Restructuring		
Countries sharing attribute (%)	83	70	22	52	83	52

Table A2.2 Urban Water Reform Index *(continued)*

Attribute	*Policy oversight*				
Country	*7. Tariff approval oversight*	*8. Investment plan oversight*	*9. Technical standard oversight*	*10. Regulation monitoring oversight*	*11. Dispute arbitration oversight*
Benin	0	1	1	1	1
Burkina Faso	1	1	1	0	0
Cape Verde	1	1	1	1	1
Chad	1	0	0	1	0
Congo, Dem. Rep.	1	0	0	1	1
Côte d'Ivoire	1	1	1	1	1
Ethiopia	1	0	0	1	0
Ghana	1	0	0	0	1
Kenya	0	1	1	1	1
Lesotho	1	1	1	1	1
Madagascar	1	1	1	1	1
Malawi	0	0	0	0	1
Mozambique	1	0	0	1	1
Namibia	0	0	0	0	0
Niger	0	0	0	1	1
Nigeria	1	1	1	1	1
Rwanda	0	0	1	1	0
Senegal	0	1	1	1	0
South Africa	1	0	0	0	0
Sudan	1	1	0	1	1
Tanzania	0	0	1	1	1
Uganda	1	0	1	1	0
Zambia	1	1	1	1	1
Subindex			Policy oversight		
Countries sharing attribute (%)	65	48	57	78	65

(continued next page)

Table A2.2 Urban Water Reform Index *(continued)*

Attribute / Country	Private sector involvement							Urban water reform index (%)
	12. Private de jure	13. Private de facto	14. Private sector management	15. Private sector investment	16. Absence of distressed private sector participation	17. Absence of renationalization	18. Private ownership	
Benin	0	0	0	0				51
Burkina Faso	1	0	0	0				58
Cape Verde	1							
Chad	0	0	0	0				68
Congo, Dem. Rep.	0	1	1	0	0			76
Côte d'Ivoire	1	1	1	0	1			16
Ethiopia	1	0	0	0				38
Ghana	1	1	1	0	1	1	0	40
Kenya	1	1	1	0	1	1	0	74
Lesotho	0	0	0	0				78
Madagascar	1	1	0	0	1			50
Malawi	1	0	0	0				71
Mozambique	1	1	1	1	1	1	0	35

Namibia	1	0	0	0		1	0	84
Niger	1	1	1	0	1	1	0	36
Nigeria	1	1	0	0	1			80
Rwanda	1	1	1	0	0			53
Senegal	1	1	1	0	1	1	0	44
South Africa	1	1	1	0	1	1	0	73
Sudan	1	1	0	0	1			63
Tanzania	1	1	1	0	0	0	0	79
Uganda	1	1	1	0	1	1	0	74
Zambia	1	0	0	0		1	0	73
Subindex				Private sector involvement				
Countries sharing attribute (%)	83	64	50	5	79	90	0	

Source: Banerjee, Wodon, and others 2008.
Note: SOE = state-owned enterprise. Blank cells: not applicable.

Table A2.3 Specification of Regulation Index

Subindex	*Indicator*	*Definition*
Autonomy	1. Formal autonomy: hire	0 = Appointment by government/line ministry; 1 = otherwise
	2. Formal autonomy: fire	0 = Firing by government/line ministry; 1 = otherwise
	3. Partial financial autonomy/operating budget: central government	0 = Budget fully funded by government; 1 = at least a portion of budget funded through fees and/or donors
	4. Full financial autonomy/operating budget: sector levies	0 = At least a portion of budget funded through government and/or donors; 1 = budget fully funded through fees
	5. Partial managerial autonomy/vetoing instance	0 = Veto decision by government/line ministry/others; 1 = no veto decision
	6. Full managerial autonomy/vetoing instance	0 = Veto decision by government/line ministry/others; 1 = no veto decision
	7. Multisectoral	0 = Sector specific regulator; 1 = multisectoral regulator
	8. Commissioner	0 = Individual; 1 = board of commissioners
Transparency	9. Publicity of decisions: reports only	0 = Regulatory decisions not publicly available; 1 = regulatory decisions publicly available through reports
	10. Publicity of decisions: Internet only	0 = Regulatory decisions not publicly available or available only through reports; 1 = regulatory decisions publicly available through Internet
	11. Publicity of decisions: public hearing only	0 = Regulatory decisions not publicly available or available only through reports/Internet; 1 = regulatory decisions publicly available through public hearings

Accountability	12. Appeal	0 = No right to appeal regulatory decisions; 1 = right to appeal regulatory decision
	13. Partial independence of appeal	0 = Appeal to government/line ministries; 1 = appeal to bodies other than government/line ministries
	14. Full independence of appeal	0 = No recourse to independent arbitration; 1 = possibility to appeal to independent arbitration
Tools	15. Tariff methodology	0 = No tariff methodology; 1 = some tariff methodology
	16. Tariff indexation	0 = No tariff indexation 1 = some tariff indexation
	17. Regulatory review	0 = No tariff review; 1 = periodic tariff review
	18. Length of regulatory review	0 = No tariff review or review lower than every 3 years; 1 = multiyear tariff review (greater than or equal to 3)

Source: Banerjee, Wodon, and others 2008.

Table A2.4 Regulation Index

Attribute of regulatory agencies	*Attribute of regulatory agencies*							
	Autonomy							
Country	*1. Formal autonomy: hire*	*2. Formal autonomy: fire*	*3. Partial financial autonomy/ operating budget: central government*	*4. Full financial autonomy/ operating budget: sector levies*	*5. Partial managerial autonomy/ vetoing instance*	*6. Full managerial autonomy/ vetoing instance*	*7. Multisectoral*	*8. Commissioner*
Benin	0	0	0	0	0	0	0	0
Burkina Faso	0	0	0	0	0	0	0	0
Cape Verde	0	0	1	1	1	0	1	1
Chad	0	0	0	0	0	0	0	0
Congo, Dem. Rep.	0		0	0	1	1	1	1
Côte d'Ivoire	0	0	0	0	0	0	0	0
Ethiopia	0	0	0		1	0		0
Ghana	0	0			0	0	1	1
Kenya	0	0	1	0	0	0	0	1
Lesotho	0	0	0	0	0	0	0	0

Madagascar	0	0	0	0	0	0	0	0
Malawi	0	0	0	0	0	0	0	0
Mozambique	0	0	1	1	1	0	0	1
Namibia	0	0	0	0	0	0	0	0
Niger	0	0	1	1	1	0	0	1
Nigeria	0	0	0	0	0	0	1	0
Rwanda	0	0	1	1	0	0	0	1
Senegal	0	0	0	0	0	0	1	0
South Africa	0	0	0	0	0	0	0	0
Sudan	0	0	1	0	0	0	0	1
Tanzania	0	0	1	0	0	0	0	1
Uganda	0	0	0	0	0	0	1	0
Zambia	0	0	1	0	1	0	0	1
Subindex					Autonomy			
Countries sharing attribute (%)	0	0	36	19	26	4	27	43

(continued next page)

Table A2.4 Regulation Index *(continued)*

	Attribute of regulatory agencies										
	Transparency			*Accountability*			*Tools*				
Country / *Attribute of regulatory agencies*	*9. Publicity of decisions: reports only*	*10. Publicity of decisions: Internet only*	*11. Publicity of decisions: public hearing only*	*12. Appeal*	*13. Partial independence of appeal*	*14. Full independence of appeal*	*15. Tariff methodology*	*16. Tariff indexation*	*17. Regulatory review*	*18. Length of regulatory review*	*Regulation index (%)*
Benin		0	0	1	1	0	1	0	0		25
Burkina Faso	1	1	1	1	0	0	1	0	1	1	52
Cape Verde	1	1	1	1	1	0	1	0	1	1	76
Chad	0	0	0	1	0	0			1		33
Congo, Dem. Rep.	0	0	0	1	0	0	1	0	1	0	44
Côte d'Ivoire	1	0	0	1	1	0	1	0	1	1	35
Ethiopia	1	0	1	0			1	0	0		29
Ghana	1	1	1	0	1	0	0	0	1	1	54
Kenya	1	1	1	1	1	0	0	1	1	0	60
Lesotho	1	0	0	0			0	1	1	1	27

Madagascar	0	0	0	1	1	0	0	0	0		17
Malawi	1	0	1				0	0	1		25
Mozambique	1	0	0	1	1	0	0	1	1	1	56
Namibia	1		0					1	0	0	21
Niger	1	1	0	1	1	0	1	0	1	0	61
Nigeria							1	1	0		17
Rwanda	1	1	1	0			1	0	0		46
Senegal	1	1	1	1	1	0	1	1	1	0	60
South Africa	0	0	0	1	0	0	0	0	1	0	15
Sudan	1	0	0	1	0	0		1	1	1	48
Tanzania	1	1	1	1	1	0	1	1	0		68
Uganda	1	1	1				1	1	1		50
Zambia	1	1	1	1	1	0	0	0	1		59
Subindex		Transparency			Accountability			Tools			
Countries sharing attribute (%)	81	48	50	79	69	0	60	41	70	54	

Source: Banerjee, Wodon, and others 2008.

Table A2.5 Specification of SOE Governance Index

Subindex	*Indicator*	*Definition*
Ownership and shareholder quality	1. Concentration of ownership	0 = Ownership diversified; 1 = 100% owned by one state body (central government or municipal government)
	2. Corporatization	0 = Noncorporatized (uncorporatized state owned enterprise); 1 = corporatized
	3. Limited liability	0 = Nonlimited liability; 1 = limited liability company
	4. Rate of return policy	0 = No requirement to earn a rate of return; 1 = requirement to earn a rate of return
	5. Dividend policy	0 = No requirement to pay dividends; 1 = requirement to pay dividends
Managerial and board autonomy	6. Hiring	0 = Either manager or board has not the most decisive influence on hiring decisions; 1 = either manager or board has the most decisive influence on hiring decisions
	7. Laying off	0 = Either manager or board has not the most decisive influence on firing decisions; 1 = either manager or board has the most decisive influence on firing decisions
	8. Wages	0 = Either manager or board has not the most decisive influence on setting wages/bonuses; 1 = either manager or board has the most decisive influence on setting wages/bonuses
	9. Production	0 = Either manager or board has not the most decisive influence on how much to produce; 1 = either manager or board has the most decisive influence on how much to produce
	10. Sales	0 = Either manager or board has not the most decisive influence on what to sell; 1 = either manager or board has the most decisive influence on what to sell
	11. Size of board	0 = Number of members of board lower than a given threshold (< 5); 1 = number of members of board greater than a given threshold (> 5)
	12. Selection of board members	0 = Board members appointed only by government; 1 = board members appointed by shareholders (either group of shareholder; all shareholder; other)
	13. Presence of independent directors	0 = No independent directors in the board; 1 = at least one independent director in the board

Accounting and disclosure, performance monitoring	14. Publication of annual reports	0 = Annual reports not publicly available; 1 = annual reports publicly available
	15. International Financial Reporting Standards (IFRSs)	0 = IFRSs not applied; 1 = compliance to IFRSs
	16a. External audits/existence of financial external audit	0 = No operational or financial audit; 1 = at least some form of external audit
	16b. External audits/existence of operational external audit	0 = No operational or financial audit; 1 = at least some form of external audit
	17. Independent audit of accounts	0 = No independent audit of accounts; 1 = independent audit of accounts
	18. Audit publication	0 = Audit not publicly available; 1 = audit not publicly available
	19. Remuneration for noncommercial activities	0 = No remuneration of noncommercial activities; 1 = remuneration of noncommercial activities
	20. Performance contracts	0 = No performance contracts; 1 = existence of performance contract
	21. Performance contracts with performance-based incentive systems	0 = Performance-based incentive systems; 1 = existence of performance-based incentive systems
	22. Penalties for poor performance	0 = No penalties for poor performance; 1 = penalties for poor performance
	23. Monitoring	0 = No periodic monitoring of performance; 1 = periodic monitoring of performance (at least semiannual)
	24. Third-party monitoring	0 = No monitoring of performance by third party (private sector auditor); 1 = monitoring of performance by third party

(continued next page)

Table A2.5 *(continued)*

Subindex	*Indicator*	*Definition*
Outsourcing	25. Billing and collection	0 = No billing and collection outsourcing; 1 = billing and collection outsourcing
	26. Meter reading	0 = No meter reading outsourcing; 1 = meter reading outsourcing
	27. Human resources (HR)	0 = No HR outsourcing; 1 = HR outsourcing
	28. Information technology (IT)	0 = No IT outsourcing; 1 = IT outsourcing
Labor market discipline	29. Restrictions to dismiss employees	0 = Restrictions to dismiss employees only within public service guidelines; 1 = restrictions to dismiss employees according to corporate law or contract
	30. Wages: compared with private sector	0 = Wages compared with public sector; 1 = wages compared with private sector (or between public and private sectors)
	31. Benefits: versus private sector	0 = Benefits compared with public sector; 1 = benefits compared with private sector (or between public and private sectors)
Capital market discipline	32. No exemption from taxation	0 = Exemption from taxation; 1 = no exemption from taxation
	33. Access to debt: versus private sector	0 = Access to debt below the market rate; 1 = access to debt equal or above the market rate
	34. No state guarantees	0 = At least one state guarantee; 1 = no state guarantee
	35. Public listing	0 = No public listing; 1 = public listing

Source: Banerjee, Wodon, and others 2008.
Note: SOE = state-owned enterprise.

Table A2.6 SOE Governance Index

Attributes of SOEs		*Ownership and shareholder quality*					*Managerial and board autonomy*							
Country	*Utility*	*1. Concentration of ownership*	*2. Corporatization*	*3. Limited liability*	*4. Rate of return policy*	*5. Dividend policy*	*6. Hiring*	*7. Laying off*	*8. Wages*	*9. Production*	*10. Sales*	*11. Size of board*	*12. Selection of board members*	*13. Presence of independent directors*
Benin	SONEB	1	1	0	0	0	1	1	1	1	1	1	0	0
Burkina Faso	ONEA	1	1	0	1	1	1	1	1	1	1	1	0	0
Cape Verde	ELECTRA	0	1	0	0	0	1	1	1	0	0	1	1	0
Chad	STEE	1	1	0	0	0	1	1	1	1	1	0	1	0
Congo, Dem. Rep.	REGIDESO	1	0	0	1	1	1	1	1	1	1	1	0	0
Côte d'Ivoire	SODECI	0	1	0		1	1	1	1	0	0	0		
Ethiopia	ADAMA	1	0	0	1	0	1	1	1	1	1	0	0	0
	AWSA	1	0	0	1	0	1	1	1	1	0	0	0	0
	Dire Dawa	1	0	0	1	0	0	0	0	1	1	1	0	0
Ghana	GWC	1	1	1	0	0	0	0	1	0	1	1	0	1
Kenya	KIWASCO	1	1	1	1	0	0	1	0	0	0	0	1	1
	MWSC	1	0	0	0	0	1	1	1	1	1	0	1	1
	NWASCO	1	1	0	1	0	1	1	1	1	1	0	1	1
Lesotho	WASA	1	1	0	1	0	1	1	1	1	1	1	0	1
Madagascar	JIRAMA	1	0	0	0	0	1	1	1	1	0	1	1	0
Malawi	BWB	1	1	0	1	1	0	0	1	1	1	0	0	0
	CRWB	1	1	0	1	1	1	1	1	1	1	0	0	0
	LWB	1	1	0	1	1	0	0	0	1	1	1	0	0
Mozambique	AdeM Beira	1	1	0	0	0	1	1	1	1	1		0	
	AdeM Maputo	1	0	0	1	1	1	1	1	1	1	1	1	0
	AdeM Nampula	1	1	0	0	0	1	1	1	1	1		0	
	AdeM Pemba	1	1	0	0	0	1	1	1	1	1		0	

(continued next page)

Table A2.6 SOE Governance Index *(continued)*

Attributes of SOEs		*Ownership and shareholder quality*					*Managerial and board autonomy*							
Country	*Utility*	*1. Concentration of ownership*	*2. Corporatization*	*3. Limited liability*	*4. Rate of return policy*	*5. Dividend policy*	*6. Hiring*	*7. Laying off*	*8. Wages*	*9. Production*	*10. Sales*	*11. Size of board*	*12. Selection of board members*	*13. Presence of independent directors*
	AdeM Quelimane	1	1	0	0	0	1	1	1	1	1		0	
Namibia	Oshakati Municipality	1			0	0	0	0	0		0			
	Walvis Bay Municipality	1			0	0	1	1	1	1	1			
	Windhoek Municipality	1			0	0	0	0	0	1	0			
Niger	SEEN	0			1	1	1	1	1	0	0	1	1	1
	SPEN	1	1	0	0	0	1	1	1	0	0	1	0	0
Nigeria	Borno	0	1	0	0	0	1	1	1	0	0		1	
	FCT	1	0	0	0	0	0	0	0	1	1			
	Kaduna	0	1	0	0	0	0	1	1	0	0	0	1	0
	Katsina	0	1	0	0	0	0	1	1	0	0	0	1	0
	Lagos	0	1	0	0	0	0	1	1	0	0		1	
	Plateau	0	1	0	0	0	0	1	1	0	0		1	
Rwanda	ELECTROGAZ	1	0	0	1	1	1	1	1	1	1	1	0	0
Senegal	ONAS	1	0	0	0	0	1	1	1	0	0	1		1
	SDE	0			1	1	1	0	1	0	0	0	1	0
South Africa	Cape Town Metro	1	0	0	0	0	0	0	1	0	0			

	Drakenstein Municipality	1	0	0	0	0	0	0	1	0	0			
	eThekwini Metro (Durban)	1	0	0	0	0	0	0	1	0	0			
	Joburg	1	1	1	0	0	0	0	1	0	0	1	0	
Sudan	Khartoum Water Corporation	0	1	0	1	0	1	0	1	1	1	0	0	0
	South Darfur Water Corporation	0	1	0	1	1	1	1	1	1	1	0	0	1
	Upper Nile Water Corporation	0	0	0	0	0	0	0	0	1	1	1	1	0
Tanzania	DAWASCO	1	1	0	1	0	1	1	1	1	1	1	0	1
	DUWS	1	1	0	0	0	1	1	1	1	0	0	0	1
	MWSA	1	0	0	1	0	1	1	1	1	1	0	0	0
Uganda	SONEB	1	1	0	1	0	1	1	1	1	1	0	0	1
Zambia	LWSC	1	1	1	1	1	1	1	1	1	1	1	0	1
	NWSC	1	0	0	1	1	1	1	1	1	1	0	1	1
	SWSC	1	1	1		1	0	0	1	0	0	0	1	1
	Subindex		Ownership and shareholder quality							Managerial and board autonomy				
	% of utilities sharing attribute	76	65	11	45	27	65	71	86	64	57	49	40	40

(continued next page)

Table A2.6 SOE Governance Index *(continued)*

Attributes of SOEs		*Accounting and disclosure, performance monitoring*											
Country	*Utility*	*14. Publication of annual reports*	*15. IFRSs*	*16a. External audits/ existence of financial external audit*	*16b. External audits/ existence of operational external audit*	*17. Independent audit of accounts*	*18. Audit publication*	*19. Remuneration for noncommercial activities*	*20. Performance contracts*	*21. Performance contracts with performance-based incentive systems*	*22. Penalties for poor performance*	*23. Monitoring*	*24. Third-party monitoring*
Benin	SONEB	1	1	1	1	1	1	0	0	0	0	1	1
Burkina Faso	ONEA	1	1	1	1	1	0	0	1	0	1	1	0
Cape Verde	ELECTRA	1	0	1	1	1	1	0	0	0	0	1	0
Chad	STEE	0	0	1	1	1	0	0	1	0	1	0	1
Congo, Dem. Rep.	REGIDESO	1	1	1	0	1	1	1	1	0	0	0	0
Côte d'Ivoire	SODECI	0	1	1				1	1	1	1	0	1
Ethiopia	ADAMA	0	0	1	0	0		0	0	1	1	1	4
	AWSA	0	1	1	1	1	1	1	0	1	1	1	0
	Dire Dawa	0	0	0	0	0		0	0	0	0	1	1
Ghana	GWC	1	1	1		1	1	0	1	0	1	1	0
Kenya	KIWASCO	1	1	1	1	1	1	0	1	1	1	1	1
	MWSC	0	0	1	1	1	1	0	0	0	0	1	1
	NWASCO	1	1	1	1	1	1	0	0	0	0	1	1
Lesotho	WASA	1	1	1	1	1	1	0	0	0		1	0
Madagascar	JIRAMA	0	1	1	0	0		1	0	0	0	0	1
Malawi	BWB	1	1	1	1	1	1	0	1	1	1	1	1
	CRWB	1	0	1	0	1	1	0	0	0	1	1	1
	LWB	1	1	1	0	1	1	0	0	1	1	1	1
Mozambique	AdeM Beira	1	1	1	1	1	1	0	0	1	0	1	1
	AdeM Maputo	1	0	1	1	1	0	1	1	0	0	0	1

	AdeM Nampula	1	1	1	1	1	1	0	0	1	0	1	1
	AdeM Pemba	1	1	1	1	1	1	0	0	1	0	1	1
	AdeM Quelimane	1	1	1	1	1	1	0	0	1	0	1	1
Namibia	Oshakati Municipality	0	0	1	0	1	1		0	0	0	0	1
	Walvis Bay Municipality	1	0	1	0	1	1	0	1	0	0		1
	Windhoek Municipality	1	0	1	1	1	1	0	0	1	1	1	1
Niger	SEEN	1	1	1	1	1	0	0	1	1	0	0	0
	SPEN	1	1	1	1	1	0	0	1	1	0	0	1
Nigeria	Borno	0	1	1	0	1	0	0	0	0	0	0	1
	FCT	1	1	1	0	1	0	0	0	0	0	0	1
	Kaduna	0	1	1	0	1	0	0	0	0	1	1	1
	Katsina	0	1	1	0	1	0	0	0	0	0	0	1
	Lagos	0	1	1	0	1	0	0	0	0	0	0	1
	Plateau	0	1	1	0	1	0	0	0	0	0	0	1
Rwanda	ELECTROGAZ	0	0	1	1	0	0	0	0	0	0	0	1
Senegal	ONAS	0	1	1	1	1	1	0	1	0	1		0
	SDE	0	1	1	1	1	0	1	1	1	1	1	1
South Africa	Cape Town Metro	1	0	1	0	1	1	1	1	1	0	0	0
	Drakenstein Municipality	1	0	1	0	1	1	1	1	1	0	0	0
	eThekwini Metro (Durban)	1	0	1	0	1	1	1	1	1	0	0	0
	Joburg	1	1	1	0	1	1	1	1	1		1	1
Sudan	Khartoum Water Corporation	1	0	1	0	1	0	1	1	1	0	0	0

(continued next page)

Table A2.6 SOE Governance Index *(continued)*

Attributes of SOEs		*Accounting and disclosure, performance monitoring*											
Country	*Utility*	*14. Publication of annual reports*	*15. IFRSs*	*16a. External audits/ existence of financial external audit*	*16b. External audits/ existence of operational external audit*	*17. Independent audit of accounts*	*18. Audit publication*	*19. Remuneration for noncommercial activities*	*20. Performance contracts*	*21. Performance contracts with performance-based incentive systems*	*22. Penalties for poor performance*	*23. Monitoring*	*24. Third-party monitoring*
	South Darfur Water Corporation	0	0	1	0	0		1	0	1	0	0	0
	Upper Nile Water Corporation	0	0	0	0	0		0	0	0	0	0	0
Tanzania	DAWASCO	1	1	1	1	1	1	1	1	1	1	1	0
	DUWS	1	1	1	1	1	0	1	1	1	1	1	1
	MWSA	1	1	1	1	1	1	1	1	1	1	0	1
Uganda	SONEB	1	1	1	1	1	1	1	1	1	1	1	0
Zambia	LWSC	1	1	1	1	1	1	0	1	0	0	1	1
	NWSC	1	1	1	1	1	0	0	1	1	0	1	1
	SWSC	1	1	1	1	1	1	0	0	1	1	1	0
	Subindex	Accounting and disclosure, performance monitoring											
	% of utilities sharing attribute	65	67	96	57	88	64	32	49	51	39	57	65

Table A2.6 SOE Governance Index *(continued)*

Attributes of SOEs		*Outsourcing*				*Labor market discipline*			*Capital market discipline*				
Country	Utility	*25. Billing and collection*	*26. Meter reading*	*27. Human resources*	*28. Information technology*	*29. Restrictions to dismiss employees*	*30. Wages: compared with private sectror*	*31. Benefits: versus private sector*	*32. No exemption from taxation*	*33. Access to debt: versus private sector*	*34. No state guarantees*	*35. Public listing*	*SOE governance index*
Benin	SONEB	0	0	0	0	1	1	1	0	1	1	0	55
Burkina Faso	ONEA	0	0	0	0	1	1	1	1	0	0	0	58
Cape Verde	ELECTRA	1	0	0	0	0	1	1	0	0	0	0	37
Chad	STEE	0	0	0	0	0	1	1	0		1	0	44
Congo, Dem. Rep.	REGIDESO					0	1	1	0	0	0	0	52
Côte d'Ivoire	SODECI	0	0	0	0	1	1	1	1			1	63
Ethiopia	ADAMA					0	0	0	0	1	1	0	45
	AWSA					1	0	0	0	1	1	0	50
	Dire Dawa					0	0	0	0	1	1	0	29
Ghana	GWC	0	0	0	0	0	1	1	0	0	0	0	42
Kenya	KIWASCO	0	0	0	0		1	1	0	0	1	0	56
	MWSC	0	0	0	0	0	1	1	0	0	0	0	37
	NWASCO	0	0	0	0		1	1	0	0	1	0	57
Lesotho	WASA	0	0	0	0	1	1	1	1	0	0	0	56
Madagascar	JIRAMA	0	0	1	0	0	1	1	1	1	0	0	46
Malawi	BWB	0	0	0	0	0	1	1	1	1	0	0	54
	CRWB					0	1	1	0	0	0	0	54
	LWB	0	0	0	0	1	1	1	1	1	0	0	57

(continued next page)

Table A2.6 SOE Governance Index *(continued)*

Attributes of SOEs		*Outsourcing*				*Labor market discipline*			*Capital market discipline*				
Country	*Utility*	*25. Billing and collection*	*26. Meter reading*	*27. Human resources*	*28. Information technology*	*29. Restrictions to dismiss employees*	*30. Wages: compared with private sectror*	*31. Benefits: versus private sector*	*32. No exemption from taxation*	*33. Access to debt: versus private sector*	*34. No state guarantees*	*35. Public listing*	*SOE governance index*
Mozambique	AdeM Beira	1	1	1	1	0	1	1	1	1	0	0	69
	AdeM Maputo	0	0	0	1	1	1	1	1	1	1	0	68
	AdeM Nampula	1	1	1	1	0	1	1	1	1	0	0	69
	AdeM Pemba	1	1	1	1	0	1	1	1	1	0	0	69
	AdeM Quelimane	1	1	1	1	0	1	1	1	1	0	0	69
Namibia	Oshakati Municipality	0	0	0	0	0	0	0			1	0	20
	Walvis Bay Municipality	0	0	0	1	0	0	0	0	1	1	0	44
	Windhoek Municipality	0	0	0	0	0	0	1	1	0	0	0	31
Niger	SEEN	0	0	0	1	0	1	1	1	1	1	0	61
	SPEN	0	0	0	1	0	1	1	1	0	0	0	46
Nigeria	Borno	0	0	0	0	0	0	1	1	1	0	0	34
	FCT					0	0	0	1	1	1	0	39
	Kaduna	1	0	0	0	0	0	1	1	1	0	0	33
	Katsina	0	0	0	0	0	0	1	1	1	0	0	29
	Lagos	1	0	0	0	0	1	1	1	1	0	0	41
	Plateau	0	0	0	0	0	0	1	1	1	0	0	31

Rwanda	ELECTROGAZ	0	0	0	1	0	1	0	1	1	1	0	50
Senegal	ONAS	0	0	0	0		1	1	1	0	1	0	51
	SDE	0	0	0	0	1	1	1	1	1	1	0	60
South Africa	Cape Town Metro					0	0	0	1	1	1	0	35
	Drakenstein Municipality					0	0	0	1	1	1	0	35
	eThekwini Metro (Durban)					0	0	0	1	1	1	0	35
	Joburg	1	1	0	1	0	1	1	1	1	1	0	66
Sudan	Khartoum Water Corporation	1	1	1	1	0	1	1	1	1	0	0	59
	South Darfur Water Corporation					0	1	1	1	1	0	0	56
	Upper Nile Water Corporation					0	0	0	1		0	0	17
Tanzania	DAWASCO	0	0	1	0	0	1	0	0	1	0	0	54
	DUWS	0	0	0	0	0	1	1	0	1	1	0	52
	MWSA	0	0	0	0	0	0	0	0	1	0	0	37
Uganda	SONEB	0	0	1	0	1	0	0	1	0	0	0	52
Zambia	LWSC	0	0	0	0	1	1	1	1	1	1	0	73
	NWSC					1	1	1	1	1	0	0	75
	SWSC	0	0	0	0	1	1	1		0	0	0	52
	Subindex	Outsourcing				Labor market discipline				Capital market discipline			
	% of utilities sharing attribute	23	15	21	28	25	67	73	67	70	42	2	

Source: Banerjee, Wodon, and others 2008.
Note: IFRSs = International Financial Reporting Standards; SOE = state-owned enterprise.

Table A2.7 Specification of Rural Water Reform Index

	Specification	*Definition*
Rural water agency	Is there a specialized rural water agency?	Yes = 1, no = 0
Rural water policy	Is there a specific policy or strategy for the rural water sector?	Yes = 1; no = 0
Map of rural water points	Is there a current map of the rural water points?	Yes = 1; no = 0
Dedicated budget/fund	Is there funding available to specifically support rural water services?	Yes = 1; no = 0
Cost-recovery policy	Is there a cost-recovery policy for rural water services?	Yes = 1; no = 0

Source: Banerjee, Wodon, and others 2008.

Table A2.8 Rural Water Reform Index

	Rural water agency	*Rural water policy*	*Map of rural water points*	*Dedicated budget/ fund*	*Cost-recovery policy*	*Rural Water Reform Index (%)*
Benin	1	1	1	0	1	67
Burkina Faso	1	1	1	1	1	83
Cape Verde	0	1	1	0	0	33
Chad	0	1	0	1	1	50
Congo, Dem. Rep.	1	0	0	1	0	33
Côte d'Ivoire	1	1	1	1	1	83
Ethiopia	0	1	0	1	1	50
Ghana	1	1	0	1	1	67
Kenya	0	0	0	1	1	33
Lesotho	1	1	0	1	0	50
Madagascar	0	1	1	1	1	67
Malawi	0	1	0	1	0	33
Mozambique	1	1	0	1	1	67
Namibia	1	1	0	1	1	67
Niger	0	1	0	0	0	17
Nigeria	1	1	0	1	1	67
Rwanda	0	1	0	1	1	50
Senegal	1	1	0	1	1	67
South Africa	0	0	0	1	1	33
Sudan	0	1	0	1	1	50
Tanzania	0	1	1	1	1	67
Uganda	1	1	1	1	1	83
Zambia	0	1	0	1	0	33
% of countries sharing attribute	46	83	29	83	71	

Source: Banerjee, Wodon, and others 2008.

Table A2.9 Specification of On-Site Sanitation Index

Indicator	*Definition*
Existence of an accepted definition of sanitation	1 = Existence of accepted definition; 0 = No accepted definition
Existence of sanitation policy	1 = Existence of policy/strategy; 0 = No policy/strategy
Existence of hygiene promotion program	1 = Existence of hygiene promotion program by the government; 0 = No hygiene promotion program by the government
Households responsible for investment finance	1 = Households responsible for financing sanitation investments; 0 = Otherwise
Government/private sector/utility/NGO/CBO responsible for technical assistance	1 = Either municipal government/private sector/water utility, NGO/CBO responsible for technical assistance; 0 = Otherwise
Government/private sector/utility responsible for desludging	1 = Either municipal government/private sector/water utility responsible for desludging; 0 = Otherwise
Government responsible for regulation	1 = Either central/local/municipal government responsible for regulation; 0 = Otherwise
Existence of cost-recovery requirement for on-site sanitation	1 = Requirement for cost recovery; 0 = No requirement for cost recovery

Source: Morella, Foster, and Banerjee 2008.
Note: CBO = community-based organization; NGO = nongovernmental organization.

Table A2.10 On-Site Sanitation Index

Country	*Existence of an accepted definition of sanitation*	*Existence of sanitation policy*	*Existence of hygiene promotion program*	*Involvement of utilities in on-site sanitation*	*Existence of a specific fund for sanitation*	*Existence of cost-recovery requirement for on-site sanitation*	*On-site sanitation index (%)*
Zambia	0	0	0	0	0	0	0
Nigeria	1	0	0	0	0		20
Congo, Dem. Rep.	1	0	0	0	1	0	33
Lesotho	0	1	1	0	0	0	33
Niger	1	0	0	1	0	0	33
Benin	1	0	1	1	0	0	50
Ghana	1	1		0	0		50
Malawi	1	0	1	0	0	1	50
Mozambique	1	1	1	0	0	0	50
Rwanda	1	1	1	0	0	0	50
Sudan	1	0	1	1	0	0	50

Ethiopia	1	0	1	1	1	0	67
Senegal	1	1	1	1	0	0	67
Uganda	1	1	1	1	0	0	67
Namibia	1	1	1	1	0		80
Cape Verde	1	1	1	1	0	1	83
Côte d'Ivoire	1	1	1	0	1	1	83
Tanzania	1	1	1	1	1	0	83
Burkina Faso	1	1	1	1	1	1	100
Chad	1	1	1				100
Kenya	1	1	1	1	1	1	100
Madagascar	1	1	1	1	1	1	100
South Africa	1	1	1	1	1	1	100
% of countries sharing attribute	91	65	82	59	36	37	

Source: Morella, Foster, and Banerjee 2008.

Reference

Banerjee, S., Q. Wodon, A. Diallo, T. Pushak, H. Uddin, C. Tsimpo, and V. Foster. 2008. "Access, Affordability and Alternatives: Modern Infrastructure Services in Sub-Saharan Africa." AICD Background Paper 2, Africa Infrastructure Country Diagnostic, World Bank, Washington, D.C.

Morella, E., V. Foster, and S. Banerjee. 2008. "Climbing the Ladder: The State of Sanitation in Sub-Saharan Africa." AICD Background Paper 13. World Bank, Washington, DC.

APPENDIX 3

Performance Indicators of Selected Water Utilities

Table A3.1 Access to Utility Water

		Access, private residential water connection (% of population)						
Country	*Utility*	*1995–99*	*2000*	*2001*	*2002*	*2003*	*2004*	*2005*
Benin	SONEB						24.6	25.0
Botswana	DWA			35.0				
	WUC							
Burkina Faso	ONEA	15.4	16.3	21.9	22.5	22.8	23.2	24.8
Cameroon	SNEC							
Cape Verde	ELECTRA		34.3	36.7	37.9	42.2	45.2	46.3
Chad	STEE							
Congo, Dem. Rep.	REGIDESO							19.0
Congo, Rep.	SDNE						22.8	24.2
Côte d'Ivoire	SODECI	28.5	30.2	29.7	29.4	30.1	30.2	29.9
Ethiopia	ADAMA					28.2	30.9	32.3
	AWSA							
	Dire Dawa						17.8	18.9
Gabon	SEEG							
Ghana	GWC			9.0	9.1	8.5	9.0	8.8
Kenya	KIWASCO						11.4	10.0
	MWSC			32.5	36.3	33.7	34.2	34.5
	NWASCO						37.4	50.9
Lesotho	WASA							33.7
Liberia	LWSR						2.7	3.0
Madagascar	JIRAMA	11.6	11.4	11.7	11.7	12.2	12.6	12.7
Malawi	BWB	23.0	22.9	22.5	22.4	25.0	24.0	25.3
	CRWB		17.8	18.0	17.6	17.9	18.8	20.4
	LWB					33.2	32.1	35.6

Mali	EDM		18.6	20.1	24.7	25.6	26.3	27.2
Mauritania	MSNE						59.1	63.0
Mozambique	AdeM Beira				11.5	11.6	11.4	10.7
	Adem Maputo				23.5	23.8	25.2	25.5
	Adem Nampula				7.3	8.1	7.7	8.1
	AdeM Pemba				14.5	14.6	15.1	15.8
	AdeM Quelimane				4.9	4.8	4.2	4.7
Namibia	Oshakati Municipality							49.3
	Walvis Bay Municipality	100.0	100.0	100.0	100.0	100.0	100.0	100.0
	Windhoek Municipality		79.4	78.1	76.6	74.9	74.3	73.1
Niger	SPEN/SEEN							
Nigeria	Borno							
	FCT							10.0
	Kaduna		50.0	51.4	50.8	50.8	50.8	48.2
	Katsina							
	Lagos				3.0	3.0	2.9	3.0
	Plateau							
Rwanda	ELECTROGAZ	11.2	11.2	11.2	11.2	11.2	11.2	11.2
Senegal	SDE		56.9	57.9	60.8	61.5	63.7	65.8
Seychelles	PUC						96.5	96.9
South Africa	Cape Town Metro			85.6	86.6	89.0	90.6	92.4
	Drakenstein Municipality			87.0	87.9	88.7	89.5	90.3
	eThekwini Metro (Durban)			94.6	94.9	95.2	95.5	90.1
	Joburg			85.2	86.1	86.9	87.6	88.4
Sudan	Khartoum Water Corporation							26.8
	South Darfur Water Corporation							10.5
	Upper Nile Water Corporation							38.4

(continued next page)

Table A3.1 *(continued)*

Country	*Utility*	*Access, private residential water connection (% of population)*						
		1995–99	*2000*	*2001*	*2002*	*2003*	*2004*	*2005*
Tanzania	Arusha							
	Babati							
	Bukoba							
	DAWASCO							
	DUWS							33.9
	Iringa							
	Kigoma							
	Lindi							
	Mbeya							
	Morogoro							
	Moshi							
	Mtwara							
	Musoma							
	MWSA					16.5	21.1	20.1
	Shinyanga							
	Singida							
	Songea							
	Sumbawanga							
	Tabora							
	Tanga							
Togo	TdE		38.9	39.9	40.9	40.7	40.5	
Uganda	NWSC		15.1	16.0	17.1	21.4	22.8	27.1
Zambia	AHC-MMS							

CHWSC							
CWSC							
KWSC							
LukangaWSC							
LWSC	16.3	22.1	20.5	24.1	22.3	18.5	23.4
MulongaWSC							
NorthWesternWSC							
NWSC						55.1	60.1
SWSC			36.5	36.1	40.6	53.2	58.9
WesternWSC							
Country typology							
Resourch-rich							30.4
Middle-income							76.0
Fragile states							17.3
Nonfragile, low-income							25.5
Level of water scarcity							
High							37.4
Low							36.1
Size of the utility							
Small							35.5
Large							37.5
Overall							36.8

Source: Banerjee, Skilling, and others 2008.

Table A3.2 Distribution Infrastructure

Country	Utility	Kilometers of water mains per 1,000 population (km/1,000 capita)							Kilometers of water mains per 1,000 water connections (km/1,000 connections)						
		1995–99	2000	2001	2002	2003	2004	2005	1995–99	2000	2001	2002	2003	2004	2005
Benin	SONEB						1.4	1.4							
Botswana	DWA														
	WUC														
Burkina Faso	ONEA	0.9	0.9	1.1	1.1	1.1	1.2	1.2	36.2	36.1	32.1	32.6	32.5	33.5	32.7
Cameroon	SNEC														
Cape Verde	ELECTRA		1.6	1.6	1.5	1.5	1.4	1.4							
Chad	STEE														
Congo, Dem. Rep.	REDIGESO							0.7							50.1
Congo, Rep.	SDNE														
Côte d'Ivoire	SODECI	1.5	1.5	1.4	1.4	1.4	1.4	1.3							21.9
Ethiopia	ADAMA							0.7							9.6
	AWSA	0.7	0.7	0.7	0.7	0.7	0.7	0.7							8.4
	Dire Dawa														
Gabon	SEEG	2.5	2.4	2.5	2.6	2.5	2.4	2.3	18.1	17.4	17.9	18.7	18.0	17.5	16.8
Ghana	GWC			0.3	0.4	0.4	0.4	0.5							
Kenya	KIWASCO						0.2	0.2						13.7	14.7
	MWSC														
	NWASCO						1.0	1.0						11.3	10.6
Lesotho	WASA														
Liberia	LWSR						0.1	0.1						25.0	22.5
Madagascar	JIRAMA	0.6	0.6	0.6	0.6	0.6	0.6	0.6	24.0	24.3	23.7	23.7	22.9	22.3	22.1
Malawi	BWB	1.5	1.4	1.4	1.3	1.3	1.3	1.2	24.7	24.3	24.0	23.3	23.8	24.3	22.6
	CRWB		3.7	3.6	3.6	4.8	5.1	5.6		115.9	112.9	113.7	151.6	155.8	160.5
	LWB	1.8	1.8	1.7	1.7	1.7	1.6	1.6						45.7	43.8
Mali	EDM														
Mauritania	MSNE														
Mozambique	AdeM Beira				0.1	0.1	0.1	0.1				4.0	3.8	3.8	3.9
	Adem Maputo											0.5	0.5	0.4	0.4
	Adem Nampula				0.2	0.2	0.2	0.2				11.2	10.1	11.2	10.9

	AdeM Pemba				0.3	0.3	0.3	0.3				10.9	10.5	9.8	9.1
	AdeM Quelimane				0.2	0.2	0.2	0.2				19.6	19.0	20.8	17.6
Namibia	Oshakati Municipality							0.4							
	Walvis Bay Municipality	7.0	6.7	6.4	6.2	6.0	5.8	5.5	36.8	35.6	30.3	29.6	28.2	28.3	27.1
	Windhoek Municipality							4.5							29.9
Niger	SPEN/SEEN	1.0	1.0	1.0	1.0	1.0	1.1	1.1			30.8	30.6	28.3	29.7	29.8
Nigeria	Borno		0.2	0.2	0.2	0.2				7.3	7.3	7.2	6.5		
	FCT														
	Kaduna			0.7	0.7	0.7	0.7	0.7						23.5	24.3
	Katsina				0.3	0.2	0.2	0.2						16.6	18.0
	Lagos				0.2	0.2	0.1	0.1				16.5	16.3	16.0	14.5
	Plateau					1.3	1.1	1.1					61.9	62.8	67.9
Rwanda	ELECTROGAZ	1.3	1.3	1.4	1.2	1.2	1.1	1.2							60.4
Senegal	SDE		1.5	1.5	1.5	1.5	1.5	1.5		24.3	23.6	22.8	22.3	21.8	20.8
Seychelles	PUC						3.9	3.9						14.7	14.3
South Africa	Cape Town Metro														
	Drakenstein Municipality			3.0	3.0	2.9	2.8	2.8			13.4	13.0	12.7	12.3	12.0
	eThekwini Metro (Durban)			4.0	3.9	3.9	3.8	3.7						17.6	17.2
	Joburg														
Sudan	Khartoum Water Corporation							0.4							10.6
	South Darfur Water Corporation							0.1							12.1
	Upper Nile Water Corporation							0.2							3.2

(continued next page)

Table A3.2 *(continued)*

Country	Utility	*Kilometers of water mains per 1,000 population (km/1,000 capita)*							*Kilometers of water mains per 1,000 water connections (km/1,000 connections)*						
		1995–99	*2000*	*2001*	*2002*	*2003*	*2004*	*2005*	*1995–99*	*2000*	*2001*	*2002*	*2003*	*2004*	*2005*
Tanzania	Arusha														10.9
	Babati														17.3
	Bukoba														17.5
	DAWASCO														
	DUWS							0.7							4.7
	Iringa														16.1
	Kigoma						1.8	1.2						25.2	25.7
	Lindi														43.8
	Mbeya														16.7
	Morogoro														15.8
	Moshi														20.5
	Mtwara														38.6
	Musoma														18.0
	MWSA					0.6	0.6	0.6					15.8	15.1	16.1
	Shinyanga														30.2
	Singida														25.9
	Songea														29.7
	Sumbawanga														35.9
	Tabora														25.6
	Tanga														22.4

Togo	TdE		1.9	1.8	1.8	1.8	1.8			40.7	41.1	39.9	39.6	39.1	
Uganda	NWSC		0.9	0.8	0.9	1.0	1.2	1.3	28.3	27.2	25.1	23.9	24.5	26.4	22.6
Zambia	AHC-MMS														
	CHWSC														
	CWSC														
	KWSC														
	LukangaWSC														
	LWSC	1.5	1.9	1.9	2.1	1.8	1.4	1.5			67.8	62.6	58.7	54.3	46.2
	MulongaWSC														
	NorthWestern WSC														
	NWSC						1.7	1.7						24.8	23.1
	SWSC					1.4	1.4	1.4						18.7	17.0
	WesternWSC														
Country typology															
Resourch-rich								0.9							23.0
Middle-income								3.2							20.1
Fragile states								0.7							31.5
Nonfragile, low-income								1.0							25.2
Level of water scarcity															
High								1.2							29.6
Low								1.4							22.1
Size of the utility															
Small								1.4							25.9
Large								1.2							19.5
Overall								1.3							24.7

(continued next page)

Table A3.2 *(continued)*

Country	Utility	Metering ratio (%)							Nonrevenue water (%)						
		1995–99	*2000*	*2001*	*2002*	*2003*	*2004*	*2005*	*1995–99*	*2000*	*2001*	*2002*	*2003*	*2004*	*2005*
Benin	SONEB													25.6	23.8
Botswana	DWA								23.9	21.4	23.4	24.4	24.4	26.1	27.9
	WUC											14.1			12.6
Burkina Faso	ONEA	97.4	97.5	97.9	97.9	98.0	98.1	98.2	19.5	17.1	15.9	14.0	15.2	17.0	18.3
Cameroon	SNEC														37.0
Cape Verde	ELECTRA									26.4	23.5	28.4	29.7	30.3	31.2
Chad	STEE														
Congo, Dem. Rep.	REDIGESO							28.6	45.2	38.8	36.4	38.5	44.2	37.6	40.7
Congo, Rep.	SDNE		18.6	18.7	17.9	19.3	19.5	21.0		27.7	27.7	27.8	27.7	27.8	27.7
Côte d'Ivoire	SODECI							100.0	14.2	17.7	17.5	18.8	20.2	21.7	21.7
Ethiopia	ADAMA						90.2	90.1							42.7
	AWSA								24.0	32.2	34.3	30.0	26.9	33.6	36.8
	DIRE DAWA														21.6
Gabon	SEEG								13.3	15.8	14.9	15.5	16.7	16.3	17.6
Ghana	GWC										52.0	58.0	57.0	53.0	
Kenya	KIWASCO						48.6	58.2						68.3	71.4
	MWSC										52.6	41.8	40.7	34.8	38.3
	NWASCO													40.0	37.8
Lesotho	WASA												28.1	27.9	27.8
Liberia	LWSR						52.5	65.1						7.0	28.8
Madagascar	JIRAMA	97.4	97.2	97.1	97.1	97.1	97.1	97.1	31.2	32.5	32.4	35.9	36.0	32.8	33.5
Malawi	BWB					42.7	32.9	22.6	34.3	35.6	34.0	45.8	43.6	47.0	51.1
	CRWB									28.6	26.2	26.3	28.5	18.7	16.7
	LWB							98.1	39.6	32.9	39.2	16.8	17.1	16.6	22.1
Mali	EDM				96.0	96.0	96.0	96.0				36.7	32.1	29.8	26.7
Mauritania	MSNE						100.0	99.9						30.4	32.0
Mozambique	AdeM Beira				68.0	99.2	98.5	99.9				52.1	54.2	53.1	60.1
	Adem Maputo				100.3	99.8	99.3	98.2				57.8	62.4	54.4	62.1
	Adem Nampula				100.0	100.0	99.8	100.0				27.2	43.2	45.1	44.1
	AdeM Pemba				100.8	102.6	97.7	99.1				50.9	52.9	51.2	45.0

	AdeM Quelimane				108.1	100.7	113.7	100.0				26.5	26.3	36.8	35.2
Namibia	Oshakati Municipality									12.4	28.9	24.5	34.7	28.2	20.8
	Walvis Bay Municipality	100.0	100.0	100.0	100.0	100.0	100.0	100.0	16.4	25.8	27.1	18.1	11.5	10.7	16.0
	Windhoek Municipality									19.8	18.1	18.4	20.2	10.5	13.8
Niger	SPEN/SEEN			96.3	96.2	96.9	97.1	96.8	15.8	20.9	22.6	17.2	17.4	16.9	18.8
Nigeria	Borno														
	FCT							23.6							80.0
	Kaduna						7.7	16.1		39.1	38.3	51.1	68.4	58.0	21.2
	Katsina						3.2	6.5				30.0	29.0	56.5	14.4
	Lagos											67.1	66.7	60.4	56.5
	Plateau					5.8	7.2	23.6				27.6	33.2	33.3	23.5
Rwanda	ELECTROGAZ							98.7	44.6	54.2	48.9	44.6	50.6	43.8	38.3
Senegal	SDE		111.6	116.2	112.9	115.9	116.6	117.3		25.6	22.3	21.5	20.1	19.9	20.1
Seychelles	PUC						46.1	45.0						16.7	20.3
South Africa	Cape Town Metro							60.3			10.0	20.2	36.5	16.4	18.0
	Drakenstein Municipality							60.7			12.9	12.9	12.3	14.3	11.6
	eThekwini Metro (Durban)						57.1	66.4			30.1	30.9	31.2	29.1	32.1
	Joburg							52.4			39.4	43.7	39.3	32.8	30.9
Sudan	Khartoum Water Corporation														40.0
	South Darfur Water Corporation														48.9
	Upper Nile Water Corporation														29.0
Tanzania	Arusha						90.1	100.0						34.0	34.6

(continued next page)

Table A3.2 *(continued)*

Country	Utility	Metering ratio (%)							Nonrevenue water (%)						
		1995–99	2000	2001	2002	2003	2004	2005	1995–99	2000	2001	2002	2003	2004	2005
	Babati							22.3							50.6
	Bukoba						63.9	62.0						60.0	60.0
	DAWASCO														
	DUWS							27.9						31.0	31.0
	Iringa						58.5	74.4						54.0	53.0
	Kigoma						36.1	34.8						40.0	49.0
	Lindi						11.1	18.4						86.0	75.0
	Mbeya						35.5	38.7						37.0	43.0
	Morogoro						64.9	91.8						39.0	37.5
	Moshi						100.0	82.8						60.0	33.0
	Mtwara						66.8	74.7						52.0	43.0
	Musoma						23.7	42.2						66.0	63.0
	MWSA					104.5	100.0	100.0					57.0	50.0	48.9
	Shinyanga						22.8	45.9						46.0	39.0
	Singida						33.8	36.9						56.0	49.8
	Songea						13.3	32.9						31.0	34.0
	Sumbawanga						33.8	38.4						50.0	48.0
	Tabora						59.4	68.7						28.0	28.0
	Tanga						100.0	99.5						34.0	34.0
Togo	TdE		100.0	100.0	100.0	100.0	100.0			28.4	35.4	26.5	24.3	28.0	
Uganda	NWSC	79.2	83.1	84.3	89.1	91.9	93.6	94.5		43.5	42.6	40.4	39.2	38.2	34.5
Zambia	AHC-MMS							15.0							32.0

CHWSC										60.0
CWSC					98.0					29.0
KWSC					7.0					57.0
LukangaWSC										
LWSC	32.6	33.6	38.6	38.1	33.3	58.7	57.8	59.5	55.7	56.0
MulongaWSC					16.0					61.0
NorthWestern WSC					86.0					45.0
NWSC						41.6	55.0	50.0	36.6	36.8
SWSC					73.0	51.8	49.4	50.5	56.0	56.0
WesternWSC					17.0					44.0
Country typology										
Resourch-rich					33.5					41.5
Middle-income					64.1					21.9
Fragile states					64.5					30.4
Nonfragile, low-income					73.8					40.1
Level of water scarcity										
High					60.5					33.3
Low					64.4					39.6
Size of the utility										
Small					61.2					39.4
Large					68.5					30.7
Overall					63.3					37.3

Source: Banerjee, Skilling, and others 2008.

Table A3.3 Treatment

Country	*Utility*	*Samples passing chlorine test (%)*						
		1995–99	*2000*	*2001*	*2002*	*2003*	*2004*	*2005*
Benin	SONEB							
Botswana	DWA							
	WUC							
Burkina Faso	ONEA			99.0	99.0	99.0	99.0	99.0
Cameroon	SNEC							
Cape Verde	ELECTRA							
Chad	STEE							
Congo, Dem. Rep.	REDIGESO		36.0	39.0	36.0	46.0	32.0	36.0
Congo, Rep.	SDNE							68.0
Côte d'Ivoire	SODECI	90.0	90.0	90.0	90.0	90.0	90.0	90.0
Ethiopia	ADAMA							100.0
	AWSA							
	DIRE DAWA							
Gabon	SEEG							
Ghana	GWC					85.5	91.1	80.5
Kenya	KIWASCO						99.0	99.0
	MWSC							
	NWASCO						84.0	84.0
Lesotho	WASA							
Liberia	LWSR							
Madagascar	JIRAMA							
Malawi	BWB	99.9	99.8	97.8	99.8	99.9	99.9	99.8
	CRWB		90.0	91.0	89.0	87.0	90.0	93.0

	LWB	100.0	100.0	100.0	100.0	100.0	100.0	100.0
Mali	EDM					95.6	97.1	0.0
Mauritania	MSNE							
Mozambique	AdeM Beira				100.0	100.0	100.0	83.0
	Adem Maputo				100.0	100.0	83.5	99.1
	Adem Nampula				100.0	100.0	62.6	76.6
	AdeM Pemba				71.1	71.0	100.0	100.0
	AdeM Quelimane				100.0	100.0	100.0	100.0
Namibia	Oshakati Municipality				95.0	95.0	95.0	95.0
	Walvis Bay Municipality	99.0	99.0	99.0	99.0	99.0	99.0	99.0
	Windhoek Municipality							99.9
Niger	SPEN/SEEN							
Nigeria	Borno							
	FCT							100.0
	Kaduna							50.0
	Katsina							
	Lagos							
	Plateau							
Rwanda	ELECTROGAZ	100.0	100.0	100.0	100.0	100.0	100.0	100.0
Senegal	SDE			98.6	96.6	99.3	98.6	95.1
Seychelles	PUC							
South Africa	Cape Town Metro							
	Drakenstein Municipality							
	eThekwini Metro (Durban)							
	Joburg							
Sudan	Khartoum Water Corporation							100.0
	South Darfur Water Corporation							70.0
	Upper Nile Water Corporation							40.0

(continued next page)

Table A3.3 *(continued)*

		Samples passing chlorine test (%)						
Country	*Utility*	*1995–99*	*2000*	*2001*	*2002*	*2003*	*2004*	*2005*
Tanzania	Arusha							
	Babati							
	Bukoba							
	DAWASCO							
	DUWS							
	Iringa							
	Kigoma							
	Lindi							
	Mbeya							
	Morogoro							
	Moshi							
	Mtwara							
	Musoma							
	MWSA					93.0	95.0	98.0
	Shinyanga							
	Singida							
	Songea							
	Sumbawanga							
	Tabora							
	Tanga							
Togo	TdE		99.8	99.9	99.9	99.8	99.8	
Uganda	NWSC							
Zambia	AHC-MMS							

CHWSC						
CWSC						
KWSC						
LukangaWSC						
LWSC	95.0		80.0	74.0	83.0	81.0
MulongaWSC						
NorthWesternWSC						
NWSC		100.0	100.0	100.0	97.5	99.2
SWSC			96.0	98.0		95.0
WesternWSC						
Country typology						
Resourch-rich						78.1
Middle-income						98.0
Fragile states						63.0
Nonfragile, low-income						88.7
Level of water scarcity						
High						85.9
Low						84.1
Size of the utility						
Small						90.3
Large						65.5
Overall						84.8

Source: Banerjee, Skilling, and others 2008.

Table A3.4 Staffing

Country	Utility	Collection ratio (% of connections billed)							Employees per 1,000 water connections (number/1,000 connections)						
		1995–99	2000	2001	2002	2003	2004	2005	1995–99	2000	2001	2002	2003	2004	2005
Benin	SONEB						93.3	115.9							
Botswana	DWA														
	WUC														
Burkina Faso	ONEA	100.0	100.0	100.0	100.0	100.0	100.0	100.0	9.7	9.7	7.7	7.0	6.8	7.0	6.2
Cameroon	SNEC														
Cape Verde	ELECTRA				95.9	84.2	94.4	98.3							
Chad	STEE														
Congo, Dem. Rep.	REDIGESO	32.6		36.1	36.6	43.7	52.2	70.0							18.0
Congo, Rep.	SDNE		79.0	0.0	83.0	81.0	83.0	88.0		5.3	4.9	7.9	7.7	7.2	7.0
Côte d'Ivoire	SODECI		171.0	158.1	158.1	128.1	143.2	136.3							2.8
Ethiopia	ADAMA					139.2	152.5	140.1							
	AWSA			83.6	85.0	70.6	71.2	83.8							
	Dire Dawa													17.7	16.1
Gabon	SEEG								8.2	7.8	7.4	7.0	6.5	5.9	5.5
Ghana	GWC			77.0	74.0	75.0	75.0	75.0							
Kenya	KIWASCO						77.3	96.7						20.8	20.7
	MWSC				111.2	90.3	74.2	101.8							
	NWASCO						73.9	91.8						10.0	9.0
Lesotho	WASA														
Liberia	LWSR						57.0	63.0						12.6	16.4
Madagascar	JIRAMA														0.8
Malawi	BWB					100.0	100.0	100.0					15.2	15.0	13.7
Malawi	CRWB									40.8	39.3	42.0	46.4	43.3	41.3
Malawi	LWB													20.6	18.4
Mali	EDM				96.0	96.0	96.0	96.0			7.7	5.9	6.0	5.7	5.3
Mauritania	MSNE						95.0	104.6						22.8	21.8
Mozambique	AdeM Beira				100.0	100.0	100.0	100.0				23.4	21.0	19.0	19.2

	Adem Maputo			100.0	100.0	100.0	100.0				8.5	8.3	7.2	6.6
	Adem Nampula			100.0	100.0	100.0	100.0				19.2	17.4	14.9	14.9
	AdeM Pemba			100.0	100.0	100.0	100.0				24.1	24.2	21.9	21.4
	AdeM Quelimane			100.0	100.0	100.0	100.3				25.7	24.3	26.0	23.3
Namibia	Oshakati Municipality													
	Walvis Bay Municipality							11.6	11.0	9.6	9.3	8.4	8.4	7.1
	Windhoek Municipality													3.4
Niger	SPEN/SEEN		79.6	88.7	93.6	92.1	87.6			9.0	8.4	7.3	6.6	6.8
Nigeria	Borno								18.5	18.3	18.0	16.7		
	FCT						20.0							31.2
	Kaduna												23.5	23.6
	Katsina												9.5	14.4
	Lagos										11.0	10.4	9.9	8.7
	Plateau											31.8	30.0	28.3
Rwanda	ELECTROGAZ			120.0	121.0	116.4	74.5							38.6
Senegal	SDE	88.8	89.7	89.0	89.4				4.4	4.1	3.8	3.8	3.7	3.5
Seychelles	PUC					98.7	100.0						19.7	19.2
South Africa	Cape Town Metro												3.2	2.9
	Drakenstein Municipality						100.0				4.1	4.0	2.8	2.8
	eThekwini Metro (Durban)												4.2	4.0

(continued next page)

Table A3.4 *(continued)*

Country	*Utility*	*Collection ratio (% of connections billed)*							*Employees per 1,000 water connections (number/1,000 connections)*						
		1995–99	*2000*	*2001*	*2002*	*2003*	*2004*	*2005*	*1995–99*	*2000*	*2001*	*2002*	*2003*	*2004*	*2005*
	Joburg														2.1
Sudan	Khartoum Water Corporation							62.5							10.9
	South Darfur Water Corporation							49.3							19.2
	Upper Nile Water Corporation							8.3							9.4
Tanzania	Arusha														
	Babati														
	Bukoba														
	DAWASCO														
	DUWS						98.1	105.4							3.8
	Iringa														
	Kigoma														
	Lindi														
	Mbeya														
	Morogoro														
	Moshi														
	Mtwara														
	Musoma														
	MWSA					90.5	97.2	94.8					14.0	11.8	11.4
	Shinyanga														
	Singida														
	Songea														

	Sumbawanga														
	Tabora														
	Tanga														
Togo	TdE		97.4	63.5	87.1	72.1	54.5			15.4	15.5	14.6	13.7	12.3	
Uganda	NWSC	100.8	110.5	103.2	109.9	101.6	100.2	99.7	26.2	20.2	16.2	11.5	10.6	9.5	8.6
Zambia	AHC-MMS							82.0							
	CHWSC							76.0							
	CWSC							81.0							
	KWSC							65.0							
	LukangaWSC														
	LWSC				66.5	80.2	80.0	77.0			14.5	13.1	12.9	12.1	10.5
	MulongaWSC							58.0							
	North WesternWSC							94.0							
	NWSC							81.0						9.9	9.5
	SWSC							57.0						11.7	10.6
	WesternWSC							76.0							
Country typology															
Resourch-rich								65.0							14.5
Middle-income								99.4							5.9
Fragile states								89.8							12.4
Nonfragile, low-income								98.5							14.8
Level of water scarcity															
High								83.0							16.0
Low								88.0							10.3
Size of the utility															
Small								84.1							16.3
Large								91.9							6.6
Overall								86.0							13.1

Source: Banerjee, Skilling, and others 2008.

Table A3.5 Financial Performance

Country	Utility	Debt service ratio (ratio)							Operating cost coverage (ratio)						
		1995–99	2000	2001	2002	2003	2004	2005	1995–99	2000	2001	2002	2003	2004	2005
Benin	SONEB						22.1	44.2						1.0	1.2
Botswana	DWA														
	WUC														
Burkina Faso	ONEA	17.5	17.2	8.5	9.5	12.1	5.8	5.1			1.0	1.1	1.1	1.1	0.9
Cameroon	SNEC														0.8
Cape Verde	ELECTRA														
Chad	STEE			113.2	19.6	34.5	20.0	35.3			3.0	3.7	2.6	3.0	4.2
Congo, Dem. Rep.	REDIGESO	1.7		2.0	2.6	4.2	7.2	11.2	0.1		0.1	0.3	0.4	0.3	0.6
Congo, Rep.	SDNE					178.9	172.6	194.6			0.0	1.0	0.9	0.8	0.7
Côte d'Ivoire	SODECI									1.1	1.0	1.0	1.0	1.0	1.0
Ethiopia	ADAMA												1.9	1.8	1.1
	AWSA								1.1	0.5	0.5	1.0	0.8	1.2	1.0
	Dire Dawa														
Gabon	SEEG								1.0	1.1	1.1	1.1	1.2	1.1	1.0
Ghana	GWC														
Kenya	KIWASCO													1.0	1.0
	MWSC												2.5	1.4	1.4
	NWASCO						218.3	51.9						1.4	2.6
Lesotho	WASA					9.2	11.9	38.5					1.3	1.2	1.2
Liberia	LWSR						182.8	30.1						1.3	1.0
Madagascar	JIRAMA														
Malawi	BWB					9.8	7.6	9.3					1.0	1.0	1.0
	CRWB														
	LWB														
Mali	EDM														0.6

Mauritania	MSNE					41.5	36.1					1.0	1.2
Mozambique	AdeM Beira									1.0	1.2	1.4	1.3
	Adem Maputo									0.8	0.6	1.0	0.8
	Adem Nampula									1.0	1.1	1.3	1.5
	AdeM Pemba									0.4	1.0	1.4	0.8
	AdeM Quilimane									0.6	1.3	1.3	1.3
Namibia	Oshakati Municipality										0.8	1.1	1.3
	Walvis Bay Municipality												
	Windhoek Municipality	5.2	5.6	5.6	5.3	5.9	5.2	1.1	1.1	1.1	1.3	1.1	0.9
Niger	SPEN/SEEN		5472.1	69.3	26.7	12.7	12.6		1.6	0.8	0.8	1.0	1.0
Nigeria	Borno												
	FCT												
	Kaduna												
	Katsina									0.9	0.5	0.6	1.1
	Lagos												
	Plateau												
Rwanda	ELECTROGAZ					1.5	3.5			3.7	3.4	1.7	0.8
Senegal	SDE				4.2	3.9	3.5	0.8	0.9	0.9	0.9	1.0	1.0
Seychelles	PUC											0.5	0.5
South Africa	Cape Town Metro		4.9	4.6	3.8	3.8			1.0	1.0	1.1	0.9	0.9
	Drakenstein Municipality				5.2	6.9					1.6	1.9	1.3
	eThekwini Metro (Durban)				2.3	2.6	2.5				0.7	0.7	0.7

(continued next page)

Table A3.5 *(continued)*

Country	Utility	Debt service ratio (ratio)							Operating cost coverage (ratio)						
		1995–99	*2000*	*2001*	*2002*	*2003*	*2004*	*2005*	*1995–99*	*2000*	*2001*	*2002*	*2003*	*2004*	*2005*
	Joburg														
Sudan	Khartoum Water Corporation														0.9
	South Darfur Water Corporation														1.0
	Upper Nile Water Corporation														0.0
Tanzania	Arusha														0.9
	Babati														0.6
	Bukoba														0.8
	DAWASCO														
	DUWS													1.0	0.9
	Iringa														0.8
	Kigoma														0.6
	Lindi														0.4
	Mbeya														1.0
	Morogoro														0.7
	Moshi														0.7
	Mtwara														0.9
	Musoma														0.6
	MWSA												1.1	1.4	0.9
	Shinyanga														0.5
	Singida														1.4
	Songea														0.4
	Sumbawanga														0.9

	Tabora													1.2
	Tanga													1.2
Togo	TdE	59.6	51.0	36.9	43.9	83.0			0.7	1.3	0.8	1.3	0.7	
Uganda	NWSC	4.4	3.5	3.0	2.9	4.8	4.7	0.9	1.1	1.1	1.1	1.1	1.2	1.2
Zambia	AHC-MMS													0.9
	CHWSC													0.5
	CWSC													1.1
	KWSC													1.5
	LukangaWSC													
	LWSC										0.8	0.8	0.9	1.0
	MulongaWSC													1.0
	NorthWesternWSC													0.7
	NWSC													1.0
	SWSC													1.1
	WesternWSC													0.9
.Country typology														
Resourch-rich							115.0							1.1
Middle-income							15.4							1.0
Fragile states							20.7							0.9
Nonfragile, low-income							19.0							1.0
Level of water scarcity														
High							22.2							1.2
Low							41.2							0.9
Size of the utility														
Small							17.6							0.9
Large							51.5							1.0
Overall							30.5							1.0

Source: Banerjee, Skilling, and others 2008

Reference

Banerjee, S., H. Skilling, V. Foster, C. Briceño-Garmendia, E. Morella, and T. Chfadi. 2008. "Ebbing Water, Surging Deficits: Urban Water Supply in Sub-Saharan Africa." AICD Background Paper 12. World Bank, Washington, DC.

APPENDIX 4

Tariffs

Table A4.1 Structure of Domestic Tariffs

Country	Utility	Type of tariff	Metering ratio (%)	Minimum consumption (m^3)	Fixed charge	Number of blocks	Size of first block (m^3)	Size of nth block (m^3)	Price of first block ($)	Price of nth block ($)
Benin	SONEB	IBT	89.1	0	No	2	5	5+	0.41	0.85
Botswana	WUC	IBT	n.a.	0	Yes	4	10	25+	0.43	1.61
Burkina Faso	ONEA	IBT	98.2	0	Yes	3	6	30+	0.39	2.13
Cape Verde	ELECTRA	IBT	91.2	0	Yes	5	7	20+	0	1.2
Chad	STEE	IBT	n.a.	0	No	3	8	300+	2.67	4.67
Congo, Dem. Rep.	REGIDESO	IBT	28.2	0	No	4	10	40+	0.05	0.12
Congo, Rep.	SDNE	IBT	17.3	0	No	3	25	65+	0.2	0.3
Côte d'Ivoire	SODESI	IBT	100	9	No	3	7	20+	0.19	0.42
Ethiopia	AWSA	IBT	n.a.	0	No	4	5	30+	0.26	0.44
	ADAMA	IBT	90.1	0	No	4	5	50+	0.14	0.34
	Dire Dawa	IBT	n.a.	0	No	2	20	20+	0.52	0.73
Ghana	GWC	IBT	n.a.	0	No	4	10	60+	0.18	0.52
Kenya	NWASCO	IBT	n.a.	0	No	5	10	60+	0.6	0.6
	KIWASCO	U-shaped	58.2	0	Yes	4	5	24+	0.29	1.18
Lesotho	WASA	IBT	98.2	0	Yes	2	10	10+	0.03	0.08
Madagascar	JIRAMA	IBT	97.1	0	Yes	1	10	30+	0.3	0.61
Malawi	BWB	IBT	22.6	5	No	0	0	0	0	0
	CRWB	Flat	n.a.	0	No	4	15	85+	0.71	3.48
	LWB	IBT	98.1	0	Yes	3	4	40+	0	0.52
Mali	EDM	IBT	96	0	No	3	20	61+	0.2	1.09
Mozambique	AdeM Beira	IBT	99.9	10	Yes	3	9	30+	0	0.66
	Adem Maputo	IBT	98.2	10	Yes	3	9	30+	0	0.71
	Adem Nampula	IBT	100	10	Yes	3	9	30+	0	0.58
	AdeM Pemba	IBT	99.1	10	Yes	3	9	30+	0	0.57
	AdeM Quelimane	IBT	100	10	Yes	3	9	30+	0	0.57

Namibia	Oshakati	IBT	96.5	0	Yes	3	10	40+	0.26	0.92
	Walvis Bay	IBT	100	0	Yes	3	6	45+	0.8	2.46
	Windhoek	IBT	n.a.	0	Yes	4	6	40+	1.01	1.94
Niger	SEEN	IBT	96.8	0	No	1	0	0	0.39	0.39
Nigeria	FCT	Linear	23.6	0	No	2	30	30+	0.16	0.19
	Kaduna	IBT	16.1	0	No	3	30	1,000+	0.19	0.28
	Katsina	IBT	6.5	0	No	6	5	500+	0.44	1.09
Rwanda	ELECTROGAZ	IBT	98.7	0	No	4	20	60+	0.37	0.73
Senegal	SDE	IBT	117.3	0	No	2	15	15+	0.22	0.47
South Africa	Drakenstein	IBT	60.7	0	Yes	7	6	1,000+	0	1.86
	eThekwini	IBT	66.4	0	Yes	3	6	30+	0	1.77
	Tygerberg	IBT	60.3	0	Yes	6	6	50+	0	1.86
	Johannesburg	IBT	52.4	0	No	6	6	40+	0	1.4
Sudan	Khartoum Water Corporation	IBT	n.a.	0	No	1	0	0	0.64	0.64
	South Darfur Water Corporation	Linear	n.a.	0	No	1	0	0	0.59	0.59
	Upper Nile Water Corporation	Linear	0	0	No	3	20	40+	0.37	1.46
Tanzania	DAWASCO	IBT	70.5	0	No	2	5	5+	0.39	0.52
	DUWS	IBT	27.9	10	Yes	3	14	25+	0	0.51
	MWSA	IBT	100	0	Yes	3	24	75+	0.24	0.28
	NWSC	Linear	94.5	0	Yes	1	0	0	0.65	0.65
Zambia	LWSC	IBT	33.3	0	Yes	5	6	170+	0.25	0.55
	NWSC	IBT	n.a.	0	No	4	6	50+	0.25	0.37
	SWSC	IBT	n.a.	6	No	4	10	50+	0.3	0.47
Simple average									0.31	0.95
By utility size										
Small									0.29	0.92
Large									0.2	0.66

Source: Banerjee, Foster, and others 2008.
Note: IBT = increasing block tariff.

Table A4.2 Domestic Tariffs at Various Levels of Consumption

Country	Utility	Connection fee	Minimum consumption (m^3)	Fixed charge	Price first block	Price last block	4 m^3	5 m^3	6 m^3	8 m^3	10 m^3	20 m^3	30 m^3	50 m^3	100 m^3
Benin	SONEB	202.00	0		0.41	0.85	0.41	0.41	0.48	0.57	0.63	0.74	0.78	0.81	0.83
Burkina Faso	ONEA	204.90	0	2.05	0.39	2.13	0.90	0.80	0.73	0.75	0.76	0.78	0.79	1.33	1.73
Cape Verde	ELECTRA	24.24	0		2.67	4.67	2.67	2.67	2.67	2.93	3.09	3.88	4.14	4.35	4.51
Chad	STEE	0.00	0		0.22	0.47	0.22	0.22	0.22	0.22	0.22	0.28	0.34	0.39	0.43
Congo, Dem. Rep.	REGIDESO	0.00	0		0.05	0.12	0.05	0.05	0.05	0.05	0.05	0.06	0.07	0.08	0.04
Côte d'Ivoire	SODECI	256.35	9	0.16	0.00	1.20	0.04	0.03	0.03	0.02	0.06	0.30	0.45	0.57	0.71
Ethiopia	AWSA	14.44	0		0.19	0.42	0.19	0.19	0.19	0.21	0.24	0.30	0.34	0.37	0.40
	ADAMA	8.89	0		0.26	0.44	0.26	0.26	0.27	0.28	0.29	0.35	0.38	0.40	0.42
	Dire Dawa	43.33	0		0.14	0.34	0.14	0.14	0.15	0.17	0.17	0.19	0.22	0.24	0.29
Ghana	GWC	0.00	0		0.52	0.73	0.52	0.52	0.52	0.52	0.52	0.52	0.59	0.65	0.69
Kenya	NWASCO	34.41	0		0.18	0.52	0.18	0.18	0.18	0.18	0.18	0.23	0.24	0.31	0.40
	KIWASCO	104.72	0		0.60	0.60	0.60	0.60	0.60	0.60	0.60	0.48	0.46	0.47	0.52
Lesotho	WASA	208.20	0		0.29	1.18	0.40	0.37	0.39	0.41	0.43	0.64	0.79	0.94	1.06
Madagascar	JIRAMA	0.00	0	0.30	0.03	0.08	0.11	0.09	0.08	0.07	0.06	0.07	0.07	0.08	0.08
Malawi	LWB	0.00	0	2.42	0.30	0.61	0.91	0.79	0.71	0.61	0.54	0.49	0.48	0.53	0.57
	BWB	0.00	5	0.48	0.00	0.52	0.12	0.10	0.16	0.24	0.29	0.40	0.43	0.47	0.49
	CRWB	76.04	0	2.33	0.00	0.00	0.58	0.47	0.39	0.29	0.23	0.12	0.08		
Mozambique	AdeM Beira	239.25	10	3.83	0.00	0.66	0.96	0.77	0.64	0.48	0.38	0.44	0.48	0.55	0.61
	Adem Maputo	239.25	10	3.83	0.00	0.71	0.96	0.77	0.64	0.48	0.38	0.53	0.58	0.64	0.67
	AdeM Nampula	239.25	10	3.83	0.00	0.58	0.96	0.77	0.64	0.48	0.38	0.42	0.45	0.50	0.54
	AdeM Pemba	239.25	10	3.83	0.00	0.57	0.96	0.77	0.64	0.48	0.38	0.40	0.43	0.49	0.53
	AdeM Quelimane	239.25	10	3.83	0.00	0.57	0.96	0.77	0.64	0.48	0.38	0.40	0.42	0.48	0.53

Namibia	Walvis Bay	0.00	0		0.71	3.48	0.71	0.71	0.71	0.71	0.71	0.83	1.06	1.38	1.87
	Windhoek	238.36	0		0.80	2.46	1.45	1.32	1.23	1.26	1.27	1.30	1.31	1.43	1.94
	Oshakati	23.66	0	3.85	1.01	1.94	1.97	1.78	1.65	1.53	1.46	1.41	1.46	1.57	1.76
Niger	SEEN	245.88	0	1.02	0.26	0.92	0.52	0.47	0.43	0.39	0.36	0.47	0.50	0.60	0.76
Nigeria	FCT WB	235.29	0		0.39	0.39	0.39	0.39	0.39	0.39	0.39	0.39	0.39	0.39	0.39
	Kaduna	15.69	0		0.16	0.19	0.16	0.16	0.16	0.16	0.16	0.16	0.16	0.17	0.18
	Katsina WB	47.06	0		0.19	0.28	0.19	0.19	0.19	0.19	0.19	0.19	0.19	0.21	0.22
Rwanda	ELECTROGAZ	146.72	0		0.44	1.09	0.44	0.44	0.46	0.48	0.50	0.52	0.59	0.65	0.92
Senegal	SDE	153.68	0		0.37	1.46	0.37	0.37	0.37	0.37	0.37	0.37	0.65	0.92	1.19
South Africa	Drakenstein	325.01	0	1.52	0.00	1.86	0.00	0.00	0.00	0.25	0.25	0.38	0.42	0.57	0.85
	Tygerberg	203.60	0	2.02	0.00	1.86	0.00	0.00	0.00	0.34	0.35	0.52	0.72	0.94	1.40
	eThekwini	337.13	0	6.89	0.00	1.77	0.00	0.00	0.00	1.08	1.04	0.96	0.94	1.27	1.52
	Johannesburg	339.95	0		0.00	1.40	0.00	0.00	0.00	0.15	0.24	0.56	0.77	0.98	1.61
Sudan	NWC Khartoum	137.06	0		0.37	0.73	0.37	0.37	0.37	0.37	0.37	0.37	0.37	0.37	0.52
	NWC South Darfur	198.74	0		0.64	0.64	0.64	0.64	0.64	0.64	0.64	0.64	0.64	0.64	0.64
	NWC Upper Nile	6.36	0		0.59	0.59	0.59	0.59	0.59	0.59	0.59	0.59	0.59	0.59	0.59
Tanzania	DAWASCO	20.55	0		0.39	0.52	0.39	0.39	0.41	0.43	0.45	0.48	0.50	0.50	0.51
	DUWS	16.60	0	3.95	0.00	0.51	0.99	0.79	0.66	0.49	0.40	0.40	0.42	0.45	0.48
	MWSA	15.81	0	1.11	0.24	0.28	0.51	0.46	0.42	0.38	0.35	0.29	0.28	0.27	0.26
Uganda	NWSC	30.58	0	0.92	0.65	0.65	0.88	0.83	0.80	0.77	0.74	0.70	0.68	0.67	0.66
Zambia	SWSC	33.49	0		0.30	0.47	0.30	0.30	0.30	0.30	0.30	0.31	0.33	0.35	0.41
	LWSC	50.00	0	1.24	0.25	0.55	0.56	0.50	0.45	0.42	0.39	0.34	0.33	0.35	0.36
	NWSC	0.00	0		0.25	0.37	0.25	0.25	0.25	0.25	0.26	0.27	0.28	0.30	0.34

Source: Banerjee, Foster, and others 2008.

Table A4.3 Cost Recovery at Various Levels of Consumption

		4 m³					10 m³					40 m³				
Country	*Utility*	*Price of 4 m³*	*O&M cost threshold*	*Capital cost threshold*	*Meets O&M cost threshold*	*Meets capital cost threshold*	*Price of 10 m³*	*O&M cost threshold*	*Capital cost threshold*	*Meets O&M cost threshold*	*Meets capital cost threshold*	*Price of 40 m³*	*O&M cost threshold*	*Capital cost threshold*	*Meets O&M cost threshold*	*Meets capital cost threshold*
Benin	SONEB	0.41	0.70	0.80	No	No	0.63	0.70	0.80	No	No	0.79	0.70	0.80	Yes	No
Burkina Faso	ONEA	0.90	0.75	0.80	Yes	Yes	0.76	0.75	0.80	Yes	No	1.12	0.75	0.80	Yes	Yes
Cape Verde	ELECTRA	2.67		0.80		Yes	3.09		0.80		Yes	4.27		0.80		Yes
Chad	STEE	0.22		0.80		No	0.22		0.80		No	0.38		0.80		No
Congo, Dem. Rep.	REGIDESO	0.05	0.70	0.80	No	No	0.05	0.70	0.80	No	No	0.07	0.70	0.80	No	No
Côte d'Ivoire	SODECI	0.04	0.63	0.80	No	No	0.06	0.63	0.80	No	No	0.53	0.63	0.80	No	No
Ethiopia	AWSA	0.19	0.32	0.80	No	No	0.24	0.32	0.80	No	No	0.36	0.32	0.80	Yes	No
	ADAMA	0.26	0.32	0.80	No	No	0.29	0.32	0.80	No	No	0.39	0.32	0.80	Yes	No
	Dire Dawa	0.14	0.18	0.80	No	No	0.17	0.18	0.80	No	No	0.24	0.18	0.80	Yes	No
Ghana	GWC	0.52		0.80		No	0.52		0.80		No	0.63		0.80		No
Kenya	NWASCO	0.18	1.13	0.80	No	No	0.18	1.13	0.80	No	No	0.29	1.13	0.80	No	No
	KIWASCO	0.60	0.49	0.80	Yes	No	0.60	0.49	0.80	Yes	No	0.45	0.49	0.80	No	No
Lesotho	WASA	0.40	0.16	0.80	Yes	No	0.43	0.16	0.80	Yes	No	0.88	0.16	0.80	Yes	Yes
Madagascar	JIRAMA	0.11	0.70	0.80	No	No	0.06	0.70	0.80	No	No	0.08	0.70	0.80	No	No
Malawi	LWB	0.91	0.57	0.80	Yes	Yes	0.54	0.57	0.80	No	No	0.51	0.57	0.80	No	No
	BWB	0.12	0.41	0.80	No	No	0.29	0.41	0.80	No	No	0.45	0.41	0.80	Yes	No
	CRWB	0.58	0.23	0.80	Yes	No	0.23	0.23	0.80	Yes	No	0.23	0.80		No	No
Mozambique	AdeM Beira	0.96	0.51	0.80	Yes	No	0.38	0.51	0.80	No	No	0.53	0.51	0.80	Yes	No
	Adem Maputo	0.96	0.73	0.80	Yes	No	0.38	0.73	0.80	No	No	0.62	0.73	0.80	No	No
	AdeM Nampula	0.96	0.35	0.80	Yes	No	0.38	0.35	0.80	Yes	No	0.48	0.35	0.80	Yes	No
	AdeM Pemba	0.96	0.53	0.80	Yes	No	0.38	0.53	0.80	No	No	0.46	0.53	0.80	No	No
	AdeM Quelimane	0.96	0.42	0.80	Yes	No	0.38	0.42	0.80	No	No	0.46	0.42	0.80	Yes	No
Namibia	Walvis Bay	0.71		0.80		No	0.71		0.80		No	1.26		0.80		Yes
	Windhoek	1.45	2.08	0.80	No	No	1.27	2.08	0.80	No	Yes	1.32	2.08	0.80	No	Yes

	Oshakati	1.97	1.44	0.80	Yes	No	1.46	1.44	0.80	Yes	Yes	1.48	1.44	0.80	Yes	Yes
Niger	SEEN	0.52	0.46	0.80	Yes	No	0.36	0.46	0.80	No	No	0.52	0.46	0.80	Yes	No
Nigeria	FCT WB	0.39		0.80		No	0.39		0.80		No	0.39		0.80		No
	Kaduna	0.16		0.80		No	0.16		0.80		No	0.17		0.80		No
	Katsina WB	0.19	0.06	0.80	Yes	No	0.19	0.06	0.80	Yes	No	0.20	0.06	0.80	Yes	No
Rwanda	ELECTROGAZ	0.44	0.51	0.80	No	No	0.50	0.51	0.80	No	No	0.63	0.51	0.80	Yes	No
Senegal	SDE	0.37	0.85	0.80	No	No	0.37	0.85	0.80	No	No	0.78	0.85	0.80	No	No
South Africa	Drakenstein	—	0.70	0.80	Yes	Yes	0.25	0.70	0.80	No	No	0.51	0.70	0.80	No	No
	Tygerberg	—	1.21	0.80	Yes	Yes	0.35	1.21	0.80	No	No	0.83	1.21	0.80	No	Yes
	eThekwini	—	1.56	0.80	Yes	Yes	1.04	1.56	0.80	No	Yes	1.14	1.56	0.80	No	Yes
	Johannesburg	—	1.50	0.80	Yes	Yes	0.24	1.50	0.80	No	No	0.87	1.50	0.80	No	Yes
Sudan	NWC Khartoum	0.37	0.28	0.80	Yes	No	0.37	0.28	0.80	Yes	No	0.37	0.28	0.80	Yes	No
	NWC South Darfur	0.64	0.49	0.80	Yes	No	0.64	0.49	0.80	Yes	No	0.64	0.49	0.80	Yes	No
	NWC Upper Nile	0.59	0.73	0.80	No	No	0.59	0.73	0.80	No	No	0.59	0.73	0.80	No	No
Tanzania	DAWASCO	0.39		0.80		No	0.45		0.80		No	0.50		0.80		No
	DUWS	0.99	0.42	0.80	Yes	Yes	0.40	0.42	0.80	No	No	0.44	0.42	0.80	Yes	No
	MWSA	0.51	0.19	0.80	Yes	No	0.35	0.19	0.80	Yes	No	0.27	0.19	0.80	Yes	No
Uganda	NWSC	0.88	0.60	0.80	Yes	Yes	0.74	0.60	0.80	Yes	No	0.67	0.60	0.80	Yes	No
Zambia	SWSC	0.30	0.30	0.80	No	No	0.30	0.30	0.80	No	No	0.34	0.30	0.80	Yes	No
	LWSC	0.56	0.27	0.80	Yes	No	0.39	0.27	0.80	Yes	No	0.34	0.27	0.80	Yes	No
	NWSC	0.25	0.20	0.80	Yes	No	0.26	0.20	0.80	Yes	No	0.29	0.20	0.80	Yes	No

Source: Banerjee, Foster, and others 2008.

Table A4.4 Structure of Nondomestic Tariffs

Country	Utility	Connection charge	Industrial			Government/ public institutions			Commercial			Comparison of commercial to residential price		
			Fixed charge	Number of blocks	Price first block	Fixed charge	Number of blocks	Price first block	Fixed charge	Number of blocks	Price first block	Residential price at 100 m³	Commercial price at 100 m³	Ratio of commercial to residential price at 100 m³
Benin	SONEB		No	1.00	0.85	No	1.00	0.85	No	1.00	0.85	0.828	0.850	1.027
Burkina Faso	ONEA		Yes	1.00	2.13	Yes	1.00	2.13	Yes	1.00	2.13	1.729	2.151	1.245
Cape Verde	ELECTRA		No	1.00	0.78	No	1.00		No	1.00	0.78	4.509	4.533	1.005
Chad	STEE		No	2.00	0.22	No	2.00	0.22	No	2.00	0.22	0.433	0.433	1.000
Congo, Dem. Rep.	REGIDESO		No	1.00		No	1.00	0.00	No	3.00	0.01	0.040	0.006	0.144
Côte d'Ivoire	SODECI		Yes	4.00	0.48	No	1.00	1.07		4.00	0.48	0.707		
Ethiopia	AWSA		No	1.00	0.42	No	1.00	0.42	No	1.00	0.42	0.397	0.422	1.064
	ADAMA											0.424		
	Dire Dawa											0.294		
Ghana	GWC		No			Yes					2.20	0.687	2.198	3.199
Kenya	NWASCO									4.00	0.18	0.403	0.435	1.078
	KIWASCO	Yes								5.00	0.60	0.521	0.479	0.920
Lesotho	WASA	Yes	Yes	1.00	0.69	Yes	1.00	0.69	Yes	1.00	0.69	1.060	0.690	0.651
Madagascar	JIRAMA					No	2.00	0.23				0.078		
Malawi	LWB		Yes	2.00	0.49	Yes	2.00	0.45	Yes	2.00	0.49	0.572	0.540	0.944
	BWB											0.494		
	CRWB													
Mozambique	AdeM Beira		No	2.00	15.69	No	2.00	15.69	No	2.00	15.69	0.606	4.395	7.247
	Adem Maputo		No	2.00	16.75	No	2.00	16.75	No	2.00	16.75	0.674	4.689	6.960
	AdeM Nampula		No	2.00	13.88	No	2.00	13.88	No	2.00	13.88	0.542	3.885	7.173
	AdeM Pemba		No	2.00	15.02	No	2.00	15.02	No	2.00	15.02	0.530	4.207	7.935
	AdeM Quelimane		No	2.00	15.22	No	2.00	15.22	No	2.00	15.22	0.528	4.261	8.065
Namibia	Walvis Bay		No	4.00	1.99	No	4.00	1.99	No	4.00	1.99	1.869	1.993	
	Windhoek	Yes	No	1.00	1.63	No	1.00	1.63	No	1.00	1.63	1.945	1.628	0.837
	Oshakati	Yes	Yes	3.00	17.70	Yes	3.00	17.70	Yes	3.00	17.70	1.758	36.810	20.934
Niger	SEEN		No	3.00	0.85	No	1.00	0.87	No	1.00	0.87	0.759	0.871	1.148

Nigeria	FCT WB	No	1.00	7.84	No	2.00	0.47	No	1.00	0.78	0.392	0.784	2.000
	Kaduna	No	3.00	0.55	No	2.00	0.19	No	2.00	0.55	0.181	0.549	3.030
	Katsina	No	1.00	1.57	No	2.00	0.20	No	1.00	1.57	0.221	1.569	7.092
Rwanda	ELECTROGAZ	No	3.00	0.44	No	3.00	0.44	No	3.00	0.44	0.921	0.691	0.751
Senegal	SDE				No		1.62			1.62	1.193	1.616	1.355
South Africa	Drakenstein										0.848		
	Tygerberg	Yes	1.00	0.82	Yes	1.00	0.82	Yes	1.00	0.82	1.401	0.841	0.600
	eThekwini	Yes	1.00	0.88	Yes	1.00	0.88	Yes	1.00	0.88	1.518	0.953	0.628
	Johannesburg										1.606	0.375	0.233
Sudan	NWC Khartoum	No	1.00	0.73	No	1.00	0.73	No	1.00	0.73	0.519	0.734	1.415
	NWC South Darfur	No	1.00	1.41	No	1.00	1.41	No	1.00	1.41	0.636	1.407	2.212
	NWC Upper Nile	No	1.00	1.35	No	1.00	1.35	No	1.00	1.35	0.587	1.346	2.292
Tanzania	DAWASCO	No	3.00	0.57	No	3.00	0.57	No	3.00	0.57	0.510	0.573	1.123
	DUWS	No	1.00	13.04	No	1.00	13.04	No	1.00	13.04	0.484	1.767	3.649
	MWSA	No	1.00	0.47	No	1.00	0.28	No	1.00	0.40	0.264		
Uganda	NWSC	No	1.00	1.05	No	3.00	0.80	No	1.00	1.05	0.660	1.050	1.590
Zambia	SWSC												
	LWSC	Yes							3.00	0.37	0.359	0.587	1.633

Source: Banerjee, Foster, and others 2008.

Table A4.5 Structure of Sanitation Tariffs (Only Utilities with Wastewater Responsibility)

Country	*Utility*	*Connection cost*	*Tariff part of water bill*	*% of water bill*	*Fixed fee*	*Block tariff*
Burkina Faso	ONEA					Yes
Cape Verde	ELECTRA					
Côte d'Ivoire	SODECI	Yes				
Ethiopia	AWSA					Yes
Kenya	NWASCO					Yes
	KIWASCO	Yes				Yes
Lesotho	WASA	Yes	Yes	0.85		
Madagascar	JIRAMA					
Namibia	Walvis Bay				Yes	Yes
	Windhoek					
	Oshakati	Yes			Yes	
Nigeria	FCT WB meter					
Senegal	SDE with sanitation					Yes
South Africa	Drakenstein					
	Tygerberg					
	eThekwini					
	Johannesburg					
Sudan	NWC Khartoum					
	NWC South Darfur					
	NWC Upper Nile					
Tanzania	DAWASCO		Yes	0.80		
	DUWS	Yes	Yes	0.40		
	MWSA	Yes	Yes	0.50		
Uganda	NWSC	Yes	Yes	0.75		
Zambia	KWSC		Yes	0.30		
	LWSC	Yes	Yes	0.30		
	NWSC		Yes	0.30		

Source: Banerjee, Foster, and others 2008.

Table A4.6 Structure of Standpost Tariffs

Country	*Utility*	*Official standpost price (US$/m³) (1)*	*Unofficial standpost price (US$/m³) (2)*	*Official piped water price at 4 m³ (US$/m³) (3)*	*Ratio of unofficial to official standpost price (2)/(1)*	*Ratio of official piped water price at 4 m³ to official standpost price (3)/(1)*
Benin	SONEB	0.41	1.91	0.41	4.66	0.99
Burkina Faso	ONEA	0.51	0.48	0.90	0.94	1.76
Cape Verde	ELECTRA	—	9.44	2.67	—	—
Chad	STEE	—	—	0.22	—	—
Congo, Dem. Rep.	REGIDESO	0.05	1.02	0.05	20.40	0.93
Côte d'Ivoire	SODECI	0.45	0.93	0.04	2.06	0.09
Ethiopia	AWSA	0.19	0.87	0.19	4.55	1.02
	ADAMA			0.26		
	Dire Dawa			0.14		
Ghana	GWC	3.64	5.51	0.52	1.52	0.14
Kenya	NWASCO	—	1.73	0.18	—	—
	KIWASCO			0.60		
Lesotho	WASA	n.a.	2.58	0.40	n.a.	n.a.
Madagascar	JIRAMA	0.14	1.24	0.11	8.60	0.75
Malawi	LWB			0.91		
	BWB	0.29	1.16	0.12	4.00	0.41
	CRWB			0.58		
Mozambique	AdeM Beira			0.96		
	Adem Maputo	0.31	0.98	0.96	3.17	3.09
	AdeM Nampula			0.96		
	AdeM Pemba			0.96		
	AdeM Quelimane			0.96		
Namibia	Walvis Bay			0.71		
	Windhoek	1.41	n.a.	1.45	n.a.	1.02
	Oshakati			1.97		
Niger	SEEN	0.24	0.48	0.52	1.97	2.13
Nigeria	FCT WB			0.39		
	Kaduna	—	—	0.16	—	—
	Katsina WB			0.19		
Rwanda	ELECTROGAZ	0.44	1.79	0.44	4.07	1.00
Senegal	SDE	0.54	1.53	0.37	2.83	0.69
South Africa	Drakenstein			0.00		
	Tygerberg			0.00		
	eThekwini			0.00		
	Johannesburg	n.a.	n.a.	0.00	n.a.	n.a.
Sudan	NWC Khartoum	0.92	1.15	0.37	1.25	0.40

(continued next page)

Table A4.6 *(continued)*

Country	*Utility*	*Official standpost price (US$/m³) (1)*	*Unofficial standpost price (US$/m³) (2)*	*Official piped water price at 4 m³ (US$/m³) (3)*	*Ratio of unofficial to official standpost price (2)/(1)*	*Ratio of official piped water price at 4 m³ to official standpost price (3)/(1)*
	NWC South Darfur			0.64		
	NWC Upper Nile			0.59		
Tanzania	DAWASCO	0.58	0.87	0.39	1.51	0.67
	DUWS			0.99		
	MWSA			0.51		
Uganda	NWSC	0.39	1.40	0.88	3.63	2.28
Zambia	SWSC			0.30		
	LWSC	0.19	1.67	0.56	9.03	3.02
	NWSC			0.25		

Source: Banerjee, Foster, and others 2008.
Note: n.a. = not applicable.

Table A4.7 Scorecard on Efficiency, Equity, and Cost Recovery

Country	Utility	Cost recovery			Efficiency			Equity			Equity score	Efficiency score	Cost-recovery score	Total score
		1	2	3	4	5	6	7	8	9				
Cape Verde	ELECTRA	1	1	1	1	1	1	1		1	3	3	2	8
Chad	STEE	0	0	1	1	1	1	1	1	1	4	3	0	7
Benin	SONEB	1	0	1	1	1	1	0	0	1	2	3	1	6
Namibia	Oshakati	1	1	1	1	1	0			1	1	3	2	6
Namibia	Windhoek	1	1	1	1	1	0	1		0	1	3	2	6
Nigeria	Katsina WB	0	0	1	1	1	1		1	1	3	3	0	6
Rwanda	ELECTROGAZ	1	0	1	1	0	1	1	1	0	3	2	1	6
Burkina Faso	ONEA	1	0	0	1	1	0	1	0	1	2	2	1	5
Ethiopia	AWSA	0	0	1	0	0	1	1	1	1	4	1	0	5
Ghana	GWC	1	0	1	1	0	1	0		1	2	2	1	5
Kenya	KIWASCO	1	0	1	0	1	1		1	0	2	2	1	5
Lethoso	WASA	1	0	1	1	0	1	1	0	0	2	2	1	5
Namibia	Walvis Bay	1	0	0	1	1	1		1		2	2	1	5
Nigeria	FCT WB	0	0	1	1	0	1	1	0	1	3	2	0	5
Sudan	NWC Upper Nile	1	0	1	0	1	1	0	0	1	2	2	1	5
Sudan	NWC South Darfur	1	0	1	0	0	1		1	1	3	1	1	5
Tanzania	DAWASCO	1	0	1	0	0	1	0	1	1	3	1	1	5
Uganda	NWSC	1	0	0	1	0	0	1	1	1	3	1	1	5
South Africa	eThekwini	1	1	0	0	1	1		1	0	2	1	2	5
South Africa	Johannesburg	0	0	1	1	1	1		1	0	2	3	0	5
Kenya	NWASCO	0	0	1	0	0	1	1		1	3	1	0	4
Nigeria	Kaduna	0	0	1	0	0	1		1	1	3	1	0	4
Senegal	SDE	0	0	1	0	0	1	0	1	1	3	1	0	4
South Africa	Tygerberg	0	0	0	1	1	1		1	0	2	2	0	4
South Africa	Drakenstein	0	0	0	0	1	1	1	1		3	1	0	4
Zambia	NWSC	0	0	1	0	0	1	1		1	3	1	0	4

(continued next page)

Table A4.7 *(continued)*

Country	*Utility*	*Cost recovery*			*Efficiency*			*Equity*			*Equity score*	*Efficiency score*	*Cost-recovery score*	*Total score*
		1	*2*	*3*	*4*	*5*	*6*	*7*	*8*	*9*				
Ethiopia	Dire Dawa	0	0	1	1	0	1		0		1	2	0	3
Ethiopia	ADAMA	0	0	1	0	0	1		1	2		1	0	3
Mozambique	AdeM Quelimane	0	0	0	1	0	0	1	0	1	2	1	0	3
Niger	SEEN	0	0	0	0	0	0	1	1	1	3	0	0	3
Sudan	NWC Khartoum	0	0	1	0	0	1		0	1	2	1	0	3
Zambia	SWSC	0	0	1	0	0	1		1	2		1	0	3
Côte d'Ivoire	SODECI	0	0	0	0	0	1	0	1		2	0	0	2
Congo, Dem. Rep.	REGIDESO	0	0	1	0	0	1	0		0	1	1	0	2
Mozambique	AdeM Pemba	0	0	0	1	0	0		0	1	1	1	0	2
Malawi	BWB	0	0	0	1	0	1			1	1	0	2	
Malawi	CRWB	0	0	0	1	1	0	0			0	2	0	2
Malawi	LWB	1	0	0	1	0	0			0	0	1	1	2
Tanzania	DUWS	0	0	0	0	0	0		1	1	2	0	0	2
Zambia	LWSC	0	0	0	0	0	0		1	1	2	0	0	2
Mozambique	AdeM Beira	0	0	0	0	0	0		0	1	1	0	0	1
Mozambique	Adem Maputo	0	0	0	0	0	0		0	1	1	0	0	1
Mozambique	AdeM Nampula	0	0	0	0	0	0		0	1	1	0	0	1
Tanzania	MWSA	0	0	0	0	0	0		1	1		0	0	1
Madagascar	JIRAMA	0	0	0	0	0	0	0			0	0	0	0

Source: Banerjee, Foster, and others 2008.

Note: IBT = increasing block tariff, LRMC = long-run marginal cost, O&M = operations and maintenance.
The scorecard is compiled on the basis of cost recovery, efficiency, and equity criteria. The scorecard adds the score against each criterion. The utility scores 1 against a specific criterion according to (1) Cost recovery: O & M cost recovery; (2) Cost recovery: Capital cost recovery; (3) Efficiency: No fixed charge or minimum consumption charge; (4) Efficiency: Metering ratio is higher than sample average (77%); (5) Efficiency: The price of the last block meets the capital cost; (6) Equity: Small piped consumers (at 4 m^3) pay less than average piped consumers (at 10 m^3); (7) Equity: Stand-post consumers pay less than small piped consumers (at 4 m^3); (8) Equity: Connection cost as a share of GNI per capita is lower than sample average (27%); (9) Equity: Residential consumers pay less than nonresidential consumers at 100 m^3 of consumption.

Reference

Banerjee, S., V. Foster, Y. Ying, H. Skilling, and Q. Wodon. 2008. "Achieving Cost Recovery, Equity and Efficiency in Water Tariffs: Evidence From African Utilities." AICD Working Paper 7, World Bank, Washington, DC.

APPENDIX 5

Affordability of Water and Sanitation

Table A5.1 Contribution of Food to Total Spending

		Expenditure budget (2002 US$)								Share of household budget							
Country	*Year*	*National*	*Rural*	*Urban*	*Q1*	*Q2*	*Q3*	*Q4*	*Q5*	*National*	*Rural*	*Urban*	*Q1*	*Q2*	*Q3*	*Q4*	*Q5*
Angola	2000	102	112	37	22	56	85	121	194	46.32	45.80	58.92	58.22	59.48	56.66	53.80	38.78
Benin	2002	48	45	54	26	38	44	51	66	55.22	60.70	49.59	62.07	64.20	62.23	60.15	47.84
Burkina Faso	2003	58	55	70	33	44	53	62	80	47.92	54.20	35.57	67.88	66.00	61.90	55.60	36.30
Burundi	1998	47	45	91	13	29	39	54	81	71.83	76.80	43.47	71.84	77.13	77.67	78.33	66.29
Cameroon	2004	69	65	85	31	46	58	76	106	61.71	65.80	52.06	63.98	66.12	66.30	66.12	56.86
Cape Verde	2001	62	59	68	43	52	61	61	75	50.68	69.49	38.23	68.23	64.55	61.56	56.92	40.51
Congo, Dem. Rep.	2005	79	64	117	33	50	65	83	126	71.43	66.50	79.85	72.90	74.30	73.92	74.57	68.45
Congo, Rep.	2002	60	40	85	20	39	49	63	96	27.73	29.06	27.18	28.99	33.79	33.11	33.26	23.99
Gabon	2005	175	150	181	34	164	202	215	205	39.19	57.69	36.77	35.99	51.43	47.28	43.06	32.51
Ghana	1999	94	83	113	41	67	85	105	131	55.71	60.29	50.82	63.56	61.95	59.98	56.88	51.47
Guinea-Bissau	2005	81	72	103	35	55	65	81	138	54.41	52.25	58.59	49.44	53.71	54.55	55.50	54.84
Kenya	1997	87	81	109	42	62	77	97	119	62.35	70.03	47.30	76.96	76.42	74.72	70.91	51.77
Madagascar	2001	173	157	220	69	106	135	184	294	61.15	66.64	51.65	74.13	76.02	73.60	70.28	51.13
Malawi	2003	39	37	59	20	27	33	40	61	56.53	59.76	45.31	61.82	62.26	61.80	60.53	50.94
Mauritania	2000	114	88	150	55	79	102	125	169	50.76	50.16	51.26	59.95	58.19	55.45	53.97	44.66
Morocco	2003	191	168	209	84	138	183	237	375	43.09	54.16	38.37	52.60	51.81	48.50	44.19	35.65
Niger	2005	84	78	112	31	47	61	79	155	67.83	73.39	53.93	62.56	67.46	69.38	68.76	67.72
Nigeria	2003	43	42	45	17	32	42	50	59	50.08	57.32	43.88	55.82	61.25	60.54	56.73	40.95
Rwanda	1998	57	51	116	22	37	47	61	108	56.70	67.05	35.08	71.73	73.47	71.97	67.04	44.72
São Tomé and Príncipe	2000	127	110	141	58	81	95	120	217	60.57	70.66	55.48	77.64	75.57	71.99	68.68	51.73
Sierra Leone	2003	55	52	61	27	42	52	61	97	50.73	62.61	38.18	61.62	63.73	61.49	55.40	38.62
Tanzania	2000	39	36	51	20	29	36	42	56	65.92	68.83	59.38	71.78	70.58	71.33	68.60	60.60
Zambia	2002	62	60	67	26	42	54	67	99	63.00	74.57	49.58	70.99	72.50	0.00	70.20	54.38

Source: Banerjee, Wodon, and others 2008.
Note: Q = quintile. Year refers to year of the survey.

Table A5.2 Spending on Water Services

Country	Year	Expenditure budget (2002 US$)								Share in household budget							
		National	Rural	Urban	Q1	Q2	Q3	Q4	Q5	National	Rural	Urban	Q1	Q2	Q3	Q4	Q5
Angola	2000	1	1	0	0	0	0	1	2	0.3	0.3	0.0	0.2	0.3	0.3	0.2	0.3
Burkina Faso	2003	0	2	0	2	2	2	0	0	0.2	2.2	0.0	5.0	3.0	2.8	0.2	0.0
Cameroon	2004	7	10	5	1	2	2	3	10	5.9	10.3	3.1	1.6	2.2	1.8	2.2	5.3
Cape Verde	2001	2	1	2	2	2	2	2	2	1.6	1.2	1.1	2.5	2.2	1.8	1.7	1.1
Chad	2001	9	4	11	3	4	6	8	14	2.5	1.7	2.6	3.4	2.7	2.6	2.8	2.1
Congo, Dem. Rep.	2005	2	1	3	1	1	1	2	3	1.9	0.9	1.7	1.8	1.7	1.4	1.7	1.6
Congo, Rep.	2002	2	1	4	1	1	2	2	4	1.1	0.6	1.3	0.9	1.2	1.3	1.3	0.9
Côte d'Ivoire	2005	4	2	4	3	4	4	4	5	1.9	1.3	1.6	3.2	2.7	2.3	1.7	1.2
Ethiopia	2000	1	1	1	1	1	1	1	1	1.5	1.5	1.3	2.0	1.6	1.6	1.5	1.2
Gabon	2005	11	6	11	1	8	9	13	12	2.4	2.4	2.2	1.4	2.4	2.1	2.7	1.9
Ghana	1999	1	0	2	0	1	1	1	2	0.7	0.2	0.7	0.1	0.5	0.4	0.5	0.7
Kenya	1997	2	1	3	1	1	1	2	3	1.7	0.8	1.5	1.6	1.7	1.2	1.3	1.3
Madagascar	2001	1	1	1	3	0	1	1	1	0.4	0.4	0.3	3.7	0.4	0.4	0.2	0.2
Malawi	2003	0	0	3	0	0	0	0	1	0.7	0.2	2.5	0.2	0.2	0.3	0.3	1.2
Mauritania	2000	11	5	14	1	5	11	10	14	4.9	2.9	4.8	1.6	3.7	5.8	4.2	3.6
Morocco	2003	9	4	10	5	6	8	9	14	2.1	1.3	1.8	2.9	2.2	2.0	1.8	1.3
Mozambique	2003	3	2	3	1	1	1	2	5	4.5	3.8	2.7	4.0	3.0	2.6	3.2	3.2
Niger	2005	5	4	7	2	3	4	5	7	4.1	3.7	3.2	4.7	4.5	4.3	4.6	2.9
Nigeria	2003	1	1	1	1	1	1	1	2	1.5	2.0	1.3	3.6	2.4	1.7	1.3	1.1

(continued next page)

Table A5.2 *(continued)*

		Expenditure budget (2002 US$)								*Share in household budget*							
Country	*Year*	*National*	*Rural*	*Urban*	*Q1*	*Q2*	*Q3*	*Q4*	*Q5*	*National*	*Rural*	*Urban*	*Q1*	*Q2*	*Q3*	*Q4*	*Q5*
Rwanda	1998	8	4	8		1	1	1	9	8.1	5.6	2.6		2.9	1.6	1.5	3.5
São Tomé and Príncipe	2000	5	0	10	0	0	1	1	18	2.6	0.2	3.8	0.1	0.2	0.9	0.5	4.2
Senegal	2001	4	2	5	2	2	3	4	6	1.9	1.4	1.7	2.0	1.7	1.8	1.8	1.5
Sierra Leone	2003	2	1	2	0	0	2	2	2	1.5	0.7	1.1	0.3	0.3	2.9	1.8	0.6
South Africa	2000	6	1	8	1	1	2	4	13	1.0	0.4	1.2	0.8	1.0	1.2	1.2	1.0
Tanzania	2000	2	2	1	1	2	2	2	2	2.9	4.6	1.3	3.0	4.9	3.7	2.9	1.9
Uganda	2002	3	2	3	1	1	2	2	5	3.1	3.1	2.1	4.3	3.0	2.7	2.4	2.1
Zambia	2002	2	0	3	1	1	1	1	4	2.5	0.5	2.0	1.6	1.3	1.3	1.5	2.4

Source: Banerjee, Wodon, and others 2008.
Note: Q = quintile. Year refers to year of the survey.

Table A5.3 Affordability of Piped Water at 5 Percent Budget Threshold for Urban Households

(% of households for which 5% of household budget is less than the cost of minimum consumption)

	Cost of minimum consumption (US$)																		
Country	*1*	*2*	*3*	*4*	*5*	*6*	*7*	*8*	*9*	*10*	*11*	*12*	*13*	*14*	*15*	*16*	*17*	*18*	*19*
Benin	0.0	0.0	0.0	2.0	3.0	4.0	7.0	12.0	21.0	33.0	41.0	45.0	53.0	60.0	65.0	71.0	75.0	82.0	85.0
Burkina Faso	0.0	0.0	1.0	4.0	8.0	20.0	24.0	34.0	42.0	47.0	56.0	62.0	69.0	72.0	75.0	78.0	82.0	85.0	88.0
Burundi	1.0	7.0	17.0	29.0	45.0	53.0	67.0	72.0	76.0	82.0	86.0	90.0	94.0	97.0	99.0	100.0	100.0	100.0	100.0
Cameroon	0.0	0.0	0.0	0.0	0.0	0.0	0.0	0.0	0.0	1.0	1.0	2.0	4.0	7.0	11.0	17.0	21.0	27.0	34.0
Congo, Dem. Rep.	0.0	9.0	31.0	49.0	67.0	79.0	87.0	91.0	98.0	98.0	99.0	99.0	99.0	100.0	100.0	100.0	100.0	100.0	100.0
Congo, Rep.	0.0	0.0	0.0	0.0	1.0	3.0	3.0	5.0	9.0	12.0	17.0	21.0	23.0	28.0	33.0	35.0	36.0	43.0	49.0
Côte d'Ivoire	0.0	0.0	0.0	0.0	0.0	1.0	1.0	2.0	3.0	3.0	5.0	5.0	7.0	7.0	8.0	10.0	15.0	19.0	23.0
Ethiopia	1.0	40.0	73.0	87.0	93.0	95.0	98.0	99.0	99.0	99.0	99.0	99.0	99.0	99.0	100.0	100.0	100.0	100.0	100.0
Ghana	0.0	0.0	1.0	2.0	3.0	7.0	10.0	11.0	23.0	30.0	36.0	46.0	50.0	55.0	61.0	67.0	76.0	80.0	85.0
Guinea-Bissau	0.0	0.0	1.0	6.0	22.0	38.0	56.0	65.0	73.0	81.0	85.0	89.0	89.0	91.0	92.0	93.0	96.0	96.0	98.0
Kenya	0.0	0.0	0.0	0.0	4.0	5.0	13.0	20.0	28.0	36.0	49.0	62.0	67.0	72.0	77.0	78.0	80.0	83.0	86.0
Madagascar	0.0	0.0	5.0	16.0	23.0	28.0	38.0	47.0	53.0	61.0	64.0	68.0	74.0	78.0	82.0	85.0	86.0	89.0	90.0
Malawi	0.0	2.0	13.0	32.0	49.0	66.0	71.0	78.0	81.0	87.0	90.0	92.0	93.0	93.0	94.0	94.0	95.0	95.0	95.0
Mozambique	0.0	0.0	5.0	16.0	20.0	32.0	41.0	47.0	52.0	59.0	64.0	68.0	72.0	75.0	76.0	78.0	82.0	84.0	85.0
Niger	0.0	1.0	4.0	11.0	20.0	28.0	41.0	55.0	61.0	70.0	74.0	79.0	86.0	89.0	92.0	93.0	93.0	95.0	96.0
Nigeria	0.0	3.0	7.0	10.0	18.0	23.0	27.0	35.0	46.0	57.0	69.0	78.0	85.0	89.0	93.0	95.0	96.0	97.0	97.0
São Tomé and Príncipe	0.0	0.0	0.0	2.0	5.0	13.0	20.0	29.0	36.0	46.0	57.0	64.0	72.0	77.0	78.0	81.0	84.0	87.0	87.0
Senegal	0.0	0.0	0.0	0.0	0.0	0.0	0.0	0.0	0.0	0.0	0.0	0.0	0.0	1.0	1.0	1.0	1.0	2.0	2.0
Sierra Leone	0.0	0.0	2.0	4.0	7.0	16.0	23.0	30.0	40.0	44.0	49.0	54.0	57.0	62.0	65.0	67.0	69.0	71.0	73.0
South Africa	0.0	0.0	0.0	0.0	0.0	0.0	0.0	0.0	1.0	1.0	1.0	1.0	1.0	1.0	1.0	1.0	1.0	1.0	1.0
Tanzania	0.0	1.0	1.0	8.0	15.0	25.0	38.0	55.0	69.0	75.0	84.0	89.0	94.0	96.0	97.0	98.0	98.0	99.0	99.0
Uganda	0.0	2.0	5.0	17.0	32.0	45.0	55.0	65.0	77.0	82.0	88.0	90.0	94.0	96.0	96.0	97.0	98.0	98.0	98.0
Zambia	0.0	0.0	1.0	4.0	11.0	18.0	28.0	35.0	41.0	50.0	55.0	58.0	61.0	67.0	72.0	76.0	78.0	82.0	84.0

Source: Banerjee, Wodon, and others 2008.

Note: Year refers to year of the survey.

Reference

Banerjee, S., Q. Wodon, A. Diallo, T. Pushak, H. Uddin, C. Tsimpo, and V. Foster. 2008. "Access, Affordability and Alternatives: Modern Infrastructure Services in Sub-Saharan Africa." AICD Background Paper 2, Africa Infrastructure Country Diagnostic, World Bank, Washington, D.C.

APPENDIX 6

Funding Gap for Water Supply and Sanitation

Table A6.1 Water and Sanitation Expansion and Rehabilitation

US $ million (Annual)	Water					Sanitation					Total		
	Expansion	Rehabilitation	CAPEX (Expansion + Rehabilitation)	OPEX	Total	Expansion	Rehabilitation	CAPEX (Expansion + Rehabilitation)	OPEX	Total	CAPEX	OPEX	Total
Angola	158	70	228	88	316	75	58	133	125	258	361	213	574
Benin	131	40	171	86	257	16	5	22	3	25	193	90	283
Botswana	22	42	64	70	134	3	3	6	1	7	70	71	141
Burkina Faso	65	45	110	44	154	44	3	47	7	54	157	50	208
Burundi	30	30	60	15	75	28	1	29	1	30	89	16	105
Cameroon	101	126	227	110	337	44	40	84	13	97	311	123	434
Cape Verde	4	2	5	3	9	5	1	6	9	15	12	12	24
CAR	54	40	94	43	137	10	7	17	2	19	111	45	156
Chad	36	31	67	21	88	44	7	51	6	57	118	27	145
Congo, Dem. Rep.	785	259	1,044	395	1,440	97	82	179	20	199	1,223	416	1,639
Congo, Rep.	90	38	129	54	182	22	8	30	4	34	159	57	216
Côte d'Ivoire	119	80	199	134	332	250	62	312	130	442	511	264	774
Equatorial Guinea	7	1	8	4	12	2	4	6	1	7	14	4	19
Eritrea	56	32	88	37	125	18	2	20	2	22	108	39	147
Ethiopia	542	153	694	337	1,031	123	33	156	19	175	850	356	1,206
Gabon	20	16	36	31	68	4	1	5	1	6	42	32	74
Gambia	17	13	30	14	44	10	5	15	17	31	45	31	76
Ghana	135	131	266	127	393	64	6	70	9	80	337	136	473
Guinea	20	42	62	25	88	18	9	27	8	35	89	33	123
Kenya	767	437	1,204	534	1,738	89	87	176	22	198	1,380	556	1,936
Lesotho	11	15	26	14	40	8	4	12	3	15	38	16	54

Liberia	34	18	52	23	74	24	7	30	17	47	82	40	122
Madagascar	290	97	387	151	538	55	2	57	17	75	444	168	612
Malawi	63	70	133	45	178	8	20	28	3	31	162	47	209
Mali	89	77	166	74	240	31	31	63	8	71	229	82	311
Mauritania	27	22	49	22	72	6	4	10	1	11	60	24	83
Mauritius	14	27	41	47	88	3	3	6	19	25	47	66	113
Mozambique	107	53	160	55	215	73	66	140	15	155	300	70	370
Namibia	58	71	129	126	255	12	4	16	19	36	145	145	290
Niger	112	54	166	46	212	45	2	47	6	53	213	52	266
Nigeria	875	259	1,134	426	1,560	448	244	692	88	780	1,827	514	2,340
Rwanda	35	16	51	21	71	27	7	34	4	38	85	25	110
Senegal	101	53	154	95	249	40	9	50	43	93	204	138	342
Sierra Leone	103	31	134	50	184	15	1	16	2	18	149	52	202
South Africa	563	565	1,128	1,057	2,184	319	204	523	613	1,136	1,651	1,670	3,320
Sudan	634	583	1,217	601	1,818	127	113	239	33	273	1,457	634	2,091
Swaziland	9	6	15	9	24	3	5	8	1	9	23	10	33
Tanzania	410	211	621	248	869	84	71	155	29	184	776	277	1,053
Togo	235	109	344	123	467	171	6	177	23	199	521	146	666
Uganda	58	98	156	36	191	72	65	137	20	157	293	56	348
Zambia	139	95	234	102	337	36	46	82	52	134	317	154	471
Zimbabwe	81	159	240	131	371	34	12	46	10	56	286	142	427
Total	**7,225**	**4,327**	**11,553**	**5,686**	**17,239**	**2,617**	**1,352**	**3,969**	**1,432**	**5,401**	**15,522**	**7,118**	**22,640**

Source: Briceño-Garmendia, Smits, and Foster 2008.

Table A6.2 Indicative Water and Sanitation Spending Needs

	US$ (million per year)			*GDP (percentage per year)*		
Country	*Capital*	*O&M*	*Total spending needs*	*Capital*	*O&M*	*Total spending needs*
Angola	361	213	574	1.18	0.70	1.87
Benin	193	90	283	4.50	2.09	6.60
Botswana	70	71	141	0.66	0.68	1.34
Burkina Faso	157	50	208	2.90	0.93	3.83
Burundi	89	16	105	11.21	1.97	13.18
Cameroon	311	123	434	1.88	0.74	2.62
Cape Verde	12	12	24	1.18	1.21	2.38
Central African Republic	111	45	156	8.22	3.35	11.57
Chad	118	27	145	2.01	0.46	2.47
Comoros	—	—	—	—	—	—
Congo, Dem. Rep.	1,223	416	1,639	17.22	5.85	23.08
Congo, Rep.	159	57	216	2.61	0.94	3.55
Côte d'Ivoire	511	264	774	3.12	1.61	4.74
Equatorial Guinea	14	4	19	0.19	0.06	0.25
Eritrea	108	39	147	11.11	4.04	15.15
Ethiopia	850	356	1,206	6.91	2.89	9.80
Gabon	42	32	74	0.48	0.37	0.85
Gambia, The	45	31	76	9.73	6.68	16.41
Ghana	337	136	473	3.14	1.27	4.41
Guinea	89	33	123	2.73	1.03	3.76
Guinea-Bissau	—	—	—	—	—	—
Kenya	1,380	556	1,936	7.37	2.97	10.34
Lesotho	38	16	54	2.65	1.15	3.80
Liberia	82	40	122	15.44	7.51	22.94
Madagascar	444	168	612	8.81	3.33	12.15
Malawi	162	47	209	5.67	1.66	7.33
Mali	229	82	311	4.31	1.54	5.86
Mauritania	60	24	83	3.25	1.28	4.53
Mauritius	47	66	113	0.75	1.05	1.80
Mozambique	300	70	370	4.56	1.07	5.63
Namibia	145	145	290	2.33	2.33	4.66
Niger	213	52	266	6.40	1.58	7.98
Nigeria	1,827	514	2,340	1.63	0.46	2.09
Rwanda	85	25	110	3.57	1.05	4.62
São Tomé and Príncipe	—	—	—	—	—	—
Senegal	204	138	342	2.35	1.59	3.93
Seychelles	—	—	—	—	—	—
Sierra Leone	149	52	202	12.29	4.29	16.59

(continued next page)

Table A6.2 *(continued)*

	US$ (million per year)			*GDP (percentage per year)*		
Country	*Capital*	*O&M*	*Total spending needs*	*Capital*	*O&M*	*Total spending needs*
South Africa	1,651	1,670	3,320	0.68	0.69	1.37
Sudan	1,457	634	2,091	5.32	2.32	7.63
Swaziland	23	10	33	0.88	0.37	1.25
Tanzania	776	277	1,053	5.49	1.96	7.45
Togo	521	146	666	24.18	6.77	30.95
Uganda	293	56	348	3.35	0.64	3.99
Zambia	317	154	471	4.31	2.10	6.41
Zimbabwe	286	142	427	8.36	4.15	12.51
Sub-Saharan Africa	**15,522**	**7,118**	**22,640**	**2.42**	**1.11**	**3.53**
Low-income, fragile	3,282	1,249	4,531	8.55	3.25	11.80
Low-income, nonfragile	5,682	2,128	7,810	5.15	1.93	7.08
Middle-income	1,990	1,996	3,987	0.73	0.74	1.47
Resource-rich	4,605	1,759	6,364	2.07	0.79	2.86

Source: Briceño-Garmendia, Smits, and Foster 2008.
Note: GDP = gross domestic product, O&M = operations and maintenance, — = not available.

Table A6.3 Existing Financing Flows to Water and Sanitation Sectors

	US$ (million per year)								GDP (percentage per year)							
		Capital								Capital						
	O&M				PPI				O&M				PPI			
Country	Public sector	Public sector	ODA	Non-OECD financiers	PPI	Household self-finance	Total CAPEX	Total spending	Public sector	Public sector	ODA	Non-OECD financiers	PPI	Household self-finance	Total CAPEX	Total spending
Angola	—	—	15.80	70.37	0	—	—	—	—	—	0.05	0.23	0.00	—	—	—
Benin	15	11.43	59	0.00	0	13	83	98	0.35	0.27	1.37	0.00	0.00	0.30	1.93	2.28
Botswana	95	172	1	0	0	—	172	268	0.91	1.64	0.01	0.00	0.00	—	1.64	2.55
Burkina Faso	17	2	37	0	0	33	72	90	0.32	0.03	0.69	0.00	0.00	0.61	1.33	1.65
Burundi	—	—	11	0	0	—	—	—	—	—	1.40	0.00	0.00	—	—	—
Cameroon	48	36	23	1	0	19	79	127	0.29	0.22	0.14	0.01	0.00	0.12	0.48	0.77
Cape Verde	1	11	9	0	0	—	21	21	0.06	1.11	0.91	0.02	0.00	—	2.05	2.11
Central African Republic	—	—	1	0	0	—	—	—	—	—	0.10	0.00	0.00	—	—	—
Chad	0	1	27	1	0	10	39	39	0.00	0.01	0.47	0.01	0.00	0.17	0.66	0.67
Comoros	—	—	1	1	0	—	—	—	—	—	0.27	0.24	0.00	—	—	—
Congo, Dem. Rep.	—	—	48	2	0	62	—	—	—	—	0.68	0.02	0.00	0.87	—	—
Congo, Rep.	28	19	0	1	0	—	20	48	0.45	0.31	0.00	0.02	0.00	—	0.33	0.79
Côte d'Ivoire	54	13	1	1	0	92	107	162	0.33	0.08	0.00	0.01	0.00	0.56	0.66	0.99
Equatorial Guinea	—	—	1	0	0	—	—	—	—	—	0.01	0.00	0.00	—	—	—
Eritrea	—	—	6	12	0	—	—	—	—	—	0.64	1.26	0.00	—	—	—
Ethiopia	123	74	92	0	0	94	260	383	1.00	0.60	0.75	0.00	0.00	0.76	2.11	3.11
Gabon	—	—	12	0	0	—	—	—	—	—	0.13	0.00	0.00	—	—	—
Gambia, The	—	—	7	3	0	—	—	—	—	—	1.45	0.56	0.00	—	—	—
Ghana	53	23	98	0	0	31	151	204	0.49	0.21	0.91	0.00	0.00	0.29	1.41	1.90
Guinea	—	—	14	1	0	—	—	—	—	—	0.42	0.04	0.00	—	—	—
Guinea-Bissau	—	—	1	0	0	—	—	—	—	—	0.45	0.00	0.00	—	—	—
Kenya	12	34	97	2	0	23	155	167	0.07	0.18	0.52	0.01	0.00	0.12	0.83	0.89
Lesotho	7	3	14	2	0	2	21	28	0.48	0.20	1.01	0.12	0.00	0.17	1.49	1.98

Liberia	—	—	4	0	0	—	—	—	—	—	0.73	0.00	0.00	—	—	—
Madagascar	0	5	19	0	0	46	70	70	0.01	0.11	0.37	0.00	0.00	0.90	1.38	1.39
Malawi	15	3	16	0	0	6	25	40	0.53	0.12	0.54	0.00	0.00	0.22	0.88	1.41
Mali	26	7	34	1	0	—	42	68	0.48	0.13	0.64	0.02	0.00	—	0.79	1.27
Mauritania	—	—	10	29	0	—	—	—	—	—	0.55	1.57	0.00	—	—	—
Mauritius	—	—	9	6	0	—	—	—	—	—	0.14	0.10	0.00	—	—	—
Mozambique	4	9	55	0	0	35	99	103	0.07	0.13	0.84	0.00	0.00	0.53	1.50	1.56
Namibia	131	12	6	0	0	3	21	152	2.11	0.19	0.09	0.00	0.00	0.05	0.33	2.44
Niger	11	28	23	1	0	3	56	66	0.32	0.85	0.68	0.03	0.01	0.10	1.67	1.99
Nigeria	14	355	100	0	0	295	751	766	0.01	0.32	0.09	0.00	0.00	0.26	0.67	0.68
Rwanda	6	0	17	0	0	20	37	43	0.25	0.00	0.71	0.00	0.00	0.85	1.56	1.81
São Tomé and Príncipe	—	—	0	0	0	—	—	—	—	—	0.14	0.00	0.00	—	—	—
Senegal	5	9	37	14	0	49	110	114	0.05	0.11	0.43	0.16	0.00	0.57	1.26	1.32
Seychelles	—	—	1	0	0	—	—	—	—	—	0.09	0.07	0.00	—	—	—
Sierra Leone	—	—	8	0	0	—	—	—	—	—	0.65	0.00	0.00	—	—	—
South Africa	1,874	115	60	0	2	—	177	2,051	0.77	0.05	0.02	0.00	0.00	—	0.07	0.85
Sudan	—	—	12	5	7	—	—	—	—	—	0.05	0.02	0.02	—	—	—
Swaziland	—	—	1	0	0	—	—	—	—	—	0.05	0.00	0.00	—	—	—
Tanzania	15	33	143	4	1	28	209	224	0.10	0.23	1.01	0.03	0.01	0.20	1.48	1.59
Togo	—	—	2	0	0	—	—	—	—	—	0.08	0.00	0.00	—	—	—
Uganda	1	1	47	3	0	41	93	—	0.01	0.01	0.54	0.04	0.00	0.47	1.06	—
Zambia	35	67	47	1	0	9	123	158	0.48	0.91	0.63	0.02	0.00	0.12	1.68	2.16
Zimbabwe	—	—	1	0	0	—	—	—	—	—	0.03	0.00	0.00	—	—	—
Sub-Saharan Africa	**3,112**	**1,252**	**1,227**	**163**	**10**	**2,125**	**4,778**	**7,890**	**0.48**	**0.20**	**0.19**	**0.03**	**0.00**	**0.33**	**0.74**	**1.23**
Low-income, fragile	128	30	105	20	0	165	313	441	0.33	0.08	0.27	0.05	0.00	0.43	0.81	1.15
Low-income, nonfragile	307	243	783	55	2	451	1,533	1,840	0.28	0.22	0.71	0.05	0.00	0.41	1.39	1.67
Middle-income	2,186	324	101	8	2	206	641	2,827	0.81	0.12	0.04	0.00	0.00	0.08	0.24	1.04
Resource-rich	188	717	238	80	7	522	1,564	1,753	0.08	0.32	0.11	0.04	0.00	0.23	0.70	0.79

Source: Briceño-Garmendia, Smits, and Foster 2008.

Note: CAPEX = capital expenditure, GDP = gross domestic product, O&M = operations and maintenance, ODA = official development assistance, OECD = Organisation for Economic Co-operation and development, PPI = private participation in infrastructure, — = not available.

Table A6.4 Annual Budgetary Flows (*not* Traced)

Country	*US$ (million per year)*	*GDP (percentage per year)*
Angola	—	—
Benin	26	0.61
Botswana	267	2.54
Burkina Faso	19	0.35
Burundi	—	—
Cameroon	84	0.51
Cape Verde	12	1.17
Central African Republic	—	—
Chad	1	0.02
Comoros	—	—
Congo, Dem. Rep.	—	—
Congo, Rep.	46	0.76
Côte d'Ivoire	67	0.41
Equatorial Guinea	—	—
Eritrea	—	—
Ethiopia	197	1.60
Gabon	—	—
Gambia, The	—	—
Ghana	75	0.70
Guinea	—	—
Guinea-Bissau	—	—
Kenya	46	0.24
Lesotho	10	0.68
Liberia	—	—
Madagascar	6	0.11
Malawi	18	0.64
Mali	32	0.61
Mauritania	—	—
Mauritius	—	—
Mozambique	13	0.20
Namibia	143	2.30
Niger	39	1.18
Nigeria	370	0.33
Rwanda	6	0.25
São Tomé and Príncipe	—	—
Senegal	14	0.16
Seychelles	—	—
Sierra Leone	—	—
South Africa	1,988	0.82
Sudan	—	—
Swaziland	—	—
Tanzania	47	0.34
Togo	—	—

(continued next page)

Table A6.4 *(continued)*

Country	*US$ (million per year)*	*GDP (percentage per year)*
Uganda	2	0.02
Zambia	102	1.39
Zimbabwe	—	—
Sub-Saharan Africa	**4,364**	**0.68**
Low-income, fragile	158	0.41
Low-income, nonfragile	550	0.50
Middle-income	2,509	0.93
Resource-rich	906	0.41

Source: Briceño-Garmendia, Smits, and Foster 2008.
Note: GDP = gross domestic product, — = not available. Nontraced spending refers to all available spending in the sector.

Table A6.5 Public Infrastructure Spending by Sector and Institution

	US$ (million per year)				GDP (percentage per year)			
	OPEX		CAPEX		OPEX		CAPEX	
Country	On-budget	Off-budget	On-budget	Off-budget	On-budget	Off-budget	On-budget	Off-budget
Angola	—	—	—	—	—	—	—	—
Benin	0.00	14.85	0.00	11.43	0.00	0.35	0.00	0.27
Botswana	72.50	22.85	169.87	2.02	0.69	0.22	1.62	0.02
Burkina Faso	0.00	17.50	0.00	1.64	0.00	0.32	0.00	0.03
Burundi	—	—	—	—	—	—	—	—
Cameroon	0.08	48.25	4.55	31.41	0.00	0.29	0.03	0.19
Cape Verde	0.64	0.00	8.71	2,47	0.06	0.00	0.87	0.25
Central African Republic	—	—	—	—	—	—	—	—
Chad	0.19	0.00	0.78	0.00	0.00	0.00	0.01	0.00
Comoros	—	—	—	—	—	—	—	—
Congo, Dem. Rep.	—	—	—	—	—	—	—	—
Congo, Rep.	1.90	25.60	14.55	4.31	0.03	0.42	0.24	0.07
Côte d'Ivoire	6.97	47.37	12.96	0.00	0.04	0.29	0.08	0.00
Equatorial Guinea	—	—	—	—	—	—	—	—
Eritrea	—	—	—	—	—	—	—	—
Ethiopia	122.92	0.00	74.34	0.00	1.00	0.00	0.60	0.00
Gabon	—	—	—	—	—	—	—	—
Gambia, The	—	—	—	—	—	—	—	—
Ghana	3.55	48.99	3.68	18.83	0.03	0.46	0.03	0.18
Guinea	—	—	—	—	—	—	—	—
Guinea-Bissau	—	—	—	—	—	—	—	—
Kenya	12.28	0.00	33.56	0.00	0.07	0.00	0.18	0.00
Lesotho	1.47	5.41	1.67	1.18	0.10	0.38	0.12	0.08
Liberia	—	—	—	—	—	—	—	—
Madagascar	0.29	0.00	5.32	0.00	0.01	0.00	0.11	0.00

Malawi	0.75	14.32	0.96	2.37	0.03	0.50	0.03	0.08
Mali	3.51	22.03	2.07	4.73	0.07	0.42	0.04	0.09
Mauritania	—	—	—	—	—	—	—	—
Mauritius	—	—	—	—	—	—	—	—
Mozambique	4.29	0.00	8.57	0.00	0.07	0.00	0.13	0.00
Namibia	13.16	118.25	2.37	9.27	0.21	1.90	0.04	0.15
Niger	0.02	10.72	1.83	26.61	0.00	0.32	0.06	0.80
Nigeria	14.37	0.00	355.49	0.00	0.01	0.00	0.32	0.00
Rwanda	0.64	5.25	0.05	0.00	0.03	0.22	0.00	0.00
São Tomé and Príncipe	—	—	—	—	—	—	—	—
Senegal	1.30	3.33	9.35	0.00	0.01	0.04	0.11	0.00
Seychelles	—	—	—	—	—	—	—	—
Sierra Leone	—	—	—	—	—	—	—	—
South Africa	1,543.27	330.31	82.21	32.65	0.64	0.14	0.03	0.01
Sudan	—	—	—	—	—	—	—	—
Swaziland	—	—	—	—	—	—	—	—
Tanzania	10.81	3.94	32.66	0.00	0.08	0.03	0.23	0.00
Togo	—	—	—	—	—	—	—	—
Uganda	0.77	0.00	0.76	0.00	0.01	0.00	0.01	0.00
Zambia	28.59	6.50	66.28	0.47	0.39	0.09	0.90	0.01
Zimbabwe	—	—	—	—	—	—	—	—
Sub-Saharan Africa	**2,216.17**	**895.78**	**1,072.60**	**179.53**	**0.35**	**0.14**	**0.17**	**0.03**
Low-income, fragile	16.37	111.31	30.46	0.00	0.04	0.29	0.08	0.00
Low-income, nonfragile	163.85	143.30	176.09	66.73	0.15	0.13	0.16	0.06
Middle-income	1,691.14	494.38	274.59	49.34	0.62	0.18	0.10	0.02
Resource-rich	67.75	120.61	662.89	54.32	0.03	0.05	0.30	0.02

Source: Briceño-Garmendia, Smits, and Foster 2008.
Note: CAPEX = capital expenditure, GDP = gross domestic product, OPEX = operating expenditure, — = not available.

Table A6.6 Size and Composition of Funding Gap

Country	US$ (million per year)			GDP (percentage per year)		
	Capital expenditure gap	*O&M expenditure gap*	*Funding gap*	*Capital expenditure gap*	*O&M expenditure gap*	*Funding gap*
Angola	—	—	—	—	—	—
Benin	106	72	177	2.46	1.67	4.14
Botswana	0	0	0	0.00	0.00	0.00
Burkina Faso	72	28	100	1.33	0.52	1.85
Burundi	—	—	—	—	—	—
Cameroon	230	74	305	1.39	0.45	1.84
Cape Verde	0	7	7	0.00	0.68	0.68
Central African Republic	—	—	—	—	—	—
Chad	79	27	105	1.34	0.45	1.79
Comoros	—	—	—	—	—	—
Congo, Dem. Rep.	—	—	—	—	—	—
Congo, Rep.	117	25	143	1.93	0.42	2.35
Côte d'Ivoire	320	166	486	1.96	1.02	2.97
Equatorial Guinea	—	—	—	—	—	—
Eritrea	—	—	—	—	—	—
Ethiopia	567	224	792	4.61	1.82	6.43
Gabon	—	—	—	—	—	—
Gambia, The	—	—	—	—	—	—
Ghana	185	83	269	1.73	0.78	2.50
Guinea	—	—	—	—	—	—
Guinea-Bissau	—	—	—	—	—	—
Kenya	1,162	516	1,678	6.20	2.76	8.96
Lesotho	12	7	19	0.82	0.48	1.30
Liberia	—	—	—	—	—	—

Madagascar	322	144	466	6.39	2.86	9.24
Malawi	117	28	144	4.09	0.97	5.06
Mali	126	38	165	2.38	0.72	3.10
Mauritania	—	—	—	—	—	—
Mauritius	—	—	—	—	—	—
Mozambique	171	56	226	2.59	0.85	3.44
Namibia	107	12	119	1.72	0.19	1.92
Niger	147	39	186	4.41	1.17	5.58
Nigeria	966	448	1,414	0.86	0.40	1.26
Rwanda	41	17	58	1.73	0.69	2.43
São Tomé and Príncipe	—	—	—	—	—	—
Senegal	69	98	168	0.80	1.13	1.93
Seychelles	—	—	—	—	—	—
Sierra Leone	—	—	—	—	—	—
South Africa	604	0	604	0.25	0.00	0.25
Sudan	—	—	—	—	—	—
Swaziland	—	—	—	—	—	—
Tanzania	512	237	749	3.62	1.67	5.30
Togo	—	—	—	—	—	—
Uganda	179	49	228	2.05	0.56	2.61
Zambia	158	97	255	2.14	1.32	3.46
Zimbabwe	—	—	—	—	—	—
Sub-Saharan Africa	**8,648**	**3,225**	**11,873**	**1.3**	**0.5**	**1.8**
Low-income, fragile	2,627	993	3,620	6.8	2.6	9.4
Low-income, nonfragile	3,673	1,612	5,285	3.3	1.5	4.8
Middle-income	312	0	312	0.1	0.0	0.1
Resource-rich	2,696	1,393	4,089	1.2	0.6	1.8

Source: Briceño-Garmendia, Smits, and Foster 2008.
Note: GDP = gross domestic product, O&M = operations and maintenance, — = not available.

Table A6.7 Reducing the Funding Gap

	US$ (million per year)								GDP (percentage per year)							
				Gain from inefficiencies								Gain from inefficiencies				
Country	*Total spending needs*	*Spending traced to needs*	*Gain from inefficiencies*	*Capital execution*	*Operational inefficiencies*	*Cost recovery*	*(Funding gap) or surplus*	*Potential for reallocation*	*Total spending needs*	*Spending traced to needs*	*Gain from inefficiencies*	*Capital execution*	*Operational inefficiencies*	*Cost recovery*	*(Funding gap) or surplus*	*Potential for reallocation*
Angola	(574)	—	—	—	—	—	—	—	1.87	—	0.00	—	—	—	—	—
Benin	(283)	98	8	0	2	6	(177)	0	6.60	2.28	4.27	2.46	1.67	0.13	4.14	0.00
Botswana	(141)	141	26	6	3	18	26	126	1.34	2.55	0.17	0.00	0.00	0.17	0.00	1.20
Burkina Faso	(208)	90	18	0	14	4	(100)	0	3.83	1.65	1.92	1.33	0.52	0.07	1.85	0.00
Burundi	(105)	—	—	—	—	—	—	—	13.18	—	0.00	—	—	—	—	—
Cameroon	(434)	127	2	2	—	—	(305)	0	2.62	0.77	1.84	1.39	0.45	—	1.84	0.00
Cape Verde	(24)	12	5	2	3	0	(7)	9	2.38	2.11	0.68	0.00	0.68	0.00	0.68	0.87
Central African Republic	(156)	—	—	—	—	—	—	—	11.57	—	0.00	—	—	—	—	—
Chad	(145)	39	1	1	0	—	(105)	0	2.47	0.67	1.79	1.34	0.45	—	1.79	0.00
Comoros	—	—	—	—	—	—	—	—	—	—	0.00	—	—	—	—	—
Congo, Dem. Rep.	(1,639)	—	150	—	53	97	—	—	23.08	—	1.37	—	—	1.37	—	—
Congo, Rep.	(216)	48	25	0	4	22	(143)	0	3.55	0.79	2.71	1.93	0.42	0.36	2.35	0.00
Côte d'Ivoire	(774)	162	127	3	3	121	(486)	0	4.74	0.99	3.71	1.96	1.02	0.74	2.97	0.00
Equatorial Guinea	(19)	—	—	—	—	—	—	—	0.25	—	0.00	—	—	—	—	—
Eritrea	(147)	—	—	—	—	—	—	—	15.15	—	0.00	—	—	—	—	—
Ethiopia	(1,206)	383	32	0	9	23	(792)	0	9.80	3.11	6.62	4.61	1.82	0.18	6.43	0.00
Gabon	(74)	—	21	—	1	21	—	—	0.85	—	0.24	—	—	0.24	—	—
Gambia, The	(76)	—	—	—	—	—	—	—	16.41	—	0.00	—	—	—	—	—
Ghana	(473)	204	1	1	—	—	(269)	0	4.41	1.90	2.50	1.73	0.78	—	2.50	0.00
Guinea	(123)	—	—	—	—	—	—	—	3.76	—	0.00	—	—	—	—	—
Guinea-Bissau	—	—	—	—	—	—	—	—	—	—	0.00	—	—	—	—	—
Kenya	(1,936)	167	90	18	40	32	(1,678)	0	10.34	0.89	9.13	6.20	2.76	0.17	8.96	0.00
Lesotho	(54)	28	8	0	1	7	(19)	0	3.80	1.98	1.76	0.82	0.48	0.46	1.30	0.00
Liberia	(122)	—	1	—	1	—	—	—	22.94	—	0.00	—	—	—	—	—
Madagascar	(612)	70	76	1	13	62	(466)	0	12.15	1.39	10.47	6.39	2.86	1.23	9.24	0.00
Malawi	(209)	40	25	0	14	10	(144)	0	7.33	1.41	5.43	4.09	0.97	0.37	5.06	0.00
Mali	(311)	68	79	0	8	70	(165)	0	5.86	1.27	4.43	2.38	0.72	1.33	3.10	0.00

Mauritania	(83)	—	5	—	5	—	—	—	4.53	—	0.00	—	—	—	—	—
Mauritius	(113)	—	—	—	—	—	—	—	1.80	—	0.00	—	—	—	—	—
Mozambique	(370)	103	41	2	18	21	(226)	0	5.63	1.56	3.75	2.59	0.85	0.32	3.44	0.00
Namibia	(290)	152	19	0	5	14	(119)	0	4.66	2.44	2.13	1.72	0.19	0.22	1.92	0.00
Niger	(266)	66	13	0	1	12	(186)	0	7.98	1.99	5.95	4.41	1.17	0.38	5.58	0.00
Nigeria	(2,340)	766	161	75	52	34	(1,414)	0	2.09	0.68	1.29	0.86	0.40	0.03	1.26	0.00
Rwanda	(110)	43	9	0	9	0	(58)	0	4.62	1.81	2.43	1.73	0.69	0.00	2.43	0.00
São Tomé and Príncipe	—	—	—	—	—	—	—	—	—	—	0.00	—	—	—	—	—
Senegal	(342)	114	59	2	0	57	(168)	0	3.93	1.32	2.59	0.80	1.13	0.66	1.93	0.00
Seychelles	—	—	12	—	0	12	—	—	—	—	1.61	—	—	1.61	—	—
Sierra Leone	(202)	—	—	—	—	—	—	—	16.59	—	0.00	—	—	—	—	—
South Africa	(3,320)	1,847	870	0	400	470	(604)	204	1.37	0.85	0.44	0.25	0.00	0.19	0.25	0.08
Sudan	(2,091)	—	103	—	47	56	—	—	7.63	—	0.20	—	—	0.20	—	—
Swaziland	(33)	—	—	—	—	—	—	—	1.25	—	0.00	—	—	—	—	—
Tanzania	(1,053)	224	80	13	47	20	(749)	0	7.45	1.59	5.44	3.62	1.67	0.14	5.30	0.00
Togo	(666)	—	3	—	3	—	—	—	30.95	—	0.00	—	—	—	—	—
Uganda	(348)	—	—	—	—	—	—	0	3.99	—	2.61	2.05	0.56	—	2.61	—
Zambia	(471)	158	58	14	21	23	(255)	0	6.41	2.16	3.77	2.14	1.32	0.31	3.46	0.00
Zimbabwe	(427)	—	—	—	—	—	—	—	12.51	—	0.00	—	—	—	—	—
Sub-Saharan Africa	**(22,640)**	**7,890**	**2,877**	**168**	**1,259**	**1,450**	**(11,873)**	**0**	**3.53**	**1.23**	**2.08**	**1.35**	**0.50**	**0.23**	**1.85**	**0.00**
Low-income, fragile	(4,531)	441	471	6	106	358	(3,620)	0	11.80	1.15	10.36	6.84	2.58	0.93	9.43	0.00
Low-income, nonfragile	(7,810)	1,840	685	39	265	381	(5,285)	0	7.08	1.67	5.13	3.33	1.46	0.35	4.79	0.00
Middle-income	(3,987)	2,637	1,037	8	492	537	(312)	189	1.47	1.04	0.31	0.12	0.00	0.20	0.12	0.07
Resource-rich	(6,364)	1,753	522	137	172	214	(4,089)	0	2.86	0.79	1.93	1.21	0.63	0.10	1.84	0.00

Source: Briceño-Garmendia, Smits, and Foster 2008.
Note: GDP = gross domestic product, — = not available.

Reference

Briceño-Garmendia, C., K. Smits, and V. Foster, V. 2008. "Financing Public Infrastructure in Sub-Saharan Africa: Patterns and Emerging Issues." Background Paper No. 15, Africa Infrastructure Country Diagnostic (AICD), World Bank, Washington, DC.

Index

Boxes, figures, and tables are indicated with *b*, *f*, and *t* following the page number.

P

Q

R

Y

Z

ECO-AUDIT

Environmental Benefits Statement

The World Bank is committed to preserving endangered forests and natural resources. The Office of the Publisher has chosen to print ***Africa's Water and Sanitation Infrastructure: Access, Affordability, and Alternatives*** on recycled paper with 50 percent post-consumer waste, in accordance with the recommended standards for paper usage set by the Green Press Initiative, a nonprofit program supporting publishers in using fiber that is not sourced from endangered forests. For more information, visit www.greenpressinitiative.org.

Saved:

- 8 trees
- 3 million British thermal units of total energy
- 781 pounds of net greenhouse gases (CO_2 equivalent)
- 3,761 gallons of waste water
- 228 pounds of solid waste